THE WINTER HEART

Frances Casey Kerns

The Winter Heart

a Colorado Epic

A Troubadour Spectacular

Futura Publications Limited
A Troubadour Book

A Troubadour Book

First published in Great Britain by
Futura Publications Limited in 1979
Copyright © 1978 by Frances Casey Kerns

This book is sold subject to the condition that it shall not, by way of trade or otherwise, be lent, re-sold, hired out or otherwise circulated without the publisher's prior consent in any form of binding or cover other than that in which it is published and without a similar condition including this condition being imposed on the subsequent purchaser.
ISBN 0 7088 1642 8

Printed in Great Britain by
Hazell Watson & Viney Ltd
Aylesbury, Bucks

Futura Publications Limited
110 Warner Road
Camberwell, London SE5

For some of our very own and very special beautiful people,

Lyn Ryder
Bob Swift
The Fransons, Richardsons and Stoddards

PROLOGUE

1838

Angus Maxwell, aged twelve, stood alone by the ship's rail and shivered. It was an evening in late May. A fresh breeze, cold in the north Atlantic, snapped and bellied the sails of the *Maid of Liverpool*. Clouds dashed across the moon's face, making the light uncertain. No one was near Angus and he shuddered more for that reason than from the cold. He had suitable clothes for the cold, but there was nothing to shield him from his aloneness. It came over him in debilitating waves. Tuttle, whom his father, the Earl of Brendeen, had chosen to go along to look after him, lay sick in his bunk. Tuttle had been seasick since before the ship actually sailed from port. Angus had determined to treat this whole thing, the beginning of the rest of his life, as an adventure. But on this raw night, under the cloud-scudded sky, he admitted within the depths of himself that he felt alone and young. The moors and mountains of Brendeen, the gentle English countryside where he had been at school, and London, where the Maxwells had their town house, were all so far away. His brothers and sisters—all older than Angus except for little Hope—his stern, omniscient father, his gentle, sad mother, were getting farther away with each swell mounted by the *Maid of Liverpool*. What lay ahead was completely unknown: America, Pennsylvania, an aunt, uncle and cousin he had never seen.

"Very few younger sons have a chance at this sort of opportunity," his father had pointed out to his mother. "Philip offers, if the boy works out, to make him a partner in the business one day. What is there for him here, with three older brothers?"

"'It's so far away, Duncan," she had said sorrowfully. "Perhaps we'd never see him again. He's so young."

"Nonsense, Catherine. We can't let sentimentality stand in the way of good sense. The boy is quite old enough to be giving some attention to his future."

In the ship's bow, Angus held his face up to the wind, and his eyes stung. It was an east wind; it had passed over Scotland. He imagined that over all the distance he could smell the damp of the spring night in the mountains. He had not realized how much of Brendeen had been absorbed into his being. Now it seemed each of his senses had its own particular and vivid memories.

"Write to us often, son," his mother had pressed him gently. "And if you're not happy there . . ."

"He'll make the most of this," his father had said brusquely, "and be content enough." He turned to Angus. "Don't let yourself be too concerned with being *happy*. That's the way women think. Concern yourself with contentment, satisfaction; those are real things that can be had. They come from a man's being proud of who he is and of what he does. There's always been great pride simply in the name of Maxwell. Don't ever forget that. One day, your name will be a part of the name of your uncle's company, Maitland and Maxwell.

Always plan and work toward that. Your mother would keep you a child, but we'll not allow that."

Angus started as a figure materialized near him on the deck. It was one of the sailors who had come up unheard and had been invisible until clouds suddenly cleared the moon.

"What are you doing here?" asked the man. "You're a passenger." His accent was Highland Scots, and Angus was more grateful to hear it than he would have cared to admit.

"I just wanted to stand up here and—don't I know you? You're a MacWinter, aren't you?"

"Aye, I am. Gavin MacWinter, and you're the laird's lad. You shouldn't be here. It's not the passenger area."

Gavin was tall and slender, with broad shoulders and a rather craggy face, unruly sandy hair and clear, sharp blue eyes. He was eighteen.

"You knew I was on this ship," said Angus. It was half-question, half-statement, and hauteur was in his voice now. No matter how his spirits might lift at sight and sound of someone from home, his father was the laird, Earl of Brendeen, and this young man was the son, one of many children, of the earl's chief shepherd.

"No, I didn't know until now," Gavin said coolly. "I've little to do with the passengers."

"What *do* you do?" Angus asked quickly. His tone was casual, faintly patronizing, but he needed desperately to go on being with this near-familiar person, just for a little while.

"I'm an ordinary sailor," Gavin said, "and I'll be on watch soon enough. For now, I'm going to get out of the wind."

He moved back from the rail into the shelter of a deckhouse, and Angus followed hesitantly. Gavin, filling a rank pipe, looked speculatively at him in the next patch of moonlight. Angus was a stocky boy, tall for his age, with brown hair and steady, calculating hazel eyes like the laird's. Why had the boy followed him? They had nothing in common.

Gavin said, without much interest, "You're traveling alone, then?"

"No, I have Tuttle with me," Angus answered quickly. "Maybe you remember him from—from home."

"The laird's man? The valet?"

"Yes. He's my man now, but he's been seasick all the voyage. . . . You left Brendeen a long time ago, didn't you? I've heard the people talk about you."

Gavin had crouched down out of the wind, and Angus felt awkward, standing before him. Gavin had no right, Angus thought irritably, to sit down so casually in his presence. He recalled from remarks of his father and older brothers that the MacWinters were a proud, independent lot. He remembered that Mary MacWinter, Gavin's mother, was a favorite with his own mother, someone she sent for when extra workers were needed at the Hall, someone whom she occasionally visited while out walking or riding. Once, several years ago, Angus had been caught by a rainstorm near the MacWinter cottage and had gone inside for shelter. It had been a warm, cozy place, crowded with people, full of talk and laughter. Mrs. MacWinter had fussed over his wet clothes, unself-consciously, as she would have done with a child of her own. The casual warmth of everyone's attitude toward him had made Angus vaguely uncomfortable. He was only seven or eight then, but already well aware that, as the laird's son, he was due some deference, not the same treatment as one of the shepherd's family. Yet he had been reluctant to leave, once the rain stopped. Now, feeling awkward, he squatted beside Gavin in the shelter.

Gavin had answered, "I've been away the most part of five years."

"Being an ordinary sailor?" pursued the boy.

"Aye, most of the time. I went out as a cabin boy first. It's the way to start."

"How old were you?"

"Thirteen at the beginning. About your age."

Angus was gratified at being taken for a year older than he actually was, and by the knowledge that he was beginning the rest of his life a year younger than MacWinter had begun. He said, "Have you been to America before?"

"Aye, to Boston, New York and Charleston, but never beyond the coasts. Now I'm—"

"I'm going to Pennsylvania," cut in the boy. His restraint, his sense of class and station all but dissolved momentarily in the need for and pleasure in talking to someone. "You see, Philip Maitland, who married my father's sister, has a fine business there, and he asked that one of us be allowed to come and learn it. My oldest brother will be the next earl, of course, the second will go into military service, and the third into the church. It's a fairly new business, but it's already made my uncle a very wealthy man. They have only one son, my aunt and uncle. His name is Philip too, and he's a grown man now. All of them want some other member of the family trained in the business."

"You're to be a kind of steward, then?" Gavin said. He smiled faintly in the darkness, anticipating the boy's outrage.

"Certainly not," said Angus crisply. "I'm to be a partner. There are coal and iron mines, and there's to be a steel mill. Have you seen anything like that?"

"No."

Angus felt smug. "My father has, and my oldest brother. My mother's people live in the English Midlands where there are mines, but we don't visit there often. My mother likes Brendeen much better than her old home. In fact, she'd rather be there than London or anywhere."

"Lady Catherine's a fine woman," Gavin said. "My mother always speaks well of her."

"And why wouldn't she?" demanded Angus curtly.

"We 'people' don't have always to speak well of the gentry, just because we work for them," Gavin said coolly, and there was a silence.

But Angus could not bring himself, quite yet, to go back to the tiny, cramped cabin. He said rather stiffly, "Why did you go away from Brendeen? in the first place, I mean. I suppose your father apprenticed you or some such thing?"

"I went because there are already too many of us on the land and because I can live without Brendeen and the family. My brother Colin is older than I am, and he had the choice to follow our father as shepherd. There was never money for an apprenticeship. A cousin of ours from Glasgow got me onto a ship where he was a sailor."

"Then it wasn't lonely for you," said Angus confidently, "not with your cousin there."

"My cousin was a sour, mean man, harder to please than anyone else on the ship. Oh, aye, I was lonely, right enough. I used to hide in the hold sometimes, so no one would see me cry. I missed Brendeen and my people that much."

Angus felt surprised and uneasy at such an admission. He tried to see Gavin's expression, but the clouds were with them again. Surely he must be embarrassed at having said such a thing, though his tone seemed casual and matter-of-fact.

Angus said tentatively, "I suppose you'll go back to the Highlands one day, when you're old and have saved a little money?"

"Ah, no," Gavin said softly. "I'll not likely see Brendeen again, but I won't be spending the rest of my life at sea either. This is my last voyage."

"What will you do then?"

"I'll be staying in America this trip. Beyond that, I don't know. I'll find work with no trouble."

"But you'll be—a foreigner, with no family or anything."

"Aye, but there'll be a lot of people like that in America. With so many others being foreign and alone, I'll not likely be given much notice. It's a grand place, you know, a free country where not nearly so much attention is paid to class and the likes of that. It's got every kind of land you could think of, a living for every kind of people. There are the great mountains, far to the west, that I'll see before I'm through."

"What makes you think you know so much about it?"

"A ship I was on for three years had a man named MacLean as first mate. He was born in America. He talked about it and he taught me to read his books."

"That's not the name of the mate on this ship."

"No, he's dead now, but he was as fine a friend as a man could wish for. He had no family left anymore, and he gave me his chest of books and things when he was sick that last time. In America, you see, there's not much of a gentry set apart from the common people. Each man is considered equal under the law."

Angus scowled and said pompously, "I don't believe that and neither would my father. Wherever he is, a man belongs to the station he was born to."

"Have you ever seen a baby, newborn? It doesn't look any more like an earl than a shepherd."

Now the boy was angry and he said coldly, "There's a good deal to one's station besides looks."

"Aye, well, I'm going to a new country and so are you. Now I've told you about free and equal, you won't be so shocked when you come up against it."

There was another silence. Then Angus asked stiffly, "Have you been to school at all?"

"Only with Mr. MacLean."

Angus said enthusiastically, "I was at Brisbane

Academy for four years. My brothers went there too. It's near London . . . Did you learn anything besides reading?"

"Writing, some navigation, a bit of mathematics. I learned to think."

Angus peered at him. "How do you mean, think? I don't understand you."

"To wonder about things, to question and try to understand on my own. Mr. MacLean said it's the most important part of an education."

"I've always done well with Latin and all sorts of things," boasted the boy. "I'll go on with my schooling, of course."

"So will every man if he knows what's good for him, but it doesn't have to be inside a school."

Angus did not understand and felt more and more impatient. "When you first spoke, I thought how much like home you sounded. Now I realize you're not much like the Brendeen people at all."

"Nor are you, but then the laird's sons never are, are they? They go to England for their education and the rest of what they come to be. The Maxwells are all but absentee owners to Brendeen."

"That's not true, and you—"

Gavin cut in curtly, "*You* sound nothing like Brendeen. You sound like an Englishman."

"And so I am," Angus said coldly. "We all are."

"If you mean your family, that's so. If you mean all the folk at Brendeen, just because of the Alliance, you're daft. *I'm* a Scot."

"The Alliance!" Angus cried. "Do you know how long ago that was?"

"Aye, I do, and it makes no difference."

"You sound as if you think an Englishman's not as good as a Scot."

"You were born at Brendeen, weren't you? You should know that for yourself. In America, Englishmen aren't so highly thought of either."

"What do you think *is* highly thought of, then, since you know so much?"

"What sort of person each man is, how much pride or strength or courage he's got, or hasn't got. Each man starts with the chance to make his own way, live as he chooses."

Angus said haughtily, "I know something about America too. I know there was traitorous rebellion and revolution against England not much more than sixty years ago. That's how far your free and equal country is from being just another British colony."

A shrill piping and the sound of the ship's bell drifted to them on the wind. Gavin got to his feet. "It's my watch now. I hope you won't find America too hard for you."

"And I'm sure *you* will," said Angus shortly. "You're living in some sort of dream while you call other people daft."

They walked more or less together until they reached the companionway for Angus's cabin. He said, again in a patronizing tone, "When do you think we'll be in New York?"

"Maybe a week if this wind should hold."

"Perhaps I'll see you again," the boy said stiffly.

"Aye, maybe," Gavin was walking away, scarcely looking back.

Angus moved slowly, feeling irritable and dissatisfied. He was a cheeky one, that MacWinter. Angus's father was well rid of him at Brendeen.

When the boy lay in his bunk, which felt clammy and smelled of mildew, he realized that the numbing loneliness had left him. MacWinter had made him feel uncertain, angry and a good many other things, but at some point during their conversation, the loneliness had evaporated. It might come again, but he sensed it would never again be quite so bad. He was going to be all right in America. He would do well, his father and uncle could be proud. Most important, he himself would take pride in his person and acts.

"You will have," his father had pointed out, "a chance to found your own line of the Maxwell family in a new country. It can be as important as you care to make it. Remember from the very beginning that you won't be building just for yourself, but for your sons and their sons as well. Keep in mind always that the future is a great deal more than just tomorrow."

It was strange to Angus, the thought that he would some day be someone's father. It would come, though, and he would make a place in this new country that any son would be proud to try to fill. The Maxwell name would always be something to be reckoned with; he'd see to that. As for this "all men are equal" nonsense, there was as much difference between a Maxwell and a MacWinter, wherever they were, as between daylight and dark. It would be amusing if this Gavin were to end by coming to him one day, to ask for work in his uncle's—his—company. That prospect made Angus smile and relax, and soon he began to doze. One day, the company title would read *Maitland and Maxwell*, or perhaps *Maxwell and Maitland*. This Gavin, who tried to seem so proud and sure of himself and his equality, would never have his name, nor his son's, as part of the title of anything.

1844

Looking back later, Gavin saw that it had been an unusual day, right from the beginning. For one thing, the air was very still in the semi-desert valley, which was naturally a windy country. It was spring, and normally sparse plant life was lush and at the height of its reproductive cycle. Along the stream called the Rio del Oso, willows and cottonwoods were not yet in full leaf and their pollen filled the air. There was a fresh smell from new grass and a sweet, poignant one from wild flowers. Insects were busy and plentiful. Birds' eggs were hatching and the harried new parents were frenetically active. Spring lambs, calves, colts were ebullient under the strong, bright morning sun.

"If you want to stay and work here," old Diego Echavarren had told Gavin, "go to the main house in the morning and see Don Francisco. He wants to see any stranger who asks for work on the hacienda, and he may be interested in you because you are a foreigner. I think he will let you have the job. We need another man with the livestock, especially with the sheep, now that it is almost time to take them to summer pasture. Our young men here are not so interested. Even my own sons don't want to do this kind of work."

Gavin smiled faintly as he rode slowly through the growing heat. He, too, had not wanted to do this kind of work with his own father back in Scotland. In the past six years, he had done many kinds of work and had seen a great deal of the United States. He had found an enclave of Scots in the southern Appalachians and had stayed there for some time, but the life of a hill farmer was not what he sought. He moved on west and ultimately worked as a freighter along the Santa Fe Trail. The first time he had come into this harsh, beautiful mountain country, he had wanted to stay, to settle down at last. The land had a vivid personality, a quiet, aged and ageless indifference and attraction. Gavin set about trying to learn Spanish in preparation for staying, though he made two more trips back east. This year, on his arrival in Santa Fe, he had found that an extra man was needed to help get a small herd of cattle north, to the hacienda of Don Francisco Arragon.

They came north from Santa Fe, into the big, semi-arid valley called the San Luis, which held the head-waters of the Rio Grande, and Gavin felt, strangely, happily, that he was coming home. They left the main stream and followed up El Rio del Oso toward the great western range of mountains, along whose peaks lay the divide of this great continent. Gavin knew he must stay here.

The Hacienda de Nuestra Señora de las Montañas had its main house on a heavy swell of ground where the great valley rose up to the western mountains. The house looked more like a fortress from the outside, and indeed it had been used as a fortress at times during the past hundred and fifty years. Below the hill on which the house stood was the mission church of Santa Filomina and a scatter of houses and shops that were the heart of the hacienda's life. Three miles to the east lay the little village of Quintana.

The tiled roof of the great house shone in the sun; the adobe walls were two feet thick. From the front, the place seemed closed and deserted. The great doors, through which a carriage could pass to the main court-yard, were closed and brooding. There were only deep slits for windows, and they were blind and silent. The slope below the front of the house was covered with various weeds and grasses, flourishing briefly with the spring, and dotted with cactus.

Gavin knew enough not to approach his business from the front of the house. Swinging wide of it, he rode toward the rear, where he found a different world. The slope at the back was terraced, watered by a little stream that came out of the house itself, and it supported a large vegetable garden and orchard. Below, in the shallow valley beneath the great brooding mountains, were the hacienda's hay and grain fields, irrigated by the Oso. Summer pasture for the sheep and cattle lay well into the mountains, in meadows where the snow-melt was only now ending. The peaks both to west and east, were still white with snow, brilliant in the morning sun.

Gavin was casually passed from servant to servant deeper into the house, until he stood in the large central courtyard. "You must see Señor Alfonso," a boy had told him importantly. "He is the one who will say if you can see the *patroń*. I will find him and tell him you're waiting."

Gavin waited. In the center of the courtyard the little stream's source, an artesian well, bubbled up into a stone-lined pool where a great willow tree grew, its top reaching high above the surrounding roofs. The court was paved with reddish flagstones and surrounded by shadowed galleries, which opened into still more shadowed rooms and passages. Vines climbed luxuriantly on the galleries' columns; flowering shrubs flourished in large, ornate clay pots; caged birds sang and flirted their feathers.

He did not see the girl sitting in the shade of a gallery. But she, holding her piece of delicate embroidery work, watched him enjoying the patio.

"You wanted something, señor?" she asked softly as he walked slowly round till only a few yards separated them.

Gavin couldn't suppress a slight start. "I'm here to see the *patroń*," he said hesitantly, aware that his Spanish was not very good.

"I think my uncle is not back yet," she said. "He went out to ride over the fields. You are new here."

"I can come back another time," he said. "I want to work on the hacienda."

"What kind of work?"

"I am a shepherd."

She said, smiling happily, "Oh, this is not where a shepherd should wait to ask for work. Señor Alfonso, the *mayordomo*, will be upset about it. When he comes, let him think you are someone more important than a shepherd."

"I think I should leave and begin all over," Gavin said uneasily.

As his eyes adjusted from the outer brightness, he saw that she was very pretty and very young. She had a fair-skinned oval face, a mass of shining black hair down her back, beautifully delicate hands which relaxed on the embroidery work in her lap, and great, mischievous dark eyes looking at him quite candidly. She was small and perfect, her smile ingenuous.

"Don't go, please, until you tell me where you learned to speak Spanish so very badly."

Gavin, feeling big and clumsy and awkward, flushed and looked at the ground.

"Forgive me," she said contritely. "I didn't mean it rudely. They always tell me I'm too forward and outspoken. If you sit down and talk with me, Alfonso won't know you're only a shepherd. He won't be upset, and my uncle should be back soon. I think you are English."

Gavin admitted it reluctantly, not knowing, in Spanish, how to differentiate between Englishmen and Scots. To his surprise, relief and embarrassment, the girl switched to a charmingly accented English.

"My mother's father was an Englishman. She taught me the language just for fun. My name is Maria."

He told her his name and, feeling very clumsy, sat down.

"I myself was new here last year," she told him placidly. "My father was much younger than Uncle Francisco, who is his half brother. He lived in Spain, my father, from the time he was a little boy. He married there, and I am the only child. My mother died five years ago, and two years ago, my father. Uncle Francisco is known, even in Spain, for his generosity and graciousness to poor relatives; so, when I finished my schooling with the sisters, it was agreed that I should come here. You have been looking startled since I first spoke to you. Why is that?"

Gavin blurted, "I thought Spanish girls were so carefully watched over and shy and . . ."

She laughed softly, delightedly. "You are right, of course, and Rosa will be here any moment. She will be shocked that we are talking together, though not as shocked as another *dueña* might be because Rosa is so used to me. My father gave me more freedom than most girls have, and my uncle is very tolerant. How do you come to be here?"

Gavin told her, in more detail than he had meant to use. All at once, he found he liked talking to her. He ended by saying, "I like the country around here. It's better than all the rest of the United States I've seen."

"But this is not the United States," she pointed out soberly. "This is Spanish territory. The Arragon family holds this great hacienda as a land grant from the king of Spain, made more than a hundred and fifty years ago."

"Someday I think this may be part of the United States," he said slowly. "There is such a great need—a kind of madness—for expansion in Americans."

"I don't know much about the United States," said Maria, cutting a thread with tiny scissors and going on with her work, "but I think the country here will always be Spanish. It *feels* Spanish, and very old, not new and raw and brawling the way I've heard it is in the United States. I like it here too, very much. People told me I would be unhappy with such a provincial life, but I am not."

An old woman came scurrying from the mouth of a dim passage, chattering Spanish like an angry, frightened bird. Maria said to her calmly, "This man is Mr. MacWinter. He speaks very little Spanish and he is waiting to see my uncle. It's all right, Rosa. He's only been here a moment."

Glaring, dubious, Rosa sat down protectively close

to the girl. Gavin again felt awkward and constrained.

Maria said easily in English, "Most men who are shepherds have not traveled about the world as you have, I think. Why are you only a shepherd?"

"There's nought wrong with being a shepherd," he said defensively. "It's a job that needs filling here and I can do it. I want to stay and it's one way I can earn my living. The reason I decided to leave Scotland for good was this very thing—people classifying each other: a shepherd, a cobbler, a fine gentleman, a servant—like that—and believing a man can be nothing more nor less than what his father was born to. I don't like that; it's wrong. I'm as much of a man—a human being—as the man who owns this hacienda." Gavin had grown very intense, almost forgetting Rosa, and Maria thought him very handsome. He asked earnestly, "Do you understand what I'm trying to say?"

"I think I do," she said soberly. "It's the way I've heard they think in the United States, but I've told you, this is not the United States. My uncle is a kind, just, fair man, but he hasn't much liking for the Americans. I think you should only ask him about the work and not tell him about these—ideas."

Rosa was tugging at Maria's sleeve, trying urgently to find out what was being said. Her duty as a proper chaperon was sorely frustrated when the young people spoke in a language she could not understand. Patiently, Maria gave her a summary of the conversation. Rosa disapproved and stared menacingly at Gavin.

Using English again, Maria said to him earnestly, "What you are saying, that people are all the same underneath, is something like what I have heard Father Gomez say. He is a young, new priest at Santa Filomina, our little church in the valley. I have heard him talking with my uncle, saying that *peones* and *patrones* are the same in the sight of God. I think maybe they are, for God, but for my Uncle Francisco, they are not. You must take care what you say to him. It's a good thing your Spanish is no better, I think. If you do a good job, whatever your work, it won't matter to him that you have these thoughts, once you have been here a while. I can see you don't like what I am saying. I think your pride and your tongue have made trouble for you before. If you like it here, then wouldn't it be worth *not* saying certain things?"

Gavin smiled, shy again. "I suppose I could hold my tongue, but you see, I like the idea of freedom of speech too."

"Everyone can have free speech in his own mind," she said nodding. "Sometimes, on the outside, he must give in a little to the people he is living with. Are you Catholic?"

"No."

"What, then?"

"My people are Presbyterian. I've not been inside any church for a long time."

"What is Presbyterian?"

"Ah, it's just—another kind of religion." He sensed she would not like his views on religion at all and managed to keep them to himself.

"Maybe you will be converted if you stay here. The Church is very important to us; it's a part of everything. I could never marry someone who wasn't Catholic."

He was startled. Her dark eyes twinkled at him.

"I don't mean you," she said calmly. "It's just that marriage is something I must think of. I don't want to be just the poor orphaned niece and cousin here for the rest of my life, a maiden lady. I could never be worthy enough to take vows, so marriage is all that's left to me, and it's often on my mind, as you can imagine. I'm seventeen. My mother was married two years when she was my age. Even in the kind of world you say you want, women are not as free and equal as men, are they?"

Taking his agreement with this for granted, she

turned to Rosa and said blithely, "We are talking about the church."

Trying to follow her lead, Gavin said, with more ease than he felt, "But you'd never marry a shepherd?"

"I might," she said casually, smiling. "I am neither *peon* or *patroń* here, you see. There are very few men of my station."

"You could never do it," he said teasingly. "A shepherd's wife must cook, keep her own house . . ."

"And be a mother many times over," she said calmly. "I can do those things; I want to do them. Learning to cook and keep house was part of my education at the convent. My uncle is not so generous that he expects every poor relative will lead as easy a life as he or his children."

"He'd let you marry a shepherd or—the likes of that?" Gavin was incredulous.

"He might, if there was no one else. Now you sound as if you are putting people in classes." Her voice was vibrant, her eyes sparkled with laughter. "And would you become a Catholic, if there was no other way? The priests here have always been good at converting heathen."

Gavin felt his cheeks flushing. She was far better at her casual game—at what must surely *be* a game—than he was. He said lamely, "I might—later—if there was no other way. But this is no way to talk, lass."

"What is *lass*?" she asked softly.

"It's only—the same as girl."

"I like it better," she said candidly. "For someone who wants to believe that people are all the same, you seem to me very shy. You must not be upset, though. We are only talking about—what is the word?—possibilities?"

Gavin nodded gravely, his face still more ruddy than was normal. "All right," he said defiantly, "suppose there is the possibility that I'd want to talk with you again, some other time? Would your uncle allow it?"

"I think he would," she said quietly, "if Rosa is with us, of course. I usually sit here about this time of day when the weather is warm. Oh, there is Alfonso. I think you shouldn't let him or my uncle hear much of your Spanish. It will probably improve in time. Father Gomez speaks some English; enough, I'm sure, so that you could take instruction—if you ever wanted to."

She gestured to Alfonso, who was just coming into the court from the opposite gallery. Gavin stood up, feeling a little bewildered.

She said softly, pensively, "*I* am very proud—and strong-willed."

"Aye," he said dryly, grimly, "I'd never doubt that." And suddenly they were both laughing.

Maria said relentlessly, "You are a handsome man when you laugh, almost as handsome as when you blush. Would you treat a wife like one of your sheep?"

"I'd try to see to it," he said sternly, "that my wife kept a civil tongue in her head."

Her light, soft laugh followed him across the court, and she turned to explain to the outraged Rosa. Gavin thought confusedly, But *was* she teasing? What an unusual, irritating, beautiful girl. I've scarcely ever felt so stupid. It would surely be best if I never saw her again. Still, on the other hand . . .

1855

Angus Maxwell looked for his mother's letter among a case of papers. His business in New York was all but finished. If the ship she had mentioned was scheduled to dock before he left, he would do as she had asked. It was a good feeling to be able to do something that pleased his mother. In his seventeen years in America, Angus's mother was the one person in Scotland that he still missed. He knew that the greater part of a man's filial respect was due his father, that a father as knowledgeable, sensible, and respected as the Earl of Brendeen deserved a great deal, even from a fourth son, even—Angus couldn't help thinking—from a kind of outcast. It was his father who had accepted his Uncle Philip's offer, had seen where Angus's best interests lay. Of course he had been right. Angus only hoped that when he had children of his own, he might be as wise and objective. But still it was his mother who stayed in his memory, bringing to it some slight warmth.

Angus had finished an adequate education under his uncle's guidance, working holidays in the business, and the Maitland Company had continued to prosper. In addition to the mining interests, they now had a fine steel mill in Pittsburgh. It was not one of the larger mills, but one noticed by people in the industry. Angus had been full-time in the business for almost nine years, and he was, for all practical purposes, running things. His uncle was not well; and his cousin, Philip II, thirteen years older than Angus and with two almost grown sons of his own, had no interest in the business, aside from collecting dividends. The elder Philip had had papers drawn that would, on his death, give Angus a concrete share in the company, though at present he drew only a salary. Angus had thought of it as his company for years. He did not expect that his uncle would leave him a very large share and he wished he could lay his hands on a great amount of capital, feeling certain that the second Philip could be easily persuaded to sell him a larger percentage of the business. Angus had so many new things—ways of keeping down costs, expansions—in mind.

During his stay in New York, Angus had met a man called Frank Fitzroy, a common, crude sort for whom he had no liking, but whose thinking on matters of business ran in the same direction as Angus's own. Fitzroy was very nearly rabid on the subject of railroads, and he knew a great deal about their construction and operation. Angus, of course, had not simply taken the man's own word concerning his knowledge. He had verification of it from men he trusted far more than he would trust Fitzroy. The man had no money of his own, though he asserted he would have it after the war between the states, which so many people, including Angus, already considered a foregone conclusion. Fitzroy would be worth a sizable salary, should the Maitland Company expand into railroading. Angus was slightly repelled, and at the same time attracted, by the man's practical, outspoken views on business matters generally.

"A man invests his money to make more money," Fitzroy had said during their first talk. "Why else would he do it—invest and take risks and all such as that? There's no use mealymouthin' a lot of morals. Men are in whatever business they're in because they want to make a profit. Me, I'm gittin' into shippin' right now. That and railroads will be big returners when the politicians and the real big-money boys decide it's time to fight this war that's supposed to be over slavery. An' steel'll be another big winner: guns, ammunition, rails. If I had all the money I mean to have, I'd invest some in steel. Can't do it, though, not now. I'm already spread too thin."

Angus and his uncle agreed that there should be a certain decorum in business matters, a kind of surface philanthropic attitude. Fitzroy called this hypocrisy or worse. Both attitudes accomplished the same ends ultimately, but having a man like Fitzroy in one's employ might mean accomplishing those ends much more quickly, while staying true to one's own personal code.

The company had almost become Angus's entire life. It was in his thoughts waking or sleeping. He had already seen satisfactory growth under his management and he would see a great deal more, particularly if this war materialized. Someday, he would have to make a proper marriage so that there would be a son to carry on, a fine son to be proud of, one who would be of the same mind as his father. A man with any foresight could not ignore his own mortality; he must be aware, as Angus's own father had said, that the future includes more than just tomorrow. But there was plenty of time for marriage and children; he was only twenty-nine. He planned to be directing the company before many more years. A wife, if she were anything like the pushy, frivolous wife of the second Philip, would not be an asset. Angus determined that he would never get involved with a woman like that. All he would ask from a wife was some capital, children and to be left alone to do his work in peace. A wife was, of course, the simple, plausible answer to his need for money. Marriage, when it came, would be a union of mutual benefit. That was the only sort of alliance that was sensible. It was the basis of his parents' marriage, of his aunt and uncle's. If he could perform his duties to wife and children as well as his own father had done, surely no one would have grounds for complaint.

Angus thought again of his mother, of how her eyes had been red-rimmed from weeping from the time when the earl had received Uncle Philip's letter to the day when Angus had actually sailed for New York. She still wrote him several times a year, and though he was a little remiss in answering those letters, he was glad of them. Someday, if the pressures of the business should allow, he might go back again, to London, or even to Brendeen. Perhaps, when he had a son . . .

Angus found the letter he had been searching for and verified the name of the ship, the *Atlantis*. She was on the boards as due to arrive today. He left his hotel and found a cab.

His mother had written, "You remember Colin MacWinter, your father's chief shepherd at Brendeen? He was ill for some time, and his son, another Colin, took over the job. The elder Colin died last spring and the family has decided that Mary, the mother, and Annie, the youngest child, should go to America to live with the second son Gavin. Mary is very uneasy about the trip, as well she may be. It seems that besides the voyage, they must travel over a great part of the continent to reach Gavin's home in what Mary tells me was, until recently, Spanish territory. Gavin married a Spanish woman some years ago and has a number of children. Mary has decided to go because Gavin has written her that so many things are different where he lives and that his young sister stands a far better chance of making a good marriage there. Gavin must, I think, have gone to America about the same time you did. I fear he is building his poor old mother's hopes up out of all proportion. Certainly you have not led us to believe things are so drastically different in the United States. I write you all this because you said in your last letter that you expect to be in New York for a part of February and March. You have no reason to remember, but I was always fond of the MacWinter family, most particularly of Mary. She is a good, honest, hardworking woman who, while knowing her place and keeping it, shows her own sort of pride, personality and initiative. If you should be in New York when the *Atlantis* arrives, perhaps you might spare the time to help them make their way from the ship to whatever conveyance the next stage of their journey may entail. I'm sure it would be a relief and comfort to poor Mary to have someone from Brendeen, and of our family, to see them on their way."

Riding through the bustling traffic and the raw, bleak March day, Angus recalled that he and Gavin MacWinter had met on the *Maid of Liverpool* when he had come to America. The memory was slightly embarrassing, for it had been he who sought their conversation. He had been so young then, and experiencing more loneliness than he had known could exist. Still, he should have been able to find appropriate company among the passengers, or to get through the bad time in solitude. Angus recalled dimly that on the ship Gavin had been cool and offhanded, almost condescending to him, the earl's son.

Though it was rather a nuisance, Angus liked the idea that Lady Catherine had made this request of him. No doubt Mary MacWinter and her young daughter would travel as far as they could by rail before taking to coaches. He fervently hoped these arrangements had already been made in detail so that he need become no more involved than seeing them safely and quickly from one means of transportation to another. In two or three days, he would be ready to return to Pittsburgh, and his mind was filled with present business and future plans.

"Mary MacWinter," said the first harried steward he questioned, "—is she a first-class passenger?"

"I would hardly think so," replied Angus coldly. A number of people had already left the ship. Perhaps he had missed them.

"Then you might ask Arthur, the one just coming on deck there. My work is among first class."

Arthur was a much younger man, with an eye for a pretty face. His tired, determined smile vanished for a moment, out of respect for the old lady.

"Oh, yes sir, I do know who you mean, and I'm very glad someone's come, for Miss Annie's sake. She said there would be no one. You see, Mrs. MacWinter died at sea, poor soul. We buried her on the sixth day out—a brain seizure, the doctor said. One minute she seemed well enough and the next she was gone. It was almost that fast, and the young lady's all alone. She's still below. A Mrs. Foster has kept her company, you might say, since the mother died, and she's helped to care for Mrs. Foster's children."

Angus scowled and wondered what he was getting into. No one had mentioned the girl's age. Would she be able to fend for herself on the rest of the journey? Of course she would; she'd have to. There was no help for it.

He was somewhat surprised and more uneasy when he saw the girl. She was small and rather fragile-looking, with a narrow, piquant face, very pale now and drawn, but quite pretty. A mass of light brown hair was in braids round her head. Her blue eyes were large, wistful and sad. Her figure was, very nicely, a woman's, though she seemed a child.

"Oh, thank you for coming, my lord," she said fervently in her pleasant little voice. "Lady Catherine told my mother she'd be writing, but we never expected you'd find the time to do this."

"I'm very sorry to hear about your mother," Angus said stiffly. "Have you considered that, with these circumstances, the best thing might be for you to go back to Brendeen?"

"Oh, sir, I couldn't!" she said, looking frightened. "My mother wanted us to go to Gavin. There are already so many MacWinters at Brendeen. I couldn't go back. I have no money for that."

"Do you realize, young woman, how much of a journey is yet before you?"

Angus himself had no real concept of the distance at

that time. His knowledge of the country extended to little west of the Mississippi.

"I have a letter from my brother," Annie said determinedly. "He tried to write us about everything on the trip. I was a tiny bairn when he left home and I don't remember him at all, but I'm sure he's a fine man. He planned everything for us and sent money and tickets."

She searched for something in a small bag. Her speech, the heavy burr of Brendeen, was pleasant to hear again. It brought Angus the unusual feeling of nostalgia in the midst of his irritation that her presence might involve more than he had bargained for.

She said, "Here it is, my lord, my brother's letter."

"There's no need for me to read your personal letters, and you needn't call me 'my lord.' "

She nodded. "We always called all Lady Catherine's children and grandchildren lord and lady. It will be hard not to, but Gavin wrote that there are no lords and ladies in America."

"And how were you to go on with your journey from here?" asked Angus.

"It's all in the letter, my—Mr. Maxwell. Please do read it. Gavin wouldn't mind, and I know you'll understand far better than I do, how I'm to go about what comes next."

He saw that her baggage was collected, then found that the train she was to take was not due until the next morning. With poor grace, he asked about a room for her at his hotel. No doubt this would make a theme for gossip among the hotel's staff for weeks. He was doubly irritated when the vacant room proved to be across the hall from his own two-room suite. He had had in mind something in the vicinity of his manservant's room, but decided that to point this out would be tantamount to denying something that had never been true in the first place.

As the luggage was being brought up, he said stiffly, "You haven't a great deal of luggage, considering the move you're making. I'm sure half of it must be your mother's, though. You'd do well to get rid of the extra. It would mean less for you to see to on the rest of the trip."

"Ah, no, I couldn't," she breathed, appalled but apologetic. "I *want* to have her things, the few clothes and all. Most of this is household goods we were bringing for me, for the time when I'll marry—things like blankets that my mother made herself, from the wool of Brendeen sheep."

"How old are you?" he asked awkwardly. The hotel servant had finished with the baggage and they stood alone in the corridor, near the open door to her room.

"I'll be seventeen soon," she said; then worriedly, "I mustn't take more of your time, Mr. Maxwell. I'll go in now. You're so very kind, but I *will* pay for the room. I've the money for it. You saw in my brother's letter where he said we might have to wait over at several places."

"And what would you have done if I hadn't come to the ship?" The question sounded almost threatening.

Annie's eyes were suddenly filmed with tears, but she did not lower her head or look away. "I was just helping Mrs. Foster get together the last of her things, and the children's, when you came. Then I was going to see to my own things and find a kind-looking person to ask for directions. But I'm so glad you did come. You see, I've never been all on my own or away from home before. I know my mother watches over me from heaven. Perhaps she had to do with your coming, if you'll pardon my saying so, sir. My mother was such a kind, good—" She choked and could not go on.

"Mmm, yes," said Angus, embarrassed. "Get some rest now—or something. I've work to do. I'll see you have some supper when it's time."

Angus forgot Annie MacWinter immediately, immersing himself in the study of some reports. Eventually, Tuttle, the old valet, came to ask his intentions concerning supper.

"Oh, and, Tuttle," Angus remembered as the man was leaving, "see that something is sent up to the young woman's room."

When the waiter brought his tray, Tuttle was still not back, so Angus answered the door himself. Across the hall young Annie had also come to receive her supper tray. She looked small, sad and alone, though she tried for a brave smile. Taking the covers from dishes, Angus thought, Why not? This is not Brendeen, after all, and it wouldn't be as if I were spoiling the girl, giving her false notions of herself. I'll never see her again after tomorrow. She tries to put a good face on things, but underneath she must be very frightened and lonely.

Tuttle returned just then, and Angus asked him to go and ask if Annie would like to take her supper in his sitting room.

She came in a bit reluctantly, as Tuttle brought her tray. Her flushed, diffident face said as clearly as any words that she had never dreamed the day might come when she would sit down to a meal with the earl's son, and that she hadn't known how to refuse what seemed like presumptuousness on her part. She had, after all, seen Lady Catherine take tea with her mother in their cottage on several occasions; and Gavin had stressed, in each of his rare letters, that almost everything in the United States was different from what they were used to at home. She was more than a little in awe of this man, though. He seemed so chilly, so certain of himself and of everything he said or did.

Angus was preoccupied, applying ideas from his afternoon's reading to his own business affairs. He was all but oblivious to the food he ate. They talked scarcely at all. Annie's entire body was stiff with self-consciousness. She ate little and was seeking the best and most polite words with which to excuse herself when Tuttle returned with the newspapers Angus had sent for, and with a letter.

"This just arrived for you, sir. I believe it came on the same ship as the young lady. I'll go and have my supper now, sir, if there's nothing more?"

Angus nodded, glancing absently at the letter. Tuttle had closed the door before the letter abruptly demanded Angus's attention. It was from Angus's sister Hope. Except for an occasional brief note added to his mother's letters, none of the other family members had written him before. And why had this letter been sent here, to the New York hotel, rather than to his regular address in Pittsburgh? Apprehensive with premonition, Angus opened the letter, his fingers gone cold.

After waiting a long while, casting frightened glances at his changing face, Annie said faintly, "Sir? Has something very terrible happened?"

Angus started. He had forgot her presence. "My—my mother has died," he said, still unable to take it in. "It was very sudden, a severe lung fever. There was just time for them to get me word by the *Atlantis*. They've sent another letter on to Pittsburgh, in case I missed this one."

"Oh, Lady Catherine!" breathed Annie. "I'm sorry, so very sorry."

Still holding the letter, Angus got up and went to the window. A dismal drizzle had begun, winter ungraciously giving way to spring. Annie stood tensely, biting her lip, trying to find the right thing to do or say. He was not the icy person she had believed. She had seen the expressions of hurt and sadness on his face. He was unaware of her again, would not want her presence. Still, she could not just slip away; that seemed too impolite, too unfeeling. Her eyes filled with tears as she remembered all too clearly her own mother's death—the numbing, confusing shock of its suddenness.

She said diffidently, stammering, "I thank you for asking me to have my supper here, Mr. Maxwell. It's always good not to be alone. I'll go now, sir, and I'm truly sorry. Many and many loved Lady Catherine."

Angus gave no immediate indication he had heard. When she reached the door, she looked back. He had turned from the window, still seeming dazed. She was sure the light glinted on tears in his eyes. Annie went out, closing the door without a sound.

Angus could not think why the news was so hard for him. His mother was not a young woman, had not been young for many years. Death was bound to come. She would have been buried several days ago. Hope had written that she had asked to be buried at Brendeen. After a long time of standing at the window, seeing nothing, thinking little, Angus went back to his papers, but he could muster no concentration.

A hotel waiter came to collect the supper things. Angus was too abstracted to wonder what conclusions the man might draw from the fact that the young woman's tray was here with his own. Tuttle returned and was dismissed for the night.

Angus stood again at the window for a long while. It seemed that all that was warm, good, worth remembering about his childhood and Brendeen was gone with his mother. It was like having a part of himself unexpectedly and mercilessly pruned away, as if now he had no past before his twelfth year.

Finally, he turned and began automatically to gather the papers and put them away. He would not be capable of any more work tonight. Perhaps he could sleep. He went into the bedroom, changed into his nightshirt, then, without remembering the movements, found himself once more at the sitting room window.

A crushing sadness and loneliness had begun to burn through the initial half stupor. He had known some such intense feelings once before, during the days of his voyage to America. He had worked hard to forget that uncertainty, fear, resentment, aloneness, desolation; had refused to admit, once the worst was past, how strong those feelings had been. Those had been the baseless feelings, apprehensions of a child. Now, with childhood so far behind him, with his last link to it lying in the sparse, grudging Highland soil, those weak, juvenile emotions were all but overwhelming him. Now, he knew, he would never go home again. Perhaps he never would have anyway, but it had been a thing he thought of sometimes, with a little pleasure and anticipation. With his mother gone, his entire reason for looking forward to a return disappeared. He had loved his mother. There had been respect for his father, fear, some desire to emulate the man. There had been toleration, fondness for his brothers and sisters because they had, by accidents of fate, been born into the same family. There had been respect and admiration for his uncle, and gratitude—though Philip had always looked on him as just another kind of investment, and he was certainly getting a sizable return on his capital. . . . But there had been love for his mother, and he knew there was not likely to be love again, for loving was a risk, the exposure of too many vulnerabilities. Surely one was better without it.

To know he was utterly alone was the worst of his feelings now, as it had been on the ship so long ago. Sometimes this solitude could make him feel very strong, very sure and capable; but now it was suffocating, awesome in its power to wipe out everything else.

He remembered that there was a bottle of whiskey in the cupboard. He had had a cold when he arrived here and had bought it for that reason. He was not a drinking man and considered those in any degree dependent on alcohol weak and ineffectual. Tonight, he tried to shrug away his prejudices. Whiskey was good for medicinal purposes. Tonight he sorely needed its propensity for dimming feelings, for casting everything temporarily in a haze of tolerability, or better yet, oblivion.

Much later, there was a knock at his door. Tuttle, he supposed foggily. Good. On this one occasion of a lifetime, he just might send the man out for another bottle.

"I—I could see your light under the door," stammered Annie. "I was—worried about you."

Angus had stepped back from the door on opening it, feeling sure Tuttle would be standing there. Annie could hear voices and laughter down the hall. She knew that people would be passing by in a moment, and Mr. Maxwell seemed not to be aware that he was standing there in a nightshirt, where he would be plainly visible from the hall. Trying to pretend that she, too, did not notice, Annie stepped timidly in and pushed the door shut until the people should have passed.

"You were worried?" Angus was saying thickly, musingly. "About me? Why was that?"

She knew now that he had been drinking, a good deal, by the look of it, but that only made her feel more empathy, more concern. Some might think, from the cold brusque dourness of him that he was a little less human than others, but that was not so. He had loved his mother. Even though he hadn't seen her for so many years, her death had been a terrible blow.

Annie's eyes filled with tears as she answered him unevenly, "Because I know how it feels when your mother dies."

A flood of new feelings swept over Angus; gratitude was uppermost among them. He was not wholly alone this time after all. He took three quick, unsteady steps, and the girl was in his arms.

Angus very soon came to think of the period that followed as his thirty hours of madness. Annie MacWinter arrived from Scotland on a Tuesday. That night they comforted each other. She was sweet, concerned, caring. When he, giddy with whiskey and her tender nearness, took her hand and led her to the bedroom, her shock and fear were short-lived. She gave in first with acquiescence, then with what seemed real pleasure. She was a virgin, modest and shy, but without real fear.

Angus woke early the next morning, his head all but splitting. The girl was there beside him. His memory of the night was not altogether clear. He went into the sitting room and finished the whiskey. As soon as Tuttle appeared, he sent him out for more. Annie, when she woke, was painfully shy and self-effacing.

"I'll go back to my room now," she whispered, barely audibly. "It will soon be time for my train."

"No," said Angus, his first word of the morning to her. "You won't leave today. We'll be married."

"Oh, Mr. Maxwell!" she gasped in horror, flushing more deeply. "Such a thing never entered my mind. You're the laird's son and I'm—I'm nobody."

Angus had known then he was being foolish, endangering everything he had intended for his life, but his sense of morals, of the propriety of things was very strong. She was a good, sweet girl, and he would be in the wrong if he did not marry her.

On the next morning, Thursday, he woke again to her presence, knew she was his lawful wife, found his folly and stupidity incredible. Of course he hadn't *had* to marry her. Whatever had possessed him? Physical lust, he answered himself grimly, and shuddered. To think that a man of his strength of character should give way to such an animal weakness. That was the folly, but the stupidity had been his insisting on marriage. He got quickly out of bed.

What was he going to do? he asked himself a little later, more calmly. How could he ever again begin to go about righting this disaster? He could never take a girl of Annie's station to Pittsburgh. The Maitlands, their friends, all his business acquaintances would be appalled, outraged, incredulous—as he was. Yet she was his responsibility now, not just someone his mother had mentioned, to whom he might be helpful in passing. She was his wife, an encumbrance—no, a millstone—an almost unbearable indication that he could still have moments of weakness, of insanity, forgetting all he had planned and worked for, willing to throw it all aside because of a pang of sorrow and loneliness and a whim of the flesh.

She could go on to her brother, he thought suddenly with a surge of partial relief. He would take her there. No one in the East need know. He would notify them in Pittsburgh that an emergency had come up, something having to do with his family. The trip was likely to take months. It would be particularly long at this time of year, with all the inconveniences of spring, but there was no help for that. He owed the girl something in consideration of what she had given up for him.

Passing through the bedroom, he could do no more than glance at her as she still slept. She was a good, sweet girl, but he resented her, even felt contempt and active dislike for her, as well as for himself. . . . Yes, he would see her safely to the far western territory where her brother lived, would see to it that she would be provided for. She would understand, would want to go to her brother. It had been she, after all, who had been shocked by the prospect of marriage. He would have no trouble forgetting her; it would be far easier than overlooking his own blind stupidity. He would go on, then, with his life as it had been, or as nearly as he could with this shameful, embarrassing, bitter secret always with him. It came to him that now he could never marry properly. He would never have a son to go on with the business. He rinsed his mouth and spat bitterness and defeat.

BOOK ONE
1870-1877

I

1870

"I don't want him—them here," said Gavin MacWinter, scowling. He was fifty now, his shoulders a little stooped, gray liberally streaking his sandy hair. His big hands were gnarled from years of work; his face was weathered and beginning to show deep lines. His blue eyes squinted a little at things close up. He had come into the house in mid-afternoon for a cup of tea because he was restless with worry and irritation.

"It can't harm any of us just to give them supper," said Maria reasonably.

She was mixing pastry to make meat pies and, as always, thought of Gavin's young sister Annie, who had taught her, years ago, how to prepare most of Gavin's favorite foods. During the years they had been married before Annie's coming, Gavin had mentioned, occasionally and with a wistful note, foods that had been familiar to him back in Scotland. When Maria had asked him how they were made, he hadn't really had the slightest idea. Since Annie's brief stay—she had been with them a few days less than a year when she died—their meals had been mixtures of the Spanish foods Maria liked and the generally blander, more ascetic diet Gavin preferred. Their children were bilingual—bicultural in their tastes for food as well as in language and everything else.

"You know how I feel about Angus Maxwell," Gavin said shortly, "because you feel the same. I didn't ask them here. I was *told* they'd come. I don't know any reason to expect we'll care any more for his wife than we do for him."

Gavin's speech still carried the strong burr of the Highlands, though it had been more than thirty years since he had seen Scotland. Maria had picked up some of the burr in the twenty-five years of their marriage and, combined with her Spanish accent, it made her English a bit unusual and very charming. When she was feeling any sort of deep emotion, and particularly when she was angry, arguing with her husband, she fell back on Spanish without thinking about it. Gavin still spoke Spanish rather badly, though he understood it well enough, and they would argue in their native tongues—she in Spanish, he in English—sometimes briefly and explosively, sometimes smolderingly, for days at a time. Still, they felt theirs was a good life, a good marriage; there was even a perverse enjoyment in the frequent arguments. They admired and respected one another, though it might not be immediately apparent to an outsider, and their love was a great, warm presence that filled their home and engulfed the children. They had shared a great deal and gradually made their own particular accommodations to the differences in their backgrounds and cultures, from which had come a mixed way of life peculiarly their own.

"I want to see what Angus's wife is like," said Maria, pouring boiling water into the teapot. "We'll never have another chance for that. Maybe you should try to forget about . . . Annie and that time, Gavin. Angus does come from your old home in Scotland, and you never see anyone else from there. Wasn't he the son of your *patroń* there?"

Gavin made an impatient gesture. "Not *patroń*, laird."

"Oh, aye," she said and made a flourishing, careless gesture of dismissal with the kettle.

"And laird or *patroń*," he said, unmollified, "I never lived with the foolish notion that I *belonged* to anyone, nor that if someone stood higher than me in some job or owned the land I worked on, it meant I had to like and respect him."

"Your father was his father's shepherd"—she couldn't resist the opportunity to tease him—"just as you are chief shepherd here on the hacienda."

"My father was willing to let himself be a servant to the laird. I'm my own man and no servant to your Uncle Francisco. Do you think he or your cousin Francisco have ever believed I'm that? Have *you?*"

She had returned to rolling the pastry dough, and she smiled fondly with her face turned from him. "No, Gavin. I think no one has ever believed he might own you. Years ago you told me you and Angus were on the same ship when you came to live in America. You have never talked about what he was like then. It must have been very hard for him, a little child, being sent so far from his home."

"He was not a little child. He was, I think, twelve or thirteen. I didn't see much of him on the ship, not that I recall, any more than I saw much of him when we were both living at Brendeen. I suppose it wasn't easy for him, coming to a new country, to people he didn't know, but I don't think anything's changed him in his whole life. He was set into his father's mold before he was born. You know he was sent here—back east, that is—because the earl's sister and her husband had only the one son, and they wanted a kind of business insurance, should anything happen to their own lad. He's not done badly for himself, if half what he'd have us believe is true."

"But think of him then," she said with compassion, "a boy, being used for business reasons. What cold people they must have been!"

"Aye, that they were, still are, and Angus the coldest fish among them."

"Annie certainly admired him," Maria said sadly; "she thought he'd done well."

"Och!" Gavin said angrily and his voice broke a little. "What could she know? Naught but a bairn herself, she was then."

"She was seventeen when she came over," Maria pointed out gently. "You've said he was only twelve."

Gavin frowned fiercely. "I was talking about a boy coming away from home. You're talking about a wee girl alone, whose mother had died on the ship, who was daft enough to marry someone without a moment's thought, someone who seems to have felt from the beginning that he was marrying far beneath himself, someone nearly twice the lass's age."

Maria poured out the tea. She didn't care much for tea, but would have a cup with him today. Gavin had gone to the little hotel in Quintana last night to talk with Angus Maxwell, and he had not yet told her much about their conversation. Maria knew something was worrying him greatly, that he would get around to telling her, but it seemed to be taking a long time and to be hard for him.

Gavin said fervently, "If only he hadn't been in New York when the ship docked. If only he hadn't heard from his mother that Ma and Annie were coming. If only Ma hadn't died on the voyage . . ."

"Gavin," she said with consternation, "I've never known you to say 'if only' so much. What's done is done, and if those things hadn't happened, we'd not have Thorne."

He looked away from her, his expression dark and

sad. Finally, he said, "I suppose, after all these years, I can see it was a thing that might happen to any man, being carried away by a pretty girl; but Angus, proud and haughty as he is, should have shown more self-control. He knew, if not from the very beginning, then certainly by the time they reached us here, that he'd made a terrible mistake, for himself and all his business plans. Our poor wee Annie was never the wife for him. In the few moments we saw them together more than fourteen years ago, in all she said afterward, it was clear the little mouse was awed, terrified by the man."

"I'm glad you managed to say so little of what you thought in front of your sister for the short time she was with us. She was such a dear, sweet, trusting little girl and she did admire him somehow. I think she always truly believed he'd come back someday for her and the baby."

"Bringing her here was the only kindness I've ever known him to perform," Gavin said wearily. "But she'd be living now if it weren't for Angus Maxwell. She hadn't got her strength back after the boy was born when the fever came on her. She'd be living, with a *good* husband and a fine lot of children."

Maria took one of the little cakes Jean and Meg had made before leaving the house, and bit into it pensively. She had grown plump with the years, but her figure was remarkably good for a woman who had borne twelve children. Very little gray showed in her black hair, and her dark eyes were still as quick and expressive as they had been on the first day Gavin had seen her. A few wrinkles lined her smooth face, but they were more from smiling than from sorrow. She had a great capacity for adjusting to circumstances, necessities, without losing any of her self, of what she was or had been. She never let Gavin forget that her father had been an Arragon and her mother had been of an equally aristocratic, though poorer family in

Spain. Yet, when they married, she had seemed to take easily and naturally to all the work of a wife and mother with no servants. Gavin looked on her lovingly now as she looked out the kitchen window.

Maria couldn't wait any longer. She had to know what the truth was, and if he didn't tell her soon, she knew, he might decide to try to keep it from her as long as possible. She said, trying to keep the tone casual, though her breath came hard, "Angus is here about Thorne, isn't he?"

"He is," Gavin said shortly, harshly, looking down at his hands. "You must have known that since we heard he had come yesterday."

"You've not told me anything that was said when you saw him last night," she said gently.

Gavin looked out across their vegetable garden to the sparse, dry pasture, where only a few lean cattle were looking for grass in the afternoon's blazing heat. His eyes moved on up to the near western mountains with their cool-looking cover of green. The sheep were there now, high up on their summer pasture, under the care of young men who worked under Gavin's guidance. If Angus Maxwell hadn't arrived in Quintana yesterday, Gavin would have been up on the slopes today, checking on the animals and the trustworthiness of the boys. Joe, Gavin and Maria's eldest son, now twenty-four and with his own family, was in charge. He was a fine, self-assured, deliberate young man, one of whose chief ambitions had always been to follow his father. It was the younger boys who concerned Gavin. No doubt he should leave it all to Joe, but he was far from ready to stop working, to stop having charge of things himself. Gavin was most interested, most curious to know what Thorne might be up to and how Joe might be handling him. He smiled a little, as he almost always did, over the boy's lively carelessness, but then his smile twisted into a frown of anger and helplessness. Thorne was not, after all, his and Maria's child, though they had considered him one of their own since Annie had died.

Gavin said abruptly to his wife, "Angus wants to see the lad. He's thinking of taking him away."

"Taking him away," she said slowly, painfully. "I knew it was bad when you came home looking so dour last night, but I didn't quite think it would be that."

"He's no right," Gavin said fiercely, then clenched the muscles of his jaws.

"What does he want Thorne to do?" She had to hear it all.

"Go to a school near where they live in Pittsburgh, then, if he pleases them, go on to college, take a share in all the businesses Angus has a hand in. His company is thinking of building a railroad up through the valley from Sante Fe and on to Denver. He's here looking over the country. Maybe we'd never have seen the man again if he hadn't had business so nearby. Maybe he'd have gone on with forgetting the lad was ever born. They're already working, I've heard, on lines to several of the new mining towns."

"We have no mines in our valley yet," Maria said absently.

"No, but some new people have come in, farming, since this became Colorado Territory. What we raise here could be used in Santa Fe, even more in Denver and those high mountain towns where most of the mines are."

"And what does Angus's wife say?" pursued Maria. "Has he just told the poor woman, after all these years, that he has a son? Elizabeth—that's her name, isn't it?"

"I have no notion what he's told her, lass. I didn't see the woman last night, when I was *sent* for. I suppose it's that Angus has given up on having children by her. He hinted that she's lost more than one, seemed to feel she did it on purpose, to make things difficult for him. He married her just a few months after our Annie died—the fine, proper wife with money to bring him. Now it seems that he's bitter over this marriage as well."

"I feel sorry for her," Maria said. "She couldn't have had a happy or easy life with him. He seems—or seemed to me the two times I've met him—to be bitter about a good many things, a hard, dour, driving man . . . but, Gavin, we have to think about this, about Thorne. Angus never agreed Thorne was to be ours—he never seemed to want to begin discussing it; but he hasn't completely ignored the boy. When he was here that time on business several years ago, you let him understand we didn't want his money for raising Thorne, but he did arrange to have the school and the teacher's house built in Quintana. He's paid Mr. Gaynor's salary all this time. I'd rather have seen our children have all their education from the church school, but Santa Filomina's is too poor to do a great deal, and the school at Quintana has been good for all the children here."

"I don't know why you think that is grounds for his expecting to take the boy now," Gavin said shortly, "for his just turning up one day when the lad's almost grown, and . . . I told him Thorne is happy here, that he wouldn't want to go."

"What did he say?"

"Nothing, just ignored everything but his own point. He's every bit as high-handed as the old earl ever was, fourth son though he may be."

"Does he mean to tell Thorne he's his father?"

"I think not."

"What other reason can he give?" she demanded. She went on without waiting for an answer: "It's a good thing we haven't completely deceived the boy. It would have been so easy to let him believe he was our child, instead of making up that story about his father's having died before he was born."

"But we've lied to him, all the same," Gavin said unhappily.

Maria poured him some more tea and he stared into the cup without seeing it. "At least, I suppose it was wrong of us to tell him his mother married a distant relation, but one of the MacWinter clan, just to keep the same name. We might have let him think his name was something else."

"And what good would that have been? Thorne would have wanted to know what his name was, if not MacWinter. Jose and Ian, Carmela and Jeannie all remember when Annie came to us, when Thorne was born. We went over it all so many times, Gavin, before deciding just what to do. If we had said his name was Maxwell, the older children would certainly have put things together—Thorne, too. You've just been talking about Angus's company moving nearer to us. Maxwell is a part of the company name. If Thorne had found out and Angus had never wanted to claim him, think how hurt and embarrassed he would have been."

"It mightn't have mattered to him," Gavin said. "You know our Thorne."

"I do," Maria said softly, smiling, "and maybe he wouldn't have cared, but we tried to think of him first when we were deciding how to handle it all those years ago, and I'm trying to think of him now, not just of how this makes us feel. He could have so many opportunities, Gavin—all the schooling, chances to know about so many more people and places. You know what Mr. Gaynor has always said about him."

"Aye, that he's a good mind if he cares to use it. But much of the time he doesn't seem to care to, and who's to say that's not his right?"

"Maybe it will be his right when he's a grown man, but he's not that yet, and it's up to us to think of what's best for him until he is."

"You're thinking of the Maxwell money now, isn't that it?" he snapped. He knew he was being unjust to her and that increased his anger. "You'd be willing to see the boy taken from here, from us and the children and all he knows, because he might—"

"Did I say that?" she demanded vehemently, her eyes sparkling. "Did I say anything that *sounded* like that? I tell you, I'm trying to think of Thorne. If Angus asked him and he were to choose—"

Gavin cut in tersely, "I don't think it's to be a matter of his choosing, not with Angus. Did we choose to raise the lad? I don't recall that we were ever asked any more than we were asked if Annie could live here after she was Angus's wife. I don't think she ever *chose* to marry. Where Angus is involved, it's always Angus who chooses. I think what he has in mind to do now is to take the boy—on trial, you might say—and it'll never matter to him what Thorne may want, nor anyone else."

"You really think he still won't let Thorne know he's his father?"

"Aye, I think he won't, not until he thinks he can know how the lad is going to turn out. That way, if he doesn't like what he has, he can drop him. He told me last night he wants to see Thorne, that they'd be coming here for supper. There was no invitation from me; you can count on that. It's likely Angus doubts that the lad, or any of us, has proper table manners. He said he's to go on up the valley tomorrow, to be back in a few days. He means to take Thorne away with them then."

Maria sighed, frowning. "You're right, he'll never go . . . unless we—"

"We'll have no part in forcing the boy," Gavin said hotly.

"No," she agreed. "Anyway, with that one, force is the last thing to be used. He's like the little fish the children try to catch in their hands. He can wriggle away from anything, and the tighter the trap, the faster he can get out of it." She smiled for a moment, thinking lovingly of the boy, then said thoughtfully, "Angus's wife, Elizabeth, must know. I think she doesn't usually make these trips with him. When he came here before, the time he decided to start the school, he'd never have mentioned her if I hadn't kept asking questions. I wonder what she can be like."

"Who gives a damn about that?" cried Gavin, exasperated.

Maria said, with gentleness he did not expect or want just now, "It's hard for me, Gavin, thinking we might have to give him up. I know it's worse for you. Thorne has always been your favorite."

He scowled, making a gesture of denial.

"Of course it's true," she said reasonably. "Children, like all other people, are different, and parents wouldn't be human if they didn't prefer some things about one above some things about others. The others are like you, or like me, or like us both. We can usually know something of what they will do or think. There's never been a way of predicting anything with Thorne. He can be so stubborn one moment, seem lazy and irritating, and the next be so agreeable, hard-working, sweet. I think we've both tried—we certainly should have—to give him a little more because he's not had his natural parents."

Gavin said thoughtfully, reluctantly, "I can see the old earl in him—and Angus. He looks nothing like them, but there's his determination—stubbornness—at times. There was nothing lovable, or even tolerable about his lordship's perverseness. He used to come home to Brendeen after being away months or even years, and overturn everything his people, stewards and such, had been working on, especially if they were good, sensible things. Thorne didn't get his willfulness from his poor mother, but it's of a different sort from the old earl's or Angus's. Ah, Maria, he's a fine lad—most of the time. At times I can't wait to see what he's going to do or say about a thing. He can be more aggravating than any of the others. There's no *making* him do anything, yet if it suits him, he'll do more. . . ."

"He can be so winning," she agreed, smiling. "He'll be a very appealing man."

"Not if Angus—" Gavin began. "I don't want the lad subjected to that man, and subjected is what it would be. Angus understands no other way. We should have tried harder—*I* should have—to see that there was a little more—bend to the boy. He goes his own way too much. The world won't be easy for him. Maybe he could adjust better if he hadn't been let to be so self-willed."

"They're all that," Maria pointed out. "I don't know how your children could be any other way."

"Aye," he said caustically, "*you're* such an even tempered biddable lass. They could have got none of it from you."

"I don't know anything about your Earl of Brendeen," she said coolly. "Thorne has always reminded me of you. I don't know how you think we could have brought him up any other way than we have done. He's been his own person from the time he was born. If you're thinking that Angus Maxwell would—well, break him—I don't think anyone can do that. Mr. Gaynor, poor man, tried very hard to make Thorne fit into some mold, and it certainly never got him anywhere."

"Claude Gaynor is a far cry from Angus Maxwell," Gavin said wearily. "But, aye, I am worried about the lad's being damaged. He's young yet, and things bother him sometimes, more than he cares to have anyone know. What's it going to do to him if he has to go away now, with no decent explanation? What are we to say to him if Angus refuses to tell him the truth?"

"I don't know," she said slowly. "I just don't know." After a silence, she went on almost absently, "You know, *querido*, I wasn't complaining when I said he's your favorite. I love him very much too."

Gavin tried to shake off some of his concern. "And which is your favorite?" he asked with a teasing, though wintry smile.

Maria drew herself up, her eyes widening indignantly. "I? *I* am a mother. Mothers have no such things as favorite children."

Gavin laughed briefly while she frowned at him. She went on with the main theme of her thoughts, choosing to ignore his lack of understanding. "I can't think what we're to do if Angus means to try to force him to leave here without knowing the truth. Even if he did know, there'd still be so much he can't understand yet. Maybe he'd blame us somehow."

Gavin got to his feet, unable to bear inactivity a moment longer. He had thought of all these things. His thoughts had run in sleepless circles all through the previous night.

"I'm going to see to mending the wool shed roof," he said curtly and was out the door in two strides, just as the four younger children came brawling in.

The children—Dougal, Carlos, Jesus and Laurie—had been playing in the shade of the cottonwoods along El Rio del Oso, and the two youngest were muddy to their knees.

"Ay, madre!" cried Maria with more irritation than was her wont. "Look at your clothes! Change them at once." She saw then that a finger of Laurie's, her *niñita* of four, was wrapped in a dirty rag with a spot of blood on it.

She scooped the little girl into her arms. "What happened, my baby?" Her voice was a tender croon. "Oh, tell Mama what has happened to the tiny finger."

Ranald MacWinter found his cousin Thorne sitting on the bank of the stream in the little side valley where Joe had sent him with part of the large flock of sheep.

Ranald said, without getting off his horse, "Jean and

Meg have come to get us. They'll be here in a minute, with Gordon. We're to go home."

"Why?" asked Thorne, who had looked up only briefly from his book. He was often too restless to be a good sheepherder, but today had been pleasant. The book had to do with pirates. He had borrowed it from Ranald, who'd got it from Mr. Gaynor's school library. In his enthusiasm for the story, Thorne had forgotten to have any lunch, had forgotten his charges, the sheep, for most of the day. He stood up now, remembering them. They were mostly resting in willow shade, and he could see only about half the number he was supposed to have, but he assumed the rest were there, concealed in shdaow. Even if he could have seen them all, he did not have that sixth sense that Joe and his Uncle Gavin shared, of knowing that all of his flock was there without counting them. Thorne simply assumed nothing was amiss and looked back at Ranald.

"A man called Angus Maxwell has come, with his wife. He's from Scotland, a long time back, one of the Earl of Brendeen's sons. The girls say he wants to meet all of us. I don't know exactly why. I guess because he used to know Papa and the family."

Ranald was a young image of Gavin, tall at fifteen, his fair skin burned and freckled by the sun, his sandy hair tousled. One might not have guessed the two boys were related, though they were rarely far apart. Thorne was dark-skinned, with black hair standing up crisply from a wide forehead. His eyes were of such a dark blue that they only showed their color by contrast with his thick, straight black lashes. His nose and chin were strong and determined, his mouth wide, rather full and petulant, redeemed by a captivating smile, with teeth very white against the dark skin. Ranald was a handsome boy. Thorne would have to grow up to the rugged good looks of his face.

"Come on," Ranald said. "We can all ride down together."

The others came up then, Ranald's older and younger sisters and Gordon Gaynor, the teacher's son, who was Ranald's friend and had spent last night with him at the sheep camp.

"Aren't you ready?" demanded Jean. She was eighteen, the promised bride of Porfirio Romero, the blacksmith's son, to be married in the fall. What she considered an enviable position had made Jean more imperious and demanding than ever with the younger children.

"I can't go just yet," Thorne said.

"Why not? Joe said you could. He's sending Juanito over to look after your sheep. Come *on!* Do you think you're Little Boy Blue, or what?"

"I have to wait for Folly," he said with a maddening refusal to be hurried.

"Folly! Well, call him, for goodness sake. If that stupid dog has wandered away somewhere, we're not about to wait until he decides to come back."

"He's just over there," Thorne said lazily, pointing to where the willows were thickest. He handed the book to Ranald and said casually, "Folly's with Patrona."

"Oh, God!" breathed Ranald.

"Well, *call* him," commanded Jean, exasperated. "And get ready to go. Don't just keep standing there. Meg and I have to get back. We can't wait for a dog to visit with his friends."

Thorne grinned at her, turned to go for his horse and said, without looking back, "They're not exactly just visiting. They're breeding."

Jean was momentarily taken aback. Gordon was embarrassed, his fair skin suffused with red. Meg put her hand to her mouth in a gesture of mock horror and to stifle a smile. Ranald was frankly frightened. They all moved their horses closer as Thorne began saddling his own.

"Thorne," Ranald said, "Joe will kill you. Patrona is Papa's best sheep dog . . ."

"It's not my fault," Thorne said calmly, "*or* Folly's. She came over here."

"Nobody wanted you to keep that dog," Meg pointed out. "Papa said Folly wouldn't be any good with sheep or for anything else, and he hasn't been. He's some kind of throwback or something."

"Still, Papa gave him to me," Thorne said placidly, tightening his cinch. He called Gavin Papa along with the rest of the children. "Not every dog or every person can be good with sheep. Folly was born, so he must have a right to live, and to make the best of it."

"Joe will have fits," Jean said righteously. "So will Papa."

"The way to keep that from happening," Thorne said, "is not to let them know this has happened."

"But the puppies!" Meg said impatiently. "Don't you think they'll know?"

"Maybe, then, but that's a long time away. Patrona's been bred to Bravo. Maybe nothing of Folly will show up in the pups."

The two dogs came from the thicket then, first the trim, compact bitch—black, with brown and white markings—followed by the huge male, who looked more like a black wolf than a sheep dog. Both of them were panting hard, looking tired and content. The dog shouldered the female in a possessive, playful gesture, and they both went to the stream's edge to drink.

Gordon carefully turned his eyes away from the dogs and felt his face growing hotter again. He liked being with the MacWinters; Ranald was his best friend, but they often disconcerted him.

Jean fidgeted impatiently and her horse stamped. "Thorne, please come on. Meg and I have to get back to help Mama with the little ones and supper."

"You could have stayed home," he said ungraciously,

but whistled to the dog and let his own restless horse move off with the others.

Gavin had always explained the difference in looks between Thorne and the rest of the children by calling him a Romany boy. It was, he said, a strain that had been introduced into the MacWinter clan so far back that no one knew who the bearer had been, and it cropped out at least once in every generation. Thorne was different emotionally as well. Usually he seemed placid and carefree, refusing to think of tomorrow, to plan anything or to take any responsibility. Somehow he got the work expected of him done while seeming, exasperatingly, to be doing nothing. He had occasionally what the family called his "black moods"; they seemed to come on without reason, stifling him in a heavy sadness and depression. He wanted to be by himself at those times, silent and brooding and would go somewhere alone, hide if necessary, and give himself up to thoughts, feelings and questions that rarely came to him in his normally carefree state. When his mood was black, Thorne's temper could be a startling thing.

As the four of them rode along, Thorne said with a small frown, "I don't remember anything about this Mr. Maxwell. Papa talks about the family, but who is this one exactly? Why has he come here?"

"It's Angus Maxwell," said Meg. "The one that was a boy and came over on the same ship as Papa did."

Jean said, "He's been here before. When I was about nine, I remember he came, and then we found out he'd decided to start the school at Quintana."

"He's here now," Ranald said, "because his company's thinking of putting a railroad through the valley. Joe and some others were talking about it the other night. The company's called—let's see—Maitland, Maxwell and Fitzroy, I think. They have steel mills and mines and railroads and I don't know what else."

"He paid for the school," put in Gordon, "and he

still pays my father, who talks about him fairly often."

"If you ever listened," said Ranald to Thorne.

"But I still don't know why he's here, at our house," said Thorne, vaguely uneasy. "I hope he's not decided to start another damned school. Why did we have to be sent for?"

"They're not at our house yet," said Meg. "Mr. Maxwell and his wife are staying at the hotel in Quintana. Papa went there to talk to him last night. I guess he just wants to meet all the family because he and Papa used to know each other."

They rode in silence for a time, Gordon Gaynor frowning. Last night, he and Ranald had stayed awake a long time, talking, dreaming about their futures. Sooner or later, he supposed, Ranald would tell Thorne the things they had said, ask Thorne to share the plans. Gordon had never liked Thorne, had tried to avoid him and, tacitly, to persuade Ranald to do the same. But Ranald would never stop admiring his cousin. Gordon and Ranald were both serious boys who enjoyed reading, thinking and an occasional sober discussion. Gordon considered Thorne disruptive and was envious of his and Ranald's unshakable closeness. "A Thorne in the flesh," Gordon's father had frequently called the boy when he was a student.

Ranald noticed that Gordon looked angry, and asked his sisters, "Can Gordon stay at the house for supper?"

"He usually does," said Meg, and gave Gordon a friendly smile.

"Well," said Jean with decision, "at least Gordon's fairly clean. You other two will have to take baths. You look and smell too much like sheep. The Maxwells are rich and very proper people. Mama will want us all to make a good appearance."

"We wash every day," Ranald pointed out, though he knew it was hopeless. "There's plenty of water up there where we're working."

"I mean *hot* water," said his sister firmly, "and soap."

Thorne glanced round for his dog, then said to Jean reflectively, "I wish that you had married 'Firio last fall—back when he really *wanted* you."

Elizabeth Stebbins Maxwell was a nervous, shy woman who looked several years older than her thirty-seven years. Because of her innate quietness, her preference for avoiding people and issues, she was thought by many, including her husband, to be not very intelligent. Elizabeth had been brought up by her father and a few elderly, whaleboned governesses in a narrow, sternly delineated New England world. They had thought of her as a sweet, docile, untroublesome girl who never gave cause for alarm or upset, whose nature, like her skin, hair and eyes, was pale and bland.

Elizabeth had married Angus Maxwell in 1857, when he was thirty-one and she was twenty-four. Angus's and Elizabeth's fathers had agreed that it would be a suitable match and so it had been done. The elder Maitland had just died, and Angus was seeking investment capital when he found Hiram Stebbins and his daughter. Elizabeth had not been consulted; it had not even occurred to her, since she was rarely consulted about anything.

Elizabeth had never accompanied her husband on a long business trip like this one to the Colorado Territory. But three days before he was to leave, Angus had said to her, "I think you might come along this time."

Elizabeth would have preferred staying behind in Pittsburgh, which—if anyone had ever cared to know—she had never liked much. Left in peace at home, though, she could have read the books she liked, could have played the piano now and then without fearing to disturb Angus, could have done her needlework, with no one but the servants around whom to be uneasy.

With her husband away, there would have been almost no worry that anyone might call; people had stopped calling on Elizabeth years ago. With Angus gone, a little of her guilt would have been temporarily relieved, the guilt of not having been able to produce a living child.

She had come along unprotestingly, however, and had spent hours and days in trains and stages and narrow, not-very-clean hotel rooms, waiting to be told why she had been brought along. When Angus talked to her about business, which was almost his sole subject with anyone, she listened carefully and tried to learn, though she rarely asked a question or made a comment that seemed worth his bother. She felt miserably inadequate and longed for the safe haven of home, wondering if it was true what people said, that losing the babies could damage one's mind.

She liked the scenery of the mountain country and, without any apparent flicker of notice, found some of the people they encountered interesting. She wanted to come along to the MacWinter house this evening because Angus, earlier, had mentioned in passing that they had "a brood of children."

As a girl, Elizabeth dreamed of becoming a teacher in some small, out-of-the-way country school. Her father would not hear of it, so she never broached the subject. Almost the only thing she dared hope for from marriage was a large family in which she might be able to lose herself. Instead, there had been three miscarriages and a baby who had lived only long enough for the mother to hold it briefly in her arms. Among children, alone with them, Elizabeth could be almost happy, but she would never have a family now. On the doctor's recommendation, Angus had stopped coming dutifully twice a week to her room at night. Another attempt at pregnancy could be fatal to her, the doctor had said. Secretly, she was relieved that Angus might never come again; in the depths of her heart, she feared and disliked him, and his absence was one of the few reliefs in her hard, strictured life.

Though she seemed to others only rather vaguely aware of her surroundings, Elizabeth noticed a great deal. She was, for instance, surprised and strangely pleased by the unusual architecture of the MacWinter house. Gavin had built it himself, with a little help, just before he and Maria were married. It was a combination of styles from several countries and times, framed in rough heavy timbers, and rather inexpertly squared. The walls were adobe brick; the roof was slate—and everyone on the hacienda had laughed at Gavin for the effort that finding the stone and getting it to the site had cost. Twice the wedding had been postponed because of that roof. The house was built in the form of a "dog-trot cabin," a style Gavin had seen often in the southern mountains. Maria had yearned for something built around a courtyard, but Gavin had judged that for a house without servants, a covered, central porch would be much more practical. So there were two large rooms, the porch between them. One room, Maria proudly called *la sala.* Except for the parents' sleeping apartment, curtained off at one end, this room was not often used. The kitchen, and in summer the porch, were the family's eating, gathering and working places. A steep-ceilinged loft above each room provided adequate sleeping places, one for girls, one for boys. Elizabeth took in a good deal of this, wondering a little at the strangeness, as she stiffly offered her hand to the two people whom Angus tersely introduced. She missed nothing about the children she saw, a little girl and three boys standing almost in a line at the back of the porch, peeking diffidently at the strangers. Briefly, through the kitchen door, she saw a young woman and a girl working, glancing out at them with shy smiles.

The adults went into the parlor and sat down. Elizabeth was not the only one feeling awkward. Maria and Gavin felt no welcome for Angus, and his wife seemed cold and aloof.

After a bit of stiff conversation, Jean brought in the wine that had been cooling in the well since noon. Maria saw Elizabeth notice the fine glasses that had been a wedding gift from her Uncle Francisco, and she saw her watch small Laurie who followed Jean as far as the door. The stern, stiff face softened and grew tender with a gentle smile. Poor woman, Maria thought, warming toward her, she's not feeling any better than we are; she's very unhappy.

Gavin had said little since the visitors' arrival, and that had barely been civil. Maria felt she must do something. These people, whatever their reason for coming, were guests in the house and no purpose at all would be served by her being a surly hostess.

She said, with a brightness and interest she did not feel, "Gavin says you may be going to build us a railroad, Angus."

This gained her a scowl from Gavin. He felt no compunction to try to put these people at ease.

Angus was irritated that his first name should be so casually and naturally used here. In his mind, Gavin would always be the son of the earl's shepherd and this woman, with her strange accent and rather pushy ways, was only Gavin's wife. Angus decided he would try to be gracious and democratic to ease things a little, because he was sure they were going to make more of this situation than was necessary. Besides, it was always easy to talk about the business.

"We may use this valley as a route between Denver and Santa Fe, yes," he began stiffly. "My company has been interested in railroads for about ten years. We bought several short lines back east and linked them together into the Central Western, which now runs from Pittsburgh to Chicago. I was out here ten years ago, with a man who works for me, Frank Fitzroy, looking over the possible prospects for railroads just after gold was discovered and this country had begun to be called Colorado Territory. The war came along just after that, but we've begun work now. Fitzroy is in Denver, overseeing out lines there. We plan to build west from Denver, possibly to the Pacific, though it's more likely we'll link up with someone else's line west of the mountains. We already have branches open to two of the gold mining areas."

Maria had been only half listening, but she said with pert politeness, "Will you join your railroads together, the one back east and what you're doing here?"

"Not necessarily. In the mountains, we build to a smaller gauge because the smaller locomotives and cars can negotiate sharper curves and steeper grades. I see the West as an excellent place for investment right now, though the great part of our business will always be conducted in the East. We have a steel mill, mines, a great many interests. A company needs diversification in these days if it's to prosper and interest investors. Our roads in this part of the country will be called Intermountain Rail Lines. What a railroad would do for this valley is to give it a real link with the outside world, bring some progress here at last."

He turned his frosty, tolerant glance to Gavin, who was shifting irritably. Scowling then, Angus looked back to Maria, continuing to point out the advantages a railroad would bring to a backward people. Finally, in a brief pause, Maria, smiling a little, trying to look as if she appreciated his conversation, said, "Please excuse me now. I must go to the kitchen and see if my girls need me."

Shocked by her own daring, Elizabeth blurted, "Oh, please, may I come with you?"

As they went onto the porch, Maria saw the other woman look hungrily to the children playing near the grape arbor. She paused a moment, pretending the interest might be for the vines.

"Gavin and I disagree about grapevines," she said

candidly. "They don't often bear here because the growing season is too short, but I love them. Gavin does not."

In the kitchen, mother and daughters discussed supper preparations, moving about efficiently from shelf to fireplace, to cupboard to table. Elizabeth sat where she had been bidden, in a large rocker with comfortable cushions. She answered Maria's observations on the weather with a nod, and her polite questions about the long trip from the East with brief sentences.

Finally, Elizabeth said with an abruptness that made the words seem forced, "Angus—my husband—said you have a large family. They—they're beautiful children."

Maria said casually, "Oh, these are not all. We have three older than Jean who live away from home now. There are three grandchildren so far. Jean will be married too, in the fall. And we have two boys between Jean and Margarita, Ranald and—and Thorne."

Maria paused at the boy's name, suddenly tense herself, waiting for something to show in the other woman's face. All she saw was the expression of wistful pleasure that had been on Elizabeth's face since they had left the parlor. No, she doesn't know about Thorne, thought Maria, decisively moving a pot. She loves children and is unhappy because she has none. Also, I think she doesn't like her husband. How much easier she is away from him.

Elizabeth said shyly, "Please tell me all their names."

Like a little girl, Maria thought. I don't believe she has ever talked much, to anyone. She began to chatter warmly, never loath to talk about her children.

"Well, our children have very different names, first a Spanish one, then a Scots. You see, Gavin and I could never agree on how they should be called, so I named one, then he named the next. Mine are names like our oldest son's: José Alesandro Enrique Juan de MacWinter y Arragon, in the Spanish way. His father and the other children often call him Joe. Then the second boy Gavin named for his own grandfather, Ian. Just Ian MacWinter, nothing more. Our first daughter I called Carmela Rosa Clara Feliz. The next one, named by her father, is Jean here. I did not know, in the beginning, how this would be with the church, but Father Gomez says it doesn't matter, so long as they are christened. After Jean, we have Ranald and Thorne, then our Margarita here, who is about to let the soup boil over. The four younger ones are called Dougal, Carlos, Jesus and Laurie." She smiled rather grimly, remembering. "There was some trouble with Gavin over Jesus's name, but it *was* my turn and Gavin got over it. He calls the child Jess and that's a shame. Such a fine name, Jesus, but," she shrugged eloquently, "what can you do?"

"Eleven children?" breathed Elizabeth.

Maria nodded, then said soberly, "We had two others."

"Oh," said Elizabeth, feeling their kinship. She couldn't help thinking, Why is it, though she has surely known sorrow too, that this woman should be blessed with eleven living children while I. . . .

Ranald and Thorne came in then, carrying pails of milk. Ranald looked shyly at the floor while being introduced to Elizabeth; Thorne gave her a brief, quizzical stare. She was rather relieved when the boys quickly went outside; they were almost young men, not children. But it was the little ones who captivated her. Maria had begun to give some details about the grandchildren.

On the porch, Thorne said restlessly to Ranald, "If they wanted to look at all of us, why isn't Joe here with his family? Why not Ian and Carmela?"

"I don't know," Ranald said impatiently, dropping down on a low bench. "What difference does it make about these people? Stop nattering. We got to come home to a good supper and beds for a change, didn't we? I wonder where Gordon's gone."

"I'm not nattering." Thorne took a riding crop from the wall and began trying to kill flies with it. "I suppose he—Mr. Maxwell—is in the parlor with Papa. Gordon must be up at the big house in the library. He usually goes there when he comes out here, and you know he never stays around when we have chores to do."

"I guess I'd better go get him for supper if he doesn't come back soon. Gordon came up yesterday and spent the night at my sheep camp."

When Ranald had been silent for a moment, Thorne turned to look at him, waiting for what he seemed to want to say.

"We talked about a lot of things."

"Well—what? You always talk."

"About what we'd like to do later, when we're grown. Gordon wants to be a lawyer. He also wants to marry Meg."

Thorne stopped flicking the crop for a moment and laughed. "Meggy's twelve years old."

"She's thirteen," said Ranald.

He shrugged. "All right, thirteen. And what do you want to do? Have you got a wife chosen?"

"No. I don't know exactly what I want to do, except—there are so many things I'd like to learn about. I want more schooling."

"No vows?"

Ranald flushed. For some reason, it had been he his mother yearned over as a possible candidate for the priesthood. The subject had always made him uneasy and, in recent years, angry. "Well," he said challengingly, "what are *you* going to do?"

"Nothing," said Thorne, grinning, "no school, no wife. For now, I guess I'll herd sheep and wait to see what happens next."

"You don't half do anything. You don't care enough about anything to want to make any plans."

Thorne paused and considered this soberly. "Yes, I do care. I care about things here, the valley and the mountains, most of the people. Someday, I think, I'll go away. I'll see everything I can—the oceans, ships, other kinds of people, other ways to live; . . . but then, after that, I guess I'll come back here."

"How will you earn money for all those travels, and what will you do to make a living when you come home?"

He shrugged. "Somebody always needs something done and will pay for it. I could herd sheep all over the world, if nothing else turns up."

"You're *not* a shepherd."

"Still, I've been working at it for most of two years, since I finished up at Mr. Gaynor's school. I'm not a lot of things, Ran, but that doesn't mean I can't do them. Hey, Carlos, could you bring me a drink of water? This bucket's empty."

"Nope," said the little boy.

"All right, then, that's the last time I do your share of the chores."

"Oh, all right, Thorne, but I don't want to go in there where that lady is."

"Neither do I. You could get some water from the well, couldn't you?"

"They had wine in the well today," announced Dougal as Carlos went away, swinging the empty bucket.

"They did?" asked Thorne. "Is it still there?"

"Jeannie took it out," said Jesus. "Nobody could have any, not even Jeannie. It was just for big people."

"I'd like to go to Harvard or Yale or Princeton"—Ranald pursued his own thoughts as the younger boys drifted away—"one of those old, really good schools that Mr. Gaynor talks about."

"Why?" asked Thorne. He sat down finally, ready to listen.

"To learn all I can about—well, just about anything."

"You'd have to go to some other school first, wouldn't you? You can't just go straight from Quintana to college, I guess. There have to be other ways than schools for learning things."

"I'm going to talk to Papa about it. I know we don't have money for anything like that, but maybe he can think of ways I could earn some."

"We could go to work in the gold mines."

"They'd never take us. We're too young."

"We could say we're older. I doubt age matters."

"I don't like dark, narrow places," said Ranald regretfully.

"Then we could go panning for gold, some new place where no one has looked before."

"Hardly anyone who does that ever finds much," Ranald said absently. He looked at Thorne earnestly. "But come with me when I go away. I don't want to do it by myself."

Thorne turned to take the water Carlos had brought. He thanked the boy, drank some and passed the dipper to Ranald.

"I don't think I could do that, Ranald," he said slowly. "All that schooling . . ."

"You like learning too. It's just that you don't—"

"Don't want any more from a school."

Ranald said, "Mama and Papa would be so proud if two of us went to college."

"They'd be proud if one did. You're the only one who wants to, so far. Anyway, I'd have thought Gordon would be going with you."

"Maybe he will, but—I'd rather have you, even with the trouble you're always into."

"I'm not."

"You will be when they find out about Folly and

Patrona, if not before that. Gordon will go to college for sure. Mr. Gaynor's been saving money for a long time. This fall he'll leave for a prep school. He's sixteen, a year older than me. Maybe it wouldn't ever really happen, but we could try it together, you and I, couldn't we?"

"Is Gordon going to speak to Papa about Meg before he leaves?"

"No, he's not, Thorne, and—"

"Is he going to speak to Meg?"

"If I hear one word about that from anybody else, I'll know who's been talking too much and I'll tell Joe about Patrona's pups."

Laurie had come up onto the porch. "I got a new corncob dolly," she said, holding it up for their inspection. "Meg helped me make her. See how pretty?"

"Has Mama seen her?" asked Ranald, wanting to continue his own conversation.

"I know what, Laurie," said Thorne. "Why don't you take your dolly to show that new lady in the kitchen? She likes dolls, I bet. Ask her why she came here."

"She came to eat supper, Thorne," said the little girl reasonably. "I guess she gets hungry, like we do."

Laurie drifted toward the kitchen door, murmuring to the doll.

"Where are you going?" Ranald asked as Thorne stood up, looking determined.

"In there," he said, gesturing at the closed parlor door. "I want to see this man and let him look at me, and then take my supper away from the house somewhere."

"Why, will you say you just walked in? If Papa wanted us going in and out, he wouldn't have the door closed."

"I can think of a reason. It makes me feel—funny or something, to have a stranger come here to—look us over. I want to have done with it. Are you coming?"

Ranald shook his head.

In the kitchen, Maria was discussing food when Laurie came in. It could hardly have been called a conversation. Maria was doing almost all the talking, but Elizabeth had grown far less tense. Laurie held the doll up for her mother to see. She glanced bashfully at the strange lady through her thick lashes.

"Oh, what a nice doll," said Maria. "Is it a new baby?"

"It's not a baby, Mama. See what kind of dress she has on."

"Yes, you're right of course, *chica*. Why don't you let Mrs. Maxwell see? No, Laurie, go close. Mrs. Maxwell would like to hold the doll, I think."

Jean and Meg had begun to set the table, and Maria turned to the fire, busy with several things.

"It—she's—a beautiful doll," murmured Elizabeth under the sounds of crockery and silver. "Would—would you sit on my lap too? You could tell me your dolly's name and how you made her."

The child acquiesced, and Elizabeth was suffused with warmth and longing as she held the soft, compact weight of her.

"Meg helped me make her," said Laurie. "My brother told me to ask why you came here."

"Why—" Elizabeth could feel her face growing hot, but she couldn't risk losing the child's nearness for want of an answer. "Why—I came because—I wanted to see you."

"You did?"

"Yes, and your new doll."

"Mama told us before that your home's far away. When you used to be far away, did you know I was here?"

"I thought—I hoped you might be."

"Oh," said Laurie, smiling, flattered. "I thought you were just hungry."

Most of the way back to Quintana in the livery

buggy, Angus and Elizabeth were silent, as they often were together. On this night, Elizabeth was not tense with the imagined need to make polite conversation with her husband. Her mind was taken up with going over the evening, especially the short time when the women and children had been alone in the kitchen . . . the little girl—oh, the darling little girl!

Angus was thinking of the boy who had walked so boldly into the parlor, and of the past.

Annie had not told him, before he left her at the hacienda, that she was pregnant; thinking about it later, Angus assumed she had not known herself for some time. When he was at last back in Pittsburgh where he belonged, he was able, almost, to forget the stupid folly of his marriage. Annie sent him a few letters. They were sweet, dutiful, pathetic—asking nothing of him, grateful for the financial support he provided. She wrote him about the baby only after it was born: "He's a strong little boy and very beautiful. I will name him Thorne if you do not object. It was Lady Catherine's maiden name and I think the baby looks something like her." Annie did not even know that Thorne was Angus's own middle name, but he never used it. Though he chafed at her giving it to the child, he made no protest, because that would have meant more correspondence with her.

Angus was very nearly incredulous at his good fortune when Gavin's brief note came, telling him Annie had died. He spent a few moments regretting the death, for the girl's sake—she had been so very young—then Angus went on with plans for the future, which had, in a sense, been restored to him.

Then Philip Maitland died. Angus knew old Mr. Stebbins, who had capital to invest, but who kept subtly insisting that his daughter Elizabeth went with the money. Angus had been left little in shares by his Uncle Philip, but with the Stebbins money, he could immediately own one third of the company. He set about marrying Elizabeth.

He did not want a wife of great social accomplishments. Such a woman would have been always chattering and mooning over parties, shopping trips, vacations and such. When Angus entertained, or allowed himself to be entertained, it was always strictly for business purposes. His only concession to social living was the declaration of his staunch Presbyterianism and a fairly regular attendance at church. Being seen there helped enhance his business reputation; discreetly large and regular contributions to the church helped even more.

He was not disappointed, then, when Elizabeth showed no inclination to things social. Leave all that to the Maitlands. Angus's wife, after his instruction, planned his meals and saw that they were properly prepared, though she was as timid as a rabbit with the servants. She rarely went out with him, or even sat at his own table when he had guests.

In the first months of their marriage, Angus had known vague feelings of displeasure, which ultimately crystallized into a constant, nagging irritation with everything the woman did and seemed to be. His home was usually comfortable enough. Certainly, Elizabeth gave him no trouble, except for the slight but constant feelings of displeasure. As time went on, he knew she was a little frightened of him, but that was as it should be, it could prevent many misconceptions and misunderstandings.

All he asked of her was children . . . a child . . . a son. . . .

Angus met Frank Fitzroy again. Fitzroy had become a wealthy man, due to the war between the states and he wanted a share in the company. It was the only grounds on which he would come to work for Maitland. Philip III and his brother Peter were taking an interest in the business by then. Allowing Fitzroy to buy shares was against Angus's better judgment, but his money would enable them to begin buying up what would later be the Central Western Railroad; and Fitzroy, who knew all aspects of railroading, was a man they sorely needed if the company was to venture afield from mines and mills. The business was reorganized after the war ended. It became Maitland, Maxwell and Fitzroy. It was perhaps the greatest pleasure of Angus's life to see his name a part of everything at last. It strengthened his wish, his need for a son. Even a son of prim, timid, simple-minded Elizabeth's could be taught the value and importance of what Angus was working to build.

In 1860, Angus took time out from his trip with Fitzroy to the gold fields to spend a brief hour at the hacienda. Gavin was openly hostile, as he had been when Angus had brought Annie home. Maria seemed to expect that Angus would show a parental interest in Annie's child. She went into long explanations about the boy's Catholic christening and the story he had been told about his parents, informing Angus that, except for herself and Gavin, everyone believed Thorne's name to be MacWinter. When he saw the boy, not quite five then, all Angus felt was a mild irritation that he should immediately see a resemblance to Lady Catherine and her people.

Later, Angus decided to have a school built and to supply it with a teacher. The hacienda—that whole part of the country, it seemed to him—was a place of poverty and deprivation. A good primary school would be a great benefit, and, when word of his philanthropy got around, it would do no harm to his reputation.

Years passed and there were no children in the Pittsburgh house, only little, miserable funerals and a growing pall of sorrow and futility. Following the doctor's counsel about no more children for Elizabeth, Angus too was relieved that there need be no more attempts. Yet why had he worked so hard since his boyhood? Why had he given up everything else for the business? He had years still left to him, but what would there be of Maxwell when those years were over?

But he *had* a son. The thought, the admission flashed upon him almost like discovery. The boy's mother was of yeoman stock, granted, but no one else need know about that. Surely the boy, after proper handling and training, would be no worse than one from Elizabeth's weak, sickly, inbred, attenuated line. Angus felt something akin to enthusiasm about the idea. He would go and look at the boy, and for once, he would take Elizabeth along. She deserved something—poor, rabbity, useless woman.

"What did you think of them?" he asked her abruptly, when their buggy had almost reached Quintana.

Elizabeth started. "What? Oh. Oh, yes. They were—very nice."

Angus was not particularly pleased with the boy, but that was no disappointment; he had not expected to be pleased. No child raised by Gavin and his silly Spanish wife could be expected to fit his needs at once. His displeasure had been evoked from the outset, when the boy walked into the parlor, looking so bold and arrogant. They might at least have tried to teach him civility. Gavin had introduced him unwillingly.

Angus said coldly, "Perhaps you'll sit down for a moment since you're here. It happens I've come to see you."

Thorne continued to stand, looking at him boldly. "Why have you?"

"It would be more polite to sit down, as you've been asked, and let me get on with that."

There was a premonition of fear in the boy's eyes as he looked to Gavin.

Gavin's helpless anger was almost out of control. He said harshly, "Sit down, lad."

Thorne went slowly to a chair near his uncle.

After a little silence, Angus went on, "I've discussed

you with the teacher—Gaynor, I believe his name is. I understand you're reasonably capable when you care to apply yourself."

Thorne watched him silently.

"My wife and I have no children. As you probably know, Mr. MacWinter's family in Scotland has lived on land owned by my family for many years, generations."

Thorne's glance flicked to Gavin, and the boy might have been tempted to smile, except that some foreboding had been growing in him all the afternoon.

"I've had a particular interest in—you children for some time," Angus was continuing. "I had the school built here, as you must know."

Only silence.

"I should like you to come east with us when we start the return trip in a few days. You can finish your education properly there, and perhaps work your way up, to a degree, in my business."

The boldness had left the boy's face. As he looked slowly from one man to the other, he grew pale.

Finally he said softly, "But why?"

"Can't you say any more than that?" demanded Angus. "I'm sure you have no idea of the opportunity you're being offered."

"But I—don't want it, sir."

Angus said bitingly, "*You* can't know what you want. How old are you? Fourteen? You have no concept yet of what life means, the things that are important. You can go to a good preparatory school, a fine college, study—well, business administration, perhaps. I'll decide about that later, when we see where your talent lies, *if* you have any."

Thorne looked beseechingly at Gavin, who could say nothing, but tried to offer support with his eyes.

"If you want someone to—educate and things like that," the boy told Angus with more spirit, "why not ask Ranald? He wants those things—a lot."

"And what is it you've thought you wanted?"

"I—don't know."

"You've not thought about your future at all?"

"Well, I . . ."

"That's enough," Gavin said curtly to Angus. "Give him time to think over what you've already said."

"In a moment," replied Angus coldly. "In addition—"

Thorne broke in, saying incredulously to Gavin, "I haven't got to *go?*"

"I'd like you to listen to me," Angus said sharply. "Along with your schooling and work, there could be a good deal of travel. I should think any young man of your age would be interested in the railroads we have built and are building. You might learn something of that end of the business while enjoying yourself at the same time. I assume you like to enjoy yourself?" He half smiled.

Thorne, looking frightened, said urgently, "If any of us is to have a—a chance like this, it ought to be Ranald. We were talking about things like this just before, and he really wants—"

"Who is Ranald?" Angus asked impatiently.

"My brother, a year older than I am. He—"

"I wasn't aware you had brothers."

A flush crept up Thorne's cheeks. "No. He's my cousin." He turned suddenly upon Gavin, a dawning horror in his eyes. "Is *that* why? He wants to just come here and take one of us, and because you're not really my parents, you . . ."

"It's not that, Thorne," Gavin said firmly, his eyes pleading for an understanding that could not come. "None of the others is more a child of ours than you are. You were born here, in this house, and you've been our own since your mother died."

Angus said relentlessly, "You've been told about your father, that he died on the way here from Scotland before you were born. He was also someone my family had known for a long while. He would want you to take advantage of any opportunities. You may take my word that life has few enough of them."

Another silence.

"I'll tell you what I might consider," said Angus, sounding grim, but believing he was achieving lightness. "I suppose I can understand something of your reluctance. You think of the loneliness and strangeness of beginning a new sort of life, though I can assure you, you would be far too busy to have time for such things. However, I can take your cousin as well, both of you on trial. Call him in here and we'll see if he's any more aware of what is being offered than you seem to be."

"No," Gavin said between his teeth. "We'll say no more about it for now. Thorne, go along, lad. You and I will talk later."

The boy fled.

After a time, Angus said with disapproval, "That's a nervy pup."

"He's a fine boy," muttered Gavin. "You really mean not to tell him?"

"Of course he won't be told," snapped Angus. "It seems to me he's already too full of his own self-importance. You might have tried to see to it he learned something of proper respect and appreciation."

"For what, man?" cried Gavin, his fists closing hard. "Is it respect and appreciation you want, when you've hardly admitted to yourself who his father is?"

Angus said nothing for a moment, trying to put down a wash of anger. Was it any wonder the boy was churlish?

"And what about your own son?" he finally asked calmly. "Is it true he wants higher education and a good job—to try to better himself? Surely you can't make shepherds of them all. It occurred to me when he was mentioned that my taking this—uh—Ranald might be my way of making up to you what you've been out on—the other one."

"The lad's name is Thorne," Gavin said, "and you owe me nothing. He's my sister's son. You can't even speak his name, let alone admit to him or to yourself—"

"He'll be told what he needs to know when the time comes, *if* the time comes. I will not have him getting a lot of high-flown notions about his place in life until it's clear whether or not he's capable of filling it. I'll thank you to keep entirely out of the matter."

Gavin said vehemently, "He'll never go with you."

"He'll have no choice," Angus replied quickly, coldly.

"Man, he's not a bairn!"

"He's also some years short of reaching a majority. If you try to thwart me in this, if he's led to think he can refuse to come and there'll be an end to it, I'll have you in court."

"Then he'd know who you are," Gavin pointed out almost mildly.

"Yes, and it would go harder with him for knowing. Now, as I say, I'll be willing to take the other boy as well, if he meets my approval more than the one I've seen, and that would not take much doing."

"You can take—" Gavin had begun fiercely when Maria knocked at the door and came in to tell them supper was ready. They had not continued the conversation.

Now as the hired buggy drew up before the seedy little Quintana Hotel, Angus, helping Elizabeth down, said to her, "I'd like you to wait up. I'll only be a few minutes taking the buggy back. There is something I must tell you."

Returned from the livery stable, he poured himself a small glass of brandy, which he had drunk on rare occasions for some years. He went to his wife's room. This hotel had no private sitting rooms, and aside from the bed, there was nothing for them to sit on except dusty straight chairs.

Angus said with no other preliminary, "The boy Thorne—are you aware which one of those children he is?"

Elizabeth tried to recall. "Yes," she said, relieved that she could remember. "The dark one. He and two others—one is the teacher's son—took their food outside. I remember he didn't smile. Later, one of the girls mentioned that no one seemed to know where he'd gone. The little children—"

"I suppose he disappeared to sulk," Angus broke in. "They've spoiled him, but I think it's not too late for change. Now, Elizabeth, what I'm going to tell you will be a shock, but you must simply accept it. It was begun and ended before I knew you."

Tersely, he told her about Annie MacWinter and his own almost-fatal mistake.

"She died less than a year after I left her here with her brother," he finished. "She had a child, the boy called Thorne."

He paused, but as usual Elizabeth said nothing. She was not looking at him directly, but he had seen her face flush blotchily, then grow pale.

Angus said with reluctance, "He looks a great deal like my mother and her people. Only one of mother's children, a sister of mine who died, had those black looks. I had intended leaving him here, to his own devices; but, as you can produce no children, I must think of the future, of my name. We will take him back with us, perhaps Gavin's boy as well. . . . Do you understand what I'm saying, Elizabeth? There will be—well, if not children, at least young people in our house at last."

"All right, Angus," she said softly.

Disgusted, as usual, with her unresponsiveness, he left her with a curt good night.

Elizabeth sat up for a time, hardly aware of some late roisterers in the dirt street under her window, trying to fit these new facts into the simple, narrow scheme of her life. It had been a surprise, of course, that Angus had had a wife before her, and a child. She felt no jealousy, no resentment. What she found shocking was that he could have ignored the boy for all this time. But then, Angus being Angus, she supposed that should not surprise her either. Even now, the boy was not to know the real, the complete reasons for his being taken from what had been his home, from all he knew.

She got up and undressed slowly, slipping as she had always done into the plain, voluminous nightgown before removing her underclothes. She blew out the light and lay down, still very much preoccupied.

The thought of an adolescent boy, perhaps two of them, in the Pittsburgh house made her squirm with almost paralyzing shyness. What would she *say* to them? If only they were tiny children! Oh, that dear little Laurie with her dirty corncob doll. A child like that, she could give her . . . Why couldn't he have gone out, when the doctor had told him she could never produce a child for him, gone out and found a sound, healthy woman *then* to bear him a child, a little child he could have then presented to her? Hot, difficult tears squeezed between her lids. Why was she torturing herself about it? she thought hopelessly. Whenever the child had been born, whoever its mother, Angus would have appropriated it for himself, everything about it. He would never have allowed it to be Elizabeth's child.

II

During most of the winter and spring of 1870, before Angus came, Thorne had been in a line shack on the south edge of the hacienda with Diego Perez. Diego was an irascible old vaquero who, because of rheumatism, needed help with the job assigned to him. Thorne had wanted work. He had finished with Mr. Gaynor's school; home chores, helping with the sheep in summer were not enough. A man—someone becoming a man—must be able to earn his own way. The wages paid to him were minuscule, but they were his first and he was proud of the money.

His and Diego's duties were to watch out for cattle, particularly after a storm, to keep them from drifting off hacienda land. Otherwise, the animals might have gone all the way to Mexico, putting their backs to a north wind the way they always did. Also, they kept an eye on the calving in the spring. It was nothing compared to the work of lambing time in his uncle Gavin's bailiwick.

Diego was very fond of talking, and being alone all that time with a youngster gave him more opportunity than he had had for years. He chastised and corrected his protégé on every tiny detail of the work. He told long, often salacious stories of his past, which Thorne absorbed eagerly. He sang songs. Sometimes it was obvious that the old man was in physical torment; at other times, Thorne felt he was being lazy, taking advantage of age and experience to shift the work to him, but he didn't mind. He took on the job in his careless, pleasant way, so that it seemed to Diego the boy was doing little and ought to have to work harder if he was ever to learn anything. Thorne thought, without complaint, Some day I'll be old like Diego, and there'll be some kid I can push work off on while I stay by the fire.

When they came back to the main ranch, it was May. The lambing, like the calving, was over. It was a beautiful spring, so tender and soft and gentle that it almost hurt. Maria made a fuss over Thorne because he'd been away. Ranald had been working at the main house, helping with early gardening chores. He had only one more day there before going to work with his father, tending sheep. He persuaded Thorne to come along and help.

Don Francisco, Maria's uncle, was now a senile old man who would drool into his sparse white beard and shout inane, unintelligible commands in his cracked old voice. Thorne saw him briefly, sitting in the sun in one of the small courtyards. The son Francisco, himself nearly sixty, was not often at home. The war and treaties of more than twenty years ago had been a great blow to the main branch of the Arragon family. They still felt this valley and their land grant should have its primary orientation with Santa Fe, with Mexico, with Spain. They would never stop resenting having been made a part of the United States. The younger Francisco liked to dabble in politics and spent a great deal of his time in Santa Fe. A younger brother, Ramon, was chiefly in charge of the hacienda.

Another younger brother, Esteban, who had never married, spent his time at the hacienda in reading and study. Gordon Gaynor, the teacher's son, sometimes worked with him at the house, making notes of Esteban's philosophies, taking his dictation of letters to other professional students and professed thinkers. Thorne had seen them, Esteban and Gordon, walking in the main courtyard. Later, Thorne was resetting some flagstones, and eventually he became aware of the man's eyes on him. Esteban had sent Gordon into the house to make a copy of something.

"Who are you?" asked Esteban, coming up to Thorne. "A new gardener? I think I have seen you before."

"My mama—my aunt—is Maria Arragon, the old señor's niece."

Esteban frowned, said mockingly, "Yes, the cousin married to the shepherd. You're a different-looking boy. I remember having seen you at some time. Do you have Indian blood?"

"No, señor. Sometimes my family calls me *gitano*, gypsy."

Esteban kept looking at him in a close, thorough way that made Thorne uneasy.

"Your Spanish is good, mostly correct, but then a cousin of ours should be able to teach that to her children, even if she has married an English shepherd. Do you work here in the house? How long have you been working here?"

"My cousin has worked here through the spring, señor. He asked me to come today to help finish up his work. These stones are done. I was just going to—"

"You needn't make such long answers. 'Yes, señor,' is quite enough for one of your station. What is your name?"

"Thorne MacWinter, señor."

Esteban smiled at him. His lips looked wet and there was a strangeness in his eyes. "Have you seen the library here? It's quite fine for this forsaken part of the world. Young Gaynor is about your age; he is able to appreciate it."

"I saw it once, señor. It was the old *patrón's* birthday and we were all invited here."

"You are a brash, disrespectful boy. I tell you, yes or no is sufficient answer unless I ask for more. Would you like to see the library again? It has been a practice with my father and brother to let a few young people such as you borrow some of the less valuable books from time to time. Could you be trusted to give proper respect and treatment to books? I have serious doubts of it, but wash your hands and come with me."

Thorne did not want to go. The main house had never held the interest for him that it generated in Gordon and Ranald. Esteban Arragon was, however, strangely, undefinably fascinating to him. It was not a pleasant feeling, but he wanted to understand it, to know what it was. The man watched him wash his hands; there was no choice as to whether or not he would go.

The library was a huge, dim place, cold after the bright spring day outside. Thorne listened politely as Esteban told him some of the books were hundreds of years old, had been copied out by hand, that the family had always taken pride in its library, had continued to stock new books through the generations, though it was becoming less and less intellectual, turning most of its interests to cattle, sheep, the growing of crops and other such peasant matters.

"My father never read a book through and is proud of it," said Esteban. "My brother is almost as bad, concerned with the dirty trivia of politics."

Thorne heard the words, but was not concerned with taking them in. He had become engrossed in studying the spines of books. He had never been an avid reader, often not even an interested one, but a place like this study was interesting, a little awesome.

Esteban pulled a book from a shelf. "This is in English. I speak and understand English very well. Here, read something. Let me see if you *can* read."

Thorne felt awkward and irritated, but he did as he was told. Esteban snatched the book from him in mid-sentence.

"Yes, you can read, after a fashion. Try something from this one in Spanish."

Thorne complied rather absently, wondering how he was to escape outside, to the soft spring air and dazzling sunlight.

"Now," Esteban broke in on the reading, "translate what you have read into English."

Thorne was tired of being tested, or whatever it was the man had in mind. He obeyed mechanically; it was easy. All the MacWinter children spoke the two languages interchangeably.

"Not entirely correct," said Esteban critically, "though perhaps there is something to be said for parents who speak different languages. You do as well as the Gaynor boy, better than his father. That man, who calls himself a teacher, has never been able to speak Spanish well or to translate easily. The cousin you say works here, can he do this?"

"Much better than I can, señor. Ranald likes books."

"Yes? And what do you like?"

Thorne could think of nothing to answer because of the look in the man's eyes. Esteban was smiling faintly and there was something disturbing about the smile as well.

"You may choose a few books to take away with you, to borrow. Take them from those shelves over there."

Thorne was loath to stay a moment longer, but the opportunity to see new books was rare, and he did like reading, if the books were the right kind. To his surprise and pleasure, most of the books seemed filled with adventure and daring. In his pleasure at leafing through them, he almost forgot Esteban's presence.

"Your cousin is the tall boy with reddish hair, isn't he?"

Thorne started. The man had come very close to him. He nodded, glancing back at the book in his hands.

"Answer when you're spoken to," said the man

curtly. "You must learn respect and decent manners if you are to come here."

Thorne closed the book and raised his eyes slowly. He did not like looking at the man.

"The Gaynor boy is no longer satisfactory," Esteban said petulantly. "He whines and expects special treatment. You are too dark, too like a peasant for my taste, but variety is a good thing. Here," he held out a thin, beautifully bound book. "Let me see if you can read this."

Thorne wanted no more of this game. Into his mind flashed a place he knew by the Rio del Oso, willow-shaded, where he could lie quietly and watch new-fledged dragonflies over the water. There was so much—almost everything in his world—that did not include borrowed books. Still, before he accepted Esteban's latest test-book, he laid three books of his own choosing on a table at the end of the shelves. There ought by rights, he thought, to be something to show for all the time he had spent here. He opened the book to its title page, then looked back at the man.

"I can't read this, señor. It's a language I don't know."

"It's French," said Esteban smugly. "Go on, turn over the pages. Perhaps you'll come upon things you understand."

Impatiently, uneasily, Thorne turned the thick creamy sheets. Then he stopped, shocked, appalled, fascinated. "Mother of God!" he murmured automatically, not knowing he spoke.

Esteban, watching him avidly, was smiling. "So you see, it's not always necessary to understand the language. Go on, look further. Have you a girl? Do you make love to girls? . . . I've told you to answer when you're questioned."

"No." Thorne's face was burning. With old Diego's winter stories and these pictures, he was coming to feel adult and he wasn't sure he wanted to.

"Perhaps you don't like girls," suggested Esteban. "I find them dirty and distasteful. Here, look farther."

He took the book and found a page himself. Now Thorne felt sick. He had heard of things like this, but only in vague hints. The pictures made it all quite clear. He turned his burning face away from the book. Esteban was watching him eagerly, his hands trembling.

"I could teach you a great deal. If you behave yourself, you might live here in the house for a time."

"I have to go," Thorne gulped, but he was cornered at the meeting of two bookshelves.

"It's time I had a change," the man was saying musingly. "Your coloring is something like an Indian peon's, and I see a wildness in you, though I think you will be able to learn quickly."

He reached out for the boy's crotch. Thorne struck Esteban's soft abdomen, so hard his hand ached. He ran to the big ornate door and felt a moment of terror at finding it locked. Then he saw the big key on a nearby table. Esteban was crumpled on a chair, sobbing. Thorne, key in hand, felt a great, fierce contempt for the man. It eclipsed his fear and shock. Deliberately he went back to the end of the row of shelves and took the books he had chosen.

"May you rot in hell!" gasped the man brokenly. "Someday you will know what it is to yearn and suffer. You—"

Thorne let the heavy door fall shut, cutting off the string of epithets. Once outside, he ran the mile to the MacWinter house. His heart was pounding, but not from the running. He did not go to the place in the willows to watch dragonflies. This was not a time to be alone, to think. He threw himself into the work of helping Gavin with heavy spring chores. When Maria and the girls began to prepare supper, he filled all the buckets from the well, then cut, split and carried a great deal of wood into the house.

"Well, *hijito*," said Maria, "what has brought all

this on? No one even asked you to do these things."

"He knows," said Meg, unimpressed, "that we're having his favorite things for supper. He wants to get extra helpings without anyone saying anything."

Thorne was having a drink of water, and Maria tousled his hair in passing. "He can have extra helpings. Sometimes we have not had much else, but there has always been enough food in this house for extra helpings. This one has been away from us; he will be going away again, to summer pasture with the sheep. You are growing up, Thorne. All of you change too fast for me. Perhaps you learned some things during the winter? Though with old Diego Perez, I don't like to think what most of them might be."

Ranald came home then, climbing up to the boys' bedroom to change his clothes. Had Esteban found Ranald? The afternoon's incident colored all Thorne's thinking.

The smaller children were all over the porch now. Gavin sat there, waiting for supper, which Maria said would take another half hour. Thorne shifted uneasily under his uncle's quick, sharp glance. He felt Gavin must know something of what had happened, and now, suddenly, he had to be alone. He scrambled up to the bedroom for clean clothes.

"How did you like it up there?" asked Ranald with a casualness that, just now, seemed incredible and ludicrous. "I've sort of liked some of it. I wish we didn't have to go up tomorrow to start getting things ready for the sheep. Gordon's supposed to go on working for Señor Esteban. I guess they'd throw Esteban out if he wasn't a son of the house. He likes to play at being a smart man, a very deep thinker. Nobody seems to put any stock in anything about him."

Thorne made no response. He felt sick, his face and hands clammy.

"Did you bring those books home? I couldn't think at first where they came from. How did you manage to get them? Gordon's the only one I know of who's been allowed to use their library. Did you—"

"I'm going to have a bath in the Oso," Thorne said curtly. His body seemed to clamor for cleansing.

"Well, wait a minute. I'll go with you."

"No, I don't want you to."

"What's wrong with you? You've been looking like a thundercloud ever since you came up here. What have *I* done? I can take a bath whenever I like."

"If you come with me, I'll drown you," Thorne said, not quite joking.

Ranald looked after him frowning, then shrugged.

At the Oso Thorne, who felt dirty by association, scrubbed his skin viciously. It had come to him, after leaving the main house, that Esteban might do something by way of reprisal for the punch in the stomach. After a short time of anxiety, he realized, without quite knowing why, that Esteban's situation must make him almost helpless to do such a thing. "Someday you will know what it means to yearn and suffer," the man had said. Remembering, Thorne knew there had been pain in the eyes, not just the pain of having the breath knocked out of him. The boy did not understand, felt nothing but contempt and revulsion for the man, but his own feeling of uncleanness was leaving him. It was not his problem, nor anyone's he cared about; he was getting some perspective. He ducked his head and stayed under till his chest ached, scrubbing at his thick hair. The water was muddy with spring runoff and numbingly cold. He came up gasping and let himself face the question about Ranald. It was all right. Ranald didn't know about Esteban Arragon. If he had, he could never have kept it to himself; he always told Thorne the secret, important things.

Thorne came up out of the water, shaking, his teeth chattering. Gordon was another matter, he thought grimly, rubbing himself hard with a towel. "The Gaynor boy is no longer satisfactory. He whines for special treatment." Gordon must be just like Esteban in the ways he . . . Or did he do those things in the pictures in order to get other things? This latter seemed even worse, more repulsive. How could anybody let himself be brought to do those things, just to have access to a few books? Thorne, numb fingers fumbling with shirt buttons, shook his head violently and with decision. He would not let his thoughts be haunted by that man, those pictures. He was shivering with the late sun behind clouds, but more urgent than the cold was his ravenous appetite.

After supper, Gavin took down his bagpipes for the first time in a long while, and went out to the porch. He had learned a little of the pipes from the blacksmith at Brendeen; and once he was settled in at the hacienda, as soon as he could collect enough spare money, he had commissioned his brother in Aberdeen to send him a set of his own. "It's only something I've always wanted," he had told Maria. "Last year, you wanted that grand furniture for the room. Nobody uses it unless the priest comes, but it's brought you pleasure. I mean to have the pipes."

Maria looked pained now, as she always did when the pipes began to wail, but she laughed when, kitchen in order, she came onto the porch and watched the children attempting the jigs Gavin tried to teach them.

Meg said, "Sister Teresa says the pipes are a joke the Irish played on the Scots a long time ago, and the Scots still haven't caught on." Maria and the children laughed. Gavin did not.

He said soberly, "I could show you the steps of the dances better, but there's none else to play."

"I can," said Ranald boldly, "well—a little."

He made the attempt valiantly, and they all were pained, though Gavin's jig was admirable.

"Much more of that and the floorboards will break through," said Maria, not with reproof.

"I've built a solid house," Gavin assured her smugly.

"Come now, lass—before Ranald renders anything more, show us some of your dances."

Maria had taken Laurie on her lap. "No, Laurie's sleepy—aren't you, *chiquita?* We'll just sing some songs." And they asked, all together, for their various favorites.

In the morning, Thorne and Ranald went up to the sheep's summer pasture. The flocks would not be driven up for a week or so, but there were things to be done. They cleaned out two springs, then began to rebuild a rough, temporary cabin where Joe, who would be chief shepherd for most of the summer herding, would live with his family. A large pole corral also needed mending and rebuilding.

One evening Thorne set snares, and the next morning they held two rabbits. While he was cleaning them, Gordon Gaynor came riding up.

"Well," Ranald greeted him warmly, "we can use an extra hand."

"Señor Esteban has decided to go away for a while, to Mexico City," said Gordon easily. "I stopped by your house. Meg and some of the little ones may be riding up here later, to see how you're doing. Hello, Thorne, or is this one of those days when you're not speaking?"

"It must be one of those days," Thorne said coldly, renewed contempt rising up in him. He flung rabbit entrails to Folly and another dog that had accompanied them.

Ranald looked at him quizzically. He said to Gordon, "We've got bark cut to put a new roof on the cabin. Want to help? How long can you stay?"

"Till tomorrow. Sure I'll help, if you show me what to do."

Thorne finished with the rabbits and hung them up. What he knew about Gordon—what he thought he knew—shouldn't change anything. He had never liked Gordon much, but Gordon couldn't—what was the word?—corrupt anybody that had good sense, and

Ranald had sense enough. Still, Thorne wanted to be no nearer Gordon than he had to be just now. Two people were supposed to be up here working. Well, two people were on top of the cabin. There were other things he might have done, but he stood idle, contemplating the sky; it was likely to rain soon. Medium heavy clouds were eddying around the peaks he could see, and the air felt chill, damp, heavy, undecided. Finally, shrugging, he crawled into the shelter of boughs he and Ranald had made to sleep in. Folly came after him, sniffing for more rabbit. At Ranald's urging, Thorne had brought along the books from the Arragon library. Until now, seeing the books among his things had made him uncomfortable. Well, that was silly. Today was a good one for reading. Vaguely, he was aware of Ranald's calling for him from time to time, but it didn't disturb him much.

A long time later he heard the other two boys come to the camping place for a drink of water.

Gordon was saying, "If you ask me, he's sulking because I came up here. He never has liked me. I think he's jealous that we're friends."

Ranald, uneasily suspecting Thorne was in the shelter, hearing, said, "No, it's nothing like that, Gordon. He just likes to be by himself sometimes. Everybody does. He—"

"He always has been jealous," Gordon said firmly. "I know he's family to you, but I don't understand why you always stand up for him. He's common. He's proud of being ignorant and . . ."

Ranald had come round to the open side of the lean-to and bent to peer in. "You are in there," he said resignedly.

Thorne grinned at him, saying loudly, "Is anybody looking for me? for a fight or something?"

"*I*'ve been calling you to come help with that roof. It's started to drizzle."

"I know. I can hardly see to read, especially when you stand there and block most of the light."

"Well, damn it, we didn't come up here to read."

"It seems a good thing to do, though. If I came up on that roof, I might get common and ignorant, and somebody might fall off."

Ranald made an impatient gesture. "You know Papa's going to be coming here in a day or two. If we're not through with these things . . ."

"What?" said Thorne loudly. "Will he send us to work in the Arragon library?"

Ranald looked at him uncertainly. "If you won't work on the roof, do something about that corral, can't you? You'll have to cut poles and then—"

"I know that, Ranald," Thorne said crossly, standing up as much as he could under the boughs. "Don't tell me what to do or how to do it. I'm proud of my ignorance, you know, and it isn't as if I have to be a stupid shepherd. I was offered a job the other day, at the main house."

"What job? You didn't say— "

Thorne had walked past him in time to see that Gordon's face was scarlet. Turning away, Gordon looked as if he might cry. Thorne knew no compassion.

"Will you tell me what's going on?" demanded Ranald, his voice low and angry.

"I'm going to work on the corral," Thorne said mildly, still more loudly than necessary. "Everybody else here is older than I am, wiser, learned in the ways of—"

"Oh, stow it," said Ranald, exasperated. "You're daft. If you'd just get off your butt *and* stop talking." He went back to the cabin, shaking his head.

Thorne took one of the horses to a grove of small trees where he cut poles and made them into a bundle for the horse to drag back. He was making fine progress when he realized how hungry he was and came back to make up the fire for cooking.

The drizzle was light and intermittent, but it seemed to be growing colder.

Ranald, coming down for more rolls of bark, said, "I guess Meg or anybody from home won't be coming, a day like this."

At that moment, the dogs raised their ears and barked. There were three of them, riding up fast, laughing—Meg, Carlos and Dougal.

"We just wanted to come," Meg said happily, "even if it did look dreary up here. It hadn't started raining at home when we left. Carlos and Dougal wanted to fish, and I thought you'd have done enough work on the cabin that it would be shelter from the rain. Have you? Hello again, Gordon."

"Let me take your horse for you," said Gordon with a shy gallantry that made Thorne grimace as he spitted the rabbits.

"There's enough of the roof done to cover you," said Ranald.

"I hope you've brought food," Thorne said. "Two rabbits are not going to go very far among six people, not as hungry as I am."

"Look at the basket the boys are bringing. *Full* of food. Mama knew you'd be starving up here. But I know rabbit isn't all you've got. We packed enough to last you a month before you left home. You know, Thorne MacWinter, you've got about as much graciousness as a badger. I don't believe either of you is the least bit glad to see us."

"Sure we are," said Ranald dryly. "It's been so *long* since we left home."

Meg had the same fair, clear skin as her mother, the same lovely oval face. Her hair was a rich dark brown, hanging in fat braids down her back. Her eyes were brown, large, dark and soft. Her figure had begun to develop only recently, and she was shy about it.

She said, only half banteringly, "If it were just you two, if it weren't for Gordon's being so nice and thoughtful, I might just turn right around and go back home, *with* the food."

"No," said Thorne, urgently seizing the basket from the smaller boys. "Let me see what you've brought first. Here, you cook the rabbits, Meggy. Girls are always better cooks."

She stepped quickly away, shaking her head. "Oh, no, I didn't come up here to take care of you. And I don't know about cooking over a campfire, not anything. *You're* the one who's good at that. I know it will be the best rabbit I ever tasted."

"You hate rabbit," he said dryly, "and if you think you can flatter me into—"

"Oh, my goodness!" she cried in feigned horror. "It's raining harder, I think. I mustn't get all wet on my day of rest. I'll go under the part of the roof that's done, and someone will surely be good enough to bring me my lunch."

"Someone'll be good enough to throw you in the creek," Ranald said grimly. "Do something to help. This is a work camp. You had no business coming if you just meant to priss around. Dougal, you and Carlos gather some more wood."

When lunch was over, the two younger boys persevered in their intention to fish, though mist and drizzle continued. Ranald decided the rest of them might spend a little longer in the shelter of the partial roof.

"It's not good for you to go right to work on a full stomach," he said, justifying his decision.

"It's a whole lot worse on an empty one," said Thorne, lying back lazily in a shadowed corner.

"Maybe it will snow," mused Gordon. "I guess it's not too late up here, even now. Sometimes I hate the weather in this country."

Meg said, "You talk about the weather in *this* country, as if it were a foreign place, Gordon. It's your country too."

"In a way," he said soberly. "But I like to think of New England as my real country. I was born there, you know, near Boston. A few summers Dad and I have gone back to visit; we lived there till I was seven. It's where my mother's buried. There, when winter's done, you can count on its really being over, and there's real spring and fall. Here, it just usually goes from bitter cold to boiling hot and back again."

"You've seen all those places—haven't you?" said Ranald wistfully, "—like Lexington and Concord and Bunker Hill."

"And Boston Harbor," added Meg, "where they threw the tea."

"And I've been to Washington," Gordon said readily, "seen all the important places there. Dad and I have been to most of the eastern states."

"Maybe you could make another trip," said Thorne, and yawned.

"There are important places here," pointed out Meg, "or near here. Santa Fe's awfully interesting. You remember, Jeannie and I went there two years ago with Mama, when Ian and Madalena were being married in the cathedral."

"You've told us about Santa Fe two hundred times," said Ranald.

She ignored him, saying to Gordon, "Spanish soldiers and priests were around here a long time before the pilgrims came to New England, you know."

"Yes, there's history in this part of the country too, but nobody makes anything of it, mostly. I mean, places aren't set aside for people to visit, things like that. Dad says maybe westerners will appreciate their heritage someday."

Meg said soberly, "I guess I wouldn't really want to live anywhere but around here. It might be awfully—different." Then, more lightly, "It just keeps getting colder. Maybe it will snow up here. We got most of the garden planted yesterday."

"Here," said Gordon quickly, "have my jacket if you're cold. I don't need it."

He put it around her, and she said primly, "Thanks, Gordon. It's too bad my brothers couldn't learn manners and politeness when they went to school."

"We haven't got jackets on," observed Ranald, unruffled. "Is anything going on down below that we ought to know about? Has Rafaela had her baby? Isn't there anything besides getting the garden planted?"

"If Joe and Rafaela had a new baby, I'd have told you first thing. But there is something you two boys better think about. Father Gomez came for supper last night."

"What's there to think about?" asked Thorne. "He eats at our house more than at his own, and I mean *more*, while he always talks about moderation."

"He talked to Mama about how you boys don't go to confession or come to Mass."

"I did at Easter," Ranald said. "That's not so long ago."

"Well, it's too long, and Thorne didn't, even then. When have you?"

"I don't know. There was no church where Diego and I were living."

"There was plenty of chance when you came home. You do too know. Anybody keeps track of a thing like that. Mama's going to talk to you and so is Father. You'd better worry about your own condition sometimes, instead of leaving it for other people to do. Gordon goes regularly—don't you, Gordon?—and he wasn't even born Catholic."

Thorne looked so long and hard at Gordon that his face began to redden again. Turning back to Meg, Thorne said lightly, "Maybe I don't sin. In that case, there's nothing—"

Meg's mouth dropped open. "Everybody does," she said hotly, emphatically. "How can you even think a thing like that? *That's* something you need to confess.

God heard you say that. He knows if you even think it."

"I can't help what I think."

"Papa doesn't go to church much," said Ranald, "and neither do any of us boys as we grow up."

"Papa's a good man," she said a little uneasily, "the best there is in the world, but he didn't have the chances we do. We were born into the Church. Papa didn't find it till he came here to live. Papa would never say a thing like that—that he doesn't sin. Everybody knows people are born in sin and they have to be always—"

"All *right*," said Thorne impatiently. "Don't you know I was teasing? I sin—sometimes, I guess, but I don't have to tell Father Gomez about it, nor anybody else."

Meg still looked concerned. "All anybody can do is ask forgiveness and try to be better. Suppose you were to die. Of course you have to tell Father Gomez."

"Father Gomez is a hundred years old. He started training to be a priest when he was seven or something. What do you think he really knows about being young? about anything? about—living?"

"He's a *priest*," she said firmly. "He can talk with God, ask for—"

"Why can't I talk with God, if I want to? We're always supposed to pray. Why does forgiveness have to be always strained through Father Gomez or somebody? You said, just before, that God heard me say I don't sin. If He hears everything, knows everything, why go to a priest?"

"Or even a church," said Ranald thoughtfully. "Not that I think—"

Meg said vehemently, "You'd better *not* think that, Ranald MacWinter. Thorne's just trying to stir up trouble."

Thorne got up, shoved his hands in his pockets and moved restlessly about the small room's brush-strewn dirt floor, frowning thoughtfully. "What I really think is that God doesn't give a damn."

Meg gasped, and a little silence followed.

"About what?" asked Ranald, marshaling nonchalance.

"About—if we sin or go to confession or get confirmed or—anything."

"You've been with Diego Perez too much," Meg said. "You know God knows about every sparrow. He knows how many hairs are on your head."

"He may know," Thorne said soberly, "but how could He *care?* How could He have the time? If He's busy running the world, what could it matter to Him if I have a wicked thought?"

There was another silence. Gordon was sneering slightly, as he often did when Thorne talked. Ranald was trying to decide if Thorne was serious.

"Don't you pray?" Meg whispered, looking at him hard.

"Ah, no," he said softly. "It's a long time since I've thought there was anything important enough about me to bother anybody else with."

"Prayers *are* answered," she said stoutly. "If you want something and deserve it, God hears."

"How am I supposed to know what God may think I deserve, *if* He knows I exist? I'd rather try to get what I want myself than wait for that."

"*That's* the reason for confession and Mass and everything," said Ranald, "—so we can try to understand God a little."

"If God is so grand and mighty that He made the world," Thorne said slowly, "then Father Gomez doesn't understand Him, nor does anybody else. Look at clouds sometime. Somebody responsible for clouds wouldn't want to be thinking about me, even if I were really evil."

"He loves everybody," Meg said fervently, "even you."

"If He loves people, just *people*, because they're alive, what does He care if we're Catholic or—or Chinese?"

"You'd better straighten out, Thorne MacWinter," she said ominously. "Mama would be worried to death if she knew you were talking like this."

"Papa wouldn't."

"You never heard Papa talk anything *like* the way you've been."

"No. When anything about religion comes up, he tells us to talk to Mama or the Father or the sisters. I think that's just to keep the peace. I don't think he really—"

"I can't believe your nerve!" Meg cried. "First you think you can tell what God's like, then you're going to tell us what Papa thinks."

"I'm only saying what *I* think. It's nothing to get mad about. Everyone has to think something, or they damn' well ought to."

Thorne looked through the doorway, up at the clearing sky. He said slowly, "Why were we made and given choices if God's just waiting to see us make mistakes? That makes Him seem so—small and petty—like a person. Somebody who made those mountains can't be just sitting in heaven, in the noise from all those prayers and the smoke from all those candles, waiting to say, 'Aha, I caught you, Thorne MacWinter! *You're* going to hell.' "

Meg was flushed with anger and concern. Ranald was soberly speculative.

Gordon said, with a touch of derision, "And what do you think He *does* say?"

Still with his back to them, Thorne said slowly, "Nothing. I think He can't be bothered with whether I'm good or bad."

"You're awful!" breathed Meg.

Thorne turned to face them and was suddenly a little

shy. Smiling deprecatingly, he said, "Let's talk about something else. This is giving me a headache."

Meg, looking as if she would cry, shook her head sadly and said to Ranald, "You still pray, don't you?"

He nodded, looking a little embarrassed. "I couldn't not, I guess."

"And you do, Gordon?"

"Yes," he said fervently, "very often."

Thorne said in exasperation, "If you believe in it, Meggy, if it's the right thing for you, you haven't got to ask them or anybody else to back you up. *Your* belief is what ought to count for you."

"You're scary," she said, her lip trembling.

"Sometimes," he said slowly, "it's scary to think." He shrugged. "It looks like the rain's over. I'm going back to work on the corral."

Carlos and Dougal came up from the creek then, with a good string of fish. Ranald suggested the fish be left for supper, but the younger boys were adamant about taking them home. Meg, still looking troubled, came to see that everything had been gathered into the basket they had brought. Gordon went to get her horse and came back with his own as well.

"I guess I'll be riding down with them," he said to Ranald.

"I thought you were staying till tomorrow."

"I haven't spent much time with Dad lately. He isn't very well, and I could be some help to him with all he has to do here at the end of the school year."

"Are you going away somewhere to school next fall?" asked Meg.

"Yes, I think it's time I did that."

"You'll be awfully smart one day," she said, trying for lightness. "Maybe you'll never come back here to live, once you've had all that schooling. We'll be too stupid for you."

"Oh, no," Gordon said very seriously, looking only

at her. "You said earlier that you wouldn't want to live anywhere else but here. I guess, really, I feel that way too."

III

Thorne was alone in Gavin's small barn. He had come there to be alone, but he wished he could be busy, wished there was some urgent task he could not ignore, something that required great physical exertion or complete mental concentration so that he need not think. In the few days since Angus Maxwell had invaded his home and made the announcement that he intended to take Thorne away with him, Thorne's thoughts had been so frantic, so repetitious and obviously so useless. Angus, his announcement, and what had followed were all such threatening, bewildering, painful things. Tomorrow was the day Angus had named for his return. Thorne was trying desperately to make himself accept and be reconciled to the fact that for reasons he could not imagine, there would be no help for him from his aunt and uncle. Hoping for aid, pleading for it in all the ways he could without actual words, proved to be of no use. They could not—or would not—even tell him *why* this thing was to be allowed to happen. He had given up the hope of even an explanation now. The only way it seemed possible, then, for him to go on being was to submit his life, to a degree, to this cold, stiff stranger who obviously disliked him, and whose inexplicable power was so frightening. Thorne needed solitude for adjusting to the situation, which he must try to accept if it were not to destroy him. Since they could not help or explain, Thorne could not bear being near Gavin or Maria, seeing their sad, wistful faces, having to feel their need for reassurance, while trying to hold his own pain, anger and confusion in check. Nor did he want the company of anyone else. Ranald, to whom he might have turned in other circumstances, spent these days trying to persuade his parents that he, too, be allowed to go to Pittsburgh. *Allowed*. Such a bitter word to Thorne. Thorne had always wanted solitude for working things out; for learning the multiplication tables as a small, determined boy; for thinking, later, of the great truths that were as old as mankind and wholly new to each discovering adolescent. The family teased him sometimes, tolerantly, about black moods. Today's solitude would solve nothing. The answers he kept seeking with such confused desperation were not within himself, and he had not been asked about this decision, apparently had no choice in the matter. There was nowhere to turn. All he could choose was company or solitude. He must be alone; and he had never before known the full, jarring meaning of alone.

There were four stalls in the barn. None had been occupied for weeks, so the place did not even need cleaning. Somehow, that added to the heaviness of his sorrow. It was warm, the late afternoon sun pushing heat against the west wall reinforced the dusty, dry smell of old hay. In another week they would be cutting this year's first hay crop, filling this loft for the winter needs of the milk cow and Gavin's horses. Then the barn would be filled with the very essence of summer —new-cut hay with the smell of the sun and wind and rain in it. And I won't be here, Thorne thought. Never before had he tried to imagine these things—home—going on without him. It's as if I'm going to die, he thought, trying automatically to swallow whatever it was that kept blocking his throat. They must know what it's like for me, and still they mean to let him take me.

Someone was coming up to the open door. He heard no step, but saw a shadow. Meg came in and paused, taking a moment to adjust to the barn's inner dimness. She carried an egg basket.

Thorne stood still, scarcely breathing. Don't see me, he willed fiercely. I won't talk to you. Leave me alone. All of you. . . .

She was pretty—Meggy. It seemed that out of the misery of this catastrophe he was seeing everyone with new eyes—a stranger's eyes? Had he, without knowing it, been considered a stranger all along? Perhaps he had never been an integral part of the family—had not belonged at all.

Meg started slightly, thinking she detected someone there in the warm shadows. "Thorne?"

Defensively, he made a slight movement, saying nothing. She tried to see his face.

"Have you seen that old speckled hen coming in here?" Meg asked. Her voice sounded stiff, unfamiliar to her. She had been shy with him these past few days; she was frightened, not understanding what was happening to him, feeling as if she could never have known a person to whom such a thing could happen.

Thorne did not answer, and she said, "I'm trying to find her nest. She's hiding eggs somewhere again. Dougal said he's seen her around this barn and I thought the loft, the hay . . ."

She could see more clearly now. His face was not sullen or angry as it might have been in the past if someone had interrupted one of his treasured reveries.

Thorne was thinking, It's been that same hen for three years now, hiding her nest every spring. Now I'll never know where she hid it this year. His face looked strangely soft, vulnerable, seemed about to crumple with his misery and aloneness.

Meg put down the basket, took a step toward him.

"You don't want to go," she said, and now the stiffness in her voice came from trying to hold back tears. Then, quickly, she took the steps that remained between them, flung her arms around him, no longer able to stop her tears. "Oh, *don't* go! I don't want you to. He can't—no one can *make* you go!"

She held to him fiercely, and her tears wet the thin material of his old worn shirt. Thorne's body, for an instant, was taut with the fear that she could make him let go of himself. The thought of giving way was fearsome; if it happened, he might never be able to recover. Meg's words, her tears, her anguished nearness meant that she understood—some of it, at least—and though he had believed he wanted an undeniable indication of such understanding, it proved a terrible threat to the trembling strength of his will. Meggy cared.

She was sobbing. "*Why* are you going?"

"I—I have to," Thorne said and his voice broke. His voice had been breaking a great deal this past year. It was his age.

"I asked Mama," Meg said, sounding angry now, resentful, puzzled. "She just talked about the schools and things, but those aren't reasons, when you don't want to go. I love Ranald too and I'll miss him awful, but he wants to do this. Well, just let *him* go and you stay."

Thorne, to his embarrassment, was almost painfully aware of Meg's body against his own, and his face began to burn. Still, he could not, quite yet, force himself to draw away from her.

Meg had grown taller during the past year. She was maturing in other ways that often made her feel awkward and self-conscious, but she was not thinking of that now. Of all the family, Thorne was nearest to her in age. Only twenty months separated them. There had always been Thorne. How could life go on in any of the good, old, familiar ways if he was gone away?

She must hold him here, physically if necessary, must protect him and so herself.

Thorne was saying slowly, his voice all but toneless with trying to disguise the tumult of his feelings, "He won't do that, take just Ranald. I have to go too." He must get away from her. She was a threat, a danger, in even more ways than he had believed at first. But she cared; she loved him. The comfort that brought was as threatening as all the others' attitudes put together. He wanted the comfort so very much.

Meg cried again, *"Why?"*

"I don't know."

"Well, if he doesn't want to take Ranald, then Ran doesn't *have* to go. Just tell him—all of them—you won't. *I*'ll tell them. Ran will understand; later he will, if he doesn't right now. He wants to believe you want this, just a little even, but later he'll—"

"No, Meggy, don't say anything—not to anybody."

For the briefest moment, with her head against his shoulder, Thorne laid his cheek against her hair. Heavy braids wound round her head now, but yesterday he had watched her, not fully aware of her at the time, drying her hair. She had just washed it with rainwater. Most of the water from the rainbarrel, softer than that from the well, went for washing Maria's and the girls' hair. He recalled so clearly how she had lain on her back on the porch with the great skein of rich brown hair hanging over the edge, highlighted in early morning sunlight. Meg had been reading a book, her face still, eagerly absorbed. He remembered uneasily and with a kind of delight new to him, how her budding breasts had pressed eagerly against an almost-outgrown dress. He thought now that her warm hair still had the smell of the sun in it, and the rain. Oh, he could not leave! —go from here, from everything! Dying would be better, easier than giving it all up.

Meg lifted her head and looked at him urgently, her beautiful brown eyes misty, pleading. "You don't want to go. I saw what your face was like when I came in here. I've never known you to be like this, just not—*doing* anything. Mama and Papa just don't understand yet how *much* you don't want to. They think—"

"They *do* know," he said, speaking almost levelly now, more quietly. "Don't ask me why again, because I don't know why, and saying it over and over doesn't do any good—can't change anything. I just think—I know I have to do it."

"They'd never let somebody like that awful man . . ."

"Meggy, will you just, please, leave it alone?" The words were harsh. She felt the tremor in his arms.

More bewildered than ever, she said with conviction, "Well, if they really *won't* do anything, there's Father Gomez. I know he'd be able to talk to them, or think of something. I'll go, right now, to Santa Filomina's, and pray about it. Then I'll ask him—"

"It won't make any difference," he snapped, growing angry, "and I don't want him around."

Thorne dropped his arms from around her, and Meg stood back a little, angry too now. "You can't just let this happen—" Then eagerly, "I know! Run away. Yes, run away. Hide in the hills somewhere until Mr. Maxwell goes away. I can slip away and bring you food. Up in the woods around Pinon Creek or—"

"I can't," he said dully, but with finality. "They want me to go, Pa—Uncle Gavin and Aunt Maria. If I hid now it wouldn't be any good, because that way I could never come back here later."

"Why couldn't you come back? That just doesn't make any sense."

"I'm telling you, Meggy, I don't know why about any of it," he cried. "I wish you'd just . . . Ah, Meggy . . ."

His arms went round her again. He needed her caring so desperately, conveyed by her touch. No less puzzled, Meg held him again and they stood there, bewildered together, holding each other against the terrible uncertainties that had so mercilessly become a part of life.

Thorne remembered then that Ranald had said Gordon meant to marry Meg. The idea made him angry, and the anger was a good thing, over the soreness of his misery. Just who did Gordon Gaynor think he was? Meg would never have the likes of him! Even without that—thing with Gordon and Esteban Arragon . . . How did Gordon dare to think, to imagine that his sister . . . But Meg was not his sister . . . Again Thorne felt the blood rising in his face and strange stirrings in his body.

Thorne drew himself away sharply, just as his dog, Folly, who had been searching for him, ran into the barn, panting, waving his black-plumed tail. Folly put his paws on Thorne's shoulders, and Thorne held him there, using the dog to hide his face from Meg.

"There is something," she kept insisting, pleading. "I know there has to be something to do about it. Let me help. Oh, Thorne, don't try to be by yourself. You haven't got to be alone."

"You can't do anything," he said tautly. He was badly shaken and tears welled into his eyes.

"Don't get *mad,*" she wailed, hurt by what sounded like anger in his voice. "Don't you know I just love you and I want you here? Why do you have to get mad about that?"

Folly pulled his paws free and sat down complacently. Thorne dropped down beside the dog. Meg mustn't look at him.

Meg, in the tender exposure of her caring, could only think he sounded sullen as he said curtly, "I'm not mad, Meggy. It's just that, sometimes, there are things that nothing can be done about. I'm glad to know you don't want me to go. Thanks for telling me that. Will you—could you—take care of Folly for me? No one will want him now. He doesn't really belong—"

He could bear it no longer, dared not risk another

word. He sprang to his feet, fiercely signaling the dog to stay, and blindly ran from the barn.

IV

1871

During their first year in Pennsylvania, Thorne and Ranald attended Pine Glen, a select boarding school where only Angus's name got them in, with their unlikely educational background and unknown learning potential. Ranald did very well, liking all the studies, adjusting easily to the regime. He did not necessarily agree with everything in their new life, but this was a great step along the road he longed to follow. Thorne, on the other hand, was in constant rebellion. Some of the classes weren't bad, he thought, but most of the rules were—the fussy, prim way in which everything was supposed to be done. He made no effort to live by a clock or by what seemed to him the mere whims of the masters, a little group of prissy old men. He made no serious trouble; simply, he refused to conform. There came to be an almost-weekly session between the headmaster and Angus, followed by long harangues from both—most of which the boy found he could shut out —followed by punishments such as demerits and the restriction of privileges, both at school and in the Maxwell house. Thorne had a great facility for avoiding or ignoring these restrictions, or for successfully pretending that what was withheld mattered not at all.

In the spring, when Thorne was all but failing in a few of his studies, Angus allowed himself the brief indulgence of shouting at the boy, banging on the desk in his study. "Just who do you suppose yourself to be, abusing your situation like this?"

"I'm going to school," Thorne pointed out with his maddening calm. "I go every day. I've not failed anything yet and I won't."

With constant reproofs from Angus and their teachers, both boys had lost a good deal of the Scots-Spanish accent in their speech, though it was a favorite irritant of Thorne's to drop into Spanish with Ranald when he wanted to be annoying. Ranald, who tried to be accommodating, was usually embarrassed, sometimes angry.

"You're an ingrate," Angus said. "They keep you on at Pine Glen only because of who *I* am."

"Well, they haven't got to do it, and I don't need to be told when to go to bed, when to go to the toilet, when to breathe."

Angus was silent, trying to put down his fury. He *would* subdue this obstinate, insolent boy, bring him to heel, make him appreciate all he was being given. Thorne had shamed him enough with his loutish, willful behavior. Angus had a great deal more to do than spend his valuable time in consultations at Pine Glen. The boy had been very nearly ruined by lack of proper handling, but that would be corrected, and soon. Ultimately, he would be fit for something like his proper place in life. He might never know who he actually was. If not, it would be his own fault—because he behaved more like the shepherd's than the earl's grandson. Two things saved the boy in Angus's eyes, kept him fighting for improvement: He showed an interest in some aspects of the business, casual and careless though that interest was; he had an adeptness for acquiring knowledge about what interested him; and he was a challenge, irksome, infuriating, but Angus was not a man to accept defeat easily. He would see the whelp broken first. He found a grim satisfaction in pitting himself against the boy and would have been secretly disappointed had Thorne capitulated.

"So Pine Glen is too disciplined for you," said Angus coldly, settling on the decision he had been considering for months. "You're going to see what true discipline is, young man. This summer you'll go out and work under Frank Fitzroy, and you'll work as the commonest laborer, which I suspect is exactly what you were meant to be. In the fall, you'll be enrolled at Smoot's Military School. We'll see what you think of discipline and Pine Glen then."

Thorne liked the summer's work more than anything since leaving home. Hard work had never bothered him. In fact, he scarcely noticed it, once the aching soreness of muscles was past. Frank Fitzroy became his friend, allowing him to go along on a trip west of the divide. Thorne found something to like about or to learn from most of the men with whom he worked, Irishmen, Chinese, rough Americans. They, in turn, delighted in his plucky, audacious gameness.

Frank Fitzroy, the newest partner in Maitland, Maxwell and Fitzroy, owned twenty percent of the company. Fitzroy, a tough, wiry man, full of energy, was the one who ran the railroad division of the company—no matter what Angus Maxwell and the Maitlands wanted people to think. He personally directed any new road from the surveying to the running of trains, keeping a constant check on all details. Men working for him said, "You give old Fitz the number of an engine, even a freight car, he can tell you where it is and what it's hauling right that minute." That was an exaggeration, but he did watch every aspect of the railroading interests carefully and delegated authority with reluctance. The lines had good superintendents, good men working under them. Fitz had chosen many of them personally, his chief criterion being that they have railroading in their blood. He sometimes thought that it was almost a disease, but under his management, no one stayed long unless he was infected. Fitz didn't look for highly educated men, even for management jobs. He preferred those who had worked their way up from grader or tracklayer or brakeman. His people were, according to Maitland and Maxwell, an uncouth lot, but they always kept a construction project going or the trains running. For two years now, Fitz, who disliked everything about office work, had managed to be in the West during good weather, overseeing work on the new Intermountain Line.

Fitz was the sixth of fifteen children. Only eight of them lived, and it was a wonder even those were able to exist under the grueling poverty in which they had grown up. His parents had a tenuous hold on a poor mountain farm in West Virginia. The father was a drunkard who made his children work almost as soon as they could walk: a lazy, belligerent man, constantly complaining about his hard lot, and never loath to lay on a whip, a harness strap, a handy piece of board. The mother was an ineffectual, pathetic, exasperating woman. Frank left home when he was thirteen. He went down into the tidewater country of Virginia, where he immediately became aware of the differences that existed among people. There were black people and white people, but the difference that counted with him was that there were important people and, in huge numbers, people who were all but nothing. He saw the huge, poor majority, black and white, living next to those few who were wealthy, who were so very secure. Fitz decided he would, somehow, become a member of that select group who never had to worry about where the next meal was coming from. He had no formal schooling, could barely write his name legibly, but he began to believe, as he did his various menial jobs, that at least some of these wealthy pompous people were, under a polished veneer, no smarter than he was.

He went north and became enthralled with the new business of railroading, soaking up detailed knowledge like a sponge. In the early fifties, he returned to the South with some money he had made from various ventures and with a knack for being convincing, despite his rough ways and bad grammar. Chiefly through his efforts, track mileage was substantially increased in the South before the Civil War was begun. He first met Angus Maxwell on a trip to New York. He had no liking for the man, but immediately saw that his interest in railroads, in the money that was to be made from them, would be useful. Fitz thought, Here's a company just itching to expand, one that couldn't be better for me and a railroad. They've got mines to supply coal their engines could burn, a mill that could make steel rails; they haven't found anybody in the world that knows anything about the building and operation of railroads—except me. But I'm not ready; I can't do it yet. If Maxwell's company isn't still waiting when I get to it, plenty of others will be.

What Fitz wanted to do, besides make money and get a railroad running, was to go to the West. He listened to everything he could hear about that country, and he decided that he could accomplish all his goals there. The mining areas and other settlements needed railroads even more than the East—it was so far from one place to another in that vast, just-opening country.

He exploited every potential of the Civil War. Most of his money went into blockade-running ships. He managed railroads, saw to shipments of guns and ammunition. Occasionally he was paid by both sides at the same time. He was a wealthy man when the war ended, and the Maitland Company was still in his mind.

In 1860, he indulged himself by going as far west as the mining areas near Denver. On his way he met Angus Maxwell again in Chicago. He let Maxwell come with him. The man claimed to believe that building railroads in the Rockies would be impossible, but Fitz saw the gleam in Maxwell's eye when they figured potential profits on freight.

By the time Fitz got to Pittsburgh after the war, Maxwell was a partner with Maitland, and Fitz decided he should be a partner too. He had money to invest, and it was always better to look after one's own interests than to work for someone else's. He knew of some short lines that could be bought, and how to go about linking them by extending a single line from Pittsburgh west to Chicago, or to the Mississippi, or to the Pacific. He was by then enthralled by and fully convinced of the practicability of transcontinental railroads. The current partners balked at having his name added to the company title. However, his capital would be most useful, were they to expand, and they still knew of no one else so wise in the ways of railroads. When they finally capitulated, Fitz could not be found for several months. He had gone to see California.

For a few years, Fitz was busy and content with putting together the Central Western, but the West had a strong hold on him. He disliked going to Maitland and Maxwell with his plans for western roads. Those plans were too dear to him, his dreams. However, if he sold everything he had, including the Virginia plantation he had bought for taxes after the war, he could not take on the West alone, not the way he wanted to do it. The company had made huge profits from the war, and he hammered at the other partners until, at last, they too began to believe in his dreams—not the dreams of conquering those great mountains with grades and curves and tunnels, but dreams of the money that was to be made by providing that country with rails. By 1871, they had a good stretch of main line running west from Denver, right through the middle of those inaccessible mountains. From the main line, there were two branches to two of the highest-producing mining areas. Construction on a third branch would begin in the spring.

When Angus first sent Thorne to work under him, Fitz had thought Thorne a funny kind of worker. Often, he seemed to be shirking so that the other hands were irked and impatient with him. Fitz had felt that way too, until he watched him closely and kept an exact reckoning of what the boy did. He found then that Thorne, a boy, was doing almost a man's share.

At first, Fitz resented taking him along. He was not going to be Angus Maxwell's kid-watcher. When he began to detect the boy's humor, his interest in railroading and his capacity for hard work, however, their relationship improved. Fitz realized almost from the beginning that Thorne was no pampered rich boy, sent along—as Angus had put it—"to be taught a lesson about what work is."

After several weeks, Fitz even took Thorne with him on a trip he made to check out a pass west of the continental divide. A pass had been chosen where the Intermountain line would cross the divide, but there were two possible routes to be used down from the pass on the west side.

"What do you think?" Fitz had asked after they had ridden over both routes. He said it just to make conversation, not because he expected the boy to have anything to offer. "Myself, I expect we'll run 'er down that first one, Wisconsin Creek."

Thorne had grown sober and thoughtful. He said a little diffidently, "It's longer that way."

"Well, yes, but there's that falls in the other canyon, drops more than thirty feet. We'd have to do a lot of blastin', use a shelf road a good part of the way instead of goin' along the creek. It'd cost a whole lot more."

Thorne grinned deprecatingly. "I guess I forgot to think about cost." Then he looked defiant. "But I wasn't thinking of a shelf road either."

"You wasn't?" Fitz said tolerantly. "What then?"

They were in camp, supper over. Thorne got up and began walking around, looking eager.

"You could put a tunnel beside that falls in Hungry Man Canyon, an angled tunnel, you know, with a good grade that would bring the track up with the upper part of the creek."

Fitz was pleased. He frowned, thinking about it, then began to smile. "You reckon that'd work?"

"I don't see why not, but I—don't know much about things like that. Would it be as expensive as a long stretch of shelf road?"

"Might not be if the rock was sound inside there, an' it'd save twenty miles over the other way."

The boy, eager now to impart information, said, "These streams in the mountains don't look like much, but they flood almost every year. They get really high. Track laid along them, the way it almost always is, will be washed out over and over."

"When you've had a lot more experience," said Fitz, stern but not displeased, "it may be you'll be the one to figger out what we can do with track *but* foller a stream in this kind of country. Nobody else has come up with a better way so far. I don't reckon you've got an idy ready right now?"

"No, sir," Thorne said, grinning, a little deflated. He sat down again, taking up the bridle he had been mending by firelight.

After a little silence, Fitz said casually, "You aimin' to be a railroader for life?"

"I don't know. It's something I like."

"How'd you come to have that funny way of sayin' your words? Accent, I guess they call it."

"It's not as funny as it was a year ago," Thorne said dryly. "We're supposed to get rid of it, Ranald and I."

He told Fitz, then, a little about his aunt, uncle, and cousins, about the hacienda.

Fitz said, "If I ain't bein' too forward, how come Angus to pick two boys from 'way out in Colorado Territory to be the ones he wanted to train an' all?"

Thorne was silent a moment, frowning at knotted rawhide. "I don't know, unless it's because he knew my uncle when they were boys in Scotland."

"Well, how do you figger it's workin' out?"

He said slowly, softly, "I don't think it is, for me. I don't think it ever will. It's all right for Ranald, maybe, but Mr. Maxwell doesn't like me, and I . . ."

Fitz lit his pipe. "Did your uncle sign some kind of papers? Are you boys apprenticed or like that?"

"No, sir."

"You ain't got to sir me, son."

"We're supposed to—always," he said with a small grim smile. "I guess I ought to stay in practice."

"An' you always do just like you're supposed to, I expect."

The dark eyes sparkled, but he said, "There weren't any papers that I know of. Are people supposed to do that when they . . ."

"Well, I don't know much about that kind of thing. I've just wondered what kind of deal this is, about you boys."

"I—don't know either."

"You git homesick, I expect. That sounds like a good place you come from, real nice family."

Looking at the bridle, Thorne said quietly, steadily, "I never wanted to go to Pittsburgh."

Fitz waited, but there was no more. "We'll be buildin' a line down that way, likely start next spring. An' we'll prob'ly run that branch to Star Gulch. Then I've bid on a short line in Montana, just from some silver mines down to where there's smelters. You could do a lot of railroadin' with this company, figger your angled tunnels and all like that."

"I have to go to school, I guess."

"I heard you didn' do right well this last year."

"I never have done right well."

"Don't like school?"

"Not most of it. This fall I have to go to Smoot's. I've heard it's about the hardest there is, some ways."

"I've heard some things about it myself, an' I never was one for schoolin' either. It seems to me like you're in some kind of a fix. I don't see why you can't go back to the Rio Grande, back home, if you want to, but you do what you can to stick with what you have to. We'll see about workin' together summers. You ever want a real year-round job, you can come to me, if you don't git too educated an' important for it."

"I'd like to work for you all the time. I'd like to start right now, only he wouldn't let me. He might fire you if you—"

"I don't work for Angus, if that's who you mean," said Fitz, laughing. "Great God, boy, he can't fire me."

"He'd—make some kind of trouble. He's got everything planned."

"You ain't afraid of him?"

The head went up, the dark eyes glinted in the firelight, but he said quietly and with bewilderment that was obvious to Fitz, "My—uncle and aunt thought I should go with him, take advantage of what he offered. I think I have to stay with him for now because I—don't really understand any of it."

Fitz nodded, but felt no less puzzled. "Why is it he won't let you be paid for what work you do this summer?"

"A lot of reasons," Thorne said readily. "He didn't like much that I did at school last year. He says learning a job is better payment than money, and I'm learning. I've cost him a lot—school, board at their house, things like that. I think he thinks that if I got paid, I'd spend it. He doesn't much like to see money spent."

Fitz smiled, then said seriously, "You know, if you

was to come to want a fine education and such, this could be real good for you, parts of it anyway. Angus ain't a easy man to git along with or suit, but from little things I've noticed about you, different times, I've got a notion you don't ease the way any for him."

Thorne looked at him intently. "I didn't make him take me. I didn't even ask him, or think about it. Besides, he hates me as much as . . ."

Fitz said quietly, "You ain't got to leave off things in the middle when you're talkin' to me. Not when we're by ourselves. I won't back you up in a lot you say, maybe, but that don't mean you can't say what you want to."

Thorne grinned. "I wish his three older brothers would die tonight and he'd be called back to Scotland to be the earl."

Fitz laughed. "That's pretty much what they call goin' around Robin Hood's barn about it. Listen, when we git back to the workin's, other side of the mountains, I'll give you a few days off, a little money. Nobody in Pittsburgh has to know. You can go down an' see your folks."

Thorne looked at the fire. Finally, he said levelly, "I guess I'd rather not."

"Well . . . whatever seems right. Hand me some whiskey, will you, out of that pack yonder? Cold does come on up in here, even if it is the middle of summer. You had a drink before, ain't you? Here, take a swaller."

The boy swallowed the raw liquor almost like a seasoned drinker. He grinned, rather sickly, and said, "If I could still have some days off, though . . ."

"Well? What would you do?"

"Go to Denver."

"Denver ain't near as big as Pittsburgh, if you're aimin' to see a city."

"The men talk about it a lot."

Fitz spat into the fire, grinning. "I ain't goin' to do

nothin' to help a snot-nosed kid start whorin' around an' the likes of that, if that's what you're after. How old are you anyway? Fifteen?"

"Once you said," recalled Thorne blithely, "that you ran away and were completely on your own when you were thirteen."

Fitz grunted. "That was a whole diff'rent thing. Now I just may be beginnin' to see why you ain't to have no money in your pocket. Hand over that whiskey bottle now an' git to bed."

It was a grim December day with an almost-freezing drizzle and a diabolical wind that sifted the rain into any slight opening in the clothing. Frank Fitzroy hunched down into the collar of his heavy coat and pulled his dripping hat lower. He was at the Central Western yards in Pittsburgh. Standing around railroad yards should not really have been a part of his life anymore. But he had some small business here and used that as an excuse to come down to check things out personally.

Fitz took the battered hat off his gray-sprinkled red hair, beat some of the water out of it and scratched his head, scowling. The Central Western seemed like a milk run now. Anybody could handle it. By the time the good weather came, he would be back in the West where he wanted to stay. He was watching a switch engine, wondering why the engineer wasn't using more sand to get better traction on the wet rails, when he caught a glimpse of someone, a boy, dodging between cars some distance away. Fitz was curious, thinking it was someone he should recognize, and he began to run. He looked into several freight cars before finding the right one.

"Well, Thorne, goin' somewhere?"

The boy huddled—cowered—in a corner in a way that hurt Fitz to see. He had no overcoat, no hat, and his hands were bluish with the cold. He was not only wet, but muddy. He said nothing, but looked at the man with eyes like those of cornered foxes Fitz had seen.

"You won't git far dressed like that," said Fitz practically. "I guess it's cold about ever'where here, the middle of December."

Fitz had come to like this boy. Angus was too hard on him; Angus was too hard on anybody if he could get to them, sober and somber, unable to appreciate anyone but himself.

"I was about to go find some coffee. Better come along. This car here won't be moved before tomorrow, goin' to Chicago for hides."

Fitz swung down, and in a moment the boy followed, his eyes down, not sullen but resigned, trying not to shiver. He looked drained and hopeless, beaten and sick. It hurt Fitz. He had never seen him look like that, though God knew he had had reason. Thorne coughed rackingly as they crossed the yards to a switchman's shack. Strong, bitter coffee simmered on a little stove. Though it was a crude, drafty shelter, it seemed warm after the raw outside air. Fitz found two cracked cups. There was a bench made of stacked railroad ties against one wall. He sat down, leaving the end nearest the stove vacant. Through the past summer, Fitz had often wished his own young son might be something like this boy, though there was little chance of it. Why was it Angus seemed so determined to destroy everything the boy was? Why did Angus, so impatient with anyone or anything that didn't immediately go along with him, keep on with this one?

"Set down, son. Maybe I can help someway."

Thorne sat, holding the coffee cup between his hands, not drinking, trying only to absorb its warmth. His teeth were clenched so they couldn't chatter.

"You've quit that school, I reckon," Fitz said casually.

To Thorne, the answer seemed obvious enough. He

still said nothing. All he did lately seemed to end in frustration and misery. Still, if he had to be caught, he'd rather it were by Fitz than anyone else here. Fitz was an exacting, demanding man where work was concerned, but he was fair and he never lectured. There was nothing about him remotely similar to Angus Maxwell. Thorne liked the railroad part of the business. If that was all there was to it . . .

Thorne coughed again, and Fitz thought, He's sick and it's no wonder, out in this weather without fit clothes, but that's not the only problem—somethin's botherin' him bad. That school that fool Angus put him in this year would be enough to break most, from what I've heard. I won't rush him. At least we're out of the rain here.

Fitz said casually, "Looks like this rain'll turn to snow before long. Was it Chicago where you wanted to go?"

"I'm going home," Thorne said hoarsely and coughed.

"Yes, I thought you might be on your way to Colorado, but I don't see how you'll make it—no food that I noticed, no decent clothes for this weather."

Thorne began to cough uncontrollably, sloshing coffee, almost cold now, over the sides of the cup.

"You never struck me," Fitz went on when the paroxysm had subsided, "as bein' a one would steal, and sure not beg. Had you figgered a way to git what you need?"

"I can manage," Thorne said dully. He *had* thought about those things, but not much. What he wanted most, what he had to have, was freedom from Smoot's, the military academy he had been forced to attend this year. Once freedom was attained, it seemed he would not much have minded freezing to death in the boxcar.

Thorne had heard of Smoot's when he was at Pine Glen. The boys there discussed rumors about it as they might, when younger, have told ghost stories in the dark. They said being sent to Smoot's was the same as being sent to prison. Blithely, Thorne had told a worried Ranald that he had got through a summer of "punishment" all right; he could manage Smoot's.

But the military school, conducted very much in an ancient style, was an incredibly shocking revelation. Every instant of the boys' lives was planned and regimented, completely out of their hands. They rose before dawn for a long march, carefully guarded by the monitors and masters, and they marched in formation to classes and meals. They participated in mandatory sports at set hours and in prescribed ways, and six days a week there were lengthy military drills. They marched to chapel on Sundays for an excruciatingly long service, then spent the rest of that day in the enforced reading of edifying books. Studies were conducted at specified times, under watchful eyes. Food and sleep were Spartan and insufficient. There was no heat in the dormitories. Conversation between the boys was not allowed during meals or when passing from one activity to another. There was a brief "recreation hour" after supper, but that, too, was conducted in a preordained, invariable way. Parents were strongly discouraged from visiting, except on graduation day. Students left the school, if permission was granted, only at Christmas, Easter and for summer holidays.

One night, the boy in the bed next to Thorne's whispered hopelessly, "This is where you get sent when nobody cares about you anymore—nobody. That Devil's Island I've read about can't be worse than this." He was a year older than Thorne. Both of them, at that time, had been at Smoot's almost two months. The other boy muffled his face in his thin pillow and cried wrenchingly.

Thorne had tried to think of something flippant to whisper, something that might cheer the boy a little, but his throat felt tight and closed. Throughout his life up to now, he had known only momentary fear, a matter of being startled or briefly worried over something. At Smoot's, they lived in fear, and Thorne was beginning to feel afraid.

At first, he tried to smile at the regulations, make sport of the masters, deny the very existence of Smoot's with carefree comments. But every slight infraction brought immediate, humiliating punishment. There were canings and lashings, and it was the rule that no one speak to the boy being disciplined, sometimes for many days. Open ridicule by the masters and the trusted, toadying head boys or monitors, and isolation —during study and recreation periods and at night in a narrow, dark, silent cell in the basement of the school building—were all part of the system for breaking rebels. At Smoot's, no master wrung his hands, clicked his tongue and sent for parents.

Thorne was strong in mind and body. Outwardly he refused to be crushed, making biting comments and surmises behind people's backs, talk at which some of the other boys could laugh in relief, and which others reported. He remained defiant in the small ways he could find, and was almost constantly under some punishment. Students were not expelled from Smoot's. Boys were sent there because they were disciplinary problems, and the school had a reputation for its dubious success.

Some of the boys were completely brutalized. Thorne tried to run away more than once, was always caught and given several punishments. He would never have thought, in his wildest dreams, that a place like this could exist, a place whose chief purpose seemed to be to humiliate, to crush out the last traces of humanness. He began to have nightmares of suffocating, of being caught in a bear trap, of drowning. Finally, then, there had been one last horrible night. In the morning, hoping that if he were caught he would be killed, Thorne had managed to escape.

When Frank Fitzroy found him, Thorne had been hours in the icy drizzle, running and hiding. The police helped to find and return runaways from Smoot's. Thorne had known where he was going, without really having to think about it, but he had had to take a circuitous, fear-filled route. The coffee cup no longer felt warm to his stiff fingers, and his shaking would not be kept inside.

"Well," said Fitz, speaking at last as an engine spun its wheels outside, trying to gain purchase on the wet rails, "I'll do what I can to help. You can have what little money I've got with me, but there's a lot more you'll need, clothes, a blanket or two—such as that."

Thorne coughed.

"Why don't you come back with me to my place first, warm up, have a decent meal, maybe a night's sleep?"

The boy's eyes were still frightened, distrustful. He put up his hand to push back dripping black hair, and Fitz saw the deep gash and dried blood from the wire cut. Thorne's cheeks were darkly flushed, and he had to breathe through his mouth. Fitz shot out a hand and touched his forehead. Thorne started reflexively, cringing away, ready to run.

"Now don't bolt on me," said Fitz in a bluff attempt at gentleness. "I was just seein' if you've got a fever, an' you have—a high one, I'd say. How long you been sick?"

Thorne said hoarsely, "Mr. Fitzroy, just let me go."

"I thought we got around that Mr. Fitzroy business a long time back. You just be easy. I expect it's been a rough time for you. I know a little about Smoot's, you see."

Fitz cursed Angus Maxwell while the boy coughed.

"Stand up there to the stove, son. See can you take in a little heat. When you've got so's you can stop shiverin', we'll go up to the hotel. I've got a buggy out at the gate. There's a blanket in there to keep off any more rain, maybe keep you from freezin' plumb to death."

Voices came to them from outside, men shouting to each other. From the few words Fitz caught, he knew they were not trainmen. He went to the door, looked out, then left the shack.

Thorne huddled on the bench, shaking, coughing, dizzy. Those men were looking for him. Someone must have noticed him coming into the yards. His heart beat heavily, but he found he was almost disinterested about whether they found him or not. He could not face running anymore, not in the cold rain and mud. His empty stomach knotted, and his vision blurred and swam. When Fitz returned, alone, his hand on Thorne's arm seemed a nuisance, his words meaningless and very far away.

Fitz had three rooms at the Ohio House. Belle Evans shared them with him. Fitz had a wife, Amanda Jane, who had married far beneath herself shortly after the Civil War. He had bought up her ruined plantation down in Virginia, rebuilt the house and begun reclamation of the land. Amanda Jane would not live in Pittsburgh, and that suited Fitz. They had never made any secret of their mutual dislike; besides, Fitz was not in Pittsburgh either, any more than he had to be. He had a stepdaughter in Virginia, twelve years old she was now. Her father had been killed early in the war. And Fitz had a son, Ted, who was five. Just recently, he had chosen a good tutor for Ted, and he intended the teacher should stay. Amanda Jane would object to him because he was a Yankee, but it was Fitz the teacher had to please. He controlled his wife's whims and prejudices by an ever-present, rarely spoken threat to sell the plantation, Fern Hill. It was no idle threat, and Amanda Jane knew it. In a few years, Fitz would put his boy into a good school, pension Belle off and have the boy with him for holidays.

Belle was a plump, comfortable, not-overly-bright woman whom Fitz had found in a whorehouse in a western mining town. She was simple, warm and generous, in bed and out. Now, Fitz sent her out to see if she could buy a few clothes that would fit Thorne. He had already asked that hot water be brought.

"I'm not much for baths myself," he explained apologetically to the boy, "but you're pretty muddy, and it might be the hot water'll help you warm up."

Thorne undressed obediently, in a haze of consciousness. Fitz, seeing the scars and fresh welts on his back, looked away, grinding his teeth.

"I'll wait in the other room. If you git dizzy agin, you holler."

What did the parents—no, it was an aunt and uncle—but what did they mean, turning a fine boy like that over to Angus? The other one, Ranald, seemed to be doing all right. He seemed to be no milksop either, but he operated under a cloak of docility and agreeableness, and he took a lively interest in almost everything. Angus seemed to forget Ranald's existence most of the time, but he could never see Thorne left alone. A proud, high-spirited boy like that . . . Fitz thought he'd better send for a doctor. He didn't know what he'd do yet about notifying Angus.

He knocked at the door and went back into the bedroom. Dressed in one of Fitz's nightshirts, Thorne lay huddled under the covers, shivering and coughing.

"How did you happen to pick on today to leave that place?" Fitz asked casually. He felt sure the boy had been through something pretty bad and hoped it might help him to talk about it. "I never figgered you to stay there this long, but you sure could have picked a better day than this one for leavin'."

Thorne thought he could never talk about those last

hours. Recollection of the date flashed through his mind and he tried to smile.

"Today's my birthday," he croaked. "Does it matter, I wonder, about anything, that I'm sixteen?"

Frank Fitzroy was admitted to the Maxwell house by a prim, elderly maid in a uniform so stiffly starched that he wondered what she would do if she had to bend over. She knew who he was, but made him wait in the hall, as was proper. The hall was cold. Angus owned mines, but was careful of coal. The drizzle had begun to freeze last night and now had turned to snow.

"Hello, Frank," Angus said stiffly, offering a chilly hand. "Is there something wrong?"

Fitz, scarcely touching the proffered fingers, went to stand before the tiny study fire. "Yes, somethin's wrong." He wished he had a drink. He'd bet this place was never really warm in winter. "Thorne's down at my place, been there since yesterday. The doctor's been twice. The boy's got a right bad case of lung fever —pneumonia—high fever, cough, a lot of trouble breathin'. The doctor says he ain't been fed right, ain't had proper rest, for months, maybe. He's pretty sick, Angus."

"What's he doing with you?" Angus was vaguely relieved but he felt there need be no real concern over the boy's health. He knew Thorne to be as strong as a horse. Someone had come from Smoot's yesterday, to his office, to notify him Thorne was missing. Angus had contacted the police, telling them he thought the boy would attempt to leave for the West. As today passed with no word, he had begun to believe he might have got away. If so, he would have him back, would go all the way to Colorado again, if necessary. It was humiliating to find the boy had gone to Fitzroy. The man was a necessary adjunct to business, but Angus wanted nothing to do with him otherwise. Certainly, he wanted Fitzroy to have no knowledge of his own personal life.

"We come acrost each other is all," said Fitz noncommittally, observing that Angus seemed unaffected by the fact that the boy might die. "Have you got any idy what they've done to him at that school? Don't you know what that place is?"

"I don't think," said Angus coldly, "that anything about my private life should trouble you, Frank. Since you have become involved, though, I will say that the boy has been a disciplinary problem ever since he came here. I'm a busy man, as you know. I can't watch and guide and correct him constantly myself. His going west with you last summer was by way of a punishment. You didn't help matters by letting him get away with whatever he chose."

"He didn't git away with anything, except bein' a boy, fifteen years old. Durin' work time, he done a man's share, soon as he caught on an' got broke in."

"Well," Angus said harshly, " 'broke in' is just what he is not. I've had regular reports from Smoot's. His behavior has grown progressively worse since September."

"Good God, no wonder! The things I've heard about that place—"

"Now he's run away, the worst possible offense against the school and against me. He's run away and come sniveling to you."

"Thorne's not a one to whine, Angus. He's not said a word of complaint about anything. Don't you realize I'm tellin' you he may die?"

"I suspect you're being an alarmist, Frank. Smoot's begins its Christmas holiday next week. I suppose they needn't take him back there immediately. I'll have my carriage sent to your hotel for him."

Fitz made a detaining gesture as Angus would have risen. Angus, with a slight sigh of mock patience, waited.

"He ain't to be moved. The doctor says so—Dr. Daniels. If he hadn't said that, I don't know that I'd be here, tellin' you about the boy. I mean to see he has a halfway chance to git through this. I thought you might be interested to know he's not out in this weather, hidin' from them convict guards from Smoot's."

"I can assure you that Elizabeth and the servants here can give him the care he needs."

Fitz had taken a cigar from his pocket. He lit it with slow deliberation while Angus frowned in disapproval and irritation.

"When the doctor tells me he's able to make the trip up here, I guess there's no way for me to stop you from takin' him; but I'll tell you this, Angus: If you don't ease up on the kid, if you send him back to that what they call a school, I'll contact his relatives out in Colorado, let them know about the treatment he's havin'."

"You're an inveterate meddler," Angus said icily. "This conversation has gone on long enough."

"Yes, it has, but you ought to keep it in mind."

Fitz crossed the room and let the door slam behind him. Angus sat very still. He had not wanted to send the boy to Smoot's. Why must Thorne make things so difficult? Would he never realize and appreciate his good fortune in being here? What would it take to make him come around, build a basis for respect and understanding? Perhaps this illness would make him think a bit, bring him closer to a man who had only his best interests at heart.

Ranald had come home to the Maxwell house that evening to begin his Christmas vacation from Pine Glen. He sat with Elizabeth in the family parlor, pretending to read a book while she moved her knitting needles aimlessly, making few proper stitches. Angus had told them only that night at supper, of Thorne's disappearance from school. Ranald was frightened. He knew Thorne—once Thorne had made up his mind to get away from Smoot's, he would freeze to death rather than go back or allow himself to be found. Ranald tried to think only of how self-sufficient Thorne was, how well he could manage if he wanted to. He would be in the country now, sheltering with some farmer; maybe he was already on his way west somehow. He would never come here. But could he manage? Suppose he was without shelter? Suppose he was hurt, afraid? Thorne afraid?

The two boys had not seen one another since the end of summer. But Ranald had heard incredible things about Smoot's from other boys at Pine Glen. Ranald felt that Thorne's being in the East at all was his fault. Thorne had been curious about the venture, but he probably would not have come if Ranald hadn't wanted it so desperately. Ranald, feeling a little ashamed of the fact, had been scarcely affected by his parents' sadness at their going. Thorne had talked often of going home, or running away. He had liked some of the things at Pine Glen, had become almost obsessed by math and drafting, spending his study time on those subjects only. He had liked working with Mr. Fitzroy last summer. . . . But what had they done to him at Smoot's? If only Thorne could be a little less stubborn. If only he could keep quiet, *seem* to go along with things and people, whether he actually agreed with them or not.

At supper, Mr. Maxwell had said grimly, "Well, he's made himself a new bed. He'll just lie in this one." Ranald decided he would go searching when the others were in bed. He had thought of two or three places that were good possibilities, but if Mr. Maxwell knew of his plans, he would forbid him to leave the house.

Elizabeth started and gasped at the sound of the doorbell. She was so weighed down by apprehension that it constricted her chest. Where was the boy? It was so terribly cold!

During the past year and a half, Elizabeth found the feelings that had grown in her more than a little remarkable. Adjusting her life to the boys' presence had been surprisingly easy and not unpleasant at all. They were eager, high-spirited, interested and interesting, polite, considerate young people, particularly when Angus was not present. The house had taken on life and zest. Elizabeth found great secret pleasure in the belief that she had come to know them far better than Angus had.

Before they had left Colorado, Angus decided they would all travel for most of the two months before the boys' school should begin. Angus had never before taken a vacation. They had gone about the eastern United States and Canada in one of the company's private railroad cars, observing and studying the construction and operation of various other railroads. At first, Elizabeth had dreaded going along. She had no interest in roadbeds, bridges, tunnels, and all the rest of it. But the boys enjoyed it, except for some restlessness during Angus's lengthy lectures and discourses; and, now and then, one of them would glance or smile at her in such a way that made her feel a part of their close relationship, their pleasure in the trip, their tolerance of Angus.

Initially, Elizabeth had preferred Ranald. He was the one who was most overtly polite, thoughtful, considerate. She liked his looks. The tall, broad-shouldered, sandy-haired, blue-eyed, grave-faced boy woke echoes in her of some long-ago, almost forgotten dream. Thorne's unpredictability made her uneasy. He had a way of closing people out with a facial expression. Gradually, however, as Angus and Thorne had more and more confrontations, as she saw the boy beaten but not defeated, Elizabeth's feelings toward him changed. Ranald could go along, give in readily if a thing mattered little to him, let the storms pass over while he stayed beneath the surface. Thorne could not seem to help fighting and struggling over almost everything; Thorne could even thwart Angus.

For instance, there was the matter of church attendance. It galled Angus that the boys had been brought up as Catholics. He talked about it when they finally reached Pittsburgh. "In this house, Catholicism is an abomination. I realize it's the only religion you've had, but now you will learn something else."

Ranald had balked, saying mildly enough, "Sir, I try to be a good Catholic. My mother wouldn't want me to do anything else. I'd like to find a Catholic church here that I can go to."

To Elizabeth's surprise, Angus all but ignored this to say to Thorne, "And you?"

"I never tried to be very good," said the boy with a careless grin. "Sometimes I still go to Mass or confession, but only because Mama—Aunt Maria—thinks it's important. I'm not really much of a Catholic—or anything."

Angus sighed. "I've asked you, time and again, to be more careful of your pronunciation. You must get rid of that ridiculous accent. Very well, then. You will come to church with us tomorrow and every Sunday you are in this house."

When it was almost time for services on the second Sunday, Thorne had said, politely enough, "I'd rather not go at all, sir, or maybe I could go with Ranald to see what St. Anne's is like."

Angus said sharply, "You will go upstairs and dress at once. We've never been late for church and it isn't going to begin now."

"I could tell you why I'd rather not go," Thorne offered. "Last time, the minister talked about—"

"I haven't the slightest interest in your analysis of a sermon. Get ready—now!"

There was further argument, but ultimately Thorne came with them. He began by sitting in the Maxwell pew, staring deliberately and solemnly at other parishioners, like a small child. Angus nudged him, frowned. Thorne then took a small book from his coat pocket and began to read. Angus confiscated it. There was a hymn. Thorne stood up for it with the rest of the congregation, sat down when it was over and, eyes half-closed, a dreamy smile on his willful mouth, began tearing tiny notches along the edges of hymnal pages. Things went on like that through what seemed to all three of them a very long service. Back home, Angus lectured for fifteen minutes and sent the boy to his room without Sunday dinner. Thorne departed with the comment, in a pleasant voice, that he wasn't hungry anyway.

Then Angus decided Thorne was to make a profession of faith by standing before the congregation to be sprinkled with baptismal waters, so proclaiming himself "saved" and a member of the church. There was strife over it for days. Finally, Thorne stood there, with a few others, to receive the minister's blessing. At first, he stood with his eyes down, his face hotly flushed. Then, during the prayer, his head came up sharply, jaw muscles clenched, and with slow deliberation, he crossed himself. Elizabeth's eyes, which should have been closed, caught the movement, and she could not quite suppress a gasp. Angus did not see, nor did the minister. A few other parishioners did see, and when talk of it reached Angus, he denied it firmly, but Thorne did not accompany them to church again.

Elizabeth admired the boy's strength and courage. Life would have been so much easier for him, for all of them, if he had given in, as she did, or if he had seemed to give in, like Ranald. She might have come to fear him, as she feared Angus, but he never gave her reason. His struggle was with one person. Thorne was usually polite and deferential with Elizabeth. Words did not seem to come so easily for him as for Ranald and he kept more to himself, but on a few occasions he had talked wistfully to her about home and the MacWinter family. Once he showed her a little drawing sent to him and Ranald by Laurie. Neither of them were able to decipher it, and they laughed over it together.

Once the school year began at Pine Glen, Ranald had been happily caught up in activities and studies, completely involved with present and future, though he obviously loved and missed his family. Thorne, despite appearances of carelessness or belligerence, was bewildered and lonely. Elizabeth could sense that, and certainly she could understand it. Would Angus have to give up eventually and send the boy away? She had found herself dreading such a time.

That night at supper, when Angus told them of Thorne's having run away from Smoot's, she found her closed, circumscribed heart aching with a flood of love and concern. Now the doorbell rang when they expected no one, and she and Ranald heard someone being taken to Angus in his study. A long time seemed to pass. Finally, when she could bear sitting still no longer and had got up to fuss with some small ornaments on a shelf, there was a knock at the parlor door. Elizabeth could not speak. Ranald said, "Come in."

Frank Fitzroy entered, went directly to the fireplace and emptied the coal scuttle onto the small fire.

"Pardon me, Miss Elizabeth, but I never did plan to die by freezin'. How are you, ma'am? Ranald? I thought you'd both want to know that Thorne's with me, down at the hotel. I happened to find him yesterday at the railroad yards—"

"Yesterday?" said Ranald. "I thought it was only today that he—got away."

Fitz shook his head. "He's there with me, an' I thought you ought to know he's right sick."

"Oh!" breathed Elizabeth as Angus opened the door.

"I'll get a coat," Ranald said hurriedly, "go with you—"

"You'll stay right here," Angus said coldly. "Take

that coal that hasn't caught off the fire. There's no excuse for waste."

"But, sir, I have to see him—know what's wrong—I—"

"I've sent for the carriage. I intend to go down myself."

"Angus—" Elizabeth began pleadingly.

"And *Mr.* Fitzroy," Angus was saying with cold fury, "I'll thank you to leave this house. I'm quite competent to tell my household what it needs to know, and in case you weren't aware of it, you've overstayed your welcome."

Fitz's chin shot out, but he tried to speak calmly. "I didn't come here 'cause I wanted your company. If it wasn't for these others, I'd see you in hell before I let you in down there at my place."

Thorne all but lost memory of several days immediately following his sixteenth birthday, while he stayed in Frank Fitzroy's rooms at the Ohio House. In moments of near-consciousness, he knew what a terrible, painful struggle breathing was. He meant to stop—it was too hard to go on—but as he lapsed deeper into coma, his chest went on laboring to expand and contract. He dreamed many things. Often the dreams were twisted horrors, incredible combinations of realities.

He dreamed of Gordon riding away with Meg, of Gordon taking Meg to Esteban Arragon for some unspeakable purpose, which Thorne knew but could do nothing to stop, could neither move nor call out. He came closer to consciousness, struggling to do something, almost remembered where he was, knew that someone was bathing his face with a cold cloth, knew that he was cold, that breathing did not seem worth the constant effort it cost, that he had been dreaming and that there was another dream he must not know again.

He sank slowly away from the room at the Ohio

House then, into the other dream—the nightmare that had been very real indeed. The boy in the bed next to his at Smoot's Military School, the boy who had compared the school to Devil's Island, was named Fergusson. Thorne had never known his first name. Fergusson smiled wanly at him on that last night. Thorne had just been released from solitary confinement again; and Fergusson, in the dim light they were allowed to use for going to bed, acknowledged him, which was about as much as he could do by way of welcome.

Later that night five boys, some of those who had been longest at Smoot's, beat and raped the gentle boy in the bed next to Thorne's. It was done almost in silence, so as not to alert the "watch." Everyone else was or pretended to be asleep. Thorne got up and fought them fiercely. Two were beating him while the other three held him, all vowing it would be his turn next, when the watch came. The older boys said Thorne had started the fight. The injured, humiliated Fergusson kept silent and Thorne said nothing. The watch, ominously promising a hearing in the headmaster's office first thing in the morning, marshaled them all back to bed.

Thorne slept little. He was afraid to sleep. But he did not hear when Fergusson got up and hanged himself.

On the way to the headmaster's hearing the next morning, Thorne broke away from the others. He ran as he had never run before. He did not feel the wire of the fence cut him, did not feel the grasping hands he kicked away. For a little while, he outran the fear of the school and everything it had nurtured in him.

But it seemed the awful dream had begun almost immediately and that the dream would stay with him always.

He dreamed over and over of what the others had done to Fergusson. He saw the boy's body hanging, turning ever so slightly, the ghastly, distorted face. . . . Then there were variations. He dreamed Esteban Arragon was somehow involved with Smoot's; he dreamed Ranald slept in Fergusson's bed.

"It's all right, it's all right," murmured Belle Evans a little desperately, trying to keep the boy in bed and covered.

Fitz looked in, rushed to the bed. "Here now! Lay still, son. What is it? What's the matter?"

"He's out of his head," Belle said pityingly. "He's been like this before, when you wasn't here. Oh! I wish we could do somethin' that would help. He's awful sick, Fitz."

Thorne saw them dimly, heard their words in a fuzzy way. He tried desperately to hold onto them because their being meant the other thing was a dream—had really happened, but only once, not over and over and . . .

He dreamed again of home, of Papa's helplessness in the face of Angus Maxwell's arbitrary decision to take him away. Gavin had said to him finally, tensely, "I think you might try going with him, lad, see what it's like." Thorne had not known what questions to ask, and there had been no answers. He simply could not believe it was going to happen.

Maria, with tears and an attempt at sanguinity, had said, "But think of it, *hijo*, a chance to go to college. You will be a very important man one day. Oh! We will miss you so!"

Thorne wanted to cry out to her that he had no wish to be an important man. How could a stranger come here, to his home, and simply decree that he had to go away? How could they let Angus do it? The fact that they could not or would not help him, that they would not explain why there was to be no help, hurt him more deeply than he had ever imagined he could be hurt. His pain, bewilderment and helplessness were so nearly unbearable that something had to be done.

Thorne did what he could. He determined to resign himself to what seemed the inevitable. He determined, too, that once he was grown up, his life would be such that he need never feel helpless again. Never again, he vowed, would he allow himself to be hurt so deeply.

Ranald, when he heard of Angus's offer to take him as well as Thorne, had said very little, but Thorne knew. The longing was there in Ranald's face. When Thorne finally resigned himself to going, Ranald had been ecstatic, though he tried not to let it show.

"It's not Mr. Maxwell," he said effusively, "it's *you* that are giving me this chance. If it weren't for you, it would never have come for me."

"Chrissake," Thorne had muttered, embarrassed, miserable.

Gavin, alone with the two of them, had said, because he felt he must say something, "You're MacWinters, both of you. See you don't forget it. Perhaps you'll gain from this—I hope so—but don't let anything, anybody, wear you down or tear you down. Live so you can have pride in yourselves."

Do we have to stay with him? Thorne pleaded with his eyes. How long do we have to stay? But he could not speak and Gavin said no more.

All the younger children begged him not to go, but it was the worst with Meg. On the day before Angus would be returning for them, she found Thorne alone in the barn. She burst into tears and flung herself upon him.

"Oh, Thorne, don't go! *Why* do you have to? Ranald wants it, but you—can't you run away and hide till those people go away? I'd bring you food. Oh, *please!* I don't want you to go."

He was embarrassed, but held her awkwardly, feeling, through her questioning, a closeness he could never feel again with the others.

Belle Evans patted Thorne's cheek, smoothed his hair, longed to be helpful.

"Let Belle put this other pillow under the poor head, sweetie," she babbled. "You can breathe easier if we prop you up."

"Meggy?" he whispered hoarsely.

"What, sweetie? Is there somethin' you want?"

"No, no ma'am," he said wearily, realizing where he was. "Could you just—leave me alone?"

Once or twice, he thought Ranald or Elizabeth had come, and he wondered bitterly how Angus had allowed them to visit him. It seemed Fitz was always in the room, but Thorne had no memory of Angus's brief, stiff visits. He dreamed many times that one or another of the staff from Smoot's had come to take him back.

But then one day he was better. The fever relented, his chest began to clear. He woke and asked Belle to open the curtains. She was overjoyed by at last being able to do something he wanted. The light was blinding—sun on dirty snow. It was almost Christmas, he recalled. What was it like at home now? . . . Why hadn't he died? . . . After a time, food was brought, and smelling it, he found he was ravenous. I can't really want to die, he thought tiredly, not if I'm this hungry.

Two days later, he was taken back to the Maxwell house. Ranald sat in his room, trying to make conversation. Elizabeth was in and out, trying to see that he had everything he might want. The servants, three of them besides the coachman he had already seen, came up to welcome him back. The old Irish cook hugged him and cried.

"It's good you're home, Mr. Thorne! I'm makin' a fine supper."

"With fritters, Bridie?" Thorne disengaged himself, trying to do it unobtrusively, so as not to hurt her feelings. He wanted no one to touch him now, to get close to him, perhaps not ever again.

"All the fritters even you could want," Bridie said, laughing.

Ranald was talking, again, about the past few months at Pine Glen when Angus opened the door and came in.

"I see you've come back," was all he could think of to say.

There was no need to answer that. He had sent the carriage, hadn't he? Thorne lay still, hating him.

Angus said, "I've talked with them at Smoot's. You've behaved disgracefully, have shamed me, which is what you seem set on doing. I didn't ask them to take you back. You may go to Pine Glen again at the end of the holiday, but our Holly Mine is quite near there. You're to go there on Saturdays and other holidays to work. Get up now and dress yourself. Supper will be ready in ten minutes."

"But he's not strong enough to come down for supper yet, sir," Ranald protested. "The doctor said he's to—"

"We'll have no carrying of food to bedrooms, not for one who's just managed a carriage ride across town."

"You won't do it, will you?" asked Ranald when Angus was gone.

"Get up for supper?" Thorne said dully.

"Well, that too, but I meant work at the mines, go back to Pine Glen, all of it. You won't stay on here, will you, once you're well?"

"I don't want to think about it."

"There's something I have to say to you, Thorne. I've been selfish as hell, making you stay when you never wanted to, because *I* wanted to. I don't anymore, not after the way he . . ."

"Yes, you do and it doesn't matter to me if you're selfish. Who's not?"

"But Smoot's and all of it. You never did anything to deserve that. Let's go home, the way you've talked about, as soon as you're well enough."

"No."

Ranald stared at him, seeing a different, older, closed face.

"Why not?" he said, vaguely frightened.

"I don't know, Ran. I don't know if I can ever go home again. I don't want to talk about it—or anything."

"I—I'm sorry, Thorne." He put out his hand imploringly and Thorne drew back from it.

"Why should you be sorry?" he asked curtly, pretending he had not seen the hand.

"About—well, what I helped to cause, the military school and all. We heard a boy died there the night before you ran away. I've heard things about that place. I can tell it was really bad."

"You can't tell anything. I learned more there than I ever will at any other school," he said coldly. "You've just been talking about the things you've planned to do at Pine Glen the rest of this school year. We'll stay."

"Damn it, you make me feel three inches high. I don't want you making sacrifices for me."

This time he put his hand on Thorne's shoulder, and Thorne wrenched away violently.

"Don't touch me!" He sounded anguished, but began to cough, and Ranald could not see his face. Finally, Thorne had control of himself again and said carelessly, "Don't talk about sacrifices and crap like that. You're being—melodramatic. I'm not about to make any sacrifices. I never have. We can stay. I tell you it doesn't matter. Now go away."

Ranald hesitated miserably. "You're—not coming to supper?"

Thorne shook his head and turned away. Both of them knew Bridie would see he had food, even if it were to mean her job.

Thorne was not hungry. He was more exhausted than when the fever had first left him. He didn't want to fight anymore, didn't care about anything. He dozed and dreamed agonizingly of the hanged boy's face. "This is where you get sent when nobody cares about you anymore—nobody," mouthed the swollen lips and horribly protruding tongue.

Thorne woke, gasping and shaking. He stifled his breathing in the covers until it was normal again, thankful no one had been in the room. There are worse places than this house, he thought dully. I suppose that's what he intended I should learn. And nobody *has* to care about me. Meggy does—she did then—but it doesn't matter one way or the other. *I*'m not going to care, that's the important thing, not ever again—about anything.

V

1877

Thorne made his way slowly through the noisy, crowded First Chance Saloon in the raw new railroad town of Graham, one Saturday night at the beginning of July. The place was hot, gritty underfoot, with dust coating everything. He had been working near the Arkansas River, but Fitz had sent for him. He felt tired and wilted from the heat and the irritations of the work they were doing, but withal satisfied, pleased with his job.

Thorne had found college no more interesting or worthwhile than his previous schooling. During his last year at Pine Glen Preparatory, he had decided that if he must have higher education, civil engineering would be his chosen field. Subjects related to engineering came to him easily, and he had liked most of his part-time work on railroad projects. Angus Maxwell had been strongly opposed to his getting an engineering degree. In the summer preceding his third year at college, Thorne had become more impatient, feeling he could not tolerate spending much more time as a student. He wanted to put into practice what he was learning, wanted to work, to be independent. He determined to finish with school as soon as possible and was ready for graduation in January of 1877, rather than in June. In some subjects his marks were barely acceptable, and in one or two of those he had gotten some assistance from Ranald, who also covered for him when he was out late or chose to cut classes. Grades held no importance for Thorne. He was, at long last, through with school, working with Fitz and other men for whom he had respect, doing work he liked, learning eagerly.

When he first came west this year, straight from college, there was not much construction work because of the severe winter weather. So Fitz, in a private business car, gave him a tour of Intermountain's growing network. The main line had its eastern terminus at Denver, where it connected with the Union Pacific and other major transcontinental lines. Its western end was Bethany, Utah, where it joined another lesser but promising road, the Great Basin and Pacific. The Intermountain main line was now triple-railed throughout, so that it could carry both narrow-gauge and standard-gauge trains. Two of the three branch lines to mining areas—one of them completed as recently as four years ago—were now virtually shut down. The gold had run out there, but new strikes had come. They were now in process of building narrow-gauge lines to a new gold field whose center was called Amity, and to a silver boom area called Silver Valley. A short line had been built in Montana, and Fitz had bid on the construction of another in Idaho. Graham, where Thorne stood at the bar wearily waiting to be served, was the point from which they were finally going to put a road over the divide between the Arkansas and Rio Grande drainages.

For years there had been trouble over this line—court suits, private and public fights. Intermountain's competitor, Rocky Mountain and Pacific, was first to begin a line south from Denver, but they ran short of money in the bad economic year of 1873. Meanwhile Fitz, who felt he had first rights on the mountain country and who took competition very much as a personal affront, had a line started from Santa Fe. It ran north, more than halfway from Santa Fe to the Arkansas, but work on it had to be halted because the Rio Grande–Arkansas divide (which they now called Brenner Pass in honor of the chief engineer), the Arkansas Valley, and any right-of-way routing on north to Denver were hotly contested grounds. Colorado, newly a state, was in Fitz's opinion getting "nitpicky, persnickety, goddamn' childish an' downright unreasonable," with new laws that tried to control and claimed to make equitable the construction and operations of railroads. But Fitz had friends in politics, and the company had interests in a few influential newspapers. Fitz was never deeply concerned that things might not eventually work out his way, but the time and trouble required for ponderous legal machinations frustrated and exasperated him. He had never been forced to endure such delays before—had never really believed such laws and restraints would come to the western country. It was all but impossible for him simply to wait while others, complete outsiders, took their time to decide what he might or might not do with his own business.

Finally, it had been decreed that, though Rocky

Mountain and Pacific had prior claim to right-of-way south from Denver, they should, for considerations, share it with Intermountain as far as the little town of Haviland on the Arkansas River. From there, RM&P had sole right to continue south, along the edge of the plains east of the Sangre de Cristo Range. Intermountain could go up the Arkansas to a point where it could turn south and cross over the watershed divide to link up with its already established line up the Rio Grande Valley. Intermountain had to relinquish any claims to right-of-way for trackage to serve a mining area called Carter Creek, over which the two companies had also been disputing and feuding.

When the court decisions finally came down, Fitz grunted with exasperation at the unnecessary delay; then he chortled. "We don't want no line out there east of the mountains an' as fur as Carter Creek goes, we'll git along without it. We're haulin' plenty of ore. This here line they're aimin' to *let* us have, from Denver to Santa Fe through the Rio Grande country'll be a steady money-maker, nothin' your dividend takers can swoon over, but a good, dependable business. If RM&P builds on into Santa Fe from the east, they can move trains faster between there an' Denver, 'cause we got more mountains to go through; but we'll be servin' a whole new territory, farmin' an' such, not just mines an' boom towns that may peter out tomorrer or the next day."

The commissions' and courts' decisions had not been finalized until the late spring of 1877, though due to inside information and his own obstinacy, Fitz had already begun grading and tracklaying along the Arkansas. During the time that work was halted or nearly so, bad blood had built up between the two companies and their employees. They still made trouble for each other whenever possible, though considerable distance now lay between their railheads.

Thorne, thinking that now he had a place at the bar,

he might as well wait for a second drink, heard his name being called. He turned so that Fitz, sitting at a table in a corner with another man, could catch his eye. Fitz gestured that he should join them, bringing a new bottle. Thorne nodded and turned back to wait his next chance at ordering and paying. He tried to think of something besides the crowding and noise, remembering now where he had seen the man sitting with Fitz. It had been yesterday and they had met because of what Thorne knew to have been skullduggery by someone from RM&P, and which the other man had seemed certain was a mistake of Thorne's.

Yesterday, while Thorne was working under the head surveyor, Bill Buckmaster had sent him to look over grading progress along a little creek called Chavela. He was riding well above the stream and roadbed, looking down on the men and their work. It was a good position for an overall view, and he saw at once that something was wrong. The early afternoon heat was incredible, and he dreaded going down into the miniature canyon where even less air was stirring. The sun seemed to have him pinned against the dripping, choleric roan horse. The heat reflecting up from the rocky ground was almost as intense as that glaring from the sky, and it drew the water from his body in streams. The sweat evaporated immediately, leaving his skin caked with a fine residue of salt that stung his eyes and burned his face, and he kept, unthinkingly, rubbing at its irritation. Even his lungs seemed enervated, stifled and scorced by the blistering heat. The sky was empty of all but the merciless, inescapable sun.

But the roadbed, a near inferno where the men toiled with shovels and dumpcarts, was not right. Through Thorne's mind as he still hesitated, dreading the additional dust and heat, came the unwanted thought, This is the kind of work overseeing Angus might do. It was enough to make him turn the reluctant horse down toward the grading. He frowned at the angle the roadbed was taking and, looking up, saw a man, riding down from the opposite direction, bellowing.

"Christ almighty!" came the strong Irish voice, directed at the work foreman. "What's your name? What the hell do you think these men are doing? Would you stand by and let them run the roadbed into the creek? Look where it's going, man!"

"My name's Simmons, Mr. Murphy," the foreman was saying as Thorne rode near them. The man spoke wearily, as though he had given his name several times before. Thorne thought the big, black-haired Irishman must be Tom Murphy, the new work superintendent whose appearance Fitz had been awaiting for a month.

Simmons said defensively, "I see where it's goin'. I reckoned there was to be a bridge or—"

"Bridge, hell!" roared Murphy. "Look at the man-hours you've wasted. You'll have to go back down there to where you let it start angling toward the water. A bridge! I don't see any stakes on the other side of the stream, do you?"

"Well, sir, no, but we was follerin' the stakes *here*. You can see 'em yourself, just like they was when we started work this mornin'."

"Yes, I see 'em, been seein' 'em all along, an' they lead into the stream, but you ought to have known something was wrong. Who in hell set them stakes, I'd like to know."

"I did," Thorne said, moving a little nearer. He felt a little lightheaded with the heat and the intensity of Murphy's glare. "Not like this, though. They've been moved."

Simmons, the foreman, looked at him in relief, but Tom jeered, "Moved, is it?"

"It's not the first time. RM&P, the other railroad company, does something like this anytime they have the chance."

"And what's supposed to be done in return, *if* any stakes were moved here?"

"The same sort of thing, I suppose. That's not been my job."

"What is your job, and who might you be?"

"I'm a surveyor. I *might* be almost anyone."

He tried a tentative grin. Simmons snickered nervously, but there was no change in Tom Murphy's glowering look, so Thorne said, a little abashed, "My name's MacWinter."

"All right, MacWinter, what's to be done about these stakes and the wasted work here?"

Thorne turned his horse back toward where the roadbed had gone awry, Tom Murphy following menacingly.

"I just came down off the hill," Thorne said. "The stakes go on as they're supposed to up around that curve." He pointed, sighting.

"You're in Buckmaster's crew, are you?" asked Tom, seeming dubious.

"Yes, sir."

"Well, yes, *I* can see where it goes on, MacWinter, *you* can see; but sometimes graders may not be as bright and farsighted as we are. Mostly, their job is to follow stakes and other such surveyors' marks. It seems to me you'd better tie up that horse somewhere and drive them some stakes to work by." His tone was still caustic.

Thorne wanted to defend himself, his properly done work, but said only, doggedly, "I'll *re*locate the stakes, Mr. Murphy."

"Well," mused Tom now as Thorne made his way to the saloon table and placed the fresh bottle in front of Fitz, "so this is the one? Yes, Fitz, we've met."

He showed nothing now but a rather reserved friendliness, offering his hand to Thorne.

"Set down, set down," Fitz ordered impatiently as Thorne hesitated. "You've got the right now to set with the big boys, if you're asked. Yes, Tom, this is him. Next partner in MM&F, I'd guess."

Thorne looked at him, surprised. Inexplicably, he felt a shiver in the heat and found it hard to keep uneasiness and irritation out of his voice as he said carelessly, "Not me, Fitz."

Fitz said complacently, "I been tryin' to figure for seven years what it is you're supposed to be bein' groomed for. I can't figger anything else it might be. From what I've just been hearin' about, though, you're never likely to make a surveyor, pointin' the goddamn' roadbed into a creek an' not even comin' out on the other side. That's your college man for you, Tom."

They were laughing at him. After a moment, Thorne shrugged slightly, grinned and drank his whiskey.

"Anyway, boy, Tom Murphy is a man I'm glad to see. You've heard me speak of him. We used to know each other back east, an' it ain't been easy, persuadin' him out here. You want a railroad built, all you need to do is find Tom Murphy an' git him on it. Tom's just been tellin' me—first chance we've had to talk—that his wife died too, back this last winter. Left him with a little girl to raise. Where'd you say she is now, Tom?"

"She's with me—here in Graham. I partitioned off part of a work car for her. Nancy's not but ten, but she's my girl; I'd never leave her very far away. Right now, she's over with that woman runs the restaurant; maybe not the best company for a young one, but Nancy's ma taught her right. She's a fine one, my Nancy."

Fitz said, "I remember seein' her before she could walk. I was about to tell you, before we was interrupted, that I've got my boy Ted here with me this summer." Fitz spoke of his son with none of the pride and warmth Tom had showed for his daughter. "You're a lucky man, Tom, for havin' a fine woman like Mary for your wife, even if it wasn' for nearly long enough.

. . . My wife, now, Amanda Jane—well, we never expected to git much out of that marriage, an' I reckon we got about what we expected. When she died last fall, hell, I was just mostly relieved 'cause she always put up some argyment about whatever I wanted to do with my boy. Maybe you've heard about it: Amanda Jane was married before. Her first husband was killed just after the War started. He was a Stuart, a fine, upstandin' southern gentleman—I been told that a good many times. They had a little girl, born in '59; a real southern lady she is now, just about what her mother wanted, I think, in spite of the fact that ever'thing else in the South is different now from what it was before the War. Cherish is her name, Cherish Charm Stuart. Amanda Jane never wanted me to adopt her, change her name to Fitzroy. She's in England now, Cherish is, gettin' polished or whatever it is they git at what I understand is about the finest girls' school there is. She'll be back to Pittsburgh late this fall. I'm not just sure what I'll do with her—can't keep her in one school or another for the rest of her life. She'll want to go back to Fern Hill—that's the plantation in Virginia—but I'm there even less than I'm in Pittsburgh, an' I reckon you can't have a young girl livin' with or without her stepdaddy without some kind of chaperone. I found a real fine colored girl named Dahlia in Jamaica, back when me an' Cherish's ma was first married. Got her to come an' be nurse to both young'uns. But your society don't accept such as that for the only companion to a young lady."

Fitz poured from the bottle, looking perturbed and irritated. The saloon seemed to be quieting down a little. Tom, becoming occupied with a large pipe, decided to change the subject.

"That's quite a grade we've got to make from here up to the summit. Is it about the same on the other side?"

"Under four percent, ain't it, Thorne? 'Bout the

same on the other side, except it ain't got to go down as far. You wait, Tom, till you git into the real mountains on some of them small-gauge lines. You'll see curves, grades an' such will curl your toenails, make you feel like if you can git a railroad through there, you must be some kinda special man." He turned to Thorne. "Listen, before I fergit it, I asked Bill Buckmaster to send you here because Brenner has said you can go with him Monday, over on the other side. It'll be good for you to foller along with the chief engineer, you two bein' about the only educated ones of us I know of. Don't do or say things will make him think you're tryin' to tell him his business. If they's one thing I got, it's men workin' for me that already knows their business. I'm damn' lucky to have got Brenner, an' he won't take none of your sass. Well, don't frown. Jesus Christ, I thought you'd been bustin' to work with him. He might maybe teach you somethin'. Here, drink this."

Tom said, "What's this other road I hear you're building?"

"Runs out of Denver, northwest up in the big hills to a place called Amity. We're buildin' another one to a place called Silver Valley. Both are narrow-gauge, but this Amity one looks like a real bitch. *There's* some work you could git your teeth in, Tom. I want to send you up there, soon as we git things runnin' right down here. How many tunnels that Amity road got, Thorne?"

"What?" He had been daydreaming about going back to the hacienda for a visit.

"How many tunnels, goin' up to Amity?" Fitz said impatiently.

"Six, I think. No, seven."

"How you ever goin' to run a railroad if you can't even keep count of your tunnels?"

"I'm not going to be running any railroad," Thorne said simply.

The air was heavy with tobacco smoke; Fitz's eyes were hazed with liquor. He studied Thorne closely, intently, as though it had just occurred to him that he should concentrate on sizing the boy up. After a moment, Thorne shifted uneasily under the scrutiny. He detested being stared at.

There was no longer a hint of banter in Fitz's voice as he said thoughtfully, "You like the work, son. You've always said you do."

"I do, but . . ."

"Well, somebody's got to foller after me, an' I shore can't believe it's goin' to be Ted. Angus or the Maitlands don't know anything about railroadin', except for some of the paperwork an' dividend sharin'. Somebody'll have to run things, an' it just may be you could handle it—when you're a good bit older."

Thorne felt embarrassed and uncomfortable. He always did when Angus was mentioned, or his own future brought up. He said, so softly that Fitz leaned nearer to him, "Angus would die before he'd even think of me in charge of anything. Besides, I don't want—"

"Angus *will* die," Fitz affirmed strongly, "just like I will, though he may not believe it. I've thought for some time that this is what we must've been workin' up to all along. You know Angus don't waste money. If he buys a newspaper, he expects somebody to wipe with it, once it's been read, so he can think of that paper as an investment."

This confidentiality on Fitz's part was an indication of a stage of drunkenness. Thorne glanced uncomfortably at Tom Murphy and was relieved to find him turned away from their table, watching two men in what looked to be a fast-warming argument over a girl. Fitz continued to peer at him earnestly, waiting for a response.

Thorne began, "Ranald—"

"Don't give me Ranald. You always do that. Ranald's a fine boy, none better, but you set right there an' tell me how much int'rest an' know-how he's got for the railroadin' end of this outfit. Ranald's aimin' at the mill office, always has been—aimin', it seems like, at what Angus meant for you to do. Ranald'll make a dandy manager, a better one than Angus, an' he's better suited to runnin' nearly anything, managin' it, than you are. A body can depend on Ranald, always count on him. Now this what I been tellin' you ain't a thing for you to worry over. *I* ain't about to turn nothin' over to nobody, but you ought, maybe, to have it in the back of your mind right along. I have. Here, drink this."

He turned to Tom and said heartily, "Yessir, that Amity road'll suit you, all the tunnels an' such. I want you to help me pick the best hard-rock crew ever was put together. We let contracts, you see, for the buildin' up there. One contractor's gone bankrupt an' another one's about to, over one tunnel. They've had slides, water, rock that ain't much more'n sand—I don't know what all. I've decided, when this last contractor gits out of the way, that we'll handle it ourselves. It's what ought to have been done in the first place. Maxwell an' the Maitlands favors lettin' out the construction work, but I shore don't. Never have. It's damned tricky, though, to keep hold of a real good hard-rock crew. What I've been thinkin' would be the thing to do, is put together a crew of the best men we can find, then try to hang onto 'em, no matter what we're doin'."

Tom looked interested but doubtful. "That kind of worker just knows one thing. What would you do with 'em when you didn't need drillin' or blastin' or the like?"

"We've got construction work enough now to last a good long time. If we was to ever run short on their special jobs, we could—I don't know—put 'em on section gangs, keep payin' 'em more than reg'lar section hands to hold onto 'em. What are you grinnin' about?" he demanded of Thorne.

"The unions back east would go into convulsions if they heard an idea like that."

Both the older men scowled at him, and Tom said hotly, "I'll not work where there are unions, or likely to be unions. That's one reason I decided to come out here."

"An' I," snapped Fitz, "won't be askin' no union who I can hire for what, or how much I ought to pay 'em. I reckon you picked up some kinda socialist crap with all that schoolin'. See what comes of it? Nothin'. Here, drink this."

Still smiling, Thorne said, "I can't, Fitz. I've had enough. It's too hot to be drunk."

"Well, what are you in here for if it's not to git drunk? I promise you agin, like I have before, I'll see you drunk at least one time 'fore I die."

"You sent for me. That's why I'm here. Was that all you wanted? to tell me I can work with Mr. Brenner? Thanks for—"

"Oh, shit, don't be thankin' . . . Truth is, Brenner asked for you. Probably he done it to git you off Buckmaster's hands after that surveyin' job Tom caught you at. You goin' to the whorehouse tonight, are you?"

"I don't know about that. There's a cantina opened up the other side of town, where I've heard there's some good Spanish music. It's been a long time since I've heard any that's good."

"You mean them cryin' songs with guitars an' such?"

"There are happy songs too."

"Buckmaster told me about that trouble you helped to settle for a gradin' crew last week. What was that, exactly?"

"Just that that one crew didn't have anyone who spoke much English, not even their foreman. It was a special Saint's Day for them; they were expecting to go to Mass, so they wanted to take off work."

"We ain't startin' none of that."

"I know, and they knew it too. Their priest had come to where they were grading to see if he could fix it for them, but he didn't have much English either."

"Buckmaster told me they went ahead and worked. What did you do?"

"I asked the priest to arrange another Mass, one they could come to after work."

Fitz peered at him again closely. He seemed about to speak several times before he finally grinned and said, "Well, you oughtn't to miss the whorehouse. There's more than one now, I reckon, but the others don't count for nothin', once you been to Daisy's. An' speakin' of goin' places, after you've worked some with Brenner over on the other side, whyn't you take off awhile an' visit your folks? Seems to me I remember you said, months back, that you meant to git that done before it's time for you to go traipsin' off to foreign parts. Go ahead, drink it."

"I told you, I've had enough."

"An' I ask you how the hell can you set, dry, in a saloon?"

Thorne stood up, smiling. "I came because you sent for me. I thought that since I was here, I ought to stay a little and see what I could take in. I've been learning, sitting at the feet of the master and—"

"Oh, quit that smartass talk," ordered Fitz fondly. "Git us another bottle over here an' then go do—whatever it is you college men do for Saturday nights."

Almost two weeks later, Fitz, looking over new roadbed, accompanied by his bored and sulking ten-year-old son, came upon Thorne, alone, staring up at the western mountains.

"That's some grade you're lookin' at there," he observed. "Surveyin', are you?"

Thorne turned and smiled at them briefly. Fitz thought that Angus would not be happy if he knew the responsibility he and Brenner and Buckmaster had allowed the boy to take on this summer. So far as Fitz had seen, there was nothing Thorne could or might do that would afford Angus real pleasure. It seemed so clear to Fitz that Thorne had been born to railroading, could carry the whole company with his abilities and railroads someday, if that should be necessary. But that wasn't enough for Angus. He had been pouting for years now because the boy had insisted on an engineering degree rather than one in business administration, which Ranald had chosen with alacrity.

Thorne, looking back to the mountains, said, "There's a little canyon, just there, that we could get trains through."

"I don't see it myself, but supposin' you did, then where?"

He shrugged. "Does that matter? I thought we just wanted to lay rails."

"It's a good thing to see," Fitz said soberly with a glance at his young son's petulant face. "For a man that cares about that kind of thing, it's a right proud feelin'. But whyn't you settle for runnin' this here on down to the river, somethin' like Brenner's had it planned? That way, it might maybe meet up with the line we already got, comin' up from the south."

"There's no challenge in that."

Fitz laughed. "I can't see yet what he's got in mind for that little stream yonder. Bridge or trestle?"

"A bridge. The bed's all but dry now, but in some springs it'll carry a lot more water than the river has at this time of year. You can see the high-water marks in the willows along there, and other places. It's almost unbelievable. That is—I think Mr. Brenner planned a bridge for it. I'm not the engineer."

"Well, I reckon you'll have to do till a engineer comes along. I just run onto Brenner back up yonder an' asked him to go to Graham and take that train for Denver. I want him to look over that mess up towards Amity an' tell me what he thinks. I told him you'd manage things here while he's gone. Won't likely be more'n a week or so."

Thorne looked at him sharply. Fitz was not teasing. He was surprised, more than a little taken aback. "I heard Angus telling you last winter that I'm not to be given any decision-making powers till I've—"

"Proved yourself," cut in Fitz. "Well, Angus ain't here, an' he ain't ever been runnin' the railroads—don't matter what he thinks he's doin'. Just let him an' the others see they turn out enough rail for us back in Pittsburgh. 'Course, you can't put in a bridge down there if Brenner's got a trestle on his plans, but you can be chief engineer here for a little while. Don't worry about it; I'll help you. I thought, till I come on some of your crew a little while back, that you might have left already to see your people. You decided not to see 'em, have you?"

Ranald had been back to the hacienda three times in the seven years since they had left. This, if he made it, would be Thorne's first visit. He wanted desperately to go, but even more desperately at times, he feared going.

"I still—want to go. Maybe when Mr. Brenner comes back . . ." Then he said impulsively, "I was thinking Ted might want to come."

Ted looked a little less cross and bored. He had heard there were other boys of about his age at Thorne's old home down the valley, and he thought things might be a little better there for a few days. Ted disliked being with his father, who seemed no more than a critical stranger, and he had no interest whatever in the building of railroads. But Ted did not like Thorne MacWinter either. He did not understand and resented his father's attachment to the young man.

Thorne was wondering why he had asked to take Ted along. So far as he could recall, the thought had never entered his mind until he spoke it. It was partly, he knew, because what the boy was and was not, irritated, disappointed and saddened Fitz. At times, Thorne felt more than a little sorry for them both; but was he so uneasy about going home that he must take a stranger to divert attention? What made him so afraid—ashamed?—to face the people he wanted most to see again? He had never wanted to leave, would still give double the past seven years to be as he had been before the advent of Angus Maxwell in his life. *They* were the ones. They had let him, made him go, simply by doing nothing to help him to stay. The bitterness of that might never leave him. Yet, when he let himself think about it, he was miserable with longing for the familiar places and people. His feelings about the hacienda would, it seemed, never be more than a bewildering, painful tangle which he saw no hope of unsnarling. Unless . . . maybe they would tell him something now, his uncle or aunt, that would answer the questions he still did not quite know.

Fitz was saying, "I reckon Ted can go with you, but you better git 'er done as soon as Brenner gits back. Ain't you supposed to be back east in three weeks or so to go with Ranald to Europe? Europe! God! That's just what we need on the roads out here, a bloomin' world traveler."

"It's likely to be the only vacation Ranald or I will ever have," Thorne said. "I still don't understand how Angus ever came to make such a generous offer."

Fitz said, with a not-quite-concealed grin, "I expect even he felt like celebratin' a lot when they said you could graduate. You ain't never tried to keep him from worryin', have you? An' then there's Ranald; *he* done things ought to be celebrated, first in this subject, second in t'other." He sobered, feeling angry. "An', by God, Angus owes you boys somethin'. Both of you have worked summers and other times free for him all these years."

"Not free," Thorne corrected drily. "We've had room and board all that time, and the schooling. We're supposed to study railroads in Europe, and mines and mills. He's getting together a list and wants written reports."

"Don't you study one damn' thing," Fitz said hotly, " 'lessen it's how to have yourselves one ringtail time."

"That's what I mean to do."

"Well, are you gonna show me now how a real-live, college-trained engineer operates?"

"Maybe I will if you play your cards right—after I eat."

Finally, with young Ted Fitzroy, Thorne rode away down the valley, not hurrying. As he rode along, he thought of the work, of future work, of Fitz, of people he had known at college, of anything to avoid thinking of home. He must expect nothing, must count on nothing. Everyone, everything would be so changed after all this time. *He* was changed, but through all the changes he had wished, painfully, that everything might be as he remembered, as he still so often dreamed.

They arrived at the half-timbered adobe cabin near supper time. It looked smaller, a strange kind of house; the sheds and barns and fences were weathered, old, some needing repair or replacement. Thorne tried not to be aware of anything that differed from his memories. His welcome was warm, clamorous, tearful.

"Ranald said you'd be coming this summer," said Maria, holding him, her breath catching on a sob. "But we were almost giving up hope. It's almost August. Ay, *hijo*, it's been so long!"

"I've been working," Thorne mumbled, more than a little embarrassed by the demonstrativeness.

"Look at how you've grown!" she cried, rubbing determinedly at her eyes. "And so handsome! How many girls are after you for a husband?"

"None," he said, finally able to disengage himself gently. He was not handsome; he knew that better than anyone.

"Of course he's grown, lass," said Gavin gruffly, refusing to let go of Thorne's hand. "What would you expect after all this while? You and Ranald are about the same height now, aren't you, lad?"

"Ranald's still taller."

"Oh, Thorne," said Maria, wistfully and with fresh tears, "why haven't you come back to us before?"

Gavin threw Maria a look which said plainly that she should not have asked the question. The two of them had discussed—how many times in seven years?—why the lad would not come back. He blamed them for Angus's taking him away, that was obvious. And why shouldn't he? They could tell him nothing, could not give him the reasons for things having happened as they had. What *could* the boy think, except that they hadn't wanted him? Gavin secretly had given up hope long ago of seeing Thorne again. Now that he was here, he would not see him made uneasy by discussion and questions about things that were none of the boy's doing.

An abrupt silence had fallen. Maria and the younger children, grown incredibly, were waiting, watching Thorne. He said lamely, "I've been—busy. I've wanted to come."

"Look here, then," Gavin said, more loudly than was necessary. "It's your old Folly. You remember the dog, lad. You asked Meg to look after him for you. Well, she has. Meg's gone over to Joe's, and she must be on her way back now. The old dog trails her everywhere."

Everyone paid attention to the dog, and he wagged his tail, looking gratified. Maria declared unequivocally that the dog remembered Thorne. Thorne felt sure he did not. How could he? Why should he? Folly was smaller than he had been in memories, and now his muzzle was gray, and he moved with grave dignity rather than the puppyish frolicking so dear to Thorne's dreams. Somehow, seeing the dog was very difficult for him.

They sat down to a delicious supper, with Maria loquacious and proud of all the things from the garden. There had even been enough grapes last year to make some wine. She brought out a bottle for this occasion, remarking, by way of a reminder to Gavin, that as she had always said, the vines *were* worthwhile. Eating eased the situation for Thorne. It was something concrete to do, along with the talking and the thinking. The others were too busy now to watch him so eagerly, and Thorne could look at them in quick, hungry glances.

Maria and Gavin looked much older to him. Maria had only a few threads of black left in the gray of her hair. Gavin's hair was white, his face deeply lined; he obviously had trouble seeing things clearly at close range.

The younger children were hardly children any more. Baby Laurie was eleven, very pretty, and the three boys were big, sometimes awkward adolescents. And Meg . . . Meg was beautiful. Her beauty startled Thorne, brought him a strange kind of shyness, almost awe. Ranald had said she was growing up pretty, but Thorne had been able to think of her only as she had been at thirteen. Actually, she was not so much changed. At thirteen, she had been tall for her age, and she had not grown much taller. Her face and figure had taken on most of their adult fullness by the time she was thirteen; but now, he thought, everything was—completed. She was not a little girl anymore, and she was beautiful. Did she have any memory of that last day when she had begged him not to go? Of course, it had meant nothing to her, not compared to the meaning and solace he had wrung from it all these years.

They told him many things during supper, and Thorne was delighted with and fascinated by their accent, by the ability, which he had lost, for intermingling Spanish and English without thinking about it. Their language and pronunciation were not, as he and

Ranald had been told by Angus and teachers, ignorant-sounding, provincial, unintelligible; they were fascinating, unique. The older children were scattered now, with their families: Jean in Denver, Ian in Santa Fe, Carmela gone all the way to California. Joe, Rafaela and their children would certainly come over from their own house as soon as they heard Thorne was home. There were eight grandchildren altogether now.

The younger children, having overcome a slight initial diffidence, put in a few words, when they could, about their own interests and activities. The boys showed a reserved friendliness for Ted Fitzroy, who was, as usual, slightly condescending, waiting impatiently for a turn to talk and boast, eager to be away from the adults and to try to make himself the center of attention.

They told Thorne about the hacienda and the rest of the community, about new Anglo farmers coming into the valley, and about what had turned out to be a minor gold strike up to the northwest. They talked about people Thorne had known: who had died, who had married and had children. Maria mentioned that Esteban Arragon had died the previous year while on a long visit to Spain. She told Thorne in detail about the new church of Santa Filomina that was to be built, about the new priest, Father O'Malley, the first priest they'd had who was not Spanish. Maria gave Thorne a searching glance and he knew she must inevitably ask when he had last gone to confession, taken communion.

Thorne answered their questions briefly, asked his own, which brought far more detailed answers. He finally relaxed. It was, after all, so good to be there. The small, aching sadness in him, because of the separation he could feel between them and himself, was understandable. He knew he was the one responsible for maintaining the distance—a margin of safety, perhaps—he had changed much more than they. They were his family, eager to take him back as a part of themselves, but it would always be in the back of his mind that they had stood by, unwilling or unable to help him in his most desperate time of need. He never doubted that there was something more than he knew involved in the situation; and now, as seven years ago, he wanted to be told what it was, but he could not ask. He was thoroughly glad now that he had come, but this was no longer his real home. Perhaps he would never again have a true home. Home was not just a place; it was a whole spectrum of feelings, and that spectrum had shattered when Gavin and Maria had withdrawn, leaving him on his own to face Angus Maxwell when he was too young and totally unprepared. They had all deserted him—all of them but Meg, who had questioned his leaving as he had, who had cried and begged him to stay.

When the meal finished, the younger children went out to the porch while the grown-ups sat on around the table, Maria not nearly done with talking. Meg brought the wine bottle to refill their glasses. She had said little during the evening, but her clear-skinned, fair face and dark eyes held a kind of radiance, a quiet joy. While filling his glass, she paused for a moment, resting a hand shyly on Thorne's shoulder. Maria went on with what she had been saying, but Thorne stopped hearing her as he looked up into his cousin's face. Meg met his eyes only for an instant, with a little smile that seemed slightly unsteady. Her lovely, gentle eyes radiated warmth. Thorne put up his hand to cover hers, but she withdrew and crossed the kitchen to begin scraping pots from the stove.

Thorne, for no reason immediately evident to him, slept badly that night. Through the morning, he helped Gavin with various tasks around the place, finding pleasure and comfort in the familiar things that brought back a flood of memories.

"You've not really told us much about yourself,"

Gavin said hesitantly, as they rested briefly, smoking, in the shade of the barn.

"There's not much to tell. I like engineering work, seeing things planned and built. I suppose I'll go on working for MM&F as long as Frank Fitzroy is around. It won't be many years, I think, before Ranald is general manager. Maybe he's written you that there has been some talk lately about moving most of the company's interests west, but Fitz is the only partner who's completely in favor of that. Ranald is popular, liked by all the partners and everyone else he meets. You must know what his grades have been."

Gavin looked at him for a moment, wistful questions still in his eyes. Thorne, avoiding the look, thought, Ranald is your son; I'm not. He disliked himself for the residual, unconquerable bitterness, but it would not be completely put down.

Joe's family came to the house for lunch. Thorne, a little less noticed now, his presence a little less novel, could for the most part keep silent, letting their talk, their existences flow around him with quiet enjoyment. After lunch, as Maria was finishing up in the kitchen, he went in and asked for a little food to take with him.

"I thought I'd take a ride," he said. "Maybe I won't be back by the time supper's ready."

Maria, chattering away, packed him a lunch. She watched him yearningly as he left.

Thorne rode slowly, once he was out of the valley, trying to live entirely through his senses: completely experiencing the feel of the hot sun on his shoulders and bare head, the slight breeze that fingered his face and hair like a familiar old friend; hearing the brawling little stream, birdsong, the fussy chatter of squirrels and chipmunks; seeing every facet of the bright sky, small fluffy clouds, mountains standing up indomitably to make a sheltering horizon; breathing the heat-increased evergreen scent—even the dust raised by the horse's hoofs smelled better than dust anywhere else;

savoring the taste of the cold fresh water when he was thirsty, and of some strong, acid huckleberries he found a little later. This was where he really belonged, physically as well as emotionally—alone, nostalgic, wistful, but not really unhappy.

After several hours, he realized that the others might be hurt if he spent too much of the day away from them. Reluctantly he turned back, the low sun pressing heat against his back and shoulders. Not far above where the little creek he followed met the Oso, he saw a horse tied beside the trail, and a moment later, saw Meg sitting on a log. His heart gave a heavy lifting beat of pleasure, but somehow he was not surprised that she had come.

"I thought you might be up here," she said in greeting, getting up and moving a little way toward him, out of shadow. "Up here along Piñon Creek used to be one of your favorite places."

As Thorne halted his horse, it lowered its head to crop at a dry bunch of grass. He said inanely, "You've grown up."

Meg blushed and made a gesture of negation. Not quite meeting his direct, approving look, she said, "Have I changed a lot, do you think?"

"You're—beautiful."

She had not expected that. She flushed more deeply and asked, "Do you want to rest awhile?"

He dismounted, tying his horse near hers, saying, "I suppose I ought to try to get back in time for supper."

"They don't really expect you. You don't have to go out of your way to be polite and thoughtful, you know. This is home, your family."

"And you?"

She frowned slightly. "If you mean, was I being polite or impolite to follow you like this?—I don't know. If you mean, will they expect me for supper?—I ride sometimes, by myself. It's a pleasant, restful thing to do. Laurie's big enough now to help Mama, and there aren't so many to do for as we used to have."

"Aunt Maria gave me bread and meat and cheese before I left. Do you want some?"

She shook her head and there was sadness in her eyes as she said softly, "I suppose it was bound to be this way, but it sounds strange that you don't call them Mama and Papa any more."

Thorne looked up, following the flight of a magpie that seemed to explode out of the willows. Meg moved to resume her seat on the log, and after a moment he came and sat beside her. There was a long silence between them. The creek ran quietly here.

"Thorne, why haven't you come home before?" Her voice was low, pleasant, full of concern. They were looking away from each other.

"You've heard from Ranald what I've been doing—that I've been busy," he said, trying not to sound curt. "What I want to know is why you're not married. I know that you were twenty in April. Are you going to be an old maid?"

"I asked my question first," she said, not smiling, refusing to banter.

"Ranald mentioned that there were a lot of boys the last time he was here, especially Gordon Gaynor. Surely some of them have asked you."

"I don't want to be talked to like a little girl," she flared, "'—Tell me about your little life, honey.' If that's what it takes, though, to get you to talk, I'll tell you. Yes, some have asked; Gordon has. I'm waiting for the one that seems right, even if it means not finding anyone, being an old maid. You must know I spent three years at the convent school in Santa Fe. This past spring, I took the teacher's examination and passed very nicely. Mr. Gaynor hasn't been well for a long time. He's asked me to help with the Quintana School in the fall. It's part of the state system now, you know. If I weren't going to work for him, I could find another teaching job easily enough. There aren't nearly enough teachers around here, and hardly any who speak Spanish."

"The state will never let you teach in Spanish."

"Maybe not, if they know about it, but I can understand the Spanish kids, talk to them, help them more with English."

Thorne found that he was thinking with anger and resentment of Gordon Gaynor, recalling his knowledge of the secret of Gordon and Esteban Arragon. Esteban was dead. Most likely, Gordon had never been truly homosexual; Thorne now knew that there were some who pandered to the needs of those unfortunate men without being one of them. Whatever Gordon's circumstances might be, Thorne resented his proposing to Meg. Ranald had told him long ago that Gordon's carefully laid plans included marrying her.

Unconsciously, Thorne clenched his teeth as he said coolly, "How much law school does Gordon have left? Two years? One?"

"I thought you'd seen him a couple of times back east," she said, sighing, resigning herself to his line of conversation for the time being.

"Ranald has."

"And what were you doing when Gordon visited?"

"Once I was making up a history exam. The second time was at Easter vacation. Ranald went to visit a friend of his in Boston. I was with Fitz, working on a bridge collapse on the Central Western near Chicago."

"You like Mr. Fitzroy very much."

He nodded and there was another silence.

She said softly, "Why haven't you come home?"

Thorne rolled and lit a cigarette. His movements were quick and jerky. She couldn't tell whether he was feeling more uneasy, or more irritated.

"Uncle Gavin says wool prices—"

"I answered your question."

A strong gust of wind ruffled the trees and died away.

"Ranald has told me," she went on persistently, with a gentle relentlessness, "that for the first year in Pittsburgh, he thought all the time you'd leave, come back home to stay. He's told me how hard it's been for you, the way Mr. Maxwell is; and he knows some of the things about that awful military school you had to go to, about the boy who—died there, about how sick you were that time. He was sure then you wouldn't stay."

"You don't need me to tell you anything," he said, trying to smile.

"I—none of us, sometimes not even Ranald—have known much from *you* in all this time. You've almost never written, and when you did, it wasn't about you; it was just—about things."

Thorne drew in smoke and exhaled slowly, looking down at the gliding surface of the stream. It had never been easy for him to talk about matters that were strictly personal. For one thing, he had been convinced long ago that hardly anyone wanted to hear them, that people preferred talking about themselves or about more objective matters, that he was the only one truly interested in his own feelings and experiences, and that perhaps even he was wasting interest on them. Growing up, striving to screen himself protectively from the bewilderments, pain and frustration of a life that had been forced upon him, he had all but lost the ability, certainly the wish, to talk seriously about himself with anyone. Meg's eyes, soft and intent, were on his face. He had never had anything to fear from Meggy.

She said, "You've grown up too, of course, but I can't really tell for sure how much you've changed. There's a—a closed look about you now; it almost seems a hardness, and I know that's not really you. Why didn't you come home? Especially after that terrible school? How could you bear staying there?"

"We didn't stay there," he said slowly. "We went

back to Pine Glen for another year and a half. I didn't leave that time, partly because I—couldn't seem to collect the energy just then; I didn't care enough—I still thought about running away, to almost anywhere. I worked in the mines when I wasn't in school. All the rest of the time we were at Pine Glen. When there was any spare time at all, I was tired."

"Why hasn't Ranald been made to work the way you have? He doesn't understand that himself."

"He has worked. Every summer—"

"He's been given mostly office work, things like that. You've had to go into the mines—hard work, driving those big nails they use on the railroads—"

"Spikes."

"—always such hard work, and not just summers. Ranald says they almost killed you."

He smiled ironically. "No one's ever come close to doing that. It's made me strong and I've liked some of it. I mean to be a good engineer."

"You could be good, the best, at anything you wanted," she said with conviction, and put her hand gently over his. Her voice broke a little. "I can't bear it that people have been cruel to you."

"No one's been cruel," he said lightly. "Even driving those big nails isn't a bad job."

"Please don't make fun of me or of yourself," she said. "You've gotten awfully good at hiding things; maybe you even hide them from yourself, but I don't think you really believe Mr. Maxwell hasn't been cruel, or, at the least, completely unreasonable with you."

After a moment, he said thoughtfully, "There was a man at Pine Glen, a new teacher, when I went back there after Smoot's. He'd been an engineer, mostly working on turnpikes and canals, but he was hurt in a stage accident and couldn't walk very well. Since I always liked math and planning things on paper, he'd let me come to his office, if I had the time, and fool around with drafting and things. He talked a lot about the work he'd done, and I could see how good it could be, to plan things and then be a part of seeing them done."

Thorne found he was uncomfortable now and drew his hand away from Meg's, trying to be unobtrusive about it, using that hand to put out his cigarette. Her real and obvious concern might prove a path for release, but any real revelations about himself also made him vulnerable, and he was very wary of that. Also, her caring and nearness were making him uneasily aware of her warm femininity.

"Ranald said Mr. Maxwell didn't want you to go into railroading—not *just* railroading, I mean."

Thorne drew a breath through his teeth, not yet defensive enough to stop talking. "I don't know why, but he's wanted me to learn about all parts of the company, the thing Ranald has really wanted and is doing. I worked in the mill our first summer in college. I suppose he wants someone who can take it all over eventually, someone under his direction, someone who's supposed to be grateful enough just to do as he's told. Ranald is great with management; he even manages to get along, most of the time, with Angus. I never want to *run* anything, except whatever construction projects I may plan. . . . Mr. Corelli, the teacher I was talking about, told Angus I could be a first-rate engineer. He said I was bright and—some other things. Angus almost strangled him. That was just before graduation at Pine Glen. I had begun to want the training and the degree by then, though I didn't really like school any better, and it seemed to be lasting forever. Angus kept talking about business administration, saying he wouldn't pay for engineering school, but I thought he would, when it came down to it; and I thought I ought to stay on, because it had begun to seem to me that he—well, owed me the education—or something."

"What happened to Mr. Corelli? Have you been back to see him?"

"What? Oh. He died, more than two years ago."

"Thorne, isn't there anyone back there, besides Ranald, who—loves you?"

He looked away, feeling his cheeks grow hot.

"Isn't there anyone you care about?"

"I don't know what you mean." His voice sounded sullen.

"Yes, you do. You're lonely and—unhappy. With all your camouflaging, I can still see it. Mama and Papa can. You've gotten—hard; at least, you try to believe you have."

"Ah no, Meggy." The words were barely audible.

"You like Ranald—maybe you love him—and there's that Mr. Fitzroy you talk about, but I've had the feeling that if both of them were to disappear, you'd try to believe they hadn't really mattered. What about Mrs. Maxwell?"

"Elizabeth is—nice."

"I know you don't like him at all, and it's no wonder, but—"

"I hate him," he said softly, levelly.

"But you're going to stay on with his company."

"I'll be working for Fitz. Maybe I'll never see Angus again after this fall. I could go to work for somebody else, but not with the kind of job, the responsibility Fitz will give me right away. Angus is only one partner in MM&F. I've come to feel that he—that the company—owes me the job I want, if I do it well."

"But what about *you*? What about other *people*? Is the job going to be your life, then?"

"I don't think I'd put it just that way. I have to earn a living. I'm really just beginning now. I'd like it to be something I can be proud of." He smiled at her. "Do you go at Ran like this when he comes home?"

"A little, maybe, but you're not Ran."

"Somctimes, I guess, I've wished I was. You know

about his college grades. And people usually like him on sight. He always knows the right thing and tries to do it. He's always been like that."

Gently, Meg took his hand and slipped hers into it. Her hand was warm, strong for a woman's, it seemed. He smoothed the long, tapered fingers down and looked at them.

"I hope it goes beautifully," she said, "—your running the railroads."

"I'm not going to be—"

"I hope, for once, it's a thing you really, truly want."

There was another silence. Thorne was not as uneasy now with the talk as he had been; he felt no need to argue or protest or point out things that seemed obvious. To his chagrin, he found himself thinking of the few women he had known in the college town. It was embarrassing to think of them while sitting here with Meg.

"Will you be working out here again when you come back from Europe?"

"Yes."

"Can you come home more often then?"

"When you say 'out here' I think of the West. It's a big country, Meg. We've got lines or projected lines other places than Colorado."

Her eyes were sad as she looked away. "Thorne, why did you have to go in the first place? I never have understood."

"Nor have I," he said slowly. "I was just thinking that you might be able to tell me. I was wondering if they might have said something. I was such a kid then. It seemed as if I had to do as I was told, and there wasn't any choice. I remember you said I should run away, but I wouldn't have been very—successful at running for the rest of my life, and I don't think I ever could have come back here if I'd run."

"Of course you could. It was plain to all of us you didn't want to go with the Maxwells, and none of us wanted you to, except Ranald, and he certainly would have understood."

Thorne picked up a stick with his free hand and drew aimless grooves in the sandy ground. The sun was dropping behind the mountains. A little finch in the brush across the stream sang a sweet song to the evening.

Thorne had not meant to say any more on the subject. The memories of the emotional pain and confusion were almost as vivid as the original feelings had been. His voice was not quite steady. "Why didn't they just say I needn't go?"

Meg pressed his hand, blinking at unshed tears that burned her eyes. "I wondered," she said softly, "and I've asked. They—saw what you were, what you could be. They wanted to do the right thing for you, for your future. They love you, Thorne. They never meant you harm, or sadness or—you do know they love you?"

"I know." His voice was quiet.

She turned her compassionate eyes to him, but he was looking away. She thought he looked tired, older than he was, trying to hold onto his mask of indifference.

"If they'd dreamed you'd be hurt the way you have been—"

"I haven't been hurt," he said, sounding angry. He stood up abruptly, dropping her hand and walking away from her. "You always had too much imagination."

Meg sat still as he walked about restlessly for a time. Finally, he came back to stand before her, most of the indications of struggle gone from his face.

"We ought to go." He could look at her directly now.

"Don't be angry." She had remembered his eyes so clearly through the years, the dark depths, looking intensely blue by contrast with the thick black lashes.

"I'm not angry."

"You were. Why do you have to hide things like that—feelings—even from yourself?"

"This deep, soul-searching stuff gets out of my range pretty quickly, Meg. It always has."

"You're still hiding. Why can't you be yourself, the way you always used to?"

"I am *not* hiding. I think I'm hungry."

She had stood up, her brown eyes flashing. "We used to talk," she challenged. "Sometimes, we had serious conversations."

"We've been talking," he said dryly. "We used to have quarrels, too, and you always seemed to take them seriously."

"Well, quarrel, then. Do things that are *you*. You want to talk about your work, the weather, politics, wool prices, anything that doesn't come too close to you. You've been doing that ever since you came back—that and a lot of listening. You're home now. You don't have to be afraid here."

"Meggy, I don't—"

"Have you decided that you have to have a heart made out of—of stone—or—or railroad spikes? You used to talk, sometimes, about birds and trees and stars. Sometimes, we saw cloud pictures, do you remember? . . . Mama told you last night she's always prayed for you. Well, so have I, and now I want to pray even more because I know that what's happened to you scares me. All the years, the education and things haven't really changed Ranald, except that he's grown up. He's still someone familiar, my brother, someone I can know again each time, as soon as he comes home. I think it was awfully hard for you to come here, that you're still not altogether sure you should have come. Oh, Thorne, have you been hurt so badly you can't love anymore, or let yourself *be* loved by us? Do you have to stop believing you care about anything? Don't you see how beautiful the sunset is this very minute? You haven't stopped noticing things like that?"

Tears had begun to spill from her eyes, and his arms went round her, trembling.

"Don't cry, Meggy. Please don't." The words were muffled, choked.

"I can't bear thinking of you as trying to be hard and mean like—the way Mr. Maxwell seems to be."

"Don't say that," he said harshly. "I'm nothing like him. I never will be."

"You used to be so happy and—and carefree. That got you in trouble sometimes, but we all loved it because it was you. Now, most of the time you've been home, you've seemed like a stranger, someone we never really knew and who doesn't want to be known. It's no wonder, I guess, if you hate us because you were taken away, but you're—"

"Meggy, I don't, I can't." A coldness inside him was melting. It hurt, as other things had hurt; but with the pain came a great and fearsome joy. "I knew, before I went away, that I loved you. So many times since then I've dreamed . . ."

His hands held her arms, caressed her face, wiping at the tears. He held her again, hard against him, seeking her mouth with his.

"Thorne . . ." Meg was experiencing tumultuous feelings, of which she had known only hints before, and she was frightened. She had not meant anything like this to happen. Thorne's hard, strong body pressing against her warmly, urgently, made her dizzy.

She turned her face away from his, struggling. "Please let me go. I didn't mean . . ."

"I'm not cold," he said pleadingly. "You're right, I suppose, I've tried to be, but it mostly doesn't work out right for me. It—it hurts to care sometimes. Meggy, please love me, really love me. I haven't known how much I need you."

His arms still held her, but loosely. She had stepped

away from him a little. She was tall and needed to raise her frightened eyes only a little to meet his. He was pale, his dark eyes burning. His face was open now, wholly vulnerable.

She looked away, whispering miserably, "I was talking about—loving parents—brothers and sisters. I don't want to hurt you. I'd do anything—almost—to make you happy, but . . . oh, Thorne, that would be so wrong. We—"

"You're not my sister. I'm not your brother."

"But we're cousins and we—"

"Why is what I want—want more than the whole world, a bad thing? I can't feel it's wrong, if you want it too. Why does it have to be a sin and a crime to try to be—"

"Let me go," she said gently. His hands were still clasped together behind her. She tried to smile. "Maybe you haven't changed so much after all. You still want to follow whims and—"

"It's not a whim. I've thought of you so much, all these years, of you more than anyone here or anywhere. I knew I loved you that day when you cried and begged me not to go. I haven't let myself think much about it, because I was afraid . . . Meggy, can't you *feel* that I love you?"

He drew her against him again, and she pushed at him, calling on anger to bolster her frightening weakness.

"Don't!" she said fiercely. "If you try to force me, I'll—"

He dropped his arms and she stepped back, stumbling a little over a broken branch. His hand came up to steady her, but she regained her balance and he did not touch her.

"I wouldn't force you," he said miserably, his breath coming with difficulty. "God, Meggy, I'm not like that. Please—want me, love me."

She stood there trembling too much to be able to

move farther away. She did love him, and not wholly as a brother. For as long as she could remember, she had loved him differently, and more than she loved any of the others. She had treasured those feelings, while keeping them, for the most part, away from the surface of her conscious mind, not willing to explore or question, or quite even to admit them. Were those feelings the real reason she had followed him today? Oh, God, no! It was wrong and wicked, what was happening to them. She had come because something in him worried her, made her afraid for him. She sensed that portentousness even now in his candid face, his ardent words and pleading eyes. He must not be hurt again, not by her. She put out her hands to him, closing her eyes.

Thorne, trembling in the grip of more than physical desire, was infinitely gentle and tender with her. He spoke shakily, words he could never have dreamed he would say to anyone, words of love and reassurance that exposed his own feelings so completely. He tried to soothe her conscience, to free it by saying over and over what he truly believed, that there could not be wickedness or even wrong in their love. Her body was slender, strong, beautifully developed. His hands were gently insistent, and his trembling increased as she began to respond to him, to relinquish all thought of anything else.

When it was finished, they lay still for long, beautiful moments. Meg's fingers moved a little, unconsciously, in his hair. There had been pain for her, in the beginning, but even the memory of it was all but erased in a flood of other feelings. She had been helpless but strong, protected but turbulently powerful, in the thing the two of them had caused to happen.

Thorne moved lethargically, murmuring her name, smiling faintly, lying beside her on the rough ground. He felt his life was changed now, that he had been rescued from some strong current over which he had little control. He didn't want to think just yet of the details of this major change or of what might result from it. He wanted to think of nothing—only Meg.

"Are you all right?" he asked with contrition. "The ground, I didn't notice was so hard."

"It doesn't matter." She spoke and moved dreamily, pushing down her clothes, turning in his arms to fit her head to his shoulder.

"Life—Nature—is unfair to women in all kinds of ways," he said apologetically. "It's not fair that it has to hurt you, making love the first time. Oh, Meggy, I'll try to make everything better from now on."

"Thorne, I love you."

"I do see the sunset now," he said softly after a moment. "It's almost done, but it's the most beautiful sunset that's ever been. . . . Angus, some of the others have tried so hard to make me be things I'm not. I've felt, I guess, that what I am was—second best, while I've fought to hold onto it. The good part about home is that you—no one here has ever tried to make me over. I suppose that's really what it means to me—to come home—that and being with you. When can we be married?"

Meg started. Memories of all the reasons this should not have happened poured back into her mind, filling her with pain and guilt. Before Thorne realized she was upset, she had slipped from his arms with a choked sob and was running to where the horses were tied.

He got up quickly and came toward her. "Don't go. Stay and talk. We *have* to talk now. I swear to you it's all right. Meggy . . ."

Without looking back at him, she pulled her reins free, mounted the horse and rode blindly away.

Thorne finally found a chance to see Meg alone again when she was in the vegetable garden, on the third morning after their meeting beside Piñon Creek.

Her eyes, as they briefly flicked up at him, reminded him of the eyes of a scared fawn.

"Come somewhere and talk to me," he said beseechingly.

"I have to get the corn that's ready," she said, her voice sounding cold. She grasped an ear of corn and wrenched at it with both hands to hide her trembling.

"I'll help you," he said, and made short work of it. "Please don't be angry."

"Thorne, just leave me alone. Forget . . ."

"You make me feel as if . . . Is it so bad that you can't even look at me anymore?"

If I run away from him here, she thought, someone might see, and the talk and questions will begin.

"I can't forget," he said softly, earnestly. "I never want to. Meggy, I'd like to say I'm sorry, and I am—sorry as hell for the way you seem to be feeling—but you gave me almost more—joy than I could bear. I want it to be something—forever. I guess it wasn't like that for you, but I'll do anything to try to make it better—right. It's not just that I want to be with you, like that. I want whatever I am to be a part of what you are and . . ."

"Please don't talk anymore," she said shakily.

"I don't exactly—want to," he said with difficulty. "I have to, Meg. I can't just—give this up. Don't ask me to do that. I feel like a hell of a weakling, having to beg you even to talk to me, but I have to—I want to, if it'll help . . . It seems nobody's ever really listened to me, given a damn what I felt about anything. Until the other day, I supposed they never would. It's never been easy for me to talk about—things that really matter, and I'm making a bad job of it now. This—you—matter more than . . ."

"We're cousins." The words were wrung from her, making her choke, as she willed her eyes to stay dry. "We could never marry; you know that. Even if we could marry, we've already committed a mortal sin. You know that too. Why do you have to—"

"We can marry, Meg. There can be a dispensation—"

"Not for first cousins!" she cried miserably.

He clenched his teeth. "If a dispensation is so important to you, you'll by God have one. They *have* been given for first cousins. Look at all the royal families where they hardly marry anyone except cousins."

"We're hardly a royal family," she said, the hurt in her voice sounding more like bitterness and derision.

He was thoughtful for a moment before he said desperately, "Then there are other churches . . ."

"I couldn't marry outside the church," she said dully. "Thorne, it's *wrong*. Everything about it is wrong. I'm so sorry I came after you. That was the beginning, but I didn't mean . . ."

"It was *right*," he said fiercely. "It was good and beautiful. Don't be afraid of me, Meggy, or of . . . Please come some place where we can talk."

"No."

"You said you love me."

"I—I—that's as wrong as the rest of it—to feel—like that, about my cousin."

"None of it is wrong," he said angrily. Then more reasonably, "To get back to the railroad at the time Mr. Brenner agreed to, I have to leave tomorrow. I've waited this long hoping you'd—hoping you could begin to see . . ."

"Go," she said with more strength than she had believed herself to have. "Pretend nothing happened here. We both have to forget! Take the trip to Europe with Ran. You deserve something besides work and lectures from Mr. Maxwell."

"I don't want anything from him. I want to be with you, to stay here in the valley for the rest of my life, if it's what you want."

"You've got a career," she said. Her voice sounded actually cold now, and she was glad. "You've practically had to sell your soul for it, and now it's just begun."

He took a step backward, unsteadily, as though she had struck him. There was a great constriction in Meg's chest, as if a cold iron fist was closing there, but she went on mercilessly.

"You're not thinking of anyone except . . . If we stayed here and tried to get a dispensation or—or anything, everyone would know. I love Mama and Papa and the others too much to want to shame them like that."

"Then we won't stay here."

"That's not what I meant. Oh, Thorne, it's all I can do to bear living with myself after . . . Go away. Don't make it any harder."

"But you do love me."

"You're my cousin!" she cried. "Practically my brother—"

"I am *not* your brother!" Then he said more quietly, "You do love me?"

"I don't know," she said brokenly. "I don't seem to know anything anymore, except that to go on like that would be selfish and wicked. If you yell at me again, I'll start screaming. I don't think I can help it. Mama will hear and then . . ."

He looked at her steadily, quietly. She was pale and looked tired, as if she had had little sleep these past nights. He, too, had been wakeful, trying to sort out what would be the right thing to do, to say, yearning to make her believe, as he did, that their togetherness was the true scheme of the rest of their lives.

"Please come and talk to me. I'll do whatever I can to help us both be calm and—"

"No. It wouldn't change anything."

She went to pick up the big basket of sweet corn, and he snatched it out of her reach.

"Suppose I tell them?" he said fiercely, "—Uncle Gavin and Aunt Maria. They'd—"

"You wouldn't!" she gasped, but his face was so black with hurt and anger that she could not be completely sure.

"I've saddled two horses," he said grimly. "I'll take the corn in and tell Aunt Maria we're going for a ride."

When they were out of sight of the house, Thorne said, his voice unsteady and his eyes turned away, "I didn't mean to—threaten you like that. Surely you know I'd never have done . . ."

Meg had begun to cry; she did not cry often or easily, but exhaustion, mental anguish and torment were taking their toll. Now she felt with hopeless desolation that she might never be able to stop crying.

"Meggy," Thorne pleaded, trying to take her hand, "it *is* all right. I swear it. Please . . ."

"I don't want you hurt," she sobbed. "I came up the canyon because you had seemed so hurt. I only wanted to . . . and now I've . . ."

"Don't be sorry for that. I told you, I can't ever be. It's only because *you're* so hurt that I'm sorry. Please try to believe it doesn't have to be the way you're thinking. People change the ways they think about things and see things. There are other ways of thinking, other ways of living than those the Catholic Church teaches. It's not wicked for us to love each other. It *feels* too right. It's not wrong, Meggy. It can't be."

"Only because we—you—want it not to be. You could murder someone—a person could—and then . . . rationalize to convince himself it wasn't wrong."

"Think about us, about the rest of our lives . . ."

"I am!" she cried desperately. "I don't want us to end by hating each other."

There was a silence before he began tensely, "I

can't know how to talk to you. I don't know the words to persuade you to look at things—humanly, instead of from the church's point of view."

"I believe in the church," she said, tears still filling her eyes. "I have to do what's right."

"How do you know what the church says is right, *is* right? There are whole other worlds. Do you think Adam and Eve were married in the church? Do you think they took communion and . . . maybe they were cousins, too. And what about their children, those sons of Adam and Eve? They took wives, and those women must have been—"

"Stop it!" she sobbed. "You're using any argument that comes into your head and—"

"You're damned right I am, and I won't stop. Don't you see that? It means too much to me."

And he went on trying as they moved slowly along the road by the river. Meg's crying stopped, but she would not meet his eyes and her face looked determined. After a time, Thorne knew he was only repeating things he had already said. Eventually, he stopped talking.

There was a long time of silence before Meg said shakily, "I'll go back now. Thorne, I am sorry."

He said nothing, his eyes on the dry weeds between the wheel ruts. Meg found she could not quite leave him and she hated her weakness.

"I want you to be happy," she said, "more than I want anything in the world, but I can't . . . Please know I just can't. There'll be someone else and . . ."

Thorne felt sick. He shivered in the late July heat, his fists clenched, his whole body tensing with defeat.

"Come back to the house now," she said in a small, frightened voice.

His horse turned with hers. He sat silent, his eyes turned away from her. His mouth looked sullen, a closed, adamant look of self-protection on his face, trying to deny the pain.

"Thorne, please!" she burst out finally. His silence, his looking like that, was harder to combat than any words.

When he looked at her finally, his eyes were dull, expressionless. "I'll go," he said tonelessly, "today, as soon as I can."

"Not like this!" she couldn't stop the words. "You have to understand . . ."

"*Why* do I have to?" he cried, and now there were sparks of anger again in the depths of his eyes. "I don't understand. Why do you have to let *things*, precepts made up by other people, ruin . . ."

"I don't want to ruin," she pled earnestly. "It should never have happened. I was stupid. We were both thoughtless—self-indulgent—"

"*I* thought we were in love," he said bitterly.

"But we mustn't be."

"But we are." His eyes were fierce, holding hers. "*Do* you love me?"

She said brokenly, hardly above a whisper, "God help me, yes."

They were off the horses then, clinging to each other, moving almost unconsciously down to the trees along the river, both of them stumbling, weak and driven with desire. There was no gentleness now. Meg used the physical needs and urges, the all-conquering sweep of the emotion of love to drown, for these moments, the moral protests that had been so much a part of her life. She was wild with a tumult of feelings and sensations. With a will of its own, her body arched to his as she cried out with pleasure at last.

Thorne had never experienced such total joyous oblivion. When they had been still for a time, the vacuum of happiness that had seemed oblivion began to be filled with total love and contentment. He thought, Now I know what *wonderful* means. It's a shame the word's used for anything but something like this. Only maybe there never has been anything like this. He said that to Meg, holding her now gently, with an aching tenderness and gratitude.

"No," she murmured drowsily, "I can't believe anyone else ever felt just like this." But she stirred in his arms, the world beginning to intrude again.

Thorne said softly, urgently, "Don't say anything more yet. Don't think anything more."

Both were silent for a time, but for Meg it was over, the beauty being slowly drained away, to be replaced by the very real torments of guilt and shame.

Thorne, feeling her body tense, draw reflexively away from him, knew what must be happening to her. He kept very still, uncertain of what he should do or say.

Finally, he asked gently, "Won't you try to see it—us—differently? Can you let yourself try, for me? I think maybe I've never asked anyone for anything before. Nothing in the world can ever be as important to me as this."

After a long time, she said slowly, "Would you—go ahead and take the trip to Europe, give me some time?"

He lifted his head and she met his eyes for a moment. He couldn't quite believe she really meant to try. "I don't want to go away from you," he whispered, afraid to speak.

"Please? I'll try to think of it with the things you've said. I'll remember how—how it is to be with you because I won't be able not to remember. But I have to have time alone."

"I'll just go back up the valley; back to work."

"No, Thorne, you'd come back here too soon. Oh, I don't want you far away. I want you . . . but I've got to be sure I can be alone—without you—to think. Please try to understand."

He felt reprieved. This was more than he dared hope for. Finally, he nodded soberly.

"If you were so nearby, I'd be always thinking you might come back, and I couldn't concentrate on trying to be sensible, and . . ." she continued to explain.

They had stood up and were brushing dust and leaves from each other.

Thorne was facing the road, and he grinned, saying, "Maybe I ought to believe in miracles. What else could it have been that kept those horses from running away?"

They were able to laugh together, a little, as they went to catch the horses.

When they were riding back toward home, Meg said, "You'll be away till almost Christmas. A good long trip to rest and enjoy yourself and see things. You look awfully tired, you know. Mama keeps worrying about you."

"I'm not tired," he said absently. Then fervently, "Let me stay."

"Please . . ."

"Will you marry me then, as soon as I can get back?"

"Thorne, I have to have time," she began desperately.

He said wistfully, "I'd ask you not to talk to a priest."

"Don't ask for—anything else, please. Until a little while ago, I was so sure there was really nothing to be thought about. You've said people can change the way they look at things, the things they believe in, and I'm trying to believe I might be able to. I can't honestly promise more than that."

"All right. I'm sorry it has to be so hard for you. To me, it all seems so simple, and wonderful, except for leaving you."

"You should take this trip. I have to have the time."

He took her hand. "Will you write me what you're thinking?"

"The letters would never catch up with you."

"I'll have to stop off in Pittsburgh for a day or two when we're back from Europe. If you sent them in care of Frank Fitzroy—I'll give you his address there—they'd be there when I get back. It would mean a little less time I'd have to wait without hearing anything from you."

"I don't know," she said, feeling the incredible significance of her responsibility, trying to mask her uncertainty from him now, protectively.

"I'm asking for things again," he said contritely. "It's just that I'm afraid . . . Come on, race you to the barn."

"Oh, Thorne!" she whispered, "so am I afraid!" She could not urge her horse to run, could not see him clearly as his horse bolted away.

VI

It was near the end of November. Thorne and Ranald, on the train from New York to Pittsburgh, were returning from the trip to Europe. Ranald left the observation platform to get in out of the cold. Inside the car, he looked back at his cousin, standing out in the wind and smoke and the beginnings of a drizzle. Thorne had no coat, no hat. He was facing backward and, Ranald felt sure, seeing nothing. For a short time after Thorne had run away from Smoot's so long ago, his behavior had been a puzzle to Ranald; he was silent in an unaccustomed, subdued way, almost completely unresponsive to anything beyond his own secret thoughts. Now, ever since he had come east to begin the European trip, he had been enigmatic, but in a different way. There was no anger in his moodiness now. He had been, in fact, unusually affable and obliging, despite his characteristic periods of almost manic restlessness. But Thorne's periods of silent, complete abstraction puzzled Ranald. He suspected that Thorne had missed half the European tour because he hardly seemed to know or care about any of it. He would sit or stand sometimes for hours: staring, as he now stared from the observation platform of the train's last car—seeing, if anything, something very different from what his eyes looked at. In those times of preoccupation, he made no effort to keep emotion from showing in his face. He might smile quietly, delightedly for a long while, his idle eyes becoming even darker with dreaminess. Then would come an expression of extreme tension, or a soft, quiet, incredulous look, as if he were remembering, reliving some exquisite and undeserved pleasure. Since Thorne had left college in January, the boys had not seen one another for seven months, the longest they had ever been separated. Ranald had no way of knowing when Thorne had begun to behave so strangely, except that it had not been evident before he had gone west the last time. To Ranald's knowledge, there had been in Europe no women, little drinking, no real escapades of the usual kind for Thorne. In fact, at times, Ranald felt himself to be the wild one. He knew that questions and comments about Thorne's state would get him nowhere, so he had pretended not to notice anything out of the ordinary, waiting curiously to see what would come. The thought had occurred to him that Thorne's behavior could have to do with a girl, but silence and fortitude had got him nothing either. He was also, just now, hungry, and he went out again dutifully, to retrieve his bemused cousin from the cold and to bring to his attention the fact that it was late for lunch.

Both of the boys were pleased and more than a little surprised to find Elizabeth waiting for them at the station in Pittsburgh with the carriage. Early November dusk was falling as they came out into the smoky, chill air.

"How was the trip?" Elizabeth asked softly when they were in the carriage. She smiled on them both, almost without self-consciousness, and with more tenderness than she could possibly admit.

During the boys' graduation from Pine Glen Elizabeth had realized strangers would assume the boys, the tall, slender, fair one and the slightly less tall, more strongly built dark one, were her true sons. The thought, recalled again and again through the months and years, always brought a thrill of joy and pride. Boldly, she had suggested to Angus that she should meet the boys with the coachman today. She must see as much of them as possible for these next few days. She supposed Thorne would be going back west as soon as he could. Ranald had told her earlier that he intended to take rooms of his own somewhere after Christmas. She wouldn't be seeing as much of them as she had when they were in college.

"The trip was grand," Ranald had answered her. "We had good times everywhere." He mentioned some humorous details of the voyage home.

Thorne appeared to be, for the moment, freed of his immobilizing thoughts, as fully cognizant of his surroundings as Ranald had seen him in the past months. His eyes were warm and smiling as he said to Elizabeth, "You know that list we had, of mines and mills and railroads to see? We lost it, going over."

She laughed aloud, feeling only a little guilty about what Angus would think of their not having carried out instructions. "How did that happen?"

Thorne, shaking his head, said, "I think it blew out of my hand when I was at the rail being sick."

Grinning, Ranald observed, "He was sick a lot."

"Not really," Thorne said. "I just liked standing up there in the wind and spray, leaning over the water. Do you know, Elizabeth, that ships never stop moving? They're always going up and down and . . ." He put a hand to his mouth and the three of them laughed together.

Ranald said, "How are things here?"

Elizabeth sobered immediately, sighing a little; she sounded worried. "Angus has been ill. He's seen the doctor, but I'm not at all sure what was said. He says he's a great deal better now, but he doesn't look it and I don't know . . ." She looked less troubled as she went on to other things. "Mr. Fitzroy was in town for a while. His stepdaughter came back from her schooling in England this fall. He was getting his boy back in school and seeing to the house, I suppose. He's gone west again. There was some accident on one of those mountain railroads, and he had to go back sooner than he'd planned. The Peter Maitlands have a new baby, another daughter."

"Which road?" Thorne asked. He had leaned forward. "What kind of accident?"

"Is there one that has something to do with a place called Johnston Hill?" she asked, frowning as she tried to recall.

"There's a Johnston Tunnel on the Silver Valley line."

"Yes," she said, relieved. "I remember now. Something about a wreck in the tunnel, and a fire, I think."

Thorne said worriedly, "That tunnel was only opened last summer. It's full of shoring. If those timbers caught fire . . ."

Ranald nodded with concern, but Thorne turned abruptly back to Elizabeth, his eyes intent, his voice tight and vibrant.

"Fitz's house is still open, though? I mean, there's been someone there since September, hasn't there?"

"Oh, yes, I think so," said Elizabeth. "The Maitland baby looks like her mother, I think. She'll be a very pretty girl."

When they came into the house, there was a flurry and bustle as they greeted the servants and disposed of their baggage. Angus came home from the mill office, effectively quieting things down. The mere fact of his presence compelled most people to go about their appointed tasks or to find tasks if they hadn't any just at that moment.

Through supper, Ranald, encouraged by Elizabeth, talked eagerly about Europe. Years ago, he had lost his shyness of Angus. He disliked the man, but had due respect for Angus's work, for what Angus had done for him. Now, his attitude in Angus's presence was only slightly subdued, careful. He included Angus in his easy flow of conversation, turning to him as often as to the others with a smile or some other expression on his mobile face.

Angus allowed himself to be included, nodding now and then, asking a few questions, mostly about the business enterprises they were to have visited and observed. At these questions, Thorne, seeming to make a conscious effort to sit still and participate in the meal and the conversation, would step in to give glib, facile answers, which he invented as he spoke.

Elizabeth, smiling, only a little apprehensive in her husband's presence, thought this was the nicest family meal they had ever had. She wished sadly that the boys would not go away, but tried not to let herself dwell on that now.

Angus thought that, considering what he had had to work with, he had done a reasonable job with the boys. His chief regret was that Thorne was not Ranald. Thorne would always be a scapegrace, unpredictable, unreliable, hardly to be trusted or counted on. Angus sighed to himself. The boy had been like that, already molded and set before Angus had got hold of him and begun attempts at redemption. If he had dreamed that Elizabeth would not give him children, he would have had the boy with him at a much earlier date, when everything would have been simpler. Hardly anything about the boy was Angus's preference, intention or doing. It was bitterly irksome to him that he preferred Gavin MacWinter's son to his own. He felt sure Thorne had held out so stubbornly for the engineering degree, as he had done with so many other things, because he knew that it was not what Angus had intended for him. Why couldn't the boy, like Ranald, take more of an interest in the business as a whole, work in an office under Angus's supervision, at a decent respectable job? There was not really a great deal more now that Angus could think of to do for him.

For more than a year now, Angus had occasionally coughed blood. Finally, in September, there had been a rather severe attack of pain with increased coughing, and he had consulted a doctor. The prognosis was that he might live only another two or three years. It had been hard for him to accept the knowledge that a time was coming, a foreseeable time, when he would no longer be head of the company; but he was gradually accustoming himself to the idea and wondering, with a kind of grim pride in all that he had done, if the business must not surely go downhill without his guidance. Frank Fitzroy was no man for the kind of broad managerial responsibility Angus carried. Philip Maitland, III, was no more interested in the actual operations of the business than his father had been. Peter Maitland, now in his early thirties, might, if forced by circumstances, be just able to hold things together, with people like Fitzroy in the field and young Ranald being an invaluable help with administration. There had been some talk recently of moving the company's entire operation to the West, perhaps to Colorado. Fitzroy had fostered and nurtured the idea, of course. Peter Maitland seemed tempted, pointing out labor problems in the East, the growing needs and consumption of an entirely new area. There were coal deposits in the Rockies, they said, not like they had here, but sufficient. Peter had suggested, rather diffidently, that they might consider, at some time in the future, selling the Central Western and concentrating all their railroad capital on the boom lines of the West. Angus had impatiently pointed out to Peter that diversification and expansion were one thing, foolhardiness quite another. He enumerated some of the losses sustained by others in the panic year of 1873, because those companies had gone too far and too concentratedly into overexpansion in the West. He could see, though, that he was not dissuading Peter. Well, they might run MM&F into the ground when he no longer had any control, but for as long as he lived, he would see the business sensible and solvent, with steady, dependable dividends and the same kind of management.

But what about Thorne? Angus was no longer making any pretense of listening to or participating in the conversation at his supper table. There was no pinning the boy down. Even after seven years, he was still a mystery to Angus; no precedents existed for predicting the boy's attitude about anything. Angus could be sure, of course, that the boy would go against him if there was the slightest potential for disagreement. Yet he had at times been struck by the boy's knowledge of things to which he had seemed to give no attention at all and by his often casual but excellent suggestions regarding various aspects of the business. On a few occasions, Angus had been literally shocked by the thought, knowledge and practicability that must have been necessary for Thorne's ideas. If the boy would only buckle down, apply himself, exert some proper self-control over his mercurial ways, make himself more amenable to the important people, apply himself to the company as a whole and give up his childish infatuation with railroads, stop his adolescent hero-worship of Frank Fitzroy. Civil engineers could be picked up on the streets these days, begging for work. Angus blamed Fitzroy, as well as Thorne, for the boy's headstrong determination to have the engineering degree, for his refusal to be sensible or to consider anything beyond the immediate future and his own whims. From the way Fitzroy bragged, a stranger might assume Thorne was his son, and such boasting and obvious approval only served to make the boy more willful, more difficult to deal with.

Angus had not determined yet what he would do so far as his will was concerned, but he had been making other plans. He had reached a few decisions, and there was no need to delay. It was time Thorne knew who he really was. Angus had intended to wait longer to tell him, but that prerogative had been taken out of his hands. Thorne must be told now, so that Angus could gauge his response to the knowledge over the next year or two and decide how to allocate his shares in MM&F. Surely knowing his true identity would sober Thorne, mature him, and bring out the best and most sensible in him.

The others were only half through with dessert; Angus had not touched his own. He stood up abruptly, in the midst of Thorne's story of Ranald's precipitate escape from an angry Alsatian dog.

"Excuse me please, Elizabeth. I've brought home some papers I must go over." He turned to Thorne. "When you've finished your meal, I'll see you in the study."

"Angus, are you—feeling ill?" quavered Elizabeth. It seemed to her he was paler than when he had first come home.

"Oh, of course I'm not," he muttered impatiently. "I told you last week that that was all over. I'm quite well."

Forgetting he had been interrupted in the middle of something, Thorne sat frowning, pushing a piece of piecrust idly around with his fork.

"Go on," Elizabeth prompted softly, eagerly.

No one spoke, so Thorne looked up and found she was talking to him. "I . . . tell her about all our cousins in Scotland, Ran," he said absently.

Thorne had meant to go straight from the station to Fitz's house to find out whether any mail had come for him, but Elizabeth had been there to meet them, looking happy and wistful, and he could not think of an excuse that would be both acceptable to her and credible to Ranald. Now there was to be further delay with Angus. What the hell was he supposed to have done wrong this time? Whatever it was, this was likely to be their shortest interview on record.

Angus was at his desk, looking through papers. He made a slight gesture to the chair facing him where Thorne had sat so often through chastisements and excoriations. He went on with the work in hand. Thorne moved restlessly, impatiently around the cold room, with its small fire, the coal scuttle empty.

"If you must pace about," said Angus without looking up, "fix the lamp, please."

Thorne stepped behind him and turned the gas jet absently.

"Not like that," said Angus in exasperation. "Couldn't you see it was already too high? All right, sit down. I have several things to discuss with you."

Grudging each second, Thorne took the chair.

Angus looked down at the papers again. "It seems to me," he said, finally looking at Thorne, "that a young person of your years and opportunities might have learned not to slouch like that."

"Is that what I'm here to talk about—posture and deportment?"

"Hardly," Angus said coldly. "Even I must admit the time is past when one might have any hope that you could achieve either. The things I want to discuss with you may clear up some questions you may have had about the past and help you with decisions for your future. I've always remembered something my father said to me before I left Scotland. He said, 'The future includes a great deal more than just tomorrow.' "

"There's something I have to do, Angus, something I have to take care of tonight."

The boy had begun calling him Angus when he had been brought back home following the incident at Smoot's. Angus had done everything he could think of to put a stop to it, but it had continued—not frequently, only enough to be very irritating. Finally, Angus admitted to himself alone that the only way to be assured of ending the discourtesy would be to cut out the boy's tongue.

"I understand you went to Brendeen during your trip."

"You knew we meant to."

"Whom did you meet there?"

Thorne shrugged impatiently, drumming his fingers on his knee. "Uncle Gavin's brother, our uncle Douglas. He's chief shepherd now. His wife, their children other cousins and things. Look, couldn't we talk about it tomorrow? Or Ranald could tell you more. I didn't really pay a lot of attention—"

"That's quite typical, isn't it?" Angus said. "Did you see much of the country? Did you look at the great hall, at Brendeen House?"

"I saw the chimneys one day."

"Was there any talk of—your parents?"

Thorne felt a new kind of tension, that of alertness. He had realized years ago that there was so much he did not know about his parents, particularly about his father, and that somewhere in that unknown past must lie the answers to the reason he was here and not still with Gavin and Maria. Now he watched Angus warily.

"Not much," he said carefully. "They never knew my father, Uncle Douglas and the others, and it's a long time since my mother came away."

"You have other relatives at Brendeen. You didn't meet any of the earl's family?"

"No. I think someone said they were in London." He moved to stand up. "I have to go out for a little while, before it gets any later."

"Do me the kindness to sit still, please," Angus said curtly. "I shall appreciate it if you can manage the courtesy of remaining in one place and listening. I believe even you may find this important.

"When I came to Gavin MacWinter's home almost seven and a half years ago and decided to bring you here, you didn't understand. You expected that MacWinter could simply refuse to allow it, didn't you? Or that at the very least, he and your aunt could give you an explanation of what was happening? They could not do that because I was not ready to have you know the truth yet, and fortunately they had the common sense to see that any partial truths they might have told would only have confused you, and the issues, more.

"You have been misinformed about your father. He was not one of the MacWinters of Aberdeen who died on a ship coming over from Scotland. I met your mother when she arrived in New York early in 1855, because my mother had written asking me to do so. It was your grandmother, Annie's and Gavin's mother who died on shipboard. Annie arrived alone. She was insecure and frightened and—very young."

A jolt of realization shook Thorne. He stared incredulously at the man and could not seem to turn his eyes away.

"You understand what you're being told?"

He shook his head, his lips forming the word, but with no sound. The "no" was a denial of the suggestion, not a disclaimer of understanding.

"I married her the day after she arrived. There has never been a proper explanation for that, even in my own mind. All I can say is that there was a letter for me, on that same ship, informing me my own mother had died very suddenly. Annie and I had the —losses in common. She was . . . Certainly I was old enough to have known better. Let this be the best lesson you'll ever have in where too much impulsiveness and weakness can lead. Of course, I recognized my foolishness almost at once, but the thing was done; we were married. I knew the best thing I could do for her was see that she got to her brother's, which had been her destination, of course. She would have been miserable anywhere else but with people and ways familiar to her.

"When you and the other children were old enough to question matters, the MacWinters told you the story of a MacWinter of Aberdeen so that you need not be confused with a name different from the others', so you could feel at home, like one of them—"

"It's not true," Thorne said heavily. He wanted to shout his denial, to run from the room, the house, slamming doors, convincing himself these past few moments had never happened.

"I'm not in the habit of lying. . . . Perhaps you understand now why I've been willing to expend so much money, time and effort in trying to help you. I trust you can begin now to feel some appreciation, some responsibility and pride in all the Maxwell name stands for, here and in Scotland."

"You trust what you like," Thorne said through clenched teeth, his voice rising. "I owe you nothing. Why in God's name didn't you just leave me alone?"

"I have no other child," Angus said, his face and

voice fully under control. A hot pain had begun in his chest and he coughed gently, trying to relieve it.

"Then you have no child at all," Thorne said fiercely. "I don't believe what you're saying. Why in hell didn't you pick on Ranald? Wouldn't you rather try to make him be the one to swallow this . . ."

"You believe me," Angus said quietly, firmly. "I certainly would have chosen Ranald, but this is one thing you won't be able to shift to him. You see, I *had* no choice in this matter, and neither have you."

Thorne buried his face in his hands. It was the nearest Angus had seen him come to showing deep emotion in years. He drew his hands away slowly, with apparent effort, twisting them together.

He said bitterly, "You had a choice. You never had to marry her. You should have exerted your marvelous self-control and not gone to bed with her. What was she then—sixteen? You lecherous old hypocrite."

Angus said icily, "There's no excuse for talk like that, and there's no point in thinking of ways in which the past might have been different. What has already occurred is an incontrovertible fact. You are a fact; I am. Now we must see about going on from there. I couldn't allow you to stay on with the MacWinters because I had an interest in your future. I'd rather you didn't smoke in here."

"You've never had an interest in your life in anything, if it couldn't be useful to you and your damned—" Thorne had stood up. He moved abstractedly around the room, leaning against the mantel to steady his hand, holding the match to light his cigarette. He hated Angus for exposing him like this, for having the power, the withheld knowledge to make him feel so helpless while the older man sat there, cold and still, watching him almost disinterestedly. Why couldn't he leave, put an end to this? God, if there was no word from Meg now . . .

Angus was saying, "—your schooling, difficult as you've always tried to make that; your food and clothing through all these years; this trip to Europe—"

"I didn't ask you for any of that. I've never wanted anything from—"

"Kindly lower your voice. I understand that this has come rather as a shock to you, though I suspect it's not your not *wanting* to see some such relationship that has kept it from you this long. Your twenty-second birthday is next month. It's well past time you learned to control your emotions sufficiently not to shout. I also realize you will want some time to think about this, to accustom yourself to these facts, but I want to give you my entire plan now, so that you can think of it all at once. You'll stay here, in our main business office, working with me a part of the time. Since you have that ridiculous degree in engineering, we may occasionally find it useful. You can serve a kind of apprenticeship under the managers of various branches of the company, try to make up as quickly as possible the knowledge you lack in most of our fields. If you work hard and really try to behave yourself, maybe in another ten years, you will be somewhat fitted for the job I now hold. I myself was just thirty when I became a partner."

"I don't want to be a partner, not in anything—"

"As you think this over, when you become calmer, you will understand the responsibility of the position you now know yourself to hold. This is something you will *not* shrug away. I've already mentioned to a few people, including Frank Fitzroy when he was here in September, and Peter Maitland, that I'm considering your adoption. That way, your taking and using the name Maxwell will be understandable to those outside this family."

"Does Elizabeth know?" Thorne's voice was almost inaudible. He stood half turned away from Angus, holding the forgotten cigarette between cold, shaking fingers.

"Elizabeth has known since we went to Colorado to bring you here. You should be grateful to her. I believe she feels more fondness for you, more hope for your future than I feel I've had cause to find. She seems to see something more in you than I do."

"Ranald?"

"No, though I intend telling him immediately. He is, after all, a part of the household. Until tonight, only your aunt and uncle, Elizabeth and I have known the entire story."

Dazedly, Thorne had taken up the poker to push together the fire's embers. He was shivering.

"Must you keep clanging at the grate like that? I ask you once more to sit down please. There's another matter—"

He replaced the poker with a clash and turned fiercely. "No! No more matters. I've served enough apprenticeships. I won't stay in Pittsburgh, and no one is going to be led to believe my name is Maxwell. My name is MacWinter and I'm proud of it."

"You're still trying not to believe me, aren't you? Can't you see that your not wanting something to be true won't make it false? Do you actually prefer seeing yourself as the descendant of shepherds, yeomen, peasants, than as someone with a noble ancestry, at least on one side of your family? Your mother named you Thorne because it was *my* mother's maiden name."

"I know that. They've told me she was fond of her, of—of Lady Catherine."

Angus pushed a paper he had initialed across the desk. "Look at this. Has it never occurred to you what the T, my middle initial might stand for?"

"Ah, God," he breathed hopelessly.

"You look a great deal like my mother's people. She had a younger brother, I remember, who was a black sheep, always coming to her to ask for money.

Perhaps you resemble him in more than looks." Angus made an attempt to smile.

The forgotten cigarette burned Thorne's fingers, and he dropped it, bent automatically to pick it up and threw it on the coals. The cold, calculating voice kept hammering at him.

"You are a Maxwell, grandson of the Earl of Brendeen. I have books you'll want to read, about the family. . . . What's that you're saying?"

"I said I'd rather be a bastard of anyone else than—"

"But you're not. However, we do agree on something. This relationship is distasteful to both of us. I have the record of my marriage to your mother in March of 1855; you were born that December. Annie was a virgin when I knew her. You look like my mother's people. I'm convinced Annie was a faithful wife to me."

"I was christened MacWinter."

"No, that's not true. The priest put your true name in the church's book. I saw it when I was last there. He was told the circumstances of your birth and, to accommodate your aunt, I understand, let everyone think you were being christened as a MacWinter. When I mentioned that only four people knew the story, I did not include the priest because I believe Ranald said he died. You'd better stop struggling against this, accept it and try to deserve it."

"Deserve *what*?"

"*Will* you keep your voice down? I have said there are pride and responsibility involved in being a Maxwell."

Thorne moved toward the door, and Angus, trying to anticipate him, stood up. "Now, this other matter I'll ask you to bear in mind—"

"I'm bearing nothing in mind."

"You'll sit down like a civilized adult until I've finished." He lifted his hand toward Thorne's arm.

"If you touch me, I'll kill you." His voice had gone

cold, level. His eyes, looking black with the intensity behind them, seemed a little demented.

Angus dropped the commanding, restraining hand. A moment after Thorne had left, he turned slowly to a cupboard and poured himself a little brandy. When he had sat down again at his desk, he looked almost without recognition at the veined, spotted hand holding the glass. It was trembling.

Thorne had left the house without coat or hat. It was cold, but he ran easily through the streets, not noticing. *Please God, let her have sent some word. Would it matter to her if she knew this?*

Some years ago, Frank Fitzroy had had a house built in a fine new section of town. One summer, three years ago, his stepdaughter, as well as his son, came to live with him while his wife was ill. When his wife died last fall, he permanently staffed the house, pensioned off Belle Evans with a very generous settlement and set about being a respectable citizen during his infrequent visits to Pittsburgh. As often as not, a woman still shared Fitz's private car when young Ted was not with him on the road; but he did what he could, if it seemed worth the trouble, to keep up acceptable appearances for the children.

During the summer that Fitz's wife was sick and his stepdaughter was in Pittsburgh, Thorne worked in town at the mill. Not really aware of the girl, who was fifteen then, Thorne had spent as much time with Fitz as he could manage, at the office and at home. The tall, good-looking Negro woman who opened Fitz's front door to him now recognized him at once. Her name was Dahlia. She had come from Jamaica originally and spoke with a mixture of the stiff British accents of the islands and the drawl she had acquired from spending more than twelve years in the South.

"Why, Mr. Thorne! You back from your travels? My land, no coat a freezing night like this? Come in here."

"I came to see if there are any letters for me, Dahlia. Someone may have written me in care of Fitz . . ."

"Well, I couldn't say, honey. All of his mail is in his office. I'll go look. You go in by the fire. It seems to me you're looking peaked."

"I'm not cold; I've been running. Could I come with you and—"

"Well, my *goodness*, aren't you even going to say hello to me?"

The girl's voice was like honey running over something warm. She stood leaning slightly against the parlor doorjamb, showing off her full, petite figure to good advantage. Her name was Cherish Charm Stuart and she was eighteen.

"Oh. Hello, Cherish." After one glance, Thorne turned back to watch the door through which Dahlia had disappeared.

"Well? Come on," she laughed softly. "Gracious, if I'd known there was going to be a caller, I'd have tried to fix up a little, not that I believe you'd notice. What *is* it? Dahlia's right, you are peaked, and I can tell there's something big on your mind."

Cherish remembered both Thorne and Ranald from her previous stay in Pittsburgh. She had found them both interesting. Ranald's looks certainly suited her better, but Thorne intrigued her. They had both treated her as a child three years ago. Ranald had always behaved, when he had been aware of her, with cool, disinterested politeness. Thorne had responded, a few times, to her flirting in a way no other boy had. For the most part, all he had done was to look at her, but those looks had been more than enough to support her already well-bolstered feminine ego.

Thorne was saying awkwardly now, "I didn't mean to be 'calling.' I only came to find out if . . ."

"I know," she said conspiratorially. "I heard you ask Dahlia. Now who in the world would be writing you here? Why would you be expecting secret letters, Thorne MacWinter?"

The name struck at him cruelly. He could not, must not think about it yet.

"Sit down," Cherish urged from the chair where she had curled herself up. "My goodness, think what ages it's been since we saw each other. I tell you, I am so bored here, I absolutely don't know what to do. I keep wishing I was back in school. Can you imagine that? I just hate this place. Fitz won't let me live at Fern Hill, not for now, at least. He has that old frumpy housekeeper here, Mrs. Switzer, that he says is the only one he'll trust as a proper chaperon for me, and the pokey old thing won't leave this dirty town, Did you ever hear the like? *I* can't live where I want to be, ought to be, because of a *servant*. This is such an ugly town, soot and dirt, and the weather's so cold. I think it's worse than England where I was at school. Oh, Thorne, I wish you could see Fern Hill. It's the most *ex*quisite place! . . . But do tell me about the trip you've had. I wanted to make a tour of my own when I finished at school, but Fitz wouldn't let me—the same old thing again, about chaperons. He's such a fussbudget about some things, and he really doesn't have the least notion of how to be a real father. I did so want to see Paris, and I was so near. Did you go there?"

"Excuse me, ma'am," said Dahlia, coming in. "I found these, Mr. Thorne."

He reached for the letters with a feeling of drowning. "Thank you, Dahlia," he stammered, and for one awful moment was afraid he might cry. There were four letters, more than he had dared hope for, but he was compelled to ask shakily, "Are you sure there weren't any others?"

"I looked clear through the stack," she assured him warmly. "All Mr. Fitz's mail that comes while he's away gets put into one certain desk drawer."

Thorne turned the letters in his hands, hungrily reading everything on envelopes and stamps. Four! Surely that must mean she—

"Dahlia, bring us some cocoa," Cherish was saying, "and some of those—"

"I can't stay," Thorne said abruptly.

Cherish was laughing. "It seems to me, from the way you're looking, that maybe somebody ought to censor those letters before you see them. Come on, Thorne, let me see who they're from."

She held out a small, pretty hand and he stared at it. Could she possibly believe he'd let her touch these letters?

"I'll bet that grumpy old Mr. Maxwell doesn't know you're getting letters over here," Cherish teased.

"Thank you . . . Good night," he said, and was gone before she could speak again.

"Those letters were from a girl, of course," mused Cherish as Dahlia fed the blazing fire. "Damn her!"

"Why, Miss Cherish!"

"I mean it. There's not a thing of any interest around here, then *he* comes in, just to get somebody else's letters. He's interesting. I think, Dahlia, that the next time Fitz comes home, I'll get him to let us go along in his railroad car, the way he takes Teddy when he's not in school. I'll tell Fitz it's because I'm *so* interested in railroads. He'll believe that from anyone. Thorne will be close to wherever Fitz is, and I know I can make him forget any letters, any other girl, with just a little time. Where were the letters from?"

"I didn't notice," Dahlia answered righteously.

"Of course you did. Don't lie to me."

"I am *no* liar."

Cherish let it go, reseating herself with a dreamy smile. "It's time I started thinking seriously of marriage. I don't want anybody I'll get bored with. Boredom is the worst thing in the world. He seems a little

—wild, doesn't he? I'll bet I could make him tame. I'll bet I could own him."

Dahlia stared at her appalled. "Honey, people don't own one another, not even slaves—"

"I mean to own whoever I marry," Cherish said firmly, "body and soul."

"I've never heard such talk."

"And," she said with deliberation, "if he's going to get the Maxwell money some day, that just may have been my future husband you gave that other girl's letters to. Get me some cocoa."

Thorne ran again, to a streetlight some distance from the Fitzroy house. He had written Meg many times during the past months, but more often than not, he had torn up the letters because they were nothing more than desperate pleadings of his case. He sent her, not the love letters he wanted to send, but casual accounts of what he and Ranald had done and seen. They had seemed to him boring, grossly inadequate, but he had mailed a half dozen missives which, for the most part, the rest of the family could have read without suspecting anything more than his sudden emergence as a correspondent.

Quickly now, as he read, he saw that there was a pattern in Meg's letters. They were about the family, the hacienda, the weather, any generalities, until the end, where there was a more personal paragraph, relating to the two of them.

In her first letter, this paragraph said only, "I'm trying very hard, Thorne, to think of those things as if they had happened to someone else. I hope that will help me to see all sides clearly."

His heart fell. That first letter was postmarked two weeks after he had left Colorado.

The second was postmarked two weeks after the first. The special paragraph there read, "I have had a talk with Father O'Malley. I did not go to confession or tell him anything really. I should. It worries me, not being able to take communion, and Mama is wondering. I asked Father O'Malley about cousins marrying. He says it can only happen for first cousins under specific circumstances and with a very special dispensation that's hard to get. Oh, Thorne, I miss you."

His eyes burned as he skimmed what were, to him, the irrelevant preliminaries of the third letter. At the end of it, in mid-September, she had written, "I have been reading a book I borrowed from Mr. Gaynor. Mama would call it sacrilegious. It's all about thinking for oneself, not letting the mind be ruled by religion or politics or social customs without ever thinking about and questioning them. It says thinking for oneself can be hard and disconcerting, even painful, but that no one with a mind should swallow everything automatically, with no assessment of his own. You will think I'm childish and stupid, having to get advice like that from a book, but I think it may have helped me. I think you already live like that, in what the book calls true freedom; maybe you always have. Do you remember a talk we had once about God? You frightened me then and you still do. Your first two letters came yesterday, and one from Ranald. Thorne, you do understand, don't you?"

He wanted to try to understand precisely what she had meant by that question, but could not forbear tearing open the last letter. It had been mailed at the end of September.

"I can hardly bear the time between your letters. I hope both of you are having a perfectly wonderful time. Can you ever forgive me for hurting you and being so stupid for such a long time? Please come home as soon as you can." And, instead of merely signing her name, she had written, "With all my love, Meg."

Tenderly, in a daze of joy, Thorne folded the last letter and put it in his shirt with the others. His fingers were stiff with cold and he was shivering, but the smile on his lips kept growing. Meggy, Meggy! It will be all right. Everything will be. We'll *make* things right for each other.

He waked aimlessly about the quiet streets, abstracted with half-thoughts, half-plans, all of them warm and bright and beautiful. Eventually, he found himself across from the Maxwell house, and very cold. Except for one in Ranald's room, all the lights were out. Angus would have locked him out of the house many times at bedtime; but Hannah, the elderly maid, stayed up when Thorne was out until Angus went upstairs, when she would creep in and unlock the side door. Thorne let himself in quietly, locked the door and went up the back stairs.

There was no fire in his room, but coal had been brought. He started it burning and lay down on the hearth rug. Meg's name kept singing in his mind.

Tomorrow he would leave here. Maybe he could go on working with Fitz, without Angus's knowing. He could trust Fitz. If he decided not to stay with Intermountain, finding a similar job would not be hard. He would try to ignore the things Angus had said this evening. With Meggy, it shouldn't be too difficult to forget Angus entirely.

He took out the letters and read them again, more thoroughly this time. She had begun to teach at Quintana school, helping Mr. Gaynor with the younger children, who tried his frayed nerves.

After a time, Thorne wondered, idly at first, why she had not written again. Her last letter was dated at the end of September. Surely she must have known there would be time for others to reach him. He thought of the feel of her against him and his body ached. . . . Maybe, after saying what she had in the last letter, she had felt there was no need for writing anything further. He wanted her desperately. . . . Could it be that Dahlia had overlooked a letter, perhaps more than one? And that silly, snoopy Cherish might . . . He had half risen, but settled back slowly. These four letters were among the very best things that would ever happen to him. Why should he feel there had to be more?

Maybe Meg would want him not to take a railroad job. As a little girl, she had maintained adamantly that she would never live anywhere but the valley. Maybe that would still be very important to her. But suppose Aunt Maria, because of the church, could not be reconciled to their marriage? Meg had thought of all that, of course. He had some idea now of how hard it must have been for her; it was not the simple, easy matter it had seemed to him with her nearness. Would she still insist on waiting, on trying to get some special permission and blessing from the church? He smiled wryly, thinking the church would not find him deserving of any special treatment, but if Meg truly felt that approval was necessary to her happiness, he would do anything to make it possible.

There was a sound outside Thorne's door, a very light knock, and Ranald came in.

"Are you all right? I didn't know you were back until I saw your light just now."

Thorne stretched lazily. "Why wouldn't I be all right? Sit down if you like."

"I couldn't help being worried, and you look funny."

"What do you mean, funny? And what was there to worry about?"

"Mr. Maxwell told me, after you'd left, about . . ."

"I'll be leaving in the morning."

"Where will you go?"

"Back home, for a start."

"Will you go on working with Fitz?"

"I don't know. Maybe."

"Do—do you—well, mind a lot that Angus—that he's your father?"

"I think I still don't believe it. Maybe that's just cowardice, but I can't *feel* it's true."

"It explains a lot of things."

"Yes, but I'd rather they'd have stayed mysterious than . . ."

"It could be that he'll leave you everything, a third of MM&F."

"Hell, people like him never die. I don't want his stocks or money. I don't want his lectures, his cold, fishy looks. I hope maybe I can never hear his name again, once I've left here."

"I'd still like to go on in the office here."

"Well, why wouldn't you?"

"It just seems—disloyal."

Thorne smiled. "You always have to be at yourself about something, don't you—usually something you're going to go ahead and do anyway."

"I don't understand you," Ranald said slowly, searching his face. "I thought you'd be—upset tonight, over what he's said. I didn't think you'd say two words about it. You act as if it makes no more difference than if someone had told you to rewrite a paper."

"I don't *want* it to matter. I'm trying not to let it." Thorne yawned. "I wonder if there's any pie left downstairs."

Ranald was too puzzled to feel really relieved. He stretched, trying to relax. "I can't think why I've been waiting up for you. I'm tired as hell. There are some letters from home. You can come and get them if you want to see, mostly from Mama, one from Jean and one from Carmela." He stood up, stretching again, moving toward the door. "All the letters are to both of us." He turned back, remembering. "Oh! I was about to forget to tell you, Meg got married the middle of October."

Thorne was staring, his breath refusing to come. "What did you say?" His voice was choked, unnatural.

"Meg. She married Gordon Gaynor. It seemed to come as a surprise to everyone. He must have asked her a half dozen times. He had to go home from school in October because his dad was pretty sick again. Evidently he asked her again and she finally said yes. They'll be living in Cambridge till he's through with school. Then, Mama writes, he's going to go back and be the first real lawyer Quintana's had. Gordon used to say years ago, before we first left home, that he'd marry Meg some day. She sure grew up pretty. Didn't you think so? . . . Thorne?"

"No!"

"What?"

"I—I said I want to go to bed now," he mumbled, not really conscious of the words. He had struggled to his feet and stood swaying, his stricken face in shadow.

"What's wrong?" Ranald came closer. "Are you sick? You look like—"

"I told you, I'm going to bed," he said dully, then, as Ranald put out a hand, he said fiercely, "Don't touch me."

"Thorne . . ."

"I—I am sick. It's just come on all at once. I'll be all right in bed if—if you go."

"You don't feel like seeing the letters, I guess?"

"No."

"Can't I do something, bring you anything? You look—"

"Ranald, for God's sake, leave me alone!"

He undressed automatically, to lie tense and cold in his bed, trying to make his mind empty, but it would not stay closed. How could she . . .? It wasn't true.

Her letters had fallen to the floor as he undressed. After a time, he remembered them and got up to retrieve them tenderly. He began to read them again, then stopped. A small cry escaped him.

None of this night was real. But no one had made up the fact that she was married. At the end of September, she had written to him, "Please come home as soon as you can. . . . With all my love." In October, she had married Gordon Gaynor.

Thorne got up, his teeth clenched, and tore the letters into small pieces. He threw them on the embers of the fire and blew on them to make them burn faster.

After that, he lay in darkness. At some point, he thought of the brandy bottle Angus believed to be concealed in his study, but had no will to go and get it. . . . Angus Maxwell had said he was his father. Surely, no one would make up a thing like that either. Thorne pulled the covers over his face.

So many lonely, frustrated nights in this room and others! He remembered, as he had countless times before, the dead boy in the dormitory at Smoot's. Fergusson. They had all been called by last names at the military school. He had been called MacWinter. All at once, it seemed unbearably sad that he had never known, or could not remember having heard Fergusson's other name. . . . He wondered if it hurt terribly to die like that . . . Ah God, Meggy, why? Why?

When first light began to filter round the edges of the curtains, he lay watching, taut, exhausted, his eyes and head throbbing. He remembered another thing about Smoot's, or at least a thing Smoot's had brought into being. It was the vows he had made to himself: that, when he was grown up, he would live in such a way that he never need feel helpless; that no one else need love him; that he would never again care enough to let anyone or anything hurt him.

I'm such a fool! He tried to swallow the bitterness in his mouth, rubbing at his dry, burning eyes. *God, help me* keep *my word to myself this time. It's all there is in the end, all there'll ever be.*

BOOK TWO
1878-1891

VII

1878

Thorne had left Pittsburgh at the end of the previous November in a state of almost stuporous mental anesthesia. Through the endless, agonized night after hearing of Meg's marriage, he had thought of everything, all her possible reasons for the marriage, the weeks she had already lived as Gordon's wife. Angus's revelation was more or less pushed into the background, but when there was respite from thoughts of Meg, from the questioning and pain of that, Thorne's parentage would give him no peace. He slept a great deal on the trip west, his body attempting its own kind of self-protection, but it was seldom successful. He always dreamed, twisted, confused dreams from which it was very difficult to wake, even though he often knew he was asleep and dreaming.

When he reached Denver, he found that Fitz was still at the scene of the wreck on the Silver Valley Line. A locomotive had derailed inside one of the tunnels there, shoring timbers had caught fire, and the heat and smoke from their smoldering had delayed clearing and repair. Thorne did not particularly want to be with Fitz. He had gone back to Intermountain only because it was the simplest thing he could do, an automatic return, a pattern in which to direct his restlessness and need for something outside himself. At the importuning of old Ralph Jeffers, he stayed in Denver for a time, helping to clear up the paperwork that always awaited Fitz's attention. Thorne found the office work extremely distasteful, but it was new enough to him to be a challenging experience, and it occupied his mind more than an engineering job might have done. Each morning, a good deal of willpower was required simply to go back to the offices, to begin a new day. It was a distraction—the reading, questioning, considering, learning. Thorne stayed with it in a kind of dogged desperation until Fitz came back to town, then he escaped to Idaho to begin the initial platting of a short line to be built there. Winter in the northwest that year was unusually mild and open. Deep snows did not end Thorne's work there until February.

"I want you to go down on the Rio Grande," Fitz said when he was back again in Denver. "See ever'thing's finished up right down there. We'll have that all open, come spring, clear through to Santa Fe finally. There's work yet on sidin's and switches."

Thorne was feeling that he had himself fairly well in hand again, but he would not risk going back to the valley. He said, "What about Amity?"

"Tom Murphy's got overall charge of construction up there. There's not much they can do this time of year. They're mostly workin' in that number five tunnel, an' it's still nothin' but a bitch."

Intermountain had taken on construction of the Amity line the previous year and had quickly completed the number three tunnel, which had bankrupted two construction companies. Tunnel four had been simple matter, but five was worse than three. There would be two more short tunnels where core samples promised stable rock, ten miles more of track into the booming mining area where mine and mill owners —and practically everyone else—were screaming for rail service. The wagon road to town was so precipitous that no one had yet been able to bring in the heavy equipment needed for stamp mills and smelters.

"You've heard we had four men killed up there less'n a month ago?" Fitz continued.

"Yes. Maybe we ought to think about an alternate route, Fitz. Those tunnels—"

"There ain't no alternate route," Fitz said impatiently. "You know that. The only other way we might come at Amity would cost us nearly fifty miles. We'd have to go through all the crap of filin' new plats with the Commission and such. I tell you, them people up there are screamin' for the line. If we was to try for the other way, RM&P might just decide to try an' come in from the west. They're not so far from Amity that way, as the crow flies."

"Crows don't haul much freight. RM&P would have a hell of a job getting over the divide just there."

"Well, we ain't goin' to study no reroute. I have yet to give up on somethin' this big, an' I won't start now just because of some rotted-out mountain spur. The whole goddamn' number five tunnel ain't but five hundred yards long. We beat these same kind of conditions on number three, didn't we? You want to go fifty miles around, just for five hundred yards of mountain?"

"No, but—"

"Tom's got a first-rate crew now. They'll git 'er through. I aim to have all that line open by summer, an' the way things is goin', it could be it'll pay for itself, extry costs an' all, in two or three years. You just go on down south awhile an'—"

"Fitz, I'd rather do something else."

"Like what?"

"Like whatever else needs doing. I don't want to go back to the San Luis."

Fitz looked up sharply. "Well, we all do things we don't want to, different times. If you're aimin' to make boss material, you'll have plenty of stuff you'd just as soon not do."

"I'm not aiming at anything like that."

"Well, in that case, you can damn' well do like you're told."

"Harvey Stabler—" Thorne began.

"You know where Harvey's at?" Fitz demanded curtly. "Harvey's haulin' freight out of Silver Valley is where. First we had that wreck in the tunnel up there last fall, an' now the god-awfulest winter ever has been up that way. It's been so hard to keep trains runnin' up there, an' crews on, that I've nearly had to go on the roster myself. Harvey's one of my best construction foremen, an' there he is, runnin' one of them little narrow-gauge teakettles."

"I could do that," Thorne said quickly. "Harvey can handle the finish-up on the Santa Fe line better than—"

"Jesus Christ!" exploded Fitz. "I thought you didn't want that finish-up job because it wouldn't be no fit place for your civil engineerin' talents. Now you tell me you want to drive a train. You didn' learn no locomotive drivin' at college."

"I worked in a train crew most of one summer. Sam Wiley was the engineer."

"You was a brakeman," Fitz recalled disparagingly.

"I did some firing too, sometimes. It was on the run from here to—"

"Hell, I know where it was, an' you know that bein' a summertime brakeman ain't a-patchin' to engineerin' a train in the wintertime in this Christ-forsaken country."

"What's happened to Sam Wiley?"

"He's got one of the passenger runs on the main line, works from Chandler to Bethany. But don't think you can dredge up talk about old friends an' git my mind off sendin' you south. You've had your time at surveyin' an' the like out there in Idaho. There ain't much of that kind of work this time of year."

Thorne was silent, but his expression was adamant. He would not go back to the Santa Fe line.

Fitz said accusingly, "I had a letter from Ranald some weeks back."

Thorne looked at him, waiting, his face showing nothing.

"He's worried about you. Says you left Pittsburgh back last fall in bad shape, an' he ain't heard nothin' direct from you since. Has that got anything to do with you wantin' to keep away from the Rio Grande?"

"He told you?" Thorne probed carefully.

"Told me about Angus, what he really is to you. It wasn' no real big surprise. It had crossed my mind a good many times he must be your pa. There just wasn' hardly no other reason for him keepin' on with you the way he has when it was so plain he wished he could make you over. Ranald wrote Angus has told Maitlands somethin' about he's adoptin' you an'—Now son, just be easy. This looks to me like one of them hard facts, just somethin' you'll have to live with an' git used to. If your legal name's Maxwell—an' they mean to use it on papers out of the Pittsburgh office if there's call for it—well, it just is, an' that's that. Ain't none of us got a choice about the name we're born with. Bein' Maxwell can't make you no different from what you are bein' MacWinter. Is it that that's makin' you not want to see your folks down there in the valley?"

Thorne, rolling a cigarette, did not look at him or reply.

"I don't see why that would be," Fitz mused. "Seems to me like this ought to have cleared up a lot of things in your mind, about how they come to let Angus take you off in the first place. Had to, didn' they? Didn' have nothin' to say about it, really. Seems like it must have been awful hard on them, too, if they cared about you, an' I guess they did. Well, but you ain't got to see 'em. Railroad don't come within twelve miles of their place, does it? It's important, you know, to learn to take orders before you start givin' too many."

"I don't intend to give—"

"Now just don't start that. You'll be runnin' this outfit some day. I always have seen that. Maybe you honestly don't know it yet, or won't let yourself think it; but, son, if that wasn' somewheres in the back of your mind, I can't understand why you come back here, after you heard this from Angus."

"I just wanted to work. This was what I knew about. I couldn't . . ."

"Couldn' stand to try to learn somethin' else or face up to new people right then? I can understand that. But you did do somethin' new for you. Old Ralph Jeffers still can't say enough about how much you helped him out in the office in December. A body'd think you might of been Jesus come to deliver him, the way Ralph rubs his bald head an' keeps talkin'. What he's doin' is tryin' to make me feel guilty about what I don't do, but I act like I don't see it. Thorne, you act right now like somethin' caught in a trap. I can't understand you. Can't you just make the most of this? You'll inherit from Angus. That's why he wants the name business set right. I guess I know how you feel about him, but nobody on earth can deny a man the right to have his son carry his name. God, if I'd stood a chance of gittin' anything from my ole pa besides his name an' hard knocks . . . If I had a boy somethin' like you to leave things to . . ."

"Fitz . . ."

"Oh, shit, you'll never make sense to me, some ways, or to yourself either. You can have Harvey's engine up yonder. If I ain't mistaken, he'll be tickled to death to see the last of it. But just for a couple of months, maybe less. You git yourself put back together an' ready to keep on with important things, come good weather."

Thorne's mind was not on the Silver Valley run. He said bleakly, "I shouldn't have come back. I could have asked for work with RM&P, if nothing else, but at the time I couldn't seem to think straight."

"I know it was a shock," Fitz said shortly, "but surely not enough to make you go over to the competition. What in hell would you have done that for?"

"They wouldn't have known. I could just have been . . ."

"Be what? You can't be no more nor no less than what you've always been. There's people at RM&P, an' you well know it, would recognize you. Word of this—adoptin' or whatever—will git around. You think Angus might not have gone through with that if you'd gone off to somethin' else?"

"I don't know," Thorne said thoughtfully. He had not considered that possibility but wished now he had done so. His mind had been numbed by thoughts of Meg, so desperate for insulation against those thoughts, that there had been little room for more than avoiding considerations of his relationship with Angus. He said slowly to Fitz, "He'll never leave me anything. I wouldn't want him to."

"When he's dead," challenged Fitz, "an' I am, you mean to just stand back, maybe see these roads run into the ground?"

"That won't happen."

"No, it won't, an' the main reason for that is that you won't let it. Don't say no more. We could argy it all day an' neither one of us change our minds about what we think right now. These lines mean somethin' to you. Come a time when I ain't here, there'll be a lot of people dependin' on you, all the other stockholders an' such. If this reorganizin' should happen that the Maitlands talk about, there'll be a lot more stockholders than now. In some things—not many—a man's got a choice. In most things, once he's grown an' set into whatever his pattern is, he ain't really got much to say about it, not when he has to come right down to bedrock. You're a strong feller. You can swing a pick or a hammer with the best of 'em, and that ain't the only way you're strong. You got a strong will. It's a hard, drivin' thing that don't give you much rest, an' there ain't no patience in it. You'll have to take on Intermountain, if for no other reason than that you can't abide to stand by while somebody else tries it. Maybe you'll never want to do it, never want people dependin' on you, askin' for nearly more'n you got in you, but you'll do it, 'cause you can't help yourself. I'll never know why you can't just rest a little easy some of the time now, take some pride an' enjoyment in what's already been done, what you're helpin' to build."

Thorne, feeling trapped, went to the window and stared out at falling snow.

After a time, Fitz said quietly, "But Ranald seems to think there might be somethin' more."

Fitz wasn't sure Thorne would answer, but finally he said expressionlessly, "More than what?"

"More than the talk you an' Angus had, somethin' more was botherin' you."

"No."

"He wrote that you didn' seem much bothered about what Angus had to say to you. Said you went out that night after Angus told you. Cherish told me somebody'd been writin' you while you boys was off in Europe, sendin' letters to Pittsburgh in care of me. Do they have somethin' to do with it?"

"My mail," Thorne said coldly, "—my life is nobody else's business. Ranald had no right—or Cherish—"

"Now I know that," Fitz said shortly. "Ranald knows it. Both of us knew if I talked to you this way, you'd act just the way you are. We both know, too, how upset you been."

"I haven't been upset."

Fitz sighed resignedly. "All right. I didn' hear a word young Jim Ritter said about you not hardly sleepin' all the time you an' him was out in Idaho. I don't see, right now, how you're wore to a plumb frazzle an' fightin' like a sonofabitch to hang on to that tight rein you keep on yourself. I won't say no more about Ranald an' how I think you ought to let him hear somethin' from you. You know, one thing friends is for is to help when there's trouble. Sometimes there ain't a thing they can do, really, more'n just be there. With you, even that little bit ain't easy."

"Fitz, thanks," he said restlessly, "but I don't need anything."

"Oh, shit, yes! Make it hard on yourself. If you ever do git so's you can loosen up an' talk about it a little, I may still be around, an' I expect Ranald will. Now git on out of here. Go on up to Silver Valley an' play with your train. When you derail or git stuck in a twenty-foot drift, just go right on thinkin' you don't need nobody or nothin'."

Again, Thorne felt the need to escape. He wanted to be not only where no one knew or cared about his relationship to Angus, but where no one had interest or suspicions about any letters. No one must ever suspect the pain Meg's marriage had caused him, how abjectly desperate he had been in those first weeks. Thorne had little clear memory of that night in Pittsburgh after Ranald's casual mention of Meg's marriage, but he knew that only Ranald's intrinsic innocence and lack of suspicion had saved the secret.

Leaving Fitz's office, Thorne walked around the streets for a long while. In the end, he took the train for Silver Valley. He could not quite bring himself to seek other employment, or even to decide in what direction he should look. Working for another company, in another job, would have done nothing to help him in the continual effort to close his mind to the past and go on with living.

Next day, at Silver Valley, he put his name on the train crew roster. For the first time, his face hard and bitter, he wrote "Thorne Maxwell." That puzzled the men who had known him in the past, but Thorne ignored their direct questions. Eventually, word filtered down that he had become some sort of foster son to the Maxwell in the company name, but that it was better not to ask him anything about it. They continued, for the most part, to call him MacWinter, or just Mac, and he seemed satisfied with that. Those who had not known him in the past picked up the name from the old hands.

After a little more than a month as locomotive engineer, Thorne received a message to see Fitz when he brought his sorely tried little train into the Denver yards.

"Well, you look better," Fitz said when he entered the office.

"This may be the hardest job I've ever had," Thorne said with relish. He looked no less tired, but more at peace.

Fitz grunted. "I've heard some of your doin's up there, out shovelin' snow with the brakemen an' the likes of that. Other engineers is up in arms. You're spoilin' the crew. That ain't a engineer's job."

"It is on this run, if he doesn't want to freeze to death. The train's stopped more than it's moving."

"Word has come back, too, about some of the crazy chances you've took. Equipment costs money, you know, an' there ain't no way to begin to be able to pay for people's lives. Makes my hair stand up, hearin' about your craziness. Sounds like you're huntin' for ways to put Intermountain out of business up there, an' yourself too."

"Nobody's been killed, no valuable equipment lost.

We're going to have a commendation from the people up there who want to get ore out and other freight in. Anytime we've started the run, we've managed to finish it."

"Well, you oughtn' to of. It ain't natural to always git through, not in this country, this time of year. I see you been enjoyin' yourself, though. I'd fire anyone else took half the chances you have."

"Is that why you sent for me?" Thorne asked, grinning.

"Not all of it. I'm goin' up to that number five Amity tunnel tomorrow. The men are callin' it Perry Tunnel now, after one of the powder monkeys was killed up there. I want you to come along. Brenner'll be with us, an' he's bringin' a feller name of Walter Smithfield, one of your educated rock men that's been lookin' the thing over. You ought to study what they've got to say. You studied rocks like that, I reckon—can't think what they call it."

"I had some geology, but—"

"It's already fixed for somebody else to take over that engine you been runnin' into the ground. I told you when you started this that I didn' aim to have you playin' games the rest of your life. You're needed for too many other things."

Thorne was gratified to be accepted by men like Brenner and Smithfield as a junior member of their profession. He wanted to be with them and had no intention, as Fitz seemed to think, of arguing about taking the train back to Silver Valley. The physical efforts required for getting the freight through—of trying to outguess the weather, slides, erratic time tables, of not freezing to death in canyons of piled-up snow or in the windswept open stretches—had been just the sort of challenge he needed. Lives, including his own, had depended on his skill and daring; and he had found, as he had after running away from the military school, that he was not, in spite of everything, quite willing to die yet. He knew he was better. Somehow, once more, his very being had been rearranged to make the essential accommodation to the new facts of his life. It no longer required the greater part of his mental abilities to close his mind against the pain and useless attempts at questioning and negation.

Perry Tunnel on the Amity line was a bleak place on this day at the end of March. The portal to which track had been laid faced east, down a narrow, twisting canyon all but cut off from sunlight. A shoulder of Elk Mountain cut the canyon there, leaving only a narrow gorge for the creek to run through. A tunnel was essential. Tom Murphy had crews working from both ends of the bore, and those on the west end were faring only slightly better. It was a constant struggle just to keep the eastern working shored up.

"We can, by Jesus, do it," Tom Murphy said fiercely to Fitz and the engineers. "There can't be more than thirty or forty yards to go before we break through to the west."

Brenner did not come into the bore with them. He was looking into some question about snowsheds.

"Miles of sheds is what we'll need, all up in here," Fitz grumbled as they walked toward the mouth of the tunnel and felt its dampness, chilling and even ominous in the dimness and cold of the canyon. "We ought to git into the timber business ourselves, too. It would be cheaper in the long run than all that buyin' from somebody else."

"Faulty dynamite," muttered John Stanley over and over. "It was the goddamn' dynamite, had to be." Unnoticed tears cut through the dirt on his cheeks.

"Chrissake, you've said that twenty times," cried Tom Murphy. "What we need is somebody knows more about doctorin' than we do."

Tom, Thorne, and two workmen carried the improvised stretcher on which Fitz lay, now mercifully unconscious.

"We have to loosen the tourniquets," Walter Smithfield mumbled sickly, stumbling along behind the stretcher, "let the blood circulate every few minutes."

"Much more bleedin' and he can't live," Tom said fiercely.

"Charges were set, some of 'em," Stanley began over again, desperately pleading. "I told 'em we had already set some of 'em, not knowin' when they'd get here, but they wanted to go on in, an' they wasn' a reason on God's earth to think it would blow. Ain't no trustin' anything anymore. Maybe the damp could have set it off. Faulty . . ."

Thorne was beginning to feel the pain in his hands now. They had been lacerated deeply as he tried to claw Fitz free. He felt, too, the dank and utter darkness, the silence, once the explosion and rockfall had stopped reverberating finally. The silence had first been broken by men's coughing as they choked on the dust-laden air; then, while some of them struggled to find lanterns, Fitz's agonized screams had begun, and they had gone on for what seemed an interminable time. Two men were lost, completely buried, surely dead before help would get to them, though others had rushed in and were now trying to reach them at no little risk to themselves. Smithfield had been struck on the head and knocked unconscious for a short time. Fitz's legs were pinned at the leading edge of the rockfall. It seemed like an eternity before they had light, and Fitz's cries filled the choking darkness so that it seemed the tunnel must surely burst. Thorne scrambled to Fitz while it was still dark, clawing desperately at the rock that held him.

"Ah, God, Fitz, please! We'll get you out. It's got to be all right. Just please don't . . . I can't stand it . . ." The words were whispered amid chokes from dust and powder smoke and beneath the horror of Fitz's cries.

"Ask me, this place is jinxed," said one of the workmen now as they tried to hurry with the stretcher along the rough, rock-strewn floor.

"Nobody asked you," snapped Tom Murphy. "We'll all keep our heads and not start talking a bunch of nonsense. Farley," he called to one of the men with lanterns, "run on out and see there's a bed ready for Mr. Fitzroy. Make sure Davis has got steam up."

They came into daylight again; a heavy wet snow had begun to fall. In the dim canyon the nearby work cars and machinery were hazy, but Thorne was able to draw his first deep breath since the explosion. He realized he had felt a fatalistic certainty that he would never come into daylight alive. One of the men asked another what time it was. Thorne was incredulous at the reply. It had been little more than an hour since they had first entered Perry Tunnel. He began shaking, now most frightened by his own fear, shock catching up with him at last.

"Here, Stevens," Tom Murphy was callling, "bear a hand with this stretcher."

The man came and took the corner Thorne had been carrying. Thorne had not realized his pace had slowed and that he had begun to let the stretcher tilt. He stopped and stood there stupidly, staring after the bearers, not seeing them, dizzy, nauseated, his vision only a blur. After what seemed a long time of half-consciousness, the cold suddenly engulfed his face, a cold different from the cold that had gripped him after the explosion.

"Snow in the face sometimes helps," said Brenner with a kind of awkward gentleness. "Better now, are you?"

Thorne nodded. The dizziness was passing, his vision clearing. He put up his hands to brush away the last of the restoring snow and saw the blood, his and Fitz's. Jerkily, he hurried away, to the relative privacy of the other side of a boxcar, where he gave way to the nausea that had been building within him.

When he was at the steps of Fitz's car, someone caught his arm.

"Oh, I saw him!" breathed the girl through tears. "Daddy said he'll live, but how can he, looking like that? His legs . . ."

Thorne drew sharply away from the girl. At first he could not imagine who she was, half believed that she was some sort of apparition. Then he realized it was Nancy Murphy, Tom's daughter, who always lived where her father was working.

"Don't go in there, Nancy," Thorne said curtly as she raised her foot to the first high step.

"Maybe I can help," she said, her eyes filling with tears. "Are you hurt too?"

"No."

"You look hurt."

Tom came out then. "Go back to our car, Nancy girl," he said firmly. "Look at you, no coat or hat—and how long have you been out in this weather? I'll come to you as soon as I can. It's going to be all right."

"They said Sanders and Filmore are still trapped in there, and Mr. Fitzroy—"

"Go on, Nancy. They've got to move this train to get Fitz out to a hospital. Make a big pot of coffee, why don't you? We can all use that."

She went away deeply troubled, and Tom said to no one in particular, "This is no goddamn' place for a girl like that, no sights she ought to be seeing." Then, more calmly to Thorne, "You'll want to go down with him."

Thorne nodded.

"It looks like he may be goin' to come 'round again. A man like that's too strong for his own good. Somebody weaker would be out of it for two or three days, and it would be the Lord's mercy if that could happen for Fitz. If he does wake up, though, he may want you."

"His legs . . ."

"You saw them, same as I did," Tom said quietly, shaking his head. "Taylor had some laudanum. They're trying to get Fitz to swallow it now. You sure you'll be all right? You don't look it. Well, I'll not go down. There are the others to see to here, and I wouldn't leave Nancy. You tell him, if he gets so he can understand and it seems to matter to him, that we'll clear up here and get back to work as soon as we can." He gestured purposefully at the dark tunnel mouth.

"Tom, why not let it go for now, until there's time to—"

"You heard what Smithfield said in there," Tom answered shortly. "He said it can be managed if we go slow and shore properly. You know how close we are to breakthrough. I mean to see this finished."

Thorne said compulsively, "The mountain's against us. I could feel it in there. Nobody can fight a—"

Tom was staring at him. "The hell we can't! The last thing I ever figured you for is a coward. This today was an accident, and the best we can get from it is to find out why it happened and keep it from happenin' again. You know this kind of thing can happen in our work. Fitz wouldn't believe it if he heard you were talkin' that way. Are you sure you didn't get a knock on the head?"

"Ready," called the fireman, leaning out of the locomotive cab, and the train's conductor put his head out and looked at Thorne.

As Thorne went shakily up the steps, Tom called after him, "Tell him, soon as he can listen, that we'll have track into Amity by the Fourth of July."

VIII

1879

For weeks after the accident at Perry Tunnel, Fitz's life had been a precarious thing. Both his crushed legs had had to be amputated at the knees. For months afterward, he was depressed, angry, querulous, rebellious, sometimes by turns, often all at once.

At first, they had brought Fitz "home" to rooms he kept above the railroad offices. He drove away the nurses Thorne hired, male or female. His helplessness and dependence were unbearably humiliating for him, and he would have liked Thorne—who, while understanding, could be almost as irascible as himself—to act as a kind of valet until he was able to begin managing for himself. But he also wanted Thorne out managing the railroad. After the accident, the manager of the Central Western had been sent out to help with Intermountain business. As soon as Fitz was out of the hospital, he summarily sent the man back east. He lay in his bed fretting and chafing, pounding peremptorily on the floor many times a day till Thorne or Jim Ritter or someone else from the office staff came upstairs to be reminded of something they might forget or to be badgered about something already done. Thorne had got Jerry Jones (who for years had been caretaker of Fitz's private car) to come and look after Fitz. Fitz decided he "could put up with Jerry," but though he had to stay in bed, he took a new and desperate interest in everything that went on in the offices below. Thorne and Jim Ritter sometimes laughed, a little hysterically with frustration and exasperation, over the fact that neither of them would lack for exercise so long as they were kept on the stairs by the frequent banging from above.

"Fitz," Thorne said to him one day, "what difference does it make if the new main-line passenger timetables come from the printer today or tomorrow? The schedules don't go into effect until the first of next month. I'm trying to look at maps of the San Miguel area. I don't know if we have the timetables. God, you never used to care if we even had timetables."

"That was when I could git around," Fitz reminded him glumly. "I got to take interest now in what's close at hand if I ain't to lose what little sense I've got. I thought you'd be at them maps. Whyn't you bring 'em up here? When'll Brenner be in?"

In June, Fitz was more than a little taken aback when his stepdaughter Cherish arrived with young Ted and her maid Dahlia.

"Tell you the truth," he said ruefully to Thorne, "I half forgot about 'em, her an' Ted both. Ted's through school for the summer. She's shut up the Pittsburgh house without even askin' me. Says she means to find a proper house here, make a home for the family. Jesus Christ, what'll I *do* with 'em?"

"I think she's right about a house," Thorne said, feeling a little relieved. "If you have a place without stairs, you can start getting around more as you get stronger."

"That's right," Fitz said peevishly, "gang up on me. What you want, an' I know it as well as you, is to get me away from the office. Well, I tell you now, I mean to git around. I ain't goin' to be stopped from livin'. You'll not be boss around here, or think you are, much longer. What have you got to say to that?"

"I'm goddamn' glad to hear it. Now I have to go down and—"

"Now wait a minute!" Fitz said hotly. "Don't you walk out on me when you know good an' well I can't foller. A house might not be a altogether bad thing, but before I'll be talked into buyin' anything, I want your word you'll live there too."

"Fitz—"

"Listen, Thorne. This is a hellish thing that's happened to me. I ain't in no way used to it yet, maybe never will be. I *got* to be in on railroad business. It's what'll help me git well, or as well as I can git. I want to hear about it from you mornin' an' night till I git to where I can spend time at the office, maybe go out agin some on the lines. Will you do it?"

Thorne shrugged and said reluctantly, "Until you're back at work. That won't be long."

Both of them knew that "long" was a relative thing. There were times when Fitz, angry and discouraged, would give up trying, but even when he worked at it, his recovery was slow. There had been a back injury too, and it was to give him severe pain at times. His strength returned with maddening slowness.

Cherish found a house, one of the best in town, and two rooms on the ground floor were equipped for Fitz. Cherish's attentions were grudging and sporadic. She felt no sympathy and little concern for her stepfather, but she was impressed by the house and by some of Fitz's friends. She was surprised and not a little incredulous to find that Fitz was on a first-name basis with the governor of the state and a United States senator. She was a ready and eager hostess to such people. She was displeased, condescending or flagrantly rude to some of Fitz's other friends, but amid complaints and strong intimations of self-sacrifice, she did cope with the running of the household, with a great deal of help from Dahlia.

Thorne usually slept at the house, often ate there, but there were many things to attend to at the office and elsewhere. His time at the house, when not occupied by the necessities of food and sleep, was spent in detailed discussions of business with Fitz, which Thorne, for his own peace of mind, needed almost as much as the older man.

The Amity line was opened that summer. Peter Maitland came out from Pittsburgh to represent Intermountain at the lavish celebrations at the mining area. In the fall, Thorne had a kind of respite when he was able to spend almost a month in the state's southwestern mountains, where a line to San Miguel, a new boom town, was being platted.

By the time winter came, Fitz was able to wheel himself about the lower floor of his house. With specially affixed straps, he could get himself into or out of bed. He began coming into the office for a few hours several times a week. He was querulous, critical and demanding of the staff, because of pain and exasperation, and because of embarrassment over his real or imagined inabilities and inadequacies.

By mid-March of 1879, Fitz was feeling relatively well and was determined to go to Pittsburgh for a board meeting. He was equally determined that Thorne must go with him. He mentioned to Herb Alden that they would be going, casting an obstinate, defiant glance at Thorne, who appeared not to be listening.

Alden was publisher of a newspaper in which MM&F owned some stock. Thorne did not like him and neither did Fitz, but he was an impressionable man, the sort Fitz sometimes enjoyed, and the paper was useful. Fitz had been trying hard for this past year to teach Thorne, among many other things, if not diplomacy at least a grudging camaraderie with "men that might come in handy." Thorne was particularly edgy and nervous this evening. Finishing his whiskey, he refilled his glass along with those of the other two men. He had spent most of the year in the Intermountain offices, taking responsibility for decisions he still lacked experience and knowledge for making, and he was beginning to hope for some relief.

When it was time for Alden to leave, Thorne, replying absently to the publisher's small talk, walked with him to the door. As he returned to Fitz, his face was set and adamant.

"What are you lookin' so sour about?" Fitz asked innocently. "It's the Pittsburgh trip, ain't it?"

"No. Why would that bother me? I'm not going."

"You are goin'," Fitz said, exasperated, no longer pretending. "You'll go because I say so, an' quit your goddamn' pacin'. Drives me crazy."

"There's no *reason* for me to go," Thorne said. He was unusually edgy and tense this evening.

The hard determination suddenly left Fitz's face, and it seemed to crumple slightly. He said querulously, "I want you along."

Thorne drew a deep breath between his teeth and said something he had wanted to say for months. "Don't give me the invalid routine anymore, Fitz. You've played that for about all it'll stand."

To his surprise, and to his unexpected irritation, Fitz laughed.

"Worked pretty good while it lasted though, didn't it?"

Grudgingly, Thorne smiled. "You old—"

"Now, now. No call for bad language. We've found out you can fair run the business, ain't we? But there wouldn' of been no keepin' you in that office, would there, if it hadn't been that your pore ole crippled friend needed you so bad? Well, you've learned some, an' learned it fast, you an' young Ritter both. Had to, didn' you, after ole Ralph Jeffers had that stroke."

"You don't think I've been completely taken in all this time?"

"If I did, you wouldn' be the man I've thought you are. 'Course I know it's Ritter's been doin' most of the work." He went back to his current topic of chief interest to say impatiently, "It won't be just the board meetin'. You know how sick they say Angus is. Jesus, the man must of known for some while this was comin' on him. It's like him, I guess, not to tell anybody. Maitlands have had it in mind for some time to reorganize. There's all this talk against trusts; government nosey pokes, don't know their ass from a hole in the ground when it comes to business, tryin' to butt in an' say how things have to be run. You've seen the letters: how Peter's sayin' we ought to make MM&F a corporation with the mines, mill, an' railroad three separate companies, how we could double the amount of stock an' sell half on the open market. Angus never would go along with that, or with talk of relocatin' the whole shebang out here. I don't mean to say they're just buzzardin' around waitin' for him to die, but he ain't goin' to be at the meetin' this time an' all that's bound to come up. They'll more'n likely want to see about sellin' the Central Western while I'm back there, an' I can't handle that by myself, not the shape I'm in. I reckon I'll sell my house in Pittsburgh, but we'll stay there this year, through Ted's Easter vacation from school."

"Fitz, I've been telling you for months—"

"Started tellin' me New Year's Eve, didn' you?" said Fitz, grinning.

New Year's Eve was a subject of which Thorne had heard more than enough. Fitz had given a large party with a varied group of guests. While other young people danced, ate and rang in the New Year, Thorne, sitting in a corner where several older men soberly discussed business and politics, drew even deeper into himself. In fact, Thorne drank so much that in the morning he had no memory of several hours of the night, including when or how he had got to bed. Early the next morning he was called about a derailment on the Santa Fe line, and while he held his throbbing head, Fitz chortled, "I always said I'd see you drunk once, didn' I? Well, there wasn' nothin' to worry about. You didn' make no kind of fool of yourself. You just set there, gittin' quieter an' quieter, lookin' like you didn' like nothin' nor nobody around you. Looked like what my ole pa used to call black moods. I swear, boy, at times there ain't nothin'll make you cheerful."

Now, three months after the fact, Fitz still relished memories of New Year's Eve, but he stifled a grin and went on doggedly. "You don't have to stay in Pittsburgh long as I do. I'll have Jerry, and Cherish is goin' along, too. She wants to spend some time at Fern Hill. Maybe I'll go there myself for a few weeks if travelin' ain't too hard. The place is bound to need some attention. But you won't have to be gone more'n a month."

"A month?"

"Now don't git excited all over agin. You was gone about that long last fall, seein' to things down around San Miguel."

"I don't *want* to go to Pittsburgh."

Fitz said truculently, "When in hell are you goin' to quit that, Thorne? Won't you ever learn it don't matter what you want? There's a business to take care of." Then, placatingly, he said, "When we git back, me an' Jim an' the others can see to things here. You can git back in the field again."

"I mean to," Thorne said fervently, "as soon as the weather breaks."

"You see," Fitz said sweetly, "the trip to Pittsburgh'll be over an' done with, time winter's over in the mountains. It's just what you need." Then, to avoid further argument, he asked quickly, "What about that timber man? Did you see him?"

"That's tomorrow. He's to bring in all the figures on his business, and Jim and I will go look over the operation again in a few days. Maybe you could come with us, to the mill at least."

"Maybe I will. I want everything ready on that to show the others back east. We could have bought several sawmills an' a lot of timber interests with what we've already paid for ties an' shorin'."

"Owning a lumber business would make us seem more of a trust than we already are."

"Shit, I don't give a damn what we seem like. We got to go at makin' a profit the best an' easiest ways we can. That's how a man's got to think if he's runnin' any kind of business. We ain't in any of this for charity. Did you talk to Avery?"

"No, why would I?"

"Because his brother-in-law is on the Railroad Commission is why, an' because Avery owns pretty big interests in some of them claims around San Miguel, an' because I told you a week ago to make an appointment an' show him your plats."

"I don't like showing plats to the brother-in-law of a railroad commissioner so he can be sure the line is going to come close enough to his claims."

"Well, that's the way things gits done sometimes. Don't turn goody-goody on me."

"I'll have the plats copied tomorrow. You can show them to Avery."

"Listen, Thorne, it's plain enough what you think of some of these people like Avery, but try to have sense enough to take a little advice. I had to learn it myself, the hard, slow way. A lot of business, some of the most important parts of it, don't git done in a office or boardroom. There's a lot of back-scratchin' goes on. It's the way things are done, always has been, always will be. You want to start on that San Miguel line, don't you, with as little delay as possible?"

"Right now, Fitz, I don't especially care."

"Oh, hell, I don't see how or why I put up with you. You can go down there an' work on the San Miguel all through the good weather this year, an' there's that new short line in Montana . . . Goin' to Pittsburgh'll give you a good rest an' you'll be rarin' to go agin, time we git back."

"I wish to God I *could* have a rest, but I wouldn't get it in Pittsburgh!" Thorne got up to leave. "I've brought some papers home I have to work on."

"What papers?"

"I told you earlier, it's the new freight rates we're going to propose."

Fitz snorted. "I just don't see how things can go on the way they have been. There ain't nothin' right about it when a company, spendin' its own money, takin' its own chances, not askin' anything from any government, has got to have all its business messed into by this court an' that commission. It ain't no way right!" He looked suddenly eager. "Tell me agin just how that went about Rockefeller's oil people settin' freight rates so they got a kickback when other oil companies shipped on the railroad."

Thorne made an impatient gesture, but smiled faintly. "*That's* a trust."

"Well, tell it to me agin. I want it absolutely straight in my mind."

"If you get it any straighter, you're going to find a way to apply it here, and I don't want any part of it."

"We ain't big, as companies go, but Intermountain's doin' all right. Look at us, settin' here between the Santa Fe and the Union Pacific an' holdin' our own. Santa Fe's buyin' all the stock it can lay hands on of RM&P's, an' them people of Gould's keep sniffin' around us like bears after honey."

"If MM&F stock is to go on the open market, how are you going to keep Gould's people, or anyone else from buying it?"

"I don't know a lot about that kind of thing. I expect Peter an' Philip will have somethin' in mind. If they ain't, I won't agree to put nothin' on the market. Intermountain is like a child I've brought up. I ain't havin' no part of it took over by them big-money eastern fellers."

A maid knocked on Fitz's door then and ushered in a middle-aged aide from the governor's staff. Thorne excused himself quickly.

He thought of going for a walk, trying to exhaust the restlessness that grew stronger in him each day, but it was raining, a cold, heavy drizzle. Standing for a moment by the window on the landing, looking out at dripping trees, rain-dimmed street lamps, he decided to go upstairs. As he passed the door to Cherish's small sitting room, it opened and she spoke to him.

"I don't like to bother you, Thorne," she said, almost shyly, though that was hardly her usual demeanor. "But there's something we just have to talk about."

She was a beautiful woman of nineteen, with a petite and perfect figure, flawless complexion and golden hair. Her voice, when she cared to be pleasing, was a beautiful thing to hear—warm and slow and expressive, with just enough of the southern drawl left to make her irresistible to most men. Thorne, however, had heard the voice raised too often in a self-pitying whine. And the way she lingered over his name, dropping the r, but still making two syllables of it, irritated him every time she said it. Cherish's eyes almost spoiled her looks. They were a lovely, light-blue color, but disturbingly shallow, empty of expression. A smile never reached those eyes; they never sparkled with animation. She was wise to exploit the long golden lashes by lowering her eyelids, for the only expression of which her eyes seemed capable was hardness, a kind of cold, avid calculation.

In the nine months since she had come to Denver,

it seemed to Cherish, despite her efforts, that whether she had tried to be subtle or flagrant, Thorne had never really seen her. After dinner tonight, when she heard Thorne and Fitz arguing again about going to Pittsburgh, Cherish's own plans crystallized, the final pieces falling into place. Her sitting room door had been ajar since she had come upstairs, and she closed it with mixed feelings when Thorne entered. In a way, she hated him for his lack of interest, for making it necessary that things should come to this, but she also felt well in control of the situation and quite able now to have revenge for his aloofness and self-possession.

"I don't know how to say it," she said softly. "It's not—an easy thing for me. Maybe if we sit down . . .?"

She went to a love seat by the fire, glanced significantly at the empty place beside her, then looked at him through her long lashes.

Ignoring her, Thorne took a chair by the window. He had never liked Cherish; she was dishonest and deceitful, petty, and as Fitz put it, "stuck on herself." He had been relieved and grateful to her when she came from Pittsburgh and began looking after Fitz's personal interests, but aside from their shared interests in Fitz, Thorne could never think of anything they might have in common. He tried to avoid her most of the time. This talk, over which she was looking so serious, he presumed would be about a maid nipping from a whiskey bottle, the drain of the new bathtub being clogged again, or Fitz's thoughtlessness and lack of appreciation. As nearly as he could remember, these had been the subjects of their last three private conversations. She always made any situation seem as dramatic as possible.

"You see," she was saying diffidently, "It's not always so easy for a girl. It's no more the doing of one than the other, and I don't know why I should feel embarrassed or—wrong, or anything like that, but I do. Can't you—it seems like you must have some hint of what I'm trying to say."

"I'm sorry, Cherish, I don't know. Maybe if you could just find the beginning and tell me straight away—"

Cherish knew he was being patronizing, but held her resentment in check. He glanced up at the clock and she said sadly, "If you could just look at me."

She met his eyes very briefly before dropping her own. Her cheeks were flushed. The heightened color added to her beauty and gave her a look of sweetness that Thorne sensed was due to some deceptive quirk of expression and not real. He had heard too much of her almost constant nagging and raging to believe there was much of pliability, gentleness or consideration in Cherish.

"You can't even guess?" Her words were barely audible.

Thorne shook his head, beginning to frown.

"Well, it began on New Year's Eve—New Year's morning, really."

"What did?"

"Thorne, you're being cruel. Please don't. I can't stand it right now. It meant so much to me, and I thought it meant at least *something* to you. Don't act like you don't remember or don't care, not even for a joke. Just now, I guess, there's not much that would seem funny to me. I—I'm going to have a baby."

Thorne stood up, moved the draperies aside from the window, rolled a cigarette with hands that were none too steady. The words jolted him, yet somehow he was not utterly surprised. His feelings were somewhat as they had been on the night Angus admitted being his father. It was a little as if he had already known. If I suspect these things already, he thought with self-derision, why am I always so unready, so unprepared? God, what am I going to do now?

"Can't you *say* anything?" cried Cherish.

"You—you're sure?" He still faced the window and had put his hands at either side of his face, the better to look out into darkness.

"I've waited all this long time so I'd be sure," she gasped and began to cry. "I didn't want to bother our big executive with anything but facts. I've missed twice and the third time's due. Is that enough, or should I have waited till . . ."

"I'm sorry," he said contritely, turning from the window.

"Sorry!" she sobbed. "What do you think *I* am? And you've made it so hard, not a word or a look afterward. I don't believe you'd treat one of those girls on River Street the way you've treated me. When you came to my room that night, I knew you were drunk, but it did seem to mean something . . ."

She had drawn up her feet, turned sideways on the love seat and crumpled against its high back.

But Thorne was thinking, Was this what happened with Meg? Is that why . . .? He had asked the question hundreds of times and his answer was always the same: Why couldn't she wait for me to come home? And why would she marry Gordon if she were having my baby? He pulled his mind up short. The time for questioning, thinking of Meg was past—long past.

He took a step toward Cherish and said, "I was in my own room that morning. I woke up there."

"Of course you woke up in your own room," Cherish said brokenly. "I made you go back before morning. Maybe you don't care, but I won't be a subject for scandal among the servants. Are you telling me you don't remember? I can't imagine anything less flattering to any girl. Or are you trying to say I'm lying, or what, Thorne?"

"Cherish, I—I have to be honest, and the truth

is I don't remember a part of that night, going upstairs, or . . ."

Her tears increased. She sobbed like a little girl, looking small, helpless, forlorn, poignantly appealing.

"We'll be married if it's what you want," Thorne said. He had moved nearer and now tentatively touched her hair.

"Oh! she cried petulantly, "what I want! I haven't got a choice, have I?"

"I'm saying everything wrong," he said miserably. "I want to make it right."

"You can't even look at me for more than a minute," she sobbed accusingly. "You can't bear to touch me."

"Cherish, we'll both have to . . ."

"To what? Have time to think about this, get used to it, see if we think we can learn to tolerate each other? Well, I have had time to think and I don't know that I'm a bit more eager than you seem to be."

Reluctantly, feeling trapped and helpless, Thorne sat down on the edge of the love seat. Cherish's tears began to lessen. She moved toward him and he sat back, letting his arms go around her. She crept into his lap like an ingratiating child, but there was nothing of childishness in her kiss, the touch of her hands, the pressures of her body. She felt his body awaken and allowed herself a little smile, her lips hidden against his neck

Thorne said, "We could arrange things—a wedding —for next week if you like. There's that church in the next block. I can talk to the minister—"

"Oh, Thorne, I've thought and thought about it," she said with abrupt eagerness. "I've been so scared and upset all this time and could hardly do anything *but* think. Please come east. I want to be married at Fern Hill more than I've ever wanted anything in the world. We could have the wedding at Easter—it's less than three weeks from now, such a lovely time in Virginia. Our good old pastor who baptized me and

Teddy could perform the ceremony, and my dear, my only real friends could all be there. *Do* let me have that much."

"I thought—wouldn't you like to get it—have the wedding as soon as we can?"

"They won't know exactly how soon after the baby's born. It's something I've always dreamed of, a nice wedding at home, where I really belong. I suppose you're going to go on trying to be like Fitz, and you won't agree to live there, so . . . Oh! it's been such hell for me all this long time."

Thorne recognized her ill-concealed manipulations, but surely he owed her something—should feel he owed her something. He doubted he could ever give love, but there might be a chance for something between them.

"I can't be away long," he conceded with little grace.

"You *will* do it! Oh, you darling!" She pronounced it dahlin, blew her nose discreetly and looked prettily flushed and excited. "You won't have to do a thing with the plans and preparations except be there. I'll send Dahlia ahead to see that the house is open and ready. Oh, Thorne! Let's do try to be happy. I guess neither one of us wants a baby, but we did get ourselves into this. Quite a few marriages must have to start something like this, I guess. We can work it out. You'll see."

Thorne thought, There's no help for it now, no other way. By God, I can try to make the best of it. Her mouth was warm and sweet.

Cherish drew away from him, smiling softly. "I know you've got your work," she said, sighing resignedly. "You always have your work, but darling, please say at least that you don't hate me?"

"I—we can do all we can to make it come right," he said quietly. "I'll do all I can . . ."

Cherish went looking for Dahlia, found her mending

in her own room. "And you'll have to leave in a few days," Cherish finished exuberantly. "We'll make a list, several lists, of things to be done at Fern Hill."

"Yes'm," said Dahlia, puzzled, a little stunned, "I guess I'd better write things down. Right now, I'm a little dizzy. This is awful—sudden."

Cherish laughed. Her laughter was lovely to hear when it was real. "It's not sudden at all. Didn't I tell you one night back in Pittsburgh it would happen? I knew, over a year ago, that I wanted him and that I could have him. All I had to do was make him take some notice, finally. Right now, he's not the most—ardent bridegroom anyone has ever seen, but that will change."

"That seems an odd way to talk," Dahlia said slowly, looking at her carefully. "And it's an odd way you're looking, Miss Cherish. Is there more to this than you're telling me?"

"It's hardly your business to know everything," she said archly. "Besides, I don't know what you're talking about."

"It just seems like," said Dahlia, troubled, "you're looking at it all kind of—cold—the wedding, 'getting him,' all of it."

"I have to seem cold to keep myself sane," Cherish said, suddenly sober and tense. "Nobody can ever know how it's been for me, waiting and waiting while he treated me like part of the furniture—oh! it's been so long, so *hard*—trying to look after that grumpy, dirty old man and all the rest of it."

"But honey, do you love Mr. Thorne? Does he—"

"I adore Mr. Thorne," she said fervently, almost viciously. "I think he's the handsomest, most desirable man in the world. I worship the ground he walks on. There, how's that? But see you keep out of our affairs. He'll never know how I really feel."

"But, Miss Cherish—"

"I won't be—used and then forgotten the way

women are. I never want him to think he can be sure of anything, least of all me."

"Why, honey—"

"Just tend to your own business, Dahlia," she said menacingly, "I know how to handle him. Heaven knows, there's been enough time for planning."

Thorne and Cherish spent ten days at Fern Hill. It was a beautiful place, with its gracious old house which Fitz's money kept in good repair, the formal gardens for which Fitz had sent a landscaper down from New York the year after the war ended, the reclaimed fields that Fitz had turned into pasture grasses, where sleek cattle now grazed. Thorne knew nothing about matters of agriculture in this part of the country, but he rode out with the manager one afternoon and looked the place over, enjoying all of it, particularly relieved to be away from the house.

He felt stifled by the house and its immediate surroundings. For one thing, there were too many flowers, though Cherish and her guests kept lamenting those that were not yet in bloom. The air seemed too mild, too tame; a kind of too-sweet blandness, closer to decay than to ripeness, engulfed everything. The guests, all strangers to Thorne, gave him the same stifled impressions of over-abundant sensations. Fitz had, after all, not come down with them. He was exhausted from the Denver to Pittsburgh trip, and suffering from back pain. Thorne had thought of asking Ranald to come, but Cherish would have been opposed; she told him she had never liked Ranald, and it hardly seemed worth the upset to have Ranald stand with him for those few minutes at the flower-covered altar in the house's huge parlor. Seeing Ranald for a few moments in Pittsburgh while Fitz was getting settled, Thorne realized that he had missed his cousin badly during the time they had not seen each other.

The Virginians, even the young ones at Cherish's house party, spent too much of their time in reminiscences of "our dear land," by which they meant the South before the war. Their talk was cloying and wistful, slightly unreal, like the heavy, ubiquitous scent of the flowers. Thorne gathered that most of these people were now in quite straitened circumstances, though someone was always detailing for him an illustrious family tree or history. Cherish enjoyed flaunting and enlarging upon her own good financial position and Fern Hill's, though she sighed as much as anyone over the lost Confederacy. She had been not quite six when the war ended, but it seemed her mother must never have talked to her unless it was about "those dear times," or the positions of the Stuarts and Bromleighs, or the complicated interwoven life stories of the others in the county who "mattered."

One night before they were to return to Pittsburgh, Cherish, after prolonged good nights in the hall, came slowly to their room, where Thorne had gone a little earlier, gratefully savoring even a few minutes alone now.

"Oh, I *can't* leave so soon!" she began mournfully. "Can't you see how much it means to me, being here? . . . Well, can't you *say* something?"

"I have to be there for the board meeting," he said. "We've been over it all before. The first time was before we even left Denver."

"And it never has made any sense," she said petulantly. "You don't have to be at any old meeting. You never meant to come east at all until you knew you had to marry me."

He said nothing. Cherish had begun to undress with lingering slowness. She found great enjoyment, absorption, in the perfection of her own body, and of his. Her openness in physical things had shocked Thorne at first, shocked and excited. He supposed there was some of the prude in him, but he couldn't help feeling hesitant when it became clear that she wanted his body frequently and fully revealed in day- or lamplight. Physical scruples he could and would have overcome quickly enough; but Cherish also wanted, and said so, to know "every little cranny of your very soul." He had smiled uneasily when she said that and mumbled that he doubted he had a soul, but her intentions and determination dismayed him. He had an innate reticence, a need for complete and sole possession of himself that he might never be able to overcome, even with someone he loved and trusted. Cherish's insistence on seeing and handling his possessions, being told his thoughts, having almost constant physical contact, left him appalled and a little frightened. Her curiosity and need to possess were as threatening to him as his natural aloofness was to her. Even in Gavin's house, where for a few years seven boys shared the one large bedroom, they had learned from infancy a respect for each other's rights to the scant property and privacy they could attain.

Cherish crossed the room now to stand beside him where he sat on a low, too-soft chair. She drew his head against her perfect, naked breasts and ran her hands over his back. "So strong," she murmured. "All those muscles just for making love to me."

He put his arms around her, and she smiled and drew away. "Now, now, you'd do nothing but those naughty things all the time if I let you, wouldn't you? I have to brush my hair."

She enjoyed sex and made no secret of it, so long as she could feel herself the director. Her needs could be satisfied easily and quickly, but before and after those physical demands took over, "lovemaking" was purely a tool.

She sat down at the dressing table and began to brush her hair with slow, languid strokes, trying to watch him as well as herself in the mirror. Evidently, she had decided to postpone the next segment in her continuous argument for staying on at Fern Hill. She said sweetly—though for Thorne it was like being pounced on—"What are you thinking about, darling?" Her drawl grew more noticeable every day they spent in Virginia.

Thorne wandered aimlessly about the large airy bedroom, his mind drained of all comprehensible thought. What Cherish wanted was to hear that he was thinking of her. He knew that, but was tired of making up things. She asked the question anytime there was the briefest of silences. The idea of her or anyone else feeling they had a right to his thoughts added to the restless nervousness that kept growing in him.

She said fretfully, "Married people are supposed to share everything, Thorne. Don't you know that? Don't you want us to get to know each other as soon as we can?"

"It's not easy," he said, trying to sound apologetic. "I mean, I've never—shared—some things with anyone. I don't know that I ever can . . ."

"It's sweet that you're so shy," she said, not looking pleased, "but do try harder, darling. You weren't shy at all that first time, New Year's Eve, not about anything. I *am* your wife, and you mustn't ever try to keep anything from me. I'll tell you what I was thinking when I asked you. I was thinking that nearly anyone could tell in a minute that Lucy Malvern's husband is a Yankee, just from nearly anything he says. I don't mean his accent, though he's certainly got one; I mean the *things* he says."

"What things?" Thorne had no interest in what the boastful, rather simple man might have said, but he was already forming the habit of seeming to go along with her when he could, while most of his mind was occupied with other things. He had brought a briefcase of materials from which he planned to write a report for the MM&F board meeting. But each time he tried to work on it, Cherish became angrily resentful, then magnanimously resigned, and insisted on hearing details that immediately bored her, whereupon she became intent on distracting him.

She was saying, outraged, "Why just this afternoon while you were out riding, he called you a black Scot."

Thorne faced her, his eyes mildly puzzled. "Well, so I am."

"Black?" she cried in a mixture of ridicule and irritation.

"There are a lot of us," he said quizzically. "It comes from mixing with Roman soldiers a long time ago, or from some of the Normans, or gypsies, or even the Moors when they were all over the place spreading the Moslem religion."

"Oh, Thorne, not the *Moors!* Please don't ever think that again. The very idea . . . There's nothing like a black about you and nobody calls anybody a black anything—not here—you surely know that in this part of the country 'black' means nigger."

He smiled. "Should I—challenge him, or whatever it is people do when they want a duel?"

"I'll thank you not to make fun of my friends," she snapped. "I'm not surprised, though, that you have so few notions about proper behavior. You won't have to do anything about him. *I* let him know what was thought of him here. I told you they went home while you were still out riding. Poor Lucy was just broken-hearted and ready to die of shame."

"When are the others going home?"

"Why, darling, would you rather they weren't here? It's been so long since I've been able to spend any time with my friends, my kind of people. I've tried my best to give you my attention too. I know a bridegroom is entitled to his—marriage rights."

"I only wondered if they'll be staying as long as we do."

"We've had so little time here," she sighed. "Yes, some will stay to see us off, if we do go. Lettie

Brewster has said she'll stay an extra day or two and see to closing up the house. Oh, Thorne, let's stay on and have a decent honeymoon. We ought to spend more time at Fern Hill, then visit in some of these people's homes—where they could afford to entertain us—then go to Europe for a few months. I didn't get to have any kind of tour. Can't you give me *anything?*"

"There's not money for going to Europe, Cherish, even if there was the time. Someday—"

"Oh, I don't know how long I can stand always hearing 'someday.' All you ever want to think about is that old railroad. You let Fitz and nearly anybody else lead you around by the nose, but you never pay a bit of attention to anything I want. You'll never forget or let me forget we *had* to get married."

"No, I don't mean to be like that."

"Then why can't we live, have some fun while we're young?"

"You know what I earn, what I've—"

"I know you ought to have more, a lot more. Angus owns a great big hunk of the company and you're the only heir he's got. Fitz would lend you money if you'd just ask for it. Or maybe old Angus is dead by now. I hope so . . . . Well, don't you? I mean, they say he's been awful sick now, for weeks, I'm only wishing him out of his misery. *You've* said you hate him."

"I've told you, I don't expect Angus to leave me anything and I wouldn't want—"

"Thorne, you ought to be proud of being a Maxwell and what it means. I can see how nobody could like that pinched old man, but you ought to expect and *get* what's yours by rights. Why, people around here just seethed with envy when they heard you're an earl's grandson, and nephew. Goodness knows, the other side of your family's common as dirt. I wouldn't have married you, no matter what, if a MacWinter was all you were. I'll tell you a secret. I ought to just let you wait until the will's read, but I'll tell you.

Before I left Pittsburgh to go and take care of Fitz, Angus came to see me. He thought you and I ought to marry. He said he'd tried to talk to you about it, about your duty to the name and company, but you wouldn't listen. He wanted the stock combined, his and Fitz's, to keep things as much in the family as possible. He's going to leave things to you. You can count on it. He said he'd leave me a little income, too, provided we were married. Oh, darling, what are you frowning over *now?*"

She came over to where he stood by the window, pressing against him, reaching up to try to stroke the scowl from his brow. "I'm ready for bed," she murmured, "but I don't mean to go to sleep for a while."

Thorne, seeking to empty his mind, picked her up and carried her to the big, too-soft bed. He was not surprised. Even his marriage had been manipulated by Angus.

"So strong!" Cherish breathed, stroking his arms and shoulders. "You could just crush little old me, couldn't you?"

"That's not what I mean to do," he said huskily.

She laughed, but moved a little away from him, holding his hands to still them. "Look at me, darling. I just love to look at your body. Can't you enjoy me just by looking, for a little while?"

After a moment, he said honestly, "You're very beautiful."

She smiled. "You want me so much you can hardly think, can you, poor darling? We really are one, the way it says in the Bible. You can possess my body and I can . . ."

Thorne had freed his hands and she laughed again as he pulled her to him.

Immediately afterward, through quick-drawn breath, Cherish wanted to know what he had been thinking while they made love. Thorne was angered by the question, feeling more than physically exposed.

"What would I have been thinking? That was enough to fill anyone's mind."

The answer, spontaneous as it was, and spoken rather irritably, pleased her. "It doesn't necessarily fill a woman's mind, but men are such slaves to—that, aren't they? Once you get—well, ready—you're just at a woman's mercy."

Thorne drew up the covers. The night was cool; he was drowsy, replete. Cherish's seeking hands began again almost immediately, exploring, fondling. He had heard men complain of their wives' bearing intercourse like a burden, but he had never heard of one bemoaning the fact that, though his wife seemed to enjoy sex, she was never satisfied for more than a few moments, never willing simply to be quiet and grant him the privacy of his own body.

"Cherish," he said when she had not spoken for an unusually long time, "will the baby begin to show soon? I mean, it's more than three months now. You're so small and—"

Her face, which had been soft and sensual, grew abruptly hard and she jerked away from him. "You want me ugly!" she said fiercely.

"No, I only—wondered."

She lay stiffly for a moment, then lifted herself to blow out the lamp. If she left it out, it would be the first time their room had known a night without artificial light.

Cherish said coldly, "You *want* a baby, don't you? I'm not enough for you. I suppose it proves something for a man, that he *is* a man, to have other people see his wife's belly is full."

He said earnestly, "I'd like to be glad about the baby. I hope I can be some kind of decent father."

"And what about me? Don't you realize what I've already been through, what there is yet to come? You're so selfish and hateful."

He said nothing, so she went on, "I have just these

few days for enjoying myself, and you have to bring up a question about how soon I'll be grotesque and ugly. You won't even consider a decent honeymoon with me, but I'll bet you can find all kinds of time to spend with a brat."

"Even if we could go to Europe," he said, meaning to be reasonable, "it wouldn't be a good time for you to travel now. You'll enjoy it so much more later."

"Then why are you trying to make me leave here. I'll be just as miserable traveling to Pittsburgh and back to Denver."

"If you think it might be bad for you, I suppose you could stay on here."

"Without you?"

"Yes, I have to get back to the job."

She laughed grimly. "Oh, no! You won't get rid of me that easily. Married a week and you're trying to find ways to get away from me."

"I just thought it might be best for you."

"Which of those other women would you run to? And don't claim you always get drunk and never remember anything."

She reached for him again. Now her manipulations were deliberately painful, and there was cruelty in her laugh as he drew away, disengaging her hands, holding them, though she struggled and scratched him.

"Look at you," she said mockingly. "I thought it was always women who pretend they don't want it. You can't hide from me, darlin'. Pretend all you want, your thermometer down there always gives you away."

Defensiveness grew in his mind as his body gave way to an implacable, animal response. Cherish lifted herself and one of her breasts rested against his face. Thorne felt shamefully exposed as once more his body clamored for her. Cherish made a small, gratified sound as his arms went round her, but just when he would have entered her, she struggled and pushed him away.

"Thorne, don't!" she gasped, her own breath coming hard in desire. "I—I've got a backache. Maybe it's bad—for the baby, for us to keep doing this. I've heard it can cause a miscarriage."

He drew away, feeling an anger that he did not understand.

"It doesn't matter to you how I feel," she accused. "You never even *ask* me how I feel. All you're interested in is—having your way. You think you can have your cake and eat it too."

"Can I—get anything for you?" he asked stiffly. "I'm sorry you don't feel well."

"A glass of wine might help," she answered sullenly after a moment.

Thorne put on some clothes and went downstairs for the wine. In the renewed lamplight, Cherish's whole face bespoke accusation as she sipped from the glass.

"I could sleep in the dressing room," he offered tensely, desperately hoping she might want that.

She began to cry. "You see! You just—use me, and then want to get away."

"Cherish—"

"Can't you see I can't bear the thought of having a baby? It scares me to death, and you won't share any of it, can't even be bothered with trying to comfort me."

"What would you like me to do?"

She flung the glass against the wall. "Why do I have to *tell* you everything?"

"Because I don't *know*," he said, just as angrily.

There was a little silence before she said sullenly, "It might help a little if you came back to bed and held me. I think I'd like to go to sleep in your arms. At least, I'd know your body's here."

He held her and she lay quiet for such a long time

he thought she might be asleep. Then she said wheedlingly, "Thorne, who were they from?"

"What?"

"Those letters that came from you that time, in care of Fitz. Who were they from? It was a girl, wasn't it?"

"Cherish—"

"I asked Ranald about them. Naturally, *he* wouldn't say anything. Are you still in love with her?"

"No."

"Men are terrible romantics. They always think what they can't have has to be better than what they can. I don't believe you."

"All right," he said. "There's not much I can do about what you think."

She yawned. "I know that some time you'll tell me all about it. Relax, darling. You're all tensed up. My back's a little better. I'll try to sleep. And please, I've asked you before, if you wake up first, don't sneak away somewhere. I want you here in the mornings."

She slept then, with what seemed amazing speed and ease. After a long while of lying tensely, Thorne tried to extricate his numbed arm from beneath her head. Cherish moaned and threw her own arm across him, so that when he would have left the bed, she clutched at him, muttering ominously.

Thorne lay still again, rigid. Soft spring air moved through the room, heavy and sweet with flower scents, filled with the sounds of frogs and crickets. This country, he thought, was frenetic with life, attacking all the senses with a kind of raging fecundity. He thought yearningly of the mountains west of the hacienda and restlessly turned on his side away from Cherish, but she clung to him, murmuring.

"You belong to me even more than you belong to yourself. You're mine now."

He could not suppress a shudder. Gradually, her breathing deepened as she drifted back into sound sleep. After a while Thorne's eyes ached, from staring into darkness.

"Don't go!" Cherish screamed and tears began again. It was their second evening back in the Pittsburgh house. "You know I'm sick and you don't care."

"When I'm here," Thorne said wearily, "we only quarrel."

"You mean to leave me and go *there?*"

"Angus is dying. The doctor says he's not likely to live through the night, or be conscious again. Elizabeth sent word, asking me to come."

"Oh, yes, Elizabeth! Elizabeth and Ranald. Fitz and the Maitlands. Anybody, anything but me. What am *I* supposed to do? Just stay sweet and quiet, putting up with this misery you've caused? The way I'm feeling now is your fault, Thorne Maxwell. You *won't* ignore me."

"Goddamn it, I couldn't if I meant to!"

"You've spent every minute since we came back here with Ranald."

"I saw him at the office this afternoon, maybe for a half hour."

"Oh, everything was fine as long as you could get in my pants whenever you wanted to! Now that I'm sick with this damned pregnancy, worn out from the trip up here—a trip there was no need to make—you can't stand the sight of me, can't give up anything to just stay here and try to make things a little easier for me."

"Cherish, it's past ten o'clock. You need to try to sleep. If there's anything I can do, something I can bring you or—"

"You always have to be told! Can't be bothered with thinking up any little thing yourself."

"I can send for Doctor Daniels."

"I don't *want* him. Doesn't it ever occur to you that I might just want you? need you? need some reassurance when I'm so sick and afraid? . . . Send for Dahlia."

"But you told her she could have some time off. I don't know where she is."

"Couldn't you have her found? Can't you take care of anything?"

As he reached the door, she wailed, "Oh, Thorne, don't go! I'm sorry, darling . . ." Then, as he closed the door quietly, "You'll be sorry for walking out on me. I swear I'll never let you forget it!"

Thorne did not want to go to the Maxwell house. He had thought he would never enter it again, but Ranald had told him that Elizabeth, exhausted from the week's long vigil at Angus's bedside, had cried when she knew Thorne was in town, asking that he come and wait with them if he could. Elizabeth greeted him as warmly as was possible for her. She seemed exhausted but also seemed to have strengthened herself during Angus's illness. To Thorne's dismay, she insisted that he go in and see Angus. Ranald, who had been staying at the house for the past several nights, had assured Thorne that he need not see his father. Elizabeth was surprisingly adamant.

"Thorne, go into his room for a few minutes, please. You must. He hasn't been really awake since yesterday. The doctor thinks he won't be again."

"Then why," he began and drew a deep breath, turning toward the hall, more than a little angry with her.

Following him, she put a tentative hand on his arm. "Thank you. I—I think I understand how you feel, but please . . ."

Thorne's question came unbidden. "Has he ever said—Did he want me to . . ."

She dropped her eyes, not answering, and that was answer enough. Thorne walked to the closed door, her hand still on his arm.

Elizabeth said, "Ranald didn't know I was going

to ask you to do this. Don't be angry with him. Thorne, please try to understand, a little, if you can. Angus has not had a happy life."

He had nothing to reply and was even a little relieved when the nurse opened the door in front of him.

Thorne did not go too near the bed, but still he was shocked by the changes in Angus. The man was no more than wrinkled skin covering sharp bones. His face was a study in plains and hollows, with fever color in the cheeks. His hair, what there was of it, was iron gray and lifeless. His harsh, uneven breathing seemed to fill the quiet room. Thorne shivered and turned to the window. This could scarcely be the man who had gone and on so relentlessly that last night down in the study. I can stay a few minutes, he told himself firmly, to satisfy Elizabeth.

Spring stars and a sliver of moon shone faintly in the smoky sky. Thorne thought no thoughts in particular; he felt no passionate feelings. He simply stood there, for longer than he realized, listening to the breathing and the silences. His stillness was interrupted by a change in the breathing, then a harsh cough. He turned to find Angus's eyes open; they were hollow and unfocused.

"Who's there?" The voice was faint, wheezing, without timbre.

"It's Thorne," he said in a voice almost as faint.

He took a step toward the bed. Angus sighed and let his eyes close. Thorne stood utterly still for long moments. As he was about to move, to leave the room, the eyes opened again and seemed to be looking at him.

"I've had dreams lately, about Annie," Angus mused. Then he said icily, "What are you doing back here now, after all this time? You've come for the reading of the will, I suppose."

"No," Thorne said. This was, after all, still Angus, with the same implacability in the depths of pain in the hazel eyes. I won't fight with him anymore, Thorne thought. It wouldn't change anything, wouldn't matter. Maybe it never did, really. Now, he's surely dying.

Angus lifted his incredibly thin hand from the covers. It was a small gesture that required a great deal of his strength, but contained a hint of the accustomed peremptoriness in it. "Sit down," he ordered.

Thorne drew a chair a little nearer, but did not want to sit.

He said compulsively, "You shouldn't talk. It will tire you. Is there something I can get you?"

Angus's weak voice sounded irritated. "Sit down," he gasped impatiently. "How many times have I asked you to do that? How many times have I asked for just that simple courtesy?"

Feeling chilled and miserable, Thorne went to the chair, but Angus's eyes were already closing, and after some moments his breathing took on the slower rhythm of coma. The nurse returned and Thorne left the room, shaken and confused by feelings he refused to try to analyze.

The doctor looked in soon after that, on his way home from another night call. When the doctor left, Elizabeth reluctantly agreed to lie down for a while. Angus had needed nurses for weeks, but that had not made it possible for Elizabeth to rest. Thorne and Ranald, waiting in the small upstairs sitting room, talked quietly, sporadically. Some of Thorne's tensions began to ease a little. He never would have guessed that this house, even with Angus limited to one room, could seem like a haven. But it was so quiet here now, and so good to be with Ranald; he wanted to forget about Fitz's house less than a mile away.

"It's not the time to talk about it," Ranald said a little guiltily, "but Peter Maitland really does want to sell most of the company interests here, move everything to the West. We're starting to have a lot of union trouble and there are some other things . . ."

"What about Philip Maitland?"

"He doesn't want to leave. He'll help with the reorganization and handle what interests there are here. His son's not interested at all. He's living in London now."

"And Peter has only daughters," Thorne said, meaning nothing in particular.

"They'd have begun a reorganization several years ago," Ranald said, "but Angus was so opposed to it. He's been—kind of incredible—frightening—staying in the office right up till he had the first bad hemorrhage in the middle of February. The doctor told Elizabeth that Angus has known this was coming since the fall we were in Europe."

"Yes," Thorne said, "I've thought he must have known for a while."

Ranald poured coffee. "He seemed—pleased to hear you and Cherish were going to be married."

"He intended it to happen. Always planning, Angus was."

"You have every reason to be bitter. I don't mean about the marriage—I hope you and Cherish are happy. I just meant—well, the way things were when you were here last, and now . . ."

"Hell, Ran, I'm not bitter," he said derisively. "Why would I be? I'm a Maxwell. You must know what a goddamned honor that is. Do you know what he said to me, just before?"

"You mean he was conscious tonight?"

"He reminded me how many times in my life he'd asked me to sit down."

"Is that all he said?"

"He said he'd been dreaming of my mother lately; or maybe he meant someone else called Annie."

"I'm sorry," Ranald said after a moment of silence.

"I shouldn't have gone in there, probably shouldn't have come here at all. Well, I am here, so tell me a lot of things about what's been happening. It's been a long time."

Ranald wished there was more he could do than talk for a time about the company's activities and the social life of a few people Thorne had known.

Finally, he said, "Fitz has talked a lot since he's been back about the way you've been running Intermountain."

Thorne said wearily, "He ran off the manager Peter sent out to us. I haven't done anything that Fitz hasn't been in on, from start to finish."

"You sound grim."

"If I can't get out of the damned office and back in the field within three months, I'm quitting."

"That bad?"

"Worse."

"Will Cherish mind? I mean, if you have to be away a lot?"

"I don't know," Thorne said curtly, his tone indicating clearly to Ranald that that should be a closed subject.

After a long, though not uncomfortable silence, Ranald said, "I guess I haven't mentioned that I saw Meg and Gordon a month or so ago. I had to spend almost a week in Boston."

Thorne said levelly, "Hasn't Gordon finished school yet?"

"He graduated last spring, but he had a really fine job offer from a firm in Boston and he's working for them for a year or two, getting some experience. He says he may stay on another year, but that they'll probably go back to the valley then. Maybe you didn't know, Mr. Gaynor died more than a year ago?"

"I didn't know."

"Mama didn't write you?"

"I'm afraid she's given up writing me, except at Christmas time. I mean to answer letters, but somehow it just doesn't happen."

"Yes, I've noticed that. Well, Mr. Gaynor left them a little money, I guess, and the house and property in Quintana. Angus turned that over to him when the state took on the school."

"If Gordon already has a job with a good firm in Boston, why would he go back to Quintana?"

"He told me he's found he's not really cut out for living in the mainstream, that a place like the San Luis is where he really belongs, working for 'the people'. I think he's doing it because he thinks it's what Meg wants. It seems as if he'd do just about anything to please her."

"And is she very hard to please?"

"No, I don't think so. I just meant that he's really crazy about her. Really, I don't know if going back home is as important to her as he thinks. She's changed."

"How?"

"Oh, I don't know—maybe she hasn't, much. Growing up and marrying, things like that, change everyone a little I guess. She's just—quieter, more—adult, just hoping for a good life, maybe, with *where* she lives it not so important anymore. What she seems to hope for most now is babies. She mentioned more than once wanting a big family. I told her not to hope for one as big as ours. I don't see how people could afford that many kids these days."

"Gordon will be rich. Lawyers seem to have a way of coming to that, eventually."

"In Quintana?" Ranald asked, smiling dubiously. Then he said earnestly, "Listen, there's something I've been wanting to tell you . . . about this girl I've met."

Ranald talked for some time about his girl Amy, and Thorne relaxed, smiling, grateful for this secret and the memory of so many others Ranald had shared with him.

When there seemed nothing more he could say, Ranald fell silent, also smiling, toying with his empty coffee cup. Then he said exuberantly, "So we've agreed to take our time—quite a lot of time—to make as sure as we can that we know what we're doing. The truth is, though, I'm already sure."

"I sort of thought that," Thorne said dryly.

"Are you going to Chicago to see those people about the Central Western sale?"

"It looks as if I may have to. Fitz's back is giving him hell."

"Go and meet Amy if you do. I guess I may have mentioned you to her once or twice. She'll be glad to see you. Now that you're married, I won't have to worry that you'll be interested."

Tension had come back into Thorne's face, but he said, trying for lightness, "On the other hand, maybe you ought to keep worrying."

They both stood up hastily as the nurse appeared in the doorway. "There's no change," she answered their looks quickly. "I just thought I'd get a cup of coffee."

"This pot's empty," said Ranald, picking it up. "There'll be more in the kitchen. I'll get it."

The nurse went into the bathroom; and Thorne, left alone, sat down, then lay back in a deep chair. Everything was strictly relative, he thought wearily. Here, in this house that death would share soon, he felt more at ease than in the house where his wife was. Death, perhaps, made more sense than life. He had, in almost full consciousness and knowledge, married someone who meant to try to make his life more miserable, even more confused than Angus had. The marriage had to be, though perhaps he had already repudiated his intentions to try to make it a good marriage. Clearly, he and Cherish felt completely different things made for a good marriage. She wanted possession, and no one would ever have that—not with him. Surely, it was fortunate that love, or purported love had played no part in their relationship.

He thought again of his last miserable night in this house. In a way, he had managed to blame Angus, a little, even for Meg's marriage to Gordon. Thorne would never have gone away from her if it hadn't been for Angus. He had blamed Angus, or Meg, or someone, for so many things. There was no point in that, no sense. He was an adult now, and must take on full responsibility for and control of his life. No matter what might have been, his marriage was now a part of his life and would have to be dealt with. He could take the blame—or credit, if ever there should be any. If only he might do justice to the child . . . Please God, he'd never badger it about sitting down or not when he was on his deathbed.

The nurse had her coffee and returned to Angus's room, allowing Ranald to join Thorne again.

After a silence in the sitting room, Ranald said slowly, "I suppose you don't want to talk about it, but I think he does—did—care about you, in his own peculiar way."

"Well, I can agree with you that if that's true, it certainly *was* peculiar."

"Do you remember that he often talked about his father? about how right the earl had been to send him here—things like that? I've come to think he was saying the opposite of what he really felt about it, trying to say the things he thought he ought to feel. I think he was awfully hurt, as a boy, by being sent away like that, to strangers and a strange country. He spent the rest of his life trying to convince himself of what a wise thing it had been."

Thorne said dully, "He seemed to be behaving as much like the old earl as he possibly could. That's a kind of strange reaction—isn't it?—if he felt the way you've said."

Ranald shook his head. "I don't think so. We get—fixed into patterns. Most of the time, I guess we don't even know it's happened. They say people who've been beaten and mistreated badly as kids often grow up to do the same things to their children, or worse. A lot of children of drunkards become drunkards."

"And some others wouldn't touch liquor if there was nothing else to drink in the world," Thorne said, feeling inexplicably defensive.

After another period of silence, Ranald said, "I want to get back to the hacienda for a visit some time this summer. It's been a long time—for me. Will you be going?"

"I doubt that I can."

"You've said you're going to work on the new road to San Miguel. You'll have to go right through the valley every time you go back and forth to Denver."

"I'm not likely to have any time off for a while, not for anything."

Eventually, both of them fell into fitful dozes. Just after five, the nurse summoned them, woke Elizabeth. With the last of his strength, Angus still struggled—this time for breath. He died just before six.

IX

The maid called Beatrice, who had, along with a cook, been hired for their stay in Pittsburgh, hurried from the kitchen with a small tray as Thorne was hanging up his coat. She was a thin, vacuous-seeming young girl, who now looked harried, or frightened almost to tears.

"Oh, sir! I'm glad you've come back. It's been a bad night here."

"What's happened?"

"Mr. Fitzroy had the terrible pain in his back, didn't sleep all night. Jerry had me up, fixin' hot bottles an' the like, from midnight on. He went for the doctor at seven, but had to find another one because Dr. Daniels was out somewhere else. So the doctor came, for both of them. Mr. Fitzroy's asleep now, but—"

"Are you saying Jerry had to have a doctor too?"

"Oh, no, sir! Jerry didn't need a doctor." She paused before saying portentously, "It's Mrs. Maxwell needed the doctor."

"What's wrong?"

Beatrice shook her head sadly, clicking a sympathetic tongue. "She seems a little better now, but . . . . I was takin' 'er this tea."

Thorne took the tray quickly and turned toward the stairs.

Beatrice said hastily, "Beg pardon, sir, but isn't Mr. Teddy to go back to school today? Cook's givin' him breakfast in the kitchen now, but . . ."

"Where's Jerry now?"

"Asleep, sir."

"Wake him up then, please. He'll have to take Ted to his train."

"Is it a late train, sir?"

"I think it's before eleven," he said impatiently, moving away from her.

"Well, sir, the truth is, I don't know if I can have his things packed by then."

"You might have done that yesterday, or most of it."

"Well, yes, sir, but nobody really told me to, an' there's been a lot else . . ."

Thorne felt the intensity of the scowl on his face and tried to be reasonable.

"All right, Beatrice, let Jerry sleep for now. I'll be down again as soon as I can."

"Shall I pack the things?"

"Get started on them, please, as soon as you can."

"Will you be wantin' breakfast soon, sir?"

"No," he said from halfway up the stairs.

She still had something to say, and from the fleeting words he caught, he wondered, just then, how they had heard about Angus already. Beatrice was saying things like, "—sorry . . . sad . . . loss . . ."

Cherish looked very small and still in the big bed. The light in the room was dim, but Thorne could see she was very pale and drawn. He stood quietly, just inside the door. Her eyes were closed. He moved finally, almost without a sound, to put the tea tray down on the bureau.

She started slightly. "Thorne?" Her eyes opened.

"I'm sorry if I woke you. Beatrice was bringing you some tea. How are you?"

"How would I be?" she wailed. "What do you think?" She began to cry.

"She said you've seen the doctor. What—"

"It's your fault!"

"Cherish, let's not start all over again. Angus died a couple of hours ago. There are things I'm expected to do. Beatrice said Fitz was up all night with the pain in his back. Nobody's done anything about Ted's getting back to school. I—"

"She didn't tell you? You would have to be told, of course."

"Told what?" Suddenly, he felt sick. Automatically, he moved a little nearer to the bed which shook with her sobs.

"I miscarried, of course," she spat, "while you went off with your precious Ranald and Elizabeth."

After a stunned moment, Thorne dropped to his knees beside the bed, reaching for her hand, burying his face against a pillow.

Cherish snatched her hand out of his reach. "You knew I'd been feeling bad. I begged you not to leave me!"

"Was—was the doctor here then?" his voice was muffled and broken.

"Nobody was here, at the time, except for that half-witted girl going in and out. The doctor came after it was over."

"Ah God, I'm so sorry. Why didn't she or Jerry send for me?"

"I said they were *not* to send for you. I didn't suppose you'd want to be bothered."

He lifted his face and she saw that his dark eyes were unusually bright with the sparkle of unshed tears. She let him take her hand.

"Please try not to cry. It can't be good for you. I'm so sorry—" he said.

"Why?" The sharp word cut through her sobs. "You're sorry there won't be a baby, but not about me. Isn't that it? Or—no! you're sorry the marriage happened. It wasn't necessary after all."

"Please don't cry like that. You'll only make yourself feel worse. Didn't the doctor leave medicine or anything?"

"No. He's a man, after all. He just has the attitude that these kinds of things *will* happen to women and he thinks nothing in particular ought to be done to help me. He was some stranger, not Dr. Daniels."

"I'll send for Dr. Daniels."

"No!" she said sharply. "I—I can't stand to have someone else examining me and—doing those things. It's all over now. Dr. Daniels probably wouldn't do any good for me either, though I still have so much pain."

"Beatrice was bringing the tea," he said, standing up. "Did you send for it? Maybe it will—"

"Oh, for God's sake, I don't want tea! Just leave me alone if you can't do anything."

"If there's something I *can* do, I wish you'd tell me."

She mopped at her face with a small, sodden handkerchief. He brought her a large, clean one of his own.

"Fitz must have something for pain downstairs, and to help him sleep," Cherish said.

"I'll see what there is."

She lay very still while he was gone, holding the handkerchief against her cheek. Sobs still caught at her breath as she pictured his real sorrow, the abject misery she had glimpsed in his face. Maybe he would begin to love *her* now.

When she had taken the medicine, he sat down beside the bed.

She asked weakly, "When will Dahlia be here?"

After a moment's hesitation, he said apologetically, "Cherish, I didn't realize it was going to be—this bad. I don't know how to reach her, and I didn't—"

"You didn't send for her? Oh, I need her. I tell you, I want her here!"

"I'm sorry. Tell me how I can get word to her."

"How would I know, Thorne? Do I have to manage things, no matter what I'm going through? If you send a telegram to Fern Hill, somebody will know where she is. She could already be on her way if you'd done that last night when I asked you."

He stood up and she said quickly, "No, wait till I'm asleep. I can't bear to be all alone again right now."

She offered him her hand, so small and cold. He held it between both of his, very gently.

"There was a lot of blood," she said. "I'm still bleeding a lot. The doctor did say it would take me a long time to get my strength back."

"Did he say—was there a reason?"

"Of course there were reasons," she said wearily, "—the trip here from Fern Hill, when I was already feeling bad; maybe all that lovemaking at a critical time."

He said nothing, looking away from her, but she watched his profile carefully.

After a time, she said, her eyes closed. "So Angus is dead."

"Yes."

"What time did it happen?"

"A little before six."

She sobbed convulsively. "That was just about the time I was losing—his grandson."

His hands tightened on hers and seemed not quite steady. But, she thought, it was the mention of the baby that woke the emotion in him, not concern for her suffering and possible sorrow. She felt so very tired, and almost defeated.

With her compulsion for keeping silences away, she said faintly, "Did you manage to talk to Angus?"

"I didn't go there expecting, or wanting to talk to him."

"What about the will?"

"I don't know."

"Yesterday, I heard you say something to Fitz about going to Chicago . . . ."

"I won't go now."

"Why not?" she said scathingly. "The company *needs* you."

"I want to stay here now—with you."

She made a derisive, incredulous sound and drew her hand away from him.

"It will be canceled—won't it?—the business thing in Chicago . . . because Angus just died?"

"I suppose it may be."

"And that's why you've so graciously decided to give up going."

"Please try to rest."

"I hope I can sleep," she said truculently. "It's about the only comfort I'm ever likely to get."

After a few moments, she began to doze. When he was about to get up and look to things downstairs, she started a little and murmured, "I want Dahlia."

"I'm going to send for her," he said softly.

She fell into deeper sleep then, and he finally stood up wearily. She was beautiful: so young, sweet, vulnerable-looking—asleep.

All through the months of good weather, Thorne supervised work on the San Miguel line. It ran northwest out of Santa Fe, into the mountains of southwestern Colorado, which many people had called inaccessible. Cherish went with him, more or less. She refused to stay at Fitz's house in Denver, or at a hotel suite Thorne offered to get for her. She also scorned the private car he offered, where she might have been comfortable, because she said she would not be kept on a siding of some railroad camp like one of Fitz's whores. She and Dahlia stayed in the small hotels of raw little towns, and Thorne, without enthusiasm, came to her when he could.

Conditions on this job were as bad as they had ever been anywhere, and worse than most places. Crews were working from both ends of the line, using all the hours of daylight six days a week and sometimes on Sunday, trying to get all the road open so that other crews could begin struggling to keep it open to traffic through the winter. By ten o'clock on a Saturday night in late September, Thorne was so tired he felt incapable of walking from the work train to the hotel two blocks away. His eyes could hardly focus and his mind was as blurred and dull as the mountain sky was clear and bright. They were having almost constant trouble with rock slides in a part of the river canyon, and yesterday the first snow had fallen in the very high country around San Miguel.

"Mr. Thorne?" Dahlia's gentle voice came to him hazily. She had been waiting for him in the lobby. "Miss Cherish is not feeling good," she said, a little apologetically. "She was asleep the last time I looked in. Yesterday, before this place filled up for the weekend, I asked them to save another room for you. I hope that's all right. It's number five, right at the top of the stairs."

Thorne swayed a little with relief, fervently hoping Cherish would not wake and think he might be in town. Through most of the summer, he had slept in a bunk in one of the crew cars. If he used an office car, Fitz and the others in Denver felt he should do office work, but he could never keep up with all the papers they insisted he see. He felt as if he had not been physically alone for years. This place was noisy with Saturday night. The bar and dining room would be open for a long time, and the walls were thin, but he was to have a room to himself. He could lock the door to number five, forget everything.

"Some telegrams came here for you. I put them and your mail on the dresser up there," Dahlia was going on. "You're hungry, I bet."

"No," he said, grinning foolishly with the temptation to kiss her and the speculation about how she might react. "I just want to sleep—after I've had a bath."

"There's water waiting for you," she said. "You had supper?"

"I—don't seem to remember. No, I guess I didn't, but—"

"You go on and take your bath," she said with concern. "I'll bring something up there for you to eat. It's just that you're too tired to want to go in the dining room. You mustn't stop eating."

Freshly bathed and dressed in clean clothes, he was almost asleep on the bed when Dahlia knocked, but the food smelled good and he was glad she had brought it.

Setting the dishes on a rickety little table, Dahlia asked, "You found the telegrams and all?"

"Yes," he said, "Thank you."

"It snowed up there in those high mountains, didn't it?"

"About four inches. We're going to have to be done with this within a month, whether we're finished or not."

"Miss Cherish'll be right glad to know we'll be going back to Denver."

Thorne frowned, but asked dutifully, "You said she's not feeling well. Do you know what's wrong? Sit down, Dahlia, if you like."

He was sitting on the side of the bed, so she took the room's single, straight chair, looking at him earnestly.

"Nothing to be too worried about," she said, wishing someone could take pleasure in the news. "You've got a baby about three months on the way is all."

Thorne looked desolate. He said, staring at his fork, "Cherish hadn't mentioned . . ."

"Well, sir, you see she wasn't right happy about it. She tried for a while to believe it wasn't so. Now there's the morning sickness that bothers her both day and night. A lot of women feel that way—scared and sick—thinking a baby's not worth it. She'll get over it, I think, when we're settled somewhere. Maybe the best thing will be when you can be with her a little more."

He glanced around uneasily, and to Dahlia it seemed as if he expected the walls to be closing in. He said slowly, "When we were in Pittsburgh last spring, Dahlia, and I had to ask you to come back before the vacation time Cherish promised you was up . . . she was sick then . . . ."

"Yes?" she prompted gently. "I remember. It was her monthly time. She's always had a bad time with that, cramps and such. Sometimes having a baby is good for girls like that, makes their monthlies easier."

Thorne had begun automatically to eat again. He said carefully, "I was away the night when she was sickest. When I came back to the house, a doctor had been there and Cherish . . ."

Dahlia's eyes were sad. "That little girl Beatrice, hired for a maid, mentioned some of her nonsense, something about Miss Cherish having a miscarriage. That's what you're asking me about?"

He nodded.

"Well, it wasn't that," she said quietly, "just a specially bad time for her that month. She told you she was pregnant, didn't she, honey, before you got married?"

"Yes," he said, not looking at her.

Dahlia shook her head, sighing. "I thought it must be something like that," she said sorrowfully. "I remembered, after she began telling me about the wedding plans, that she had asked me all kinds of questions about that New Year's party. She went to bed nearly as soon as it struck midnight, because she didn't care for some of the people Mr. Fitz had there, but I'd stayed up, helping out with things. When she heard him tease you the next day because you said you'd had too much to drink and didn't remember how you got to bed, she . . ." the words trailed away as she looked at him compassionately.

"What did you tell her?"

"Why, that you went up to your room after a while. After you'd been gone a little while, I asked Jerry to go up and see if you were all right. He found you asleep. Helped you get some of your clothes off and under the covers."

Silence fell in the room. Music, a shout of laughter from below were suddenly loud. Thorne had stopped eating and was staring down at the dusty, faded rug. He was not surprised. In fact, he had first begun to suspect there was no baby on the very day Cherish told him of the miscarriage. Or had he known before then? The fact that he had not avoided the marriage, and that he had gone on with it when there was no longer the concrete need, was less Cherish's fault than his own. He had been so busy, though, that there had seemed no time for the battle he knew must come at the end. And now there was the fact of a real child, again complicating matters.

Dahlia refilled his cup from the coffee pot, went to

the washstand for a water glass and filled that for herself.

"I can see you're worn out," she said solicitously. "You need sleep in the worst way, but maybe we'd better talk, for just a few minutes. I didn't know—or anyhow didn't understand the whole of this until now. I should have talked to you months ago, Mr. Thorne, back in March when Miss Cherish first mentioned a wedding. I thought about it—a lot. One minute I'd think, Dahlia, it's none of your business, then the next, I'd be thinking, Well, but yes it is, too. I just didn't know what to do.

"Mr. Thorne, I was a slave in Jamaica, on a sugar-cane plantation. I worked in the house, looking after the children there, from the time I was a little tiny girl. My mama did the same kind of work before me. I even got some schooling with those little English children. The man I started living with, when we weren't much more than babies, worked in the house too. We had two little children, and both of them died of sicknesses before they were a year old. Then my man—his name was Tom—was caught in a lynching, for something he never had any part in. I couldn't stay there after that. I ran away and hid on a ship that was bound for Boston. Old Fitz was on that ship, had some kind of interest in it. When they found me, he kept them from—doing anything, and offered me work at Fern Hill. He'd just finished buying it not a month before that, and marrying Miss Amanda Jane.

"I'm telling you this because maybe it'll let you understand some of what Miss Cherish means to me—and Mr. Teddy too.

"Their mama was a kind of a strange woman. She didn't ever care about spending any time with her children, except to tell them about how grand things used to be. When I went there, Miss Cherish was six years old and Mr. Teddy wasn't even on his way yet."

Dahlia paused. Thorne was lighting a cigarette.

He sipped the coffee, rubbed absently at his tired eyes. She was a little relieved by the movements. That trapped staring at the floor had wrung her heart. This was a good boy. Cherish was the wrongest person in the world for him. Maybe there wasn't a soul that the poor baby could be good for.

She went on with determined gentleness. "I love Miss Cherish. The Lord knows she's got faults—weaknesses—and I know them. There's not any of us but what has our shortcomings, but she . . . Miss Cherish—well, she lies. Sometimes, it's hard for even me to tell what's the truth and what's made up with her. I honestly believe *she* doesn't always know the difference. It comes, I think—some of it anyhow—from the way her mama was, always living in the past when the South was in its glory and everything a lot better than it ever really could have been. It must have seemed to Miss Cherish, before she was old enough to know she was thinking about it, that the life she was living couldn't come up to that one in the stories, so she started—well, changing things, trying to make them . . .

"Somehow, too, she's come to think she knows all about men and marriage. Her mama was sick a long time before she died, and Miss Cherish used to sit with her in her room for hours. I suppose some of the ideas must have come from her, but I don't know about the rest. I do know, though, that what Mr. Fitz and Miss Amanda Jane had wasn't any kind of fit example for a good marriage, and it's all the children ever saw, close up.

"Miss Cherish loves you, Mr. Thorne. It's the truth," she said firmly, meeting his incredulous, satirical look. "It's her kind of truth and she means it.

"She first told me about it back in Pittsburgh, that fall when you two boys had just come back from Europe. She's scared to death to let you know it, and I don't know that she'll ever be able to show it in any way you can see. I know she's made your life a misery. I've thought and thought and I just don't know that there's anything to be done that could make things better—easier.

"Mr. Ted and Miss Cherish both have been spoiled rotten by the kind of life they've had, and at the same time, hurt in their minds, you know, looking at so many things—well, crooked, you might say. I don't ask you to understand because I can't hardly do that myself and I've mostly raised her, but I hope you can kind of see how it is. Maybe you can see your way clear to a little more patience and to not being so hurt yourself by the kind of life she's giving you. She makes people—harden toward her, does all the wrong things. Until just lately, there used to be times when she knew she was doing it herself and she would try to change. I'm hoping the baby will help her to be different. That *can* happen, you know." The words were a plea. Her eyes had filled with tears. "I'd give anything to see Miss Cherish find some happiness, some peace."

Thorne's face had grown hard.

Dahlia said gently, "I believe I've come to know some things about you, too. I always have been one for watching people. I believe you've had a lot of hurts yourself and you're not in any shape to put up with her—serious problems—all the time."

"I don't know how I could possibly try to—help her," he said tonelessly.

"You don't love her, do you, honey?"

"I—no. I can't."

"She wants you to," Dahlia nodded sadly. "But I know it's best for you that you don't. If you mean to try to help, let her have some of the material things she wants when you can. She's talked to me about a house of her own she'd like to have, ever since Mr. Maxwell's will was read. But the main thing is, Mr. Thorne, please don't ever leave her completely.

I don't know what might happen to her if that were ever to be. I think she feels love for me, maybe some for Ted, but you're the only person I've ever heard her say she loves. She knows she tricked you into marrying, and she's scared to death, every minute, of losing you."

"It's not her fault—the marriage," he said compulsively. "I knew, somehow, that things weren't . . . I should have—well, looked into things more. Maybe I really am a fool, looking for something . . ."

"No sir, you're not any fool," she said stoutly. "You're a good man and you've got a tender heart, though you try not to have. And you're all too ready to take on responsibilities that by rights belong to other people. I've seen you just be quiet and let Miss Cherish blame you for any- and everything. And I see how Mr. Fitz and those others are always at you to do what you don't want to do. You don't want to let your own self know what a fine man you are."

"Dahlia," he began, heat rising from his face.

"All right, now I'll hush about it," she said, with a fond smile. "We may live in the same house for years to come—I hope so because, everything else aside, I like you. You're a good man to work for—but I wanted to say, just once, what I honestly think of you . . . . You're both so young, you and her, and I'd give anything to see life easier, happier for both of you. Anyway I can help, I will, and if there's anything you think I'm doing wrong, you tell me."

She began putting his dishes on the tray. "You don't want the pie?"

"No, but—thank you."

Her eyes sparkled with tears again. "Three months ago, I'd have said the marriage wouldn't go on this much longer. I know that, for you, knowing now that there's going to be a baby can't be a pleasant thing, but try to be a little glad. You need some gladness, and it could just make a big difference. Here, let me turn that bed down right for you. You want to be called any special time in the morning?"

"God, no. I want to sleep from now until the work train is ready to leave tomorrow night."

"And you ought to," she said with concern. "If you don't see to taking a little care of yourself, you'll be sick for sure. They put too much on you, Fitz and the others, and you just keep trying to do it all."

Thorne slept almost as soon as he was stretched on the bed, but there was, as so often happened, a twisted, frightening dream. This one was of Cherish and himself and he woke gasping and sweating. The noise from downstairs was still going on.

Lying awake, Thorne wondered dismally why he could not keep the control of his personal life from slipping through his hands again and again. He had meant to separate from Cherish one day, when he could get to it, but now there would be a real child to consider. He just went on getting into bad situations, letting himself be pushed or dragged . . . well, there was no one else to blame for any of this. He was managing the work for Intermountain—just barely—and he liked most of what he was doing now. He thought, since it now seemed necessary, that he could reconcile himself, to a degree, to the marriage with Cherish. She irritated, angered, exasperated him, but he could go on being himself now. She had ceased to frighten him. There was no need for fear—not anymore. In the very beginning, he had been a little vulnerable because he had, against all odds, hoped, wished, for something from her. But that passed very quickly and the fear was only a residual thing. There was no longer any way she could touch him below the surface of his being. Only now, again, there was a child to consider.

"Ah, God," he breathed bleakly. He had very nearly believed that he had wanted the first fictitious baby, could make a decent life for it, and for himself as a father. Was it true, as he had suspected so often, that Cherish was a little insane? Was it something that could be passed on? Had it come to her from her mother, as Dahlia had seemed to intimate? Would the child—? But, whatever the child was, he was as responsible for its being as Cherish was. He could not abandon it. Still, he felt certain now, after six months of marriage, that Cherish would never let him play a father's part without incessant fighting. He wasn't at all sure of being able to go on with that, particularly if it seemed detrimental to the child . . . or was he just trying to find excuses for his potential failures before the fact?

Cherish *loved* him? That brought a small, bitter smile. There were some who had tried to imply Angus might have loved him too. . . . Still, Cherish deserved consideration from him—pity? How long could any relationship survive on pity from one side and—what she gave from the other? God, things were such a shambles! But why did he keep expecting things to come out neatly? They never had, not for years and years. There didn't have to be a relationship for him to build her the house she wanted in Denver. With him, she cried and nagged to go to live permanently at Fern Hill, knowing he would not do that. If only she would agree to their living apart, as her mother and Fitz had. But she could have a house in Denver. There was income enough now. He had been left more than half of Angus's holdings, the rest divided between Elizabeth and Ranald. He could see that everything Cherish could possibly want was incorporated into a house. Though he knew that when he was through, she would discover she had wanted something else instead. He could try a little more in other ways, too, for the baby's sake, while praying there would be no more.

Unbidden, Meg's face swam on his closed eyelids. He clenched his teeth, willing the past to leave him in peace. After a little, he slept again, drugged with exhaustion.

He was wakened again almost immediately. Cherish was there, a lighted lamp on the table. She was dropping a robe on the chair, lying naked beside him, stroking, pressing against him with her particular kind of hunger.

"No," he murmured, trying desperately to hold onto sleep. "Leave me alone. The door's locked."

"Silly," she crooned. "There are always two keys. I made Dahlia get me the extra one when she said she was going to get this room for you. You can't lock me out."

He tried to struggle free of her, but she clung, heavily, softly. His traitorous body had begun to respond to her even before he was actually conscious she was in the room.

"So tired," he pleaded thickly.

"You're going to forget that in a minute," she purred in that fearsome, gloating voice he dreaded.

Even as his body tried doggedly to give her what she would certainly later try to turn against him, he thought bleakly that there must be some decent-sounding thing to call this besides "making love." That was certainly not what this was between them, this cruel, bitter, mechanistic thing, purely of the flesh, which perhaps she didn't really want any more than he did. Even with girls like those on River Street, there had been a fleeting tenderness, a sense of sharing pleasure, and knowing that both parties would emerge with their self-respect intact and would not be set on destroying the self-identity of anyone.

Cherish lost no time tonight. Almost before the mechanical accomplishment of her orgasm was over, she said menacingly, "Dahlia told you."

Thorne moved away from her, his breath almost a sob. "She said you weren't feeling well."

"I'm a little better now. I woke up and supposed

I'd be expected to do my wifely duty. Oh, Thorne, don't smoke in here! I swear I'll throw up."

He let the tobacco pouch fall back on the table. His watch, lying there beside it, showed three forty-five. There were no more sounds from downstairs. He lay back, apart from her, all but praying for silence.

"So you know I'm pregnant again?"

"Yes."

"And you're thrilled," she said sarcastically.

"No, I'm sorry."

"Well, at least that's something we have in common." She began to cry. "There aren't words to tell you how much I hate you for this! I told you, after the miscarriage, it wouldn't be safe for me to get pregnant again for a long time, but you're so selfish! Never a thought for anything or anybody—"

"Cherish, I know there was no miscarriage. Let's not talk about it again."

She gasped. "That bitch! That nigger Dahlia has been—"

"Dahlia didn't tell me anything. I've thought for a long time it wasn't true. You don't have to dream up lies like that. Reality's bad enough. Please let me sleep now."

"You nasty, hateful thing! I knew this separate room was a mistake. If you think you're just going to ignore me, once you've had—"

"Go away, can't you! Leave me alone."

"Oh, yes, you'd like that! You'd like to forget I'm alive if you could. You think you can just excuse yourself completely by thinking I trapped you."

He sighed, sat up. "I'm not thinking anything." He reached automatically for cigarette materials. Why couldn't he just keep silent, respond to nothing she said?

"That's it!" she shrieked. "Smoke your stinking cigarette. Enjoy all your dirty little pleasures. Maybe you'll get some warped enjoyment out of seeing me vomit. I suppose it does something for your manliness to see such evidence that I'm pregnant with—"

"It must be doing something for the whole goddamned hotel," he said fiercely. "Can't you talk to me without screaming?"

She was choking with sobs. "And I suppose," she gasped a little less loudly, "you want to know why I wasn't a virgin when we married, since you know I wasn't pregnant."

"I had assumed," he said coldly, cruelly, "it was because I came to your room that time I was drunk, as you said I did, and—"

"I despise you!" she shrieked, realizing she had fallen into a trap set by herself, wild with anger.

"Go away."

She was still, staring malevolently at the back of his head. "It was in England," she said mockingly, "one of the schoolmasters—a *real* man, who knew how to make me feel—"

"Cherish," he cut in icily, "I don't care!"

"Oh, you bastard! You dirty sonofabitch! You're so cold and hard and selfish, and you don't care about *anything!* Sometimes I think you're not even human. *Nothing* can touch you . . . What are you doing?"

"You can see I'm getting dressed," he said levelly. "The work train's on the siding. I'll be there, trying to sleep, till it's time to go back up."

"And how long am I expected to stay in this hole without you?"

"You don't have to stay anywhere. Leave when you like. You do know how to make a draft on the Denver bank, don't you?"

"I won't let you walk out like this! I'll follow you—"

"You ought to get dressed first."

She was so furious that her tears stopped. She screamed something wordless as he closed the door.

He was almost convinced she would follow him and for a long time lay in dread in his work-train bunk, while a few members of the crew snored around him, sleeping off their Saturday nights.

How could Dahlia possibly imagine Cherish *loved* him? Cherish was sick—mad. Still, she was his wife. It always came back to that certainty . . . in England . . . a schoolmaster . . . maybe there were others, maybe this child she carried . . .? Or maybe the schoolmaster was a lie like the first baby. "The biggest mistake of my life," Angus had said, referring to his marriage with Annie MacWinter. *Was* he going to be like Angus? God, no! Nothing like Angus! But wouldn't it be safer to be like Angus, encased in the assurance of his own rightness, his near-perfection? Surely Angus had never suffered from self-loathing, and probably allowed himself a minimum amount of inner examination. For Angus there would never have been much hurt, bewilderment, never the feeling that his life was slipping away always just beyond his control. Was he—had he been—jealous of Angus's overt security and self-certainty? Was it some warped need of his for punishment, some madness of his own that had let him be deceived into this marriage—a conviction that, for reasons inexplicable to himself, he deserved nothing more? But punishment for what? He had done nothing worthy of . . .

Meg? Meggy, no! If she knew about all this, would she think his misery just retribution for what she had called their mortal sin? Was she suffering too, somehow, and taking perverse pleasure in it, calling it penance? "Someday," Esteban Arragon had said to him so many years ago, "you will know what it means to yearn and suffer." God, everything he was thinking now was lunacy!

He turned over, clenching cold fists, grinding his teeth in a struggle to reestablish control over himself. None of those things mattered anymore. Esteban least of all, nor Angus, Meg, how he had come to have

Cherish as his wife. Those things were past, done; nothing could change anything about them. He would go on from here. He would maintain his sanity, his identity in spite of Cherish; he had managed to do that against Angus's desires, hadn't he? He would take the pleasure and satisfaction he could find in his work, and from any other sources that might be available, he would give Cherish and the child as much as he could of what he had to give, and he would go on with life.

But is that all? cried something desperate within him. Will there never be anything more than that? No, he put the small, trembling thing down firmly. That's been a major part of my trouble all along. I've always expected—other things—more. I only knew vaguely what they were—except for those months when I thought and hoped Meg and I might . . . but I was wrong to think there could be more, deluding myself for all these years, so disappointed because I thought I wasn't getting all that I deserved—whatever the hell I thought *that* might be . . . . It must be that everyone, inside, is alone, lonely. People don't talk about it any more than I ever have, but when you're young, you get the idea there's supposed to be happiness. It's all a myth . . . . why don't people warn kids of that so they won't . . .

He made a determined, conscious effort to relax. All right, he thought more quietly, now I know. It's taken a long time and it's been hard, but I do now fully and completely know. There are no great, ineffable joys, no passions to make the earth tremble, no . . . . This is all there's to be. I can live with that. I have to, if I'm to live.

He slept.

X

1880

Meg and Gordon came home to the hacienda in June of 1880. It was a soft, cool, slightly hazy day, with more of the feel of autumn beginning than of summer. Plenty of rain in the spring made the valley lush and beautiful. Gavin had just sent the sheep to summer pasture, with Carlos and Dougal and several other boys going along to help Joe. Joe and Rafaela had a boy of their own now, old enough to look after a small flock of his own. Gavin and Jesus, busy with late spring lambing, returned to work after the initial hubbub of greetings. Gordon went along with them. Maria and Laurie had been prodigiously busy in the kitchen for some time. Not only was there Meg and Gordon's homecoming to prepare for; Ranald was coming for a few days, Jean and her family would be coming from Denver with him, and Ian's family would be up from Santa Fe. The really big meals would begin tomorrow. Finishing the pies on which she had been working, Laurie shyly made an excuse to leave and promised to return soon.

"She's meeting the Ortega boy," Maria said to Meg and compressed her lips. "They've always been friends, but I don't like them seeing so much of each other now. Nothing will come of it. Paco is not good enough for someone like our Laurie. He ought to have a job right now instead of just hanging around down along the river. I'd like to send Laurie back to Denver with Jean for a part of the summer, get them apart for a while. She might meet some fine young people with Jean and Porfirio. They have a fine truck farm, you know. Papa and I have been twice, in winter, for visits."

"They're so grown-up," Meg said sadly, "Laurie and Jesus."

Maria smiled with a touch of regret. "It always happens before we know, before we are ready. Wait until you see Dougal and Carlos. I've written you about Jesus? Father O'Malley believes he truly has a vocation. He's too young yet to make a real commitment, but he's always been more interested in books and things like that than in things that distract other boys. I'm glad they don't take them as young as they once did. How can a child of seven or eight possibly know about a thing so important as becoming a priest? It is the parents who make the decision then, and they can't judge either, even for their own child, about something so serious and personal. If the choice were left to us, I don't think Gavin would ever agree to it. Father O'Malley says that next year, if Jesus still feels as he does now, he will recommend his entrance at St. Stephen's in Santa Fe. Tell me about you and Gordon. Did you get my letter before you left, about Carmela's new baby out there in California?"

Leaving no time for reply to her question, Maria went on to detail the increasing brood of grandchildren, with wistful, meaningful glances at her third daughter. Meg and Gordon would be married three years in October. Maria felt an uneasy certainty that something must surely be wrong.

Finally, when there was a significant, expectant

pause, Meg said, "Gordon has done so well, Mama. He graduated with very high honors, and the firm he's been working for in Boston didn't want to let him go. I wish you and Papa could have seen the graduation, and Mr. Gaynor."

Maria said proudly, "Such intelligent people our children are—and marry. I wish we could have been there too. Poor Mr. Gaynor used to sit here in this kitchen, talking about his plans and dreams for Gordon. I always thought it would have been so much better for them both, Claude and Gordon, if Claude had married again after Gordon's mother died. I used to think Gordon must be very lonely, and I was glad he spent so much time here, with Ranald and all of you. And to think that someone as smart as Gordon wants to come back here to Quintana and work for the good of the people in the valley! You've written he's had offers for going into practice in the East. Such a fine husband to be proud of!"

"Yes," Meg said, looking down at a big batter bowl as she sifted flour into it. It seemed to Maria, glancing at her lovely daughter, that there was something automatic in the answer. Since their arrival, she had noticed a shadowiness in Meg's eyes that worried her. There was also an uneasiness, a wistful uncertainty in Gordon's expressive face. She could see for certain that Meg was still too thin. Meg had been like that when they married—pale, too thin, not quite wholly aware of what went on around her, even of the wedding. At the time, Maria had fretted to Gavin that it hardly seemed like a wedding, and adding to her worry, Gavin had not disagreed. But now Meg and Gordon had been married more than two and a half years. Perhaps the way they looked now, or seemed to look, was due only to the normal tensions of beginning a new life, now that schooling and temporary jobs for Gordon were over. Still, Maria felt sure there was sadness, discontent, fear in the continuing absence of a child on the way.

She put wood into the new stove, making it ready for the cake Meg was mixing, and said brightly, "Now we have three college graduates in the family. Papa and I never dreamed so many, and there are still the younger ones. I think Carlos or Dougal will never want to go to college, but there is Jesus. Laurie has talked of becoming a nurse. That won't need college, but it's a thing to be proud of—until she is ready to marry, I mean. All our children make us proud. You've written about the college classes you've had."

"I'd like to have more. Some teachers, far too many, haven't gone farther than the eighth grade themselves."

"Teaching needs all the learning you can get," agreed Maria without much conviction, "but surely what you have is enough for Quintana. Are you—planning to teach in the fall?"

"Yes. I wrote the school board months ago, and just before we started home, there was a letter saying I could have the job."

Maria said scornfully, "The teachers we've had the past two years didn't know a word of Spanish. Of course Mr. Gaynor didn't either, when he first came, and he never did really learn enough, so that it was easy for him, but he tried. These others didn't try. I've been glad, these last few years, that our children were all through with Quintana school. Since we became the State of Colorado and the State took over our school, we never know what sort of person they will send. You're right—usually they don't know nearly enough to be teaching others. I'm glad you'll be teaching—for a while. Soon, though, you and Gordon will have your own children and you'll need all your time for them. Think of it! Gordon a lawyer and you a teacher. The MacWinter family will have two of the most respected citizens in our part of the valley. If Laurie becomes a nurse—I think she won't; she'll marry—but with our Jesus a priest, with you and Gordon, Ranald and Thorne—it makes me a little dizzy trying to take it all in. Such a wonderful family!"

"You used to think Ranald might have a vocation."

Maria shrugged, smiling fondly. "That shows you that even a mother can be wrong. No, Ranald is too much the big business man. We are surprised and pleased at Angus's leaving him some of his interest in the company. I suppose you know how important Ranald is to them, especially since Angus died. They are working now to move most of their interests out here, to Colorado. Ranald is out here with one of the Maitlands to look at land, for a place to build a steel mill and for coal mining. Has he written you, Ranald, about any particular girl he's interested in?"

"Mama," Meg reproved, smiling, "all you really think about is getting us all married, then with big families."

"Those are the most important things in anyone's life," Maria said stoutly. "They're what we're put on earth for."

"Well, I don't know anything about Ranald's girls. We saw him once when he was in Boston on business, but that's been more than a year ago. He hasn't written more than three or four times in all the while since. I know he's been terribly busy."

Maria sighed. "Still, he must have time to give *some* thought to finding a wife. And he isn't nearly the only one of you children who doesn't write enough letters."

"Do you hear from Thorne?"

Maria shook her head, sighing again. "Only a little, through Ranald. I worry about Thorne; Papa worries especially. He's only been home the one time since the boys went away with Angus and Elizabeth, but he seems to be very changed. I know it was very hard for him, going away from here when he didn't want to, not knowing the reason why. I'm afraid he will never forgive us for that, though he does know now that

Angus was his father. He's all around the country, Ranald writes, building his railroads. I must have written you that he married last year, the daughter—or stepdaughter I think it is—of that Mr. Fitzroy, who's part of the company. In Ranald's last letter, he said they were expecting a baby. It's probably born by now."

Meg slid the cake into the oven, feeling a heat in her face that was not from the stove alone. "Where are they?" she asked, and even to her own ears, her voice sounded strained, curt.

Maria was pouring coffee. "Let's sit down for a while. Nothing more has to be done just now. Thorne's wife, at least, is in Denver. We've heard from Jean, as well as from Ranald, that Thorne is having a fine house built there. Jean and Firio saw Thorne once last year, not long before Christmas. It was an accident they met, all three of them down town shopping. The wife—Cherish is her name—Jean says she thinks herself quite a lady. Her picture was in the papers several times, before the baby was showing. It was on the society page, and Jean kept the clippings for me. I'll show them to you sometime. Once she was hostess at a party her stepfather gave for the governor. I have some pictures of Thorne, too, but not from the same pages or papers. His are in because of railroad business. I don't think she's Catholic, his wife. Meg, you still go to church, don't you?"

"I do, Mama."

"And Gordon?"

"Yes, Gordon too."

Maria smiled. "This Sunday, I'll have more of you children than I've had for a long time with me at Mass. I think we can even persuade Papa to come along. I do worry that some of you, when you are so busy with other things in life, won't stay faithful to the church. Thorne was never—well, you know—

and I'm not all that sure about Ranald." She shook off the worry for the moment. "You haven't said what you think of our railroad."

"It certainly makes getting here easier and faster. I was so eager to get home, but then a little surprised to be here so soon, or at least at Mixon where we left the train. It's nothing like taking stages."

Maria nodded, frowning slightly. "Since they opened the railroad, Papa and I have done more traveling than in all the rest of our years put together, but I'm not completely sure I like it. It makes a lot of things easier, cheaper, but there are too many changes too fast. A lot of new people have come into the railroad towns, into the valley farms in the last two years. Mixon, the railroad's town over on the Rio Grande, is such a rough place. They say new towns are almost always like that, but for such a very long time almost nothing changed in this valley. Gavin says I'd stop progress if I could, and he's right, but I know he'd do the same. It was partly the way life was here, the kind of steady sureness of it, that made him want to settle here finally."

"And partly that you were here," Meg said softly.

Maria smiled. "Well, the railroad isn't all bad. It just could be that Jean and Firio and the children, maybe even Ranald with them, could get here on the late train instead of waiting until tomorrow. Wait till you see Jeanie's youngest. A year old last month and the very image of Papa. I wouldn't be surprised if they have another on the way by now." She looked sad, wistful. "It just could be, I suppose, that if Thorne is in Denver, Ranald just might be able to persuade him to come along. They were always so close. I pray Thorne hasn't given that up too."

Meg said stiffly, "I suppose this must be their busiest time of year, people in construction businesses."

"Yes, only . . . I understand, I think, some of how

it's been for Thorne, not knowing the most important thing he should have known; but when years and years passed without his coming back to visit us, I said to Gavin that perhaps we'd just have to reconcile ourselves to—giving him up. I suppose Angus did all he could to keep him from coming back here, even to visit, but Thorne was a grown man some of those years, and he was out here, not so very far away. Now, since he knows about Angus and why things had to be the way they were with us . . . Well, I don't know. Maybe it's partly that his wife doesn't want to come here, but he hasn't been married all the time and . . . I don't mean to be catty, but if she gives parties for the governor and such things . . . Oh, I don't even know what I'm trying to say. I only wish . . . it seems strange, doesn't it, to think of his being called Maxwell? When Jean showed your papa those things from the papers, where they write about Thorne Maxwell, I swear there were tears in Gavin's eyes."

The Romeros and Ranald did come that evening, but very late. Though they all claimed they had supper in the railroad's dining facilities after leaving the train at Mixon, Maria insisted on putting a second supper on the table, pressing them all to eat.

When the table was respectably loaded, she sat down herself and got immediately down to cases. "Well, Ranald, are we to have any word about a new daughter-in-law?"

Everyone around the table smiled and looked to Ranald, who was doing justice to a pasty.

Gavin said with mock severity, "Maria, you wanted them to eat. Can't you leave the lad alone now, about wives, at least until he's had his supper?"

"No one mentioned 'wives,' " she said firmly. "I only asked about one. Such a fine, handsome businessman as this shouldn't think of staying single too much longer."

Meg had sat down in a shadowed corner, holding

the soft, compact bundle that was Jean's sleeping baby. He made her arms, her whole body ache with yearning. If only this were mine—ours! If we had a child, then—

"Can I get you more coffee?" asked Gordon, resting a hand on her shoulder.

"No. No, thank you."

He must know what she was thinking. He always watched her, always seemed to want to try, without asking too many questions. I should appreciate that, she thought, impatient with herself. A lot of husbands never give a thought to what their wives think or feel. The wistful importunity in his eyes, his half-apologetic attentions too often roused only irritation in her, or deepened her longing to be left alone. There was something wrong with her, more than one thing, surely. She wanted children more even than her mother could dream. Children, a child, would make her life, and Gordon's . . . Father, forgive me for I have sinned . . . Was the absence of children truly to be her penance? Such a hard, merciless punishment, it seemed, spread over the long years of a lifetime, her lifetime, and Gordon's; surely it was unjust, at least for Gordon, who had done nothing. She reached up briefly, to touch his tentative hand on her shoulder, and tears came into her averted eyes. Poor Gordon, I'm sorry! her heart cried out to him—sorry for so many things. What possible reason do I have to be impatient with you?

When she drew her hand away, Gordon touched her hair, then returned to his place by the table. In the lamplight, she saw that his face was sad and wistful.

Ranald was saying, "Well, Mama, the truth is, there is a girl. Her name is Amy Warner, and we've known each other about two years now, though she lives in Chicago and we haven't had much real time together. We're engaged—sort of, though there's not been any announcement or anything like that. We promised each other to take plenty of time making up our minds, but if things go as I hope they will, we'll be married some time this fall. Amy's father has a good-sized interest in slaughterhouses. He—"

"Oh, slaughterhouses!" cried Maria in disgust. "I want to hear about *her*."

"All right," said Ranald, holding his cup out to Jean for more coffee, "to answer your first and most important question: Yes."

"Yes, what?" cried Maria as the others laughed.

"Yes, she's a good Catholic girl," supplemented Gavin.

"I certainly hope so," said the mother, unabashed. "I have a feeling this careless boy needs a good influence. How long, Ranald, have you been thinking of these plans without letting us know? Do you love her, or are you thinking more of the slaughterhouses?"

Ranald's smile grew pensive and tender. His face, so like Gavin's, seemed to Maria to glow as he said softly, "I'm counting on our being married this fall or winter. Amy's somebody very special, Mama. Yes, I love her. I can't say how much because there don't seem to be any words for it."

When the new arrivals had done justice to the supper, Maria and Laurie went with Jean to get the children settled for the night. Meg did not want to give up the baby, but she had held him through most of the supper preparations and now felt she should contribute to the work. She began to clear the table, to wash the dishes. Gordon carried in more water for her, and as he came in, Porfirio said, "Now that the family lawyer is here, I need some advice. Do you know anything about water rights in this state? For irrigation, I mean."

"Not as much as I ought to know," Gordon said, "but I know where to find information, which ought to be a good start."

"Let's go out here," said Firio, indicating the porch

where Jesus had already gone to strum softly on an old guitar.

Ranald and Gavin sat on at the table, smoking. Meg had tea steeping for her father.

"Joe and the boys will come down from their sheep camps tomorrow," Gavin said, "and Ian and the family should be here by supper time. Maria told you, I think, when you first got here, but everyone had so much to say just then. It's the happiest time in a long while for your mama, and for me, with so many of you coming back home . . . . Ranald, did you see Thorne?"

"Yes. Mama didn't give me a chance to say anything about that. I've been in Denver for a week and he left the day after I got there, but we did go out to have a look at the house he's having built. They had a baby boy three months ago, Thorne and Cherish."

Gavin smiled, but painfully. "Maria will be sorry she didn't get that news straight away. Where's he gone to now?"

"They're building a feeder line in Utah. It'll be finished this year."

"And Thorne?" Gavin prompted gently, not quite knowing how to go on with the question.

"Well, Papa, I don't really know what to say. He's —not very communicative. He used to be quiet when we were kids, but then there'd be other times when he'd start talking and no one else could get a word in until he'd finished. Now, he—never seems to feel like talking, and there are a lot of things he just won't talk about at all. He works very hard. Everyone depends on him for decisions about the railroad and for overseeing the construction work. Frank Fitzroy says that Thorne's worth three ordinary men."

"But he likes the work?" Gavin said, seeking reassurance.

Ranald shifted his chair and nodded to Meg's offer of tea.

"He's always liked planning things, seeing them

built, finished properly, ever since we first began learning something about railroads—not that I ever learned that much. He's a fine engineer."

"Maria will say he shouldn't have left his family so soon after the baby was born."

"They needed him, on the job, I mean, because they started work out there in April and he'd already been out a couple of times before now. They've started triple-railing now, on the main lines south and west out of Denver, so that both narrow- and standard-gauge trains can use the same track. All our main-line trains will be standard-gauge when that's finished."

"Just what is the difference between the gauges?" Gavin asked.

"Standard-gauge tracks have four feet eight and one-half inches between rail centers. There are a lot of other gauges, bigger and smaller, but what's accepted now as narrow gauge is three feet wide; it makes a big difference in the size of cars and locomotives."

Ranald looked reflectively at his pipe and went on, Gavin listening only absently now.

"For several years now, Intermountain has given us our best returns, and we all hope it can do that for several more years. This reorganization and transfer of operations is even more expensive than we thought. I'll be awfully glad when we're finally ready to settle down and just stay out here, without having to be traveling back and forth so much. That's one of the reasons I've been willing to wait all this time to marry Amy. I don't like the idea of being away from my wife so much of the time."

Gavin sighed, "Thorne will never forgive us for letting Angus take him from here. Maria wants to think he feels himself to be better than we are, with his job and wife and inheritance. I suppose it's easier to think that. But I know the lad—I believe I do—and he'd have had to change more than it's possible for a person to change if he'd begun to think like that. *I* can't think such a thing of him because it would make him seem too much like Angus. We failed him then, when you were boys. Angus refused to tell him or let him be told the truth. I should have told him anyway. I was afraid that Angus would deny it if I did, and that it would only have made for more confusion. I doubt Thorne understands that, though, and I can't blame him if he feels . . ."

"I think he does understand, Papa, knowing now who Angus really was. Remember the one time Thorne did come home was before he knew."

"He should have known all of it, from the beginning. Telling half-truths, or just avoiding a subject, is always bad for everyone concerned. That one time he did come back, he asked over and over to know all of it—not in words, you know. But I was too much a coward to tell him, even then, when he was a grown man, though I've never been sure *why* I couldn't answer him. I thought, at the time, that Angus might have decided never to tell him at all, and that it would be easier for Thorne that way, after everything he'd been through already. I—hoped he'd always be a Mac-Winter, I suppose. Aye, and he does still blame us for letting Angus take him."

"I honestly don't believe he does, Papa. I know, especially looking back on it, that he was awfully hurt and confused in the beginning and for years afterward. I didn't think about it much at the time because I didn't want to. I was so pleased at going, at the opportunities, myself. It's always been hard to know what Thorne's thinking unless he just wanted to tell you, but I'm sure if he were really bitter, he'd never have come back that time. All through those years, he was almost constantly being forced to do things he didn't like, and I just can't imagine that he'd have added to them voluntarily. When he came east after being here, he said he'd had a grand time, and he talked a lot about the family and all. He's just been so busy since then . . ."

"We noticed then," Gavin said thoughtfully, "how he'd changed. When you were boys, I used to worry sometimes that he'd not take anything seriously enough. But when he was here, I noticed how seldom he smiled . . . . He did seem pleased to be here, though; at least, in the beginning. Then, after a day or two, it seemed he couldn't be away fast enough. You were here, Meg; didn't it seem so to you?"

"He was always restless, Papa," she said, barely glancing around at them as she added hot water to the dishpan.

There was a little silence, and she had to look around again, furtively, but neither of them was looking in her direction now.

Gavin said, "And how was it with him when Angus did finally tell him the truth?"

"I—don't know," Ranald said slowly. "That was a strange time. Thorne had been—well, not himself, all the time we were in Europe. Later, when I thought about it, altogether, it seemed almost as if he knew something was going to happen, some big change in his life, something like that. I don't see how both of us didn't guess that Angus was his father in all those years. Thorne has been telling me for years how naive and innocent I am. Maybe he did guess and simply refused to think about it or let himself admit it. He can do that if there's something he'd rather not think about or feel. . . .

"Anyway, Angus talked to him that night, when we'd just got back to Pittsburgh, and right afterward, Thorne left the house. Angus called me to his study and told me then. He said—well, he said he wished things were the other way 'round; he wished I was his son. He'd said that to Thorne, too."

Gavin grimaced. "A hard, cruel man."

"Yes. He never showed Thorne anything but criticism and disdain, not even when he was dying. I got on better with Angus, but I never liked him. I know of times when things have been absolute hell for Thorne, but you know how he always was. There were sometimes things he could have done to make things easier for himself."

"Aye," Gavin said, "he has an overdose of pride and stubbornness."

"I thought he would surely have gone away that night," Ranald went on, "but he came back after everyone else was in bed. What Angus had told him didn't seem to be much on his mind then. He said he didn't want to talk about it, but he didn't seem upset either. It seemed as if most of his mind was all tied up with something else. He seemed happy at first. Then, all of a sudden, he turned dark and closed the way he can. The next morning he left for Denver and he looked terrible. He didn't talk any more with Angus. I'd not have seen him myself except that I heard him moving around in his room before it was really even daylight.

"A while later, I saw Cherish and she said someone had been writing him, sending letters in care of her stepfather, to Fitz's Pittsburgh house. That was where he went that night after Angus talked to him. I've wondered and wondered about that. The letters must have been from some girl, but I can't imagine who. There was never any one I know of that he was particularly interested in. I've thought, Meg, he might have mentioned someone to you when he was home that summer. You two used to find a lot to talk about at times."

"No," she said evenly, concentrating on the scrubbing of a crusted pan.

"And it had nothing to do with this Cherish," Gavin said thoughtfully.

Ranald shook his head. "Cherish only told me, I suppose, because she was crazy to know who the letters came from and what they meant. I think, though I didn't realize it at the time, that Cherish was ready to marry him then. It seems to have been something Angus wanted—for them to marry. I feel sure that if Thorne had suspected that, there never would have been a marriage."

"You don't think much of her, do you?"

"Honestly, no. She's selfish and grasping, jealous and a snob. She doesn't know the meaning of a closed mouth."

"Thorne must see more than that in her."

Ranald gestured helplessly. "I just don't know, Papa. When they came east a year ago last spring and were on their way to Virginia to be married, Thorne just seemed to have—given up fighting for a while. Angus wasn't the only partner who wanted the marriage. Fitz seemed pleased about it too, though he admitted that Cherish was not a wife he'd wish on anyone. Of course, Fitz had already arranged to leave a good deal of his share in the company to Thorne and felt it was good that he'd be a part of the family, so to speak, and could look after Cherish's and Ted's interests from that position too."

"I thought this Fitzroy had been a real friend to Thorne. That seems a strange way for a friend to look on the rest of his life."

"Fitz," Ranald said thoughtfully, "is, I guess, the American dream of the self-made man. He came from a hill cabin in West Virginia and made his way alone, with the help of the Civil War. One of the reasons he was able to do that, is that he is a very practical man in business matters, and just about everything is business to him. He wouldn't let things like love or happiness enter into a question of business, and that's how he seemed to look at the marriage. Angus thought like that, too. Philip and Peter Maitland were pleased about it as well, strictly for business reasons. You see, with the reorganization and division of shares, what the original three partners had will be only fifty-one percent of the stock. No one likes to see it split up any more than necessary. As for Thorne, I can't believe he'd marry for reasons like that. He's said practically nothing though. He just seems—not to remember he's got a wife most of the time."

"But there's the baby now, his first son. Surely . . .?"

"I don't know, Papa. The baby's only just been born. Maybe when he's older . . . if Thorne will take the time . . ."

"Is he a Romany boy?"

"No," Ranald said reluctantly. "The truth is, I think he may look like Angus, and that's . . . well, maybe it really doesn't matter what he looks like. If Cherish has her way, he may hardly get to know Thorne; and Thorne, for now at least, doesn't seem to care. Cherish is jealous, afraid he might give the baby a minute's attention, but still nagging at him if he doesn't. She doesn't like me because she's jealous that Thorne and I are friends. It's downright embarrassing to be around her. She's at him constantly about something. To avoid saying only bad things about her, I will admit that she's a beauty, one of the prettiest women I've seen, if only she could keep her tongue still."

Gavin sighed, frowning with concern. Then, with a conscious effort, he tried to change his mood, attempting a smile.

"And this Amy of yours. What about her looks? What sort of tongue might she have?"

The sleeping arrangements were as they had been when the MacWinter children were all younger and unmarried. The women and small children were in the bedroom above the parlor, the men above the kitchen. Maria said happily that there were too many coming home now for any other disposition to be feasible. Meg was glad of the arrangement that first night, glad it was necessary that relative quiet be maintained in the women's room, so as not to wake Jean's little ones. Even so, it seemed a long while before Jean and Laurie stopped whispering and fell asleep.

Very quietly and in darkness, Meg found her clothes, dressed, and crept from the room and the house. She had to be alone, away from everyone, sleeping or awake. One place drew her; it was just at the top of the little canyon of Piñon Creek, but she must never really go there again.

Instead she went to the barn where the milk cow and her calf were shut up for the night. There was an empty stall, with clean straw. She spoke softly to reassure the animals and sat down there.

All the time she'd been away Meg had thought, when things seemed most desperate, Everything will be better back home. If I can just get through this, I'll be all right again when we're back in the valley. She saw that now as more self-delusion. Of course nothing was better here; it was all worse. But surely it would be easier, once the shock of it was past, when she was accustomed again to hearing them talk about him, when everything she saw had grown comfortable and familiar again and no longer, necessarily, reminded her of Thorne.

Meg loved Gordon Gaynor. In a way, she always had. Loves were as varied and different as people were. She had always felt Gordon's sensitive loneliness, his wistfulness in the midst of her big voluble family. Claude Gaynor had cared for his son, in his way, but he was always the teacher, serious and didactic, or dreaming his silent dreams over books and might-have-beens. Laughter had been a rare thing in Claude's house or school. Gordon had told Meg many times how he had always yearned for a real place in the MacWinter family. He had it now.

Hot tears poured from Meg's eyes. Oh, God! what

have I done? Please, please! I have to make it right for him—for us.

Once the tears were allowed to come, the time with Thorne—such a brief time, and almost three years past—came flooding back upon her. She could hold the memories off no longer. She never had been able truly to shut her mind to them, though she had believed once that it was possible. If she had truly closed them out of her thoughts, the words, the looks, the feelings could not possibly be so vivid as they were now, seeming to be things she had experienced no longer ago than yesterday. She was weak and selfish. Surely she could have done better than this—for Gordon. But maybe . . . if she let the thoughts come as they would, this one more time, then things truly *would* be better. And she must think of all of it, not just the moments they had been together, but the hours, days, weeks after Thorne had gone away. Her mind had been in turmoil then, as it was now.

Meg had asked Thorne to leave, had insisted on it, but before he had ridden quite out of sight, she was wildly demanding to herself, how could he leave me? She could not bear the doubts and fears, the desperate, short-lived hopes alone. Thorne was so sure of himself, so easily convinced that because he wanted something, it could not be wrong. Many times in those weeks of torment, she convinced herself, almost, to hate him for his strength and assurance. Then, just when she was beginning to gain strength in the conviction that he was wrong, that they were both only being selfish and wicked, memories of his strong, hard body, his quiet, insistent voice, would wash over her, and she would feel her own body and will melting. "Oh, Thorne, Thorne, come home," she would cry within herself. "I promise not to worry about anything if we can be together again."

She was not able to eat or sleep properly during

those weeks that grew slowly into months. Her parents noticed her thinness and red-rimmed eyes. Maria made her take a tonic and often felt her brow for fever. She had no doubt that Meg's irritability, preoccupation and exhaustion came from something she called "summer complaint," which had symptoms enough for several diseases. Meg felt sure the truth of what was wrong would never occur to Mama. She was not so certain under Papa's thoughtful, probing looks. But she thought it unlikely that even Papa would think of Thorne as anything other than their son—her brother.

Often, Meg could not pray. Thorne invaded her prayers . . . the words in her mind were gently overwhelmed by tender, almost swooning preoccupations with memories . . . the longing, yearning for more things to be remembered. Maria became concerned that Meg did not take communion.

"I haven't—felt like going to confession," Meg had to answer one day, color rising in her cheeks.

"I know you haven't been well," said Maria in gentle reproof, "but you've been able to keep up your work around the house, to go on getting ready for your school teaching. It would only take a few minutes to walk over to Santa Filomina's and have a talk with Father O'Malley—not confession, even. Just a talk might do you good. He's a very understanding man, the Father. I'm beginning to wonder if something is troubling your mind. I wish you could tell me, or Papa, but it may be you don't even know what it is. Father O'Malley might know best how to help you find out."

A few days later, when Meg was on the porch, peeling apples, and her parents, in the kitchen, were unaware or forgetful of her nearness, she heard her mother say, "Gavin, I'm wondering more and more if our Meg may not have a vocation."

"No," he said sharply. "Lass, you see a vocation behind every bush."

"And you act as if it would be something to be ashamed of," snapped Maria.

"Not ashamed, Maria—avoided. No, I don't like the idea of any child of mine shut away from the world for life. There are a lot of things wrong in the world, and living's not always easy, but I want them to know life, to be whole people."

"You've never even come close to loving the church. You have no idea what it could mean to be a monk or nun, the fullness of life such people can have. Do you thinks priests are shut away from the world?" Maria had, unconsciously, lapsed into Spanish. "Not all monks and nuns are sequestered. Many do mission work, teach, care for the sick. Meg already plans to teach. You can't really understand how it might be, Gavin. You're only Catholic by—association."

"I think Meggy's just been thinking long thoughts about the future—it's a time that comes on all young people—and not feeling very well in the bargain. Maybe if you just stopped making her take that foul medicine—"

"That foul medicine has kept your children strong and healthy—you too. Gavin, I don't like the idea of her teaching school now. She'll be alone, all on her own, I mean. Jean and Carmela were married before they were her age."

"Just leave the lassie alone a bit, Maria, trust her. You act as if her teaching will be a thousand miles away. She'll only be going to Quintana every school day. I won't have her pushed, not into a convent, nor marriage either. She's a fine girl . . . ."

But Meg slipped off the porch and heard no more. Oh, Papa, I'm not! If you knew . . . .

Still, Meg wrote to Thorne in what, afterward, she always considered as moments of extreme weakness. There were many more letters than the four that ultimately reached Frank Fitzroy's house in Pittsburgh. She strove to make the ones she mailed objective, friendly but casual, letters from a sister, though she was unable quite to deny herself the luxury of a small personal comment at the end of each one. Even before the school year began, she got into the habit of going to the Quintana post office almost every day. Sometimes she could not stop herself from mailing a letter.

Thorne's letters were the kind that she could and did show to the rest of the family: brief, casual, noncommittal, though more than he had ever written in the past.

"Such a fine, thoughtful young man he's growing into," said Maria. "Now I'm doubly glad he made us that visit at last, short as it was. If he hadn't come back, remembered us and his old home, he probably would not write us at all."

Meg thought, in moments of reason, that she would have been angry, had he sent her love letters, but the letters that did reach her seemed hard and cold and careless. She meant nothing to him after all. Surely, he must have known many other girls, women. The things he had said to her he might have said many times before. She strove to harden herself toward thoughts, memories, longings. Often she had long, wistful thoughts of a convent, of peace and forgiveness and safety.

One day just after the school year had begun, she asked Laurie to tell their mother she was going to stay at the school to work on papers and might not be home for supper. She got her horse as soon as the children had all gone, and rode all the way to Garcia, ten miles south of Quintana. Trembling with relief and trepidation, she entered the church there. She knew the priest was newly arrived, would have no idea who she was. She made her confession.

When it was over, she said faintly, desperately, "Father, I—I need to ask some questions"

He waited, silent.

"May—may cousins ever marry? . . . first cousins?"

"No," he said curtly.

"But—but sometimes, in royal families . . . I've heard . . ."

The priest was weary, impatient. Being sent to this large, poor, Spanish-speaking parish was something of a humiliation at his age. At least, he thought cholerically, here was a parishioner who spoke and understood English.

He said censoriously, "It would take a very special dispensation, difficult to obtain and requiring a long wait and most special circumstances. To my mind, it's incest for people so closely related to marry. I never question the wisdom of church authorities in such things, but I am pleased that so few such dispensations have ever been granted. Is this boy you have been speaking of your cousin?"

To Meg, the tone of the question seemed salacious. She had meant to broach the subject of entering a convent, but almost before she realized it, she had stammered out a lie. No, it had nothing to do with the boy she had been talking about, nor with herself. It was a question someone else, a friend, a recent convert had asked her and she had been a little uncertain of how to answer, never having thought of such a thing before.

She stumbled out of the church into soft autumn dusk, drawing deep, tremulous breaths as if she had been suffocating for a long while. There was, at last, some feeling of release and safety. She had lied and was certain the priest knew she had lied, but once the penances he had given her were done, she could confess lying to the kind Father O'Malley at their own church, could bring her thoughts about a convent up for his consideration.

Maria was upset with her for being out so late alone. Meg wanted no supper. She went to bed feeling drained and limp, thinking mercifully little. In the next few days, though, she gave up the idea of becoming a nun. God had not spoken to her, of that she was certain, not about anything. It was only fear, purely self-centered thoughts that made her yearn to seek such a haven.

Then a time came when it occurred to her that she must be pregnant. The thought struck at her just when she was getting out of bed one morning. It came fully developed, a certainty that must have been just beneath her consciousness. She fell back as if she had been struck physically, feeling cold, sick, dizzy, her ears ringing so that Laurie's voice, urgently asking what was wrong, seemed to come from very far away.

"Nothing," Meg mumbled, finding it hard to breathe. How could she have been so stupid as not to think of it before now? Her period was so long overdue; in fact, it was practically time for a second one, if one were to come. How had her mind managed just to shut out this horror for so long? They said the children of near relations were likely to be deformed . . . Oh, Thorne, how could you leave me like this? Alone to . . .

"You're so pale," Laurie was saying solicitously. "I'd better call Mama—"

"No!" cried Meg in desperation. If the discerning Maria saw her now, like this, she would surely know. Meg struggled to her feet, clutching the foot of the bed, barely conscious of anything except this cruel new knowledge. "I—it's better now." She strove to sound more calm, but could not really judge what her own voice was like. "It must just be Mama's tonic, working overtime."

She dragged herself through the days, always struggling to seem normal. Her teaching job was a godsend, though she knew she was not doing it well. It gave her some respite from the incisive, loving eyes. The nights were interminable.

They must marry, despite the tenets of the church,

despite her parents' hurt and disapproval, if she was pregnant. Even if it would mean leaving the church, spending the rest of their lives in retribution for those brief, lustful moments, dying lost and unshriven. *If* he came back . . . there must be no more of those moments, no danger of conceiving another child, a child doomed by their sin. Thorne would come to hate her. Both their lives would be torment. . . . Yet, in the depths of those endless nights and in her misery, one thought would not quite be shut out: I'd rather be with him, no matter what the reason, no matter the pain, than with anyone else. Even if there is something terribly wrong with the baby, I can spend my life in loving and caring for it because it's his . . . Thorne. . . .

As the days passed and she could not find even a glimmer of hope that she was not pregnant, she began to have fleeting hopes that the child could be normal. Perhaps, this once, in their wickedness, God could show them such mercy and love. Maybe they could go away, the three of them, far away where no one knew them, where no one could guess the real extent of their sin, and make some sort of life for themselves. If they could be granted such beautiful forgiveness, this once, it would be all the more reason why there must never again be opportunity for conceiving. Thorne would never admit to understanding that. She called up melting memories of his gentle but commanding voice, his hands which, though they trembled, were firm, insistent. . . .

Sometimes she hated him for what had happened between them, for the results which now she alone suffered. He had always been so determined, so single-minded and relentless about getting what he wanted, once he decided what that might be, giving little thought to the future or consequences for himself or others. Right now he was having his trip to Europe, wasn't he?

Doubtless blithely and sensuously enjoying himself, with no thought of her.

Then she would be flooded, overwhelmed anew with the feelings she had known with him on those two beautiful days . . . the fault was not his; it was hers, all hers. Everyone knew it was women who were supposed to show strength in such matters. She was the guilty one. Witness how her deceitful, degrading body, even now, felt like the very manifestation of yearning and sensual hunger.

Meg mailed her last letter in care of Frank Fitzroy. "Come home as soon as you can. All my love." It was like fire in her hand when she carried it to the post office. She must trust him now, to understand, to take care of things in whatever pieced-together way he could. There was no other choice now, under these circumstances. And she could trust him. He had always been strong, able, almost dauntless . . . .

Meg knew a time of relative peace then, resting, depending on Thorne, on his return, his understanding and love. It was what a part of her had yearned to do from the beginning.

"Your summer complaint seems to have cleared up," Maria said with satisfaction after Meg had known several days of this new quietness of mind. "It lasted longer than it should have, but that tonic will always take care of almost anything in time. How is Mr. Gaynor, poor man?"

Mr. Gaynor was very ill again, had had to turn the school over to Meg and a capable older student.

Before daylight on a morning around the first of October, Meg wakened to grinding pain in all her lower body. There was the warm stickiness of blood on her nightgown and sheets. At first she feared she was having a miscarriage.

But it was not a miscarriage. It was only what her mother called "a very bad time this month." Meg stayed in bed all through that weekend, cowering there, wracked with cramps, bleeding profusely, crying most of the time she was alone, and she was utterly alone now. Thorne was gone; his child, and hers, had never really existed. He must be, forever now, beyond her dreams. She made the jolting discovery that she had come to want their baby and the other, harsh and stringent, but certain and unquestionable realities which would have followed from her pregnancy. Despite fears that the child would be deformed in body or mind, she had come to want the child, to count on it.

On Monday, she was very weak and white, her eyes very dark and shadowed in her pale, exhausted face. Maria ordered her back to bed when she came down at breakfast time. The school would have to function or not function on its own.

Meg was restless, and after a time she got up again, went downstairs, then outdoors to sit in the soft, hazy fall sunshine. Temporarily, she was alone at the house. It was very quiet. Folly came and lay down near her. Thorne's old Folly. The dog was very old now, his black muzzle grizzled with gray. He moved stiffly and seemed to ask no more of life than a quiet place to lie down. Meg, too, felt quiet. Surely she had been given a reprieve, though she had all but failed to recognize it until now. It was another chance at a good and decent life, for herself and for Thorne. In a small, choked voice, she said to the dog, "You gave him up a long time ago, didn't you? You used to whine and cry, after that first time he went away, but it couldn't have been so hard for you. Now I—" Folly's dark, liquid eyes had opened, and he looked at her with what seemed to be kindness, gentle sympathy. Fresh tears threatened, but she held them back.

What had happened to her, this physical salvation, was surely a sign from God, a gift of mercy. She must not cry anymore, but find strength, work every day at steeling herself for the time when Thorne would come back. She could not, must not hide from him. She owed him honesty, must make the attempt to convince him of what she herself must never doubt again. He would not understand, would not be any more convinced than he had been in July of the implacability of the reasons why they must never marry. If there seemed no other way, after she had tried, then she must lie, hurt him, say she didn't love him, had never loved him, make him believe that. She could never make him understand about the horrors these weeks had held for her.

Meg got up decisively from the porch steps. Now she knew. She must overcome the habit of thinking in those worn, weary circles. It was over. She went into the warm, empty, peaceful kitchen, a prayer in her mind for forgiveness, for strength, for Thorne's happiness and his soul. She began to peel potatoes for dinner.

Gordon came home a few days later. He was tired and haggard from his long journey and worry over his father. Mr. Gaynor was a little better by the time he arrived, and Gavin, meeting Gordon in Quintana, asked him to come for supper.

"They must not have very good food at your school, or very much of it," said Maria, bustling to load Gordon's plate. "You look to me as if a few weeks of decent meals would do wonders."

After supper, Gordon shyly asked Meg to come for a walk. She knew why. He had asked her to marry him before. This time she said yes. It was ridiculously, unreasonably easy. There was no tumult in being with Gordon. He took her hand, his face shining with joy in the moonlight. He kissed her. Meg stood quietly, feeling a vague emptiness, a faint, gnawing longing for something lost, something she must never think of trying to recover.

Meg knew her acceptance of Gordon's proposal was a cowardly thing, an injustice to Gordon. She would make it up to him. She *could* love him and be a good wife to him. Marriage to Gordon would make it unnecessary for her to face Thorne again. Already Maria had begun a long, chatty family letter to be sent to Pittsburgh for the boys when they came back from Europe. That letter would have to include news of the wedding. Even Thorne's wild willfulness and determination would be of no avail when he knew she was married. It was a cowardly thing, a wicked cruelty, but Meg knew she might not have been able to stand up under Thorne's importunities and persuasions, had he come back to the hacienda. She loathed herself, for so many reasons; but that could be dealt with later. This, now, was Gordon's time. She turned her attention and thoughts to the plans he was eagerly broaching.

That night, when everyone else in the house slept, she cried again. She had thought some of the other times bad, but this night was incredibly miserable and utterly desolate. Thorne hid hurt so well, in anger or pretended indifference, but she knew the look of it in his eyes. She remembered when he was to be sent away with Angus Maxwell, and when she had tried to refuse to talk to him, that day in the vegetable garden. Her arms, aching, remembered his hard, strong body. Her body, strained with yearning, felt his arms holding her, holding everything else away so that she could forget it all for a brief time of fulfillment in shared joy and love. . . . Perhaps, though, he would not be much hurt by what she was about to do. There were those casual, disinterested letters. Maybe he had changed his mind long ago, but was trying to be kind about it. Oh, but he does love me! He will be hurt . . . he'll never . . .

Beginning to be numbed by exhaustion and intense emotions, Meg tried to think of Gordon, tried to promise herself she would never again think of Thorne as she had been thinking this night. Soon she would be Gordon's wife. She summoned his round, fair face, glowing with happiness as it had been earlier. She would dedicate herself to insuring the continuation of that happiness. But Thorne filled her dreams.

Meg could hardly remember her wedding. She moved like an automaton through the festive day, evidently doing and saying most of the right, expected things, because no one seemed to notice that she was not really cognizant of what was happening. When Gordon, his thin arms trembling, held her against him at the end of the ceremony, the arms she imagined were strong and muscular, steady and insistent, not Gordon's at all.

They began the trip back to Gordon's college that afternoon. His father was somewhat recovered, had been able to attend their wedding. They spent the first night in a sleazy, noisy little hotel in Mixon, twelve miles from the hacienda.

"I wish it could have been someplace better," Gordon said apologetically as noise from the bar filtered up to their room.

Meg tried to say it didn't matter, for that was true, but she found she could not speak.

Gordon's lovemaking was quick and awkward, though his love was real enough. Afterward he drew away from her, and they lay silent, not touching. The room was dark, but if Meg had had any of her customary perception and sensitivity for others, she would have known that Gordon was hurt or angry or disappointed.

As it was, she was seeing Gordon at last, despite the darkness. He was thin and narrow, and that made him look very tall. His skin and hair and eyes were of an almost uniform pale fairness. His face was surprisingly rounded with an innocuous, cherubic look which belied his real, earnest gravity and intelligence. He had, she now understood, been more apprehensive about and frightened by this night than she had. Gordon was good and honest. She was not, but she would become so again. If only the dark, strong, masterful one . . . But this was *her* mind; she could not blame Thorne for her thoughts. She *would* love Gordon and make him happy. She felt an overwhelming need to apologize to him. Of course, she never could, not in words, but there would be other ways. She bit her lips together and willed back tears.

Finally Gordon said, his voice breaking unsteadily, "Meg, was—has there been—someone else?"

Meg's body hurt with the effort not to start. "Gordon . . ."

"You weren't—a virgin." She heard the anger, accusation and deep hurt. She had thought of his discovering this, and of an overheard discussion long ago, between her mother and another woman.

Her voice sounded calm in her own ears, too calm; the answer seemed too quick and pat. "I—hurt myself a long time ago, riding a horse." A lie but, please God, the last one she would ever tell him.

Gordon laughed in relief and moved quickly to take her in his arms. "Oh, Meg, I'm so sorry. And I've been lying here, thinking . . . I was afraid . . . there's never been anyone else for me, another girl, and I—I don't know a lot of things. Please be patient and forgive my—stupidities. I love you so very much and I've waited so long. Always before you've said there wasn't anyone else, but just now I was afraid . . . I don't know what I'd do if . . ."

"It's all right, Gordon," she said softly, stroking his cheek.

There was another silence, easier this time, less tense. Music and laughter came up to them from the bar.

Gordon said, "Meg, I know you don't feel the way I do. You couldn't. I love you so much. I know you don't—really love me, not yet, but I swear it will be a good marriage. I'll do anything I can to make you happy, to nurture love and trust and . . ."

"Yes, it will be a good marriage," she said fervently, "and, Gordon, I do love you."

Gordon slept soon. Meg lay listening to the town, awake far into the night. As she finally came near to dozing, her wayward, willful mind ranged free. Thorne would have laughed tonight and he would have made her laugh, forgetting to be frightened or to worry about anything. A wedding night was a time for laughter and the shared exclusion of the rest of the world. Thorne would have—she started painfully awake. Sleep did not come again that night.

A few nights later, they had their first experience of Gordon's impotence. He was embarrassed, bitterly humiliated. Meg had no idea of what she should say or do. She was sorry for him, but for herself it didn't really matter. His lovemaking was boyish and inept; the urgency of his own body left him no room for considering her; he gave her no pleasure.

"We're both tired," she said quietly, trying to comfort him. "Let's just—get a good night's sleep. Everything will be all right again."

"Meg, I've waited so long for you," he said painfully, "dreamed so often . . . I think this—now—is partly because I still can't believe we're really . . ."

She tried to sound warm and matter-of-fact. "Well, I'm here, Gordon. I'll always be with you."

"Will you, Meg?"

"You know I will. Don't be upset. If you're not sleepy, tell me some more about the university."

His impotence came and went for no reason that was apparent to Meg. Finally, though, she realized it had to do with her. If she made moves of responsiveness, before or during intercourse, he would freeze. Is it wrong? she wondered forlornly. Don't other women enjoy it, or want to? Is it really no more than "a woman's burden," the way I heard Mrs. Ortega say to

Mama once? I must be some sort of freak, wanting more.

They never really talked about the problem nor attempted to search for its reasons. Meg blamed herself and became convinced Gordon blamed her, that she was at fault, a woman with unnatural lusts. Times between their sexual togetherness grew longer. When they came, Meg forced herself to be still and passive. After a little while, it took no effort.

They received the news of Gordon's father's death on an afternoon in January. They had been married a little over three months. Though he felt guilty and remiss about it, Gordon decided not to go home for the funeral. His father was gone; Gordon's presence could do him no service. The trip still took weeks, and it was now time for semester exams to be given. Meg did all she could to bolster him, reassure him that it was the only sensible decision in the circumstances. That night, when he believed her alseep, Gordon began to cry.

Meg lay very still, appalled, even a little frightened. She had almost never before known a man to cry. Pity welled up, and sympathy, filling her own eyes with tears. She turned and put her arms about him.

After a little, Gordon said brokenly, "It's such a lonely feeling. I know you must think I'm weak, unmanly, but I . . . I can't really remember my mother, and now he's gone. Now there's no one left . . ."

"There's me, Gordon," she said tenderly. "There are all the MacWinters. You married a family, you know, whether you meant to or not. And some day, I hope soon, we'll have our own children."

"You're so good for me." He held her close and grew more calm. Finally, he asked, "Are children very important to you?"

"Oh, yes. I hope there'll be a lot eventually."

"Why?"

"Well, because—that's what marriage is for . . . partly. I love kids. Don't you, Gordon?"

"Oh, yes!" he said, too quickly, too heartily, "but I can't help hoping there won't be any—for a while, I mean. I like having you to myself, just the two of us . . ."

Meg stood up slowly from the hay in her father's barn. She mustn't stay out here all night. Suppose she fell asleep and someone found her here in the morning? What would she say? "I had to be alone; Thorne is married and has a baby son"? Her memories, thoughts of him, had grown less tumultuous with the passage of time, but, when they came, there was still the pain.

Ten years ago, almost to the day, she and Thorne had met by accident right here in this barn. She had cried, pleading with him not to go away with Angus, with his father. She had read the misery and bewilderment in his eyes. He had held her, awkwardly, then with growing fierceness. Then he had drawn away, jerked himself free of her, and asked her to look after Folly. His voice had been tight; she had believed at the time that he was angry with her.

How is he now? Does he ever . . . Oh, God, let him be happy. Let him truly love his baby and his wife. Send them good things, and happiness. . . . Let me be what Gordon needs, and please—please! send us children. If I haven't done penance enough yet, please —must it be barrenness?

The night was lit by a full summer moon and when she came from the barn, someone was walking near by.

She gasped, unreasonably frightened. "Who's that?"

"Meg?" Gordon came to her quickly, smiling a little and looking quizzical. "What in the world are you doing out here?"

She clung to him, suddenly wanting him desperately.

"I've just been—thinking about things. I couldn't sleep straightaway."

"So have I been thinking. There was a lot of snoring in the boys' room. I want to start working on fixing up our house tomorrow. Ranald and some of the others will help, maybe."

"Gordon, there's—an empty stall in the barn, clean hay . . ." Her voice was faint, timid; her body clamored urgently.

He did not seem to understand. "It's a beautiful night. You are glad to be back, aren't you?"

"Oh, yes . . ."

"Good, my sweetheart. I hope things will be better now."

"What things?" She had begun to tremble slightly, but his arms around her remained casual.

"Just—everything. I know you weren't happy back east. You've always wanted to live here. You used to say that all the time when we were kids." His voice took on an almost shaky tone of earnestness and hope. "Meg, I'm going to be a good lawyer here, not just the kind who's out for all the money he can make. There is justice in the law and it's past time that it applied equally to the poor, the ordinary people."

She nodded automatically against his shoulder.

"And you'll have the teaching job. Your mother's right, you know. We will be prominent citizens, at least to most of the people around here." He laughed softly, absently stroking her hair.

She said, just audibly, "Gordon, please give me a baby."

She felt him tense and he was silent.

"Have I said something wrong?" Her voice was still faint, unsteady, but there was a hint of anger in it. "Is it evil or something for a woman to want a baby? After all, the purpose of the marriage act is begetting children."

"Come in now and get back to bed," he said gently and kissed her forehead.

"Gordon . . ."

He laughed unconvincingly. "What would people say? Quintana's only and leading lawyer and schoolteacher, romping around in the hay." He took her hand. "Come on back to the house, Meg. We both need some sleep."

XI

1886

"Do you want to take her awhile?" George Baxter asked Thorne, shouting to make himself heard in the locomotive cab.

"I thought you were never going to ask," Thorne yelled back, grinning.

The train, equipped with the very new, straight air brakes, was on the return trip of its maiden run. It contained only two passenger coaches, one coach for members of the board, who had been on a tour of inspection, and one coach for railroad workmen, coming down from Silver Valley to Denver to celebrate the Fourth of July.

George Baxter got down from his high seat and Thorne slipped into it.

"We got to take on water," George yelled. "Whiskey Tank's comin' up."

Thorne nodded, beginning to slow the train. He knew this line. Every curve, fill, tunnel, trestle, straightaway, cut or grade provided a memory peculiar to it alone. The Silver Valley Line was the first line he had ever really worked on, and over the years he had done many and varied jobs along it.

George watched critically as Thorne brought the engine under the spout at Whiskey Tank and stopped, a little jerkily. Thorne sat still then, listening to the chuffing locomotive, feeling its liveness all through his body. George, sensing that the other shared his own feelings for the machine, smiled, exposing blackened teeth.

Thorne, looking slightly apologetic, declined George's offer of a plug of tobacco.

"Well, I got these seegars," George said. "Whole pocketful of 'em. They come before we left out of Denver, compliments of the Railroad, to mark this here engine's first trip an' all."

"Thanks, no. I don't think I want to smoke just now."

"I reckon you had somethin' to do with the box of seegars."

"Not me. I wish I had, but I'm afraid I'm not as thoughtful as that. Even if I were, I've not had much time to think these past days with all the board members around. I think some of them still expect an Indian raid every time we come out of a tunnel."

"Easterners," sympathized George. "Flatlanders." The two words were sufficient, conveying almost exactly what they both felt, though the feelings were different. "Well, then, I reckon ole Fitz, or more likely Miss Nancy, was the one thought of seegars. Makes it seem like a feller's wife had a baby or somethin'. Come to think of it, that's a little the way it is, gettin' to engineer one of these for its first real time out. You know, I'd raise hell if anyone was to try to make me take one of them standard gauge, main-line trains. I'm right attached to these here little ole sewin' machines, an' this here's a dandy. Except, it does seem to me like she heats up, gits close to overheatin', a little fast an' often."

"I noticed your heat gauge. But I think it's just that it needs less coal than we're used to using."

George nodded and the fireman nodded.

George said, critically, but fondly, "Another thing, it seems to me like she's mighty rough. All these tea-kettles is that, but this seems extry. Maybe they could do a little adjustin' with the springs?"

"Tell them about these problems at the yards in Denver. They'll have to do a complete inspection anyway."

"You understand I ain't makin' no real complaint?"

"I do, but did you ever know everything to be just right on the first run of anything?"

George spat and grinned. "No, nor the last one either, nor very few in between."

"What about these air brakes?"

George looked a little embarrassed. "Kind of scary. You know how much we need brakes on this here down trip from Silver Valley. Well, these is nearly too good, an' I can't get over it that they don't have to be set car by car. Keep nearly forgittin' that I got to operate that there little thingamajog an' that's all there is to it."

"Yes, but I'm afraid that on a train of any length, there'd be some pile-up trouble," Thorne said. "The forward cars would be stopped and the rear ones would hit them pretty hard before the braking motivation got back that far."

As George and the fireman nodded agreement, the fireman said, "I've heard you was a brakeman one time, Mr. Mac."

"Just for a summer."

"You can tell it wasn't for long," George said grinning. "He's still got all his fingers, even all the joints of 'em. You come from a brakey, Herb. I did too. Looky there. Both of us got stuff missin'. Can't nobody hold that job for any length of time without gittin' caught in the damned couplins'."

"I've heard somebody's tryin' to make automatic ones," said the fireman. "Reckon how they figger to work that."

"Oh, somebody's always talkin' automatic somethin'," said George. "The biggest part of it never comes to anything. I'm glad of it, too, about most things. Too many changes as it is. But I do like most of the stuff that's new about this here engine." He turned all his attention to Thorne as the fireman went to shut off the water. "What do you reckon she'll be called, this machine?"

Intermountain rarely named its locomotives—all had line numbers—but the crews almost always came up with their own names for the engines. It was a small, private satisfying part of their lives and work.

Thorne said, "She'll be yours on a regular run, George. Somebody back there," gesturing toward the rear, "suggested calling her the Columbine, but—"

George snorted. "That ain't much of a name for a work horse."

"I didn't think so either. You name her, if you've got something in mind."

"You mean it'd be official?"

"Well, if it's printable."

George was pleased and a little embarrassed with his pleasure. "Well, I *have* been thinkin' about it, ever since I found out I'd be runnin' er, special trip an' regular. It seems to me like we might call 'er Nancy, if you think it wouldn' offend nobody."

"I think a lot of people would be pleased. Tom, Murphy, Fitz, Nancy herself." Thorne nodded his approval. "How much did you open 'er up coming up yesterday?"

"Well, I kep' to the limits," George said. "Always do that. I might have been tempted to let 'er out a little more, but any long grades we got, comin' up from Denver, is upgrades. About forty-five was the most we done."

Herb, the fireman, was leaning out, looking back. "I reckon we're ready. Carter's some conductor, ain't he? He ain't stuck his head out of that passenger coach with them other deadheads since he got his fancy passengers settled into the other car."

"Carter," said George laconically, "is a conductor for freight trains. Mr. Mac, you want me to take 'er now?"

"I'd like to go ahead with this for a while, if you don't mind," Thorne said.

George spat and said heartily, "Hell, why would I mind? I can play with 'er another time. If a feller like you can't run his own train, on his own railroad, I don't know who ought to."

"It's not quite all mine."

George made a gesture of dismissal. "Except for one or two, them others back yonder in the passenger coach don't know nor care beans about trains an' railroadin', long as they git a profit out of it."

"Do you want to go back in the crew car for a while?"

"Well, . . . maybe. You know we got to git off down here at Level Siding to wait for the reg'lar up-freight?"

"Yes."

"Oh, an' I noticed yesterday, down here at the Gursten Fill, it don't feel hardly right. It might a been just this rough-ridin' engine, but maybe you'd see what you think."

"All right."

George climbed down from the cab, still vaguely

uneasy about leaving his locomotive. "Be the first time in a lot of years that I've rode a train somebody else was runnin'." But he was pleased about going to the car with other crews and workmen.

Running the locomotive made Thorne feel younger, shy and proud. His pleasure in such simple things was a little ridiculous, maybe, but it was a welcome change after the past two weeks. Thorne had become literally itchy with tension, exasperation and irritation during the directors' tour. He had played no part in the decision that had sent the board of directors of MM&F on their inspection of part of the Intermountain lines. The directors had come to Silver Valley a few days ago to approve or disapprove the proposed new line to Beanpot. Several significant strikes had been made along the nearly inaccessible Beanpot Gulch this last year, and now, with a town booming there, there was promise of relatively long-term mining. The proposed route was a daring one, the only possible one that seemed feasible to Thorne, and he was proud of the plans. The straight-line distance between Silver Valley and Beanpot was thirty-four miles. The projected rail line would be just under fifty-nine miles, and still it would have more difficulties than they had overcome anywhere else. Thorne resented having to try to convince people who for the most part knew little or nothing about the mechanics of the situation, of the acceptability of something that would bring them a very respectable profit. The directors had held him captive, censuring various aspects of the roads and their operations while refusing to have things really explained. They asked the same questions, made the same inane comments over and over, until Thorne was on the point of hoping their car might be derailed and hurtled into a canyon somewhere, anywhere. No, things were not nearly as simple as they once had been, not since the reorganization. Approval of a large project was no longer a matter of how much money could be made available and of getting Fitz, Angus and the two Maitlands to agree.

"You convince them," Thorne had pleaded with Fitz, when the tour was proposed. "You're the one can talk anybody into anything. You're the one with all the political and newspaper friends—"

"I'll *talk* to 'em," Fitz cut in, "but that's about all I can do. I don't like havin' to admit it, but travelin' wears me to a frazzle. You know that. An you'd do damn' well to git friendly with them newspaper people an' politicians yourself. A man don't run a business on a island, all to himself. You'd do well, too, to try to git the trust an' respect of these board people."

"I'll ask Jim Ritter to go."

"No, you won't, neither. He's needed in the office. Besides, Jim ain't no civil engineer. He didn't have anything to do with the plattin' of that Beanpot route. For that matter, neither did the railroad commission or them officials, but you don't seem to mind too much waitin' for them to approve your plans."

"That's hardly the same thing. Why should anybody have to work to convince our people to put some of our capital into a thing like Beanpot, where we can already see big returns are practically guaranteed? I don't like begging anyone for anything, especially money."

Fitz sighed. "See if you can't think of it as explainin' or sellin', not beggin'. I know most of them don't know anything about any of the operations, but they're tryin' to learn so they'll know how to look after all the stockholders' interests. We got this here corporation thing worked out, finally: Maitland Steel, Rampart Coal, and Intermountain are all still under MM&F. Now, most of these people that'll be comin' knows somthin' about *one* of them businesses—that's why they bought stock in the first place an' got to be board members—but not hardly any knows about *all* the work we're into. You can't send Jim

Ritter, not only because he ain't got all the answers they'll want, but because it's you that'll be vice-president in charge of Intermountain when I make up my mind to quit or die. All them people know that, seems like, ever'body but you, an' that's because you're just too bullheaded to *say* you know it. Now, goddamn it, quit frownin'. I ain't tellin' you nothin' new. If you'll take my advice—which is somethin' I'm yet waitin' for you to do—you'll forgit this civil engineerin' business. Hell, you might be a engineer some day, but you ain't *never* been civil. If you want to build that Beanpot line, you go along an' nursemaid these people; after they've finished with the mines an' mill an' the rest of what they want to see about the railroads, then you, by God, sell 'em the Beanpot line. I don't know how long I been tryin' to teach you that there's a lot more to any real job than just the fun part."

Now, as he sat in the locomotive cab, Thorne thought, Well, the board's tour was almost over. Tonight there would be supper and a party for them at his own house, a business meeting tomorrow, and the next day most of them would be returning east. The tour had worn away his enthusiasm for the Beanpot line. Before, he had been proud and excited, chiefly because of the engineering logistics it would involve, but now he was almost indifferent to its approval. A few of the board members had followed him each time he moved, insisting on drawing him into conversation when he wanted to be silent, asking questions no alert child would have to ask about the roads, the trains, the workmen, the country. Thank God, they had at least been dissuaded from bringing their wives along on this particular part of the tour. "The girls" had stayed in Denver, where Cherish and plenty of people not directly connected with MM&F were eager to entertain them.

Thorne did not want to be host at the supper party

tonight. That was Cherish's idea, which she had broached to Peter Maitland and Ranald before mentioning it to Thorne. Cherish was very active socially. When it suited her, she could be absolutely scintillating, charmingly vivacious. She was a popular hostess or guest, not really liked, but popular. Socializing seemed to be her only outlet, her only pleasure, and Thorne knew he really should not grudge her her triumphs. Nor would he have, if only she would leave him out of her "events."

He had come into the locomotive cab to get away from the directors, and because he was excited about and interested in the new engine and brakes. Already, he felt almost a new person, easy and relaxed. They were just coming out of the mountains at that very definite break where rolling high plains bent and soared up to become the front range. He wanted to open the engine up to try the air brakes. He held his face out to the hot summer air, made cool by the train's velocity, and even the biting coal smoke in his nostrils was all right. He was getting acquainted with the train, sensing it with every part of his body. It felt good. He smiled. *He* felt good, and the main reason seemed to be brief freedom from the directors. Someone had written that pleasure was the absence of pain, and they were right, he decided.

It was foothill and plains country and the line ran in easy grades and long, shallow curves. He could see for miles when his eyes weren't watering from smoke or cinders. He eased the throttle open. The fireman was saying something, but Thorne couldn't hear. Herb made gestures and Thorne caught the word "Level." Level Siding was where they had been instructed to wait for the scheduled freight coming up from Denver. Well, there was another siding beyond Level—Smith's, if he remembered right. It was several miles, but he and the engineer of the up-train could see such long distances here. Besides, freights always ran behind schedule. He suddenly felt a little light-headed with pure impulse and defiance.

As the engineer, George Baxter, climbed into the workers' coach, Carter, the conductor, demanded, "Who's runnin' your train?"

"MacWinter," George said casually. "Hell, when the boss wants to take over, I ain't the one to say no." He dropped into a seat and was offered a whiskey bottle. "I oughtn' to," he said wistfully, then took the bottle. "He won't want to take 'er all the way to Denver, I guess. Oh, hell, I'm dry as a bone. Little swig can't hurt."

"Tell me some things about this railroad," said Harvey Wilcox, who had offered the bottle. Harvey had been hired recently as a section foreman. He would not begin his job until the following week, but he had come up to look over and get the feel of the section. "For one thing, I thought his name was Maxwell, that dark-headed feller I seen gittin' in the cab at Silver Valley; Maxwell, like in the name of the company. An' I can't git it straight who them others are," gesturing toward the rear coach, "an' you'd be breakin' some mighty big rules on most roads by leavin' your cab, drinkin' during work time."

"This ain't one of them roads, nor one of them companies, where ever'thing's got to be done always an' forever by the rules," George said easily. "That's one of the main reasons I've been workin' for 'em ever since they started up business out in this part of the country."

George passed the bottle on. "If the boss wants to run my train, I ain't got any argyment. Somethin' was to go wrong, it's his neck, not mine. He's the kind would take the blame—but nothin's going to happen. I remember him when he was just a shirttail kid. He's a little railroad-crazy, like anybody stays with it long. He knows lines an' trains, from when they're first thinkin' about a road on paper, right up, prob'ly to how many passengers there was on the Utah Express last night. He's into just about ever'-thing has to do with Intermountain, young as he is, an' he *knows* things—it ain't just holdin' himself in high regard 'cause he's a boss.

"It's play for him to run a train." George grinned. "I been watchin' him all day, out of the corner of my eye. Couldn't hardly stand it till he got his hands on the controls of that-there new engine, but he didn't tell me he'd take over. Waited for me to mention it. He gives a man credit."

"I've heard he's a hard one," said Harvey, unconvinced.

"Oh, he is," George nodded readily. "For one thing, that one can fair work. He's got a college degree as an engineer, the kind, you know, that plans construction work and like that. An' even now, when he's all but runnin' the main office, he'll take a hand with a dump-cart or pick or hammer if he comes on a crew that's shorthanded. Seems he can handle seven things at a time; I mean, like things he's got to think about, at his office, or plannin' a line. A man that can work like that usually don't see why ever'body else around him can't do just as much, just as fast. So there's mighty little carelessness on Intermountain roads, mighty little laziness. MacWinter and the men that work for him, supervisors an' such, can spot a slipshod job a mile off. Still, he's fair, MacWinter. Leaves a feller alone to do his job, providin' he's willin' to *do* a job."

George lit a cigar, passed the rest of his pocketful to those nearest him. "About his name," he went on to Harvey Wilcox, "it is Maxwell, I reckon. They say old Angus Maxwell, the first Maxwell in the company, dead now, adopted MacWinter. I never seen old Angus; he stayed back east all the time. That was when they had a lot of business back there. Some say Mac's his bastard. I wouldn't know about that, but it wouldn't be no surprise. Bein' a bastard don't have much to do with the kind of person a man is. Us old hands knew him as MacWinter when he was a boy. Ole Fitz used to put him to work doin' different things, summers. He never mentioned we ought to change what we call him.

"Them others, the special passengers, is the board of directors. We got the whole MM&F Company, them that amounts to anything for money, on this train. You surely know ole Fitz, the one in the wheelchair. Had to have both legs cut off years back—eight years, I guess it's been—after he got hurt in a tunnel cave-in."

"Fitz, the old crippled feller, is the one the girl goes with," said Harvey, smirking.

"Miss Nancy's Fitz's wife," George stated with a little belligerence. "You'll go ahead an' think what you want to, but she's a fine girl, that one. Her Pa's Tom Murphy. Maybe you heard of him, works new construction. He always kep' Miss Nancy with him on jobs, an' there wasn' no funny business neither. Never been anyone but Fitz for Miss Nancy. Now she travels with Fitz, when he can go, which don't happen often. She's a good girl, good to ole Fitz too, an' makin' him happy. The young feller back there, one always looks like he's been eatin' persimmons, that's Fitz's boy Ted, by his first wife. I don't know how he happened to come along on this trip. Ain't never give a damn about anything havin' to do with the railroad, nor any kind of work. MacWinter is married to Fitz's stepdaughter. I never seen her, except for pictures in the paper. She's a real pretty woman, real pretty, but she don't have nothin' to do with common folks, one of these society ladies. I've heard she wants Mac to stay home, wear a suit or somethin' all the time, go to fancy parties an' charity balls, the likes of that. An' Ranald MacWinter back there, he's a cousin to Mac, I believe. Seems to be right smart and a good feller, though I don't know him myself. He works mostly for the steel mill. Peter Maitland, he handles the office business of the mines. There's another Maitland, but I ain't sure he's even here. Them others back there I don't know anything about, except that they're directors."

Harvey laughed. "Seems to me like you know a good bit."

"Well, it used to be that when Intermountain first started an' was just small, all of us workin' for the company knowed who the big bosses was, by sight. Some of 'em we knowed personally, was friends with. When you know people, you kind of keep up, through the gossip and such. But there's precious few of us left like that, the men that—now what the hell is he doin'? Jesus Christ, he's goin' to pass up Level Siding."

The train had picked up momentum and was hurtling ahead at a frightening speed.

Carter, the conductor, snatched at his watch. "Train six is due right here in twenty-five minutes. Gowdy runs a tight train. He won't be more'n ten minutes late, if that, this near to leavin' the Denver yards."

The men in the car fell silent as the realization of the imminent danger spread. George Baxter sat forward, tensely gripping the seat in front of him, against the train's increasing speed. "Forty-five miles an hour's faster than anybody in their right mind would want to go," he muttered angrily, "an' he just passed up Level like he didn' know about it. Why didn't Herb—"

"You shouldn't have left the cab," croaked Carter menacingly.

Six minutes before the Denver train was due, they began to slow.

"He's goin' for Smith's Siding," breathed a brakeman. "Christ, we may not make it."

"I'll take even odds he gits us to Smith's," said an old section hand, more scornful of danger than the others. No one answered him.

"I hope the points on the goddamn' switch moves easy," said the brakeman.

The brakes had gone on hard now, increasing their tension.

"Jesus, them fancy passengers will be on the floor," someone else said with a nervous laugh.

The train went onto Smith's Siding, the switch was reset for the open main line and three minutes later the other train, running eleven minutes late, pounded past. Through a sooty window, George saw the frightened, questioning looks and gestures of the number six crew. In such open country, they would have been able to see this engine coming at them where they never expected it to be.

"Lord have mercy!" breathed George and fell back weakly in his seat. He was sweating and pale.

Before number six had passed through the upper switch, George's train began to move again, smoothly this time, sedately, toward the lower switch.

"I've heard he used to be a wild one," said the brakeman, passing the bottle with a shaking hand.

"Used to, hell," snapped Carter indignantly. "George, while we was stopped there, why in the devil didn' you go up there an' take the train back? If he pulls somethin' else like that again, we might not be so lucky."

"Well, Mr. Carter, you might have spoke to him yourself, bein' as you're the conductor." George's anger was brief as he admitted sheepishly, "Truth is, I don't know that my legs would have got me to the cab, the state they was in at that time. Lord God!"

The rest of the trip was sedate, uneventful, but the holiday hilarity never was regained in the work car. Carter went back to look in on the special passengers and did not return.

When they reached the Denver depot, George Baxter went up to the engine, his legs still feeling a little strange. "Jesus, Mr. MacWinter, you liked to have scared the shit out of us."

Thorne was making notes on a piece of paper and did not look up. He had not quite met the eyes of Herb, the fireman, since they had gone onto Smith's Siding. He answered George absently, "How was that?"

"Why, we were supposed to have got off for the up train at Level, not Smith's. I reminded you before . . ."

Thorne said mildly, "That's the longest, straightest stretch on the whole road to Silver Valley, George. I wanted to see your 'Nancy' open up, try the brakes. Where's Carter? He's not trying to make trouble for you?"

"He went back with the passengers. I seen him git off with them, helpin' somebody with somethin' they had to carry. Well, you sure's hell did try the brakes an' run 'er wide open."

Thorne said, "See about a clearance from the yard dispatcher if Carter's disappeared. Find out about a place to put these cars and leave this machine at the shop. You're right about the roughness; I think something can be done about it. Give this to Hal Rodriguez at the shop." He handed George the paper. "I'd like to go over myself, but I haven't got the time."

George said earnestly, "Mr. MacWinter, Carter won't give me no trouble, but the superintendent an' them up there in the Level Division are goin' to have my ass."

Thorne studied him and said, finally, looking rather like a guilty boy, "They won't know which siding we took."

George grunted. "Ever'body on this train knows. The crew on number six knows, I could pretty near see their eyes buggin' out as they passed. You don't think it's goin' to go no further?"

Thorne swung down from the cab and looked up at the troubled engineer. His teeth flashed white in his dark, soot-smudged face as he said humbly, "That was a stupid thing to do, George. I'm sorry." Then the mood that had brought on his race with the train came back momentarily. "But I knew I could get to Smith's. I didn't doubt it for a minute. You know the kind of feeling you get sometimes . . . I'll talk to the division people. I'll send them a telegram right now. You won't have any trouble, or if you do, let me know. It was just—well, something I wanted to do."

"You'd fire any engineer that—"

"Goddamn' right. Always keep to your train orders!" He went away, across the tracks, on the opposite side of the train from where the passengers and workmen had got off the platform.

"Crazy!" said the fireman, still incredulous. "I tried to tell him, yelled my head off . . . He just signaled for more coal."

"Let's git this train put up," said George. "I got to git home an' see if I can't think about somethin' else."

Thorne was more than a little embarrassed now by what he had done with George's train. He wanted to avoid Fitz just now. The trip to Silver Valley was the only one Fitz had taken along with the rest of the board. Some people said they'd never get the line he was proposing to Beanpot through. Even Fitz was dubious about one or two places. Had Thorne's own locomotive engineering convinced the board members that he wasn't mentally capable of taking on such a job? He grinned, still shamefaced. He had known, without a tremor of doubt, that he could get the train safe to Smith's. It might seem foolhardy to anyone else, but he had been sure. Besides, it had been the most enjoyable thing he had done in years. The tension built up by the past days was almost entirely gone now.

The summer heat of mid-afternoon was crushing, enervating, as he walked slowly toward the house he had built for Cherish, wishing he might have spent this holiday on a mountain siding somewhere, alone in his office car.

Cherish had got her house in Denver in the fall of 1880. Thorne drew up the rough floor plans according to the things she told him she wanted incorporated. Most of the things, that is. He had balked, for instance, at a conservatory. The house was not the biggest in town, but it was certainly one of the best, the most modern. For a few months, Cherish had been pleased with it, feeling superior to everyone else—though Thorne had heard little except her complaints. Now, after almost six years, she fretted considerably over other people's newer homes and the latest conveniences they incorporated. She was particularly enraged over the house Fitz had built last year before he married Nancy Murphy.

Thorne and Cherish had reached a kind of mutual standoff with their marriage; neither of them were able to change or adjust or give up. Cherish still nagged him incessantly about his absences from home, his lack of attention to his children and to her. The absences made life bearable for Thorne, perhaps kept the marriage together. He was securely shut away from her behind his own invisible barriers; she hardly ever knew if anything she said or did really reached him; his defenses seemed impregnable. Though she still loved him, it was a bitter, love-hate emotion which, only Dahlia knew, devastated her. Cherish went through his clothes, his papers when he came home, even while he was away, searching for something with which to accuse him.

Her brother Ted had assured her that Thorne didn't have other women, but Ted was so busy following in his father's footsteps along those lines that Cherish doubted he had much time to spare for watching Thorne. Cherish and Thorne had separate rooms, had had them since the house was built. Their sexual encounters were limited, necessarily now because Thorne was away so much and because neither of them wanted more children. Through both her pregnancies, Cherish had relentlessly railed at Thorne for her condition. Though, once they existed, she did not hesitate to use the children as weapons against him. Thorne was convinced that her pregnancy with the little girl had been a deliberate plan of Cherish's. So, because he was afraid it might happen again, he had locks put on their bedroom doors. Cherish had the locks removed as soon as he left on his first business trip after they moved into the house. Thorne replaced them, but the next time he came home he found the locks had been removed, and he was too embarrassed to put them on again. Cherish was always the one, then, to initiate sexual relations between them, coming into his room as she chose. She knew the smallest detail of everything he kept at home, the order or lack of it in the drawers and closets in his room, everything that came and went in his study, all his personal habits, though he became more of a stranger to her with each passing year. She could *not* reach him—at any rate, she rarely knew when she had reached him—and for that she hated him, and became more determined to get to him.

She taunted him often with hints that the children were not his. She did and said anything she could think of that might rouse him or make him angry. He had also balked at having a butler—in addition to a cook, two maids, a coachman-gardener, a nurse for the children, and recently a distant relative of hers whom Cherish designated as a governess. About the conservatory and butler, Thorne had simply said, "I've set up a household account for you. It's a damned generous one. You do whatever you like with it, if you can afford it." He had arranged things so that she could not touch money other than that account. He seemed able to cope with anything she attempted, with calm indifference. Despite all her prying, her persistence, her urgency to know she could get through to him, he stolidly and inexorably maintained his privacy of person and thought.

Cherish never went to his office because his work occupied him so thoroughly. She refused to attend any function such as a company picnic, feeling she was "far above" those workmen and their families whose friendship she believed to be important to Thorne. Her jealousy of them and of his job knew no bounds. It was a thing bitter as gall, and as corrosive.

Cherish's only pleasures were social activities in which she could associate with people she considered her equals. She could, when she chose, be a lively, intriguing woman. Men admired her greatly, but she had no women friends.

Though Thorne detested society affairs, Cherish tried to force him into them almost every evening when he was home. She took great pleasure in showing him off at dinners, dances, parties. He was attractive to other women, even when he did little but scowl. On the occasions when he detached himself from her at gatherings, she watched him almost constantly and stored up accusations for when they would be alone. Most of the time, though, she clung to him, figuratively if not literally, chattering constantly to others, gloating that he was actually with her. At least his objection to their social life was something he did not hide, something she could work with.

Thorne frowned as he approached the house. He did not like it, had not liked it from its inception. It was too big, too gaudy and pretentious, and of course, Cherish was there. He thought of the house and the children as Cherish's. She had wanted complete control of them, and he had given it with few qualms. He would have liked to know his children better, to be with them more, but Cherish implicitly, sometimes explicitly forbade his "interference."

Dahlia, he knew, had overall charge of the children, as she did of the household. Cherish called Dahlia her maid, explaining "Thorne, you don't call a *nigger* a housekeeper, not in *my* house, you don't!"—but Dahlia was the housekeeper and a great deal more. She told Thorne that when he was away, Cherish hardly saw the children, leaving them with the English nanny or the fluttery, ineffectual Miss Dimity or Dahlia. Miss Dimity, the governess, had nothing to teach them, since the children were now only six and three; on the other hand, she probably couldn't do them any harm. The nanny seemed a good enough, sensible woman, and he would have trusted Dahlia with anything. When he was at home, Cherish alternately spoiled the children shamelessly or punished them in some way. At times, she even managed to do both at the same time. She was constantly at him to spend time with them, give them attention, accusing him of being the same sort of father as Angus. Yet, he had only to look at them, mention them, and her jealousy flared, white-hot and vicious. It was better in the long run, Thorne decided, easier on everyone, if he left them alone, never got to know them well. Besides, he had always seriously doubted his capabilities for being a good father. He had expected to feel something when his children were born, something wonderful and satisfying, but he had felt nothing more than gratitude that the births were over and Cherish's screams of anger or pathos no longer filled the house. He had looked at each baby as Dahlia thrust it into his arms, saying, "No matter what that English nanny says, a man wants to see his babies and hold them." But there had been an absence of feeling. Vaguely, he thought about new life, the perfection that was almost always achieved, a very remarkable thing, but he might have thought that about any baby. Now, with his son six and his daughter three, it was too late. Even if he knew what to do with them, how to make them better, more well-balanced people his influence would have no effect with Cherish close by.

Dahlia opened the front door as he came up the steps. She looked puzzled. "Mr. Thorne, it's good to see you home, but Harry went down to the depot to pick you up with the carriage."

"I guess I missed him," he said. He always avoided the passenger platform and hadn't thought about Harry. He would never quite get accustomed to a carriage, to people bringing him things, picking up what he dropped, often when he would have preferred to have it left alone. He asked Dahlia "Is everything all right here?" as he removed his jacket.

"Yes, sir, pretty good. We've all been busy, getting ready for the big doings tonight."

"Are the kids—"

"Thorne!" cried Cherish, running down the stairs. "My goodness, you're so late, and look at you! Don't you dare kiss me or even touch me. You look like you've rolled in a coal pile. Do hurry and have a bath. There are so many things I need to tell you."

Watching, Dahlia felt renewed heartache for them both. Cherish had said to her recently, in a fit of anger and misery, "Even when we make love, I can feel that a part of him is shutting me out. He hates me as much as I hate him." Dahlia had said, "Honey, won't you try to just—let him be? Maybe then, after a while he'd—" "He'd forget I was alive," Cherish had shrieked. "Oh, leave me alone. Why in the world I talk to you I'll never know."

"Is there anything to eat, Dahlia?" Thorne asked.

"Oh, Thorne, we'll be having a *wonderful* supper tonight. Don't spoil your appetite for it. You haven't even noticed how nice the house looks or anything. *Do* come on upstairs so you can start to get ready."

"I'm starving, Cherish."

"I expect there's still some of that roast beef left from last night," said Dahlia.

Cherish threw her an angry look. All the servants petted Thorne, and he was usually thoughtful and considerate of them, much more so than Cherish considered necessary. She was often embarrassed by his acting as if he were on the same level as they. His attitude toward Dahlia, Dahlia's toward him, was particularly irksome. She had, from time to time, accused them both of an affair. Cherish would never know about the money Thorne had put aside for Dahlia. Shortly after Clare, the little girl, was born, the house had been in a particularly long and rigorous state of upheaval. Thorne had said to Dahlia then, "You're more of a parent to the kids than either of us is, and maybe the best friend either of us has. I want the money to be there, in case you ever decide you've damned well had enough of this."

Now, as Dahlia headed toward the kitchen, Thorne asked, "Could you bring me a sandwich, upstairs?"

"Yessir, I'll get it right away."

Cherish began to chatter as they went upstairs. "I hope you've had a good time, darling, on your trip with those people. They'll all be here tonight of course, but I invited some of the wives for a sort of women's sociable the other night. A few of them seem respectable people, worth associating with. I invited Amy, just because you and Ranald are kin, you know. I never *dreamed* she'd come. I mean, she's pregnant and showing so much. It's an out and out disgrace. So, you can imagine my surprise when I found out she meant to come tonight, with all the men here and everything. I don't understand why she came to Denver in the first place, at such a time. She even brought her three children and Elizabeth."

"It's because they plan to live here. I would have thought you'd find that out, Cherish. They're going to look for a house. Ranald's through traveling between here and Pittsburgh."

"Well, if he had any consideration, he'd have left her and those children somewhere, with her people, maybe, where she could have some peace till the next brat is born."

"Amy didn't want to do that."

"No, I suppose not. She acts like she couldn't exist without Ranald. It's Ranald this and Ranald that, till you wouldn't think she had a brain of her own in her head, and she probably doesn't."

"Was Elizabeth here? I rather hoped you'd ask them all to stay here."

"Thorne, what do you think I *am?* I can't keep up the life I live and look after houseguests like that. I know you don't think I do a thing. This is a slow time of year. *Most* men go somewhere out of town with the families at this time, but I've been busy every minute this week, and there's this dinner and party tonight I've had to get ready for. If Elizabeth and Amy had been staying here, I'd have had them underfoot, needing to be entertained. I certainly wouldn't have wanted the extra children in the house. How long have they been married?—less than six years, isn't it?—and about to produce a fourth one. Well, I suppose that's what comes of being good Catholics. As for Elizabeth, I never have understood why you're so nice and deferential to that mousy old thing. I don't understand, either, of course, why Amy and Ranald have her living with them. But I was talking about my little women's supper party, and I wanted to tell you about Mrs. Baker. She just *loves* this house." Cherish paused as another thought occurred. "Thank God that little snot Nancy went off gallivanting with Fitz. I couldn't have asked her here. It was all I could do to make myself send them an invitation for tonight. It just embarrasses me to death to even think about her."

"There's nothing embarrassing about Nancy. She's Fitz's legal wife."

She flared, "Yes, *you* would say nothing embarrassing. I've seen you looking at her, the little twirp. She wasn't Fitz's legal wife, and you know it, when they started out. She's what—eighteen or nineteen? and he's nearly sixty and crippled like that. You know what she came from, and he's turned soft in the head with age."

Thorne had stopped at his door to face her. She looked pretty standing there in a sprigged muslin housecoat, though her jealously was obvious and ugly. "I know she's going to inherit when Fitz decides to die, which will be a long time coming. That's what really bothers you, isn't it? You and Ted?"

"That's Teddy's money," Cherish said bitterly. "He's got every right to it. And I ought to have something for what I did, coming out here to take care of him, planning his parties and dinners for important people, being his hostess right up till last year, seeing his social things came off right until that little tart . . . Thorne, Ranald is your good friend; Elizabeth will let either of you vote for her at board meetings and things; if Fitz's money came to Ted and me, we could control the company."

"We'd need a good deal more than that," he said and turned. "I'll see the kids for a minute."

"Oh, Thorne, I do wish you'd get ready first. You can abide by those old railroad schedules, do anything in the world to accommodate anybody else, but you're never ready on time for anything at home."

Clare was napping. She was a beautiful child, a small replica of her mother. Stuart was momentarily alone in the cool dim playroom. Thorne sometimes thought that he might have been more drawn to his son if the boy hadn't reminded him so strongly of Angus. Stuart had the same narrow, ascetic face, the same lank, brown hair, the same sharp hazel eyes—

even, it seemed, the same smug, censorious expression. He sat now by a low nursery table with pencil and paper.

Thorne said, after a brief, unenthusiastic greeting from the boy, "You need more light. Stuart. What is it you're drawing?"

"Don't touch the lamp," Cherish cried sharply. "It only makes it hotter in here."

"It's a fox hunt," said Stuart. "Miss Dimity told me about how they used to hunt at Fern Hill and places like that. Those are the people and horses and dogs."

"I see. Where's the fox?"

"I didn't know. I didn't put it in yet, or maybe the dogs already ate it up. Could we go there sometime, to Fern Hill to live?"

Thorne sat on the floor by the low table, trying to ignore Cherish, to talk to the boy, to feel something for him. Stuart told him about going to the park with Miss Dimity. Thorne thought simply "Dim" would have been a fitting name for the empty-headed woman. Something was going to have to be done about the boy's education. Cherish would not let him go to a public school; nor would she send him to boarding school.

Thorne said, trying to be enthusiastic about it, "I drove a train today, all the way down from the mountains."

"You got awful dirty," observed the boy soberly in the drawl he'd picked up from Cherish.

Cherish laughed musically. Thorne got up and went to take his bath. He remembered the time they had talked about the baby before Stuart was born.

The conversation had taken place at the small hotel on the San Miguel line, perhaps two weeks after Dahlia had told him a child was expected. Thorne, tired as usual, was trying to compile a list for a rush order of materials. Cherish had begun with a plaint about loneliness.

"*Why* won't you come here and spend a little time with me? Sometimes I think I'll lose my mind with nobody to talk to . . ."

"I can't come here because it's so far from where we're working. I have to be at work at daylight as long as the weather holds."

"I don't see *why* you have to be at work at daylight. Are you, or aren't you the boss?"

He looked back at his papers. "I am; that's why I have to be there. I've wondered all summer why you don't try going to church or something like that. You could meet some people. There must be other women around."

"Good lord, they're trash! Why should I want to meet the people around *here?* You won't understand anything. You don't even try. Oh, I'd give the world to be back at Fern Hill."

"That could be arranged," he said absently, biting his pencil and frowning at a column of figures.

Cherish was furious at his casualness, but she tried for a moment not to let it show and changed the subject.

"What are those old papers, Thorne? Haven't you got any—clerks or whatever it takes? I don't see why you have to do them."

"These are things I need for an order that has to be made tomorrow. It's faster to do it myself than to try to tell some else how to do it."

"Oh, you can always talk about work things," she burst out. "Never about anything that interests *me.* Would you honestly just not care if I was as far as Fern Hill when your baby's born? Would you have it born in a place like this?"

"Cherish, we'll be back in Denver inside a month. The weather's going to shut us down any day now. The baby isn't due until next March."

She went to him then, pushed papers onto the floor, and snuggled on his lap.

"Thorne, if the baby's a boy, I want to name him for both Mama's and Daddy's families. Oh, they were such fine families! Two of the most respected in Virginia, right up there with the Jeffersons and the Lees. If it's a girl, I want to name her Jane Clare; Jane for Mama, and Clare for Daddy's mother. There's a story, you know, that Daddy's branch of the Stuart family is descended directly from Bonnie Prince Charlie and Flora MacDonald."

Thorne grinned. "Come on, Cherish. Those two were only together with Flora's family and in the boat going over to Skye, maybe. Uncle Gavin comes from Scotland, remember? We were raised on stories about Bonnie Charlie. Everybody named Stuart claims what you've just said, those named MacDonald too, for all I know. Charlie and Flora didn't get the chance to start a baby."

"Oh, what do *you* know?" she fumed, stiff now in his arms.

"Well, but if they did, it would have been a bastard. It would have been named MacDonald. I know they didn't marry. Or maybe they would have called it FitzStuart. Fitzroy means king's bastard, but surely the illustrious Stuarts of Virginia didn't start like that."

She jerked away and stood glaring at him. "I suppose you think the MacWinters, what you believed yourself to be, are something special. What does MacWinter mean? Nothing, that's what."

"I don't know what Winter means—what it meant when someone took it as a name. Mac just means son of . . . son of Winter . . ."

"Oh, I don't *care* about that. You'd have happily remained one of that brood and never have taken the rights and responsibilities coming to you. What do you know about good family? family pride? It's just that you have to tear down anything that's the least little bit important to me. I *will* name a boy for those families, and there's not a thing you can do to make it seem shabby. Mama's people, the Bromleighs, were very prominent too. Stuart Bromleigh Maxwell."

She didn't miss the fact that he winced slightly. Being reminded that his name was Maxwell could still do that to him.

"Why do you mind, darling?" she said sweetly. "You're the grandson and nephew of an earl. The Maxwell family has held that land in Scotland for nearly two hundred years. One of them was once married to a king's sister, I forget which king. And the Thornes, your grandmother's people that you look like, had a duke. I think it was your grandmother's aunt that married a duke of Suffolk."

"How do you know those things?" he asked curiously. "I never heard about them."

"Well, of course you didn't. Angus said he wanted to tell you things about the family, give you books to read, but you wouldn't listen to anything. He told me that time he came to see me in Pittsburgh, when he told me about his will and that he hoped we'd marry."

Thorne picked up the papers from the floor. He wrote down a figure, knowing it was wrong, erased it and began over. How much did the dead know, he wondered, about people who went on living? Was Angus pleased about the marriage? God knows, he'd never been pleased with anything else.

Now, as Thorne finished his bath and began to shave, Cherish tapped on the door, urging him to hurry. He could feel his nerves, his muscles tightening as they always did.

Cherish began talking as soon as he came from the bathroom. She had slipped out of her housecoat and was in lacy underclothes.

"I was about to dress," she said archly, "but then

I decided you might want company. You haven't been at home for more than one night in over two months. Do you realize that? Or do you care? Oh, Thorne, *why* won't you just work in the office so you can be home and have a job that the children and I can be proud of?"

The beef sandwich and a glass of milk that Dahlia had brought were on a small table. Thorne picked up the newspaper Dahlia had placed on his chair, sat down and began to eat.

He said, "There's a troupe of pipers playing at the Sheridan auditorium tonight. I'd like to hear them."

"Oh, for heaven's sake," she said scornfully. "Last time it was Spanish dancers you wanted to see, but will you ever go with me to a ballet or concert or opera? No, indeed! You have the tastes of a—well, I don't even *know* what. Will you *please*, for the lord's sake, stop reading that paper? You can't say two words to me."

He let the newspaper drop.

"I suppose you'll be leaving again soon?"

"The middle of next week."

"I suppose with Ranald living here, you'll spend even less time at home."

Thorne looked at the dress clothes that had been laid out for him, frowning. "I don't see why all this is necessary, Cherish. I mean, I suppose we have to entertain the damned directors somehow, but couldn't we just have a picnic outside or something? It's what a lot of people do on the Fourth of July. It's so damned hot."

"It is too hot!" she cried fiercely, "and I have *slaved* over this house, Thorne Maxwell, to see everything about the house was just right, bought food that would make an impression on those easterners who've come all the way out here to the middle of nowhere. You walk in and act like there was no point in any of it. I'm *trying* to help your business interests. You want that stupid railroad track to go to that stupid Peapot, don't you?"

"Beanpot," he said mildly.

"Oh, just shut up. I don't care what it is. You never appreciate anything, especially not if it's something *I* do. You are the most selfish, thoughtless, ungrateful. . . ."

"I'm sorry," he said quietly, unexpectedly. "It's just that I wish I didn't have to put on those clothes and go through an evening with a lot of people in the house, especially some of those people."

She came to him slowly and ran her fingers over his bare shoulders and back. "You don't have to put the clothes on immediately."

"This is certainly quite a house," said Ranald, finding Thorne alone in his study.

"You've said that before."

"It's not exactly gracious to remind me."

"You're not being gracious when you say it. You look at it just about the way I do, I think. Sit down if you like. I have never learned to like parties. If I see much more of Mr. Baker and a couple of those others . . . He asked me, Baker, if newspapers still reach us by coming round the Horn on ships, for God's sake. How did the idiot get here himself? Doesn't he know railroads have been transcontinental for some time now? What the hell is he doing as a board member?"

"Be calm," Ranald said, grinning sympathetically. "Mr. Baker is the proverbial pain, but he knows about steel mills. They've had a good time out here, you know, with the scenery, the excitement and anticipation of a possible Indian raid."

"Well, I wish they were off the board. People who have anything to do with decision-making ought to know not only the business they're dealing with, but the country where it is, and the kind of people who work in it."

"You're right," Ranald said, "and there's an election coming up after the first of the year. I may have said this before, but you're doing a grand job. Peter Maitland said to me that he really didn't believe the last report until he went on this trip and saw things for himself. You're doing a grand job, and you're working too hard. You have done, most of your life. I wonder if you *can* relax now."

"Are they going to go for the Beanpot line?"

"Most of them are, I think. At least—they were until that little—thing with the train, coming down. We didn't know, back there in the board members' coach, that you were playing engineer, until the conductor came back and told us. He was kind of greenish and Fitz—"

Thorne burst into a laugh. "He must have been madder than hell."

"Well, he was a little—put out, but he didn't give you away. He said to them, pretty coolly, that since ours wasn't a regularly scheduled train, we naturally had to give right-of-way and that you had 'hurried a bit' to get on the siding."

They were both laughing and Ranald went on. "The conductor kept trying to say something to set Fitz straight until he gave him a look that would have killed two normal men. The conductor shut up then, but the red of absolute fury hadn't all gone out of Fitz's face even when we got into the station. I got the idea he had something to say to you."

"I've spoken to him a couple of times tonight," Thorne said, wondering about it. "He didn't even mention the train. He looked sort of—bemused. Do you want a drink?"

As he poured two, he noticed that the small orchestra, near the closed study door, was playing:

"The joys of love are but a moment long. The pain of love endures the whole life long."

He said, "So you're here to stay?"

"We are, said Ranald, sighing. "Amy tells me she found a house she likes. She and Elizabeth and I will be damned glad to get into it, all of us together and finally settled down. The baby's due in less than a month and Amy's about worn out, but we're finally where we've been trying to get for all this time. If it hadn't been for Elizabeth, especially this summer, I don't know what Amy would have done. Our boys are not bad kids, but they're damned lively. I thought maybe it wouldn't work out when Amy started talking about asking her to live with us, but it's been great. She never—well, intrudes, yet she seems like one of the family. The boys call her Grand Maxwell, you know. So Amy was right; she mostly is. . . . Anyway, I think everyone's convinced now that the real future for MM&F is here, in the West, in Colorado. God, I'm glad to be back and to know I don't have to be travelling anymore. I don't see how you keep up the kind of pace you do. The railroad's practically carrying everything else—I'm sure you know that—until we can get the mines and mill out here into full operation."

"Don't depend on it for too long," Thorne said, lighting a cigarette. "A good deal of our freight is to and from silver mining areas, and God knows when or what the government's going to do to silver. If the bottom is knocked out of prices, those places will clear, be ghost towns in about three days. Shutting down one line wouldn't hurt us much. That's going to happen, running into so many boom towns. It already has happened, but we've got three branch lines that are there for silver."

"Somebody told me the gold they've brought out of Beanpot is assaying more to the ton than almost any that's been found in this country."

"I told you that. It's true. And they can't half operate

up there with nothing but freight wagons to do their hauling."

Ranald nodded, grinning. "We have to do what we can to help the poor souls out."

Thorne held up his almost-empty glass in a toast. "Let's drink," he said, "to two philanthropists together!"

They sat a few moments in smiling, contented silence, the sounds of talk and laughter elsewhere in the house seeming louder.

Thorne said, "They couldn't have found that gold in a more out of the way place. You saw the wagon road and the rail route. Everything we do on that line will be hard."

Ranald took out his pipe and began the ritual of filling it. "Does it ever occur to you that we sometimes seem like a couple of staid old businessmen? It's kind of a shock. Inside, I don't see myself as all that different from what I was when we first left the hacienda. But once in a while I get to thinking . . . then you do a damn' fool thing like with that train today. Those workmen, if not the directors, know you're daft now. I never doubted it. I thought you'd got over doing wild things, but then I haven't been with you much for a lot of years. You know that you could have killed about fifty people. It's the kind of thing you would have done when we were kids, if anybody'd been crazy enough to let you get hold of a train."

"I know," Thorne said sheepishly. "It's the stupidest thing I've done in a long time. But nobody was killed. Suppose we had been wiped out, the whole goddamn' board of directors of MM&F. Do you think it would have made any real difference in the world? If it had been like that, Cherish and Amy and the other women might be holding a meeting right now, trying to decide about running a road to Beanpot."

"You always did have a weird sense of humor."

"I wasn't really trying to be funny. It wouldn't have caused the earth to shift in its course. Still, there were *innocent* people on that train, and the other one."

"You're still not having any union trouble?"

"Very little, though it'll come. Fitz doesn't think so but he just won't face facts about unions. Our wages and working conditions are better than average, though, in some instances that isn't saying a great deal. Our best construction boss, Fitz's father-in-law, Tom Murphy, is death on unions. He can smell an organizer a mile down the line. There are a few others like that working for us, but the right organizer will come along one day, get enough people excited."

"You don't mind? I mean, Fitz gets so upset."

"I won't like it when it comes, but what I like, or whether or not I get upset isn't going to change the course of the world either. I don't see what's to be done about something that seems to be inevitable. I don't think it will happen for a while though."

"How long?"

He frowned. "Well—five or six years. That's not much time, is it? when you measure it in the things that get done."

There was a silence, then Ranald snapped his fingers, remembering something.

"Have you got maps here? for Beanpot? There's something I've wanted to ask you since we rode the route."

Thorne spread a map on the desk, looking eager.

Ranald studied the map. "Right here, where the canyon makes this sharp bend. As I remember, there's the shelf along there, above the stream, but I don't see how you're aiming to make that turn. It looked to me like the side of the canyon there was about five hundred feet high and pretty much sheer. That's a lot of rock to blast if you tried to make a curve you could use. Will there be a tunnel or what? You didn't say anything when we were there."

Thorne watched him soberly. "We can't blast, not much, nor tunnel. That shelf is something God almighty must have put there just for trains to run on. It's an old stream bottom, before the water cut down beside it while the old bottom was gradually being pushed up. Now it's just there, waiting for somebody to lay rails. There's almost six miles of it like that, running almost evenly at a two percent grade. A few places, we'll have to widen it a little. When I came on it, I thought I'd died and gone to heaven—till I got to the curve here. This face, this rock cliff along here, is unstable inside. We've done core samples. It's something like that up at Perry Tunnel where Fitz was hurt. The outside is safe enough, that's why it's still there, but when you go in a few feet, it's rotten. If we blasted, we'd get water, deteriorated rock, all kinds of slippage and I don't know what else. If we blasted in there and got the line through, it would be shut down more than it would be open, because of slides."

"Well, what then? A trestle running along with the creek? Even I can see there's not room for a curve like you'd need and what would you do about getting to a trestle? How far is that above the creek?"

"It's fifty-seven feet, just there. I don't want to build a trestle up that much, and I don't want to lose the height by going down to a trestle. I want to put a turntable in, a stationary turntable, just on the point. It would give us, almost exactly, the minimum radius for a narrow-gauge curve."

Ranald stared at him. "God, where did you get the idea for that? I've never heard of anyone doing that."

"No one has, that I know of, but there's no reason why it can't be done. Fitz says not. He gets madder than hell every time he thinks about it. Just ask him some time. He made me swear, before the eastern directors came, that I wouldn't mention it and I haven't. But, hell, turntables are for turning. We can get solid anchorage for the base in the stream bed, leaving plenty of spaces for flow. There'll be less area that way, for floods to work on than there would be with a trestle."

"You'd just have the trains swing out, over—nothing?"

"Well, yes, but that's what's done with them on bridges and trestles and fills. This isn't even high, compared to a lot of things, fifty-seven feet."

Ranald said quietly and with admiration, "I always knew you were revolutionary but I wasn't thinking of the word exactly in this sense. I'm sure as hell no engineer, but it seems to me it would work.

"If we don't do that," Thorne said earnestly, "I don't see, for several reasons, how we're going to come up Aspen Creek with the line at all. If we don't use Aspen Creek, we've got Ten Mile over here, but it's got some impossible things in its favor, and would add thirty miles. If we couldn't use Ten Mile, we'd have to come up from the Arkansas and I'm damned if I'll do that."

"You say the idea makes Fitz mad? Why is that?"

Thorne grinned. "Mad is not the right word, really, he gets more like wild. But I've talked about it with several people who know about things like building railroads. One is Mr. Brenner, who was chief engineer on several of our lines before he retired. One of the partners in his firm rode through there once with me to have a look. They think it ought to work fine, though they don't know that they'd do it if it was their job. It's just that it hasn't been tried yet and not many people would want to take the responsibility. Fitz gets mad because it hasn't been done and, mostly, because he didn't think of it."

Their eyes met and they smiled. Thorne poured more whiskey.

After a time Ranald said, "We haven't had a real chance for talking. Thorne, how is it with you and . . . Are you all right?"

Thorne still smiled. "I guess I don't understand,"

he said, looking down at the map he was folding.

"You know, surely, that I've always felt closer to you than to any of my brothers. You stopped being happy when we went to live in Pittsburgh. I think you still haven't—started again."

He put the map away. "I like the work, most of it."

"But—" Ranald prompted, watching him.

"But nothing, Ran. Are you out of tobacco? Try this."

"Thanks. As soon as we're settled, with the new baby and all, I want to go home for a few days. Do you think you might be able to arrange things so you could get away and come along?"

"No. I don't see how I could."

"Papa isn't at all well, hasn't been for some time. Do you hear from them?"

"Not often. I haven't had time to keep up with correspondence these past eight or nine years. After Fitz was hurt, you know. . . ."

"They don't understand, Mama and Papa, and neither do I. They truly couldn't help what happened. They couldn't have stopped Angus—"

"I know that, Ran. It's a long time past."

"They want to see you. Times, before Jeanie and her family moved away, they wanted to visit you here then, but you weren't in town."

"I'd like to have seen them," he said quietly. "I don't know that they could have come here. Cherish is not—well, once when I saw Jean, I asked her to let me know when they came, but you're right, I wasn't here at the right time."

"Do you mean never to go back? If you do, I think it would be fair to let them know that. At least it could be a certainty then."

There was a knock at the door. Thorne went to open it, held it while Fitz rolled his wheelchair in.

"I thought I'd find you two off together someplace. The womenfolks is frettin'. A couple of young ones like you ought to be out there dancin'. But pour us all a drink, Thorne. I want to make a toast. Can't make it general for all the party—might embarrass some. It's funny, ain't it, when you think about it, the things that embarrasses some folks? Here's to my new son, due to be born in December." Fitz looked shy and proud. "It's kind of like a miracle for me an' little Nancy. Grandson of a rock farmer an' a construction boss. *This* one will be a railroad man. If I'm not here, you boys are to see to it."

They drank with him, smiling, giving congratulations.

Thorne said innocently, "He'll be able to see, I guess, the varied uses of turntables and such."

"Jesus Christ," Fitz spluttered. "You're goin' to cause me a stroke if you keep on about that goddamn turntable. What I really come lookin' for you is to ask you what in the bloody hell you meant today, playin' with that train? Chrissake, you oughtn't even be let to have a job as engine wiper."

XII

1890

Thorne walked along the track, clean clothes over his arm. It was near five in the afternoon; the August heat shimmered in merciless waves between ground and sky. Storm clouds above far mountain peaks looked promising. He had been taking part in the final work of getting rails into Columbia Creek, a copper mining town in Montana. Columbia Creek was a shorter, far less challenging road than the one to Beanpot, completed two years ago; but Columbia Creek, too, was *his* road. He had just seen a locomotive with a few boxcars of priority freight, for which people had been waiting, draw up to the platform of the unfinished depot in Columbia Creek. It was a satisfying thing. In a few days, there would be a big celebration, the official opening of the road, but he would be gone by then, glad to miss it. There had been a serious freight derailment on the main line in Utah, something that required construction for temporary rerouting; he needed to look into how that was going.

Intermountain's main line reached into three states, and they had short lines in two others. Thorne's name, in gold leaf, was on an office door in the fine new Maitland Building in Denver, but he was there as little as possible. Jim Ritter handled a great deal of his office work; that which Thorne absolutely had to do himself followed his official car, where he ate and slept more than in any place not on wheels. He always spent more time than he could afford on new construction—it was the part of his job in which he took real satisfaction—but the paperwork piled up. Well, he thought philosophically, no one can do everything, be all things to all people. The Beanpot road was his real pride, but Columbia Creek was nothing of which to be ashamed. In the winter, he would be thirty-five years old. Everyone ought to have something by that age which was more or less *his* creation, something that belonged to him more than to anyone else.

The town of Columbia Creek, jammed and rowdy, filled a narrow little valley between the steep hills containing the mines. The railroad's work camp was a few miles below the town. There was a water tank and the siding on which the work cars were parked. There would be a small yard here eventually; there was not room for it in the town. The construction hands usually cleaned themselves up under the water tank, but Thorne passed it by now as being too much trouble for one man alone. The crews would not be back for a half hour or so. Fred Morley, the clerk who often traveled with Thorne, had his fingernails chewed to the elbows over the paperwork. Thorne meant to take care of some of it today. He went to the small dam, which by way of a flume fed the water tank, and stripped off his sweaty clothes in the shelter of some willows. He gasped painfully as the icy water came up around him, but it was, at least, a way to get respite from the flies, mosquitoes and other similar creatures he did not care to identify.

He wondered, scrubbing at his hair, if he could ever stop missing Fitz. Fitz had died two years ago, quickly—painlessly, they said—of a stroke. Fitz's second son had been born on Thorne's birthday in 1886 and before Fitz died, all through that summer of 1888 when they were completing the Beanpot line, Fitz, Nancy, and the little boy had been in the work camp, in his private car, just like old times. Rather in spite of himself, Fitz had developed tremendous interest and excitement over the road, with all its difficulties. Thorne had spent all the time he could with Fitz then, portentously convinced that there was not going to be much more time with him. He ate Nancy's suppers, detailed the work for Fitz, and played with the little boy. He felt more closeness to Fitz's son than he would ever know for his own children.

This summer, he had tried again, albeit half-heartedly, to get to know his own Stuart. He had brought the boy, ten now, to the Columbia Creek workings for a few weeks. First, there had been a major battle with Cherish and Stuart's interest, his wish to come, had not really merited it. Remembering Fitz, dragging his first son Ted around, summers and how little it had accomplished, Thorne did not try to force Stuart's interest in the work or the country, though he had hoped the boy would find some pleasure in being out of the city, having opportunities different from those of other summers. Stuart had spent practically all his time inside Thorne's car, reading, complaining of heat and boredom, wanting to go home. Thorne let him go, two weeks before he had meant to. There was no point in prolonging the frustration and exasperation for both of them.

He stood in the sun to dry, shivering at first, but he had walked back to his car, sweat was running again on his body, evaporating as soon as the air touched it; his hair was drying with disappointing speed and he was very thirsty. He looked hopefully at the clouds, saw a javelin of lightning, maybe even streaks of rain, lancing down to one of the peaks.

"I've been looking for you," said Ted Fitzroy peevishly as he stepped from the shade of a supply shed. "Morley said—"

"Hello, Ted," Thorne said, perfunctorily shaking the proffered hand. Thorne was not much of a hand shaker and he knew why Ted had come, the only reason he ever saw Ted now. "Hold on just a minute, will you? Let me get rid of these dirty clothes."

He went up the catwalk to his car, leaving Ted scowling. The inside of the car was stifling.

"*More* dirty stuff," observed Silas, who looked after Thorne and Fred Morley and the car. "I swear you git dirtier'n any of them others. Don't seem to me like a boss—"

"What's for supper, Silas?"

"Well, sir, you said I didn' have to cook nothin' tonight. Said you was goin' over to Mr. Murphy's an' me an' Mr. Morley could eat with the rest. I thought—"

"You're right," Thorne said. "I forgot." He turned

and called through to Morley, "Bring some of that stuff outside, Fred. It's too goddamn' hot in here to do anything."

Ted was looking more irritable. He followed Thorne to the shade of a cottonwood, where Thorne sat down on the ground, then lay back, his hands behind his head. He was very tired. A breeze was springing up whimsically from the direction of the thunderstorm; the outdoor shade had a welcome coolness, and the insects were not so bad here. Silas brought out two chairs. Ted took one of them. Thorne, not getting up, told him a little about the progress of the work. He knew Ted wasn't interested, was frustrated by the delays, but Ted damned well ought to be frustrated. Silas brought another chair and a small folding table, placing them at a little distance for Fred Morley, who came down the catwalk frowning, looking at the papers he carried, protecting them against the whims of the breeze.

Ted did not look like Fitz at all. Like Cherish, he was blond, with a fine complexion that could never take the sun. Features that made Cherish a softly beautiful woman left Ted looking weak and childish. Nobody, including Ted, knew what he ought to do with himself. His preferences were for traveling, sipping vintage wines, briefly knowing pretty women, gambling. He had had the use of a private car for some time now, but it rarely ran on Intermountain rails. Ted had always been petulant, with tendencies toward impulsiveness and drifting. These facets of his character had been more apparent since Fitz's will was made public.

Fitz had left a quarter of his assets to Ted, and Fern Hill to Cherish. Thorne had received another quarter of Fitz's interest in MM&F. The rest—half his interests in the company and everything else he owned—had gone to Nancy and little Murphy; the income being more than sufficient to provide for their needs, the capital in trust for Murphy when the boy should reach twenty-five. Thorne and one of the company's lawyers were executors of the trust. Ted had never liked Thorne. Once the will was read, he hated him.

"When did you get here?" Thorne asked him casually.

"I've been here since last night," Ted said angrily. "I had to leave my own car down on the standard gauge, naturally. I got a room in Columbia Creek, finally. I've been trying to talk to you all day."

"I wouldn't have thought I'd be hard to find."

"Well, I don't fancy trying to carry on an intelligent conversation in the middle of a work gang," Ted said petulantly. Then with a little smile, "Really, I didn't get around to looking for you last evening. I came up on the stage, since the railroad didn't seem to be running anything, had dinner at the Copper King Hotel. Then I found a little game and some other entertainment that wasn't too bad, considering this is the backside of nothing. I made the acquaintance of a man named Parsons, rather a civilized fellow."

"I hope you won something from him," Thorne said grimly. "He owns the freighting business up here, and his people dynamited a bridge of ours. It cost several weeks' work."

"I won," Ted said complacently. "He had some things to say about the railroad, about you in particular. Are you taking him to court?"

"There's nothing we could prove, not anything that would stand up in a court of law."

"You're just going to let people get away with such things?"

"Some things are inevitable, Ted. If you fight the inevitable, you're selling yourself out. So—I suppose you're just passing through?"

"I want to go to St. Paul from here. A friend of mine, a fellow I went to school with, has invited me to see Minnesota, in my car, of course. It doesn't sound particularly exciting, but things slow down everywhere this time of year. Do you realize, by the way, the exorbitant rates the other roads charge me for moving that car around? Why can't it be a matter of exchange, the way it used to be?"

Thorne sat up to roll a cigarette and to throw Fred Morley a sympathetic look, indicating that he didn't want this delay any more than Fred did. He lit the cigarette and lay back again.

"Because the Interstate Commerce Commission has said we can't do the exchanges anymore. As far as I've been able to find out, they're another inevitability, the Commission."

"But it's a ridiculous expense, and it's not as if the trains aren't going anyway. I might save money by buying my own locomotive."

"That's a thought," Thorne said dryly. "Anyway, we'd never repay your mileage in exchanges, not the way you've been traveling since you got out of school. You must know the country pretty well."

Ted frowned with distaste. "I'd have preferred to do most of my traveling in Europe, as you well know."

Thorne drew deeply on his cigarette and looked up at the bright sky through the cool thickness of cottonwood leaves.

"I've just come from Denver," Ted said sullenly. "Cherish sent you a message. She said you ought to come home now and then. She's right, of course. You're a disgrace as a family man."

"Is that what you came up here to tell me?"

"Not chiefly, but she is my sister. I've always been fond of her. I never have understood why you married her. You've certainly given her no sort of decent life. Yet she tells me she cares for you. Why don't—"

"Ted, suppose you just stick to your own business. I'm sure you've got some. You didn't take this detour to look after your sister's welfare. If that turned out to be the case, it would shock hell out of me. I've got to go to work. What is it you want?"

"Don't you dare just to try to—brush me off," Ted said fiercely. "I'm going to sell some stock. That's the chief reason for my coming all this way. I thought it was just barely possible that you'd appreciate knowing about it."

"I can't buy it. You know I've never got much cash. You should have talked to Ranald, or Peter."

"Of course I know you don't have cash. You always put so much back into the company that my sister doesn't even have enough money to run her household or bring up your children properly."

"That's not true," Thorne said mildly. His equanimity was making Ted furious.

"She's had some extra expenses for Fern Hill," he said righteously. "When she and I were down there in the spring, it was obvious quite a lot had to be done in the way of maintenance."

"Maintaining that plantation mansion for the honor of the long-gone Stuarts and Bromleighs, and so that you or Cherish can stay there for a month every year or two, is not my idea of a good business investment. But if Cherish takes money from her household account for Fern Hill, that's her business."

"I didn't offer my stock to Ranald MacWinter," Ted said peevishly. "Peter Maitland was out of town. Ranald bought some shares from me last winter and I had to listen to a lecture about holding onto them. It's none of his business what I do. I'll put them on the market before offering anything to him again."

"Well, you know, Ted, if you'd held onto all that you had in the first place, it would have provided you with what seems to me like a pretty comfortable income. Once you start dipping into capital, though, the income drops off and I would imagine that the way you've been going, you're just about scraping the bottom of the barrel now. I don't have any lectures for you. You're a fool, but I think you've at least got the sense to know it. If you need money, and you always need money, why in hell don't you go to work?"

"I was never cut out for—*this*," Ted said coldly with a scornful gesture that took in the work camp.

"Then find work in some other part of the company. God knows, I'd rather not have to work with you. All of us feel a little—responsible for you, only because of what Fitz meant to us. Your business administration degree ought to qualify you for several office jobs in Denver, if you'd bother learning them. At least then you'd have a regular salary to supplement your frequent stock sales. If Fitz were alive, you wouldn't be—"

"Oh, don't play father, Thorne. You've hardly had enough experience to qualify. Neither did Fitz. You're right, if he were alive, I probably wouldn't be traveling around in my own private car, trying to enjoy myself. He never thought enjoyment could come from anything but scrabbling for more work. You're very much like him. You recognize nothing but work. You're wasting my sister's life . . . but don't try to set me straight. Spare me that. Your straight and mine are quite different, as you surely recognize. Besides, you do owe me a great deal."

Thorne sat up and looked at him, widening his eyes. "I do? I must have missed something important somewhere along the way."

"You know very well that you own or are handling money that should have been mine, you and that—strumpet, with her brat."

"Yes. Well, Ted, we've been over this before—several times. I really haven't got the time now to—"

Ted took a deep breath. "My father opened up this country for the company, taught you everything you know, but *I* carry the Fitzroy name. There's no one else to—"

"There's Murphy," Thorne said quietly, "and his

mother. God, Ted, if you're proud of the name, of what Fitz did, I've never seen any indication of it. Fitz knew you'd run through the money. Maybe he didn't dream it could happen quite this fast, but he knew."

"How I carry my name is my business. Save your concern for your own."

"Oh, I'm not concerned about you," Thorne said coldly. "I don't give a damn about you, except that you're taking my time to—"

"I've heard," Ted said mockingly, "that he asked you to look after us when he was dying, and that 'us' even included me."

Thorne said nothing.

"Well," Ted drawled, "that sort of discussion really has no point, has it? except that he was my father—not yours. You're a fine one to tell somebody else about respect for his father and for his proud name."

Thorne simply looked at him coldly.

"At any rate," said Ted, his face flushing with anger at his own uneasiness, "my father was senile when he made that will. There was," he smirked, "—undue influence from that redhaired bitch, and his doting on that kid, who both Cherish and I have always suspected is yours."

Thorne stood up in a single easy motion. "I still don't know exactly why you came up here, Ted, but I have to get to the paperwork."

"I didn't suppose you'd want those shares sold, especially not on the open market."

"It looks as if there's not much I can do about it."

"You might want to consider a loan. Five thousand dollars right now would—"

"You've just told me you know all about my personal financial position. I'm subsidizing Fern Hill. We both know that if it weren't for that, if Cherish could have laid her hands on five thousand dollars, you wouldn't be here. I won't subsidize you, and I'll see there's not money enough for Cherish to do much along those lines. You'll have all your MM&F stock sold soon. Then you can damn well go to work; or not go to work, just as you like, I guess it doesn't take a hell of a long time to starve to death."

Ted turned abruptly maudlin. "Thorne, you were around a lot of the time. You know the kind of father Fitz was, the lousy kind of life I had, going back and forth between my parents or to some school where no one cared—"

"For god's sake, Teddy, don't whine. Yes, I do know. And I know that you've reached your legal majority. What are you—twenty-three? I can't tell you how glad I am that you were past twenty-one when Fitz died. He planned to make me your guardian if you weren't. You're supposedly old enough now to take responsibility for yourself. Don't blame Fitz or your mother or some school or me, for what you are or what you're doing. Growing up should mean taking charge of yourself."

Ted scrambled to his feet, glaring. "Goddamn you, you bastard! I didn't come here to listen to some hypocritical—I could gladly kill you."

"It wouldn't really help, Ted. It wouldn't change a thing, not for you."

"If it weren't for you—and that woman—and child . . ."

"That would be a lot of people to eliminate," Thorne said calmly and walked away from him toward Fred Morley who was waving a report at Thorne.

The trouble was, Thorne thought, angrily scanning papers, he was concerned about Ted. He had never liked him, but nothing could change the fact that Ted was Fitz's son. Fitz had counted on that, and knowledge of that made Thorne more impatient with the boy, more committed to seeing he didn't starve. He resented many of the things that Fitz and others had expected of him, but that made him feel no less responsible.

After an hour or so, Thorne had given Morley enough dictation to keep him busy for several hours. Thorne would do more himself, would probably stay up all night to get caught up with the paperwork; he felt an urgency about it, a compulsion to clear it up. He often worked at night because he had such trouble sleeping. Tomorrow, or perhaps the day after, he and Morley would leave for an inspection of the two Idaho short lines.

Thorne walked slowly toward the end of the siding where Tom Murphy's car stood. Nancy, lonely and a little bewildered, had come along with her father this summer, she and small Murphy. Tom was glad of her care and cooking. The crews were in camp now. Several men yelled and splashed under an icy shower from the water tank. The self-contained little village of cars was at the height of its evening bustle. The storm Thorne had seen in the distance had broken up or moved on, but other promising-looking clouds sped across the low sun, driven by strong upper winds.

"Thorne!" a child's voice screeched after him from the water tank. The little boy came running, a towel flapping inadequately around him.

"Hello, Frank Murphy Fitzroy," Thorne said, grinning, feeling the lift of pleasure that could come simply from thinking of the child. "And what have you done with yourself today?"

"I just had my bath, with Grandpa and the men. I'm cold now."

Murphy was not four yet, but he had begun to talk remarkably early. His blue eyes were sober and very intelligent, and his hair resembled the rather faded strawberry color Fitz's had once been. He was built like Fitz, small and wiry; he had Fitz's roundish, freckled, rather homely face. Thorne loved him, wondering, perhaps for the thousandth time, as he bent to wrap Murphy's towel more securely, why he could feel nothing for his own children. Granted, there were valid outside reasons, chiefly Cherish's interference, but what about inside—within himself? Love had welled up in him the first time he held Murph. The sturdy infant had laughed up at him then, drooling a little, and Fitz had beamed with smug delight.

"Didn't you have some shoes, Murph?"

"I left everything so I could hurry. I wanted to walk with you. Maybe Grandpa won't forget them."

"The gravel hurts, doesn't it?"

"Not me. I'm tough, Thorne. Are you going to eat with us? Before it was time to take a bath, I went with Grandpa and some others on a handcar to Columbia Creek. They have candy in a store there that came up on our train. Did you see the train?"

"I did. Did you get some candy?"

Murphy giggled. "It's under my bed, the part I couldn't eat yet."

"Well, Murph, the big job's just about over, isn't it?"

He looked somber. "Do you have to go someplace?"

"Yes, but not tonight."

"I don't want you to go, and I don't want us to live back in town. I don't ever want to be at Denver. In a few days, we can get a puppy. Did you know that? Mr. Willis's dog had seven puppies and I get to have one. I named him already. His name is Spike. He's a railroad dog."

During supper, Tom Murphy, looking uneasy, said, "Well, my gang'll be through here in less than a month. There 's the sidings to finish and such, but it won't be long. Where do we go from here?"

Cutting his steak, Thorne said, "That bridge in Utah has to be finished properly. After that, I don't quite know, Tom. There's no new construction to start on. It's not that long until winter anyway."

"You haven't bid anything?"

"There was another short line, just over the big ridge from here, but they've decided to hold off on it.

They're not taking bids. Things are pretty tight."

"Some say there'll be another money crash," Tom said with concern.

"Some are sure of it," Thorne agreed grimly. "Investors are hanging onto their money tighter every day now. I'd like to see some rerouting work done on the San Miguel line this year, but the others won't go for it, not until they see how other things are going to fall out. I've been thinking, Tom, that with no new work, we might just call your crew troubleshooters, keep them on that way."

"Well, I've mostly worked new construction for a lot of years," said the old man dubiously, but he was pleased, gratified that Thorne had been thinking of him and his men, planning so that they would not be laid off. People could say what they liked, Tom thought, about this man's conduct of his family life and of formal business; if a man was willing to work for Thorne Maxwell he would be looked after.

"What I was thinking of is a gang that can handle special problems well, like the Darby Bridge in Utah, replacing all the tunnel shoring, which we've got to do soon on the road to Amity. You'd be moving, probably more than you do now. But you know that some of our section gangs in the high country can't handle half the work they have, especially in winter. You'd be called on, sometimes, to help clear wrecks, bad ones, to get the line open as quickly as possible. It might not be a pleasant job and it would never be easy."

Tom snorted. "I don't think I've ever had a reputation for looking for the easy jobs. Who would I be responsible to? I wouldn't want some kid of a section foreman—"

"When your special crew was needed, you'd take charge of whatever section you were working on, be responsible only to me, or to Jim Ritter if you couldn't get in touch with me."

"Ritter? What does he know about construction and repair? I can't think of one job he's come out on."

"He knows a lot, Tom. It's because he stays in the office that I can be out on jobs."

"Knowing on paper and knowing on the site are whole different things," Tom said dubiously. "But you're the boss. One thing though, I'd have no union sympathizers."

Thorne took a slice of bread from the plate Nancy offered, absently smiling at her in thanks.

"You may have to one day, Tom," he said soberly. "The unions can't be all bad. The time will come, I think, when we can't get good people to work for us unless we take at least some union men. We can't be the only railroad in the country holding out against them. They're going to come, you know, and it won't matter how you or I feel about it."

"I don't see why in hell they should. This is a fair company to work for. All unions could do with it is make a mess, with their eternal rules and regulations and strikes."

Thorne thought sadly that Tom sounded a little querulous, that he was getting old and would follow Fiz long before he, Thorne, would be willing to let him go. Tom Murphy was still the best construction boss he had ever seen, never flinching from responsibility, able to think for himself and not make many demands on the engineers and supervisors.

Thorne said, "Would you want us to go into this troubleshooting idea later in the year?"

"I'll think about it," Tom said rather glumly. "You know, finishing off sidings, things like that, has never been my kind of work. I like the new main-line stuff. I been with the company thirteen years and there's always been new construction to go on to. It seems like what you're talkin' about would be like some of the finish-up work, just following along behind somebody else, trying to handle their mistakes—no challenge, no spice in it."

"Life can't be all spice," said Nancy, looking at him fondly. "You *could* retire, you know. You've saved a good bit and you've worked so hard for such a lot of years."

"Humph!" said Tom.

"Everybody ready for pie?" Nancy asked.

When supper was finished, Tom went to join the other men who were going back to Columbia Creek on handcars. One saloon in town had started offering free drinks to the railroad workers, and all the others were following suit, not to be left out of the publicity and patronage. Thorne turned down an invitation to go along. He sat on the floor building towers of blocks with Murphy, putting off his paperwork, while Nancy washed the dishes.

"I could make grand big buildings," said Murphy soberly, "real ones, when I'm big."

"You could, but I thought you were a railroad man."

"Yeah, I am, but I could do other stuff too, maybe on Sunday I could—"

Murphy's current building toppled under his hand. "Oh, shucks—damn!" he muttered.

"It's the law of gravity, Murph," Thorne said philosophically. "You can't put up a tower like that and expect it to withstand—"

"You told me about it," muttered the little boy disgustedly, "—anything that goes up, has to come down unless something stops it, but I still don't know *why* it has to. That was just beginning to look right."

"If you built a real building like that, with a tall, spindly tower, it wouldn't stand up either. Besides gravity, there'd be wind and—"

Murphy was looking at him intently. "Thorne, you don't know about pretend, do you? I wouldn't make a real building like that because I don't know how to make a real building, not yet. I like towers, and when they're pretend towers, you don't have to have gravity and things. Look, it's raining."

"All right," Thorne said, chastened, "build whatever you like. You're right."

Still looking out through the partly open door, Murphy said thoughtfully, "What would happen to rain, if it wasn't gravity?"

"Well, I guess it would just float around; only without gravity, there wouldn't be any rain because there wouldn't be any clouds."

"How could things grow then? It would be awful hot."

"There wouldn't be anything to grow, or to be hot either. Without gravity—"

He broke off as Nancy came in, taking off her apron. She said, "It's past your bedtime, Mister Murph."

"I'm not sleepy," said Murphy, pouting a little.

"You will be. Come on; say good night."

"We have to pick up these blocks, me and Thorne do."

"I've asked you so many times to say 'Uncle Thorne.' Come on, Murphy, you can pick up more than one block at a time."

"If it wasn't gravity," said the little boy, "I couldn't stay in bed; not even if I really wanted to, ever."

When Nancy came back, she stopped near the door to pour whiskey into a glass for Thorne.

"Thanks," he said. "You know I don't mind his not calling me uncle or something."

"Well, I do," she said firmly. "There are things he just has to learn, like some manners. Pa and the other men spoil him rotten."

"It's easy to want to do that, Nancy. He's such a smart little kid. I don't know if you completely realize—"

"I do," she said, sitting down with some darning, moving the lamp on the table between them to get better light. Rain fell outside, pattering on the car's roof, making a swishing sound as it passed through the leaves of the trees. "Maybe I don't know all it's going to mean, but I do realize, Thorne. He's so smart it scares me sometimes. But that's another reason not to spoil him. He already knows too much about using people, how to get around them."

"If Fitz could see him now," Thorne said wistfully.

Nancy smiled sadly. "He was always so proud of him and *he* spoiled him. I'm not sure, though, that Fitz would know, any better than I do, all about what would be best for Murph. But I think about Fitz, and sometimes I feel as if he still sees things, knows what happens with Murph."

There was a little silence. Thorne finished his whiskey.

"I'd better go," he said, putting down the glass. "The rain's about stopped, and Morley will be biting his nails again."

"Could you stay—for just a few more minutes?"

"All right."

"Do you want another drink?"

"Thanks, no."

She laid her work aside. "We'll be going back to Denver soon, Murphy and I. I've decided we've got to stay there, most of the time, after this. I think Murphy ought to have a tutor. You know he can already read some. I just feel that, young as he is, he already needs more than I can teach him. I never had any real schooling myself, just what Ma could teach me and what I picked up from a few other people. That's all right for me, but it won't do for him. He wants to learn; he'd rather learn than eat, and I want the best of that kind of thing for him."

"Well, you've got income enough to hire the best teacher around, Nancy."

She smiled a little uneasily. "I may never get used to the money. I just can't feel—comfortable about it somehow. But I was wondering . . . I know how busy you always are, but I don't know about things like that, Thorne. Would you—advertise or whatever it is that needs to be done to find the right person, maybe to start some time this fall?"

"As soon as I'm back in Denver, I'll start looking for someone."

"Would he have to live—at our house, or what?"

"That would be up to you. Maybe you'd rather have a woman to begin with."

"*I* might, but we're supposed to be thinking about Murphy, and I believe he'd do better with a man, the right kind of man."

"Then we'll find one."

After a moment, she said slowly, "Ted was here this afternoon. I saw you talking to him later."

Thorne nodded.

Nancy smiled, trying to be casual. "He asked me to marry him."

"He did?"

"This was the second time. He came to the house in Denver once, early last spring. He wants to adopt Murphy, take care of us. It's a new thing for me, you know, having someone after me for my money. I don't like it."

"I can talk to him, tell him to keep away."

"No, I guess I can handle him. Besides, he's probably left by now. He said he'd be taking the stage down this evening. I feel sorry for Ted, really. He tries, in some ways, to live up to being Fitz's son, but he's not really proud of anything Fitz was. I can understand that. I loved Fitz, but he was different with me and with Murphy. He just never could be much of a father to Ted. Well, at least Ted and I both know exactly why he wants to marry me."

Thorne got up, poured himself a second drink and sat down across from her again.

Nancy said thoughtfully, "It's a strange thing, about

families. Fitz fought his way up from nothing, as far as money and pride were concerned. Ted, if he had his way, would bring it all to nothing again; at least it seems that way. Ted says that if he'd been left almost everything, as he thinks he should have been, then he'd feel different, behave differently about the business. Perhaps he would. . . . Fitz always said you were more of a son to him than anybody else could be. I understand that, too, but I still can't blame Ted too much for feeling the way he does."

"But there's Murphy," Thorne said, making a cigarette.

"Yes," she said. "Murph is like Fitz, in some ways. I think they would always have got along. But Murphy's different, too. For one thing, he's going to be a great one for education, I think, just for the sake of learning, knowing about all kinds of different things. Fitz never felt that way and neither do you, I guess. You're both ones for wanting to see the education pay off right away, increase profits or something. Still . . . I wish you could be the one to teach Murphy, for a while."

He smiled, feeling vaguely shy. "Me? You've just said—"

"Oh, I know, and I believe what I've said, both things. Murphy needs a good, strong man in his life, one that's smarter than he is and whose authority he respects. You could teach him plenty to keep him busy, if you had the time, and could help figure out what he's most interested in. Fred Morley was telling me the other day about the books you've been collecting. He said you always have some with you, and boxes and boxes stored at the office, besides a library at home."

Thorne felt inexplicably embarrassed, apologetic. "Those at home, in the library, are just books everybody ought to have, if they can afford them. Cherish ordered them, mostly. They aren't read much. Sometimes I can't sleep. I have been reading more the past few years, I guess."

"Well," she said gently, "it's nothing to be ashamed of, is it? What I was saying is that Murphy really needs you, and you need him, Thorne. The way you feel about him, it shows in your eyes sometimes. It does me good to see you together. Fitz used to be so pleased that you—liked Murph. Fitz always felt partly responsible that you were married, with children, but still—lonely."

"No one else is to blame for—" Thorne brought the glass to his lips, finishing the drink, stopping the words. "I wish I could spend more time with Murphy. Maybe, when he's a little older . . ."

"I know Cherish hates him," Nancy said softly, looking away from him. "She's always hated me. I know she's always been jealous of your work, the people who are your friends and—things."

"She's had some justification," he said evenly, "about the work, anyway, I am too tied to it. But it's there, for someone to do. Well, I think I'll go now, Nancy."

"No, wait, please. There's one other thing, only I don't know how to say it, not to make you angry . . ."

"I've never been angry with you."

"It would be a good thing for you, I think, if you did get mad more often—just mad, without having to look for good reasons. You try too hard to look at things from everyone else's side of them. That makes you—impatient and things, but with yourself, not with other people, the way it ought to sometimes. You're way too hard on yourself, Thorne. People use that against you, and they know they can get away with it. I saw Fitz doing eaxctly that, lots of times. But the other thing I meant to say—well, you *are* lonely. So am I. Can you—know from that . . .?"

He reached across the table, took one of her restless hands between both of his, holding it gently until she brought her brown eyes back to his face.

"You'll marry again one day, Nancy. You, and Murphy, deserve that. You're just about the most—generous person I've ever known."

"It's not being generous, Thorne," she said, flushed now. "I want to marry again, if I ever find the right man, but he'll have to be awfully special. There's Fitz to compare him with—and there's you. I'm not being generous. I—I want you, you see. I always have been—fond of you, and we both—"

Thorne stood up, drawing her to her feet. She trembled faintly in his arms, and he bent his cheek down against her hair. "I really do have to leave," he said softly, stepping back, his hands on her shoulders.

"Do you—have other women?" she asked, barely audibly.

"No—not often."

She looked into his eyes again. "Is work all that to you, then?"

"It's not, but it usually makes me very tired and I can sleep nights." He took his hands from her shoulders and made another cigarette for something to do with them.

"Did you love Cherish—in the beginning?"

He stared at his hands, forgetting to light the cigarette. "No, but I haven't lied about it. I never said I did. I'm not at all sure, Nancy, that I know what love is."

"You know," she said with quiet conviction. "You've loved somebody, sometime. It's in your eyes."

Thorne tried to smile, turning slightly toward the door, away from the light. "All you Irish are dreamers," he said lightly, "romantics."

"Pa, when he's had some to drink, says all Gaels are a little bit fey, especially the red ones, like me, and the black ones like him—and you. The Scots and Irish are mostly the same people, if you go back far enough. He's told me, a lot of times, about that time when Fitz was hurt, at Perry Tunnel, about what you said about not fighting the mountain. That bothered Pa, because of the look of you when you said it. I'm trying to say that you ought to be able to understand it if I think I can—see into you. I know somebody hurt you once, almost more than you could bear. The hurt's still there, isn't it?"

"Nancy," he said slowly, "I want to—make love to you, but I can't, yet. It's a thing that takes thinking about. I guess I'm a prude, some ways, but I can't just—"

"It's Fitz, isn't it?"

"I don't know . . ."

"I told you before that I think he docs still see things. He wouldn't mind now, Thorne. But I don't mean to try to . . . Go do your paperwork," she said, smiling warmly. "There's plenty of time for us."

He took the few steps to the door and turned back. "Tell Tom I'd like to know what he decides about the troubleshooting job before I leave. Nancy, thanks for supper, for . . ."

"You know Pa'll take the job. He'd never work for anyone else." She followed him to the door and touched his hand tentatively. "Murphy and I will probably be back in Denver by the time you're through in Utah. Come see us, please. For supper or—I'd like to help . . . ."

"Yes," he said softly, "I will."

She stood watching him go down the steps and into darkness, where a light rain dripped from a heavy sky. Despite the day's heat, the air was now chilly, with portents of autumn in it. It occurred to Nancy to be glad the light was behind her, in case Thorne should look back. Her mouth was not steady, and her eyes were filled with tears. As far as she could tell, though, he did not look back. The camp was very quiet as she shivered and slid the door shut.

XIII

"Where have you been, Thorne?" demanded Cherish, rushing into the front hall the instant he opened the door.

It was October. Thorne had stayed in Denver for almost three weeks because of pressing office business. His head had begun to ache mercilessly this afternoon and he despised the pain, tried to ignore it, for he considered it a weakness to give in to tensions.

"It's not quite six," he said defensively. "I quit earlier today than I usually do."

"For heaven's sake, Thorne, give Dahlia your coat. Don't put it up yourself. Why do you think she's standing there? You never wear the nice hat I gave you."

Taking his coat, Dahlia gave him a warm, encouraging smile.

Clare ran down the stairs, shrieking. She was a small duplicate of Cherish, beautiful and petulant. "Stuart always acts like an old bully. He thinks he's smarter than anybody just because he goes to that fancy old school. And *I* ought to have something special, like he has his old school. Mama thinks so, too," she said accusingly to Thorne.

Stuart followed his sister slowly down the stairs. How had they grown so fast? Thorne wondered abstractedly. Ten and seven they were now. In some ways, it seemed to have happened almost overnight, all that time passing . . .

"I can't help it," the boy teased his sister, "because I'm older and smarter."

"See? *See?*" clamored the little girl. "He acts like that every weekend, right from the time he gets home on Friday. I wish you'd never even *come* home, Stuart Bromleigh Maxwell."

"Why," Thorne said angrily, "can't any two people in this family be together for two minutes without starting to yell?" He kept his own voice low, cold. Anything else would have increased his headache.

"We're high strung," stated Cherish with apparent complacency, "the children and I; it runs in the family. Stuart, *try* to behave like a little gentleman with your sister. And Jane Clare, I don't want to see you run downstairs like that, ever again. It certainly isn't ladylike."

"Ever since he got home," whined Clare shrilly, "he's been as hateful and nasty as he could be. He's jealous, for one thing, because I'm going to Celia's party tomorrow and he can't."

"Oh, I'm not either," cried the boy, outraged. "What would I care about some old girl's birthday party?"

Cherish spent little time with her children, Thorne knew. Still, they both drawled; her own drawl had been exaggerated during the years away from the South. It was part of the way she saw herself, a true southern lady among people who were, for the most part, barbarians.

"I just showed him my new dress for the party," Clare kept on. "He was going to spit on it."

Thorne thought longingly of the house he had just come from—Nancy's warm smile . . . Murphy, sometimes boisterous, but happy.

Stuart, his face cold and accusing, so like Angus, tossed at Clare, "You made us get rid of the dog."

Thorne had brought them a puppy, a litter brother to Murphy's pup Spike. Cherish had had a fit over the little dog's presence, and Stuart had shown no interest in the animal at the time. But Clare had begun to sneeze and sniffle almost before the dog had been brought into the house.

"If we even wanted a cat," the boy reminded his sister, "we couldn't get one, because of you."

"Well, *I* can't help it," wailed Clare, and then, her eyes moving from one parent to the other, "See? See how he is?"

"Stuart," said Cherish shortly, "you didn't care a thing about that dog and you know it. It was just a mangy little mongrel and you didn't want it. Now stop trying to upset your sister."

They had picked up the drawl from poor simple Dimity, of course. Cherish and Dimity had finally had an irreparable disagreement and Dimity, with copious tears and accusations, had gone back where she had come from last year.

"She's such a little snotty-nose," Stuart was saying, leering at his sister.

"See? See? He always starts calling me nasty names and—"

"For God's sake!" cried Thorne. "Hasn't either of you got anything to *do?* Is this how you spend your time, acting like a couple of spoiled two-year-olds? Both of you shut up. I mean it, Stuart. If you can't find anything better, then go to your rooms. If you can't stand each other, then keep apart and be quiet."

The children, slightly surprised and uncertain, turned their eyes to their mother, not missing the aggrieved look on her face.

"Do as you're told," said Cherish with a weary, resigned sigh.

"But Stuart keeps . . ." began Clare. The words faded under Thorne's withering look. Her lower lip stuck out as she trailed slowly up the stairs.

Thorne turned away from them and went to his study, closing the door behind him. Cherish angrily flung open the door and followed him. He was pouring himself a drink.

"Don't tell me," he said bitterly before she could speak. "It's all my fault, the way they are."

"It is," she said righteously. "And I don't see why you have to start cursing at them, practically with the first words out of your mouth when you walk in the door. And sending them to their rooms is a little silly, isn't it?"

"Last night, and a hundred times before last night, I've listened to discourses on how I never discipline them. What they both need is regular spankings about six times a day until they—"

"Don't you *dare* lay a hand on my children!"

He gulped the whiskey to stop the anger and frustration rising up in his throat. From the time he opened the front door he had had a feeling that something, a turning point in his life, was about to be reached. The feeling frightened him, and he wanted to do nothing that would precipitate it. With the pain in his head, he seriously doubted his ability to handle anything at all. Pouring out another drink for himself, he sat down beside the empty fireplace, deciding that a fire was what he wanted because he felt cold and ill.

Cherish, looking more aggrieved, sat down across from him. "You don't even show me the common courtesy of standing till I sit down," she said pouting, "and do you know how much you're drinking lately? I suppose I can't expect anything like respect and decent manners from you, but can't you ever be home without getting mad and having a glass in your hand?"

Thorne looked into the fireplace and saw for a moment, a picture of Maria's and Gavin's kitchen, filled with children, talking, arguing, laughing.

Cherish said with mournful resignation, "You can't even be bothered to notice my new dress. It's one from New York. As soon as I start trying to talk to you, spend a little time with you, you've got to be drinking and sulking."

"It's—nice," he said vaguely, but he meant it. It was a pretty dress, and she could be so beautiful when she let her face fall into repose for a moment. "I did notice, when I came in, but there are always so many—"

"You think I buy too many clothes," she challenged.

Eleven years, he thought, eleven-and-a-half years they had been married, and things had been like this . . . For some time now, he had been having these blinding headaches. They always came when he spent more time than he could afford in the office, and at home . . . Home. It was an alien word. He had not had a home since his boyhood, and that was a very long time ago.

Cherish, somehow a little mollified, gave him a tight smile and said brightly, "Do you want to change before people start getting here?"

Thorne drew a deep breath and said quietly, "Who's coming?" She usually wanted people in the house, or insisted that the two of them must go out in the evening. He had to admit that the evenings were a little easier to get through with other people around. If they stayed home alone, she felt they must be together, talking, which amounted to quarreling.

"Why, Thorne, I must have told you a dozen times about this evening. You never listen to a word I say. Those new people, the Fosters, are coming. He's a doctor, some kind of lung specialist, and Ted is bringing the Hampstead girl. I invited Ranald and Amy, but she said they already had other plans. I did it because I know you go on liking them, though they obviously don't like me. But since they felt too good to come to my house, I asked the Bellamys, so we could have eight people, two tables for cards after supper. There's something I want to talk to you about. If you're going to change, we can talk upstairs."

"I think I won't." The pain was beginning to ease a little. He sat very still, his eyes closed, even breathing with caution. The headaches were scary. He seemed to be frightened of a great many things these days.

At his last words, Cherish had looked upward, as if seeking guidance, or perhaps merely a witness to what she had to bear.

"Well, I suppose it's something, some kind of accomplishment, that you will, sometimes, wear clothes that look halfway respectable for the office. It would certainly be *nice*, considerate, if you changed for dinner, but I should have learned by now to know better than to expect anything."

"What is it you want to talk about?" he asked dully. He opened his eyes, automatically reaching for tobacco and cigarette papers.

"Oh, Thorne, I wish you wouldn't smoke. You know it always gives me a headache."

"I'll be glad to go outside," he said curtly.

"There you go again!" she cried. "Anytime I try to talk to you—"

"Cherish, I'm listening," he said coldly. He laid the unlit cigarette on the edge of the desk.

"Well," she said hesitantly, not looking at him, "it's about Ted."

"Christ," he muttered tiredly.

"Thorne, you don't have any idea of what that boy's going through, the humiliation he's suffered over what that old man did to him. It just gets worse and worse, and we're the only family he's got."

"He's no family of mine, and he's not a boy. He's miserable because he's run out of stock to sell. He's run through more money in the last two years than most people could spend in ten. Why is he staying in Denver now? He claims to hate it here, always has. He's going to have to break down and go to work soon, but I wouldn't think he'd want it to be here."

"Ted's not made for the kind of life you're talking about," she said, trying to sound reasonable. "He's a free spirit. Not many people can find—whatever it is you find—in just working all the time. Ted's a gentleman, a true southern gentleman."

"There aren't many of those left," he said sardonically.

Anger flashed in Cherish's eyes, but she managed to keep her voice wheedling, placatory. "It was bad enough for me when Fitz left practically everything to that—Nancy and her child, but at least I share—I have a right to share—what you have. Poor Ted has nothing."

"He *had* the stock he's sold off. It would have brought enough for him to live, comfortably on, maybe not in the manner he wants, but . . . he's sold it all, and now, obviously, he's still living on what you've been able to scrape together to let him have."

"Thorne, he's desperate," she said urgently. "He was here today, to finally tell me the whole truth about things. He wouldn't want you to know—he's too proud, like all my family—but I'll have to tell you. I don't know any other way to impress you with how serious it is. You've got to help him."

She waited, but Thorne did nothing more than reach, unconsciously, for the cigarette and light it.

Cherish sighed but went on, "Ted's been gambling—quite a lot, at some of those big racetracks back east. Naturally, he assumed the people he met there were all gentlemen, the ones he made bets with. Some of them have traveled with him in his car; he's visited in their homes . . . but now they've turned the collection of his bets over to—thugs, hoodlums, terrible people who won't wait. He knew those bets were the same as any other debts, and he meant to pay—when he could, but now they won't wait. Ted's afraid, Thorne. He didn't say it right out, but I think he thinks those people might—kill him. That's why he didn't go east again when he finished his visit in Minnesota. But two of them—those hooligans—have told him they'll be here next week. They're coming all the way out here, and they say he'd better have the money to pay them, not just a payment, but all of it, right now."

"How much money?" he said disinterestedly.

"He wouldn't say exactly. He paid them some in August, and he's been trying to take care of it; every time he could afford to, he's paid a little something, but there's still a lot to pay. They've got the IOU's he signed, those—gangsters, and they won't give him a minute's peace. Right now, he can't even afford to pay his hotel bill. Oh, that awful, unnatural Frank Fitzroy! leaving his own son practically destitute!"

"Cherish, Fitz left him what amounted to about—well, enough of a percentage, an interest in the company that he could have—"

"Oh, the company! That's all you talk about, think about. I'm talking about *Ted*, my own flesh and blood. Ted knows he's done wrong, gambling and all that. He's more than willing to begin to change some of his ways, and no one can blame him for having a little fling when he's still so young, but he *has* to pay those people off. This is all the fault of that Nancy and her brat. Ted got wild because he was so torn up over Fitz's will. I told Teddy time and time again, he ought to have contested that will."

"He was in too much of a hurry to start selling stock and spending the money."

"Well, that's done now. It can't be helped. We've got to help him get straightened out over this."

"I don't have any money to give him, Cherish, *if* I wanted to give him money. That's what you're getting at, isn't it? He doesn't need to be helped out of this. He'd just get into something else as bad or worse."

"Thorne, that's a lie. I know it, Teddy knows it,

and you know it. You could get the money with no trouble at all."

"*You* might get some of it by mortgaging Fern Hill, if you're really worried."

She gasped incredulously. "Fern Hill? Fern Hill is —*home*."

"You should be able to get quite a lot," he said speculatively, "from a Virginia bank. If you like, I'll ask one of the company lawyers to look into it, begin drawing up the papers. Besides the property, there're the cattle your manager down there will be selling in the fall. . . ."

"And what would I use to pay the bills with?" she snapped, "*and* mortgage payments? You have a fit every time I spend a penny on the place."

The pain in his head had lessened so that he no longer felt dazed. Things were coming to him clearly now, and he disliked the clarity. "I don't have a fit," he said coldly. "If I were prone to fits, I'd have died of them long before this. I don't see why you spend the money the place earns on things like completely refurnishing it. If you were living there, I might understand. Fern Hill meant something to Fitz. He was willing to carry it, because owning the place was important to him. He didn't care if it paid for itself or not. It means nothing to me and I won't pay for it."

"*Nothing* means anything to you! You have no sense of—heritage, or history or family loyalty. Your very heart's made out of railroad steel."

Thorne did not respond, not even with a look.

After a time, Cherish said abruptly, "Who would have *her* money, if she wasn't around?"

"Nancy's money, do you mean? She doesn't have anything except the income from the capital that's in trust for Murphy, unless there should be some crisis and the income's not enough."

"Well, if Murphy—if something happened to both of them . . ."

Cherish was looking at her hands, concentrating on keeping them still.

Thorne said quietly, "Then whatever is in the trust fund would be divided between Ted and me."

"*Why* did Fitz lean so on you all those years? You influenced him, too—I know you did—to get him to cut Ted out like that."

A slight shrug was all Thorne gave for reply. There was no point in talking any further. Like most of their subjects of conversation, it only came round full circle and started over again.

Cherish said, "You know as well as I do that if Fitz had ever treated Teddy the way a son ought to be treated, if he hadn't turned to you and just—forgotten Ted, things wouldn't be the way they are." After a moment's silence she asked casually, "How much would that be?"

"How much would what be?"

Her voice was unsteady with nervous impatience. "What's in the trust fund?"

"I don't know exactly, Cherish. It's variable. The accountants would have to—"

"Oh, never mind! You never give me a straight simple answer about anything. What if she married again?"

"Things would be the same as they are now. Nancy would have the income. The shares would stay in trust for Murphy."

"Oh, that ridiculous name! She *had* to name him for her common Irish father!"

"Stuart is named—"

"Just stop it, Thorne! I don't want *my* child mentioned in the same breath with . . . She's back in town, you know, even giving parties and going around acting like butter wouldn't melt in her mouth. Ranald and Amy actually *went* to one of her parties. She's living high for a shanty girl, I can tell you, flaunting herself in front of this hicky cow town. I suppose she fits right in, in a way, with all the other trash and their new money from mining and such."

"She wonders," Thorne said casually, "and so do I, if we failed to get our invitation to her party."

"I threw it out, of course," Cherish snapped fiercely. "I wouldn't be caught dead in the same house with her, and you know it. I resent her invitation coming in *my* mail. And what do you mean, she was wondering?"

"I stopped there on my way home this evening. She asked me to see about finding a teacher for Murphy and I—"

"A teacher!" Cherish cried scornfully. "Is she trying to pass that brat off as some kind of genius? She must really believe she can make a silk purse out of him, and herself too. As for you, you never have any time for your own children, not a minute for me, but you can—"

"I was there maybe fifteen minutes."

She glared at him, seething. "If *I* asked you to come home early, you'd make a point of being an hour or two later than usual. Do you know what Ted thinks about you and that—child?"

"I've heard it."

"Is it true?"

"That's not worth answering, Cherish."

"How often do you see her? Now I know why you've stayed in town longer this time."

The doorbell rang. She threw him a last baleful look and turned away, determinedly composing her face.

"Why, here are the Fosters!" she trilled, going into the hall as Dahlia let them in. "Thorne, darling, our guests are here."

Thorne sat stonily through dinner and through what seemed countless hands of cards. He despised games, especially when they had to be played with people who took them as seriously as Cherish and Ted did.

He played badly, could not keep his attention on anything for long. The pain in his head ebbed and flowed like a tide, carrying him on its waves. At times he could not really see his cards, the pain was so bad; it was a receding throb that he could almost ignore sometimes, but then, he almost wished it stronger. He didn't want to think, not of the people around him, not of—something he could feel, a threat, a thing to be feared and avoided, even in thought.

At one point, when Thorne had played his cards with rather remarkable stupidity, Louise Bellamy—she and her husband also took cards very seriously—commented tartly that he looked tired.

"Oh, my goodness, no!" cried Cherish from the other table. She had been the center of attention all evening, as she usually was, chattering volubly, laughing, getting prettily serious over her cards, flirting with the men. "Why, Louise, you know my Thorne better than that. I mean, he may *look* tired, but he never *is*. He can always find strength and time for just everything. He's had to take on helping to bring up my stepfather's child now, along with everything else he has to handle. Thorne's the little boy's guardian, you know, and little Murphy needs him more, really, than Stuart and Clare do."

The room had fallen awkwardly silent. Thorne felt their eyes on him and concentrated on dealing the cards yet again, his face growing hot, feeling angry that Cherish could still embarrass him.

Not much later, the plain but wealthy Miss Hampstead, Ted's date, said she had promised not to be too late, and Ted took her home. The other two couples left soon after. While Cherish was saying her last effusive good nights, Thorne escaped through the side door and went for a walk.

The fall air was chilly, fresh and damp. Stars shone sporadically, through rifts in heavy, fast-moving clouds. The waves of pain in Thorne's head surged and receded.

From experience, he knew the headache would not completely leave him now, not until he could get away and be absorbed by some out-of-town work for a day or two. He kept seeing his desk at the office, still stacked with things needing attention. Another weekend had begun. He'd brought home a briefcase full of work, but there would be little chance to do it. He had little trouble out on a job, or even at the office, considering several problems at once. Why were the clamorous demands of his family more than he could cope with? Because it's all so futile, he thought miserably. If I can't get away soon, I'll . . . Well, all right, what? . . . I'll go on, of course. I always have.

For a long time he walked swiftly through quiet neighborhoods, gradually finding a degree of stability in his mind, grateful for a sudden, overwhelming weariness. Yawning, he turned toward his house, longing for sleep now, for oblivion, when he saw a fiery glow against the clouds to the south. Something was burning. Heading home, he tried to concentrate on the problem Tom Murphy had come in to talk to him about today, the reshoring of tunnel five on the Amity line, the tunnel where Fitz's legs had been crushed. Nancy's words came to him: *All Gaels are a little fey.* He didn't want those words; what did they mean, and why did they frighten him so?"

He let himself into the house and went up to his room, almost without a sound. He half expected Cherish to be in his bed. Cherish still, despite everything, found some pleasure in having sex with him, though it had become little more than mere duty for him. He was relieved that he was to be spared tonight, hating himself for the knowledge that if she had been here, he might have wanted her, in that brief, rather bestial way which was all he could feel for her.

He had dropped into a fitful doze when she touched him, startling him so that his whole body hurt from the jar of suddenly tensed muscles, and his headache surged up with renewed strength.

"Darling, I didn't know if you'd come back or not," she said meekly. "I'll turn on the light. We could have a little drink together."

"Cherish, no. Please. My head aches—"

She laughed softly, slipping into his bed. "I thought that was supposed to be a woman's excuse, Thorne. All right, I won't turn on the light, but I brought a bottle. Have a little drink. That and other things will make you forget you've got a headache."

"I don't want to drink any more," he said groggily, moving away from her ubiquitous, exploring hands.

"I've been wanting you all day;" she crooned. She often said that, no matter what she had said to the contrary earlier. She drew herself up to lean over him, her breast lightly brushing his face. "Why, darling, you're as limp as a dishrag. I believe you really are sick. Well, I know how to fix that, don't I?"

"Cherish, go away." He was clenching his fists to keep from striking her. His whole body was tense to a breaking point.

She went on with her fondling, smiling a little, trying to see his face. She knew that he hated her coming to his room, hated her watching and probing into his precious privacy. She turned his aversions into her weapons and used them freely. Still, no matter what she did, she felt a part of him forever closed to her; she hated him and yet she would *make* him want her. The struggle was what she enjoyed. Her smile grew wider as his body began to respond.

"Did you think you'd used it all up on that little redheaded whore this afternoon? Or maybe that's where you went when you went out. Well, *I* have marriage rights too, and you know it, don't you?"

Thorne gripped her hands and pulled them away, hurting her, but the hands were replaced by her entire body, moving urgently against him.

"You hate me, don't you?" she murmured possessively. "It's the one thing I can always count on having from you. Well, I hate you too. Show me how much you hate me, darling."

Suddenly, Thorne was vicious, desire and frustration mingling in a seizure of emotion that made him tremble. He rose up and flung her down onto the bed, catching her hair in his fist, his other hand and his mouth cruel on her soft body. Cherish was half out of her mind with delight. He had never been like this before. She cried out in pain, in feigned fear, and finally in blissful completion.

Thorne drew away from her quickly, feeling disgusted. Still, she would not leave him, but stayed, talking incessantly, gloating over what she considered her triumph. He felt drugged by the pain in his head and by emotions that were too conflicting to be dealt with. He slept while she still talked, still touching him possessively. He clutched at the sleep with gratitude, feeling that nothing could stop it, nothing wake him, perhaps ever again.

But he did wake. It seemed a long time later, but he saw that it had been only a very short time. Dahlia was banging on his door from the hall, calling to him urgently, sounding frightened. He had heard the sounds for some time, but had been unable to make himself respond until he heard Cherish fling open her own door.

"Dahlia, for goodness sake, what is it?" Cherish cried. "You're going to wake the children and everyone else in the house. Don't you know it's one o'clock in the morning?"

Thorne got up, struggled into a dressing gown. He felt strangely heavy, sluggish, reluctant to move. In the hall, Cherish, having given Dahlia no real chance to reply, railed at her peevishly.

"I heard the doorbell, Dahlia. If it's someone from

the railroad, tell them Mr. Thorne's not to be disturbed. He's not feeling well."

"What is it?" Thorne asked curtly, opening his own door. Then, tensely, "God, Dahlia, what's happened? Here, come and sit down."

"Oh, Thorne!" protested Cherish, but she followed as he helped Dahlia to a chair.

"It—it's Effie," breathed Dahlia, wiping at her eyes. "You know Effie and Sam Shorter, that work for Miz Fitzroy? Effie's come. She rung the doorbell. She's downstairs . . ."

"Well, what about it?" demanded Cherish. "Dahlia, it's the middle of the *night*. What's Effie doing here?"

Thorne sank down on the bed, putting suddenly cold hands over his hot face. He had known. All evening he had known . . . *All Gaels are a little fey* . . . and yet he had not let himself know.

Dahlia's voice came to him from a long way off, "Mrs. Fitzroy. Mrs. Fitzroy's house burned up. The poor soul is dead. They couldn't get to her. It went up so fast. Effie says it seemed like the whole place was soaked in coal oil. Sam got the little boy out all right. They took him to the hospital, but he's all right—I mean, not burned. He breathed some smoke and was nearly scared to death, of course. And then, just after Effie came, Miss Amy called here. They woke up and saw where the fire was. Mr. Ranald went over there and told her to call us. I'm all right now. It just . . . well, I don't know what it's made me feel like. I'll go down and make Effie some coffee."

Thorne said woodenly, "Was Sam hurt? Was there anyone else . . .?"

"Just those four were in the house. Effie says that Sam got some hair singed off but that he's all right. He thought to stay and watch things over there, but Effie says there's nothing left of the house."

"Just what do you think you're going to do now?" Cherish demanded harshly when Dahlia had gone.

Thorne did not bother to answer. He dressed as quickly as he could, thinking, Ah God! I knew. I knew and I wouldn't let myself . . .

"There's nothing anybody can do now," she said, catching at his arm.

He wrenched away from her. "I can go and be with Murphy. Cherish, just how much did you know about this?"

"I don't know what you're talking about." Her voice was unsteady, and she drew back a little from the look in his eyes.

"Those things you said earlier, the questions: What would happen to the money if Nancy and Murphy both . . . My God, Ted was desperate, wasn't he?"

"How *dare* you, Thorne Maxwell, and are you accusing *me*, too? You *know* where *I* was. I was doing my marital duty for you, right there in—"

"You weren't. I saw the fire while I was out, I just didn't think . . . Ted had had plenty of time to take that girl home and go to Nancy's house."

"God! you've got a sick mind! I don't have to listen to you accuse my brother . . . Just because you've lost your favorite whore. You could have done it, if someone set the fire. Where were you? . . . I suppose you spent all summer with her, didn't you? Didn't you!"

"No," he said coldly, "but I wish to God I had."

Tears flooded from Cherish's eyes. "I always knew it! I don't want you to go out of this house, Thorne. Can't you see how you've upset me? Don't leave!"

"I'm going," he said heavily, and the decision seemed to spring full-blown into his consciousness, "and I won't be back."

"Thorne, what do you *mean?* You can't *do* this!"

He closed the door against her cries of pleading and outrage. As he stumbled down the stairs, it was Nancy's face before him. "Lonely . . ." and now her healthy, wholesome body, the body he might have loved, was . . . Again, he covered his face with his hands, standing in the lower hall. It was some foreknowledge that he was, finally on this night, going to put the decision to leave Cherish into effect—that was the thing he had been trying not to know, trying to fight it off so hard that he had not seen what she had put so clearly before him in the study hours ago. Hours he might have used to stop this, not to let it begin . . . Ah, Nancy, Nancy! I'm sorry . . .

Dahlia had come into the hall from the kitchen. He was not aware of her until she touched his arm tentatively. Then he started and his eyes frightened her.

"You want a cup of coffee before you go, honey? You look terrible."

"Which hospital did they take him to?"

She told him. "You look bad, Mr. Thorne, awful bad right now. I expect Mr. Ranald's gone to the hospital. Maybe you ought to stay here."

"Dahlia," he broke in slowly, "when you have the time will you pack some of my clothes and send them . . . well, send them to Ranald's. He'll know where I am."

"Honey, what are you talking about?" she said tautly, really frightened now.

"I'm leaving, that's all. I've told Cherish. She doesn't believe it yet."

"Mr. Thorne, don't do this. Please don't. It'll kill her."

"You told me once before, a long time ago, not ever to leave her completely, and I've always thought I could stay somehow. Well, now I can't, not anymore. That little boy, Fitz's and Nancy's boy, he's completely alone now. There's not anyone. . . . He's not even four years old yet, and they, Cherish and Ted . . . Don't you see that I can't stay here now, not ever again."

His eyes, full of pain and misery, pleaded with her.

Dahlia said quietly, brokenly, "I'll send your things, and I—I'm sorry, Mr. Thorne."

Ranald came up to Thorne as he stood by a window in the hospital corridor.

"Listen," he said worriedly, "I know you can't very well take Murphy home with you. Let me take him to our house. Amy says so too. Being with other kids will be good for him. You come too, if you want to."

"I've taken a couple of rooms at the Fremont," Thorne said. "I'll take him there as soon as he wakes up."

"Tell me what's happened," Ranald said slowly. "All of it. You look like hell—do you know that?"

"I'll be keeping the rooms at the hotel. I've asked Dahlia to send some of my things to your house when she can get to it. I'd rather no one knew, for a few days, where Murph is, especially those goddamned reporters."

He told Ranald then, of his suspicions—certainties about the fire. It was almost noon now, and he felt groggy and dazed from lack of sleep and too much of too many other things.

"I was there before the police came," Ranald said slowly, still incredulous. "They, and the firemen, said it had to be arson, the way the house went. But, Thorne, my God, you really think Ted could have done it?"

"Not with his own hands. He's too much a coward to take action like that on himself. He found somebody else to do it. Cherish knew he meant to, and I should have guessed."

"Are you sure," Ranald said with concern, "that you're not just looking for reasons to blame yourself? I mean, you feel responsible for all of them, Ted included. Fitz depended on that, and so have all the others. Maybe you just . . ."

"The doctor says Murph should be waking up

within the hour," Thorne said wearily. "I'll just take him then, try to keep things quiet for a while."

"I don't mean to doubt your word. It's just so—well, it's something you might read about, but it doesn't happen to people—people you know."

"I don't want anybody reading about it. The next person who has the gall to come up to me and identify himself as a reporter, I'm going to knock hell out of. Jesus, they're vultures. Tom will be down on the evening train from Amity. This is going to be hard for him."

"*Tom* can stay with us if he wants to," Ranald said, feeling helpless. "I can handle some of this. You haven't got to do it all yourself."

"I'll meet Tom. You come, too, if you like. I guess he'd appreciate a place to stay without having to make any arrangements."

"What about Murphy? You won't take him to the station—"

"I've arranged to have one of the maids at the hotel sort of on call for him for a couple of days. I'll have to find someone more permanent after that."

The pain in Thorne's head was all but blinding. The light from outside the window hurt his eyes; he swayed a little as he stood there. Ranald took his arm and held it when he would have pulled away.

"Come and sit down. There's nobody in there now."

Thorne allowed himself to be led. He said, after they had sat silent in the waiting room for several minutes, "When you left earlier, the doctor said Murph wouldn't wake up, so I went to look for Ted."

"And?" Ranald said reluctantly.

"He's gone. He didn't pay his bill at the hotel. I went down to the yards. He'd arranged to have his car on RM&P's midnight train to Cheyenne."

"I'm glad he wasn't there. You've told the police, Thorne. Let them handle it."

"They aren't doing anything, not about finding Ted."

"Well, I suppose they can't do much, not immediately, when he's gone to another state."

"I wish I'd found him. Finding out the truth from him wouldn't have been hard to do."

"Well, I'm glad you didn't find him, damned glad."

They made arrangements for Nancy's funeral, on Monday, asking that it be a private service; but a small crowd of reporters and other curious people gathered outside the church. Thorne was outraged, when he slipped into a back pew, to see Cherish sitting near the front of the church.

"Thorne, I've been worried to death about you," she said, low and angry, catching up with him in the stream of people leaving the church. "Where have you been staying? How's Murphy?"

"I made arrangements with the bank this morning," he said coldly. "You'll have a letter in a day or two; there'll be money, for you and the house . . ."

"And just what am I supposed to *tell* people?" she demanded, gripping his arm with both hands as he would have strode away from her.

"Anything you like," he said, trying to pull free of her.

Cherish saw that people were watching them, some who had been inside the church, and some who were now waiting for their carriages to come up for the trip to the cemetery. Ranald, who had been with Amy and old Tom Murphy, was making his way toward them. Cherish looked up at Thorne, her face soft and innocent and beautiful, but coldness, menace in her blue eyes.

"The police came to the house. The *police*, to *my* house. How on earth could you do such a thing, Thorne? They've bothered everyone who was at the house on Friday night. If you set out deliberately to humiliate me, you couldn't have been much more successful. I hope you're satisfied. And, of course, since you felt it was necessary to talk to them, *I* told them the truth about that night. After all, what *could* I do? You were out at the time the fire started. So far as I know, you were alone—wherever you were—with no witnesses." She glanced round at Ranald, who had been detained momentarily by Peter Maitland and his wife. "You'll be able to clear it up, I'm sure," she said to Thorne. "And you'll come home, sooner or later. I know you very well, you know. I really do. All these years of living with your need for your precious privacy, of your trying to keep yourself from me, but I know. You'll come back. Hello, Ranald," she said brightly, but with a touch of pathos in her face, worthy of the occasion. "I won't be able to go on to the cemetery. Clare's sick with a cold and I won't leave her so long. Here's Harry with the carriage. Give my love to Amy and Elizabeth and the children, won't you?"

Thorne did most of his office work that week in the sitting room of the two-room suite he had taken at the Fremont. He had found a girl, a sister of the hotel maid, who could stay with Murphy anytime, but for the most part he was with the little boy, trying desperately to be whatever Murphy needed. By Thursday afternoon, he made up his mind what he wanted for Murphy. He told Jim Ritter at the office that he would be in San Miguel the following Monday, to see about a short spur that was needed for a new mine there. Taking Murphy and the girl he'd hired to look after the youngster, Thorne boarded a train for Mixon.

XIV

Thorne took rooms for Murphy and the girl, Flora, and himself at the Mixon Hotel and then arranged to hire a livery horse from the stable early on Saturday morning. Flora was a young woman of seventeen or eighteen. She seemed to make no connection between Murphy and the stories that had been in the papers in Denver. She had never been more than five miles from her home in west Denver, and she enjoyed everything with abandon. She was good for Murphy, who had developed an expression in his solemn blue eyes that made him seem older than Flora.

"I want to go with you," Murphy said wistfully when Thorne explained that he would be leaving early in the morning and would probably not be back until late on Saturday night.

"It's been so long, Murph, since I've seen these people, my uncle and aunt and the others. There'll just be a lot of talk all day. I'll take you over there on Sunday, all right?"

"I wouldn't mind if it was just a lot of talk."

"Flora would. She likes to do things. She'll be glad to go with you to the railroad yards here. Or you can go watch—"

"All right," Murphy sighed. "But I'm pretty tired of taking care of Flora."

Thorne had ridden half the way to the Arragon hacienda when he turned to watch the sun rise over the great Sangre De Cristo range far away on the valley's eastern edge. It had been a long time since he had watched a sunrise, consciously and in detail. The air was wonderful, light and dry and clear; even breathing seemed easier here. He was a little giddy—just tired, he supposed. Still, since they had got off the train last night in Mixon, he had been feeling an unaccustomed sense of well-being, of calm and peace. Splashes of color glowed on the near mountains where trees and brush had turned, late this year, and even closer, the willows and poplars along the Rio Del Oso shouted autumn with brassy voices of yellow and red. He was too near the western mountains to get any proper perspective. He knew the high ridge peaks of the Sangres to the east were covered with new snow; he had seen it yesterday. It was too bright now to look for long in that direction. Thorne felt enclosed, safe here, near to peace. He had passed through the valley along the Rio Grande many times on the railroad, but it was more than thirteen years since he had been to Quintana or the hacienda. The thought of all that time having passed made him feel tired and sad and old, but as he looked to the mountains again, he thought how stable and dependable they were, and the calmness came round him again.

"Thorne!" Maria cried. Before he finished tying up the horse, Maria came running down the steps to meet him like a girl. "*Ay mi hijo guapo, querido!*"

She hugged him fiercely, pressed a tear-drenched face against his shirt. Thorne was shaken. He tried to draw away, gently, without her noticing, to finish securing the horse.

"So long, so long!" Maria crooned, stepping back to look at him through her tears. "Even those few times we went to Denver to see Jean, or Ranald and Amy, you were always away. We have never met your wife, your children."

There was no real reproach in her voice or manner,

only a wistful sadness. Thorne almost wished she were angry.

"Such a fine man you look. At least we've seen your pictures, read the things about you in the papers that Amy saves for me. Gavin will be so glad!"

Maria's hair was gloriously white in the sunshine, thick and lively. Her face was remarkably unlined, and her dark eyes still flashed with love, laughter, warmth, pride.

"You look fine," he said softly, "just—grand."

"Oh, you!" she laughed. "I'm a grandmother so many times over now that I must think hard to remember just how many grandchildren there are at any one moment."

"And Uncle Gavin?" Thorne said. "Ranald told me that he's been sick."

Maria shook her head, the smile temporarily gone. "Gavin is not very well. He has to spend most of his time in bed now. He was asleep just now, but I have surely wakened him. Come, *hijo*, see the others."

Carlos's very young wife, Josefa, stood smiling shyly in the kitchen door. A tiny girl, just walking, clung to her skirts and peeked round with great dark eyes. Another child apparently was on the way. Carlos himself was not at home just now. Maria asked if he had had breakfast and Thorne said he had, though it wasn't true. He didn't want to think of eating, only to be here, in the midst of this strange, newfound quiet that came from within him. Josefa poured coffee for him while Maria chattered.

"You won't remember Josefa, I suppose. She is one of the Muñez girls, probably too young when you left to have caught your notice. I would guess she was five or six then, and Carlos was—yes, eight, when you and Ranald first left. They are very good for us, our Carlos and Josefa. We are no longer young, your uncle and I. Joe and Rafaela and their family moved long ago, you know, to Texas. Sometimes I have trouble keeping the right count of the great-grandchildren, too. But Carlos is chief shepherd here now. There have been so many changes on the hacienda while you've been away. And all of my children so grown-up and—capable looking, and important—it scares me a little if I think too long. Isn't he fine-looking, Josefa? This is Papa's Romany lad you've heard us all speak of. But tired, *hijo*, around your eyes. Ranald always says you are working hard and don't get enough rest."

She scooped up the little girl who had made the decision to leave her mother's skirts and try her grandmother's. "But when we have a little *niña* like this small Maria with us, how can I be sad about anything for long?" She kissed the baby and put her down. "Come and see Gavin now. He'll be wanting to know who has come."

The dim *sala* was little changed. The same furniture was there for the most part, looking shabbier, but still little-used. Maria pushed back the curtains that separated bedroom from parlor and tied them back with bright ribbons. Gavin lay there, propped on pillows, his dim eyes on the gap in the curtains.

"It's Thorne, Gavin!" cried Maria. "He's come home at last. You always said so, didn't you?"

Neither of them could speak at first. Thorne, feeling small and unworthy, slowly came close to the bed. Gavin took his hand between his own hard, dry, wrinkled palms and would not let it go. He could see nothing at all now because his filmed eyes were filled with tears. There was a faint, constant tremor in Gavin's hands. Thorne had not been prepared for the changes in him, but he had no desire to pull his hand away.

"Bring a chair, Maria," Gavin said. His voice, also, was not quite steady, and it seemed weak and husky. "No, lad, let her bring it this time—here, close to the bed. Open the window curtains, too, will you, lass? I want the light now."

Thorne sat down in the chair, averting his own wet eyes. How could they be like this, always, when he had neglected and ignored them so long?

Gavin's hair was white and thin. His face was heavily lined and tired, with shadows of pain or worry in his dimmed blue eyes. Still, Thorne felt a strength, a steadiness emanating from him, a security and stability that he would never, for all those years, have let himself admit needing. Now, he just sat there, not trusting his voice, feeling the quiet sureness of Gavin's add to his own peace. With one of his hands, Gavin openly wiped at his eyes. He smiled shakily.

"Damned watering eyes," he murmured.

"I couldn't believe my eyes," Maria was chattering. "I didn't know what to say."

Gavin's smile widened. "Ah, lass, I've not known that to happen to you before."

Maria brought tea for Gavin. Finally, he relinquished Thorne's hand, but went on watching him hungrily.

"Josefa and I have planned a very special meal for dinner," Maria told them. "She is starting to cook now."

The fatted calf, Thorne thought, and his throat hurt. I don't deserve this, but it's been here, all these years. They've been here, and I've—

"Well," said Gavin into the silence that had fallen when Maria left them, "you see how she is, my Maria. She stays the same somehow, always blithe and bonnie."

"Yes," Thorne said, softly, gratefully.

"And you?" Gavin said. "Ranald has helped us to keep up with things. We know you're a grand engineer and businessman. How are things going for you now?"

"Everything's fine, now. I've had to spend some

time in the office lately, but I'm on my way to getting back out in the field again."

"I've not been able to read much for some time. Maria or Carlos or Josefa read the papers to me, the ones Amy sends. You and Ranald are—fine men. I'm glad you're both in Denver, close enough for us to be able to keep up with what's going on. It seems what we mostly read about you is that you're beginning a new line, or finishing one, or going to court."

Thorne smiled. He was vastly relieved that they seemed to know nothing about the fire yet. His plan, his chief reason for coming here now, was not going to work out, and he didn't want to have to discuss Nancy's death.

He said, "Well, that's about what we've been doing. We seem to have more court suits every year, mostly from various competitors, but things are not going badly."

"Ranald and Amy and the four kids were here last August. He talked a good bit about some improvements he hoped to begin making at the mill—additions."

"He hasn't been able to get much of a start yet. Money's tight. No one much wants to see expansion just now. They have opened up a new mine—a coal mine of ours, I mean—that looks really promising."

"And the rail line to Beanpot that Ranald tells us you're so proud of, is there still plenty of business there?"

"Well, the boom's past, but there are several other big-producing mines, which will keep things lively for a while, it seems, maybe longer than any of the others."

"I've wanted to see that road, to ride over it."

Maria bustled in again to fill their cups. "Your family, Thorne—tell us about them? Do you still have only the two children?"

"Yes, two," he said rather lamely. But he stood up and left the room and when he came back, he carried two miniatures of Stuart and Clare, painted only last spring. They had been in his study and Dahlia had packed them with the things she sent to Ranald's for him. When Ranald had sent those bags and boxes on to the hotel, Thorne had felt sad at how little, of a material nature or otherwise, he had accumulated in that house in eleven years. When he found the pictures, he knew he wanted his aunt to have them.

Maria cried again. "Such beautiful children!" She studied the pictures, wiping at her eyes. "Ranald and Amy say your wife is such a fine lady. We've got pictures of her from the newspaper too. Ranald described the children, but I was afraid we'd never really see them. I hope you can bring them next time. Elizabeth has come three or four times, with Ranald's family, you know. We like her so much. That first time, I could see I'd like her, but she was just—well, almost crushed by Angus. He could do that to people. Anyway, I was saying, maybe your wife wouldn't want to come here, it's so deep in the country, so many things and people that would be different for her, but surely you could bring the children next time?"

She stopped fussing with Gavin's pillow and looked at him so sharply that Thorne turned his eyes away to the window. "Thorne, I think you are very sad. Why haven't you come home to us before?"

"Maria, don't start on the lad now, the minute he's walked in the door," Gavin said gently.

"Gavin, I never pry," she said firmly. "You know it's not our place to interfere in the lives of any of our children. There, isn't that more comfortable?"

"I can't tell any difference," Gavin said ungraciously.

She chose to ignore him. "Carlos should be back any time, and I have a feeling Meg may come in time for dinner. She often comes out from Quintana on a Saturday; sometimes Gordon's with her. You remember Gordon Gaynor, Thorne. He's a fine lawyer, someone the whole valley is proud of. He went to court about six years ago, district court or something, in Denver, about the old Ornado land grant over on the river. I think your railroad was one of the people against him in that case; there were several. You must have noticed the new farms over there around Mixon that have come in now that they have irrigation water. Some of the children from there go to Meg's school at Quintana because it's so much better than the one Mixon has. Meg's school is not the one you remember. The state has built a fine new one. Meg's been teaching all these years, and now she needs two other teachers to help her. Meg and Gordon are very important people here."

Gavin sighed and smiled resignedly as she hurried away again. "Forty-five years I've tried to teach her that you don't have to say everything in the first hour after someone's come." He picked up the pictures Maria had laid on the bed. "I wish I could see them better."

"Clare looks like her mother," Thorne said steadily. "She's blond, with blue eyes, very pretty. Stuart is like Angus; I mean, he looks like him, quite a lot."

"I've been worried, Thorne, these past few years, that I might not have the chance to talk to you about Angus. I should have done it long ago, before he ever came here to take you. We lied to you about your father."

"It doesn't matter anymore," Thorne said quietly, and meant it. "It stopped mattering a long time ago—I don't really know when."

"Still, there are things, just a few things, that I've wanted to say. I've had a good deal of time to think of them. When Annie died, your mother, my wee girl of a sister, you were—one of ours, Maria's and mine. We wanted your name to be MacWinter, the same as the other children's, and it seemed simpler at the time . . . But you should have known the truth. I never liked the earl's family. I most particularly didn't like Angus when he came here, bringing Annie and in such a hurry to be rid of her, acting as if she were a maid or some such instead of his wife, acting as if the rest of us . . . And, well, the whole truth is, you were such a fine, bonnie laddie, and I—I didn't want you to be his son. Can you see that? You were mine, ours. Sometimes I'd forget the truth myself, for months together. But you should have known your own father was alive. I could have led you, maybe, to see a few things to be proud of, in him. He wasn't all bad, the way I've always thought of him; no man is that, all one way."

Thorne had stood up and gone to the window, lighting a cigarette.

Gavin said, "I'm sorry if the talking bothers you. It's just a thing I've felt for a long time I had to have straight, for my own sake. I'm sorry lad, about all of it."

"It doesn't bother me to talk," Thorne said and knew it to be true, for now. "I just can't talk well myself, or think, without moving around. . . . Uncle Gavin, it's not because of Angus—any of that, that I've not been back. I don't know that I know all the reasons myself, or could explain them."

"Would you want to try, just for a bit?" Gavin said urgently.

Thorne drew on his cigarette, exhaled slowly. "Those first years, before I came—home the one time, I don't know what I thought. I was—there seemed to be so much I needed to know . . ."

"And you were what—fourteen?—when you first went away? It's a critical time in a boy's life, or a man's. None of us did right by you."

"Well, yes, I thought that, but what I wanted, all those years, more than anything, was to be back here. I dreamed about the hacienda almost every night then. There were times, I guess, when I wanted to—

hate you and the others, but I couldn't . . . I could have come before I did. Partly, Angus kept me from coming with work, but there were times when I wanted to run away from him. I knew, somehow, though I couldn't understand why, that he'd come for me again, and if I ran away, that this would be the first place he'd think of looking, and I suppose I was—scared you wouldn't . . . that the whole thing could begin all over."

Thorne had turned and was looking at Gavin. Talking like this, this—ease that had come over him, was incredible. It was as if something within him, long cramped and choked, had been released; it was so strange to be at peace with himself.

"When I did come back, I was glad, for so many reasons. I knew then that you, all of you, still—cared about me and that I felt like that about the family. It was—all right to be here. I don't know how long I suspected who Angus was before he told me; it was quite a while before I let myself believe it. It was the only thing that came close to explaining things. Well, but by the time I did come home again, I'd had—a lot of things, the schooling, so much time to think, and I—thought it was time I had something for the work I'd done. I never liked work all that much when I was a boy.

"So Ranald and I had the trip to Europe, and then . . . a lot of things happened. While I was here, I wanted nothing more than just to stay, but once I'd gone away again, I—got involved with other things. Fitz was hurt—my friend, my real boss. Then I—married. Aunt Maria's right. Cherish never would have come here and I—never asked her to."

Gavin said, "Ranald has told me some of it. It's been a bad time for you, lad."

"I left her, Cherish and the children, a week ago."

"Ah, then. We'll not tell that to Maria. She needn't be bothered about it now. Amy can tell her the next time they come. Women like having those things together, between them. Will you and Cherish be able to make it right?"

"No."

"Ranald said she has put you through hell."

"No, it's not that. What we've been together hasn't been her fault. I've thought, for all this time, that I ought to stay with them. Now, it seems I never should have. I'd—appreciate it if we don't tell Aunt Maria. She—I ought to feel more than I do, about my children, at least, but I just—can't care. I know it's a hell of a thing to say. They're my responsibility . . ."

"That's another thing Ranald has worried about, your feeling so responsible for so much. It takes two people to make love, Thorne. I'm not talking about having sex. I mean, it would have required something from both you and Angus for there to have been family love between you. Just as you need something from your wife to make your marriage work."

"I never really tried," he said quietly.

"Did you love somebody else?" The words were steady. Gavin's eyes, though he could not see Thorne clearly, were upon his face.

"I thought I did, once. And I don't understand, any more than you do, why I married Cherish. There were reasons at the time, but I could have got round them . . .

"Anyway, it got to be a habit again, not coming here. I know now that I was afraid, not of the things I thought I was afraid of, so much as of wanting to stay if I came back. I've just realized, talking about it, that that was a big part of it, after a while. I was afraid that if I came, and things here still meant as much to me, then I wouldn't be able to . . ."

"To go back? To pick up all you've been carrying?"

"It hasn't been all that bad, but—yes."

"And how do you feel . . . since you've come?"

"That's a strange thing," Thorne said slowly. "Last

week, there was a day when—when a lot of things happened, and I didn't know if I could . . . it's as if something was broken then, a—a glass or something like that, that had kept me from feeling, from seeing things. I feel glad I came. I don't see how you and Aunt Maria can be glad to see me, after I haven't even written all this time, but I'm grateful. And I feel free, quiet."

"And will you stay for a while?"

"Ah no, I can't. But I won't stay away so long, ever again."

"Well," Gavin said with slow thoughtfulness, "free is the best thing a man can feel, I've always believed. And it's no good at all, doing something like traveling to a freer country, the way I did so long back, if a man's not free within himself."

"I've been wondering—is it—do people, maybe, feel quieter, like this, as they get—older? I mean, do we begin to know, or not to care, about some of the answers, even the questions? Is it easier . . ."

Gavin smiled regretfully. "Ah, lad, don't count on anything like that. I can only tell you how it's been for me, and it's not been like that. I'm seventy now, you know, and I don't like being seventy. It hasn't brought the peace of mind you seem to be hoping for. The years have brought a lot of things, some bad, mostly good; but inside me, I'm not so very different from what I was when I was your age. I'd give a lot to see thirty-five again. Not that I'd change much. I doubt I could if I wanted to, because I'd be the same person I was the first time around. It's the body grows old, not the spirit. Most of the things that puzzled me—about life, about other people, about myself—they're still there, and I'm not likely to solve much at this late date, would you think?"

Thorne shrugged. "I've always believed I would understand a lot of things someday, have them come clear for some reason. The way I feel now, I don't have to know anymore."

"It's good to see you smile," Gavin said softly. "I could see it when you turned to the light just then. You used to laugh so much when you were a laddie. When you came home that time, I thought that you were tearing at yourself for some reason. How long has it been now, since you and Ranald first went away? Twenty years? Ah God, lad, where has it all gone to?"

After a moment, Thorne, suddenly aware of what he was looking at through the window, said, "Aunt Maria's out there carrying wood. I'll go and bring some in for them."

Gavin fingered the two little paintings again. "You mean Maria to have these?"

"Yes. She can—keep them for me."

"I've often wondered if your little girl might look anything at all like Annie. But you couldn't know about that, could you? I'll ask Maria what she thinks when she comes in again. Be sure Carlos shows you the new black-face tup we've got. I doubt you'll be able to stop him—Carlos, not the ram."

Thorne filled the wood box. He was carrying two buckets of water from the pump when Meg drove up in her buggy. She was still the most beautiful woman he had ever seen, possibly more beautiful now in her full maturity, than she had been thirteen years ago. Her skin was flawless, and her rich brown hair, tied back, fell down past her waist in heavy waves; her brown eyes were soft and warm, quieter now, it seemed. Thorne looked at her from his own invisible sphere of calm. His unexpected presence startled her, but he was so calm, so matter-of-fact that he made the situation very easy for her.

Carlos came home. He and Thorne helped Gavin into the kitchen for dinner. Thorne was appalled by Gavin's wasted body; his legs in particular looked shrunken, except that the joints were swollen, slightly twisted looking, and the veins bulged out.

This kitchen was still a place of warmth and laughter, not so very different, on the surface, from what he remembered of long ago. But there were differences; for a beginning, there were so few of them together now. Sadness came into the stillness of Thorne's mind, as it had been doing now and again all through the morning. It was a painful feeling, almost a tangible reality, but not so bad that he had to barricade himself against it.

He helped Carlos with some work after dinner. When he came back to the house, Gavin was sleeping and Meg was getting ready to go to her own home.

"I'll harness your horse," he said.

"Take your own horse," Maria urged him warmly, "and go along with her. You should see what a nice house they have, and maybe Gordon will be home by now. It's been years since you've seen Gordon."

Thorne drove the buggy, holding the horse to a brisk walk, his own rented saddle horse tied behind. He looked at the autumnal trees, the fall wild flowers—weeds—blooming along the roadside. The quiet, near-empty peace still held him, and he would not question it, only let it last however blessedly long it might. He thought he could go on like this forever, holding the reins lightly, feeling the low sun hot on the back of his head and his shoulders, a light breeze, warm for so late in the year, on his face, blowing the dust raised by the buggy behind them, Meg beside him, slender and graceful, silent.

Meg looked at him in quick, covert glances. There were lines, faint ones, at the corners of his eyes and mouth, lines of rigid, unrelenting control. His face had grown so stern—no less strongly handsome, she thought, but rather formidable. His black hair was graying at the temples, and once or twice she saw flashes of hardness in the depths of his indigo eyes.

For the most part, though, it had been so easy and good, having him home. She had stopped trying, long ago, to think what that might be like. He seemed strangely quiet, relaxed. She felt, finally, that something must be said. She began to speak, had to clear her throat and start over.

"Will you be staying long? Mama hadn't got round to asking you that."

"I have to leave tomorrow."

"They'll be disappointed, Thorne. Mama thinks you've finally come for a good long visit, though she did say you didn't bring any luggage with you."

"Uncle Gavin knows. I'll tell her when I go back. They're—the most wonderful people in the world."

"Yes. They've always missed you, worried about you."

"Have you?"

"Thorne—"

"I mean," he said quickly, calmly, "as family. It's all right, Meggy. It really is. I don't know when it began to be all right—a long time ago, I suppose. Today, well, almost anything seems all right. There are a lot of things I may never understand, but I wanted you to know, if it matters . . ."

"I'm so—glad you've finally come back. They've always felt you could never stop blaming them for—Mr. Maxwell and all that happened."

"I don't blame them for anything. That stopped a long time ago, too."

"Will you—can you talk to them about it? It would mean a lot to them, especially to Papa, I think, to hear that from you."

"We talked earlier, he and I."

Thorne wished she would not try to say more. He wanted to be able to go on with his inner quietness. It was not euphoria, but neither was it depression. It was a kind of neutrality, and while it lasted, he could relax his rigid determination at thought control. Also, he could think of others, and he saw that Meg's fair face was a little flushed, knew she was uncomfortable with him. He could, out of his inner respite, spare a little effort now to help her be at peace.

Meg was saying tensely, "Mama says she's hardly been able to get you to talk about your family. Ranald and Amy tell us what they can, but . . . Thorne, are you—happy?"

"That's a strange question," he said, "I've always wondered why people ask it, because happiness—whatever it is—means completely different things to different people."

"But I meant . . . are you content, I suppose—reasonably satisfied with some of the things about your life?"

"If I'm not," he said, "it's my own doing. But I'm not really sure. Being content, things like that, I've tried not to think about too much, so I can't really say. Maybe I'll be more content, satisfied, after whatever it is that's come on me today. . . . I've tried for a long time not to expect too much of anything. I used to believe there had to be—fairness, a kind of justice in life as an automatic part of the scheme of things, those things, and hope. . . . When I finally knew that living and hope and justice just didn't go together as a matter of course, it got a little easier to . . . hell, I meant to answer you. I'm not making any sense at all."

"You don't—hope?" she asked slowly. "That has to be a part of everyone's life, surely."

As he looked at her, his eyes seemed all black in shadow, very intense. Confusion, concern for him showed in her face.

"Well, it's not not-hoping," he said, well aware of the difficulty of putting thoughts so long suppressed into words. He wanted her to understand, to stop worrying. "I used to think—a long time ago, that people, when they become adults, make their own lives, have complete control, complete responsibility. I still believe that." He smiled fleetingly over the futility of words. "It just doesn't seem to be true, that's all."

"Once," she said, "such a long time ago, we talked about God. You said people ought to have the credit, or the blame, for what they did."

"Yes. I still think that, but there have been some strange times, a few, when—things have happened to me, when I've come to some point in my life—a crossroads, the dramatists would call it—and I've seemed to know what was going to happen. It's as if I'd known it for a long time, had been moving toward it without quite knowing consciously. Then it happens and I'm not surprised. The surprising thing is always—well, how am I going to deal with it, now that it's out in the open and I have to look at it? It's a worrisome thing. It almost tempts me to try to believe in—predestination, predetermination, something like that."

"You?" she smiled incredulously.

"It's a temptation," he said a little diffidently. "It would be a simple answer to a lot of questions. Isn't it a part of how you explain things?"

"The church doesn't . . ." she began.

"I'm not talking about the church, Meggy. I'm asking about you. Or can you still, really, let the church do your thinking for you?"

"Thorne—"

"Relax. Please do. I'm not knocking the church. I just want to know, since we're talking about it . . ."

"Well," she said slowly. "I don't *think* I let the church do my thinking. It's still very important to me, the church. I believe in most of the things we learned as we were growing up, but predestination is not a Catholic teaching at all. And when you say you've stopped expecting fairness or justice, that you've tried not to hope for anything . . . that's scary. It sounds so stark and . . ."

"It's just that I don't like surprises. The ones I've

had have been bad ones. What I've expected—looked forward to, has hardly ever happened, or when it has, it's been so different, disappointing . . . I think part of the trouble was that I rarely got around to deciding exactly what I wanted, what I meant to aim for. Some people seem to be able to *plan* their lives and have the plans work out. Ranald has done that, I think. When I was young, I couldn't be bothered with things like that. I wanted a lot, but without any real idea of *what* I wanted. Things sort of got out of hand, as far as I was concerned. I lost control of my life without ever quite having had it, and I've never really got it back. I never quite got the knack of order and . . . well, it makes a good excuse anyway."

"There must have been times," she said gently, "when you resented Ranald very much. He's told me how Angus used to hold him up as an example, things like that. He still worries about it."

"I haven't resented him. Well, maybe I have, but it was no fault of his, none of that."

"Once—the other time you were home, you said something about feeling second best."

"I don't remember ever saying that, but, all right, if I'm to be honest, I suppose there must have been times when I'd have liked to have Angus's approval, but that I didn't have it—that's not Ran's fault."

"Maybe, it's not your fault either," she said gently. "Maybe it's no one's fault. There doesn't have to be fault, does there, always?"

"Well, there's always someone who has the chief responsibility . . ."

"It doesn't have to be you. Ranald and I have talked about it, about you . . . People have always leaned on you, because you're strong and you—don't run away from things, not on the surface. Even when you were a boy, blithe and bonnie, the way Papa says, we knew you weren't afraid to face things."

"But I am," he said, vaguely surprised that it seemed

not to be common knowledge. "It's easier to slide away from things, not to face them. I've always been a coward."

"You're not," she said softly, warmly. "You face—cowardice better than most people. It's a part of your strength. It began a long time ago, people using you. Papa did it, wanting you for his son. He didn't realize, of course. Ranald used you to get the things he wanted. He says Elizabeth used you, in her own way, because you would stand up to Angus and she couldn't. Angus used you, he must have had no feelings at all. Mr. Fitzroy wanted you to take on not just Intermountain but his family—everything. *I* used you. Ranald thinks your wife has used you terribly, and he says your children learned early to use your guilt. . . ."

"I left them," he said calmly, "Cherish and the children, and there is guilt. I've never been able to . . ."

"You ask too much of yourself," she said fervently, "and nothing of anyone else. Don't you know that in any relationship, both people have to be able to give. If they both can't, or won't, it's not a relationship; it's all one-sided. You won't let other people give to you. You can't accept. It's a part of your strength, but it fosters weakness in other people; it almost forces them to take advantage of you." She sighed. "What will you do now? I mean, with the rest of your life, if you don't go back to your family?"

"I won't go back. I've got the work. It's been an important part of my life for a long time."

She was silent for a time, before saying gently, "But *you*, Thorne, what about you? You're not a machine that just works. Ranald talks about how hard you work, what a fine job you've been doing all these years, but what sort of person are *you* when you're not being the engineer or vice-president in charge of Intermountain. What else do you do—with yourself?"

"I survive," he said quietly, simply.

Meg shivered, but Thorne was staring ahead, at the

horse's ears, and did not notice. The words were coming easier now. He was not so much concerned about her comfort as with this strange new experience he was having. He went on thoughtfully.

"I do what I can with what there is. I hated Angus; I suppose I always will, for the hardness and coldness of him, his single-mindedness. But I've come to see some similarities between us, though I don't *want* to see them. . . . My work is important, and it's just about all there is that lasts. At least I *have* that. It's something concrete that I can get hold of, can feel good about—or bad—and can understand. I think I don't need much more, not anymore. It's a restful thought. What about you, Meg? Are you happy?"

"Yes," she said, also feeling calm now, deeply sad, but quiet. "I suppose everyone has vague ideas of what happiness—what life is going to be like, and it probably doesn't turn out the way we dreamed, for anyone, but it's a good life I have. I love teaching, children. Gordon's a good lawyer. We have things in common, interests in—well, justice, legal justice, the rights of people who often can't afford a lawyer or even a teacher. We'll never be rich from interests like that, but there are other rewards. We may be moving to Denver sometime next year. We haven't told the folks yet, or anyone. It's going to upset Mama. If we leave, that will mean that all of us have moved away except Carlos and his family. Gordon has been asked by a number of people, to work for some unions, labor unions. I dread the thought of leaving. Things change so. Papa won't be with us much longer, the doctor says. I can't imagine Mama without him. But I think working for the unions is something Gordon will have to do, will want to do soon."

They were silent for a time, both of them thinking of Gavin and Maria, feeling their childhood and youth slipping farther away, going with the things and people they had taken for granted then, things and people that had been a great part of the stability of life, of who they themselves were, or thought themselves to be.

Thorne rolled a cigarette, lit it and drew on it deeply.

"I came here, mostly, because of a little boy, Meg. It wasn't just that I thought I ought to see Uncle Gavin and Aunt Maria. I came meaning to ask something of them. It seemed damned selfish when I thought of it, and I've gotten so much, somehow, just from being here again; but now I have to go back to trying to think what I can do for Murphy. He's Frank Fitzroy's boy, not four years old yet. His father died two years ago, and his mother was killed in a fire last week."

"Nancy Fitzroy was killed?" Her eyes filled with shock, sympathy. "Ranald and Amy have talked about her, about them, of course."

"Well, Murphy hasn't got anyone else now. His grandpa, Nancy's dad, was so broken up about it. Tom asked me to look after Murph, but I can't, not alone. He's smart, Murphy is, and—sensitive. He needs—things I don't think I can give him. I came here meaning to ask them, Uncle Gavin and Aunt Maria . . . Ranald had been telling me that Uncle Gavin wasn't well. I guess I just hadn't been able to—believe it. I can't ask them to start over again with a little boy, not the way things are for them. I couldn't ask it of Carlos and Josefa. They have their own lives, their own children, their own problems to worry about and the right to be left alone with them. Murph needs—some special attention right now, and this wouldn't be the place for him, with Uncle Gavin sick and—"

"Murphy," she said softly. Her face had taken on a soft glow, her eyes were big and wistful. She could look at him for only a moment.

He told her, briefly, about the fire, about Ted.

"Oh, Thorne, how terrible!" she breathed. Tears had sprung to her eyes.

"So Murphy needs a new life. Security, I suppose,

nothing more to do with death . . ."

"But where is he now?"

"He's in Mixon, at the hotel there, with a girl I've got looking after him. I was going to bring him here, but—"

"Thorne, I want children more than anything in the world," Meg said urgently, unsteadily. "Gordon and I both do. We just go on waiting and hoping, and nothing . . . Would you let me keep him if Gordon —Oh, I know he'd want it too. Do you think he might still be in danger? Murphy?"

"I don't think there's any more danger. Ted isn't brave, or even very bright. I don't think he set the fire that killed Nancy. He hired someone and then got out of town. I don't think he planned any further than the fire. I wouldn't ask anyone else to take Murph if I thought there was still that kind of danger. For other reasons, publicity and such, it would be better if no one knew where he was for a while. It would be no kind of life for him at all, being with me, and I'd like . . ."

"Oh, let him come to us. Let me ask Gordon. But can't something be done about Ted?"

Thorne pulled up the horse in the shade of cottonwoods. The houses on the outskirts of Quintana could be seen in the distance. The Oso, beyond the trees, made a deep placid song.

"There's no real evidence," he said. "I mean none leading to Ted. It's plain enough the fire was set, but the police don't really want to push it. I think the only way it could ever be solved is if the person Ted hired were to be found somehow. The Fitzroy family is well-known, and the Hampsteads—the family of the girl Ted was with that night—are as well-known and much more respected. They resented having their daughter questioned, even though it was done without publicity. I've raised hell myself about publicity, but it's because of Murph . . . and Nancy . . ."

"Thorne, I know it's no business of mine, but the way you look—did you . . . you loved Nancy, didn't you?"

"No," he said heavily. "She was a very special person, but I still couldn't think of her without thinking of Fitz. I guess, though, that I had begun to want to."

Meg's hands had grown cold with the nervous excitement of thinking of the child. Without realizing it, she laid one of them on his hand, holding the reins. His hand felt warm and strong in the instant before he, unconsciously and out of long habit, drew away from the touch of another person. Meg wanted to understand the intensity of his look, but her thoughts were too much occupied now with the little boy.

"Would you," she asked uneasily, "—if you mean to leave him with someone else now—would you want to have him back later?"

"I'd want that, I suppose, but I wouldn't do it, not if I knew he was happy with someone else. He doesn't need to be changing homes all the time. When he's older, a lot older, and if he were to show a real interest in the business, I might . . . well, that would be about all I could give him, really."

"It's not nearly all you're giving him now," she said gently.

He looked away at the eastern mountains, the snow there sparkling bright in the sun's almost-horizontal rays.

Meg's voice was barely audible as she said, "Please let him come to me, Thorne. I don't know what's wrong with me, that we can't have children. Sometimes I think . . ."

"Don't say it's a punishment, Meggy. You've been looking for punishment all your life. You don't deserve any."

"But I've tried so hard to . . . sometimes I can't

find any other answer, when I want children so very much." She wiped quickly at her eyes, looking down at the dusty weeds. Then she said tautly, "I think you haven't believed in God for a long time, not since we were kids, at least, not the way I do."

"Ah no. I can't think I'm that important."

"It's not just the need, the wish to be important, Thorne. God is important to me. I'm not as intense as I once was, about the Church and things like that, but believing in God—that he does know, does care—is a part of what and who I believe myself to be. Can you understand that?"

"Yes, I think I can, but this thing of punishment. You don't deserve punishment, Meggy. You haven't done anything to deserve bad things for the rest of your life. Isn't it supposed to be enough to tell your God you're sorry, to repent? Do you have to believe in something that—vicious? Shouldn't God be busy running the world?"

"Yes," she said. "I do see what you're saying, but for me to believe the way you do—it would seem to me like abandonment. I mean, I'd feel God had abandoned me if I didn't think he cared. Didn't you feel desolate, when you first began to think things like that God was too busy to look after you?"

He lit a cigarette, knowing it was time now, his mind quiet and sad.

"In that last letter, such a long time ago, you asked me to come home as soon as I could. Not long after I read it, maybe an hour or two, Ranald told me you and Gordon were married."

"Please don't, Thorne," she said unevenly. "It's not fair."

"I don't mean to be unfair," he said softly, wistfully. "Your answering isn't a condition for your having Murphy, nothing like that. It's just something I'd like to be able to understand, after all this time."

"It *is* so long ago," she said pleadingly and looked

up to find his eyes on her face, waiting, insistent. Words came from her in a rush then. "I thought I'd have to be able to explain to you some day and I have never known how I could do it. Thorne, I was so upset—a little out of my mind at times, I think. One minute, I'd be sure it had to be right—us—the next, I'd be certain it couldn't be. I couldn't sleep much, or eat, or think straight. For a while, several weeks, I thought I was pregnant, and I'd decided we'd have to get married, but I wasn't. I suppose it was just all the tension. Anyway, I'd sent you that letter before I knew I wasn't pregnant. Finding out I wasn't pregnant was like a sign to me that we'd been—forgiven, given another chance—"

"Ah, God," he groaned.

"I didn't want to hurt you," she rushed on, looking up pleadingly. His eyes, his whole face, were averted. "Please see that, Thorne, please know it. It seemed you'd be less hurt by having it ended than by going on. Don't you see we'd have ended by hating each other, with me so mixed up, feeling that it was wrong."

"I can't know that. You can't. I believed then that I could make you see it wasn't wrong. What would have happened if I hadn't gone away when you asked me to?"

"We can't know that either," she said with a hint of anger. "Oh, don't you think I knew how cruel I was being, how unfair to you and to Gordon . . ."

"And yourself?" he asked quietly.

"Thorne, I knew I couldn't face you, stand up to you, if you came home again. I was afraid of you, afraid that I was too weak and that you'd make me do something I believed was wrong. When Gordon asked me, again, to marry him, it seemed . . ."

"Deliverance," he said bitterly, his mouth a straight, hard line.

"Oh, God, Thorne, please don't! Don't you think

I've . . . Please look at me. Please forgive me. It's been so long . . ."

She buried her face in her hands. He turned and looked down on her hair, highlighted in the late sun. The calm was still upon him.

"Meggy, I stopped . . . I forgave you a long time back, I think. I'm sorry for—seeming angry. It's just that I've wanted to understand. You were probably right all along, and it would never have worked out. Everything gets so tangled, so complicated when you start trying to sort it out. We were pretty young then. Maybe, in some ways, we were just sort of products of each other's imagination. We hadn't seen each other then since we were kids. Maybe we didn't really know each other at all, as the people we were going to become. Maybe we didn't know ourselves. It's a thing I've wondered about. It's the way, finally, that I made myself believe you were right to—end it. . . . But at first, you see, that wasn't enough. I tried to think of everything that might have happened while I was in Europe. I thought you must have been pregnant and scared. I complicated hell out of every possibility, and now it seems to have been so—simple."

"But it wasn't simple!" she cried, the words muffled by her hands.

"No. I only meant . . . Meggy, don't cry." He touched her hair. "I think we need to talk about it, a little, if we're to . . . I'd like us to be friends. You're the finest person I've ever known, a stable person. It seems I can depend on your being—what you've always been."

She looked at him. There was no bitterness in his expression or tone. He met her eyes easily, but her own sight was still blurred.

"If you think you might want to have Murphy, then can we be friends? I'll want to see for myself how Gordon feels."

"He never knew, Thorne, about us."

"I didn't suppose he had, and that's not why I want to see him."

He drew the reins tight, making the horse lift its head from its roadside browse and move on toward the little town.

"I wish things could have been better for you," she said after some moments had passed. "Ranald and Amy have told me about Cherish. It seemed so hard, so impossible for you, and I always hoped that you might find someone else some day."

"I suppose Gordon's been a good husband?" he said disinterestedly. "He always wanted to be best at whatever he did, as I remember, and to be taken terrifically seriously. Gordon and I never liked each other much, you know. But it's not a thing for you to worry about, or anyone else. Our dislike began a long time before the other thing."

"Gordon and I have a lot in common," she said, sitting erect again, her eyes clear and steady.

"But no children."

"Thorne—"

"I only mean that it seems sad. I said I'd stopped expecting fairness from life, but I guess I still haven't, really. I only meant to say that it seems unfair that I have two children and you've had none."

"You didn't want them?"

"Meg, it really was a hell of a marriage. They've never been my children. I was there at the time of conception, that's all. They're Cherish's kids. That's the way she wants it, and I've let it be that way, because it was so much easier that way. It's made their lives easier, I hope, that I haven't fought her over them. At least, their ultimate welfare makes a good-sounding excuse for my neglect. If I'd cared enough about them, been able to have the feelings most fathers have, I'd have found a way, but I've hardly felt anything for them."

"You feel a lot for Murphy," she said gently.

"Yes."

"It's sad then, terribly sad, that you feel you can't keep him with you."

"Not sad for Murph, if he can be loved and have a good home."

"Our house is right over there, the white one," Meg said. "We sold the old one and had this built several years ago. There's the new school, too, through the trees."

Maria cried when she heard Thorne did not mean to stay. He promised to come back the next day for a little while, and told them a little about Murphy and Meg's wish to take him.

The next morning, he rented a buggy, and after seeing Flora onto the morning train for Denver, took Murphy to Quintana. The peace was still upon him, a kind of lassitude that made him want to sleep. He tried gently to convince Murphy that he might like living around here.

Meg was watching for them; her wistfulness and nervous anticipation were painful to see. Gordon, reading the Denver papers, held a glass in his hand. He had been drinking yesterday, Thorne recalled, and felt renewed uneasiness about him. He tried to put down the feeling, thinking that he had never been very fair to Gordon, had always felt some jealousy of him, first because of Ranald, then Meg. Yesterday, Gordon had seemed to him not much different from when they were boys, but he hadn't been so bad then. Thorne recalled the thing with Esteban Arragon, but that could have happened to any young boy. He had not known the meaning of compassion then, did not particularly want to know it now, but wanted desperately, for Meg's sake and Murphy's sake, to be fair about Gordon.

Murphy kept very close to Thorne at first, saying

little, looking frightened and worried. Thorne had told him, as they drove to Meg's, all he could think of about Meg and Gordon that might interest the little boy: about their house, the school, Meg's family near by. He said this might be a new home for him, if Murphy chose to stay. Finally, reluctantly, Murphy let Meg persuade him now to go and look at the room that would be his if he stayed.

"You won't leave?" he asked Thorne.

"I won't, Murph."

They went upstairs, and the living room was silent. It seemed to Thorne that Meg's house was a place for serenity and comfort. He saw her in everything about it.

Gordon, too, remembered boyhood, perhaps more clearly than Thorne did. He hated Thorne's knowledge of that shameful secret thing that had happened so long ago with Esteban Arragon. That, and the fact that Thorne was so sure of himself, always so complacent and sure of his own rightness.

"It's a little early for it," Gordon said, and hated the sound of apology in his tone, "but would you like a drink? A man has to relax sometime, and this is Sunday. Meg's just come home from church . . ." He was refilling his own glass. "You sure you won't have something?"

"Thanks, no. I've got the coffee."

Gordon's fair hair had thinned and grown lighter. His face was round, what people called a baby-face, but lines and wrinkles made him look older than he was, and the veins in his nose were becoming prominent under the extreme fairness of his skin. His eyes had almost no color at all. Everything about him seemed faded, subdued, as sometimes happens with people who are very light in coloring. He had a mustache, long, but thin and wispy, almost the color of his skin. I wouldn't like to look like that, Thorne thought. It was a smug thought, perhaps, but it made him feel a little more kindly toward Gordon, more tolerant.

"It will break her heart," Gordon said, glancing toward the stairs, "if he won't stay. She's counting on it. I suppose you know that."

"I've done what I can to convince Murphy that this could be the right place for him, but will it be, Gordon? I felt yesterday, and I still feel that no matter what you say, you'd rather not have him here."

"I'm only thinking of Meg," Gordon said shortly, sitting down again among his newspapers. "I don't want her hurt. After what's happened to the boy, the fire and all—it's not going to be easy. It would be hard enough—would mean making changes enough—to take any child of this age into our home. Murphy has, as you've said yourself, special problems. Meg says she told you we may be moving to Denver. I don't want us to have Murphy, if there's going to be danger of any kind."

"I don't think Ted's likely to make any more trouble."

"I don't mean just that. Take a chair, why don't you? I mean if relatives tried to take him away after Meg's got used to having him, something of that kind."

"Well, his grandfather won't do anything if he thinks Murph is all right. Old Tom moves around a lot, has to keep long working hours. He's asked me to do something. Aside from Tom, the only other relative Murphy has is Ted."

"But there's you," Gordon said, looking at him sharply.

"Me? What . . .?"

"How much interfering would you be doing? I'd feel better, talking like this, if you sat down."

Thorne moved thoughtfully to the chair Gordon indicated. "If it seemed to be working out for Murphy, I'd try to think of Meg—of both of you—as his parents. I'd have no right to interfere if things could be like that. I told you yesterday, there'll be a monthly check from his—"

"And I told *you*, I have no interest in the money. Take it, if he stays, and put it back into his trust fund. Could we adopt him? I won't see Meg get all tied up in someone if there's a chance he could be taken away from us."

"I suppose you could adopt him, eventually. I can talk to the lawyer who's coexecutor of his trust."

"I'm a lawyer," Gordon said testily.

"I know that, Gordon," he said curtly.

There was a silence. Thorne made himself a cigarette, lit it, and sipped at the coffee Meg had given him earlier. The coffee was cold now.

Gordon said belligerently, "If we do move to Denver, it will be because I'm there to represent people in various union matters. Intermountain Railways is one of the biggest companies in this state holding out against unions. I suppose you're proud of that, but what if your company goes to court one day and I'm the attorney for the opposition?"

Thorne frowned, puzzled. "I don't see what that has to do with whether or not Murphy can come to feel his home is with you and Meg."

Gordon smiled frostily. "Ranald has told us how wrapped up you are in your work. I have a feeling that trying to separate you from Intermountain would be like trying to separate church and state in a heavily Catholic county, like this one."

"If you mean, would I use Murphy—or Meg—as some kind of blackmail?—No."

"I remember you as a boy, Thorne," Gordon said coldly and paused to empty his glass. "You've always used any expedient to get what you want. Now, it seems, what's more important to you is more miles of track, laid and run your way. I understand you haven't even been able to find time for your own wife and children."

"I can't help what you remember, or think you remember from when we were growing up, and I haven't come here to discuss my personal life, though I will tell you that I stopped having any illusions, a long time ago, about being able to get what I wanted."

"Your company took that land grant on the river away from the Ornado family—"

"Come on, Gordon, I didn't come here to argue that with you. I can't help it if you lost that case, but I do have to remind you that you were opposing the federal government then, not Intermountain. The courts found the grant to be invalid."

"That's a mere technicality and you know it. The greater part of the land went to the railroad."

"Technicalities seem to be about all the law's based on."

"What if that had been the Arragon grant? Suppose it had concerned Gavin and Maria that directly? It could have, you know, if your people had chosen to route a little differently."

"Well, it wasn't the Arragon grant."

"Companies never want to be bothered with thinking about *people*, do they? You can't conceive, for instance, of men being able to demand their just rights through a union?"

"I can conceive of their wanting to stand on their own feet, get their rights for themselves."

"Some aren't capable of that and you know it."

"I know I wouldn't try to decide that for them, dictate to them what they're capable of or what each one believes his right to be. You're looking down on people as incompetents, but then all crusaders do that, don't they?"

Thorne kept his voice low and even. Gordon's rose a little and he flushed.

"What can you possibly know about your workmen? You inherited everything."

Thorne grinned, then frowned, wishing he had some respect for Gordon.

"I mean to help to see," Gordon went on hotly, "that your workmen, all *people*, get their birthrights as Americans. The common man has been deprived—used long enough by companies like yours. I mean to see such companies broken, if it takes that. You've been careful and slick, you people, but you're going to have anti-trust troubles. I know you've incorporated, ostensibly divided things up, but you're not fooling anyone. Besides the mines, mill and railroad, plenty of us know the interests MM&F has in timber and newspapers, for instance."

"All right, suppose we're broken," Thorne said reasonably as Gordon got up to pour himself another drink. "What would happen to this valley without the railroad? It wouldn't be without for long, of course. Rocky Mountain and Pacific would get hold of our right-of-way soon enough. Both the Santa Fe and the Union Pacific are doing everything they can to get hold of a voting majority in RM&P stock. *There* you have trusts."

"Lawbreaking is not a matter of degree," Gordon said, sneering. "What you're trying to say is what a fine, benevolent despot Intermountain is. Christ! the times I've heard that from company people."

Thorne couldn't help another grin. "I guess, sooner or later, all our trains do pull into a benevolent despot."

Gordon was clearly angry now. "It's hardly a laughing matter."

"You're right, it's not. But I've told you, I don't want to argue with you. I've come here about Murphy." Still, he couldn't quite not say, "Besides, I wouldn't think all this idealism would pay off too well for a lawyer."

"There are people, even lawyers, who are able to look beyond margins of profit!"

But Meg and Murphy were coming downstairs. Both the men were relieved to have them back.

Murphy came miserably and leaned against Thorne's knees. Unconsciously, Thorne clenched his fists to stop himself from touching the child, picking him up.

"It's a nice room," Murphy said, answering Thorne's question. "There's a big back yard where other kids play sometimes. If Spike hadn't got all burned up, he'd like to play in that yard. And out the window, you can see the school where Mrs. Gaynor teaches. Thorne, I want to stay with you."

"Do you want to meet our cat?" Meg asked, trying to keep anxiety out of her voice. Going into the kitchen, she called back, "Here she is, lying on the back steps, just where you and I decided she'd probably be."

Murphy went to see, and Thorne followed him, wanting to avoid any more discussion with Gordon. Gordon showed no intention of going with them.

"She's fat," observed Murphy, smiling at the big calico cat.

"That's partly because she'll be having kittens in a couple of weeks."

"She will? Where are they now?"

Meg looked at Thorne, who smiled and shrugged.

She said to Murphy, "Her name is Brendeen. That's for the place where my papa came from in Scotland."

The three of them had gone out into the sunny back yard.

"How many kittens?" asked Murphy speculatively, still stroking the cat who had begun to purr loudly.

"We can't know that until they're born," said Meg.

"What's that?" he asked, indicating a small building nearby.

"The tool shed," she said. "Look inside if you like. Can you open the door?"

Absently, her eyes following the little boy, she sat

down. Thorne sat on the step below her and looked at the ground.

"He's wonderful," she said softly.

"Meggy, Gordon doesn't like this," Thorne said hesitantly. "Surely you must see that I can't leave him here if . . ."

"It's not Murphy," she said quickly. "We talked a long time about it after you'd left yesterday. In fact, we've hardly talked about anything else. Gordon . . . doesn't want you to see Murphy, if things work out for him with us."

"He didn't tell me that—exactly. Why not?"

"It's because of the union disputes, things like that. He's come to feel the same way about Ranald and Amy. He says a child we're going to raise ought to be left alone to think as we do as he grows up, not be pulled between—well, opposing camps, until he *is* grown and can decide things on his own."

Thorne said evenly, "I'd thought of seeing Murphy sometimes, for a weekend or something like that, but . . . If he were—satisfied, staying with you, there'd be no reason I'd *have* to see him. I won't tell him that yet, but . . ."

"Thank you. You do understand, Thorne? Can you stay for lunch?"

She looked up then, met his eyes briefly and saw his misery in giving up the little boy; she began to flush at her own selfishness.

"No. I told Aunt Maria I'd come back there today. I'll be taking the bobtail tonight for Santa Fe."

"The what?"

"The bobtail. It's what we call the mail trains."

Murphy wandered back and sat down close to Thorne.

"Well, Murph, what do you think?" he said, and his voice sounded unsteady to him. The quietness inside him seemed to be breaking now. "Want to stay here and see those kittens?"

"I could, Thorne, but I'd rather go with you."

"You know I'm never around. We talked about that—"

"But I could *go* with you."

"No, you couldn't. I've told you, I won't even consider that. You have to stay put in one place so you can spend a lot of time learning things."

"My ma said you were going to find me a teacher. She said it just before . . ."

"Meg's a teacher."

"I guess I could stay here—for a little while, if I have to. Would you send letters?"

"I will."

"I'd send you some too."

"Good. Send them to Ranald's. I don't know where I'm going to be, exactly, for a few weeks. Listen, Murphy, I . . . who does that little red wagon belong to? See it over there?"

"She said it's the neighbors'. They have a boy my age."

"Well," he said, speaking with difficulty now, "why don't you take that load of dirt it has in it and put it in that hole? It looks like some dog has been back here, trying to dig up the—"

"Lilac bush," Meg finished for him.

"I can do that," said Murphy without interest. He went slowly out to the wagon, began to move it listlessly, looking small and alone. Thorne had stood up.

"Don't get up," he said curtly to Meg. "Stay with him. I can't say good-bye to him. Write to Ranald and Amy about him sometimes, will you? They'll tell me."

"Oh, Thorne," Meg began, her eyes filling with tears, but he had gone, running, stumbling, around the corner of the house.

Some six weeks later, on a snowy evening in December, Thorne hurried up the walk to Ranald's house, preoccupied with a problem that had been awaiting him at the office when he got back to town a few hours earlier. He stopped, disconcerted, staring, as Dahlia opened the door.

Dahlia had to laugh at the look on his face. "It's all right. Come on in here, honey, before you let in all the cold. Didn't anybody tell you I'd be here?"

"Yes, but I'd forgotten. I thought I'd come to the wrong house—or the right house, but for the wrong reason—Well, you know."

"I know," she said, her face sorrowful as she took his hat and coat. "They're in there, Mr. Ranald and all the family." She gestured at the closed parlor door.

"Dahlia, do you want to tell me what happened?"

"Well, sir, she just—Miss Cherish thought I'd known you meant to leave, thought I had a part in it or something. Miss Amy mentioned once, a long time ago, that if I ever needed a place to work, I ought to come here. She was just talking in fun, you know, but I came."

"Cherish just told you to leave?"

"She did, finally, a little more than a week ago."

"Dahlia, you've been a better mother to Cherish . . . and to Stuart and Clare—I'm sorry for them. You don't have to work, you know."

"Honey, I know I've got that money, and I thank you for it, again, but I *do* have to work. *You* ought to be able to understand that."

"Well, yes, only, you know Cherish is going to ask you to come back. I'm a little surprised she hasn't already done. I hope, for your sake, you won't go."

She began to cry then. "Oh, Mr. Thorne, I can't talk about it. You go on in. They're waiting for you."

"You stayed a long time," he said softly. "Thank you."

Starting away from him down the hall, she said, her breath catching on a sob, "Honey, so did you."

Thorne had to stand there for a moment, getting

himself in hand. It occurred to him that the house seemed unusually silent, considering the four ebullient children who lived here. As he opened the door, all of them, smiling, began to sing, "Happy Birthday." Thorne stopped and tried to smile, managing only to look perplexed.

"I didn't . . ." he faltered. "I hadn't thought of it. Ran, couldn't you have . . . Thank you, all of you."

Elizabeth came and kissed his cheek diffidently, leading him into the room. She was still stiff and shy—that was not likely to change for a person her age—but she was happy. She was not so far from sixty, but she hardly looked or felt older than she was when Angus died, almost twelve years ago. She was a part of a real family now, dearly loved, and so grateful for her happiness.

"You have to blow out all the candles, Uncle Thorne," Betsy, the six-year-old was saying. "Then you get a wish."

"But we can't eat the cake till we've had our suppers," cautioned Susan, who was four. "Mommy says not even you can have any till you eat up all your supper. When it was *my* birthday, *I* threw up."

Thorne laughed with the others, then, still embarrassed at being the center of attention, blew out the candles Amy had lighted on the tall white cake.

"It's all right if you whisper your wish to me," Susan assured him confidentially. "I won't tell anybody."

"All of you, go," said Amy making sweeping gestures. "Your supper will be cold. You can have cake with us later."

A little silence followed the children's departure.

Thorne turned to Amy and said, "I didn't mean to disturb the whole household. You shouldn't have—"

"Don't be silly," she said quickly, but her gray eyes were full of kindness and understanding. "Our kids are always late for supper. So are we, usually. Everybody around here likes birthdays. We couldn't let one pass without candles and cake. Also, it seems a little ridiculous for you to be staying at the hotel, as little as you're in town, and with the holidays coming. I've told Ran we shouldn't stand for it."

She gave the two men drinks and went to see about things in the kitchen. After a moment's talk about the weather, Elizabeth left them as well.

"We know it's Murphy's birthday too," Ranald said. "We sent his gift. There was a letter from Meg yesterday. He seems to be doing well, and she hasn't sounded so happy in—well, ever. Gordon's decided they will be moving here in the spring, when school's out. I don't suppose any of us will be seeing much of them, the way Gordon's come to feel. Meg feels lousy about your having to—give Murphy up the way—"

"But do you think it's going to be all right for Murphy?"

"Amy can show you the letter. I never know what happens to any mail around here. Sit down, Thorne. Do you want to see the paper? I've finished with the damned thing. I hear enough about tight money and impending chaos at the office all day. Jim was telling me just before you came in, that you're thinking about concrete for the tunnel where Fitz was hurt."

"I want to try it. It's so wet in there that shoring timbers rot. I don't remember how many times they've been replaced."

"How long will the Amity line be shut down?"

"I'm not sure. We're trying to give the people up there plenty of notice, get everything shipped in before Tom's men go to work on it right after Christmas. The snow gangs can't wait till the road's shut down."

"Yes," Ranald said grimly. "They can go over and work up toward Silver Valley and Beanpot. Have you ever thought what it might be like to build and operate railroads in the plains—the southern plains?"

"Things like that have crossed my mind from time

to time, but there wouldn't be any challenge in that. How does it go with your rolling mill?"

They talked about that for a time, then fell into a companionable silence. Thorne looked desultorily at the paper for a while, then said, not quite meeting Ranald's eyes, "Do you hear anything of Cherish and the kids? Since Dahlia's come away, I mean."

"Amy's run into Cherish three or four times—not intentionally. Evidently, she's just pretending nothing has happened. She doesn't ask about you or anything. A couple of days ago, at some women's club affair, Amy overheard her telling someone else you'd be home for Christmas. Will you have Christmas with us?"

"I've got to go to Montana soon. They should have been completely finished with work on the Columbia Creek line months ago, but there's still a construction crew up there, and we can't get a straight report from anybody about what the hell they're doing."

"You know, there'd probably be trains running, on some of the lines, if you'd try relaxing a little. Whatever is going on in Montana, will still be there after the holidays. I hoped you'd stay with us, then come with me to the hacienda to see Papa. Meg writes that he just keeps getting gradually worse, and I want to go down there the day after Christmas."

"I'll have to go back to Santa Fe after I've been to Montana. I'll stop at the hacienda then."

"He may not live that long, Thorne," Ranald said quietly.

Thorne looked down at the paper, found the print blurred. "It's probably not good for him, then, to have too many extra people around at once."

"Meg never meant you had to keep away entirely. She said you've only written twice to Murphy, and he—"

"This is the best way for Murphy, if that's going to be his home. I suppose, in some respects, it's the easiest way for me too. Have you heard anything about Ted?"

"Dahlia told us he's staying with some of his mother's people. She also said Cherish was trying to arrange to mortgage Fern Hill, and he'd given promissory notes, or something like that, against his debts. Thorne, I hadn't thought about it, specifically, until Mama wrote us after you were there in October. It's been more than twenty years since we came away with Angus and Elizabeth. You've only been home twice. It meant so much to Papa to see you, and Meg keeps trying to explain, to us, that Gordon never meant you to keep away completely . . . I remember when we were kids, you said once you'd go all over the world, seeing things, doing—whatever you were going to do, but that you'd ultimately come back home. I know Cherish would never have gone down there with you. I thought that might be part of the reason, but now you've . . . Couldn't you have stayed a few days in October—for Papa's sake, if nothing else?"

Looking at the paper again, Thorne said, "It's not safe for me to stay there. I get—well, I could like it too much."

"Is there something wrong with that?"

"Yes, I've not yet had—enough of whatever it was I meant to do. God, will you look at the damned silver prices?"

BOOK THREE
1892-1896

XV

1892

Early on a bleak April morning, Thorne stood in the open doorway of the office of Intermountain's trainmaster in Denver.

"Will the bobtail be about on time today, Ed?"

Other railroads had been struck. Enough Intermountain people had joined unions to make a strike here seem inevitable. The strike was to begin at midnight on Friday, and it was already Thursday.

The gray-haired trainmaster looked up hurriedly. "Oh, hello, Mac. They're making up the mail train now. It's going to be late out of here, but with this weather . . . I didn't know you were back in Denver. I've been told—I guess you gave the order—to keep operations as near normal as possible. They say they're just going to leave trains at the nearest depot, come tomorrow midnight. Damn' decent of 'em, to run into stations."

"I'll be going to Santa Fe then."

"All right, sir. I heard there was to be some kind of meeting down there. How's it been over in Utah?"

Thorne shrugged. "It's hard to tell yet if it's a good strike they've made or a flash in the pan. They're calling the place Oro Grande, and they want a railroad—yesterday. We couldn't really do much in the way of surveying with the weather like it's been."

"Jesus," muttered Ed, "I never saw a winter like this has been, and it don't show any signs of spring that I've seen." He looked out dolefully at a slow, greasy-looking drizzle. "I guess you heard about the snowshed collapse on the Beanpot road, up above Silver Valley? Did you file a route for the Utah line?"

"Yes, but I think RM&P may have beat us to this one. We should know about that in a few days, and I guess there's no hurry. We can't start any new construction until some of the other things are settled."

"I've heard," Ed said worriedly, "that this may last long enough to shut us down, all the way, that we might all better start looking for other jobs."

"Come on, Ed, you can hear anything, at a time like this. That sounds like union propaganda to me," he shrugged, smiling, "or company propaganda. You may *have* another job, though, look or not, if they strike."

Ed said unhappily, "Christ, I'd hate to have to go back to a telegraph office or something like that."

"Still, we'll have to do the best we can with supervisory personnel, and whoever else we can get, keep the mail going, and the freight, move whatever passengers we can."

"I heard there might be an injunction today . . . ?"

Thorne would not comment on that. He had asked for an injunction, but even if one were forthcoming, he doubted the men would honor it, not with the growing mood of restlessness and hostility he had sensed in recent months. He was attending the meeting in Santa Fe not because he thought getting together with representatives of other companies would help any of them, but because he felt he would be able to hire more nonunion replacement workers in the Santa

Fe area than in Denver, where more roads would be competing for people willing to work.

He said, "Would you have a telegram sent to Bennie Juarez in Santa Fe, Ed? Tell him I'll be wanting a narrow-gauge business car. I've got to see about that flood damage on the lower part of the San Miguel line. You might suggest to Bennie that if he's got a business car, he not lose it the way he did the last time I was there."

Ed made a note before looking up. "What'll we do if—" But Thorne had gone.

Thorne always liked walking around the big, ornate, echoing train station. Many roads used it, not just Intermountain, but its busyness made him feel proud. It was, when you knew some of the details, rather remarkable that so many activities—the running of passenger and mail services, the movement of so much freight—could be carried on as smoothly as they were and as close to schedule. Here was a further reason to resent the strike. Many people had worked many years to have this terminal functioning smoothly. All that would be wasted, lost for a time. By Saturday morning, this station would be either completely empty, or tumultuous with people trying to do jobs they knew little about; it depended on which groups struck and which others honored their picket lines. He felt mildly guilty about not staying with the main office now, but he had been in town nearly a week and could see nothing concrete to do for the next two days. In Santa Fe, he thought, he could hear what people from other companies were saying and find men to hire before the other roads got hold of them.

The bobtail, or Rio Grande Mail, consisted this morning of a mail and express car, a baggage car and two passenger coaches. Thorne had eaten breakfast in the depot restaurant and swung onto the back platform of the last coach after the train had begun to move. Scattered passengers sat in groups at either end of the coach, near the stoves. The car was an old one, and Thorne frowned at its shabbiness. The newer, more comfortable passenger coaches went on the express trains, but they badly needed new rolling stock. Money just kept getting tighter. The unions could hardly have chosen a more vulnerable time to hit them; not just Intermountain, but all railroads, like most businesses of any kind had come on harder times these past two years.

Choosing a seat near the middle of the car, at a little distance from anyone else, Thorne reluctantly opened the heavy briefcase Jim Ritter had thrust into his hands as he was leaving the office. He kept glancing up from the papers, watching the drizzle turn to wet, heavy snow as the train climbed slowly up the watershed divide south of Denver. He was less restless now, and he knew that even if there were no possibility of hiring strikebreakers in Santa Fe, he couldn't have stayed in the office any longer. The idea of a strike seemed a personal threat to him, as if he had been slapped with a gauntlet. He wanted to be out on the road, getting the feel of things, a party to some of what was happening—not just sitting in Denver, waiting for reports from other people.

There really was not enough light for the paperwork, he assured himself, and decided he would try to get some sleep.

Thorne had not seen his uncle Gavin again, alive. Gavin died in March of 1891. Thorne had gone to Quintana with Ranald and Amy for the funeral. His visit the previous autumn had been a time of such unexpected peace, but there was no peace left in March. Why couldn't he have made time to see Gavin, at least once again? He had to force himself to go into the little church of Santa Filomina and sit still through the service. Outside in the heavy, damp, miserable spring wind, they dropped wet, raw earth on a part of his life as they buried the old man. He kept a little distance between himself and anyone else, stood shivering, his eyes on last year's sere grasses.

He had thought, coming down, that he might see Murphy, but knew he should have realized Meg would not subject the little boy to the funeral. She stood there, with Gordon, at the other side of the grave. They had told Thorne Murphy was well and happy, seemed to be making a good adjustment.

Since the fall, in addition to sorely missing the boy, Thorne had had qualms about Murphy's living in Gordon's house, but had decided his own reluctance was of no particular importance. It would be Meg who was mostly responsible for Murphy. Thorne, as always, couldn't quite take Gordon seriously. He'd had to find a home for the boy quickly because he could not bear to go on for very long with the looking. Ranald and Amy would have had Murphy with them, gladly, but Thorne felt the change of living in Quintana would be a good distraction for Murphy. Besides, Thorne had made the decision to bring Murph to the valley, and he could not, at the time, seem to think beyond that. Meg would have been hurt so deeply if he had taken the child from her when his own doubts about the situation surfaced. His chief concern ought to be Murphy, not Meg, but in that strange quiet lassitude of those few days in October, he had been able to do little more than try to carry out previous plans and decisions. His mind had refused to be troubled with anything new. He had felt in October, and again in March, the sensation of losing control of his life, of having matters decided, regardless of his judgment, somehow taken out of his hands. In October, this had been rather a heady sensation. In March, beside the gaping grave, it was not.

Meg and Gordon would be going, with the rest of the family and friends, back to the house Gavin had built, gathering to comfort and bolster a strangely silent, small, vulnerable Maria. Thorne had been there for a while, before it was time to go to the church.

He had barely been able to look at his uncle's face as Gavin lay in his coffin. And Maria's quiet tears had choked him. He had been thankful for all the people then, because their presence had made it possible for him to spend most of the time in a corner of the kitchen, or, silent and miserable, with some of the other men, outside in the dreary early morning, looking up to the half-obscured mountains where Gavin had looked with love and appreciation for so many years. Thorne could not go back to the house, not again, not today, perhaps never. He felt sadly apart from the others; he thought that some of them resented him, and that he might deserve their negative feelings. He wanted to ask about seeing Murphy, but he could not bear to stay, and slipped away before the graveside service was quite finished.

Riding back to Mixon, he knew that he had wanted to see not just Murphy, but Murphy with Meg. He wanted the assurance he knew Meg would feel, that Gavin was not really in that plain coffin. It would have been comforting to hear, in her quiet white house in Quintana. He had reached Mixon just in time to get a ride back to Denver in the caboose of a freight train. . . .

Now, on the southbound mail train, a little more than a year since Gavin's death, Thorne knew sleep would not come any more easily than the abandoned paperwork. He wondered idly why he had not seen the conductor, but perhaps the man had passed while his eyes were closed. He stood up, swaying easily with the train's motion, and walked through to the forward passenger coach. The track was rough and needed work. This line was shared with RM&P, and each railroad liked to assume maintenance was the duty of the other.

"Hey, Thorne!" cried a child's voice. "Hey, here we are!"

Thorne was startled but not really surprised as he turned back to see Murphy and Meg occupying a seat in the rear of the small group of passengers at the car's front end. He felt again, briefly, that sensation of not being able to hold onto or direct anything, but he smiled, grasping Murphy's hand, catching hold of a seat back with his own free hand.

"Well, *Murph*!" he said with growing pleasure. "Look how you've grown! Hello, Meggy."

"I never supposed you'd ride your own train," Meg said, smiling, offering her hand. Her chest felt suddenly constricted, as if the breath had been knocked out of her; her heart beat fast, irregularly, as he took her hand. She said a little giddily, "I have a few complaints about the service. Is there anyone you know who would listen?"

"Oh, yes, ma'am," he said, still smiling, holding her cold hand in his warm one. "We all aim to please; that's all we ever aim for. I've got some complaints myself, like where did they resurrect these two coaches, but what's your problem?"

"I'm freezing," she said, withdrawing her hand. "Every time I look out the window, I get a little colder."

"Well, the first thing to do for that is not to look out the window. I'll see what else can be done."

With Murphy following, Thorne fed the stoves at each end of the car, then brought his heavy overcoat and put it round Meg's shoulders.

"So you're going to the hacienda."

"Yes. It's Murphy's spring holiday. Gordon had to go to Chicago, so we thought we'd spend a few days with Mama."

"How is she?"

"Her health is good, and she's been remarkable about adjusting to being without Papa. Carlos and Josefa live with her, you know. They're expecting their third child soon, and the children make Mama so happy. I'm going to try to persuade her to come back to Denver with us, but I doubt that she will, with Josefa's new baby coming. Would you like to sit down, Thorne?"

"If I sit by the window, it won't be so easy for you to look out."

She smiled and moved over. Murphy happily knelt on the seat in front, looking at them over its back.

"I wondered and wondered why you didn't come to see us," said the boy, "especially since we live in Denver now. It's a long time since we moved."

"I've wanted to, Murph," Thorne said, looking away. "I've been pretty busy."

"Mama and I kept thinking you were busy."

Thorne glanced at Meg, and she saw he shared her pleasure at Murphy's calling her Mama.

"Where are you going?" she asked.

Murphy pursued his own line of thought. "Last Christmas we were at Uncle Ranald's. We all thought you might come then."

Ranald had told Thorne of Gordon's disagreeableness, his insistence on maligning the company and making everyone else uneasy.

"I was out of town for nearly two months around Christmas time, Murphy. I'm going to Santa Fe now; then I'll be over on the San Miguel line, where your grandpa's working."

"Grandpa comes to see me about every two months," Murphy said accusingly.

"You're going to that meeting in Santa Fe," Meg said soberly.

"Yes. Not that I think there's any point in it. But maybe you'd know more about that than I do, the way Gordon's been working."

"Do you think there'll be a strike?"

"Yes, but as I said, you may know a lot more than I do."

"Even with the injunction everyone feels sure you'll get? I'd have thought you'd be in court today."

"Jim Ritter's taking a turn at the courthouse—my assistant. *I*'d have thought Gordon would be in court, rather than going to Chicago. Wasn't this supposed to be one of his big moments? What's he doing in Chicago?"

Meg had flushed. "It's probably better if we just—don't talk about it at all, don't you think?"

Thorne's eyes held hers very briefly. The light was poor, but there seemed a firm insistence, a kind of command in his dark gaze.

Murphy said, "Have you been building a new road?"

"Not just lately, Murph. Things have been a little—close for new construction."

"Those aren't Intermountain boxcars," Murphy observed, looking from the window as they edged past a sidetracked freight.

"That's an RM&P train," Thorne said. "This is shared track, a double track, so that there's a main line in both directions, and both tracks are triple-railed to handle both standard and narrow-gauge trains. When we get down on the Arkansas, you'll see where the two roads separate. That line, down below Haviland, was the first one I really felt I was taking part in—fifteen years ago, that was."

"I saw all this line when we were moving to Denver," Murphy said, "and when you and me and that girl went down to the valley that first time . . ."

Thorne looked up as the big, gray-haired conductor stopped beside them. "Hello, Smokey. It's been a long time."

"I heard you swung on after we'd started movin'," said Smokey, smiling, reaching for Thorne's hand, "but nobody told me you'd brought the family. Glad to have you, ma'am, son."

"This is Fitz's boy, Smokey," Thorne said.

Meg began, "And I'm—"

But the conductor cut in heartily, "Well, I declare. You look somethin' like ole Fitz, young man. Good to see you. I started railroadin' with your pa, thirty years ago, back in Kentucky . . ."

He went on, volubly recalling railroading in a border state during the war.

Meg's face felt hot. Again, Thorne caught her eye, and she saw the whimsical look on his face and had to suppress a smile.

Smokey finished, regarding Thorne thoughtfully, "You prepared to run this old train, Mr. Mac?"

"You're not going to strike us, Smokey," Thorne said mildly.

"Yessir, 'fraid we are, come tomorrow midnight."

"We'll be in Santa Fe well before that," Thorne said. Then earnestly, "But, you know, our wages to trainmen and conductors are just about what the unions have asked for from other roads in this part of the country. Things haven't been exactly easy for the company, the past couple of years, but we haven't had pay cuts; none are being considered."

"Intermountain's a good road," Smokey agreed, nodding readily, "but us workin' people got to stick together. It's not just better wages we're after. There's safety regulations, uniform operatin' rules . . ."

"We've got one of the best safety records in the country, *the* best if working conditions are taken into consideration—the grades and snow and all the rest that goes with railroading in the mountains."

"Yessir, I know that. I know it's somethin' you've worked hard to get, and we're as proud of it as you are. All I'm sayin' is, we're stickin' together. We'll go out to help the other fellers, like them with Rocky Mountain and Pacific. They got a lot more grievances than we have. Don't you see, it's the only way there is to get what's fair and equal for ever'body?"

"I don't see, Smokey," Thorne said quietly, intently. "It seems like biting the hand that feeds you. Most businesses are a little shakier now than they were, say, three years ago. Quite a lot have gone under just lately; you know that. Suppose you strike and we lose so much business we have to shut down. Maybe we'd never get back on our feet, the company or you men. What would you have proved then? What would be the gain?"

Smokey said soberly, "I remember you from when you was a gawky kid. I've always felt like we was friends, and there's nothin' personal against you in how I feel. There's no need for us to argue it, I know. We're just bound to be on different sides, but I do feel right strong about what we're tryin' to do—goin' to do. And you've just hit the nail on the head when you talk about bitin' the hand that feeds us, Mac. The railroad don't feed us; we feed it, the company. This is a good one, as companies go. I know that's because it's always had good top management, people like you and Fitz. You're the kind of boss that don't think of the men workin' for him as bein' like the freight or rollin' stock on your road. But the only way some of these other managers will ever come to think of people *as* people is to do without 'em for a while. For myself, I'd hate like anything to see Intermountain hurt, and I don't like to think of lettin' people like you down, but this is the only way we can go. I was at this meetin' the other night. We had this feller, Gordon Gaynor, a lawyer—maybe you've heard of him—for a speaker. He told us a reg'lar history of unions, all kinds, and how management's always fought 'em. It made you think and see how we've got to be united. Enough of us are organized now—the movement's too big for anything to stop it. I want to get this old bobtail to the other crew at Mixon. I live down there, you know, and it'll be my days off, startin' from when I turn the train over to Garcia, but I'll be on the picket lines. I've got to be." His face was friendly and his eyes asked Thorne's understanding, but he could not read the dark expression.

Smokey said, "Conductor for RM&P was tellin' me at the station back yonder that this weather just gets worse if you go south or higher. Well, I better do a little work. We're fixin' to lose most of the passengers down here at Corvela and Haviland. May pick up some more, but I kind of hope not, with this weather." He looked at Murphy and said, "Say, son, you want to come with me on my rounds? Maybe you'd like to ride the engine a little while." Smokey turned to Thorne. "He could go up there at the next stop and ride to Haviland. It ain't but about thirty minutes, or it oughtn't to be. We sure are fallin' behind."

"Who's engineering?" Thorne asked as Murphy looked eagerly from him to Meg.

"Vinegar Crawford."

Thorne grinned. "Vinegar's always been particular about having people in his cab. You might ask him if Murph can come up, but don't tell him. Ask if I can come too."

"Vinegar is a little particular about his engine and train, but I think he'll be glad to see this boy. Come on, son. You can punch tickets for me."

"Why didn't you tell him?" Meg demanded in a low voice as Smokey and Murphy went back through the coach. Thorne had turned to the window. "He thinks . . ."

He glanced at her blandly. "I didn't want to embarrass him by saying he'd made a mistake."

"Embarrass him! You weren't very careful of his feelings when it came to strike talk, trying to make him feel guilty and . . ."

"He wanted to talk about it. I didn't start it."

"And he's right," she said stoutly, "about all of it."

"And you're right," he said with equal conviction, "it's a thing we'd better not talk about."

The windows were frosting up now. Outside, wind packed the heavy wet snow in ridges along the ledges. Thorne looked out again, not really able to see anything, wondering about Meg's expression. The light was bad, but her face was soft, alive, despite the overtones of anger and irritation in her voice.

He said, "You can get a seat nearer the stove when some of these other people get off."

Meg answered, "I'm much warmer now."

He did not turn this time to try to read her expression. He was beginning to feel, under his worry about the weather and the strike, some of the strange peace and acceptance he had known at the hacienda, and he wanted to question nothing. He peered at freight cars on a siding, plastered with snow, the locomotive slipping and struggling along the icy rails. He thought about plans he had seen for central heating systems for passenger coaches, recalled with pleasure the developments he had seen in rail operations and services, wondered again why they had felt it necessary to use such ancient coaches on this particular train.

Meg was saying, "Thorne, you must surely know that, that day at our house in Quintana, when you brought Murphy, I didn't mean you should never see him again. He's missed you so, been so puzzled, and I haven't been able to give him an explanation that satisfies him. He's so perceptive and . . ."

"It's what Gordon meant, though," he said, finally turning to her. "And I think it's been easier this way, for me. Is Murphy all right now, do you think? He looks healthy enough."

"I think he's happy with us. He doesn't have nightmares anymore about the fire. He's doing so well at school, and he's—I'm so happy for having him. It's been—like a new life. But, Thorne, you left your family. You don't have anyone. . . . There was something you said, that day you told me about Murph and the fire—it's bothered me . . . I asked about you, what you did besides your job, and you said 'I survive.' It sounds so very—bleak, lonely."

He said readily, "It's not, necessarily. It can be a thing to take pride in, I guess. You must have read Thoreau; I think it's Thoreau who says, somewhere, 'Most men lead lives of quiet desperation.' "

"I didn't know you read things like that. I guess I thought you'd just read—well, trade papers, things like that. I don't remember your reading much of anything as a boy."

"I do read trade papers, and I've been trying, the past few years, to learn what I can about things like electricity and chemistry, on my own, when I can find a little time. But I've also been trying to—broaden my mind," he smiled, looking diffident. "I don't know, really, why I *have* read Thoreau. Most of what he says is so obvious. I keep thinking, here's a man whose books people buy, but the knowledge he has to impart is about things I already know."

Meg was glad of the dim light, the noise of the train. She could feel almost as if they were alone together. It gave her a warm, safe, quiet feeling. Her hand remembered the feel of his, holding it earlier, strong, gentle. He sat there, a tangible barrier to the cold that seeped in around the window, a safeguard for her against— She wrenched at her thoughts, trying to make them fall into acceptable lines. She said gently, "And are you . . . desperate?"

"Sometimes I am," he answered readily enough, "about problems I'm trying to cope with, three or four at a time, about the paperwork I can never keep up with—things like that."

"But those things aren't your life, they're just business."

"They're my life," he said quietly. "They're often more than I can handle."

"But you," she said earnestly, "I can feel your loneliness. You never want to believe you need other people. You've been so hurt, so disappointed, that you can't . . ."

"I've learned things, Meggy. I guess I'll never be through with learning things. I'm going to go and see Vinegar Crawford when we stop again. Would you mind if Murph rides in the cab for a while? Shall I help you move your things nearer the stove?"

When Thorne and Murphy returned to the coach, their hair was wet with snow, their faces red from the cold wind. They stood for a time by the stove, then sat down together across the aisle from Meg, talking eagerly. She had taken out a book from her bag. The light was too poor for reading, and the coach swayed too much, but she held the book and glanced up at them now and then. Thorne and Murphy seemed so happy to be together again, so content. They belonged together.

It was long past noon when they stopped for lunch at a diner operated by the railroad. There were dining cars on the expresses now, but not on the mail trains. Only one or two new passengers boarded the train. The few who were left gathered in the front coach.

Smokey worried aloud to Thorne about the weather. "That freight of ours we passed back at Haviland—they said they nearly didn't make it over Brenner summit up above Graham. I wish we had them new rotary snow plows I've heard about. They say they clear so much better. Look out there! Rain again, and freezin'. I'm wonderin' if we oughtn't to think about shuttin' her down at Graham, waitin' a while on the weather." He waited, expecting an answer.

"It's your train, Smokey," Thorne said easily. "You're the boss here."

Smokey was worried, unhappy. "Well, I don't think there's anything moving on this line but us and the northbound mail. We usually meet down close to Mixon, on the Rio Grande, but the Lord knows where it's goin' to be today. If we can get over Brenner, I guess we'll be in fair shape."

Murphy fell asleep, leaning against Thorne. Eventually, Thorne, too, slept fitfully. Then Meg could look her fill at them with no one to notice.

At Graham, Thorne got off to watch the locomotive's supplies of coal and water being replenished, to listen to the talk of trainmen and station agent. He noted a string of empty cattle cars on a siding, saw the locomotive that had been moving them being cooled down, and another locomotive, often used as a helper over the summit, sitting cold and still, gradually being sheathed in ice. He had a premonition about the weather, had had it all day—or was it about the weather?

"It's bad up there," the station agent was telling Smokey, looking up toward the summit, "snowin' an' blowin' like a sonofabitch."

"What's your last word from over the valley?" asked Smokey.

Lucero, the agent, shook his head. "Line's been down since before noon. I ain't had anything but word of mouth. Freight come through a while back. You must have met them. They said snow and sand was blowin' so bad up this end of the valley, they couldn't hardly tell if they was comin' or goin'. It seems to me like they may have shut the northbound mail down at Mixon. Telegraph lines to the east of here won't last much longer with this ice."

Smokey looked pleadingly to Thorne, who was standing a little apart.

Thorne said, "A helper wouldn't be much good, but you might get crews on those two locomotives, keep them fired up for a while, in case they're needed." He looked a little apologetic, shrugged and went back to the coach.

"Who's that?" asked Lucero irritably. "When did you start askin' your passengers—"

"MacWinter—Maxwell—is who," said Smokey uneasily. "Got his wife with him, and old Frank Fitzroy's boy. Well, I guess we'll try it, Vinegar," he said as the grizzled engineer came up to them. "I never did feel right about holdin' a train, especially a mail train. If we can get her to Mixon, it'll be up to the other crew. I'm down to just four passengers now, besides the Maxwells. I guess we can keep 'em from freezin' to death."

"This bastard," said Vinegar, gesturing toward his engine and speaking in the shout that had become habitual after years spent in locomotive cabs, "will travel a hundred miles, gittin' up that grade to Brenner. It's already been slippin' like a sonofabitch."

"Well, I tell you," said Smokey. "Let's back her up, about to that little bridge, come through here at a good clip and get a fair start on the grade."

"We ought to park the damned thing."

"I don't want to quit on my run, especially not with the big boss and them on my train. We'll try it. We can ease 'er back down here if we don't get over."

Vinegar spat copiously. "You just want to be sure to be home before you start the damned strike," he said and climbed into the cab, cursing.

The first part of the grade was bare, open, sagebrush hillside. The wind increased steadily as the train snaked up along the series of switchbacks.

Thorne, who was restless but not worried, saw the tension in Meg's face. He sat down beside her, taking Murphy on his lap, and told them about working on the building of this line. Meg relaxed, again feeling protected, almost free of having to think hard about anything.

When they got into the trees, the wind and snow eased up a little, but it was colder. The wedge plow was not accomplishing much, and the locomotive's traction was poor.

"We going to make it?" one of the passengers asked Smokey.

"Oh, yeah, we always make it," he said easily, but he was worried, thinking of the bare, open summit, where there was almost always high wind.

Early darkness had descended as they emerged from the belt of trees. The wind was a wild, vengeful thing, flinging snow so that it cut like driven sand. The grade was less steep, but they were still climbing at a snail's pace, the locomotive snorting, its slipping wheels sounding as jumpy and irritated as old Vinegar. Then there was a heavy jolt, and the train stopped, except that the howling wind swayed the cars.

Smokey, holding onto a seat near the stove, glanced

back to meet Thorne's eyes. It was too dark and shadowy, but he supposed Thorne knew. He went out into the vestibule. Thorne got up to follow him, getting into his overcoat, pulling on gloves.

"Me too," said Murphy eagerly, reaching for the stocking cap he always tried to avoid wearing.

"No, Murph, it's too cold," Thorne said and went out without looking back.

"Your dad a railroad man, son?" asked one of the other passengers tensely.

"Yessir, he is," said Murphy with a proud, conspiratorial grin.

The man turned up the nearest lamp. Meg was the only woman left on the train. She was tense but not afraid. All of them tried futilely to see through the iced windows.

"Well, we ain't backin' up now, and we ain't goin' forward neither," old Vinegar was bawling above the sounds of the wind and the patient chuffing of the standing engine. "This here wheel has slud off, and that goddamn' plow ain't worth a hoot. It's the way they spring the dern pony trucks. I must have had this happen a dozen times, and still nobody solves the problem. A dozen times, and not one of 'em was a *good* time. I said she's off," he snapped at Thorne who had just come up and was peering under the engine by the light of the brakeman's lantern. "You think I don't know a derailment when I feel one?"

"Let's keep cool, Vinegar," Thorne said absently.

"Cool, hell! I'm near about froze."

"We'll have to have a rerailer," Thorne said to Smokey.

"When I hauled freight," Vinegar said, "I always *had* a rerailer somewheres. Passenger conductors feels like it's sellin' their train short to hook on a work car and carry things like that. Bunch of damn' fools in charge of things now, tryin' to move trains in the wintertime without thinkin' they ought to carry ever'thing might be needed."

"He's right," Thorne said drily to Smokey. "The unions ought to put jacks and rerailers in their contracts."

"Let's go warm up and think about this," Smokey said, feeling harried.

"If we had a rerailer, it wouldn' be no good," asserted Vinegar perversely. "They ain't enough of us to handle it."

Thorne thought he was right there, too. The mail and express clerks had let themselves out of their locked car to find out what was happening. Except for a youthful brakeman, who looked so excited that he could almost be counted on to do the wrong thing if left on his own, Thorne was the only man on the train under fifty.

They tramped back into the coach to warm up and think about it.

"We've got a wheel off the rails," Smokey told the passengers.

Joe, the young brakeman, asked what time it was and Vinegar turned on him.

"You afraid you won't be no place at all in time for your strike? What'll you big union men do if you're stuck in a place like this, come Friday midnight? Carry a sign? God almighty!"

"You're not striking, Vinegar?" Thorne asked him mildly.

"Hell, no, Mac. You ought to know better than that. I got some saved; figger to quit railroadin' in a year or two. Unions ain't nothin' to me."

Meg said, "I suppose you wouldn't have anything to make coffee with? I wish I could do something . . ."

"Well, you surely can, ma'am," Smokey said gratefully. "Joe, get her the pot and coffee out of the baggage car."

Vinegar began to tell a lurid story about a stalled train on which everyone had frozen to death. Meg made the coffee. There weren't enough cups to go around, so she gave the ones there were to the train crews and brought one to Thorne.

"What will happen?" she asked softly, under Vinegar's spate of words.

"When I drink this, I'm going for help."

"Where?"

"Graham."

"What about—what about the telegraph line?"

"We checked it. It's down."

"But couldn't we just wait here, until . . ."

"Until what?"

"Well, until it's not so cold outside, or until another train . . ."

"There won't be any other trains, Meg, and this one will be buried, the way it's drifting. Everything will be all right. It's just going to take a little time."

"But it's so far."

"By the line it is. It's half the distance if I go straight down the hill."

Thorne borrowed boots from the brakeman. They were too big, and he got extra socks from his bag to fill the space.

"There's a siding here, isn't there, Smokey?"

"Yessir, all the way through the pass. I wish you didn't feel like you have to be the one to do this."

"We're past the first switch?"

"Yes."

"Well, if it seems worth the effort, you might try to clear the switch about the time you think I ought to be back. I'll get those engines in Graham, put them together, back to back, with a work car between. We'll have to use the siding to get one of them out of the way. If we can't get this one rerailed right away, we can uncouple and let the other engine take these cars down, or if that doesn't seem like the thing to do at the time, the passengers can go back to Graham in the work car."

"It's so dark," Meg breathed, not intending him to hear.

Thorne said, "Murphy, if you'd let me borrow your cap, I could wear it under my hat."

Thorne pulled the cap down over his ears, and Murphy grinned.

"It won't take too long, will it?" asked the boy, sobering.

"Things are likely to seem long, a night like this," Thorne said, "but I'll be back."

Meg put her scarf around his neck, tucking it in, pulling his coat collar over it, then drawing up the scarf to protect his face.

"Mama made this for me years ago," she said softly. "She spun the thread and wove the cloth from wool of Papa's sheep."

"It's good to have."

"I wish you wouldn't go," she couldn't help pleading.

He took her hand as she finished with the scarf, held it briefly and released it. "I have to."

Smokey followed Thorne through the car, worrying. "I wish," he said fervently, "you'd be the one talks to our union representatives when the time comes, and I wish you'd let me be the one that goes now."

Thorne said, rather tersely, "I won't talk to the unions, Smokey. We've got negotiators, the same as the unions have. Besides, how could I talk to a union? It's men I'll talk to, one at a time. Let's not worry about that now. Just stay with your train. See that Vinegar and Henry keep the engine hot."

Smokey said, "Hell, Vinegar'll keep the whole train hot. Listen at him."

The seven or eight miles to Graham were straight down the hill. Thorne slid and stumbled most of the way, trying desperately to keep his lantern from being put out. He could feel his hands, feet and face growing numb, but it did not seem very long before he had reached the level where Graham's few buildings were. Lucero, the station agent, was coming out to meet him. Snow and wind were less heavy in the little valley, and Lucero had been watching Thorne's bobbing light with consternation.

"I couldn't think what the hell the light was at first," he said. "Sorry I didn't know who you was before, Mr. Maxwell. I sent for crews, like you said, as soon as the bobtail pulled out."

"We'll need a work car," Thorne said, "jacks, a rerailer, shovels and some men besides the crews if they can be found."

Waiting for the rescue train to be readied, Thorne kept a respectful distance from the roaring depot stove. His hands and feet and face ached as they warmed; his eyes burned and watered. The soft blue scarf Meg had given him had a wide border of ice from his frozen breath.

"I had a feelin'," said Lucero with a degree of satisfaction, "when Smokey decided he'd go on. Well, they'll get the train back all right, and you can get some rest now. This is not the place it was while the line was bein' built, but the hotel's not bad. I expect you're hungry, the rest of them people up yonder, too. I could send my caller over to the hotel, git your supper ordered."

"Will there be rooms enough for everyone?" Thorne asked.

"Oh, I'd think they've got four or five empty rooms now. Not much business this time of year."

Thorne went to the door, opened it a crack and could tell, more by sound than by what he could see, that the engines and work train were coupled.

"Say, you're not goin' back up there?" called Lucero as he started to go out.

"Why wouldn't I?"

The station agent hurried after him. "Well, you look like you've had about enough of that weather. I don't know—ain't my business, of course—but if I was head of the railroad . . ."

Thorne stood out of the way in the cab, dully

watching the snow in the beam of the headlight. It swirled and spun. He felt light, a little dizzy.

When Thorne got back up to the mail train, all of the men began working. There were enough of them now, so many that they got in each other's way, but still they had a hard time clearing with their shovels so that the jacks and rerailer could be set. The rerailer was a long, monstrously heavy piece of steel, rising from ground level at both ends to rail height in its center. If they placed it properly, jacked the pony truck correctly, gave the derailed wheel a good start and moved the locomotive exactly right, the wheel would run up the rerailer and, with the requisite care and caution, could be made to slide from its top back onto the rail. Thorne and most of the other men had taken part in such operations before, but this one seemed impossibly difficult. Snow was packed around the tools as they tried to work. Their lanterns were blown out; one was blown away and completely lost. Wind snatched away their words, their very breath as they strained and struggled, making try after try. They had to go into the coach from time to time to warm up. Even old Vinegar had almost stopped talking. The coffee was gone.

Smokey said, in defeat, "We'd better get ever'body in the work car and git down off of here before ever'thing blows away."

Thorne moved about mechanically. It hadn't occurred to him to stop trying. "We'll get it the next time," he said doggedly. "I suppose it's possible the northbound mail might come up, Smokey. You ought to send somebody up with a flag to watch for it."

Meg had made her way through the car to him. Murphy was sleeping. "Thorne, your face is bleeding," she said, her voice sounding irritated in her concern. "Please don't go out again."

He tried to smile, and it hurt his burning, bloody lips. "We'll all be ready to go down to Graham after we have one more try."

Thorne woke slowly, struggling with difficulty out of a sleep so deep that its after-impression held something of fear. Usually he went from sleep to alert wakefulness all in one motion. Now his progress was very slow. He did not move. Even his eyes stayed closed; he did not know where he was. He knew he lay in a bed, in a room. He was not in a business car; it didn't feel like that. There were no sounds for him to identify. His head hurt, and it seemed to grow worse with each step toward full consciousness. He was totally exhausted, and decided that he did not, after all, want to wake up. Then he started, remembering the derailment, the people in the passenger coach, waiting for him—Meg and Murphy.

His aching eyes opened. Meg stood at the room's window, looking out at a curtain of snow that tattered and shifted with the wind. From the dingy gray light, Thorne thought it must be early afternoon. She was here. It was not a dream then. All of it was real. Meg turned and found him watching her.

"Oh! How are you?" She came quickly to the bed and stood looking down at him.

"You look tired," he said and was irritated that his voice sounded faint, weak.

"I've had some sleep," she said warmly. "I'm all right."

She laid her cool, soft hand on his forehead. His face burned, his eyes watered profusely and he wiped at them dazedly.

"Where's Murphy?"

"In there," said Meg, gesturing to a door. "He's taking a nap. No one got much sleep last night. It was after three when we got down. Do you remember any of it, after you were hurt?"

"Hurt? No." Automatically, he had put his hand to his head where the pain was, and he found it bandaged.

"You fell," she said. "Just when all of you got that wheel back on the track, you hit your head on one of the jacks. There was a lot of blood, and I was . . . the doctor doesn't think it's serious—nothing broken."

"Doctor."

"Yes, Dr. Wilson. This is his house. They didn't really have room for all of us at the hotel. The doctor keeps two rooms as a kind of hospital, so they brought you here. You and some of the others who were out got frostbite. Your face . . . but, thank God, the doctor says that won't be serious either. He says it's more a kind of burn than anything else, burned from wind and cold. I'm going to put on some more salve now."

Her hands were cool as she applied the ointment to his cheeks, mouth, and nose, cool and gentle and strong.

She said, "He says it will be sore, may peel like a sunburn, but it will be all right in time. Is the headache bad?"

Thorne had let his eyes close. He made a drowsy sound that could have been yes or no, or no answer at all, feeling the quietness stealing over him, the wish to sleep again.

Meg sounded far away. "You need to eat something if you can."

"I could be hungry," he murmured, not trying very hard to fight clear of the drowsiness.

He lay in a pleasant stupor while she was away. It seemed a long time, but he didn't mind. When she returned to the room, he struggled to open his eyes.

"What the hell is that?" he said, disappointed by the tray she carried.

"Tea and broth and crackers."

"I thought you were going to bring food. I haven't eaten for a long time. Could you get something to eat?"

"This is what the doctor said you should have first. It's food. There'll be something more later. I didn't suppose you'd be a very appreciative patient."

He sat up slowly, carefully, but still the room spun

and tilted. Meg pushed pillows behind him, gave him the small tray.

"What time is it?"

"Almost two."

"On Friday?"

"Yes."

"I was supposed to have been in a meeting at nine this morning."

"The northbound mail never came," she said. "And it just keeps snowing, though I think it may be letting up a little now. The town's cut off—no roads, railroad or telegraph."

Thorne glimpsed his face in the mirror of a dresser. His cheeks, lips and nose were red and raw, smeared with the whitish salve. His eyes were swollen and bloodshot, watering, only halfway open.

"Meg, I hate hot tea," he said petulantly. "Take this away, will you? God, I thought you meant to bring some food."

She smiled, finally convinced that he really was going to be all right. "Try to drink some of it."

"Nobody can know about the injunction," he said thoughtfully. "I suppose the strike's still on."

"I guess so. As far as I know, the mail train crew is still sleeping, over at the hotel."

Thorne smiled. It hurt his lips, but the tea and broth were hurting them anyway. "So Smokey won't get home to Mixon. It must be aggravating to be an enthusiastic union man and not be able to get to the right place in time for the strike, or to be too sleepy to care. Meggy, are you sure you're all right?"

"Of course I am. It's only that I've been so worried about you . . ."

"I'm not sick," he said irritably.

"You have a fever."

He gave up on the tea, crushed all the crackers into the broth and scowled at it. "They made this broth with a chicken that had been dead too long before they started on it."

"Thorne," she said and couldn't help laughing. "I wouldn't let Murphy make a mess like that, or talk that way."

"I wouldn't let you try to make Murphy eat this."

But he ate most of what the bowl contained and she took the tray away. Feeling tired and weak, Thorne pulled out the extra pillows while she was gone, sank gratefully back onto the bed and into sleep.

When Meg returned from the kitchen, she knew he was sleeping. Soundlessly, she came back to the chair beside the bed and sat down, deeply grateful for being beside him. When he slept, Thorne's face, discounting its burned look, was almost as she remembered it from years ago. In sleep, the lines at the corners of his mouth and eyes were almost nonexistent in this light. There was one, a line deeply etched across his forehead, following the curve of his black brows, that was not softened by sleep. Meg put down an urge to try to smooth it away. Last night, as she had helped the doctor clean and stitch Thorne's head wound, she had noticed the gray threads in his hair, pointed up by the bright light the doctor needed. Now the gray was hardly noticeable. She still felt something of fright, remembering his exhaustion and all the blood in his hair and over his face when they had carried him into the coach. But he breathed slowly and quietly now, and even in sleep, there was strength and reassurance for her in the rugged handsomeness of his face. Cautiously, she lifted her hand and with one finger touched a spiky tendril of his hair, feeling its crisp liveness through all her body.

I can't just sit here, she thought, after she had been sitting beside him for a long time. But she stayed for a little longer, to be near him, loving him. Finally, she made herself get up and go into the next room, to try to take a nap herself while Murphy slept in the other bed.

"It'll all come out all right, I guess," said Smokey, still looking worried.

Smokey had been occupying the chair for a few minutes while Murphy, who had brought him upstairs, and who couldn't seem to stop grinning, sat at the foot of Thorne's bed.

"The wind and snow's about quit. Things ought to be able to begin movin' around here by tomorrow. I sure was glad when we heard you'd waked up awhile this afternoon and seemed to be all right. We was right down worried about you after you fell. Your wife was tellin' me you felt like eatin' a good supper. Don't you give that girl no extra trouble. I guess you know what a trooper she is. And be sure you remember to buy her a new dress and coat and such. She was bloodier than you, time we got the train back down here. Well, I guess I'll git on back to the hotel. I ain't had my supper yet."

When he had gone, Murphy said, grinning, "I guess they all forgot you said I was Fitz's boy. They just keep thinking you're my dad and Mama's your wife, the doctor and everybody. I wish it *was* like that."

"Where is Meg?"

"She was going to help the lady that works for the doctor to wash up the dishes and things, so that lady can go home."

"Murph, tell me something, all right? Do you—like Gordon? Do you call him Dad?"

"Yes, I call him Dad. It's easier to do that than always say Mr. Gaynor or something else. I don't remember my real dad, I guess, though it seems like I do. I remember my real mama, but since I can't have her, this one's just as nice. It's been a long time, Thorne, since you took me to stay with them."

Thorne thought that the year and a half must seem a very long time to the little boy, as it constituted more than a quarter of his life up to now.

Murphy said, "My—dad, you know? He's teaching

me to play chess when he has time. He's got a nice set with ivory pieces. Can you play chess?"

Thorne said ruefully, "I can't even *watch* people play chess. It drives me crazy, but I'm glad you're learning, if you like it."

"I do. Sometimes I play pretty good. And I like him, too, but not as much as Mama."

"Why not?"

"Oh, he doesn't have much patience sometimes. He gets upset real easy and then he drinks. They fight sometimes. I don't mean they hit each other—but I don't like it when grown-ups yell. Sometimes he yells. I wish we could all just stay here for a long time. Thorne, next time, it won't be so long before I see you again, will it?"

The doctor came in then, a bald, bustling little man. He said, fussing, "Son, I don't think you've had time yet to be caught up on your sleep. I know your pa needs his rest. You better run on now and let me have a look at him. I've been out in the weather most all day. We all need to get to bed."

He began to take the bandage from Thorne's head. "This giving you much trouble?"

"Not much now."

"I put eleven stitches in here," he said, appraising the wound, "damned good job of it, too. You'll have a scar, but your hair'll grow back. Had to shave some of it, you know, to clean the wound and so on. It looks good. Your fever's gone down some from this morning. You had a lot of exposure last night, and blood loss, but you'll be all right in a few days. You're a lucky man."

"Yes."

A few minutes after the doctor had gone, Meg came upstairs. She sat down by the bed, after looking in on Murphy, and they were quiet for a long while. Thorne's eyes were closed, but she thought he was not asleep.

"Thorne," she said finally, softly.

He opened his eyes and looked at her, waiting.

She stood up, brought the salve from the dresser. "I'll put some more of this on, then I'll go to bed. Are you going to be able to sleep, do you think?"

"The doctor left some laudanum," he said, "but I won't need it. I'm all right now. I can put the salve on."

"I know," she said, "but I like to. Just this once more."

He was silent while she applied the medicine, but he kept watching her face and she felt her color rising.

"No one's going to know we've been—well, that they don't know the truth," he said. "Cherish knew a few people from the office, but she'd never have anything to do with the railroad. These people aren't likely to find out you're not my wife, but I can't help wondering why you haven't set them straight. I thought you were mad at me yesterday when I let Smokey assume you were."

"I wanted to stay with you, look after you. It just seemed easier not to try to explain when they already thought I was . . . Murphy thinks it's so funny."

"I don't."

"Thorne—"

"Is Murph asleep?"

"Yes."

His eyes caught hers, held them. "Stay."

"Oh, please, I didn't—"

"*Be* my wife, for as long as we're here."

"I can't," she said pleadingly. Her knees were weak and she swayed a little, trying to make herself move away, wanting so desperately not to go. "I have to think of Gordon, of . . . I've never been really fair to Gordon. He needs me and—"

"I need you," he said implacably. He sat up and put his arms around her waist. "Don't talk, Meggy, don't think. I'll try not to ask for any more than right now. You must know I love you. I thought I'd stopped long ago, but I seem not to have. Stay with me, Meg."

"Thorne, don't. You shouldn't be getting up." Her voice was small and faint in her own ears. He had got out of bed, was locking the room's two doors.

"Your head," she tried one last time, not wanting to try, only to give full sway to the feelings, the hunger that raged in her, answering what she felt in him as both of them fumbled weakly at her clothes.

"Don't worry about my head, or about anything," he said urgently. "Don't talk or think, I tell you. I haven't got a headache anymore. I don't feel anything except you and how much I want you. Ah, God, I've wanted you for so long!"

Their breath mingled, a ragged, torn sound in the room. Thorne's mouth was warm, firm, demanding. Meg responded tentatively at first, then with growing appetite. She realized that she had remembered, through all the years, the feel of him, smooth, strong, forceful; and her body clung to him now and she whimpered. The need for release and satisfaction, the knowledge that they were at hand, seemed more than she could bear. Thorne began to tremble then. He wanted to go on touching her, kissing her, making this sweet, incredibly beautiful time last forever, if they could bear the ecstasy of it, but their frantic bodies, weak, and at the same time strong with desire, were beyond the control of his will. A searing, cleansing heat bound them together. He stifled his moans of release in the pillow beside her face. Meg pressed her gasping cries into his shoulder.

The room fell silent again, except for the sounds of their tremulous, uneven breathing, of which neither of them was aware. After a long drifting time of near-stupor, Thorne drew away slowly from the sweet, strong, slender woman's body, experiencing a fresh crush of joy, knowing this was no dream, but truly Meg. He lay beside her and she turned in his arms, her cheek on his chest, her hair against his throat.

"It's never like that," she said dreamily, "except with you. I thought maybe it was something I'd dreamed, the way I remembered. Thorne, are women supposed to feel that?"

He stroked her hair with the gentleness that had eluded him earlier. "Don't always worry about what others feel or don't feel. You're you, and there's no comparison at all."

Tensions were beginning to seep in again, into the limp, surfeited quiet joy of her body. She was starting to think again, not wanting to. She said guiltily, "Your head . . ."

"I'm not sure I've got one, so I guess it must not hurt. Meggy, it's so good with you."

"I—I'd better go."

"Why?" he said, hurt.

"Murphy . . ." She drew close to him again abruptly. "I don't know why I have to be so compulsive about going, now."

"Please don't worry. Just stay here. We'll wake up before he does."

She wanted simply to lie there, at rest, surrounded by his strength and protection, to let herself go at last and completely, to do the thing she had, for so long, wanted more than anything in the world. Still, she heard herself saying, "You can't know that. You can't be sure."

"I can't be sure of much of anything," he said fervently, "except that I want you here. Just for right now, I don't think I can live if you go away."

"Don't say that. You need to sleep."

"I'll sleep."

She relaxed then. It was so good, so beautiful to give up, thinking nothing, feeling only their closeness. They were silent and still for a long time. Faint rises of wind made a low, broken moaning sound round the corner of the house. Otherwise, there was absolute quiet. The little town was wrapped in the stillness of the heavy snowfall.

Finally, Meg stirred, pulled a little away from him. They drew deep, simultaneous sighs and smiled a little shakily into each other's eyes. Suddenly, her lips trembled, and her eyes stung with unshed tears.

"It's all right," he murmured. "Meggy, believe me, it's all right."

"Last night," she said unevenly, "when you were unconscious and bleeding, it seemed to take such a horribly long time for them to get the train back here. I prayed, for you, for us. I thought that if only you could be all right, I wouldn't ask for more. Now . . ."

"Now what? Are you sorry about being here?"

"Yes, but only because . . . oh, Thorne, it will be so hard now."

"It doesn't have to be."

"We're both married to other people," she said tautly. "There are even more people that have to be considered—your children, Murphy . . ."

"My marriage doesn't count for anything. It'll never matter to my children what I do, so long as there's money in the bank. Murphy would be glad. He told me just before, he wishes we could stay here together."

"I tried to warn you before," she said heavily. "Thorne, I'm just not brave enough for a thing like that. I can never stand up to you, argue it out, try to convince you, but I just couldn't do it, not to Gordon."

"You can do it to me," he said bitterly, but he could not quite believe just now that she would do it, not while they still lay here with their bodies touching.

"Gordon is not strong. He depends on me. He loves Murphy, and me, I think, very much."

"How is he not strong? Do you mean mentally or physically?"

"His health hasn't been the best. He's sensitive."

Thorne laughed, but there was no humor in it. "If we have to talk about Gordon, tell me if sensitivity is what's making him drink too much."

She did not answer, and after a time he said drily, "Well, we're still cousins. At least you don't seem to be worrying so much about that anymore. Will there always be something to put between us, to hide behind? Are you so afraid of me?"

He had drawn away, and she turned from facing him, though he saw she had become very pale.

She said tremulously, "Thorne, there's no one who can make me feel so much a woman, so right in what I am . . ."

"That's not all there is to it—to us—is it? It's so beautiful, making love with you. It's the only thing in my life I've ever been able to think of as making love, the times with you. But that's not all, Meggy. It's only the beginning. Don't you think we could make a life—a good, whole, full life, together?"

"But *think* about it," she said. They both spoke hotly now. "You're so caught up, so involved with your work—"

"If it seems that way, it's because it's all I've had. I'd chuck it all in a minute if there was something else, something more. I don't want to think. Can't we just *be* together?"

"Oh, my love, we'd have to think sometime. If you don't care about anyone else, just consider Murphy."

"I've told you, Murphy said he'd be glad if we were together."

"He wouldn't like what other people would say, what they'd still be saying when he's old enough to understand."

"What other people? We could go away where no one would know us."

"Thorne, I can't be divorced. You know the church would—"

"Goddamn the church!"

He sat up, reaching for papers and tobacco. The pain in his head was strengthening again. His eyes ached.

Meg said miserably, still turned away from him, "The church is almost all I've had to count on, for a long time."

He said viciously, "Probably you should have entered a convent at puberty."

She answered quietly, steadily, "There have been times when I thought I wanted to do that."

After a moment, he said fiercely, "You tell me Gordon needs you. How can you think I don't? How can you think I'm strong when I keep begging you—"

"Thorne, you are strong," she said tenderly. "Everything would be all right now, I mean we could have gone on with things just the same, if—"

"Meg, everything has never been all right."

She said pleadingly, "I can never get anywhere trying to talk with you, when you've made up your mind. I thought maybe you wouldn't keep at me like this. Before, you said we should think only of now. You said you wouldn't ask more."

Thorne covered his face, and the cigarette, held between two fingers of an upraised hand, trembled.

Finally, he said more quietly, hopelessly, "You're right. I did say that."

When the cigarette burned his fingers, he took his hands down and stubbed out the butt. Meg had not moved. The covers were drawn close around her, and she was shivering.

"You've asked me," he said slowly, "who I am, what there is to my life besides the work. Well, I'll try to tell you, though I may have said it all before. There seems to be so little in the way of an answer, and I've thought about it, tried to figure it out, for so long. I never knew what I wanted when I was a kid. There were a lot of things, but they were shadows. I didn't worry about it. I supposed that they'd come clear, but they never have. I knew I wanted you, I know it again, but the rest has been . . . When we went away with Angus, I felt trapped: There was so much I couldn't understand. Well, I still feel that way, about so many things. I think I told you, that time when I brought Murphy down, that life was beginning to convince me of predestination or some such thing. Suppose I told you I felt we were *meant* to be together? I think you feel it, too, when we are together. I'm running Intermountain today because it was there, needing management, after Fitz was hurt. People took it for granted I'd do it, and I couldn't seem *not* to do it. It's been worthwhile at times, but I want to start living for something more than getting the next new line open. I wish I had an interest, a right to an interest in my kids' future. I'd like to look forward to my own future, to feeling that some of all this time has been worthwhile, has counted for something."

She turned and took his hand. "Oh, my poor, lonely love!" Her tears fell on their joined hands.

He said, his voice rough and low, "I did say, before, that we'd just think of now. Can we go back to that?"

"Yes," she whispered. "Oh, I want to, so much. I've been talking about more than now too, but I won't again. I have to be with you, while we can . . ."

"Don't be sorry," he said urgently. "It's been almost fifteen years since the last time. You'll have all the time in the world—if you won't change your mind—to confess and do penance and punish yourself. Just now, while we're together, don't be sorry."

"Darling, I can't change my mind, but I can't stop loving you, either. Let's just be happy, now, while we can.

He put out the light, turned to take her in his arms. His cheek lay against her breast, his mouth formed the word "happy."

XVI

Meg slipped into a fresh, crisp dress. She had been cleaning house since breakfast and was preparing now to go to lunch with Amy and Elizabeth. She had run into Amy while shopping a few days earlier, and her sister-in-law had said with her usual warmth, "Come for lunch on Thursday, why don't you? Just because Ran and Gordon have to take different sides in this awful strike business doesn't mean we can't see each other, or it shouldn't. It's been ages, Meg. Bring Murphy. The kids will love seeing him."

The late August weather was very hot; but the house, now that Meg had finished her work, seemed cool and dim and pleasant. She liked this rather small, practical house, set back from a quiet street on a large lot and shaded by elms. It seemed a happier house than the one in Quintana, but that was, of course, mostly because in the fifteen months they had had this house, they had also had Murphy. And now . . .

Looking into the mirror, as she combed her rich, dark brown hair, Meg felt sure there was a change in her face, a softness, a youth that had come into it over the past weeks, despite her fears and cautions, as hope had grown into certainty. This morning, as she washed the breakfast dishes, the child had moved within her. The movements were not the little flutterings she had heard other women describe, but strong, imperious thrusts of developing feet or arms or head. Because of her terror that this might not, after all, be pregnancy, she had told no one yet. Tonight she would tell Gordon. Surely, he would share some of her joy and be a little distracted from his preoccupation with union business.

For years, it had seemed to Meg that the face looking back at her from the mirror was that of a prim, no-longer-young wife and schoolteacher—a cool, practical, sadly unfulfilled woman. Now, she smiled absently at herself, relishing a flood of girlhood dreams and memories. She was thirty-five, would be nearer thirty-six when the baby was born. Some people would consider that a very great age at which to become a mother for the first time. Her only real question about it was, could she bear waiting until January? Still smiling, she gave herself an impatient little shake and turned from the mirror. Of course she could bear it. It would be a lovely time, with so much to get ready, so many hours spent in dreams and anticipation. After all, she had already waited fifteen years, and the child was her own now, more than it would ever be once it was born.

Through the open doors, she could hear Murphy impatiently crumpling paper in his room across the hall. He was determined to draw a map of their neighborhood, with all the houses, fences, streets, everything, put in proper perspective. Once he decided to do something, his perseverance could be a little frightening. He had been working at the map off and on for several days, but it still didn't seem to be going well.

"When are we going to go, Mama?" he called, sounding exasperated. Then he came and stood in the doorway.

"It's earlier than I'd thought," Meg said. "Let's wait another half hour."

"Will I have to change my clothes?"

"Since you've managed to tear your shirt, I think you might change that. The rest of you looks pretty good."

He turned away, then looked back soberly. "You look nice today," he said judicially.

"Why, thank you, Murphy."

She left him scowling over a large, fresh piece of paper, and went down to the dim, cool living room. A basket of mending sat by her chair, waiting to be done, but she did not take it up, only sat, very still, with her thoughts.

That night back in April when they had been stranded in Graham by the snowstorm had been the most beautiful, the most poignantly sad time she had ever known. She had been able, during most of the time since then, to keep thoughts of it out of the conscious part of her mind. Occasionally, when she believed herself occupied fully by other things, the memory would sweep back in a flood of warmth, love and sadness that would weaken her knees and start her hands trembling. Occasionally, too, when she was alone and quiet, the memories came more slowly, passing through her mind and body with a detailed, aching tenderness. Then she could remember completely every word, touch, thought, and she would be flung helplessly from joy to sorrow and back as she lived the time again.

Thorne had fallen asleep after their lovemaking, after they had agreed that they wanted to think only of now. In the first unconsciousness of sleep, he turned on his side away from her. Meg had known bitterness, regret, sorrow would come, but she thought innocently, as she listened to his quiet breathing, maybe it will be all right, beautiful, like this, till morning. Maybe I can know enough of love now, this night, to last the rest of my life. She crept close against his back, her whole body almost painfully aware of him, feeling his breathing, the ridges of muscle down his back, the smooth, rich firmness of his skin, the warmth of him, the solid, implacable strength. He seemed to stand between her and the morning, between her and all the rest of her life. It was wrong, their being together like this, but Thorne was right: There would be so very much time later for guilt and self-reproach. It had happened, was happening, and her mind could now almost refuse to think farther than that about the future. For this little time, she could simply be with him. He loved her still.

Meg did not want sleep. She must know, feel, draw out every moment of this night. As she heard the big clock in the lower hall of the doctor's house strike one, she thought, Time is so ineluctable, so merciless.

Before Thorne slept, she had got up to look in on Murphy, lighting the lamp again, leaving it turned low. It still burned, leaving deep shadows in the room's corners. Looking around, wide-eyed in her present happiness, Meg thought this must be the loveliest room in the world. The shadows were all friendly. Even the little, desultory moans of the wind outside added to her feeling of security, happiness, and to her delicious sense of their apartness from the rest of the world. Slowly, carefully, she drew herself a little away from Thorne and raised on an elbow. She wanted to study his face again, but it was in shadow. It seemed then that he had slipped a little away from her, and she could no longer bear his sleeping. She knew how exhausted he must be, how ill, but he must come back fully so that they could thoroughly share the little time that was left. Her body ached, melting into tenderness of remembered and rekindling desire. She lay down against him and began a slow, infinitely tender caressing. Her hands must know, must memorize all of him. He made a little sound of pleasure, moved against her, sending currents of aching pleasure through her. Then he roused slowly, started slightly, remembering, and turned to her, a sad smile on his poor raw mouth and in the depths of his indigo eyes.

"I didn't mean to sleep," he murmured, turning to her. "Ah, God, Meggy, Meggy!" The words were a reverent, incredulous, joyful whisper, and his arms seemed to stop her breath.

"You need sleep," she gasped, "but I . . ."

After a little time, he drew away slightly, leaned above her, his hands and lips gentle, insistent, leading her to a wild forgetfulness of words. Now he could hold himself back, draw every aspect of their lovemaking out to the full bliss and burning hunger of its potential. Meg had never known such utter abandonment in any of her senses. She was completely helpless, joyously yielding to his touch, swept to tremulous heights by his caresses. Through what seemed an infinite suspension of time, when it seemed they must reach the ultimate crest or become completely, irretrievably demented with their unbearable joy and hunger, Thorne would lie still, trembling, holding her with every fiber of himself, moaning with desire and fierce effort at control, at not letting go, too soon, of this burning beauty. Meg would moan, her body, freed now, would writhe against his, pleading. Then she, too, could lie still for a wild, beautiful moment, knowing their utter oneness, every nerve fiber bringing messages of him to her dazed, reeling brain. She knew then the drunken bliss of being possessed and of possessing. She thought he could not, surely, feel quite as she did and knew deliriously, nonetheless, that her power to please him was hardly less than his to awaken her to a joy she had not dreamed could exist. At last, she knew the fearless liberation of complete love and trust, and knew that he was returning what she gave in equal or greater measure. He was giving her not only his physical knowledge and strength, his total love, but his vulnerability, the most secret, private core of his being. Her gratitude, her rejoicing, would then make it seem impossible to wait another moment.

"Yes!" he cried in a wild gasp, an affirmation of all that was good and right. Meg's body moved with his, frantic, trembling. Then they shared the delirious oblivion of full, true completion, all but losing awareness, of each other, of themselves.

Finally, Thorne drew away gently and lay down beside her. She moved languidly against him, not able, yet, to be without his touch. They lay in a long, lovely mindless stupor, drugged with joy, grown full and quiet. Eventually, they opened their eyes and looked at each other for long, voluptuous moments of soft, tender speaking without words.

"You're so beautiful," he murmured huskily.

"*You* are," she answered dreamily. "How could anything be so wonderful? Do you really think people, mere mortals, are meant to feel, to know so much . . .?"

The sentence, the thought went unfinished as he held her eyes with his. Words were so pale, so paltry and they did not need them.

They slept eventually, neither of them recognizing just when the change came, from waking dream to sleep.

Meg wakened again, reluctantly. Thorne still slept, but he moved restlessly and she knew his fever had returned. She felt contrite and frightened. She counted five slow, measured strokes from the clock downstairs, wanting to scream, to try somehow to prepare battlements from which to fight back the morning light that would come so cruelly soon. Painfully, knowing the most utter loss and desolation she had ever felt, she tried to make herself leave him, to go to the bed where, by the normal rules of her life, she should awake when the morning forced its reality upon her.

Thorne wakened as she slipped from bed to begin, with trembling hands, getting dressed. His hands gripped the covers, clenched, white-knuckled fists. She could not meet his eyes.

"The pain's bad, isn't it?" she said shakily. "Your fever's up again."

"Meggy, we can work it out, make things come right. Surely . . ."

"There's the laudanum the doctor left for you," she said with a coolness that tore at all the tenderness of her that had been exposed. "Take it now. You've got to have some decent rest."

"You really mean," he said slowly, dully, "to throw away everything we could have—again?"

"Thorne . . . take the medicine, please." Her voice rose a little wildly on the last word. She felt the hysteria of abject loss coming upon her.

He sat up, catching at and holding her wrist, his fingers hard, hurting her. His eyes, still wide open to hers, held for a moment the specter of trembling, naked anguish. Then they clouded with a protective shadow of anger. She dragged her gaze away from him, wishing she were dead. He let her go.

"Is—is there anything I can . . . Would you like more water or—"

"Water!" he said brokenly. "My God! Go away!"

Mutely, unable to stop the movement, she reached out to him, but he had turned away and did not see. "Thorne," she whispered and all her plea for understanding went with the forming of his name on her lips.

"How can you be the way you were—we were, earlier, and then do this? Go if you're going. There'll likely be a stage out of this town, to somewhere, today. Take it, you and Murphy. I can't—I don't want to see you again—ever."

Vaguely, she was glad of his anger, knowing it would help, a little, to protect them both. She said compulsively, her voice faint. "It was so—wonderful. I'll never forget last night."

"Nobody," he said through clenched teeth, "can make any kind of a life from one night of memories. For Chrissake, will you go?"

At breakfast, Dr. Wilson told her he was not surprised that his patient had become feverish again. "It would be more of a wonder if there wasn't some infection," he said. "I'd rather he didn't have the fever, of course, but I don't think it's anything to worry about."

"Doctor, might there be a stage out today?"

"Well, there may be. I heard they started working yesterday on the road toward Haviland, when the snow began to let up."

"My—Thorne wants us to try to leave today, to try to get back to Denver. There's some business . . . Will it be—safe for me to leave him?"

"I don't think he's in any danger, ma'am, if he'll just rest for a few days. If you could get out to Haviland, the railroad junction, I suppose one or another of the roads would run a train on that main line eventually, even if the strike is on. They've promised to keep trains running. But it seems to me that you're far from being well yourself. You're looking very pale and tired this morning."

Forcing herself to move and speak, she made the

most plausible excuses her dazed mind could come up with, and when toward noon a stage did leave, she and Murphy were on it. The road was terrible, the trip interminable. She went through it all, numb with loss and longing, knowing that surely, in the next instant, she must give in to the pain and misery. Less than three hours after their arrival in Haviland, Rocky Mountain and Pacific's own mail train came up from the southeast, bound for Denver.

Meg had no idea how many hours they had been on the train before she came to herself a little, became aware that she could not stop shivering inside her coat, the coat which still bore faint stains of Thorne's blood, though the kind woman who worked for Dr. Wilson had given her best efforts to cleaning it. Meg was aware, too, of Murphy's dear, serious little face, of his eyes, flickering at her in worried, uncertain glances. A flood of love for the little boy engulfed her, and she knew it was necessary to talk to him about their meeting Thorne.

She said hesitantly, "Murphy, let's not—tell anyone we saw Thorne on this trip. Do you think, when we talk about it, that we could just—leave out his being there?"

He turned his attention upon her. He looked unhappy, tired, morose, puzzled; and she realized dimly how quiet he had been since they left Graham.

"Are you mad at him?"

"No. I just . . ."

"Well, I am. He wouldn't even talk to me before we left, not really."

"He was sick."

"Yes, but he could still talk. He was sick the day before, and he talked to me a lot then. He said that if the strike got finished by summer, and you'd let me, I could come and stay with him for a while. And then he wouldn't even talk about that, or anything. Would you let me go with him?"

"We'd have to ask Daddy."

"Will Daddy be home when we get back?"
"Not for a few more days, I think."
"I wish we wouldn't go back."
"We'll go to the hacienda another time, soon. You have to get back for school."
"Before Thorne got so mean, I kept wishing we could stay there, you and me and him. I guess I still wish that."
Meg could not reply, and after a silence, Murphy said more steadily, "I won't tell anybody about Thorne. I know Dad doesn't like him. Today, *I* don't like him very much, only maybe we shouldn't be going, when he's so sick. Maybe he wishes we were there now. Are you going to cry?"
But Meg did not cry, and as time passed, she felt relieved that there was so mercifully little torture for her in what she knew to be the moral wrongness of that stolen night in Graham. The next time she went to confession, it was enough to admit the sin of unfaithfulness; she seemed to come close to forgiveness, to exoneration, through prayer and penance. There was torment in the beauty and pain of memories, and her most intense residual feeling came to be love for Thorne, concern and pain for the hurt she knew he had felt. Then she had begun to suspect pregnancy, to pray for it, cling desperately to the hope of it.

Sitting now in her quiet living room, she felt the child move again, strongly, and knew a great lift of joy. It was Thorne's baby. She knew that. She remembered being so terribly frightened by this same prospect fifteen years ago, fifteen years, almost to the month. But even then, in the midst of her fear, she had still hoped for it. Now, sure knowledge brought quiet, eager joy, and gratitude, as well as the desperate, helpless feeling that she could not give back to him this hope he had given her.
Gordon had rarely made love to her in the past several years. He had little interest in a physical re-

lationship, and incidents of impotence had continued to torment him. But there had been a time in April, on his return from Chicago. He had been drinking heavily that night and it had taken a very long time. He labored doggedly, sweating, while Meg lay utterly still, impassive, as it seemed essential she do for him. Her mind had been almost blank while she waited for it to be over. She felt little more than pity for Gordon. He would probably never know the full joy of anything. Afterward, they had discussed, far into the night, his involvement in and plans for union causes.

Meg started now as Murphy seemed to have materialized suddenly before her eyes.

"Can we go now?" he was asking. "Were you taking a nap?"

"No. Well, maybe I was—sort of," she said, drawing her mind back to present realities. "I'm ready, Murph."

The pre-noon, residential streets were somnolent in the heat. It was pleasant, walking along with the little boy, from sunlight to shade and out into the sun again. Meg knew and was grateful for still another gift from that single night of love, of abandonment to pure sensuality. She had never before known such pleasure, such changes of sensation, in walking, moving from heat to shade. There seemed to be a newness on everything, a wistful beauty. And she knew it could go on like this because she would have the child, would see the world new, again and again, through the eyes of Murphy and the baby. Oh, Thorne! her heart cried. You've given me everything, my poor love, and what is there for you?

Murphy was saying with his accustomed serious expression, "School starts in ten days. I wish I could have gone with Thorne this summer, like we talked about. I keep thinking maybe he'll come and see us sometime, even with the strike. If he and Dad liked each other, maybe—or maybe Thorne just doesn't like kids much really. He never has his own kids with him, does he?"

"Murphy, grown-ups have such a lot of misunderstandings and disagreements. Children are the smart, lucky ones, because they can usually fight, or call names or cry and make an end of being hurt or angry or whatever the trouble is. Grown-ups don't usually seem able to be so clean about things. Thorne and his wife couldn't get along together, so they stopped living in the same house. She has the children with her because it's usually better for them to have one home than two, and because mothers mostly have more time to spend with children than fathers do. I think you might have spent some time this summer with Thorne, if it weren't for the strike, but you know how terribly busy he is, and there have been such awful troubles because of the strike. Has this been a bad summer for you? Are you unhappy?"

"Well, no," he said slowly, with his dear, funny solemnity. "I think I don't much want to be a grown-up."

"It's not all bad," she said, and there was another silence.

He said, "Did Dad tell you he was going to see about adopting me?"

"No. We haven't talked about it for a while. We'd like to, very much. It's only that Dad's been so busy. We've put it off because we already have you with us. Murphy, we love you so much. How do you feel about being adopted?"

"He asked that, too, when we talked about it last night. I want to live with you, but I think I'd like to stay named Fitzroy. Everybody with the railroad knows who my real dad was. When they hear my name is Fitzroy, they're always saying 'I remember ole Fitz.' I like that. I don't see it would make any difference in how much we like each other if my name got changed to Gaynor. Besides, if I got adopted, Thorne wouldn't be my—what's it called?"

"Guardian."

"Yeah. Dad says he wouldn't be that anymore, if I got adopted. I like to know he's supposed to be guarding, even if he never is around anymore. His wife and kids came back to town. Did you know that?"

"No, I didn't."

"You know when I was at Steve's house the other day, to play? Clare Maxwell came there then, to see Steve's sister. Thorne's Clare's dad, her real one. I don't like her one bit, or Steve's sister either. They're nine, I think, and they always try to act like they already know everything in the whole world. Anyway, Clare said her dad was going to come back and live with them soon. Is he?"

"I don't know, Murphy."

"She doesn't even like him, and she doesn't like to be in Denver either. Clare and her big brother don't even have to go to school yet. They have a teacher that lives right in their house. I wouldn't like that."

"I'm a teacher," she reminded him. "You're stuck with me."

"But you don't get paid to teach me things. If we had one that got paid, I bet he'd be asking me teacher questions when I was trying to eat my supper or think about something, or all the time. . . . Did you think about if I can have one of the kittens Steve's cat has? You said, when we had to leave Brendeen at Quintana, I could get a kitten sometime. That's been a long time."

"You can have one when they're old enough to leave their mother."

He grinned. "I know the one I choose. I already told Steve. It's all stripes and has rings around its tail. Would you come and see them?"

"Yes, in a few days. I want to stop in over there at the church for just a few minutes. Will you come in, or wait outside?"

"I'll come in. It's always nice and cool in there. I remember one time, walking with my other mom. I think it was somewhere around here. We saw some bigger kids and she told me they were coming from catechism class. Will I go to catechism?"

"I hope so, when you're a little older."

"Probably," he said complacently, "I'm old enough now. Miss Barry, at school last year, told Mr. Phelps I'm too smart for anybody's good. My grandpa Tom is Catholic, and Grandma MacWinter, and just about everybody. But some people aren't, you know. Is it bad not to be?"

"I think everyone has to decide that for himself, when he can. People should choose whatever religion seems best to them. Some don't have any at all."

"They don't? What does God think about them?"

"Well, I guess he wishes they didn't feel that way. I don't really know what God thinks, but I think they must be at least a little—sad and lonely, those people."

"Is Thorne Catholic?"

"He used to be." She smiled sadly. "There were enough of us MacWinters that, if we'd needed to, we'd have made a catechism class all our own."

Murphy said wistfully, "I guess it's fun to have brothers and sisters. I wish you had lots of other kids to go with me. Would it do any good, do you think, to pray for some?"

Luncheon at Amy's was a voluble, rather hectic time. Neither Amy nor Meg believed that children should be silent in the presence of adults, but they were ready to say a few words on their own account when the meal was over. The two boys were several years older than Murphy, but they agreed with rather condescending magnanimity to take him along on a reconnaissance tour of nearby fields and pastures. The little girls went off with a friend to busy themselves with a new doll house and its occupants. Amy led Meg and Elizabeth out to sit on the quiet, shady side porch.

"Tell me something," said Amy, her rather plain, sweet face suddenly very serious. "Have you got any idea when this strike will be over? Does Gordon know anything about it that he's passed on to you . . . that you can let us in on?"

Meg said regretfully, "I don't think he knows any more about that than anyone else does. It's up to the negotiators to agree on some sort of terms. Then the whole union has to vote."

Amy sighed. "Yes, I know how it's supposed to go. I just hoped you might be able to tell us something new. I've never been so sick of anything in my life. We went through organizing and contracts and the whole thing last year, for the mines and mill. It was a breeze compared to the railroad thing. Most of Ran's work, you know, is supposed to have to do with the mill, but they have a way of throwing everything together down there at the Maitland Building. He comes home, occasionally, to eat and sleep, maybe change his clothes. Otherwise, I've hardly seen him since April. He's trying to handle some of the work in the railroad's offices. It's always been hard for Thorne to stay in the office, and now he's never there. He's always out somewhere, running a train, or overseeing repairs, or being a dispatcher. Some of the union people have asked for him, time and again, to attend the negotiations, but he won't. He just keeps trying to do everything, driving himself—"

"He looks terrible," Elizabeth said worriedly. "Ranald and the others are tired, but Thorne . . ."

"He's going to kill himself," Amy said angrily. "Nobody can keep on the way he is. Some of the others are ruining their health, just trying to keep up with him." She sighed, then smiled resignedly. "I came from such a peaceable family. Daddy owned slaughterhouses. That's not romantic or anything, but it's not as grim as it sounds either. He just owned them, you know? He didn't rush around, trying to do the cattle raising and buying and butchering and the whole business. I don't remember more than two or three times in my life when he was even late coming home from the office. I'd like, just once before we're too old to enjoy anything, to be able to have a nice, long, uninterrupted vacation with Ranald. You're not a great, pushing, driving person, Meg; and it seems as if some of your other brothers and sisters know how to relax. Where do Ran—and more especially Thorne—get this terrible compulsion for work?"

Before Meg could think of anything to answer, Elizabeth said quietly, "Thorne is like Angus in that."

Amy was momentarily flustered. "I'm sorry, Elizabeth, but you know I have never been able to think of them as anything but brothers . . ." She shook her head, looking concerned, then changed the subject and found her stride again. "Are you going to have a teaching job this year, Meg? I remember your mentioning that you'd like to."

Meg smiled and said shyly, "I'm going to have a baby in January."

Amy stared, her mouth slightly open. "You *are*! How wonderful! But aren't you kind of shocked? I mean, it's been so long and . . ."

Meg laughed. "I am, but that makes it all the better."

Amy jumped up, with warm impulsiveness, and hugged her. "Oh, Meg, I'm so *glad* for you. Gordon must be just thrilled to pieces."

"He doesn't know yet. I couldn't believe it, in the beginning, and I wanted to wait until I could be sure . . ."

Amy had turned and was looking with irritation toward the front of the house. "Oh, my God," she groaned, then grinned apologetically and said, "I mean, mercy me. Elizabeth, is that Miriam Halstead coming, and Cherish with her? I knew Cherish was back, but I'd kept hoping we'd be spared. Say absolutely nothing, Meg, that you don't want twisted out of recognition and spread over the whole state."

Cherish's and Miriam's greetings were effusive with false warmth and sweetness. Amy, making no real pretense at pleasure, brought out a fresh pitcher of lemonade. Elizabeth excused herself tersely after a few moments and went into the house.

"Well, Amy," prattled Cherish with an empty, brittle brightness, "I've been meaning to visit you just forever. We've been back here since July, you know, but there's been so much to do. And I'm glad to meet Ranald's sister at last. Tell me, Mrs. Gaynor, is your husband the lawyer I've read about, who works for the unions or some such thing? My, that must make for conflict on the family front. I guess you two must have to meet in secret."

"Tell us what you've been doing with yourself, Cherish," said Amy.

"Well," she said readily, "we spent ten months in Europe. The children went to very good private schools in England. I visited people, saw things. I went to Brendeen, for one thing, to get to know Thorne's people a little, his cousin the earl, you know. And, of course, we've spent some time at Fern Hill." She explained to Meg, "Fern Hill is my old family home back in Virginia. My father's people were Stuarts, descendants of Bonnie Prince Charlie."

"Tell them about Ted," urged Miriam, her pinched face avid.

"Oh, yes!" bubbled Cherish. "Amy, you remember my little brother Teddy. Well, he was in Europe with us and he's finally married—a lovely girl, originally from Philadelphia. Her father's an importer, a fine old family. They've got a lovely apartment, Ted and Edith have, in Paris. Ted will be working for his father-in-law there and they'll be having their first baby soon." She laughed. "Almost too soon."

"Are you back to stay?" asked Amy.

"Well," said Cherish slowly, smiling, "that depends . . ."

"She and Thorne are trying to work things out," said Miriam.

Amy could not quite stop a frown, and Cherish

said lightly, "Oh, you never can tell about such things, you know, Amy. Those rumors that he'd left us came a lot earlier than it actually happened. I never could find out who started those rumors. The real truth is that I had to—well, to ask him to go, finally. He paid so little attention, all those years, to his home and family, and then I found out there was another woman. Even *I* couldn't just stand still for that. I've given him plenty of time to think it over. He's begging now, for us to get back together."

"He is?" said Amy, not bothering to try to mask the wryness of her question.

"Yes, indeed. I'd appreciate it if you didn't talk this over with Ranald. You know he's always done his best to influence Thorne against me. I expect I'll have to give Thorne another chance, once this strike is over and we have time to work out an understanding. After all, what choice, really, does a wife have? He's been rather sweet, actually, swears he can't live without me. And of course the children need their father."

"You've seen him then," said Amy, completely unimpressed.

"Why of course I've *seen* him, Amy dear. And he is *very* contrite."

"As he should be," murmured Miriam.

"When?" pursued Amy relentlessly.

"What?" said Cherish.

"When did you see him?"

"See Thorne? Why the times he's been in town since we got back, honey. Maybe he hasn't had time to see you and Ranald, but he's come to the house—*our* house—every time."

Meg had stood up. "Amy, I have to get home and start supper. Excuse me, please, ladies. It's nice to have met you both. I've heard Amy speak of you." And to Amy, who was also standing, "You'll send Murphy home when the boys get back?"

"Murphy!" cried Cherish. "Why that's *right*. Now I remember. You and your husband took little Murphy after his mother died. How is he? Oh, I'd love to see him. I was always so fond of him. Frank Fitzroy was my stepfather, you know. I wanted to take Murphy into our home, but Thorne and I were having such difficulties, just at that time."

"He's fine," said Meg, wanting only to escape.

"You have to go and start supper?" asked Miriam in feigned sympathetic surprise. "Don't you have servants?"

"I'll just go out the back way, Amy."

"I'll walk to the gate with you," Amy said.

"Amy," said Cherish with a detaining gesture, "is Dahlia here? I've heard she came to work for you. I suppose I should say just a word to the ungrateful woman. I believe she was really fond of the children."

"It's Dahlia's day off," Amy said curtly. "Excuse me, please. I'll be back in just a minute or two."

When she and Meg were out of sight of the porch, Amy beat her clenched fists together. "Those two, together, are more than anyone ought to be expected to stand."

Meg smiled ruefully. "I should have told her how much of Gordon's work doesn't get paid for—servants, indeed!"

"Yes, it would give them something to carry on to the next house. I think I'll just slip out and go along with you." Amy laughed a little. "No, really, I can't do that. Cherish is lying through her teeth. If she's seen Thorne even once, I'll eat that gatepost. He would have told Ranald . . . Well, maybe he wouldn't, either. I never know what to expect from him, but I do know for certain that we're more likely to have snow on a day like this than she's likely to get him back. I wonder what she's really up to. Oh, well, listen, Meg, let's not wait nearly so long before we get together again."

"Thank you for lunch. You come to our house next time, soon."

"Yes, but I think I'll wait now until school starts

again. That's going to be one of the happiest days of my life."

"I'll call you and Elizabeth."

"Fine, and you take good care. Meg, were we really the first ones to know about your baby? That's a very special kind of honor, it seems to me. Is it all right if I tell Ran? If I ever see him again. Oh, I know Gordon will be so happy."

"Randy and Rob know about birds and squirrels and things," Murphy said when he was about to go up to bed that night. "They showed me some nests. All the young things that were born this spring are too old to be in the nests now. Sometimes I wish we lived back in Quintana again. That's almost living in the country. Did you see a lot of baby animals when you were young, Mama?"

"Yes," Meg said. "I remember a family of squirrels that made a nest in a tree right outside our bedroom window. Every year we got to watch the little ones grow up. And there were lambs and calves and colts all over the place. We raised a fawn once. Its mother was killed by a mountain lion while she was trying to protect it. My two older brothers happened to come along and scare the lion away, and the fawn was saved. We kept her for more than a year before Papa and the boys took her back into the mountains. Remember the fawn, Gordon?"

"Yes," he said absently, scarcely looking up from the papers he had brought home.

"When you were a kid," Murphy said to him, "did you wish you were really a part of the MacWinter family? I mean, sometimes when you had to go home and be by yourself?"

"It's a good thing to be by yourself sometimes," Gordon said. "That house was always so full of talk and noise, I don't see how it kept from bursting. Go to bed now, Murphy. It's late."

Meg kissed the boy, tousled his unruly reddish-blond hair. "We love you, Murph." He went upstairs.

Gordon got up to pour himself a drink. "Want one?"

"No, thank you." She was suddenly shy of saying what she had to tell him.

"I have some things to talk to you about," he said. "First, though, do you wish we hadn't left Quintana?"

"Well, sometimes, a little. Why, Gordon?"

"Well, because you looked like you wished that, talking to Murphy. I think I'm doing important work here, Meg, work someone certainly has to do."

"I know you are. I'm proud of what you're doing."

"Are you?"

"Of course I am."

"Then I wish you and Murphy would do your part by keeping away from Ranald's family."

"I like Amy, Gordon. It's not as if we're divulging your secrets, or Ranald's. Neither Amy nor I would do that kind of thing. They're the only family I have left here."

He set his glass down sharply. "There's your goddamned cousin Thorne. He's got some of the men so stirred up, they're wearing down the organizers' morale, blowing hot and cold about whether they can hold out with this strike until they can get what's coming to them by rights. He's got a bunch of greaser scabs that will work, or pretend to work, and make plenty of trouble, under any conditions."

She was shocked. "I've never heard you call people greasers."

"Well, that's what they are."

"I'm half greaser!"

"You know very well the sort of people I'm talking about, and it just may be that your selfish, high-handed cousin has bought himself more trouble than he's bargained for, but we'll get to that later. I was going to say that I don't see why you always seem to think you have to *have* family. Can't you make yourself some new friends? Don't be so provincial."

"I have friends," she said, leaning a little toward

the lamp to thread a needle. "We haven't really had time yet to get to know each other. Real friendship usually takes a long time growing. You know that."

"You don't know Amy that well either. Visit with someone else."

"Amy's the wonderful kind of person you can get to know pretty well at one sitting. Ranald was your best friend for such a long time. I don't see why union business has to bring an end to everything."

"I was never Ranald's best friend. Thorne always got in the way, making trouble. Our people could work with Ranald now, and Peter Maitland, if it weren't for that bastard." He finished the drink. "I don't know why you didn't go ahead and apply for a teaching job here this year. I'm sorry to say we could use the money, and I think you and Murphy would both be better off if you were working."

"You do? Why?" She looked up from her mending.

"He spends too much time with you. He ought to have more friends."

There was a little silence before she said, "The strike must be very hard on some of the men's families."

"It is, and some of the sources for help are running dry. The thing should have been settled by now. All the other railroads in this part of the country are back in full operation now, with decent union contracts. We're trying to put together the biggest meeting we've yet had of Intermountain people, strikers. I've been asked to address it. I've also been approached—depending on the final outcome of all this—about running for the legislature."

"You have? Oh, Gordon, that's grand."

"Well, it won't be for two years yet. It's nothing to get excited about now. But I think I could do some good there." He got up and brought the bottle to the table beside his chair, pouring himself another drink. "What I meant to tell you, first thing, is that old Tom Murphy was killed yesterday."

"Murphy's grandpa? Oh, no! He was killed? Was it . . .?"

"Yes, it was strike trouble," Gordon said grimly. "He's been so adamantly against organization, old Murphy, heading up his renowned troubleshooting crew . . . And that gang of ruffians of his have been doing a lot more than repairing damages, though there have *been* a lot of mysterious damages lately. A trestle was blown up the night before last, up on their Amity line. There were union men there when the old man's repair crew came yesterday morning. They were picketing, of course, on behalf of the legally striking section hands. The story isn't all straight yet, but you can be sure old Tom did everything in the world he could to make trouble. There was fighting, some shooting, I'm afraid. One of our men was killed, two others seriously hurt."

"Oh!" she breathed and shuddered. "Gordon, does it have to be like this? Can anything ever be worth that kind of thing?"

"Good God, Meg, the men are struggling for their rights. If the company—your relatives—would listen to reason . . ."

"Was Thorne there?"

"I don't know where he is. His own people don't seem able to find him half the time, or they claim they can't. I wish he had been."

Another silence, and she said sadly, "Murphy has no family left now."

"At least he wasn't especially close to the old man, hadn't seen him much lately. How long is it since Tom came here last?"

"It was about a month before the strike started. March, it must have been."

"Yes. Well, I'll tell Murphy in the morning."

"Do you know anything about the funeral?"

"No, and you're not to think of going."

"But, Gordon—"

"Meg, won't you understand that I'm becoming

somewhat known? With this whole situation as it is, I won't have you seen at a company funeral."

"How can a funeral be—"

"You know very well what I mean."

He drank, and poured again into his glass. Meg, suddenly feeling angry, wondered why he bothered with a glass. She finished with the shirt and began to darn a sock.

"You shouldn't have to be working all the time," Gordon said gently. "I ought to be able, after all these years, to afford some help for you."

"Sometimes, I like doing the work. I wouldn't know how to behave with a maid."

He leaned forward earnestly. "Meg, we'll have it easier soon. Unionization *is* important. It's the most important thing this country has known up to now, and it's all for the working man. I want to be a small part of its happening. I want to be identified with this cause. It could be that I—we—could derive something material from it one day, a chance to earn far more money, a name. But even if nothing should come of it in the way of personal benefit, I'll still know it's worthwhile, doing what I can to help all those people who can't speak and stand up for themselves get what ought to be every working man's birthright."

Meg nodded, but doubt of his motives, his true fellow-feeling for all those common men, had begun to creep into her mind months ago. He seemed to set himself so far apart from them, above them. She knew his weaknesses and biases, and that they grew stronger and more numerous with each passing year. They had moved to Denver fifteen months ago, and her respect for him had suffered greatly in that time. Of course she knew most of the reasons for that were not really of Gordon's making, but what would be left for them without respect? Pity was no fit basis for any relationship. Gordon did need her for many reasons, and above all there was her almost unshakable belief in the sanctity of marriage. "Till death do us part" were not merely words. They were a sacred promise. Her marriage, and Murphy, and now there was the baby.

She said, "Murphy mentioned today that you'd said something about looking into his adoption."

Gordon looked up from contemplation of his glass. "As a matter of fact, I talked to John Blessington this morning. He's MM&F's lawyer who is partly responsible for the handling of Murphy's trust. I knew I'd be running into him today at the county building."

"Murphy would like his name to stay Fitzroy, Gordon. Is there any way we can be his legal parents and let him keep the name?"

"I suppose that could be arranged," he said petulantly, "if anything can be arranged. Just what does our young man find wrong with the name of Gaynor?"

"I don't think it's that he finds anything at all wrong. It's just that everyone identifies himself with his name, very young. He's been Murphy Fitzroy since he can remember. Being called Murphy Gaynor would make him feel strange, different, at least for a while."

"Do you wish your name was still MacWinter?"

"No, but it did seem odd for a while, being Meg Gaynor. I've had a long time to get used to it."

"He'd get used to it too, soon enough. He's very young and such decisions can't be left to a child. Does he want to stay on with us, or not?"

"Of course he does, Gordon. Where else would he go?"

"I'm not sure about any of this after my talk with John Blessington today."

She looked at him, fear shadowing her eyes. "What do you mean?"

Gordon had picked up a cigar and did not answer until it was lighted to his satisfaction. "I talked with this same attorney before about this, you remember, shortly after we moved from Quintana. Thorne had told Blessington we could adopt the boy after a reasonable trial period. I don't know what Thorne had in mind, but John and I agreed, at that time, that a year should be a satisfactory period for all of us. Today, he said that back in the spring, when he had to see Thorne about something to do with the trust, he had remembered our talk and had asked Thorne if he should contact us about going ahead with the adoption. Thorne said no."

"He said no? But maybe he only meant Mr. Blessington shouldn't contact us, that we should be the ones to do the contacting."

"He told Blessington he'd changed his mind about it."

Meg picked up her workbasket, almost dropping it because her hands shook, and searched for thread to match Murphy's trousers that needed a patch. Thorne had been so angry, so hurt, that ghastly early morning in April. Would he do that out of a need for retribution? Would he take Murphy from her? Didn't he know she had been just as hurt, just as torn by that parting? Still, Thorne had no one . . .

Gordon said ominously, "You realize what this could mean. I warned you, Meg. I never trusted Thorne about anything, never felt safe about taking the boy in. I got John Blessington to think back carefully, and he decided this decision of Thorne's first came to him about the beginning of May, *after* the strike was called. Don't you see? He planned to use your—our—feelings for Murphy in some way. Have you seen him without telling me? Has he, or someone he's sent, been trying to persuade you to try to influence me in some way that would be detrimental to the unions?"

"No, Gordon. Amy and Elizabeth are the closest I've come to any company people in months." Her hands still shook.

"Well, he's got something in mind. Just remember, please, that I told you I thought it would be a mistake to take the boy."

"Gordon, it's not 'the boy,' it's Murphy, our Murphy. Aren't you glad—"

"I *won't* be glad, and neither will you, if he's taken

away as some sort of hostage to the company's interests!"

"Thorne would never use a child like that."

"I can't believe he's fond of children or anything else. Look at the way he's neglected his own family. I can tell you, I've heard some pretty raw things about how he treated his wife. It's no wonder she left him. A lot of people—including his wife, I hear—believe Murphy is actually Thorne's child. I probably shouldn't mention such things to you, but you might as well know. The old man, Fitzroy, you know, was badly crippled and about sixty when the boy was born. Murphy's mother was no more than a young girl. They say she was still Thorne's mistress at the time she died. That could explain a lot of things, including, perhaps, reasons Thorne didn't care to mention to us about why the fire was set in her house. And why has Murphy been whining to see him all summer? I don't recall nearly so much of that in the past. Has someone talked to him? A kind of sabotage? What is it, Meg? You're so pale."

"It's nothing. Gordon, you're seeing sabotage everywhere. Murphy would tell me if he'd seen Thorne, or anyone else who's talked to him about Thorne. Oh, when will the strike end?"

"Good lord, I can't answer that. Settlement is up to the companies, to their showing some sense, a willingness to compromise and adjust to reasonable terms for settlement. But as soon as it is ended, you'd better see Thorne and try to get this settled, once and for all. Unless something comes to light before then, that is. *I* won't ask him for anything, but if you want to keep the boy—"

"*If* I want to?"

"We can never feel safe about it without a legal adoption. This sort of worry could come up over and over again. I remember what a creature of whim Thorne was as a boy. He hasn't changed at all, only become more vicious and exploitative. We can't live like that, at someone's else's mercy."

After a few moments, Gordon came and sat beside her on the sofa, bringing the liquor bottle and placing it on the floor at his feet. "I thought you'd better know these things, Meg, as they come up, but please don't look so worried. We'll try to get it worked out somehow. Ranald, at least, has always been a fairly reasonable person. Maybe you ought to ask him to talk to Thorne. I think, though, that we shouldn't do anything at all, just yet. Maybe, by doing nothing, we can find out what he thinks can be gained by this. If we should have to give Murphy up—"

"We won't," she said vehemently.

"Meg, I am glad to have the boy, but since he came things have changed. We were always enough for each other before that."

He put his arm around her shoulders, and Meg's body grew rigid at his touch. She had known all along that he resented Murphy. Of course she had, only she had not let herself make the admission consciously before this. Oh, God! her whole life seemed a tissue of refusals and hidings and lies and substitutions. Gordon resented Murphy. What would he feel for this new child? Had he been doing something, all these years, something she was too naive to know about or recognize, to deprive her of children? Now she didn't want him to know, wished desperately that she could be free of him, could take Murphy tonight and go back home, back to her mother where she could live and have the baby in love and peace. But that was unrealistic, childish. It was the first time she had ever given herself even the briefest luxury of the thought of running away, back to her mother. Oh, Papa, did you guess? You used to talk to me so longingly of Thorne. You would have understood . . . But Meg felt she was getting weak, ridiculous. She must tell Gordon about the baby, soon, before he should notice some evidence of it on his own.

"After this big meeting, in two weeks or so," Gordon was saying, "I may be asked to go to Chicago again. I hope you'll want to come with me this time. Isn't there some friend Murphy could stay with?"

"Gordon, don't drink anymore. Please. We have to talk."

"We are talking, darling, and you know how I hate it when you start nagging at me, particularly about drinking. I have to do something to relax a little."

Meg drew a deep breath, and looking down at the mending she had dropped into her lap, she said, all in a rush, "We're going to have a baby."

Gordon was silent. His arm dropped slowly from around her. Finally, she had to look at him. He was staring at her. His face was dead white, with fiery blotches on the cheekbones.

"I'm sorry, Meg, but you must be—you're mistaken," he said, and took a drink from the bottle.

"I'm not," she said, desperately trying to call back her joy. "It should be due about the middle of January. Oh, Gordon, finally, after so very long! Today I felt it move. I've waited to tell you until I could be sure—"

"I tell you, there is no baby!" He had started to tremble, and his voice was rough and loud. He drank again, swallowing spasmodically.

"I felt that way too, at first," she said with a growing uneasiness, with fear. "But it *is* true."

He said coldly, "I can't produce children. I've mentioned the very serious illness I had as a small child, before Dad and I came west. The doctors believed that it had left me sterile, and it has. Otherwise, we'd have had children long before this."

"But you can't be sure. . . ."

"I should have told you in the beginning. I know it wasn't fair not to tell you, but then you'd never have married me, would you? Or, if I'd told you after we were married, you'd have wanted one of the church's annulments for failure to produce, wouldn't you? I'm no less a man for it, and we got along very well for a long time without children."

She wanted to scream at him, to tell him it hadn't, after all, mattered in the end, that she had not truly believed even for a moment that he was the father of her child. And still, she could not take it in yet, that Gordon would be capable of keeping a thing like that from her. She said fiercely, "Gordon, there is a a baby. You must be wrong!"

"If there's a baby, it's not mine!" The thought had penetrated slowly through the liquor fog in his brain. He turned on her furiously, brandishing the nearly empty bottle.

"You bitch! You slut!" He struck her with all the strength he could muster, across the face, with his open hand.

The workbasket fell to the floor. Spools of thread, buttons, seemed to roll for a long time before they all came to rest and the room was completely silent.

Meg stood up, holding a handkerchief to her bleeding nose and moved shakily to the stairs. Her knees almost gave way before she could reach the bedroom. She lay down on the bed, trying desperately to control her dizziness, her anger, her fear. All these years, she had prayed for children, had been fully convinced their absence was her fault, some lack in her, or a punishment, and he had let her go on believing that; she had felt guiltily that she must try to make it up to him, when all along, he had known—

She cringed as something smashed downstairs. More and more frequently with the years, Gordon had had too much to drink. He had shouted at her often, in anger, frustration, disagreement, anything; had broken things, but he had never hit her, not until tonight. Suppose Murphy woke. Gordon would go on saying what he pleased, whatever might come to the surface of his half-numbed brain, whatever he might have a right to say? But Murphy mustn't hear things like that. Or perhaps Gordon would come up here, hit her again, hit Murphy . . . She could hear nothing more from downstairs. She lay rigid, for what seemed hours, waiting.

There *was* a baby and she must know the right things to do, for its happiness and protection, and for Murphy's. She had never believed this to be Gordon's child, had not wanted it to be so, but it was hers. And Gordon had been deceiving her pitilessly, all these years. That was no justification for her weakness, her wrongdoing, but it made it seem a little more likely that she could, someday, be able to forgive herself completely.

She had begun to relax a little, from sheer exhaustion, when she heard his feet faltering on the stairs. She tensed again, sitting up defensively. The room was dark. Gordon fumbled his way to the bed.

"Meg?"

"Yes?" She was surprised at the cold steadiness of her voice. How could it sound like that when she was terrified?

"Oh, Meg." He groped for and found her hand. "Meg, forgive me. Please! I didn't . . ." He dropped to his knees on the floor beside her, sobbing, burying his face against the bedspread.

His hands, holding hers, were as cold as her own, damp, soft, trembling. Her hand had its own memory, of other hands, hard with smooth callouses, warm, strong, insistent, but gentle, infinitely tender. Her eyes filling with tears, Meg tried to pull her hand away from Gordon's.

"Gordon, don't," she said desperately. "Please don't cry."

"I—I've picked up all your things in the living room," he said brokenly, clinging to her. "Please—you've got to try to understand what a shock this was for me. I know you'd never sleep with another man. I'd given up hope, long ago, Meg . . . This must be one of your miracles. Please forgive me." He sobbed loudly and held her.

"Gordon, it's late. Let's get to bed."

"You can't forgive me, can you?" There was something of accusation in his abject voice.

"Yes, I can. It will be all right."

"I saw you were bleeding, Meg. Are you all right? I never would have dreamed I could hit you. You're so right about my drinking too much."

"Please, let's just try to forget tonight. Let me go now. I'll light the lamp."

"I'm going to sleep on the sofa," he said, growing calmer. "You can't want me near you now, after what I've done and said."

Meg's relief all but drained her of the strength fear and anger had brought. She said shakily, "I'll come and make it up for you, then."

She went downstairs, leaving him alone, but he followed. His eyes were red and swollen, his hands shook. She yearned to have him stop watching her with that expression of pleading and abject apology. She saw the workbasket, retrieved, on the table, the broken bottle he had cleaned up and put into a wastebasket.

As she moved about, trying to make the sofa into a smooth comfortable bed, she could scarcely control the shaking of her hands.

"Meg, don't hate me," Gordon said softly.

"It will be all right, Gordon. Only give me a little time."

"We have been a good team, haven't we?"

He was being unfair, managing to use, in some way, her guilt to hide his own. But that was ridiculous. He didn't know about Thorne.

"Yes," she said stonily. No, he didn't know about her guilt, but he was going to manage, as he always did, to make her feel more guiltily tied to him, by this frightening, shared experience.

"Can we go on being?"

"What?"

"Meg, can we go on being a good team?"

"Gordon, I'm sure we can, but let's sleep—"

"You won't leave me? I don't mean to sleep, I mean—"

"I won't leave you," she said, feeling heaviness, tasting bitterness.

"Sit down here, please, for just a few minutes."

She had finished with the bed and seemed unable to think what else to do, so she sat down, stiffly, beside him. They were silent for a time. Finally, he took her hand and held it again, between both of his.

"Would it be utterly selfish, do you think, if I hope for a son?"

Upstairs, finally, Meg closed the bedroom door soundlessly. A few moments later, she pulled a pillow over her head as well, to stifle the sound of her own wrenching sobs.

XVII

"I been lookin' for you all over the place," called Sam Wiley, hurrying across the railroad yard to drop a hand on Thorne's shoulder. "Got spies out, even. I'm glad I caught up with you."

Sam was a big man, taller and heavier than Thorne, past sixty, but still solid, more than a little formidable to some of the people who didn't agree with him. He had a full head of crisp, lively white hair. His brown eyes were quick and observant. There was no hint of stoop about his heavy shoulders. He had been a locomotive engineer with Intermountain since its inception and had become one of the earliest, most enthusiastic, most tenacious converts to unionization.

Thorne turned at the sound of the voice and hurrying feet behind him. It was past eight o'clock on a September evening. They had put up extra lighting in the Denver yards; still the place was shadowy, a little eerie with dusk. Things were not as busy as they would have been in the daytime, but yard engines were shifting cars, and from the shops at the far side of the yards came a great clamor of banging and clanking.

"Hello, Sam," Thorne said, moving out from under the not unfriendly hand. "What do you want?"

"Let's go somewhere where we can get a cup of coffee. You look like hell, boy."

"I can't. I don't have time."

"We can't talk here. Too damn' noisy."

"You've done all right so far. I've got to move a train in a minute."

"You drivin' 'em too, are you?"

"When we can't find anyone else to do it, and when your people haven't blown the tracks to hell."

"Goddamn it, Thorne, I was the one taught you the first thing you ever knew about runnin' a engine."

"You were, but I can't see what that's got to do with anything now. Does it have some bearing on the fact that we had two engines blown up in the Chandler yards last week, half the shops there ruined, a watchman killed? Has it got anything to do with Tom Murphy's being dead—and those other people? Let's not spend time we haven't got calling up old relationships, Sam. If you people are in the dire straits I keep hearing people cry about, after five months' strike, where are you getting money for dynamite?"

"You think I'm responsible for that?"

"No. Do you think I am?"

"We could settle this real quick, Mac, if you'd just listen a little. Why won't you come to the negotiations? All of us want you there."

"I'm trying to run a railroad."

"Listen; the only holdup now is this crew business, you know, where one crew oughtn' have to work all the way down from, say, Silver Valley to here. That's ten or eleven hours for a passenger train, a good bit longer for most freights."

"Where would you want a division point?"

"Well, on that run, up there around Level somewhere, right at the edge of the mountains."

"There's no town there. Are we supposed to build you one? Crews stationed there, their families, would be wanting to deadhead into Denver every other day. And what about that second train crew? Going either way, you'd have one crew that only worked half, or less, of your eight-hour day."

"All that could be worked out, if we just kept cool and tried at it. Thorne, most of us are not so very unreasonable. The men, ones that have known you, didn't used to think you were. A lot of us in this business have known you a long time, from back when you used to come out here summers with ole Fitz."

"I told you, it's no use to bring up Fitz and old times. I think I used to *be* reasonable. I used to have this stupid notion that we were all trying to work together, for pretty much the same things. I could hardly have approved a strike, ever, but it didn't really bother me much until this Christforsaken destruction and killing started. You'd better be glad I don't go to the negotiations. I wouldn't concede the time of day, now, to your goddamned unions."

Thorne rolled a cigarette and his hands shook. He swayed a little with weariness and moved to lean against a post.

"We all worked together to make your profits," Sam said steadily, with deep conviction. "We ain't after nothin' but our rights."

"Neither am I. Neither was Tom Murphy, I guess. I'm pretty sure Tom must have thought that."

"Thorne, I'm as sorry about Tom as you are. We'll find out, in the end, exactly what all happened up there, who was responsible for things gettin' so heated up. If it was men of ours, there'll be punishment. I can guarantee you that. But you know we can't have a strike go on like this, for five months, without runnin' the risk some hotheads'll cause bad trouble, one side or the other. Nearly every other road in the country has settled now."

"Nearly every other road isn't trying to operate in this part of the country, under the conditions we have here. You want towns built so you can change crews every eight hours, by the clock—"

"I don't think you even really know what it is we're workin' for. Let me tell you—"

"I don't want to hear it, Sam. I hear about it every time I cross a picket line. I hear it in my sleep—when I can get any. I know one thing you want is all things equal, everything done in the same time, in the same way, on every train and railroad in the world. Where would that way of doing things leave *men*? Where would be the point in working for any one company, over any other? How would a workman feel he was a person in those kind of circumstances, instead of a machine? How could there be any pride, for anyone, in his own particular job? Sometimes I think *I*'m the one trying to protect you people, trying to see you're not deprived of your goddamned rights—as individual people, not as a bunch of stupid, united sheep. And I don't know why in hell I ever cared. You people talk to Ranald MacWinter, talk to Peter Maitland. They'll sit down with you. Talk to *our* negotiators. They must be some good. We're paying them enough, to come and sit in a damned conference room all day and night."

"You want to see the road go under?"

"Do you?"

"Hell, none of us wants that, Thorne."

"Then don't you threaten me. God, every day now I see something more your great equalizers have wrecked."

Sam was growing angry too. His big fists were clenched, his face reddening. "We want this ended. We got hungry kids to think about. We're tryin' to work—nearly all of us—for the greatest good for the most people. What difference is it to you, really, how long a train crew works? Hell, I know you've always worked hard, but it ain't been because you've really had to. You inherited half the company off of old man Maxwell and Fitz. You ain't *got* to be doin' any of this."

"Quite a lot of your people are crossing over the lines now, aren't they, Sam?" Thorne said coldly. "Are those men backing all this union activity—men who don't have to worry about your hungry kids—beginning to be afraid the strike will fail? that Intermountain may never *be* union? I'll tell you something, Sam, back there, as late as the first of August, I wouldn't have cared much what we settled for, so long as there was a settlement. I was tired. Now, it's getting so we're running trains, a lot of the time, with full crews. We've got a reasonable number of men in almost all the section gangs, men who are interested in working. We're moving the mail and passengers and the essential freight. They're managing in the yards. We're paying these people more than you new union men ever made for the same job, but our rolling stock is rolling. You know we're losing money on a lot of those trains, but we're moving them. You can take that report back to your people, though I suppose they know it all already. And you can also tell them that from the fifth of August, when they blew Anselm Trestle up on the Amity line, I've been the most ardent scab you're ever likely to find. If you men—just you, without your eastern and west coast organizers—had come to me, sometime back, with most of the proposals that have been agreed to, I think we could have worked it out. I wouldn't have liked some of them, but then I don't think you, on your own, would have made some of them. I've always thought most of the people who work for Intermountain were smart enough to see that all situations, the circumstances on all roads, are not the same, any more than all people are the same. Whatever people may think, I do, sometimes look at newspapers. It's never been in my mind to take the bread out of your wife's mouth, or the milk away from your kids. You've got every loose thug in the country on your hands, haven't you, now that those other strikes have been settled? Every foreman and supervisor on this road has had orders, all the while, to keep his people cool. If he hasn't been successful in that, he's been out of a job—I'm talking about us scabs now. We haven't done much yet in the way of retaliation, but if it comes, if I think it was provoked and justified, I'll be in favor of it, and people won't lose their jobs over it again."

Thorne dropped his cigarette, ground it out, realizing he must have become incoherent. Through the most recent weeks, he had talked only as much as whatever job he was doing required, speaking only sometimes when spoken to. Sam had come here, as they all did, to find Thorne, to be listened to. Thorne had not known how much he had been wanting to have a say.

Sam said gently, "You know, you ought to find a place to sit down for a while."

Thorne couldn't stop himself from going on, compulsively and with great intensity. "You're destroying what I've worked for. I know nobody gives a damn, but I designed Anselm Trestle. It was the first thing of that kind that I ever worked up, all on my own. One of those locomotives wrecked at Chandler was an engine that Brad Halliday, the chief mechanic here, and I worked up for a special order. I went back to the locomotive works myself and watched while they worked on some of the special parts for it. Fitz was superintending on the main line, over on the western slope there, not so far from Chandler, when they built that bridge at Autry Creek, the one that fell into the canyon last week, just about ten seconds after the western mail had finished crossing it. That's the main line. We've got a jerry-built, thrown together footbridge over that canyon now. Passengers walk across; mail and absolutely essential freight is carried. Tom Murphy was my friend. Is it worth all this, to anybody, to have a guaranteed-never-to-vary eight-hour day?"

Sam said, grinning a little, his deep voice soothing, "Where was you aimin' to take that train?"

"All the way to Bethany if I can't find a relief. It's more than eight hours." Bethany, Utah, was the road's western terminus, as Denver was the eastern one.

Sam said, "You're not fixin' to take on the Utah Express?"

"Why wouldn't I be? It's going to be running almost three hours late to start with tonight. They've run out of engineers, all at once, who are qualified for passenger trains."

"You're not qualified, are you?"

"No."

"What do you do at Autry Creek? Change ever'body and ever'thing over to another train on the west side of the canyon?"

"You know what we do, Sam. You've got enough people over there watching. They'll have a temporary bridge open in a few days."

"Well, I oughtn' to hold you up. It looks to me like if you don't find you a place to hide and rest, you're about to be a hospital case." There was nothing of menace or malice in his tone or expression.

"I'm not," Thorne said quietly, steadily. "I won't be."

"You can't run 'er by yourself, Mac. Not even you."

"If I have to, I can try."

"And he would by God try," said Sam with admiration as he ended a report of the conversation to a small group of other men.

Ten days later a contract was agreed on, and the members of the various unions voted to accept it. It was not what some of the less-flexible men thought it should have been, but the steady, thoughtful people like Sam Wiley were sick of even the idea of more negotiations.

In October, Thorne went back to Denver to spend some time in the office. He arrived in the middle of a Wednesday night, and going to his suite at the Fremont Hotel, where, his presence unknown to anyone in town, he slept for seventeen hours.

He woke feeling stiff, sore, and despondent, as some of the months' long tensions began to let up in him. The last thing he wanted was to be back in the office, trying to make a start at putting things back together under the new conditions. He wondered wearily how he had ever got into all this in the first place, when he kept trying to hold full control of his life. He turned over, thinking he might sleep some more.

That brief time in April seemed so long ago now, like something that must surely have happened to someone else. On that morning when he had wakened to find Meg dressing with trembling hands, her face white and drawn, and he realized she was leaving him, he had felt an intensity of pain and bitterness and anger that he had not dreamed could exist. Meg had used him, his love, in a way he could not forgive—that one night had been enough for her.

He had stayed on in the doctor's house, in a half-stupor of fever, taking what the doctor would give him in the way of laudanum to keep his body half-numbed, suffering when he roused to near-consciousness a mental agony that choked him obstructed his breathing. The next morning, against the doctor's recommendations, he got up, dressed and went to look for Vinegar Crawford. The old engineer had said he would have no part of a strike, and he was true to his word. They found two other men who seemed capable of firing the locomotives without blowing up the boilers, put two engines on the mail train and fought through the drifts on Brenner Summit. They went on to Santa Fe, where Vinegar and a trustworthy crew prepared to return north with the mail train. Thorne spent two long, hectic days initiating the hiring of strikebreakers. He then went on to the San Miguel road, spending as little time as possible there, trying to ensure that reconstruction after flood damage should go forward. He turned to Denver, as a starting point from which to plunge into the real work of trying to keep up at least the illusion of normalcy under seige.

Those first weeks after seeing Meg, he had pushed himself to the point of collapse, not simply because the work was there to be done, but in a half-demented attempt to bring on such exhaustion that he would be no longer able to think or feel. Memories of the night with Meg would return to torment him at the least likely moments. His bitterness toward her seemed a palpable thing, always with him, burning his vitals, no matter how many other things and people might be clamoring for his attention. His dreams, when he was able to sleep, were anguished.

Gradually, as he had desperately, blindly hoped would be the case, his body took over, asserting its needs, its demands for self-protection, its determination not to be destroyed. Sleep came more easily, began to be more refreshing, though there was less and less time for it. His appetite returned. More and more he could concentrate his full mental and physical abilities and potential on keeping the road in operation.

The anger that smoldered, then began to build and burn—anger toward the unions and their sympathizers, toward some of the things they were doing in the name of the working man and a fast settlement—was a welcome thing in some ways. It was cleansing, all but eradicating the soreness and anguish in him over other things.

Now, six months after that April night, he wanted to try to forget it and most of what had happened since then, to try to reassemble things, and go on to whatever the future would bring. The violent bitterness had been leached away, most of it, burned out of him by other emotions. If Meg had used him that night, then he, too, had used her. As in almost everything else, the two sides seemed about equal if you weighed them long enough and could be a little objective. But he thought he never wanted to see Meg again.

He got out of bed now, in his hotel room, to shave and dress. His eyes were bloodshot and circled with shadows like great bruises. His face was hollow and haggard, the heavy, several-days growth of black beard making him look a rugged and formidable character. He felt well enough, though drained. He had come through more than the strike in the past six months, and he looked at himself in the mirror, scowling a little, marveling dully, again, at man's instinctive, scrabbling determination to survive, no matter what the odds, even in contention with the will of the mind or the spirit.

It was a little past eight in the evening. He craved coffee badly and was almost out of tobacco, so he decided to go to Mrs. Castleton's house down on River Street. Ma Castleton frightened a lot of people, but she was very obliging, with clients she liked, about good meals and almost anything else. She and Thorne had a fondness, a platonic respect for each other. And the last time he had been there, very nearly a year ago, there had been a strikingly lovely Chinese girl he still remembered. One more night, before any of the company people should discover his whereabouts.

Ranald came into Intermountain's outer office toward noon on that Friday. Busy clerks and secretaries looked up, warmly acknowledging his nods and smiles of greeting and recognition. He walked through the little corridor that separated the inner offices. Jim Ritter was at his desk in his own office, but his door was wide open, and he was keeping an eye on the closed door across the hall. Thorne's chief assistant was a dapper dresser, a neat, efficient bald man with glasses. He was holding his head now with one hand, using the other to turn through a sheaf of papers on the desk before him.

"I take it he's here," Ranald greeted Jim softly, glancing at the closed door, which Jim seemed to be guarding with an almost hopeless exasperation.

"Jesus, yes," groaned Jim. "He's been here since eight o'clock."

"And he's—busy?" Ranald couldn't help smiling.

"Well, yes, in his way. And he's been *seeing* people. He always *sees* people when he's here. He's had the chief accountant in there, badgering poor old Stohrer to come up with money that isn't there for building a new bridge at Autry Creek. He had a talk with a complaining lady passenger who was raving in the outer office when he happened to open that door. She had wandered into a smoker on La Luz express and thought all the men with cigars and such ought to have had to move instead of her. He saw a section hand who got his back hurt during the strike, when he wasn't working, and is threatening to bring suit against the company—and the section hand's lawyer. Then he got out again and spent twenty minutes in the under-clerk's office, listening to John Hoffmeyer brag about his twin baby boys. Every time I try to get near with paperwork that's been piling up for six months, needing his attention, he says, 'You've got a power of attorney,' or some smart-mouth thing like that and yet he *sees* anybody, for anything."

"It sounds to me like things are already almost back to normal," said Ranald.

Jim sighed. His left eyelid kept twitching spasmodically and his stomach was burning from too much coffee. He felt he had to go on with his litany. "He's sent Fred Morley off to investigate a lost-freight claim. Jesus Christ, I need Fred *here*. There are plenty of other people who could have done that, whose *job* it is to do that. And, oh, yes, he's designing the new bridge for Autry. You know Hansen, that old crippled switchman who always hangs around the building here, or at the yards, or the depot, and who will try to keep anybody that even looks at him listening to his stories all day? Well, that's who's with him now. Hansen saw Thorne come in this morning and thought he'd drop in for a little talk. I was going to send for some dynamite to blast the old man out of the reception room, but Thorne saw him before I'd got to it. I don't know why we didn't buy space in the papers and advertise the goddamned open house."

Ranald, smiling in commiseration, sat down where he, too, could watch the closed door. "Well, yes, Jim, I suppose you might have done that, but as far as most of us are concerned, we're going to be buying as little advertising in most of the papers as possible for some time. The papers have absolutely torn Thorne and Intermountain to pieces these past months."

"Why have they been so rough, do you think?" Jim asked thoughtfully. "I haven't had time to read the papers, much less talk about it, but it has been kind of hellish, especially from the *Star*. Partly, I suppose, it's because Thorne has always been so antagonistic toward anybody he suspected of being a reporter."

"It's partly that," Ranald said. "That new man they've got, helping to run the *Star* is from back east, Washington, I think. Muckraking is big business these days, you know, and it's justified, at least partially. The *Star* wants Denver to have its share of sensationalism, tabloid-type news. Thorne is an ideal person for someone like this crusader to blast out of the water. He's uncooperative, completely unimpressed by the press, doesn't give a damn about anything but trying to get his job done—any job. Have you *read* the stuff, Jim?"

"I remember some of it: 'Capitalist Villain,' 'Enemy of the Working Man'—"

" 'Hereditary Rail Baron,' " Ranald took it up. " 'Arch Oligarchist.' God, I don't know *anybody* who's more of a real anarchist at heart than Thorne is."

"Well, it's seemed to me, when I've had time to think about it, that he ought to be able to sue in some cases. I don't mean for the name-calling; there's just going to be a certain amount of that, but some of the allegations, the outright claims and statements, have been libelous as hell. Have you talked to him any about this?"

Ranald shrugged. "He was passing through town a few weeks back and had supper with us. Amy, my wife, brought up the newspapers. Amy just may have been madder than anybody. She was ready to get dynamite too, use it on the *Star* and some others. Elizabeth had been literally sick about some of those things like 'In Depth Portrait of an Hereditary Rail Baron.' She thought it must surely be hurting Thorne, making him feel bad, I mean. He told them he hadn't read much of anything, that he mostly used the newspapers for starting fires. He said he wouldn't waste time reading them, not to mention considering libel suits."

Jim laughed. "He's quite a man, and nothing can touch him."

Ranald looked at him earnestly, frowning a little, running a hand through his gray-touched, sandy hair. "Almost everybody thinks nothing gets to him. They're wrong. God, Jim, I've helped out over here when I could. *I* know and *you* know what he's done these past months. He's kept the trains running and the track mostly fit to run them on, is what he's done. They never make folk heroes out of company men, though, do they?"

Jim nodded soberly. "You're right about him. I've worked with him a long time, you know, from back before old Fitz was hurt up at Perry Tunnel. It may be I know, better than just about anybody else, just how much he *can* handle, but I swear to you, Ranald," and he smiled unwillingly, "he can be the most aggravating man I've ever seen, while he's doing it. He wouldn't be caught dead *thinking* about anything as ordinary, as arbitrary, he calls it, as office routine. This place is not only an open house, it's a madhouse when he's here. I remember old Fitz saying once, 'He can fair turn out the work, but if it's paperwork, he means to see ever'body within a mile suffers from it ever'bit as much as he does.' "

"But he does it," Ranald said. "God, he does it."

Jim nodded, twitching nervously as a door closed rather loudly down the hall. "Fred Morley's been out with him some of the time, you know. Trying to keep up with him is about all Fred says he's been able to do, not much other work. Fred tells me he's been carrying a book on or by Machiavelli."

"Thorne?" Ranald said, delighted. "For God's sake, why?"

Jim denied all knowledge with a helpless gesture. "Lord, I don't know, but I'm expecting him to come up any minute with some new ideas that he's gleaned from that stuff. He does that, you know, throws out everything sometimes, starts over with a whole new system for doing something or other. And the hell of it is that once we give in and *try* it his way, it usually works like a charm."

Thorne opened his office door then for the old switchman, whose toothless mouth was wide in a happy grin.

"Hello, Ranald," Thorne said warmly. "Come in. Jim doesn't like me to keep this door open too long. He's afraid I'll suffer from a draft or something."

The dusty, battered desk top was scarcely visible under stacks of papers. There were badly worn paths in the muddy brown carpet, no drapes at the windows. An empty coffee cup and an overflowing ashtray were on the windowsill beside a drawing board, where paper for the barely begun drawings for the new bridge were spread.

"You're making a mental case out of poor old Jim," Ranald said.

"He's been trying to be certified as a mental case for fifteen years. Sit down."

Ranald kicked suspiciously at a ruptured armchair. "This place is a disgrace. Where in the world did you get all this junk? You've always had an office budget."

Thorne looked in sudden consternation at the armchair, as though he had never seen it before. "I don't think that looked like this the last time I noticed it."

"Why haven't you got any drapes or shades?"

Thorne frowned, trying to recall something. "Now I remember. We had some in the beginning, drapes, and they were always in the way. There was a man—I think it was Pete Gonzaga; do you remember him? He was waiting for me in here one day and he fell asleep with a lighted cigar in his hand, set the drapes on fire at this north window. You must remember that. Somebody called the fire department, and we must have had every piece of equipment in town blocking the street down there, after the fire was all out. I found out the light was a lot better without having to bother with the damned drapes, so then somebody must have taken the ones off the east window too."

"But this looks as if you didn't even have new furniture to *start* with."

"Well, no, I don't think we did. Somebody asked me, before the building was opened, what I wanted in the way of office decoration, so I asked Miss Welch to go out and see if she could find some secondhand stuff. She asked what I wanted to pay, and I told her, and I guess these are the things she got. Fitz used the room next door, what we use for a conference room now, when he was able to come down here. It's pretty nice, I guess. Hell, Ran, I don't need a fancy office. I try not to be here, or when I am, I don't look at drapes and things like that. We use our office budget—my share of it—for other things. The other people are all right, the ones who work here. They've got the latest machines and file cabinets and such, comfortable chairs . . . well, I think they have."

He was standing beside his desk, glancing rapidly through a stack of papers. He looked up and pushed the empty swivel chair at Ranald. "Other people sit in my visitor's chair, but if you won't, take this one."

"What other things does your part of the office budget go for?" pursued Ranald, sitting down.

Thorne was scowling at something in one of the reports. "Hell, Ranald, I don't know. We need some extra money sometimes. And right now, we need a whole hell of a lot more than we're going to get from an office budget surplus. What are you nattering about anyway? Your office is in good shape. You've seen this one before."

"I don't remember that it looked quite this seedy. Peter Maitland must surely have things to say about it."

"He never comes here. I go up and talk to him."

"Well, you know Peter's a great one for keeping up appearances. He'd say you have to make concessions to the position you hold, even if you don't care about things for yourself."

Thorne shrugged. "Maybe that's why I go up to his office when we need to talk about something." He made hurried notes on the margin of something.

Ranald said quietly, "Are you angry about the contract?"

"Which one?"

"The *union* contract, Thorne."

"No. There had to be settlement sometime, I guess. We're not ever going to get back to what we were, but there'd be no point in being angry."

"You wouldn't sign the agreement."

"But Jim did it, with his power of attorney. Ah, hell, it was a stupid principle, I know, but I couldn't sign, not after Tom and all the rest of it."

"Do you think it's really that bad? That we can't ever get back to what we were?"

Thorne shrugged. "It's not so *bad*, I guess. Companies are like people in some ways, you know. After a big quarrel, or some kind of upheaval, they can't get back to what they were, but it probably doesn't have to be a bad thing. Maybe there's something better than what we were. What I mean is not so much the adjustments we'll have to make because of the changes the unions are forcing on us. I was thinking of things like that we may as well start considering closing down the short lines. Two out of four could go right now, and we'd save money."

"You'll have to go to court ultimately, won't you, before you can discontinue all service?"

"God, yes. That's why I say we may as well begin on it soon. The Columbia Creek road in Montana is the only short line we ought to hold onto. It may be we can sell the others, but I doubt it. The mines at Columbia Creek are going to last a while, but not forever. We'll have to think about selling or shutting down the road to Amity in another year or two. I'll not like doing that. That's always been such a bastard, that line. We've got to have some new rolling stock. Track's in bad shape all over right now, with winter coming on, when it ought to have been all worked over. I'm beginning to think we may already have seen the best years for the narrow-gauge. It's sad, if that's true."

"Why don't you take a vacation?" Ranald asked quietly.

"I am," he answered blithely. "I already told Jim, it started this morning."

Thorne opened a folder stamped Urgent, Maxwell—June, 1892. "What's going on around here?"

"They've got the new mine down by Chavez open. It looks pretty good, Peter thinks. We're doing all right at the mill, not the way I'd like to see it going, but all right. Some of the changes I've wanted—new equipment and shifts in production—are coming, but you must have heard there's a shortage of money."

"Are you still cutting back on rails?"

"There hasn't been much demand for them this year. If you don't think *we're* going to be starting any new construction, it must be the same, or worse, for other roads. Really, it hasn't been bad with the mill after the strikes last year. I'm pleased enough for a while. Peter's going east to try to get a loan or two. Have you seen him?"

"Not lately, no. He'd better try to arrange big ones."

"He'll want to see you . . . today, if you've got the time. He'd like you to go east with him."

Thorne glanced up blankly. "Peter's good at asking for money. I'm not. He's good at talking to stockholders, too, and he's going to have to do that in January. I can't think where Intermountain's going to come up with anything that even resembles a dividend. . . ."

Ranald said, rather surprised and pleased by the idea, "Thorne, do you realize it's just us now, you and me, with Peter Maitland—one Maitland? I still don't really have the feel of it. I tend to keep thinking of us as if we were still kids, as if Angus and Fitz and Philip were around somewhere, waiting to jump on us for something or send us out to bring them coffee. Do you have any idea what a fantastic job you've done with Intermountain? I don't mean just this year, during all the trouble. Do you ever *read* the annual reports? The railroad's paid dividends every year since '73. Most of those years—even last year and the one before, when things were pretty tight—Intermountain had better earnings per track mile than almost any other road in the country."

"Fitz was in charge here until a few years ago."

Thorne crossed to open the door. "Jim, come and take some of this stuff, will you? . . . I've finished with this, and those. I've meant to tell you that the passenger cars they're having to use for the Rio Grande and the western mail are something to be ashamed of. The last time I was on the Rio Grande bobtail, I swear they were using the first passenger coaches that were ever made. I think we must have bought them secondhand from the Central Western, back in the beginning of time. I want construction started on a permanent bridge at Autry by the end of the month. I'll be through with the specifications for it in two or three days."

"Well," said Jim, "I guess they've got some of the basic stuff they'll need to start with, either at Chandler or Bethany, wouldn't you think?"

"They have, but I wish to God we had Tom Murphy to run the job."

Jim said, taking note of the work Thorne had indicated on the desk and sounding a little hysterical, "You can't be through with all this. You've had people in here the whole morning and—"

Patiently, Thorne flipped pages, pointing to his notes and signatures.

"Well, there's more out there," Jim said defiantly.

"Yes," Thorne said grimly. "I thought there might be, but let me empty the desk, will you? I think I've lost something, and it's probably under there somewhere."

"What is it?"

"A book of Fred Morley's. I'm sure I brought it in, to give back to him."

"The Machiavelli?" asked Jim.

"Yes, it is."

Ranald asked, "What's your interest in Machiavelli?"

"Well, he says that people pretty much get what they deserve, in the way of politicians, rulers, treatment from their governments, things like that. I expect he's probably right."

"That is the grossest, most simplistic oversimplification I've ever heard," said Ranald, laughing.

"Yeah, well, what I've mostly been doing with the book is using it as a kind of sleeping draft. Half a page and I'm out for the night. It's sort of the same reason I started chewing tobacco this summer, only that was to keep myself awake. But don't tell Fred, all right? He thinks Machiavelli was a terrifically intelligent man. He's thinking of going into politics, Fred is. But speaking of Fred, has he come back? Did he find out anything about those cars?"

"He was in for a minute. The cars may be in Santa Fe, or somewhere down there."

"What do you mean, they *may* be? *Nobody* can *lose* six boxcars."

"But with the strike . . ."

"Come on, Jim, that stuff was supposed to have been in San Francisco before the end of July. We won't use the strike as an excuse for everything. Those cars came into the yards here from Chicago at the beginning of July. Nobody knows where they've been since then. That's priority freight, not perishable, thank God. It's that old pot-bellied guy—what's his name?—Maloney. He's the yardmaster at Santa Fe, and he'd rather be goddamned than give anybody a straight answer about anything. How's the stuff supposed to have got down there anyway?"

"I don't know," said Jim, throwing Ranald a helpless glance.

"Let's wire Maloney. Tell him I said he's not to go home until he's made a thorough check for those cars, and if he finds them, he's not to go home until they're moving north."

"Tomorrow's Saturday."

"Well, what about it? And tell Chainey that those cars are not to be sidetracked when they get back up here."

"They'll have to be sent by Union Pacific out of

here. That stuff's too heavy for the temporary bridge at Autry. It's going to cost us—"

"We're in the business of moving things from one place to another, Jim. I know it's going to have to be turned over to Union Pacific, but that freight is two and a half months late. It's damned well not the shipper's fault, or the receiver's. That sort of leaves us holding the. . . . See if Miss Welch can find us some coffee, will you?"

"But there are yardmasters and train masters to take care of things like getting those cars moving. We employ several civil engineers. Couldn't you tell one of them what you want done about the Autry bridge and he would work on it? So we could get on with—"

"We're getting on with it, Jim," Thorne said soothingly. "It's all going to work out."

Thorne put his fresh cup of coffee on the windowsill and turned back to his drawings. "How's the family?" he asked Ranald when they were alone again.

"They're fine. Amy was pretty upset all during the strike, but she's getting over it. Elizabeth's having some trouble with arthritis, though she never mentions it. Rob was in a fight at school last week, and I had to go and talk to his headmaster. He's a scrapper, Rob. I'm not quite sure what to do about him. A lot just doesn't seem to get through to him, but his allowance has been stopped until November. That may make some impression. I can't believe our boys are nine and eleven already.

"Mama was up for a couple of weeks, staying with us and at Meg's. She was sorry not to see you. God, I was about to forget the important news. Meg and Gordon are having a baby in January."

The words shook Thorne oddly. He concentrated on his drawing and asked finally, "How's Murphy?"

"Seems to be fine, brilliant in school. His teachers are worried about just what they ought to do with him. We don't see them much. You know how Gordon is. Associating with me would be bad for the reputation he's making for himself. He seems to be drinking quite a lot. Mama's worried about it, and she almost never criticizes anyone her kids marry. She finds fault enough with the kids themselves, but seems to think the in-laws, generally, are above reproach. Can you come and have lunch with me now? It's what I came for, an hour or so ago."

"No, I'll see if I can send someone out for food later. You know, in this part of the building, we've got to come up with almost a whole new reorganization plan, taking into account the new regulations and all. I think I may have to go and supervise this bridge work. God knows I want to."

"Amy called me this morning. I told her you were rumored to be back. She and Elizabeth are expecting you for supper."

"Not tonight, Ran. I'm here now. I guess I'll stay awhile."

Ranald stood up. "You don't have to *live* at the office. You won't forget about seeing Peter? And be sure to go up to see him. Something has to be done about this office of yours."

Thorne grinned, not looking up. "Poverty begins at home."

"Truth is stranger than fiction," Ranald said, and they both laughed.

At the door, Ranald looked back. "Don't you ever sit down?"

"No more than I can help, if I'm supposed to be busy. Sitting down makes me sleepy."

"Well, I only came to see how you were. You still look like the wrath of God, but you seem to be cheeky and insolent enough. There's something else I was almost forgetting to tell you and I suppose you should know. Cherish has been back in Denver since some time in July. It would seem she's expecting you home."

"She is? I can't think why."

"Her story is that you've *been* home, every time you've been in town."

"I've hardly even been in town, except for passing through the yards."

"I know that, but other people don't. She's been doing a lot of talking."

"Saying what?"

"That she asked you to leave because of other women, because of Nancy especially. That you're asking, now, to patch things up with her."

Thorne looked at him grimly. "I haven't even thought of her in months."

"Well, I thought you ought to know, be warned, in case anything comes up."

"Yeah, thanks. You've brightened an otherwise damned dreary day."

Ranald came over and put a hand fondly on his shoulder. "Come to the house, first chance you get, all right?"

Thorne stayed and worked in his office until almost midnight and went in the next day, Saturday, to spend several hours. He walked back to his hotel in early, cloudy autumn twilight. He wore no coat, and a cold wind, down from the mountains, came blustering at him from every direction as it careened wildly around the buildings. He thought he might forget supper and go to bed, for weariness seemed to be sapping more of his strength now, distracting and slowing his mind, more than it had through all the hot, hectic summer.

Cherish was waiting in his sitting room when Thorne unlocked the door. She ran to him, flung her arms around him and lifted her face expectantly.

Thorne disengaged himself in surprise and irritation. "What are you doing here?"

"I knew you'd be surprised," she said, showing only slight signs of being deflated. "The manager told them to let me in. I've been waiting almost an hour."

"Why?"

"Why did he say I could come in? Because he believed me when I said I'm your wife. It's true, you know, but I got the impression I'm not the only woman who's told that story. Thorne, you look worn out. It's been an awful time, hasn't it?"

"I meant," he said doggedly, "why are you here? Why have you been waiting almost an hour?"

"I wanted to see you," she said, pouting her pretty little mouth. "Aren't you the least bit glad? Can't we sit down and have a talk?"

"About what?"

"Well, sit down, or maybe you might offer me a drink. Do you have any sherry?"

Not doubting that she had been through every drawer and cupboard and closet in the two rooms, Thorne opened a cupboard and said wearily, "I've got gin and Irish whiskey."

She grimaced. "Well, just give me a little of *something*. It's turning cold, isn't is?"

He gave her a glass and stood at the window with his own. "Was it the weather you wanted to talk about?"

"You haven't even asked about the children. They're *always* wondering about you."

"Well, what about them?"

Cherish took a sip of the whiskey, choked. "Oh, Thorne, couldn't I have some water in this? It's horrible."

Thorne took the glass and brought it back to her almost filled with water. Taking it, her touch lingered on his fingers.

"The children are well and doing nicely with their studies. They have a very good tutor now, a man I found in England. Stuart will probably be going to boarding school in less than a year. I'm sure he will be accepted at Fairchild Academy near Richmond. Some of the very best families in the South have sent their boys to Fairchild for more than a hundred years. Clare is growing into a stunning beauty. You surely want to see them, don't you? It's been two years,

Thorne. And we'll be going back home to Fern Hill again soon, unless . . ."

"Unless?"

"I wish you'd sit down, or at least have the courtesy to look at me. It wasn't exactly easy, coming here."

He went to a chair opposite hers and sat down, watching her coolly, with a taut, irritated expression.

"The important thing I came to say," she said softly, barely glancing up at him through her lashes, "is that we really ought to try again, Thorne, for the children's sake, if nothing else. I dream about you. Do you ever dream?"

"It's no good talking about it, Cherish. I don't want to try again."

"You're so cold," she said, her voice low and bitter. "Nothing ever reaches you, does it? I wish I knew why in God's name you ever married me in the first place."

He said nothing. A flush rose in her lovely face. She drank, gulping, and tried to compose herself.

"I suppose, in that case," she said stiffly, "the house here ought to be sold. The children and I loathe this town. We can't wait to get back to Fern Hill."

"All right. I'll turn it over to someone to put on the market when you leave. When it sells, the money will be put into your account. The company, at least the railroad, isn't going to be paying much of a dividend this year."

"Thorne, you planned that house, we did. Don't you have any feeling at all about anything in all those years? Remember, they started building at almost the same hour Stuart was born?"

She seemed so much quieter, so much more rational than he had expected, despite the constant recriminations that were so much a part of her behavior toward him, that Thorne was a little taken aback.

"I'm sorry," he said slowly. "It was wrong from the first. I can't think of anything that can be done now that would make any of the past any better.

Why don't you get a divorce? You're still very beautiful, Cherish. Maybe you'd want to marry again."

"Oh, that would make a fine scandal, wouldn't it? A divorce. Haven't you had enough publicity lately? The only grounds I could sue on would be adultery. How would that strike your dear old Mr. Maitland? Or your so very dear and Catholic relatives?"

"I'm not particularly concerned about how it strikes anybody."

"No, that's right, isn't it? I had forgotten, just for a minute, how you're never very concerned about *anything*." She smiled sadly. "Well, what if I were to do it—get a divorce? Who would I name? Where's your mistress? Who is she? Or should I say they?"

"There are girls on River Street who would be willing to be named as corespondent, for a fee."

"I don't think the courts accept whores, darling."

Another silence; then she said wistfully, meekly, "Have you had supper?"

"No."

"The carriage is downstairs. I more than half promised Clare and Stuart you'd come back with me for supper with us. Don't shake your head," she implored. "They're your *children*! Can't you spare them two hours now when you seem so perfectly willing to give them up without a qualm for the rest of their lives? Can't you try to give them just a few minutes of something decent to remember about you?"

She knew his guilt over the children, used it. Both of them knew what she was doing, but he went along to the house because she was quiet and subdued, for Cherish, and he thought it might be a way of avoiding something worse than supper with the children. Clare and Stuart chattered and bickered about things of which, for the most part, Thorne had no knowledge. Clare, who truly was beautiful in the soft, small, blond way her mother was, seemed to want nothing more than to get back to her friends at Fern Hill. Stuart, who was good-looking in a spare, ascetic way, was campaigning for the purchase of a racehorse. Cherish grew rather feverishly vivacious during the meal, talking gaily, fluttering her long lashes at Thorne and at the children's tutor, Nigel Mason.

After supper, Thorne found himself alone for a moment with his son and daughter. He felt awkward and self-conscious, wondering what sort of person each of them really was, wishing he had managed somehow to know them, even a little.

"If you'd ever like to come back here," he said stiffly, "we could probably work something out."

"Mama said you'd be coming back to live with us," said Clare complacently.

"No, I won't be doing that, but if either of you should want to come here for a visit one day . . ."

"She said the railroad would have to go out of business because of all the money you lost about the strike. She said we'd be poor, but we could all live together at Fern Hill. We read those things that were in the newspapers about you. They embarrassed me. I'd be embarrassed to be poor, too."

"Well, you won't have to worry about it, for a while, at least," he said sardonically, then wished he had not spoken. She was, after all, only a child.

"What would we do if we came back here?" asked Stuart scornfully. "Mama said you're going to sell the house, and we hardly know anyone here anymore."

Cherish came running lightly down the stairs then. "Isaac ought to have the carriage ready, Thorne. I'll just ride back to the hotel with you."

In the carriage, while he clenched his teeth in frustration and irritation at not being able to be free of her, Cherish said, "Are you proud of them at all?"

"They—they're a fine-looking pair of kids."

"And you've always wished they were yours by somebody else. Don't you think I've known that? What do you think of Nigel?"

"Who? Oh, yes. Do you mean as a teacher?"

"What else do you think I'd mean?"

"I don't know. How can I tell anything about that from so little time?"

Cherish smiled in the darkness and laid her hand lightly on his thigh. "It's no one's doing but your own that there wasn't more time. There could be all the time you'd want. Well, Nigel is a good teacher—and a good lover."

Thorne shifted, moving away from her hand. "Is he? Then I'm glad for you."

"And jealous? Just a bit?"

"No, Cherish, I'm not. Why don't you divorce me and marry Nigel? Wouldn't that be a better, more moral situation for Clare and Stuart, not to mention for you and Nigel?"

"Why, I don't want to marry Nigel, darling. His family is nothing. . . . I went to Scotland, Thorne, last May. I met your cousin the Earl of Brendeen and had a lovely time visiting with him and his family at Brendeen House—the Hall, you know. He asked me to come again, when *you* could spare the time, and to bring the children. I do want the children to be at least acquainted with your family, if they're not to be spared any of your time and thought. Lady Madge Maxwell is a dumpy, frumpy little old thing, but the earl, Lord Evan, is very handsome and dignified. He looks something like Angus, as I remember Angus. You're nothing like him, of course, but I can certainly see the family resemblance in Stuart."

They drew up in front of the hotel, and to Thorne's growing annoyance, Cherish said to her driver, "I'll be here for just a little while, Isaac. You can wait around the corner."

"Cherish, there's no point in any of this."

"If I'm not to see you again, there are some things that have to be settled."

"Like what?"

"Like how much money the children and I are to have, and don't tell me you've provided plenty up to this time. I wouldn't call it plenty, though it has been there—but do you think I'll just trust your bounty forever? I want some legal agreement drawn up, and it would be much easier if we didn't have to discuss the terms of it standing here in the middle of the sidewalk with people staring at us."

A light rain had begun to be flung about on the cold wind. Grimly, Thorne returned with her to his suite, and they discussed financial matters and other settlements for a time. Cherish then told him her version of the story of why Dahlia, insolent and ungrateful, had left her almost two years ago. It was a pathetic story, as she told it, and he listened tiredly, without comment. Still, remembering Dahlia's loyalty and the devoted, loving story Dahlia had told him years ago, when he and Cherish had been married only a few months, Thorne could not quite put down a small stirring of pity for Cherish. She brought so much unhappiness on herself, and perhaps she really could not tell the truth anymore from the complicated, convoluted fabric of lies that had become her life and being.

When Cherish finished her story about Dahlia's desertion, she said sweetly, "Darling, you've mentioned divorce three or four times this evening. Do you want to marry again?"

"No."

"I've worried about you, you know, during all that strike trouble. I know you must be so very tired now that it's finally all over. Wouldn't you just like to go somewhere where it's quiet, maybe with some pretty scenery, and rest for a good long time? I'd like to come with you. It wouldn't mean we were going to stay together or anything like that, you know. It's just that I think the change, and having a woman, would be very good for you. I could make you so happy, you'd forget all about the strike and everything."

"Cherish, I keep telling you, and I mean it, I'm not interested!"

She cut in sharply, "Who were those letters from?"
"Letters? What—"

"The ones someone sent you, in care of Fitz, that time you and Ranald were in Europe. I know they were from a girl. It's hard to imagine you as some kind of romantic dreamer—you've certainly never meant to show that side of yourself to *me*—but I've often thought you've kept on believing you love her. I know you never wanted to try to love me, and God! how I've hated you! But I'll tell you something. I'd rather see you dead than married to someone else. You'll never have the satisfaction of a divorce from me."

She began to sob. She stood up, stumbling, and flung herself into his arms. "Oh, Thorne, you know you're mine; and I only want, once in my life, to be able to please you. Make love to me. You know you want it. I can feel that you do."

Thorne stood up easily, holding her, and then set her on her feet. Her crying was loud in the quiet room.

"Cherish, please don't do that." His voice was flat, impatient. "Come on, now, go in and wash your face. I'll walk back downstairs with you."

After a moment, to his relief, she did go into the bathroom, her movements stiff with fury. She came back red-eyed, but seemingly composed. As he opened the door into the hall, she said truculently, "I'll make you sorry, you bastard. Life with you has never been anything but one humiliation after another. You're going to regret that, all of it."

As they crossed the lobby, she screamed, suddenly, horribly, and ran a few steps from him, looking back as if in terror for her life. Her face was suffused in a flood of tears.

"Rape!" she shrieked. "Oh, please, somebody help me. He's trying to . . ."

People rushed toward them from all sides. Thorne stood trembling, his fists clenched hard at his sides, feeling, very oddly, a little removed from the scene. It was as if he were watching from the mezzanine, and his body, here in the lobby, suddenly were no longer a real part of him. This unreal body could not quite get its eyes to focus; sounds came faintly to its ears; the heat of angry blood rose up in the face and the head felt dizzy, ringing.

People were clustered around Cherish and a group encircled her. A salesman carrying a sample case approached him, snarled something belligerent, and grabbed Thorne's arm. With a fierce backhand swing, Thorne sent the man sprawling. He could not sort out or identify any of the words that were being shouted around him, at him. The detached part of him saw Cherish being soothed by a large motherly woman, who glared over Cherish's head at him. The lobby tilted and swayed sickeningly.

"Mr. Maxwell . . ." cried the night manager, rushing toward him.

Thorne took a step, not knowing where he meant to go. Then the sounds faded; he could see nothing at all as he crumpled to the floor.

He woke in the bed in Ranald's and Amy's guest room; Ranald was sitting beside the bed, looking worried.

"How do you feel?"

"I don't know," he said vaguely. He tried to sit up then, remembering the scene in the hotel lobby more clearly than it had actually been to him at the time. He was dizzy, weak, impatient with himself.

"Don't do that," Ranald said. "Rest a while. Do you have any pain?"

"No." Thorne robbed his eyes. A dreary daylight was coming outside the windows. "What's happened to me?"

"Dr. Sharpe couldn't find much wrong with you, just total exhaustion, maybe, and some sort of shock. He said you need a complete rest. We brought you here so we can be sure that you get it."

"Cherish—"

"Never mind about that. I know about it."

"What do you know?"

"Well, that the night manager down at the Fremont probably saved you from being mobbed. The desk clerk told him that Cherish had said she was your wife earlier. That took some of the interest out of her story for all those curious people. She'd left before I got there, or I'd have beat her backside bloody."

"She came and wanted to talk about money, selling the house. A part of the time, she seemed so reasonable—for Cherish. I thought those things did need settling. I went with her and had supper with the kids and then . . ."

"You don't have to explain anything."

He did sit up then, before Ranald could stop him. "Jesus Christ, the newspapers—"

"I think we shut them up, the hotel people and I. The Fremont doesn't want that kind of publicity any more than we do. There's been enough news out of Intermountain lately."

"You talked to somebody?"

"No. Costa did, the hotel manager. I thought it would be better that way, but I did ask him to call Mr. Alden."

Thorne grinned starkly. "Alden, Fitz's old friend. Fitz always tried to tell me those people were worth cultivating." He sighed, then frowned. "I've never done a thing like that in my life."

"Like what? Talking to Alden?"

"Like passing out. What a stupid . . ."

"Myself, I thought it was a beautiful way to get out of that situation."

Thorne did not answer his smile, and Ranald said intently, "You know, by rights you should have done that, or something like it months ago. Don't you *know* you're exhausted? You're heading for some kind of breakdown; Sharpe says so too. You're going to have to be sensible, at least for a few days, give your body half a chance. Dahlia's waited up to fix you some breakfast. I'll tell her you're awake."

Thorne stayed at Ranald's until Tuesday, then went up to a mountain cabin Ranald had had built years ago. He took briefcases full of paperwork, but he rested and was mostly alone. Silas, who was his housekeeper for the business cars, went along to cook, but Silas was not a particularly communicative man and was partial to long naps. Thorne had meant to stay at the cabin only two or three days, but he let the time stretch into a week, caught in a quiet, indifferent lethargy. One day he took a book from a shelf, sat down and read it through without interruption. He could not recall the last time such a thing had been possible; he relished the wasting of time, a thing wholly new to him. He began to sleep easily at night, long and deeply.

"I guess we'll go back down tomorrow," he said finally, reluctantly, to Silas. "We must be running out of food."

"Yessir, we are," said the old man. "There ain't coffee but for another day or two, for one thing."

"Then there can't be any question, can there?"

Silas took away his dishes, looking pleased, Thorne thought. Silas did not like the mountains, had never got over being exasperated by the isolation of most of the railroad camps. He was always pleased at the prospect of going back to town.

It was snowing, a still, soft fall; and Thorne took a long walk, another thing he had not done, purely for the pleasure of it, for a very long time. The area reminded him a little of the mountains above the hacienda.

Meg and Gordon were to have a child in January. Until now, he had not allowed himself to look fully at the fact. For a time, after that night in April, he had lost the ability to control his conscious mind. He was in charge of himself now, and it was safe to think of such things. April to January . . .? Was it his child? She had wanted children so desperately, had believed their denial a punishment for her sins, and his. Had she been thinking of a child that night? Was that why, when he had said "Stay," she had stood there trembling, not going away from him? Thorne wanted, needed to believe there had been calculation on Meg's part, but the anger would not come back to him now. He knew only the heavy residue of pain and longing. She had, after all, warned him it could be no more than a temporary thing. Perhaps she had been more honest and objective, throughout, than he. A night like that, feelings which she must surely, in some degree, have shared, were not things for objectivity. Still, whatever her motives, if motives there had been, he felt now that he could live with the pain and yearning of memories, that the hurt would grow less and eventually blend into the other might-have-beens of his life. He thought, with only mild self-derision, of the times in his life, crisis times, when he had vowed never again to feel helpless. Had he really believed one ever had a choice? The most one could hope for, he supposed, was not to *appear* helpless, and even that much seemed a great deal to ask. Perhaps he had expected too much of himself, had been unrealistic. This tendency toward self-toleration, toward a kind of inner empathy, was a new thing for him, and he was not yet ready to face it directly. It made him wary within his own mind; yet it seemed to offer the prospect of some new vista, the possibility for greater peace within himself. He was not ready fully to explore the growing willingness to accept himself, and yet . . . He had always, without ever quite knowing details, expected so much. Had the expectations been of other people, of life itself? Or had they been, to a greater degree, expectations and demands of himself, subconscious specifications for thoughts, feelings, words, behavior that had been, would always be, beyond his ability? It was something to think about, to be considered some day, a blurred half-promise;

but he was wary, frightened by any prospect of promise. So many things that had looked hopeful had, in the end, brought only bitterness and disappointment.

Standing under a ponderosa pine, still, in thought, he watched a little gray-headed junco come flitting through the snow, casually, going about its daily business, undeterred and undismayed by the weather. The little bird, with efficient, matter-of-fact chirps, dipped in and perched on a small bough, dislodging a minuscule avalanche of snow onto Thorne's bare head. He looked up abstractedly, smiled at the junco with a warmth of fellow-feeling, the reasons for which he would not bother to explore. He turned back toward the cabin, walking slowly, his senses taking in and enjoying his surroundings while his mind went more or less its own way.

He wanted to see Murphy, now that he would have a little more time, and meant to do so. He would call Gordon's office, perhaps even go there, and arrange to have the boy with him for a part of the Christmas vacation in two months. Meg should not be troubled so much by Murphy's absence now, as she prepared for a new baby.

Back in the spring, Thorne had told John Blessington, the company lawyer, that he was no longer willing to consider Murphy's adoption. At the time, his bitterness toward Meg was uppermost in his mind. And Gordon was so much in the public eye, assisting with union causes and demands. Thorne prevented Blessington from contacting Meg and Gordon about beginning the legalities of the matter, almost purely for reasons of spite and vengeance. Beneath those reasons, though, had been his uncertainties about and lifelong contempt for Gordon. Murphy was obviously still uncertain about "Dad." Thorne no longer had any wish to take the boy from Meg—not for vindictive reasons, at any rate—but he would let matters stay as they were, concerning adoption, until he could feel surer that Murphy was content.

If he had never taken Murphy to Meg in the first place . . . but he had, with his eyes wide open, just so that he, Thorne, could . . . could what? Be with Meg, have a reason for seeing her? That day when he had driven her buggy back to Quintana from Uncle Gavin's, Thorne had felt and had believed himself to be so very detached, almost disinterested in the whole situation between himself and Meg. Along the road to Quintana, he had been nearly convinced that the Meg he had loved, had held to for so long, had been mostly just one more of those shadowy, hoped-for things he had wanted from life. But during that strange time of peace, had he subconsciously been scheming for a reason, an excuse to be near her, dream or no? Was there a chance that Murphy, in any way, had been a sacrifice to his own willful, blindly obstinate self-indulgence? Yes, he would go and see Gordon, though there might be hell to pay. He had heard that Gordon was much taken up with self-importance and superiority in his efforts "on behalf of the common man."

Thorne thought that he had rarely, if ever, known a "common man." Each turned out, eventually, to be at least a little extraordinary in some special, private way that was the essentiality of that man's individual being. In any case, he had no intention of taking any nonsense from Gordon, but he would try to stick to the subject of Murphy, to make a true evaluation of what might be Gordon's feelings and motives concerning the boy. If he was convinced that Murphy's situation was tenable, he would wait until Christmas vacation to see the boy, then question him—or better yet, simply let Murphy talk until he could know the boy's true feelings about Meg and Gordon. If not for Murphy, Meg might not have been on the mail train, that particular mail train, on that specific day. If not for Murphy, the tacit conspiracy to let people believe she was Thorne's wife would not, likely, have been joined. Then, that next night . . . but that night should not have happened. He could certainly have gone on coping with life more easily if it had not happened. Probably Meg's life would have been easier, too. No doubt, she had burned a hundred candles since, done the stations of the cross, a thousand Hail Marys, contributed to the poor box. Still, if that night had not happened, he would never have known the meaning of the fullness, the completeness of love. Knowing it briefly, then being deprived of it, had brought him greater suffering than anything in his life before, but it had been an experience of beauty and joy. Had Meg known any of that, felt it herself? Thorne believed she had. Without realizing it at the time, he had seen with painful clarity, had absorbed indelibly the agony of her face when she left him. And, whatever she had or had not felt for and with him, without that night, he felt almost certain, she would not be carrying a baby now. His—and Meg's . . . Ah, God!

But he shook himself emotionally, made himself go back to the question of Murphy. Had he, for two years now, left the little boy exposed to the eroding and damaging influences of Gordon's dislike? He thought that if Gordon's displeasure was all that was involved, Murphy would be able to cope with that nicely. Murphy was a coper, one who, it seemed to Thorne, was always going to land on his feet and not be dislodged from being himself or from being at least slightly complacent about being Murphy. It was abundantly obvious that the little boy was happy with Meg. Still, a child should not be thrown into the midst of adult conflicts needlessly and selfishly. Thorne felt he must do whatever was possible now to look into the situation, to rectify it, if necessary, to whatever extent that might be possible. If his uneasiness and doubt lingered, if he became convinced Murphy should not stay on with them, then other arrangements would have to be made. Meg, he knew, would be devastated if he were to take the boy. Now that his own anger and bitterness had dissolved into the less complicated, more comprehensible ache of hurt and loneliness, he had no wish to hurt her; rather, he shrank from the possibility. But he meant to consider Murphy first now—not Meg, not himself, not any sneaking, ulterior motives, not even any exigencies. Murphy he loved, to the degree that he could feel safe in loving. Murphy was far more his own child than were Stuart and Clare. He knew the boy had become Meg's child as well, in some of the same ways, but Meg would now have the consolation, should she need it, of another child.

Thorne had walked back almost to the cabin. Snow still fell, though in the past few moments, there had been a brightening. The clouds were thinning, letting the sun come through in a lambent, glowing increase of light. As Thorne paused, in a little clear space in the open pine woods, to make and light a cigarette, a shot shattered the stillness. The bullet thudded into a tree in front of him, knocking a stinging chip of bark into the snow. Violently startled, acting reflexively, Thorne wrenched himself around toward where the shot had come from. He saw a man carrying a rifle, running away, stumbling in too much haste. Not really thinking of what he was doing, Thorne flung himself into swift pursuit. He saw the man fall, tripped by a branch or something under the snow, the rifle ejected from his hands as if by a spring.

"His name is Gaylord Milton," Thorne said calmly in Ranald's living room on the evening following their return from the cabin. "He's admitted setting the fire that killed Nancy. He also had to do with some of the dynamitings, during the strike, and not just against Intermountain."

"Why?" said Ranald. "Who in hell is he?"

"Nobody, really, with personal grudges or anything

like that. It seems he's just one of those people you hear about who'll do anything for the right price. Business has been pretty good for him around here, I guess. Ted paid him for the fire, and there have been several good fees since."

"Who . . .?" began Amy. Then, worried and frightened still, she was not sure what she had meant to ask, and she began over. "Was he shooting at you because of the unions, or . . ."

"He seems to have been willing to talk pretty freely to the police, once they had him," Thorne said, nearly relaxed in his chair. "He says he doesn't really know who paid for the dynamitings. Apparently that was a cloak and dagger thing, with blindfolds and picking the money up at the third telegraph pole past the Garfield switch or some such thing. As for taking a shot at me—well, Cherish seems to have kept his card, or got it again from Ted. She hired him, paid him half the money before she left for Virginia and promised to send the rest if the results were good."

"My God!" Ranald exclaimed softly. Just for this moment, he was more appalled by Cherish's vindictiveness than by his cousin's apparent and exasperating calm in the face of the matter.

Elizabeth, to her irritation and chagrin, began suddenly to cry. After an instant of surprise, Amy went to sit on the sofa beside her, a comforting arm around her.

"It's just that I've worried so about him for years," she gasped brokenly, appalled as much by the rising hysteria in her voice as by the fact that she was saying anything. "He will never take care of himself properly, exposing himself to—just anything, living all those years with that woman we've all known was insane, working until he's ready to drop and then . . . then acting as if nothing at all has happened, has ever happened. . . ."

Thorne's eyes had widened in puzzlement and surprise. Ranald was looking at him meaningfully, but he couldn't understand the meaning. Amy was glaring at him with command. He sat for a moment, trying to understand what he had done wrong this time. Then, not quite sure why, he stood up and went around the end of the couch where Elizabeth sat and put a tentative hand on her shoulder.

"It's all right," he said awkwardly. "It really is, you know. He's not going to have a chance to try anything. In one of the dynamitings, on RM&P's Brandon line, a man was killed. That, I think, is what they mean to try him on."

Just for a moment, Elizabeth pressed her wet cheek against his hand. Then she wiped her face and blew her nose, flushed at her display and at having become the center of attention. But still she was a prey to impulse, just for another moment more. She took Thorne's hand with both her own, turned to look up at him.

"You are incredible," she cried accusingly, trying to smile with trembling lips. "You are incredible and absolutely impossible. People are just wasting their feelings if they worry about you, want to take care of you. I love you and other people love you and you just stay so—*impossible*!"

She dropped his hand, drew herself up determinedly and said, in something of a return to her normal stiff primness, "I—I think I'll go up to bed now, if you'll all excuse me."

"Shall I come with you?" asked Amy warmly.

"No," said Elizabeth. "Thank you, dear, but I think I'd just like to be—alone for now. Please forgive me, all of you. I just don't know what happens to me sometimes—giving way like that . . . I just—well, good night."

Thorne looked at the empty doorway when she had gone, then glanced, still uncertain, at Ranald and Amy.

Amy said shortly, "If you're pretending not to understand, Thorne Maxwell, then stop it, right now. If you *don't* understand, then don't look at me like that. The thing just isn't explainable if you have never seen it, known it for yourself. She's completely right, you know. You are hopeless. Oh, sit down, will you. I want to know more about this, and I see it'll have to be pried out of you, bit by bit. Can't they prosecute Ted and Cherish?"

Thorne returned to his chair, still disconcerted. He had thought he was being very cooperative and informative about all of it.

"I don't know," he said. "They're looking into it. Ted lives in France, you know. I don't think there's any chance of anything more like the fire or hired assassins coming after me with a rifle. Most people only come across one Gaylord Milton in a lifetime."

Ranald got up to make drinks. Looking round from the liquor cabinet, he said, "You'll have to know something. Dahlia left with Cherish."

"My God, why?"

"Cherish asked her," said Amy angrily. "She called Dahlia here at the house, asked her to come see her. Dahlia told me about it. I couldn't tell her not to go. Dahlia's a grown woman supposedly in possession of her senses, but I knew right then how it would end. During these past two years, we've all come to love Dahlia. She's the dearest person in the world, certainly the best we'll ever know who's willing to work for this mess of a family, but I've always known she'd go back if Cherish even so much as looked like she'd ask her. She loves Cherish and the children."

Thorne said sadly, "For Dahlia's sake, I wish to God she'd been able to keep away, but I'm relieved, thinking of Stuart and Clare. Since Silas and I brought Milton down—I've been wondering what I ought to do about the kids."

"You don't think they're safe with her?" Ranald said, "—with Cherish?"

"Well, I don't know. Clearly, she's not stable. I've known that for a long time, but I don't think I was ever quite ready to think she'd do something like try to hire a killer. It seems there must be something I can do about the kids—for them."

"You'd have to go through the courts to get them away from her."

"Yes, and that might be worse for them than if I just left things alone. The thing is, I don't really know if I'm more concerned about doing what's right for them, or about making things easier for myself."

"Oh, good grief," said Amy wearily. "You never make anything easy on yourself. You're always tearing at yourself, and I can't honestly believe you don't know that."

"If you'll take some advice," said Ranald dubiously, "I'd say leave it alone for a while. If the law doesn't go after Cherish for trying to have you killed, maybe she'll go on being no worse a mother than she has been all along. If anybody rocks the boat, it seems pretty likely to me, from what we know of her, she's likely to take it out on the kids, or anyone else who happens to be handy."

"I've told them I wouldn't bring charges. I will against Milton. If he hadn't been so damned clumsy in the snowy woods, I wouldn't likely be sitting here. But I wouldn't prosecute Cherish."

"Oh, Thorne, for the lord's sake, why not?" cried Amy, her exasperation not diminishing.

"For the reasons Ran's just said. Because she's Stuart and Clare's mother. Because, to be completely honest, it's easier that way." He sipped his drink and smiled ironically. "They tell me Milton is looking for a lawyer. He doesn't know any. Maybe Gordon will defend him."

Amy said, still very much concerned, "And what will you do now?"

Thorne looked at her, mildly surprised again, quizzical. "Well, I've had a good rest. Thanks for the use of the cabin and for taking care of me before that. Now I guess I'd better try to see if I can still run a railroad."

XVIII

1894

In the year following the railroad strikes, a new and promising gold discovery was made in another isolated part of the Colorado Rockies. The place, originally called Despair Gulch, grew quickly into the boom town of Cornucopia, with names like the Bonanza Saloon, New Chance Creek and the Oro Plenty Mine marking its existence. Cornucopia was a straight sixty miles from the nearest railroad. It would take more than a hundred miles of track for Intermountain to reach the new boom area. Thorne did a quick initial survey and filed it, feeling something of the old excitement in the challenge of a prospective new line. Building to Cornucopia would not be as difficult as getting a road to Beanpot had been, but it would have problems, as mountain lines always did, and he was eager to get on with it.

Intermountain was still operating under straitened circumstances. Getting track to Cornucopia seemed a necessity, a partial answer to some of the company's more recent and pressing problems. Another money-making road could put the company on its feet again, not just in paying debts and dividends, but in giving those old hands—workers and company people—a renewed interest in and respect for Intermountain and their own jobs. It could be a little like the old days again. But they could not even begin the new work without outside financial help.

At Peter Maitland's request, two eastern financiers named Calfcart and Eisenberg came west in the early summer of 1894, to appraise everything that made up Intermountain's assets; they were carefully considering a large investment.

Thorne spent time and effort on Eisenberg and Calfcart, trying hard and conscientiously to answer their questions in ways that would best serve the company's interest. He accompanied the men on a tour of the Intermountain main lines to the west and south, and over the narrow-gauge road through Silver Valley to Beanpot, then north to Amity. He went with them by stagecoach on the hectic, torturous trip in to Cornucopia, watched them as they weighed the enthusiastic, near-rabid optimism of Cornucopia's boosters and promoters. Peter was with them, too, on most of the trips. He was no longer young, and not a well man. His wife had died some years before; the last of his daughters was now married and gone from home. The corporation, MM&F, was his chief interest now and he wanted to see things going well. The traveling tired Peter, but he did not trust Thorne alone with the easterners.

"Who can guess," Peter had worried to Ranald, "what he might take it into his head to do? I suppose there would be nothing I could do to stop him if he decided to try to beat another train to a siding, the way he did that other time, but if he chooses to be haughty and uncooperative, perhaps I'll be able to smooth it over a bit."

But Thorne was determined the roads should make their own impressions, that the easterners should see they were promising propositions, well-founded and well-run, that they should be convinced that money put into yet another mining line would be money well and wisely invested. He set about his "poor but respectable" program by appropriating the company's oldest business cars for use on the tour, rather than the newer, more comfortable and luxuriously appointed ones he would ordinarily have used. He made sure the coaches were painfully clean. Privately, he cautioned division superintendents and others who were to make any part of the trip that they must do all they could to convince the easterners of Intermountain's great worthiness and, at the same time, of its need for money.

Murphy went along on the Calfcart-Eisenberg inspection trip. Since Christmas of 1892, he had spent a part of all the longer school vacations with Thorne. Thorne was convinced Gordon had no liking for the boy, but also he sensed Gordon's wish to please Meg, and believed Gordon was not likely to do Murphy any harm.

At the Fremont, on the morning after their return to Denver, following the inspection trip, Murphy leaned in the doorway, watching Thorne shave. His freckled face was thoughtful, as usual.

"I wish I could have black whiskers like yours when I'm grown up. I'd grow a great big beard."

"You won't have," Thorne said absently, stretching his mouth out of shape for ease with the razor. "They'll be red. No, strawberry."

"Well, probably people with strawberry colored whiskers shouldn't grow beards. I know I'm not handsome," said Murphy philosophically, "but there are other things."

Thorne's mouth was still contorted so Murphy was not aware of the grin. "Like what, Murph?"

"Oh—like being a nice person, or even if you're not 'specially nice, like knowing how to act so people think you're nice. Maybe if somebody's not handsome, he could have real good manners, or do good things for people, or make them *think* he was doing nice things. It doesn't bother me, what I look like. Nobody gets to be everything. Do you think I look like my dad—my real dad?"

"Not only do you look like him, you are like him. Right now, what you were just saying, I can imagine he said almost the same thing when he was a boy."

"Are we going to have breakfast with those men, Mr. Calfberg and Mr. Eisencart?" Privately, between the two of them, they had been mixing up the names for weeks. It gave Murphy great pleasure, and he smiled conspiratorially.

"Let's try to believe they'll be sleeping late this morning. I don't want to see them again just yet."

"Yeah," said Murphy fervently, "they talk all the time."

Thorne washed the lather from his face and went into the bedroom to finish dressing.

Murphy said, "I never saw so much of the road before, like we did this time. I kept wishing all those other people didn't have to be around all the time."

"So did I. Maybe we can spend another week or two together before school starts again. You've still got almost two months of summer vacation."

Murphy put a book into an open suitcase and closed it. "What I really wish, lots of times, is that I could be in two places at once."

"If you want to spend the rest of the summer at home, I can understand that. You never *have* to come with me, Murph."

"I want to come with you, but I was just thinking, Melissa's kind of cute, sometimes, now that she does things besides wet her diaper and cry and sleep and eat. She tries to talk a lot now, things like that. She likes me to play with her. Sometimes she's a pest, but not always. You should see her."

"She'll have grown in the time you've been away. Babies change fast."

"You knew me from when I was a baby, didn't you?"

"I did. Have you put your jacket in there someplace, with your things?"

Murphy looked at him patiently. "If I waited for you to remind me, I'd have left the jacket at Cornucopia."

"All right, wise kid. I'm only trying to do my duty by you."

"Like a father?"

"Something like," Thorne said and put his own dirty clothes into a laundry bag.

After a little silence, Murphy said, "I know I wasn't cute the way Melissa is, when I was a baby. She smiles or laughs almost all the time, and she's always running around. Why won't you come to the house, ever? You could come home with me this morning, just for a little while, to see what Lissa's like."

"We'll find a cab for you after breakfast. I have to get to the office and have one last conference with those men."

"Will they lend you the money?"

"I don't know, but I think they will. I'm going to be very glad to see the last of them."

"I heard you telling them about those lines that are closed down now. You said Intermountain might never be like it was in the first twenty years. Will it still be there when I grow up?"

"Oh, yes, Murph, I don't see why it wouldn't be. Not the way I can remember it, but something pretty good. Things have to change. It seems they always have to get more complicated, less free, but if you want to be a part of Intermountain, it will still be something you can be proud of. Are you ready for breakfast?"

In the dining room, Murphy pursued the topic he considered uppermost just now. "Grandma Maria may be here visiting us now. Will you come to see *her*?"

"I guess I'll have a chance to see her at Ranald's."

"Rob and Randy and Susan and Betsy have three

grandmas, counting Grand Maxwell, but she's not really your mother, is she? You know, Thorne, you've never been inside our house here. Is it because you don't like Dad?"

Thorne hesitated. "Yes, Murphy, it is. It's better for all of us if Gordon and I keep away from each other."

"But you always send a cab for me and then send me home in a cab. You could come some time while he's at work, just to see Melissa and visit with the rest of us."

"I don't like doing things behind someone's back."

Murphy frowned intently. "I guess he would find out. He really doesn't like you either."

Thorne said slowly, "And how do you two get along?"

Murphy stirred sugar into the cup of coffee Thorne always allowed him to have. "Me and Dad? We get along all right. Sometimes I think he likes me quite a lot. Sometimes it seems like he forgets we're all around, even when we're there in the house together. That's when he's been drinking a lot, or has brought a lot of work home. Sometimes, I think he likes me better than Melissa. He doesn't like it when she's noisy or anything."

"And you—do you like him?"

"Well, yeah. But he always acts like what I do and say is a little bit silly, like being a grown-up is the most important thing in the world. Sometimes he yells and things, but dads do that. Mostly, he's sorry later, after he's been upset. A couple of times," he said uncomfortably, "he was so sorry he cried. I didn't know what to do then. Once, when he was *real* upset, he said if you wouldn't let them adopt me, I ought to live with you all the time. Is it because of the strike you don't like each other?"

"We were never good friends, even when we were kids at Quintana. Sometimes, people just don't get along."

"Do you write letters to your kids?"

"No, I don't, Murph."

"I remember when I went to live at Quintana, you sent me two letters and then you didn't send anymore. In one of them, you said you would not have much time to write. Would you send me letters now if I didn't see you, and keep sending them till we got together again?"

"I'd want to."

"Don't you want to write them to Stuart and Clare?"

Thorne lit a cigarette. "I can't explain to you why I don't. For one thing, I don't understand it all myself. I'm ashamed that I never really got to know them, but this is the way things are. I hope they're all right with their mother, that they'll grow up reasonably satisfied with their lives. They don't seem to miss me very much either."

"Well, I guess that's all right. If you had them, I probably couldn't spend time with you, or not much anyway. And I don't want to be adopted. The way things are now, it's like you're my dad too, you know. Can I call you sometimes?"

"You know you can. Murphy, I'd like them to adopt you, in some ways. Maybe you and they would feel better about a lot of things if they did. It wouldn't have to change our spending time together."

"Dad said it would. That time he got awful upset, he said I either ought to live with you all the time, or they ought to adopt me and I'd never see you again. It usually makes him mad when I go with you, and he doesn't want me to talk about what we do or things like that. I don't want to be adopted, Thorne. I don't want my name to be Gaynor. Mama told me once about how you had to change your name after you were grown up. I still don't understand why your real father left you all that time and let you think your name was MacWinter."

Thorne stood up. "Look what time it is. I have

to get going, Murph. Let's go bring your things down and see if we can find a cab."

Ranald came into the Intermountain offices that morning shortly before Thorne arrived. The clerks and secretaries looked eager and cheerful; even Jim Ritter was smiling.

"Come and see," said Grace Welch, ushering Ranald into Thorne's private office. "Some of us were here most of the night. The carpet wasn't put down till late yesterday afternoon, and we wanted to stay and have everything ready for this morning. You know, he never operates on a schedule, Mr. Maxwell. I mean, we often don't know when he's going to be in town. But this time we knew to expect him back last night."

Ranald looked appreciatively at the new carpet, drapes and furniture, the freshly stained walls and sparkling windows.

"This does justice to a top executive's office," he said, grinning. "You've all done a fine job."

Miss Welch said with pleasure, "That's almost exactly what Mr. Maitland said. He knew this was going to be done, you know, so he dropped by too. He'd only just left when you came in." Shyly, she said, "I brought the potted plant from home this morning. It makes a little touch of—well, warmth, I think."

"Very nice," said Ranald. "And what about the books? Where did they come from?"

"Why, they're Mr. Maxwell's. He's been bringing them down here, two or three at a time, and storing them in one of our file rooms in the basement. Melvin Howard, the receptionist's husband, made the shelves. He's an excellent carpenter, and we all just knew Mr. Maxwell wouldn't want any more money spent than necessary."

Ranald grinned. He couldn't help recalling all that

saved coal in the hearths of the Maxwell house in Pittsburgh.

"He's coming!" someone called softly.

They hurried back into the outer office, closing Thorne's door.

Thorne spoke to his staff and to Ranald in a preoccupied manner. "Jim, Calfcart and Eisenberg will be here around eleven. Mr. Maitland will be down, Ranald, a few other people. I'm glad you left this report copy at the hotel for me to see. For Chrissake, go to accounting and tell them to get another one ready. By ten-thirty."

"I don't see how they can get another one ready—"

"You read this? All right. What I want them to do is stop projecting on the basis of the way things were five or six years ago. It's not five or six years ago, and we've got to have financing. If we don't have it, or can't prove we're going to get it, we'll have to forfeit our route claim. We'll be in default on that if we haven't started work by the first of August. There's not time to get any other money people out here, and I don't want any more of these kinds of visits. Tell them in accounting that they're not making a report to soothe stockholders. Or maybe you'd better get Stohrer in here so I can tell him. No, I don't want to waste his time and mine listening to him. He knows better than to send me something like this. I want last year's facts, and this year's, so far as we have them. Those two men would recognize this as a doctored up mess in about two minutes; anybody would if they knew anything about the year of ninety-two. We're not trying to *sell* the road, for God's sake. If Stohrer lets another cake icing bunch of statistics out of his office, he can take early retirement. This makes me think he's ready. Ran, do you want to come in for a while? Have some coffee?"

All of them except Jim, who had left, crowded eagerly, silently behind Thorne as he opened his door. They smiled, nudging each other, each trying for a look at his face. Thorne was looking into a folder Jim had thrust upon him. As he looked up at the shining walnut expanse of the new desk, he was finally aware of change. He turned his eyes slowly about the room, looking bewildered. The office staff glanced at one another in humorous anticipation.

"Just what the hell is this?" Thorne said, not smiling.

"Mr. MacWinter and Mr. Maitland approved it," said Dean Graham quickly. Graham was Jim's assistant.

"Mrs. MacWinter chose the furnishings before she went east to visit," said Miss Welch nervously. "We did take the liberty of bringing up your books from the basement. They add to the room. We thought..."

"How long has it been—like this?" demanded Thorne in real consternation. "Where's the old stuff?"

"We did most of it last night," said Graham. "They didn't finish with the carpet until—"

"And what have you done with the other things? The junk. Where is it?"

"It was put out to be—picked up," Dean said. His face had flushed. Everyone had begun to look uneasy, disconcerted.

"Picked up! Do you mean by the trash haulers? Jesus Christ, that was my last card. Harper, you can run. Go see if it's still there. If they've taken it . . . I want everything back in here, the way it was, before those two men come here at eleven."

The staff dispersed quickly, disappointed, irritated. Thorne stood on by the desk, scowling around the fine-looking room.

Miss Welch hovered. She said mournfully, "You don't even want the plant?"

"What plant? They can shove this stuff into the conference room for now. What happened to that big tobacco stain that used to be just there on the wall? Christ, I never saw such a prosperous-looking office! Send down to the yards, Miss Welch, for some people to help move things. Oh, hell, no! The unions would have a fit. Why did you people do this? I haven't got time—"

Abruptly, Miss Welch crumpled into a brown leather chair, sobbing.

"We thought you might be—pleased," Ranald said curtly. "They've worked pretty hard . . ."

Thorne stared at the sobbing woman. Grace Welch had been head of his office staff since the opening of the Maitland Building, and before that, she had worked in Intermountain's old offices. She had, on occasion, come nearer to being Thorne's nemesis than anyone else in the office. It was extremely rare for her to exhibit emotion of any kind. Word of this present phenomenon would spread all through the building, well before lunchtime.

Thorne said awkwardly, "Miss Welch—Grace—if it's . . . I know you don't like people to swear, and I've told you I respect that in you, but I don't think you ought to try to impose your standards on everyone else. Some times, I *have* to swear, and you'll just—"

"Oh, hush!" she wailed. "It's nothing to do with swearing. It's—*this*," she said, suddenly furious, waving one hand at the room and wiping at her eyes with a handkerchief held in the other. "We thought you'd appreciate it."

"Well, look—it's really very nice, and I do appreciate it. Tell the others so, will you? The thing is that I've been counting on this place being scroungy. You see, I've been trying to convince those financiers we need money. I want them to see that Intermountain is solvent and doing nicely, but that it could stand a great deal of refurbishing. Now they're going to think, aren't they—Miss Welch—if they walk in here to a grand, brand new office, that I've been having them on? We'll put it all back, just like this, when they've left. Don't be angry . . ."

Sniffing reproachfully, she got up. "I'll ask Polly

to bring your coffee," she said and left with great dignity.

Young Harper had rushed back, breathless. "The dray was just coming," he said. "I got there in time. Do you really want that *rug* back up here?"

"I most especially want the rug. I've been counting on the rug."

Ranald could not keep his face straight. "You'd better come to my office while things are being moved."

"No, I'll help here."

"You should look over the folder I gave you," said Jim Ritter from the doorway. "Stohrer says you'll have one copy of a very rough report within an hour. Graham tells me he's rounding up people to help with the moving. What the hell is he talking about? What moving?"

Ranald's office was tastefully and comfortably decorated, and it was quiet. They sat having coffee while Thorne scanned the papers in the folder.

"I saw Peter last night," said Ranald. "I was at the Regents' Club and he came in for a drink. He says you've done a grand job with these men."

"I haven't liked it. It's damned hard to find a balance when you're trying to seem both comfortably secure and on the edge of destitution."

"Peter and I both know you haven't liked it. I'm a little—surprised you put so much thought and work into it."

"A few years' worth of money from a line to Cornucopia would be good for all of us, even if a lot of the profits do go east."

"Something you said gave Peter the idea you think railroads have had their day."

"Well, I don't think that at all. Our main lines should do a good business indefinitely. What's to replace them? But the narrow-gauge roads may never be quite the way we remember them. Some will have to be shut down eventually. Others will have their traffic reduced to just a few trains a week. I remember when we opened the Amity line, there was a washout of a fill up there one day and in the time it took the section gang to get the track safe again, there were six trains waiting in one direction and four in the other. The first year we opened up Beanpot, we averaged five passenger trains a day through Silver Valley—that's including the winter. But big mining strikes and boom towns can't go on forever."

"It hasn't been easy for you, spending so much time with these men, asking for money."

"I never expected it would be easy, and I don't like having more of the control of the railroad going out of our hands. That's been happening, though, for a long time. I'm glad Fitz didn't have to see too much of it."

"Or Angus," Ranald could not refrain from adding. "He would have liked outside influences even less than Fitz did. But the railroad's been on such sound footing, almost from the start. We've shifted money around, you know, using its profits on behalf of the new mines and the mill. If we hadn't done so much of that, you might have the money you need now. You should have been left alone more, to continue the grand job you're doing."

"I have been left alone," Thorne said drily. "Much more talk like that and somebody's liable to get the idea we're running a trust here, when *we* know that what we have is three independent companies."

He made notes on a sheet of paper.

"It could be, though, that a line to Cornucopia will be our last narrow-gauge one. With new equipment, it gets easier to put standard-gauge through the mountains. It takes a lot more blasting, a lot more of everything, but the bigger trains make more money, even using four or five engines for grades and such. Some people from Nevada came to me when we were in Utah this time. They need a short line out there, through some really rough country. I told them we weren't interested in bidding, though I'd damned well like to have done it."

"You've always enjoyed the building most."

"Yes, it's the best part for me, but I suppose a time has to come when maintenance—improving what you've got—is more important, or ought to be more important. How are things going at the mill?"

"Great. I was hoping you'd come down with me and have a look sometime soon."

"Yes, I want to. How's Elizabeth? I didn't think you'd be able to manage for a month without Amy and the kids."

"Elizabeth's pretty well, and you're right, I couldn't have managed if she hadn't been there. I can't tell you how *quiet* it's been in that house. There have been times when I've thought I'd give almost anything for some peace and quiet, but after the first few days, the quiet wasn't half as good as I'd thought it would be. They'll be back next week, thank God. I'm hoping Amy and I can get away for a few weeks somewhere, once school starts again. We haven't had much in the way of trips, except when there were business reasons. Did you know Mama's here now, at Meg's?"

"Murphy thought she might be."

"I'm going there for supper tomorrow. They'll want you to come, too."

"I want to clear up as much as I can here," Thorne said, finishing his coffee. "If we can get firm word that this loan is approved, we can be ready to start grading toward Cornucopia in a couple of weeks. There are going to be some interesting problems on the line."

"I'd like to see the plat maps. Why don't you come home with me tomorrow? We could have supper at Meg's, then look at the maps at home afterward. Elizabeth wants to see you too."

"I don't think I can, tomorrow. I'll try to see Aunt Maria some time before she leaves, but not tomorrow.

I'd better go now and see if they've got my rug down. You know, I don't think I'd ever really looked at that office until you were in there bitching about it, some time back. Then, on this trip, when I got the idea it might be an asset for what I've been trying to prove to these men, I discovered that every grim detail of it was etched on my mind." Thorne paused with his hand on the door. "Do you think I could borrow a little of one of your secretaries' time?"

"Sure. Why not?"

"I'd like to ask her to arrange for a supper party somewhere, for all my office people. They've—stood for quite a lot over the years, you know."

The following afternoon, as Thorne stood by his office window, listening to young Graham's explanation of a new freight rate schedule and why it should be implemented at once, one of the male secretaries knocked and entered. Before he could speak, he sneezed; the air in the room was hot and torpid and thick with suspended dust, from its recent moves.

"Excuse me," he said. "There's a lady to see you—your aunt, she says, Mrs. MacWinter."

Thorne went to the door. The staff enjoyed Maria's voluble rush across the outer office at sight of him, her fervent hugging and kissing of their boss, who looked more than a little embarrassed in their presence.

Thorne attempted to establish Maria immediately in one of the sleek new chairs, but she wanted to walk around the room to examine everything, talking all the while.

"You have to take care of all this," she marveled, indicating the stacked desk . . ."Ranald's desk never looks like that. But what a fine new office. Ranald told me about the surprise for you. I have never seen you at work, you know."

He grinned, picking up a pen with a flourish. "I could let you watch me sign something," he offered, "or maybe give an order, if I could get anybody to listen."

She laughed, walked round the desk and tiptoed to kiss his cheek again. "They've told me how you won't dress properly for coming to an office and how you never want anyone here to think you do any work. *I* think you look wonderful. Do you realize, *hijo*, that I have not seen you since Gavin's funeral? I've been keeping a scrapbook of things about my children. A lot of it is taken up with clippings about you, from the time of the strike."

"That's not much to make a scrapbook from."

She looked fierce for a moment. "Ranald and Amy, and Meg too, have explained how the newspapers always like to find a villain and how they were glad to choose you because they said you wouldn't co-operate with them. I keep those things, and each time I look at them, I am reminded of what a fine man you really are. You see, their writings have the opposite effect from what they meant to do. I can see, though, why they might have been angry with you. You've always been such a stubborn boy."

"Stubborn, maybe. It's a long time since I've been a boy. Would you like some coffee or anything, Aunt Maria?"

"No, *querido*, thank you. I only drink one or two cups in the morning now. It's a very irritating thing when your body starts running your life. I'm not ready to be old yet, but sometimes my body feels it must remind me."

She sighed, but not unhappily, as she went to sit in the chair he offered. "You will always be a boy to me, I suppose. It's very hard for me to make myself believe that any of you is more than a boy or girl. Ian's second daughter is to be married this fall. Maybe I'll go to Santa Fe for the wedding and a visit. Maybe I'll go on from there to visit with Carmela and Jean and their families in California, and on the way stop off in Arizona to see Jesus. He should be settling into his new parish by now, his first parish, among Indians."

Thorne sat down behind his desk and lit a cigarette. Sitting with idle hands made him nervous. He was glad to see Maria, but she was going to ask him for something, and he thought he would not be able to give it.

He said, "You look so well, Aunt Maria, *bonita, linda, hermosa*."

She laughed. "Gavin would say you always did have a way with your tongue, if you cared to bother. You look good too. Before, the few times I've seen you, you've looked tired, but I know there's something in you that drives you to work too hard, always. The gray in your hair is becoming. Thirty-nine in December, isn't it? Well, if you were sixty-seven, as I am now, you'd see how very young thirty-nine is. Also, I've been looking at poor Gordon lately. You and Meg and Ranald all look so much younger than he does. I don't understand it, but something very bad has happened to Gordon since they came to live in Denver. He's aged so terribly, and now most of his hair is gone. I don't suppose you've seen him recently."

"No."

"Something troubles him. Ranald and Meg say it is his new activities, working as the unions' lawyer; they say that he carries a great deal of responsibility. I know Gordon has never been able to laugh much, or even smile. For one with a heavy load, a laugh now and then can do a great deal to keep a man young and not so burdened. I'm not convinced that the job is all there is to it. He drinks too much, too often, and always seems edgy and worried." She shifted in the chair, using a physical effort to change the talk to happier things. "They say you haven't seen the baby either, little Melissa. Thorne, she's a year and a half now; and for a part of the time, you are living in the same town with them. All of us are your family. I just can't understand why you seem to try to hold yourself apart from us, try *not* to see us. I used to think maybe you felt you had risen above us, that perhaps your wife helped you to believe that. Gavin always said you wouldn't think like that, and I suppose I thought it partly to ease my own conscience—about what Angus—and we—did to you as a boy. You see something of Ranald and Amy, but the rest of us . . ."

"Aunt Maria, Gordon doesn't want anything to do with me. I can't—"

"He feels the same now about Ranald, but Ranald and his family still see Meg and the children when they can. Meg needs you, Thorne. She needs us all."

He stood up and went to his drawing board. "Why?" he said evenly, taking up ruler and compass. "What's wrong?"

"She's a wonderful girl, our Meg, trying to make the very best of everything about her marriage. Oh, she never talks about it, never complains, but I can see how things are, how they have been over the past few years. She just needs to know, always, that she can depend on any of us who are nearby to *be* her family. Meg's a strong, brave woman, but anyone needs the support of people who love them. At some times that need is greater than at others, and it's what families should do—be there."

Thorne almost spoke, a few bitter words, but he concentrated on the paper where he was drawing nothing recognizable. Maria could not see his face.

She said, happily now, "And you must see that little girl. So sweet, very lively and full of joy. Gavin would have called her a Romany lass. Her looks come from that strain he liked to talk about in the MacWinters. She's very beautiful, and she's made Meg's life so much fuller, she and little Murphy. Maybe you don't know how desperately Meg has waited for children."

Maria frowned again, in deep concern. "And Meg needs the joy the children have brought. I don't know what she might do if . . ." She shrugged, trying to shake off her worry. "Anyway, I did want to see you in your office, and I've come to take you back for supper. I asked Ranald last night if he would send his carriage for me, late this afternoon, thinking I could come down here, and then the three of us could go home together, for supper at Meg's."

"I can't do that," he said quietly. "Gordon—"

"Gordon will be at a meeting tonight. Do you know he's planning to run for the legislature? He seems to be making plenty of money now, and getting some of the things people work for all their lives. So, I just don't understand why he is like he is. Well, there's no use going on and on with that. You will come, Thorne. I won't hear of anything else. These days, I only rarely get a chance to be with three of my children at once. If you start looking for excuses, you'll break my heart."

Thorne, his face composed, looked up finally to meet her eyes and found them full of tears.

Ranald hugged his sister while Murphy rushed to Thorne, talking eagerly, showing him a new drawing. Maria looked on, smiling complacently.

"We'll have supper on the table in a few minutes. I'm glad to see you," Meg said. She looked toward Thorne, who had become absorbed with Murphy, back to Ranald and said softly, "Both of you."

"Didn't I tell you I'd bring him?" Maria demanded gaily. "As I recall, Murphy made me a little bet about it. Where's the baby, Margarita?"

Meg said, a little stiffly, "She finished her supper just a little while before you came. I asked Lupe to take her upstairs so we can eat in peace. Maybe she'll take a short nap. She can come down again later."

"But she always sits at the table with us when Gordon's not—" Maria broke off. "Well, as long as the boys see her before they leave."

Maria did most of the talking during the meal. Meg could not resist a few covert glances at Thorne. She had tried to refuse herself even a dream of how she might feel at seeing him again after more than two years. He looked well and seemed very calm as he devoted his attention to Murphy and Maria. Once, when her eyes inadvertently met his, she felt again the strength of his look, thought there was a shadow of anger in the depths of his eyes and was grateful for it. Oh, but seeing him meant so much. It was enough to make her feel, for now, small and quiet, as if she could almost let someone else take over everything.

"Come upstairs and see my room," urged Murphy impatiently when he had finished with dessert. "You never have, and I've been wanting to show you. It's nice."

Thorne glanced at Meg. She smiled and said easily, "I wish I had a nickel for every time Murph has wished he could show you his things."

They went upstairs, and after a few moments of looking around the room, Thorne sat down on the edge of the bed with Murphy to see if he could help to figure out a new game the boy had been given. They heard small feet running in the hall, and the little girl dashed in.

"Lissa!" said Murphy grinning. "You climbed out of your bed again."

"Bed," she said and shook her head vigorously. She had stopped near the door at sight of the stranger, momentarily still and solemn.

Thorne looked at her and could not take his eyes away. He saw black hair that was thick and curled a little. Meg's hair was brown, Gordon's that weathered straw color. He saw the lovely shape of Meg's face, but with smooth, clear, dark skin. Slowly, the little girl moved toward him, and beginning to smile impishly, leaned against his knees. Thorne looked into blue eyes, so dark a blue they might have seemed black without the contrast of long, thick, straight black lashes. Without quite realizing what he was doing, he held out a hand, and the baby put up her arms to him. A tremor ran through him as he picked her up.

"Lissa, this is Thorne," Murphy was telling her. "Can you say Thorne? She likes everybody," he added.

Melissa had been watching Thorne's face pensively, paying no attention to Murphy. A mischievous smile curved her full mouth once more, and a tiny finger came straight at Thorne's eye. Gently, she touched the lid he had closed reflexively. "Nose," she said quite clearly, and the three of them laughed together.

"That's her favorite game right now," said Murphy with pride. "She knows it's not your nose. She just likes to tease."

She touched Thorne's lips, "Ear!" and laughed again. He held her close and the pain in his chest made breathing difficult. This was his child, the only child he had ever felt was truly his own.

"Come on, Melissa. Can't you say Thorne?" Murphy kept urging.

Thorne laid his cheek against her hair. She was still for a moment, making a soft hum, a loving sound; then she struggled purposefully to stand up on his lap. She fingered his hair for a moment, then abruptly let herself go completely limp, so that Thorne made a startled grab to prevent her falling.

"That's another game she plays," said Murphy, through the little girl's laughter. "She's always so sure someone will be there to catch her, and she just lets go."

Melissa stopped laughing suddenly, and smiling into Thorne's eyes, said gaily, strongly, "Torn."

"Hello, Mama," said Murphy, looking toward the door. "Lissa got out of bed by herself again."

Melissa, looking with mischief at her mother, snuggled into Thorne's arms again. "Torn," she announced.

Thorne looked at Meg, and she could not meet his eyes. She had come upstairs several moments ago, at Maria's urging, had heard them in Murphy's room. She had been standing in the doorway, unable to bear making her presence known. They were so beautiful together, so painfully right—the three of them, together.

Abruptly, Thorne put the baby down. She did not object, but began immediately to play peek-a-boo with Murphy.

He moved to the door, his eyes black now with the tempest of emotion. Meg moved aside, more than half afraid of him.

"Do you have to go?" called Murphy, coming after him, disappointed. "Are you going to—"

"Yes," he said harshly. "There are other things I have to do."

"Can I come up to Cornucopia with you soon? I heard you're getting the money from those men."

"Talk it over with your parents," Thorne said coldly. His face had been hot. Now it felt drained of blood, numb, cold.

There was a little crash from the bedroom, and Murphy turned back. "Oh, Lissa, why did you knock that down? You're not even supposed to touch it, you know that. Get out of the way now so I can fix it."

Thorne went downstairs, seeing and hearing nothing.

Meg caught up with him in the front hall. She kept a little distance, trembling, but felt she must say something. "I know you didn't want to come here, but thank you for thinking of Mama. She's wanted—"

"She's mine," he said hoarsely.

Meg's frightened glance went to the closed door of the living room. "Thorne—"

"Was this what you had in mind that night? In Graham? Was it?"

"Oh, don't!" she beseeched him. "I love her more than anything in the world. She's brought joy to everything. She's my salvation—"

"I thought you'd settled what was to be your salvation seventeen years back. If not, I'm damned glad to know I could be of service. That makes everything absolutely—"

"Oh, God, Thorne, please! I love—"

They had kept their voices low instinctively, but both of them were trembling with an anger that tried desperately to mask all the other feelings, the pain too excruciating to be borne. Meg, vaguely believing she understood what Thorne's feelings were, tried to stifle her own. After all, as she had reminded herself so often, she had the children, and they made separation from him just bearable. If he felt remotely as she did, and had nothing at all, no one . . .

"I've given up everything," Thorne said in a kind of ecstacy of bitterness and fury. "I don't know why I have, but that's the way it's been. Tonight, I know what it means, giving up everything, and I can't do it again. She's mine. I want to have them, both of them!"

Meg took hold of the newel post for support. "You can't!" she gasped.

He cried softly, brokenly, "Ah, God, of course I can't! I never can!"

He wrenched open the front door and was confronted by Gordon, supported by two others, on the steps. The strangers stared, surprised, uncertain, at Thorne's terrible face, flushed and fierce.

Gordon, swaying slightly, smiling slackly, said, "Well, I didn't expect to find you here."

"Mr. Gaynor wasn't—uh—feeling very well," murmured one of the men uncomfortably.

Gordon stood unsteadily away from them, smiling. "Thanks, Bill, Harry. I'll do as much for you some time." And to Thorne, "Where's Meg?"

"I'm here," she said shakily, looking past Thorne's shoulder.

The two men went away down the walk. Gordon stepped inside, stumbling on the sill. "Little unsteady—oops." He swayed, and Meg tried to support him. Hating him, knowing for the first time in his life a true wish to kill another human being, Thorne grasped his arm as Gordon would have drawn Meg, too, off balance.

"I'm all right," Gordon said irritably. "Just a little—relaxed. Yes, that's it, relaxed, have to do something . . . but my mind—my mind's as clear as a bell. You two have been arguing. What's it about? Do we have other guests, Meg? I mean, besides your dear mother?"

Meg closed the front door as Ranald and Maria came from the living room. Gordon stepped away from Thorne, held to the back of a heavy old straight chair. "Well," he said scornfully, "two-thirds of the executive force from MM&F. Hello, Mama Maria, I suppose I have you to thank for these others' being here? My meeting broke up early tonight. I wonder what does go on around here when I'm not home." His eyes settled finally on Ranald. "Let's go and sit down, shall we? It's been a long time since we've had a real talk, or a drink together. I could use a drink."

"Gordon—" Meg began, but she turned at a sound from the stairs. Murphy was there, holding Melissa's hand as the little girl took slow, concentrated steps downward.

"Murphy," Maria said peremptorily, "go back upstairs. Take the baby."

Glaring at the boy, Gordon said angrily, "What is it you want *now*?"

"Lissa wanted to come down," Murphy said quietly, but with a touch of defiance.

"Well, go away, both of you. This is a time for adults. I think we can manage, this once, without you two little bastards."

Meg's hand went to her mouth. Maria glared at Gordon.

Ranald said softly, "Thorne, help me get him into the living room, will you?"

"I'll help you," Thorne said, not bothering to lower

his voice. "I'll knock hell out of him, and then you can drag him wherever you like."

"He's drunk—" Ranald said.

"Good God, I can see that. I was just leaving."

"No, don't go yet," Ranald said, putting an urgent hand on his arm. "This may need two of us before it's done."

Meg was saying, "Gordon, go up to bed. You'll feel better—"

"Oh, leave me alone," he answered her peevishly. "I'm ready now, after all these years, to spend some time with my boyhood friend—friends. Are you going to begrudge me even that?"

The children were still on the stairs, Melissa objecting more and more strongly to Murphy's quiet but determined efforts to take her back.

Suddenly, Gordon was shouting. "Can't you keep those goddamned brats out of my sight *ever*?" He had lunged up a few steps and now hit Murphy a hard, solid slap in the face, which made the boy sit down hard and all but knocked Gordon off his feet. Ranald and Thorne moved together, dragging Gordon down into the hall again. Meg had got past him somehow. She snatched up Melissa, who had begun to cry, put her free hand on the shoulder of Murphy, who had not.

"Go upstairs with them, Mama," Ranald said, in passing. "We'll see what's to be done about him."

Thorne let go when they had passed into the living room, clenching his fists spasmodically, leaving Ranald to half carry Gordon to the couch. Slumping down, Gordon began to cry.

"Get me a drink, for Chrissake," he sobbed, not looking up. "A man has to do something. It's all ruined. All she's thought about for years is those goddamned kids."

Ranald looked to Thorne, who would look at nothing. His face was black with fury and contempt.

"Find something," Ranald ordered urgently. "He'll

pass out soon enough. I'd like to hurry it a little. Gordon, for God's sake, calm down. You know this is no way to behave."

"Sometimes," Gordon gasped, "I wish to God I had the strength to kill them all, and myself. Meg's so *good*, like her dear mama. It's more than a man can stand, living with a martyr. And the kids—"

"You've got your own little girl upstairs," Ranald said sternly, coldly. "Murphy's been your child for four years. Can't you pull yourself together and try to show them a decent father? God, Gordon—no, here, lie back. Here's a drink. You've got this far, you may as well go the whole way. How often does this sort of thing happen?"

"I keep *thinking* when I'm sober," Gordon whined, gulping. "You think I'm just a—nothing now. Well, Meg does too, has for years, maybe for longer than even I've known. That's not my daughter, Ranald. She's no more mine than the boy is."

"Drink," Ranald said coldly. "Much more talk like that and I'll beat your face in."

Thorne had found the bottle, thrust it roughly at Ranald before drawing back into the shadows across the room. Gordon drank from it again, convulsively.

"No, it's true, Ran. God, I've got to tell somebody. All this time . . . I can't father children. I've known that since I was a kid. There was an illness I had. It's not possible. She wanted me to think there'd been some goddamned miracle, and Christ knows I've *tried* to believe that." He drank again, his face wet, his breath coming harshly. "I should have told her from the first. I know that now. With her misguided senses of pity and loyalty and duty and *goodness*, she probably would have gone on with the marriage. But at least then, maybe she'd have been more careful, more discreet about her sluttish affairs. Children, that's all she could ever think about. I wasn't enough for her, right from the start. She wasn't a virgin, you know.

Children! That's the important basis, after all, for a fine Catholic marriage, isn't it?"

"Gordon, shut up. Just lie back and shut up. If you were sober, I would kill you."

"Can't I talk to anybody?" Gordon wailed. "I've got to talk to somebody. Can't you understand that? Your lovely, sweet, long-suffering sister is what they delicately call in books a trollop. I've loved her since we were little kids. I still love her, but what I'm telling you is God's truth. There comes a time when everybody has to accept the truth, try to face it, learn to live with it, because it doesn't go away. Oh, I know what you think of me, but why not? *She*'s known for years what a weak coward I am. This is killing me, I tell you. All that time before the baby was born, I tried to believe it was mine. I could almost believe something had happened to me that the doctors hadn't figured on. But it was born, and as it came to look like—Anybody would know. That kid—"

"God *damn* you," Ranald said fiercely between clenched teeth.

But Gordon was oblivious to the menace of the tone, to the rough hands that shoved him back onto the couch.

"It's good old Thorne's kid," he cried in a spasm of anguish. "Take a good look at her. You won't find anyone in the world the baby looks more like. He's always had everything. Remember how he always came between you and me? You always chose him when there had to be a choice. So did Meg. So did everybody, even Don Esteban, when that was the only way I had of making any real money in that godforsaken valley. Everybody always chose him, and it seems Meg just goes on choosing him. God knows how much they've managed to be together, using us, making fools of us all. The precious baby must have been conceived when I had to be away in Chicago that time. She wouldn't come with me. Oh, no! Had to stay here because of Murphy's school." He laughed with an ugly gasping, rending sound. "First, he brought her one of his bastards, ready-made, then he did even more, obliging son of a bitch, to give her a second one. And that happened just at the time of the beginning of the strike, when I was working so hard to . . . she, my *wife*, was—consorting with the enemy. Oh, Jesus, Jesus!" He was sobbing again, wildly, hopelessly.

Ranald had moved away a little distance from Gordon, to stop himself from hitting him. His face was white, his blue eyes burning with fury. "I've got to get out," he said in a choked voice. "If I have to hear much more of this from him . . ."

Ranald put a hand on Thorne's rigid arm and they both went into the hall. Ranald closed the door on Gordon's hoarse misery, his arm trembling. Meg was there, crumpled like a broken thing on the bottom step of the stairs, her face in her hands.

Taking a fresh grip on himself, Ranald went to her. His hand was gentle on her shoulder. "Meggy . . .?"

"Mama's with the children," she said dully, not raising her eyes. "I came down because I thought—well, sometimes it seems I can do something to—help him. Usually, when he gets like this, I can . . ."

"Usually? Does this happen often then?"

"Not like this," she said abstractedly, "not with other people around and—"

"Meg!" Gordon was calling, pleading. "Meg, please, for Chrissake . . ."

"I don't think he can get up," Ranald said as she started. "Whatever he can or can't do, you're not to go in there and listen to any of that . . . I want to know, right now, how long this sort of thing has been going on."

"Ranald, he's sick," she said heavily. "He doesn't know what he's saying."

"My God, I can see that! He's pathetic, but you can't live like this."

"He's never hit one of the children before."

"And I guess that's supposed to make everything just fine," Ranald said angrily. "I want you to go and get together what you'll need, and all of you come to my house, for tonight, at least. In the morning, we'll see what's to be done."

"I can't leave him," she said brokenly, her face still covered by trembling hands.

Unnoticed, Thorne stumbled out the door and sank down on the stone steps. They were still warm from a day of sun. The night was bright with a full moon and streetlights. It was still almost too warm for comfort, though Thorne shook convulsively. The initial battering of emotions had passed, leaving him feeling empty and broken. He felt incredibly tired, drained, and so cold. He yawned, a reflex of nervous tension; the muscles in his jaws clamped rigid and felt as if their fibers were being ripped apart. In a while, Ranald came out and sat down near him.

Ranald decided that the silence on the steps had gone on too long between them. Finally, he said, compelled to say something, "He passed out—fell off the sofa and passed out. Meg and Mama are getting the kids ready to come to the house. I've called for John to come back with the carriage. Christ almighty, I wonder how long it's been like this for her?"

Thorne couldn't stop the harsh words. "No one has forced her to stay."

"She believes in marriage," Ranald said quietly, "in the vows, the ideals of it, I suppose. I can understand that, because I happen to believe too."

"Maybe Gordon's right about martyrs. Yes, it runs in the family, stronger in some. Why in hell are you going to take them away if you believe so goddamned strongly in 'for better, for worse' and the rest of it?"

"Gordon needs help," Ranald said doggedly. "A doctor, some kind of cure. I never dreamed things had got like this."

"Murphy needs help for those damned great fingerprints on his face."

"Thorne, try to get hold of yourself. You know how drunk Gordon was. I know that doesn't make any of it right, but he had no idea what he was saying or doing."

"The hell he didn't, Ranald."

After a moment's silence, Ranald said, still quietly, "I wonder if I should come back here to sleep tonight, in case he . . . Will you—"

"You're crazy! That must run in the family too. I won't do anything. Do you hear me! Nothing!" Thorne's voice broke and he stopped, gulping painfully at a dry mouth.

Another silence. Through the open front door, they heard the baby begin to cry upstairs.

Ranald said gently, "Along with everything else, she's afraid you will take Murphy away from her after this."

"And well she may be."

"Thorne, the kids have kept her going. That's plain enough to see now. She says Gordon won't remember much of this in the morning, but that he'll be sorry as hell."

"That'll be just grand," he said with searing bitterness.

"She doesn't need, maybe can't stand the extra worry of being afraid you're going to take Murphy away."

Thorne dragged himself to his feet and stood glaring down at Ranald.

"I'm leaving," he said tautly. "Tell Meg, if you like, that I won't stand for Murphy, at least, living like this. With Murphy, I do still have the choice. I won't take him tonight because I can't yet."

As Ranald stared up at Thorne's terrible face, his own turned white again. "Thorne, it's not—true?"

"Some of it is," Thorne said, his tight voice very low. "I've loved her since we were kids. Once, a long time ago, before she married Gordon, I thought she might marry me. It was the thing I wanted most in all my life. The only thing that I've ever been sure of . . ."

Ranald stood up slowly, shaking again, feeling stiff and sore, an empty bottomlessness inside him.

"He was telling the truth? You—you and Meg . . .?"

"No, he wasn't telling the truth. It's not been the way he said, but you'll have to believe whatever you choose."

"Thorne, the two of you are cousins! Meg's been another man's wife all this time . . ."

"Those things have come to my attention from time to time."

Ranald's hands clenched. "I'm warning you, don't be so goddamned cute. It's your child?"

"I don't suppose I should be the one to say."

"God*damn* you! She's my sister . . ."

Ranald struck him then, a hard, bruising blow to the mouth, hurting his knuckles against the teeth. Thorne staggered back, his own fists pressed convulsively against his thighs. Blood ran from his lips.

"This makes me wonder," Ranald said coldly, following to stand close, "if other things are true, too, like what almost everyone has believed about you and Nancy."

"Wonder," Thorne said harshly. "You just goddamned well go ahead and wonder."

He turned, a hand to his mouth now, and walked away, stumbling into the tree shadows.

XIX

1896

Thorne went restlessly out of the workcar, away from the incessant frettings and complaints of Virgil Webb, the Amity division superintendent. He stood on the racketing little platform, leaning out slightly to the frigid smoky air. There had been a snowslide last night, at the east portal of tunnel five, and they were going to assess the damages. The snowsheds, the rear car and caboose of a freight train had been carried away. Thank God, no people had been lost. They were taking a section crew and a work train with an extra troubleshooting crew to try to get the line open again as soon as possible. Webb had good reason for complaint. This division had always been Intermountain's most difficult, even though it did not contain their highest summit or their longest tunnel. Its grades were no worse than those on other narrow-gauge lines, but there always seemed to be some trouble on the Amity road. Webb's litanies served no purpose except to relieve Webb himself. They offered nothing toward a solution.

Squinting against the cold air and stinging smoke, Thorne looked toward the laboring locomotive. Since the age of fourteen, Thorne had held a great love and admiration for these narrow-gauge trains, for the lines themselves. Since construction on it began, he had held a particular respect for the Amity line, though it had defeated him many times. Tunnel five had been the site of Fitz's crippling accident. That tunnel had finally been lined throughout with reinforced concrete. He had rerouted the line at the sites of several repeated washouts, had altered grades, had even come up with new construction for snowsheds. But now Thorne's newly designed snowsheds were at the bottom of the canyon.

A stretch of railway could set a man back countless times, bring all his crafty schemes to nought, and it was still a challenge. It might bring disappointment, irritation, anger, disgust, but it rarely brought pain, hopelessness. Service to Amity consisted now in only three trains a week, yet it required almost as many section hands in winter as it had when five or six trains had moved daily. The line had shown no profit for the past four years, and each year they lost more money on it. With improvement, the wagon road, which served the quietly dying town and the isolated ranches on the way there, could carry the freight and the few passengers. It was past time for starting to close down the line. Then the line would feel it had won, beaten him finally, and Thorne would not particularly mind that. It was only that bringing the contest to a close was an end to something, a palpable end to a period of his life.

The Beanpot and San Miguel lines would eventually go the way of the Amity road. Business decreased on them a little more each year. The Cornucopia line, finished three months ago, in October of 1895, was doing a tremendous business, but that would pass eventually, as it had passed for the others. The heyday of the narrow-gauge lines was over, though there could be a brief revival. Intermountain's main-line business was very good, profitable and steady. There would always be operating problems, dispatching mix-ups, track damage from floods and slides, an occasional wreck. Anyone could handle things like that, anyone with a little of the proper background. The time of great expansion was passing—and as it waned, the challenges for Thorne became more ordinary and less intriguing; their significance was dwindling.

He shivered, pulled up his coat collar, brushed a cinder from his hair. Soon now, he would go away. Where, he did not know, nor did it particularly matter. He was not needed here, never had been really. Someone else could have done his job, all of it. His whole life had—if one were to be scrupulously honest—been unnecessary. There had been brief times when he had believed, as had Ranald and Peter, that he was indispensable to Intermountain and so to MM&F, that his talents, knowledge, abilities and propensity for work were in some way unique. To go on for long, a man had to feel there was something worthwhile about himself or about what he was doing.

After he had decided what to do about this latest snowslide, he would go back to Denver and see if he could put things in order for the next head of Intermountain, make financial arrangements for his children's future, turn Murphy's trust over entirely to John Blessington and the bankers, or perhaps to Meg. If only Murphy were going away with him . . . If only there could be something to show for all these years, something—someone—to provide a purpose to the past and to bring continuity between it and the future. . . .

On the morning following that crushing evening at Meg's house a year and a half ago, Thorne had gone to Ranald's house and had taken Murphy away with him. The boy's face was discolored with bruising, his eyes bewildered and sad.

A maid let Thorne in. Ranald, she explained, had already left for the office. Thorne had counted on that; it was why he waited until almost mid-morning. There had been nothing to prevent his coming earlier; God knows, sleeping had been no deterrent. He had not slept at all. The maid asked him to wait in the living room and went upstairs. The house was very quiet. Maria came in, looking tired and sad.

"Don't do this to Meg, *hijo*," she said pleadingly. "She has enough to bear. You must know Murphy is as much hers as any child could belong to and be loved by its natural mother."

Thorne was obdurate, scarcely speaking. Finally Maria left him, and after a few moments Elizabeth came in.

"I don't know a great deal about what happened last night," she said gently, "but I have heard enough to be able to understand why you don't want Murphy living in Gordon Gaynor's house, for now, at least. But, won't you let him stay here with us? Ranald and I talked it over before he left. Amy and the children will be back in a few days. It would be good for Murphy to be with the children, a distraction. If he were here, Meg could see him and Murphy could see her and his little sister. He loves the baby very much. Thorne, Meg is nearly frantic. I know you're thinking of Murphy's welfare, but don't leave her out of it."

Ultimately, Elizabeth too had to give up. Meg came down to the living room. She was white and drawn, her eyes a little wild. She had been sitting on her stairs the night before, outside the partly open door of her living room, and had heard almost all of what Gordon had said. When, later, Ranald came upstairs looking furious and stricken, she knew that he and Thorne had fought, or at least had quarreled, perhaps irreparably. Now, seeing Thorne's bruised and swollen mouth, which added to the set, implacable look of his eyes, she could not speak to him, could not beg forgiveness for the many things, could ask for no concessions, could not plead again, for understanding or even tolerance.

They stayed there for a few moments, Thorne

walking irritably about Amy's bright living room, Meg—feeling small and more than a little unreal—almost cringing near the door. Neither of them looked quite directly at the other until he turned, caught her eyes and held them for a moment, the look of his own eyes like a vise, fierce, crushing her to submission, almost to nothingness. He turned from her then, with an unconscious gesture that seemed an impatient dismissal, and went upstairs to find Murphy himself.

The women had, evidently, known what the outcome of this morning would be, even while they pleaded for his reconsideration. Murphy had two bags packed. Someonc had obviously been back to the Gaynor house. Murphy was willing to go with Thorne, but he was solemn and wide-eyed, not inclined to frivolous conversation. Meg, if she was still in the living room, was not visible from the hall. As Thorne opened the front door, both he and Murphy were painfully aware of a squeal of Melissa's gay laughter, floating down to them on the warm, still summer air.

Thorne had to stay for another week of work at the office. He arranged for Murphy to spend the days pleasantly at a day camp. It was inevitable that Thorne and Ranald should see one another occasionally, in the corridors of the Maitland building. Their eyes never met, and they passed by as strangers.

As soon as he could get away, Thorne took Murphy and went west to oversee the final surveying, the beginning of grading and other construction on the line to Cornucopia. They camped out for most of the rest of Murphy's summer vacation, living and working with various crews. The worry and perplexity left Murphy's freckled face as he learned to enjoy the changing railroad life.

Thorne accompanied Murphy back to Denver three days before the opening of school. They sat together in the observation section of Thorne's business car. Thorne frowned over papers, Murphy grew more sober with each mile.

Finally, the boy asked hesitantly, "What will I do now?"

Thorne looked up slowly. "I've been thinking we'd look for a small house somewhere in town. I could find a good housekeeper, and she'd be with you when I have to be away."

"I wish we'd done that in the first place, right after my mother died."

"I'm sorry, Murphy. I've—there have been a lot of mistakes—"

"That's what I'm trying to tell you," Murphy said doggedly. "It wasn't a mistake for me to live with them. I liked it. The thing is, if I never had done it, I couldn't know I liked it."

"You don't want to go back?" Thorne demanded, finding he was more irritated that incredulous.

"Well . . . yes. I want to be with them and keep seeing you whenever I can. People say a thing about having your cake and eating it too. I guess I understand now what that means."

"Living with them and seeing me is one thing, but I won't stand for . . . Murph, had Gordon hit you before that night? I'm not talking about spankings. Had he—"

"No, and he was awful sorry about that one time. He came to Uncle Ranald's house that morning before you came to get me. Uncle Ranald had gone back to our house for the night, and when he came over to eat and change his clothes for work, Dad came with him. Dad and Uncle Ranald both looked very sleepy. I don't know what really happened that night. I don't know why everybody was so very quiet and sad in the morning. Dad was glad to see us and he was nice. Everybody has things they're sorry about. He promised it wouldn't happen again, socking me or any of it, whatever the rest of it was. He even said he wasn't going to get drunk anymore, ever."

"That was just the heat of the moment, Murph.

It wouldn't be an easy thing for Gordon to stop drinking."

"No, but he did say that, and I think he meant it. When people tell me things, I always believe they mean them, unless they tell me or show me they don't. When I say something, I mean it—right at that time I do. People change their minds, because they want to or have to sometimes, but I think they mostly mean what they say—when they say it."

Thorne was silent for a moment; then he had to ask, "Has he hit—Melissa, or—your mother, like that?"

"Not Melissa," said Murphy with a firm fierceness. "He may have hit Mama sometimes, but I never saw him. After he hit me, I could think back to times when he might have hit her, but not with me around. . . . Thorne, I mostly like to have a little sister, and I like to be with Mama. Gordon's all right. Sometimes I like him a lot. He didn't mean anything that night, not anything—well, you know—final. Everybody gets really mad sometimes."

Thorne felt shattered. He left Murphy waiting for answers or at least responses, and went into the small office of the business car. Fred Morley had gone out for a cup of coffee. The office was empty. Thorne stood by the window, one hand lightly bracing his swaying posture as the train moved slowly up a canyon. He tried to sort and straighten his thoughts, to be reasonable, though God alone knew why he tried anymore.

All right. I want Murphy with me; I always have wanted that, but I can't spend much time with him, not even evenings eighty percent of the time. I *could* arrange to be with him more; I could rearrange my job, work in a different way, reevaluate, look for the priorities. But I can't do that right away. The Cornucopia line has been started, and it has to go along now as quickly as possible. There's not time to arrange for someone else to superintend the construction, and

I have to see my job—myself—as one priority. I can't get away from that. So I wouldn't be with Murphy in a house we'd share; not while the good weather holds. If I'm not to be with him, then I want to know that he's safe from unnecessary stress and harm, from having somebody several times his size knock him around in a stupid, cowardly, drunken rage. There's more to it, though.

How much of my wanting to hold onto Murphy is because of the baby? How much of the anger toward Meg, the getting at her through keeping Murphy, is because I saw that little girl? I saw her that once, and I know now that there is a child in the world who's really mine. I fathered her that night in Graham, in the middle of a snowstorm, and now I feel like a father, God help me. I want Melissa. If I could get her, no matter what the means, I'd do it. I'd kill Meg with the pain of it and take the baby.

He had closed his eyes and begun to sweat in the close warm air, feeling physically sick in the renewed onslaught of mental agony. But, be fair about Murph. God, yes! Be reasonable! I'll never have that laughing, mischievous little girl. If I can show any sense, and if I'm careful, I'll never see her again. I'll never have Meg. I've never had Meg, not really, not wholly. Ranald is lost to me now. I know his morals. He never tries to force them on anyone else, but for himself, for the way he looks at other people, other things, he's as inflexible as Meg, as quietly certain of the rightness of his position. He might understand, a little, if I tried to tell him all of it; but I won't do that—I can't, and, even if he did understand . . . No, things would never be the way they were before. I have to try to ignore these other people, stop letting them figure in things. It's only with Murph that I have any choices at all, any opportunity for trying to make the right judgments, equitable decisions. Murphy wants to go back to them. He loves his family and that's as it should be. I'll have to let him go. I have to be fair with Murphy. Taking any of the rest of the bloody impossible situation out on him isn't going to make anything at all come right. It would only make things drag on longer. Someday, when I can bring myself to face it all and do what's necessary to bring some order to things, I'll take steps myself, instead of waiting for the course of events to push me. Yes, someday, as soon as I can, I'll go away. That won't change things, won't put an end to feelings, to wishing things might have been different, but it's something I can do for myself, something I'll have to do, eventually. Something I have to do . . . so, again, there's really no choice.

So, on his first day back at the office, with Murphy staying at the hotel, he asked Miss Welch to call Gordon's office, to ask if the Gaynors would come and talk with him.

Meg came alone that afternoon, looking pale and tense and frightened.

"Where's Gordon?" Thorne said coldly, with no other greeting.

"He's in Haviland about a case," she said tensely. "He won't be back before the weekend. Thorne, Murphy . . ." She bit her lips together to stop their trembling and to force back tears.

"Murphy wants to come back and live with you."

"Oh, God, please let him!" she whispered.

"Not with Gordon—"

"Gordon says he doesn't remember much about that night, but he does remember hitting Murphy. He's heartbroken—"

"I'm sure of it," he said with flat, cold irony.

"He's stopped drinking. He hasn't had a drink since then. He had never been like that—hitting Murphy or . . . Well, he doesn't seem to remember anything after he hit Murphy."

"Let's not tell him. Let's, at all costs, protect Gordon from—"

"I've done what I could to try to make Ranald

understand. I know you two fought that night, and he thinks—"

"Don't try to tell him anything. He won't *be* told, any more than you ever would be. I don't need your help with Ranald, or want it. I don't need Ranald. You've got your hands full, it seems to me, with redeeming Gordon."

"Thorne, I haven't meant to ruin your life. I didn't *set out* to make things happen the way they have. I have so many things to be sorry for, so sorry I can't . . . I'd give anything if—"

He made a sound of anger, a violent gesture of dismissal. "Spare me contrition. Pray about these things. That's the ultimate answer, isn't it, to everything? When something gets to be too much for you, you turn it over to the good fathers or to God, and then you seem really to believe you're relieved of the responsibility, of . . .

"I asked you to come here to talk about Murphy. Only Gordon's the one I wanted to see, to look at, so I could try to judge what his behavior is going to be toward Murph. I would have asked that you *not* come, except I wanted you to see Gordon with me, so that if something comes up later, you can't say I'm being unfair to Gordon, or committing some other kind of crime with no justification. After this, I don't intend to see you ever again, and you'd better pass it on to Gordon that there'd damned well better not be any reason for me to feel I have to see you, either of you, but especially not—"

He broke off, and she sat there humbly, her hands gripped together. Goddamn it! Why wouldn't she get mad? Why did she always seem to feel that she deserved punishment? He lit a cigarette.

"Murph can go back with you. He's at the hotel. I've told him you or Gordon might be picking him up this afternoon. Murphy's promised to tell me if things—go wrong again. It's a condition of his coming back. I wanted to tell Gordon that if there's any more abuse like that, I'll kill him. Meg, you're a fool to stay on there. Don't you know the chances you're taking with—"

"I've told you, he's stopped drinking," she said heavily, and with a touch of impatience, or defensiveness, or anger.

"Has he stopped hating? Will he ever be able to do that? God knows, he's got reason to hate. He said that night you're a martyr, and he's right about that. Do you enjoy it? Do you feel holy and selfless and sanctified and—forgiven? Just what is the price of forgiveness? How do you really know when you've paid enough? Is there some great burst of light, or angels singing, or what? Is it—whatever it is—worth risking those kids—"

"Oh, Thorne, please! How much do you think I can stand?"

"Hell, forget it. I can't stop you. I never did convince you of anything. But I guess that's just how it has to be, isn't it? I'm wrong, selfish, greedy, immoral, always wrong, and you've got the absolute, indubitable right on your side, God-given perfection—"

"Oh, Thorne, I—"

"All right. I'm off the main subject again. Let's just skip the rest of it, forget the past, all of it, and think about Murph and the future. I'll want to go on seeing him at vacation times. I'll ask one of the secretaries to call you, give you plenty of notice, the way we've been doing. I won't consider an adoption, not ever, but if Murph wants to be with you, and if Gordon can manage to restrain himself . . ." He couldn't hold back the fierce, desperate question, "How do you mean to handle it when he starts beating the baby?"

"He—Gordon is—you have no—"

"Yes, that's true. I have no right, have I? It's not my affair, is it? You'll excuse me now, Mrs. Gaynor. I have quite a lot of work to take care of."

At the time, he had been grateful for his anger. It

had carried him nicely through the interview. Her pleading, humiliation, helplessness, pain under his taunting, gave him a measure of questionable satisfaction while she was there, even for a time afterward. It was an advantage he had, something that he need not relinquish, along with Murphy and everything else. Only that, too, turned out not to be wholly true. In time, he came to be ashamed of his words and conduct that afternoon.

Now, in the bleak cold of a clouding January afternoon, Thorne stood on a platform of the work train as it made its way up the narrowing canyon toward the snowslide. They passed the buildings that were bunk- and cookhouse for the section crew who lived there through the winter. The engineer brought the train up as close as he could to the havoc that was left where the snowsheds had been. Virgil Webb came out of the car, with Adolfo Constanza, the replacement work foreman, and John Berry, the permanent section foreman, came wading and plowing toward the train, followed by the crew, who had been doing what they were able to do with shovels. The men looked harassed, worried and tired.

Thorne swung down, tramped through deep snow to the front of the locomotive, and stood there in a small, relatively clear space, looking at the devastation. Uprooted trees and great boulders were scattered in the snow where the sheds had been. He could see the ends of a few timbers sticking out down the steep slope to his left. Most of their efforts here lay buried under deep, quiet whiteness on the canyon bottom far below. To his right, up the shoulder of Elk Mountain, there was a scar, the wide path of the slide.

"Sure went to hell, Mr. Mac," said John Berry with a weary hint of apology.

"But nobody was hurt?"

"We knew she was coming. I'd meant to dynamite this morning, blow 'er down, *our* way, and then clean up. It warmed up a lot in the night—one of them damned chinook winds. Train two was late, got held up by a sprung rail a couple of sections down, but I guess you know about that. They didn't get up here until about two this morning. When the train came through, it shook 'er loose up there. You can see where she started from. Jesus! I don't think I ever in my life heard such an awful noise, and us in bed, nearly a mile away. I hope I never again hear anything like it. I guess it wouldn't have been as bad as all that if it had been daylight, if we'd been ready for it. Carlson had all his train crew in the cab of the engine. They didn't have to look out for no other trains and was trying to get warmed up. The engine had got in the tunnel, thank God, when the slide hit." He looked down ruefully. "There's a good bit of lost freight down there. We dug the crew out. They wasn't in real good shape, what with all the smoke that had built up in the tunnel before we could get it opened up. We took 'em to our bunkhouse and that's where they are now. Getting the men out is about all we've been able to do. Most of our machinery and tools, you know, we kept up here, under the sheds. And will you look up there, at that godforsaken sky! It'll be snowing again before dark."

"You men get in the cars," Virgil Webb was calling. "There's food. You can warm up, and get some rest. John, we've brought an extra section crew, some of the troubleshooters, and everything we could think of that might be needed. What would be your guess as to how long it'll take to get the line open again?"

"I couldn't hardly make a guess," Berry said disconsolately. "The tracks are bound to be tore to hell under that. That was some force. Look at the trees it brought down."

"Hold on a minute, Dolfo," Thorne called to the foreman of the relief crew. "Let's not have anything unloaded yet. John, you say it's number two's engine in the tunnel. What about up above there? Is there another train at Amity?"

"No, sir. Two makes the round trip, up one day, back down the next; that is, when she can run to schedule. I guess there might be a few freight cars up there is all."

Thorne looked up once more at the mountainside, thinking of the threat, the terror he had known inside this same mountain when Fitz had been hurt, screaming in rending, terrifying agony. The mountain had never meant to threaten him, nor any mortal. It could not be bothered with such pettiness. He was not afraid now. His mind had grown quiescent. No, it was better yet: His mind, heart, spirit, soul—whatever made up his thoughts, his feelings, his very being—was growing acquiescent. He would be able to handle things now, to go on. Things were not going to be all right, but after yet another year and a half of slipping, mentally and emotionally, from shadow to shadow, he felt he could now cope, could go on to the next phase—alone. The endings would be hard. The aloneness he had never—despite what he had believed in the past—quite been able to believe in; but now, he thought, once he had the will to accept it fully, his aloneness might turn out to be something dependable, something he could count on, just as he could count on the merciless, indifferent implacability of Elk Mountain.

Thorne turned. John and Adolfo and Virgil were all looking at him quizzically. The standing locomotive made the sounds of a large, tired, and complacently panting animal.

He said casually, "Get your people in the train. We'll pick up the train crew down at the camp. We'll—leave it."

"What?" cried Virgil, staring. "What do you mean, leave it?"

"Can anybody use the telegraph wires? Good. Go into the tunnel and tap in. Let them know at Amity that they're going to have to settle for being cut off a little longer. I think I know of a freighter we can contract with to take in the supplies they'll absolutely have to have for the rest of the winter."

"They've let that stage road go to hell, Mr. Mac," John said. "It ain't even been plowed once this whole winter."

"The freight outfit I'm thinking of keeps sleds and dog teams. It'll cost us like hell to keep our obligations that way, but probably no more than it would cost us to clean this up and go on trying to keep the road open. We'll just leave it till summer, and then see."

Virgil Webb was worrying about his job, the jobs of all the Amity line employees. He gave Thorne a final, puzzled, disgusted look and started plowing his way along the side of the train again. He could think of the things he needed to say better while sitting near the stove inside the car.

Thorne had turned again to the destruction. The man, going to send word to Amity, was making his way, as much on top as he could stay, toward the shoveled ramp that the men had dug for getting the train crew out of the tunnel. Thorne did not watch his progress, for the snow drew him, the steep white slope down the canyon bottom, the steeper slope of the mountain above. There was a finality in the scene, a kind of cleanness, perhaps even rectitude, of a very harsh sort.

"When I saw you get down from that train," John Berry said, marveling a little, "I thought, now there'll be the devil to pay. I thought you'd be mad as hell."

"Why would I be, John? Maybe I've been fooling myself, but I've always tried to be at least half reasonable."

"Well, you know, it ain't got anything to do with reason or no reason, really. It just happens to a feller sometimes, getting mad as fire. The new way of building sheds that you and them others come up with, and we built these here two-and-a-half years ago. I thought, and it seemed like you thought, that construction was strong enough for nearly anything. *I* was mad—I'll tell you that."

"At least nobody was killed."

"Yes, there's that, and I'm thankful for it, of course . . ."

"If *people* had done this," Thorne said musingly, "or if they—someone—were responsible for letting it happen, then I'd be mad. I could *do* something then. But the snow, the mountainside, the weather—those things just don't give a damn. They do the natural things, the way they have for a million years; and the puny little things we do, the indestructible snowsheds—we ourselves, John, just—don't matter. Anger in the face of something like that is—useless, or worse than useless, isn't it?"

John watched him uneasily. "Well, sir, that may be, and probably is, but me and the others been mad, and goddamn' cold. What I thought, too, when I saw you'd come up, was that you might have already figured a way to reroute this, go around this tunnel, even this canyon. There's nearly always been more trouble, just in this stretch through here, than in any other section Intermountain's got."

"Somebody may want to consider that next summer," Thorne said absently, turning back toward the work car.

John followed him slowly. "Mr. Mac," he said quizzically, "you sound to me like somebody that's fixin' to shut down a railroad. I don't mean just for this week, or the rest of the winter . . ."

Thorne glanced back at him, smiling ruefully, but it was all right. He welcomed the resignation he was feeling, the quiet.

"It is shut down," he pointed out rather absently. "I wasn't called to a consultation about it or anything."

"Well, sir, that's surely so, but I meant—shut down, permanent."

"I don't know, John. That will have to be considered too, later. Come on, let's get moving before it starts snowing again and we can't get back down out of the canyon."

The quietness had come on Thorne again. It had begun that late afternoon under the shadow of Elk Mountain, and while he still felt too much sadness to call it peace, it was better, preferable to some states. For the first few nights of this current stay in Denver, he had slept deeply, a blessing that had not been allowed him since that night of Gordon's pitiable, sobbing, drunken maunderings, that night when he had seen his small daughter. All the old turmoils had come on him that night, increased in intensity, a thing he would never have dreamed possible; they were accompanied by new tortures: He *had* seen the baby, and he would never again see Ranald or Ranald see him, not in the old and much-treasured ways that had girded their friendship, their brotherhood for forty years. The pain, the fear of not being able to withstand the pain, had been worse for him through the weeks immediately following the night at Meg's—worse, even, than in that long ago April when they had left Graham in opposite directions. As before, anger and pride—emotions more acceptable than naked, trembling anguish—had sustained him for a little while. He had had the new construction on the line to Cornucopia, and that helped him go on living. Usually, he was rather proud of the strength of his body. Though he was thirty-nine when the Cornucopia job started, he could still swing a sledgehammer or a pick close behind the lead men in any of Intermountain's crews. At times, though, during the first summer of that work, he would have given a great deal to be physically weak and vulnerable. But he had adjusted his being as best he could to go on living. During that summer, and without his conscious knowledge, he had begun to consider the possibilities of going away, to put so much physical distance between himself and the people he loved that there would be no chance of their seeing each other. The decision had crystallized slowly, but now it was firm, final. He slept well and worked purposefully at the office for several days.

Once the decision was made, he was restless and wanted to get on with it. It was not that he expected any joy or even relief to come from a physical change. God willing, he would expect nothing, ever again. It was only that he wanted to have done with it all.

Courting sleep, he read. Two books lay on the table beside his bed at the Fremont. He had read them both through, with hardly a memory of their contents. At a little past three this morning, he had finished a third book. Wearily, submissively, he got up, dressed, and went for a long walk through the quiet winter streets, where the desolate, lonely, predawn cold gripped him. In it, he gave up the last of his hope.

From the beginning, his thoughts about leaving had, against his will and better judgment, included Murphy. He had not quite been able to banish or subdue such half-thoughts as: Murphy and I will . . . We can . . . He will like. . . .

Murphy had maintained for several months that Gordon had stopped drinking. Then, when he came to spend a summer month with Thorne last year, he had said sadly, "I guess he has to drink. It seems like he can't do anything now without his hands shaking, unless he's had some drinks. He doesn't live with us, but I guess I told you that on the phone. He moved away in the spring. I think Mama asked him to move away. He still comes back to talk to her, but he doesn't stay. I guess he's awful—sick."

No, he could not take Murphy. Murphy was Meg's child; she was his mother, and that was only as it should be. It was even more than likely that the boy would refuse to go with him if asked to make the choice. Thorne felt he should never have allowed the involvement between himself and Murphy to continue so strongly. Maybe he should have never seen the boy again after leaving him in Quintana more than five years ago. He had meant not to see him again, but then there had been the train trip that stormy April . . . He was always meaning or not meaning something to happen, but whatever he tried to prepare for always turned out to be on the wrong front. He had, all this time, been forcing Murphy to live the kind of life he had lived, a confusing life of divided loyalties and divided identities. No, let him stay with Meg. She could give him love and precepts to live by. If Murphy were very very fortunate, those precepts might be worthwhile, satisfying to him. Besides, Thorne didn't have the strength now, nor the fortitude, to broach the subject to the boy, to try to explain—any of it. He could not have Murphy any more than he could have small, laughing, vivid Melissa, any more than he had ever, really, had their mother.

So he would go anyway, without them. Did that matter anymore? What had he ever had? But how could he know, if he had never had anything, how very much he had lost? Well, never mind that. With that kind of question lay madness. All right, he had finally faced up to the thought of disconnecting his life from Murphy's. There was little else left to be done. He wanted to be through with it, on his way, moving.

Thorne found himself walking in a part of town that was completely unfamiliar. That was ridiculous. Denver was not some large, alien city. He knew it all—he had thought he knew it all. The strangeness frightened him out of all proportion till he recognized a corner two blocks later. In the block after that, light spilled from the window of an all-night diner, and the light was welcome because the sidewalk was so icy and uneven. He looked at the stones, great slabs of reddish sandstone, and of a beautifully pebbled conglomerate rock. People never realized how fortunate they were to have such creations of nature, the works of thousands and millions of years, to be used to avoid walking in mud. Thorne was glad he could think that, pleased that his senses would still register such things. He was going to get through this, all of it. He started back toward his hotel.

At a corner several blocks from the hotel, in a dark, still neighborhood, with the pre-daylight cold a damp, sepulchral presence, he slipped on an icy spot and fell, scraping and badly bruising his cheek as it struck a lump of frozen slush. He lay there far longer than the hurt warranted, wanting rest, oblivion, freedom. People were sometimes killed in falls. People died of stress or overwork. In books and songs, people could die of broken hearts, always, it seemed, with ample time first for a detailing of their grievances and for recrimnations against those who had caused them pain. Some people did not wait for the fall or the broken heart. He thought of the dead boy at Smoot's Military School. What had been his name? God, how could he not remember that? He felt a miserable sense of his own coldness, that he could not remember.

A train whistle blew then, an engine, signaling to a flagging brakeman, or was it a switching signal? Thorne struggled to his feet, feeling self-conscious and foolish, a little blood running down his face, holding desperately onto the train whistle and the remembered muted, blended coloring of the rocks in the slabs of sidewalk.

The next afternoon Thorne sat idly in his office, the bruised place on his cheek stinging and burning as he touched it absently and remembered last night, still upbraiding himself because he could not remember the name of the boy at Smoot's.

He opened a desk drawer and withdrew a glass and bottle. He had rarely been able to achieve real drunkenness. He almost always got sick before he could attain numbness, oblivion. Today, quietly and steadily, he had worked at it, wanting to think of the sandstone sidewalk, the train whistling in the dark early morning, rather than of hangings and heartbreak. It was late afternoon. Perhaps he'd spend tonight on River Street, go there straight from the office. On River Street sleep, eventually, might be possible.

Once he had truly believed that becoming an adult meant the end of being manipulated from the outside, by . . . what—Fate? and by other people? "You care about nothing," Angus had said to him. "Nothing is of any real importance to you. You respect nothing. You're an unnatural person." But he had cared! God, he had cared so much, knowing all the while how dangerous caring was, how it placed him at the mercy of others, aware that caring was a kind of self-indulgence, a luxury of the moment, which always called, sooner or later, for payment. God, if these years had been luxurious, then let him for the rest of his life have the poverty of hopelessness!

Was everyone, deep down, a quaking, cowering, vulnerable fool? Did everyone, on attaining something that had been a goal, large or small, have it turn to ashes in their hands and cry within themselves, "But I thought . . . I wanted . . ."? Was this all there was?

He looked down at the few sheets of paper on the desk before him. Waiting to be finished was his part of the annual report to stockholders. He had a few other things to clear up, but now that the peak years of new construction were past, Jim Ritter could doubtless run the company. There was talk, even, of selling most of the construction equipment, of contracting out any new work in the future. Well, he could leave things fairly well in order with the business. For years he had longed to run away, to hide, to pretend many things were not true. Now that he was on the verge of going, admitting he could not take the blows life had to deal, he felt an urgent need to prove he was not really running, that he was capable of leaving at least a modicum of order behind.

He had seen John Blessington, the attorney, shortly after his return from shutting down Amity. John had papers drawn; Thorne signed them and asked him to wait two weeks before notifying the other people concerned in the arrangements. Yesterday he had talked for a long while with Peter Maitland, asking for and receiving Peter's assurance that nothing would be said about the conversation for a few days. To discuss any of these matters with Ranald was still impossible.

Thorne sighed and emptied his whiskey glass. More than a month ago he had had his fortieth birthday, and there were all these *things* that involved him, rather like physical bonds. How had he come to be so very involved? Well, forty years of living surely meant some involvements, if it meant nothing else.

Jim Ritter knocked and entered the office. "Accounting has just sent down those final figures you wanted for your part of the stockholders' report."

Thorne took the papers, laid them with the others. "Have a drink, Jim?"

"Well—all right, sure, why not?"

Jim looked at him with concern. This man, who was always so full of restless energy, whom he had been trying unsuccessfully to pin down for so many years, had, as far as Jim knew, been sitting at his desk all day. Sitting! Thorne Maxwell. Hadn't even had any lunch sent in. He was quiet; he looked sick. The whole office staff had been subdued this past week, sensing that they ought to move quietly, speak softly.

"Sit down," Thorne was saying. "It's almost quitting time. I'll take these things back to the hotel with me. I didn't get very far with my part of the report, but you'll have it Monday."

"*I*'ll have it? Aren't you going to the meeting?"

"Ah, no. I've always missed them whenever I could."

Jim sipped his whiskey, wanting to do or say something, having no idea what that something should be. He cleared his throat. "Looks like the weather's going to give us a January thaw."

Thorne looked absently to the window: bright sun on the city's uneven January snow. It seemed incredible, yet comforting, that the sun should go on rising and setting. The light hurt his tired eyes. He turned back from it and lit a cigarette.

"About train twelve," Jim said, compulsively going on with business as usual, "on the Beanpot line. You were going to make a decision about taking it off or not."

"Train twelve," Thorne said absently.

"You know the freight we've been—"

"I'd think, from the figures, they could do without it up there, at least during winter. The freight contracts can be kept without it."

"All right," Jim nodded. "What about the crews?"

"Yes, the crews. We haven't come up with any permanent answers about what to do with the Amity people either. Right now, I just can't . . . See what you can come up with for them, Jim, you and Dean. I don't know."

"Well, then there's that stretch of main line that was damaged in the flooding early in the winter. They've been running over pretty patched up track down there. You mentioned something about heavier rails. Should we get them and get the work started?"

"All right."

"I'd expected you'd go down there before now—Thorne, you don't look—"

"Come in," Thorne called, answering a knock on his door.

Grace Welch entered, immediately caught sight of the almost-empty bottle, the glasses they held. She frowned and said primly, "There's a Mrs. Maxwell outside, Mrs. Elizabeth Maxwell."

Scowling, Thorne tried to pull himself together. "You told her I'm here, I suppose."

"Well—sir, you *are* here, and you've always seen anybody who came to see you."

He stood up and went to the door, as Jim returned to his own office.

Elizabeth, shy and awkward, sat on the edge of a leather chair. The past fifteen years had been joyous ones for her, being with Ranald and Amy, and especially with their children. She had come to see her previous life much more clearly than she had been able to while living it. But she could never stop worrying over this dark one, who always worked too hard, felt things too deeply, struggled too desperately to let nothing show. She knew a little about his marriage, his work. The rest of his life was closed to her, but she was aware that it was unhappy. She thought she had never known him look as unwell as he did today, not even when he had been so ill after running away from military school, or when Angus had finally told him the truth about his parentage, not in all those months of the railroad strike when he had driven himself to the very limits of physical endurance. She had not seen him since the morning after his and Ranald's estrangement. She knew very little about the rift between them, but if she was ever to be any real help to him—to them—it must surely be now.

Sounding brusque, but feeling only tenderness and concern, she said "What happened to your face?"

"I fell on the ice." Thorne knew why she had come. Obviously, Peter had not kept his word about their conversation. He would have preferred not to have to deal with Elizabeth, but it should not be too difficult. He had, at least, had a comfortable amount to drink, all through the long afternoon. He had gone to stand by the window, and not noticing, he let cigarette ashes drop onto his clean empty drawing board.

"Peter Maitland came to see us last night."

"Yes, I thought he must have. He'd told me he wouldn't do that." Thorne looked from the window, squinting as the bright light hurt his eyes.

"He didn't mean to betray you, or anything of that sort. Actually, he only talked to me. He felt he should check on some of the things you talked about, see if arrangements could be made so that he could know about them, before you go away. You've asked him to take care of a good many things. He wanted to check, for instance, on whether or not it was agreeable to me for him to take over my proxy for voting my stock. He said it had been borne in upon him more and more all day what your leaving was going to mean to the company. He was concerned about you, about your family. He also told me you've asked him to see about having Maxwell dropped from the company name, substituting MacWinter."

"Ranald's worked hard," Thorne said defensively. "He'll go on working hard. I think it would mean a lot to him to have his name a part of the company. Elizabeth, I hope to God you haven't told—"

"I told Ranald and Amy you planned to leave right away, none of the details Peter told me. Thorne, we've made a great many demands on you over the years. The beginning of it was when Angus and I, for our own reasons, asked you to be our son, after you were already—formed, when you were nearly fifteen. That would have been an impossibility for anyone, particularly anyone who had had a good life up till then, with people like the MacWinters. After that, there were years of struggle between Angus and Frank Fitzroy as to your interests, what your life would be. I know how it must have been for you when Frank was hurt. It was the very chance he had been looking for, though, to force you to take on the railroad. I know how hard you've worked, for the good of all of us, never wanting to be an executive, an administrator, never wanting all this responsibility. We couldn't help coming to know some things about Cherish. I know the demands she made; most of them were too extreme for any human being to meet. I hope you've found some things, a few at least, that made you feel the work has been worthwhile. You mean a great deal to—to us, not because of the work you've done, but because . . . Still, I can understand, in part how you'd simply want to go, once you'd made the decision, without telling anyone, listening to any more arguments. But we are your family, we—"

"I suppose Peter told you, then, that I asked him to be co-executor of Murphy's trust, and of funds I'm having set up for Stuart and Clare. Altogether, it was a great deal I asked of him. I don't quite know how things, so many things, have come to be so complicated. But Peter said he didn't mind, and he said he wouldn't . . ."

"He said your asking him to say nothing was the only really difficult thing you asked. He just couldn't feel it was right—for any of us. He doesn't understand, Thorne. Neither do I. He says you've given up all your stock, one way or another."

Thorne was silent.

"Where are you going?" She pressed her lips together to keep them from trembling.

"I'm not sure yet."

"Peter said you seemed to be planning to leave very soon—for good."

"Yes."

"Thorne, you're vital to the company. Peter thinks they can't—"

"I'm not vital, Elizabeth. Nobody's indispensable. Suppose I died? They'd manage."

"But why did you mean to go like this—without saying anything to any of us?"

"Because it's easier," he said with a trace of anger. "But, since you're here, will you agree to the corporate name being changed? It's going to need a general vote or something, but I did ask Peter to check with you before going on with it—if he decided to agree, that is. You're the only Maxwell left."

"I'm not," she said gently. "There are two of us."

"Ah, no. I never wanted the name. I never really wanted most of this." He gestured, taking in the office, the building.

"Well, it's something I shall have to give a lot of thought to. I think you must know how much Ranald and his family mean to me, and I know you're right: Having MacWinter as a part of the title would please Ranald a great deal. Still, I think of Angus. I had such a cramped life, Thorne, growing up and afterward. It's only since Angus died, since I was able to have—a family of my own, that I've been able to expand myself a little, think more widely, perhaps understand some things. If I had been another sort of woman, Angus might not have been quite as he was. I feel more—tenderly toward him now than I did while he was alive. I think I understand some things about him. He never got over the very deep hurt of being sent away from his home and family as a sort of—business investment. Strengthening the company, having his name perpetuated were so important to him, for many reasons.

"I know you never wanted to become so involved with the company and in other ways," she said with a gentleness that was hard for Thorne to hear. "Angus saw the kind of strength and staying-power you had. He'd never have complimented you on it. I doubt that he ever really admitted it to himself, but he recognized it—I think, depended on it. He—admired Ranald, though he always harbored such a great resentment for Gavin. That resentment was all out of proportion, and the idea of having MacWinter replace Maxwell in the company name would be—disagreeable to him, to put it mildly. Angus gave up so very much for the Maxwell name. You know, there are similarities between you and—your father, though they have found different ways of expression, for the most part. Please don't be angry. In his way, I believe, Angus was proud of you. Your similarities were the main reasons you never could get on together. Shake your head all you please; he did depend on you. That was the chief cause of his not being able to show you anything but criticism. He couldn't bear the thought that Angus

Maxwell, whatever the reason, would be dependent on anyone . . . I'm terrible with words. I want to make you see what I mean about Angus—and you."

"It doesn't matter," Thorne said stonily.

"It does," she said, with more vehemence than was usual in her stiff, prim speech. "Being sent away from home like that, as a business proposition, Angus never learned—compassion, least of all for himself. He always saw his first marriage as a mistake, a sign of weakness. In his second, which was far more proper and profitable, I couldn't give him children. He wanted children. I think they were even more important to him than higher production figures and the like. Then some of the same kinds of thing happened to you. We took you from a far happier home than ours was. You weren't even told the reason for more than seven years. Surely, things would have been a little easier for you if you'd known. Certainly it would have been fairer to you and to your aunt and uncle. *Your* marriage was a sad and difficult thing, you could never be close to your children. Don't say anything, please. This is hard for me, but I've begun. Let me finish, since I'm here. Do you remember that I tried once, years ago, to talk to you about your marriage? I was worried that that woman was going to drive you insane. You snapped at me. You said the wrongness of the marriage was all your fault, and you left the room.

"*That*'s the difference between you and your father. Both of you could handle great amounts of work, take responsibility for them; but Angus either never did, or at some point stopped, feeling any responsibility for human relationships. He could always see the faults in the other person and feel completely justified in his own stand and behavior, whatever it was. As a result, I'm sure, of the harsh things that happened to him as a child and young man, Angus grew ever more cold and unfeeling. You haven't been able to be like that, though you've tried very hard to make people believe you're—not to be touched."

Thorne went to his desk for a fresh cigarette, looked wistfully at the whiskey bottle and turned away.

"Have a drink," Elizabeth said gently. "I've never objected to drinking. In fact, you might offer me just a sip."

Her hand shook as she accepted a glass. She noticed his care in not letting their fingers touch; and this gesture, which she saw as a naked and pathetic attempt at self-protection, brought tears to her eyes. Thorne returned to the window.

"I have no right to criticize Angus or anyone else for coldness," Elizabeth said tautly after a moment. "I'm far from being a warm person myself, on the surface. It's the kind of upbringing I had, and a kind of protection I don't seem able to do without. I wish after these years with the family that I could be different, could show more of the things that matter most to me. It really isn't a weakness, but knowing that and living it are wholly different matters. I think you understand what I mean.

"When you boys first came to us, I resented you both, though most especially you. It wasn't because you were Angus's son by another woman, but simply because I hadn't had you from the time you were a tiny boy. I did want children so much. After a very short time, I wished I were truly your mother. I saw what Angus meant to do with you—to you—and how you could stand up to him, fight him and often win, even though you were still a child, or very nearly so. If you'd been my son, he would never have allowed me much part in your upbringing, but being your mother might have made me a little different in some ways. And while you were small, I could have . . . No, you were far better for having spent those first years with the MacWinters. That's what saved you, saved you and hurt you so badly at the same time, made everything so mixed up and confusing for you."

She sipped at the whiskey, shuddered faintly at its burning strength.

"When Peter said you were leaving, I wanted to rush to you last night, at your hotel, and plead with you not to leave. I know what you're like, once you've made up your mind to something, and though I'd give anything to keep you nearby, I don't think this is a mistake, not for you. Perhaps you can find—something this way. I did want you to hear, from me, my thoughts about the name of the corporation, and I wanted very much to see you again. Still, if those two things had been all of it, I probably wouldn't have come. Some time back, little Susan said, 'Grand Maxwell is like a loaf of bread, all crusty on the outside, but . . .' " Elizabeth smiled a little, her eyes burning again. Then she said a little desperately, "Thorne, be—friends again with Ranald before you go."

He was silent. She could not see his face, only that his knuckles were growing white as he gripped his glass.

"I don't know what happened between you two the summer before last. Amy doesn't either, for certain. It's no one else's business, obviously, but the two of you are brothers. Amy and I tried again to talk to Ranald about it after Peter left last night. I know Maria has tried too. I told him he can afford a quarrel—an estrangement, far better than you can. He has a happy home and family; he'll be going on with the company. Thorne, don't leave with things like this between you. Are you trying to punish yourself, giving up everything like this? You don't deserve anything of the sort."

He said curtly, "Evidently your talk with Ranald got you nowhere. What makes you think I'd be any more willing?"

"There's some sort of major production problem at the mill. Ranald's been down there every day this week, as I'm sure you know. He left this morning long before daylight. Come home with me for supper. He'd be so very relieved to see you. I could see that in his eyes; so could Amy. One of you has to begin the giving, moving toward something better. Let it be you. Must you always be so stubborn, when it hurts you more than anyone else?"

"I can't," he said with finality. "You're wrong in what you think saw saw in Ranald. He wouldn't want me in his house."

"Please," she said painfully and her chin shook.

"No," he said, calmly now. "I'm sorry, Elizabeth. I can't do it. Why don't you come somewhere and have supper with me? It's time to go home now."

She gathered herself together, more emotionally than physically, and with a great effort. Sho had not really believed she could persuade him. Why should she have been able to? "I don't know," she said bleakly. "I suppose I could call Amy from here, tell her I won't be back for a while . . ."

Thorne dropped the empty whiskey bottle into the large wastebasket, gathered papers into a briefcase. He never expected to see this room again and found he was glad to have someone, anyone here with him in the last moments. He had hated the office for all this time, and yet . . .

"When will you leave?" Elizabeth asked timidly.

"Sunday maybe, or Monday. I still have a little work to finish."

"And you really don't know where?"

"I've thought of several places, possibilities."

"It doesn't even matter?"

"Where doesn't matter much. I guess I'd like building things, railroads, roads. There's not going to be so much of that kind of thing around here anymore. Frontiers are over, almost everywhere. I have to work."

Elizabeth had come over to the desk, hesitated, and looked at the telephone. For almost the first time in her life, she put her arms around another adult. Her misted eyes hidden from him, she said shakily, "Yes, my dear, you have to work. I know about that. I thought—hoped—I might be able to do something for you—help a little, for the first time in my life."

"Elizabeth . . ." His hand rested briefly on her back before he gently disengaged himself.

She had to collect herself all over again, dabbing in impatient embarrassment at her eyes. "I'm sorry, Thorne, but I think I'd better go on home after all. I'm only making things harder for you, not easier the way I'd hoped I could."

XX

On Saturday afternoon, Meg was in her kitchen making frosting for Melissa's birthday cake. Murphy was decorating the living room for the party. Three years old, her baby! It made Meg feel sad, wistful and tender. Three years ago on this day, there had been snow, literally torrents of snow. Now it was raining, a dismal winter drizzle that seemed to penetrate and chill everything, with the temperature hovering only a few degrees above freezing. A bleak day for any sort of party, but wasn't there some saying about winter's children being the truly happy ones? Certainly Melissa was happy so far—bright, vivid, irrepressible. Meg wondered how she had ever lived without Melissa and Murphy. What had there been to life before they came?

Her little girl looked more like Thorne every day, at least the way Thorne had once looked, with a quick infectious smile and sometimes dreamy eyes, even the same endearing shrugging of the shoulders.

Gordon saw those things all too clearly. Maria commented, each time she saw the child, on how strong that particular strain was in the MacWinters, that dark, careless, lovable Romany strain. Meg wondered wearily if her mother were really as innocent as she seemed. Maria had been upstairs that night when Gordon had made his accusations, but how could anyone who knew the whole family so well not see it? Certainly the likeness had become clear to Ranald. Meg had not seen her brother since the morning after Gordon's revelations. Meg had tried to keep away from his family as well, out of consideration for Ranald's feelings and wishes; one more thing to try to gloss over for the children and for her relentlessly insistent mother.

Meg meant, though she had told no one yet, to move back to Quintana when school was out in the spring. The house there was rented, but she would ask the tenants to move, and she'd give the Denver house to Gordon to do with as he pleased.

Quintana would be a better place for the children, and perhaps it was far enough away from Gordon's work that he would not come there, crying, pleading, promising. Meg had recently written to the school board about a teaching job. If one was not available, she could get work in a store or somewhere. She would do almost anything now to get away from Denver. Why had she stayed so long, when the situation, the very place became more crushingly depressing with each day?

She had begun teaching again in Denver in the fall of 1894. Gordon had made more money in the previous two years than he had ever made before. They had had Lupe working for them for a while, a girl from a hacienda family who wanted a job in the city. Then money grew short again, for a number of reasons, and Meg had needed to work. She also did it to distract herself from all the other difficulties. She was teaching in a grammar school made up almost entirely of Spanish-speaking children. It was a rather rewarding job, and she had Murphy and Melissa. Mrs.

Pratt, a neighbor, an irascible elderly widow who happened to love children, looked after Murphy and Melissa on the weekdays. She did not have to be told details of the situation, asked for no explanation from Meg as to why she did not want the children available to Gordon.

At first, Gordon had kept his word about drinking. He had stopped completely for several months. But when he was not asked to run for the legislature, he began again. It started on New Year's Eve, at the end of 1894, and very rapidly got beyond the point where it had been the previous July.

On a day late in March, Meg returned from her school to find Gordon already home from the office. His words slurred a little, while his nervous hand clutched spasmodically at a glass of whiskey; he told her sullenly it had been a bad day. When Meg wanted to go for Melissa, he ordered her to leave the little girl with Mrs. Pratt, to let him have some peace, at least until supper time. Murphy arrived from school, bringing a friend. Gordon shouted at the boys to keep out of his house. He went on drinking, but slowly, in a brooding, ominous silence.

At supper, he demanded that Melissa be taken from the table and put to bed because of some slight infringement of his rules for mealtime behavior, which were arbitrary and subject to change for every meal at which he was present. He forbade Murphy to leave the table when the boy would have gone, but there was no way in which Murphy could be forced to eat the rest of his meal.

When both children were at last upstairs, Meg, tense and uneasy, sat at the cleared dining table, trying to go over papers from her classes. Gordon came back from the living room, glass in hand, to begin berating her for her lack of feeling for him, for the children's recent behavior, for her very existence. Hoping to placate him, thinking he must fall asleep soon, Meg went into the living room, ready to listen, concerned about what had gone wrong during the day.

A large suit Gordon was handling was not going well; and the litigants, a union of growing importance, were not pleased with the way Gordon was handling it. The firm's elderly partner, whom Gordon had always counted on replacing, was bringing out a nephew, a recent law school graduate, from Boston. Meg tried carefully to express her sympathy in ways that would not increase Gordon's anger. But as his voice grew louder, his invective more violent, she said compulsively, "Gordon, the children. Please, let's not wake them."

It was a mistake. She knew that as she said the words. All his fury and frustrations were directed to her again. She had no feeling for him and his problems, he began, had never had any real feeling for him, for anyone except herself. It was her fault his work went badly, her doing that he had never had anything he wanted. If not for her and her children, he might have amounted to something. She had never let him have his chances. He had never wanted to return to Colorado after his own graduation from law school, but had given up all his dreams for her, and what had she ever done in return?

He no longer noticed what, if any, responses Meg made to his recriminations. Shouting, stumbling about the small room, he bitterly went over the years again. Meg waited, growing frightened, feeling a good part of the responsibility he insisted was hers. She felt there was something of madness in his eyes.

Gordon went on drinking, gulping straight from the bottle now whenever it caught his attention. He would not sit down, would not give in to the drowsiness that threatened to overtake him. When she finally suggested meekly that he should rest, his answer was a wordless half-scream of fury.

At last, past midnight when he had detailed his grievances over and over, he began to demand to know how many lovers she had had and when, accusing her of impossible feats of unfaithfulness, shouting at her every vile name he knew. Then he stood over her and violently slapped her face, first one side, then the other until her head rang.

Terrified, Meg was able to escape his clumsy movements, but there was nowhere for her to go. If she ran upstairs, he might follow. She dared not leave the house.

After more loud, violent vituperation, he stumbled away to the kitchen. Surely, she thought, he must be exhausted, must finally collapse. But after a few moments of slamming about out of her sight, he returned with a large knife. He would show her, would prove his strength and manhood. His voice ominously low and steady, he told her once more of his suspicions of her motives and morals; but, he said finally, things had gone completely wrong with their marriage, his job, himself, only after the children came, when he had really begun, finally, to see her for what she was, behind her religion, her morality. He would kill the children, and they, just the two of them, would be together again. She would pay for the rest of her life for all she had done to him. He had never earned her respect with his sacrifices; now he would have it through fear.

At another time, Meg would have gone on trying to soothe him, convinced he would be unable to climb the stairs, would crumple in tears or unconsciousness in the next moment. This evening, she was convinced he meant to try his drunken best to carry out his threats.

Gordon's face was bloated and terrible in its rage. The knife seemed to grow larger, steadier in his hand. His voice rose again in conviction and determination as he moved heavily toward the stairs. In the hall, being careful not to confront him directly, she grabbed a small heavy lamp and struck it desperately against the side of his head.

Gordon fell, and after a still, terrible moment, Meg feared that she had killed him. Holding her own breath, she found that he still breathed. Blood trickled from under his head. She wanted desperately to go for help, but suppose he came to. The children . . .

Shaking now so that she could scarcely stand or direct her hands, she took the knife and the other knives from the kitchen and dropped them into a garbage can outside the back door.

Gordon was conscious again, after minutes that were the longest of her life. He was quiet, incoherent, dazed with alcohol and pain, exhausted with the long emotional tension, his intentions of moments before forgotten. In her own daze, Meg washed and bandaged the cut on his head, helped him to the couch and sat trembling on the stairs until heavy snores came from the living room.

She went upstairs then, carried a restlessly sleeping Melissa into Murphy's room and huddled there. Murphy, who always slept deeply, roused a little to ask what was wrong, but he heard Meg's reassurances only dimly before sleeping again. It seemed hours before Meg's trembling began to relent, before she could conquer the nausea that kept rising in her throat. She felt that winter dawn might never come again.

Finally, she had to face Gordon again.

"I used to believe we had such a good marriage," he lamented pathetically. "Once I—"

"A marriage is one thing," Meg said, trembling, determined, "but the children—"

"Oh, Christ, yes, the children," he said truculently. "Neither of those children is mine. Meg, don't you love *me* at all? Didn't you ever?"

"The children are here," she said firmly. "They've come into our world, and I love them. They need my protection and care. Grown-ups—you—are supposed to be able to get along on your own. I can't go on like this, being frightened for all of us. I won't let the children live like that. You'll have to leave, Gordon, or I will. If I'm the one to go, you'll never find out where I am."

"I'm not leaving. A man can't be thrown out of his own house. At least I do know the legalities of it."

"Then the children and I will go. I'll give notice at school today."

"I won't give you a penny. It's all you've ever wanted me for, to provide money for raising someone else's bastards," Gordon whined, and poured himself a drink.

"I know how unfair I've been to you," she said shakily. "If you'd been honest with me from the beginning, about not having children, I might have been able to give up hoping, to try to count on something else . . . And, of course, if I'd been honest with you, we might have . . . Gordon, please don't drink now."

"It seems to me the least you can do now is not start your holier-than-thou nagging about liquor," he said querulously. "Thanks to your breaking that lamp on me, I've got a splitting headache. I drink because of you. The work I'm trying to do won't stand the scandal of a separation. But my job, anything to do with me, has hardly ever been worthy of your consideration."

"If I go, I'll leave town. If you just move out of here, take a room or an apartment somewhere, I don't see why anyone, not most people anyway, has to know we're separated. I'll do everything I can to keep people from knowing."

Finally, he did leave, filled with anger and self-pity. The people whose opinions he said mattered most knew very soon about their separation—because Gordon told them.

He still came to the house far too often, with pleadings, accusations, promises. He waylaid Murphy several times after school, trying to persuade or threaten the boy into "taking up for me with your mother." Meg was afraid of Gordon, but pity overcame a great deal, pity and a crushing sense of guilt over what Gordon had come to be.

She looked from her kitchen window now at the bare, dark, dripping trees, feeling so weighed down, physically and emotionally, that she scarcely seemed able to finish stirring the cake frosting. Melissa had been sent to take her afternoon nap at Mrs. Pratt's, while party preparations went forward. In a half hour or so she would be home, then her specially invited friends would arrive and the darkness would be banished to the most shadowed corners by the laughter of little children. Was she, Meg asked herself guiltily, asking too much of Murphy and Melissa? Wasn't she putting too much responsibility on their small shoulders, responsibility for her happiness, such as it was, for her very sanity?

She rarely went to church now. Some time back, she had stopped being able to find much in the way of respite from prayer and penance. Thorne hated her. It had been in his eyes, that night he'd seen Melissa. But it was, after all, a kind of miracle that his love had lasted through all the years it had been able to survive. If only she could tell him how grateful she was for Melissa. But that was insane. How could that help him, make up to him for his not having a family. If only he would not believe she had deliberately used him that night in Graham.

She had not left Denver before now because of Thorne. She felt a panicky need to stay somewhere as near to him as possible. Sometimes he was at the Fremont, and strangely enough, when she knew he was there, she often slept better, seemed to have more courage for facing things. That made no sense, of course, but neither did so many other things.

Meg started at the faint sound of knocking at the front door. Oh, God, she just couldn't bear Gordon today, wheedling or bullying, casting a pall over the baby's birthday. Trying to keep weariness or apprehension out of her voice, she called to Murphy, asking him to go to the door because she could not leave the frosting. Already, she had almost managed to scorch it.

"How are you, Murph? Is your mama home?" It was Amy MacWinter's warm, vibrant voice.

"I'm in the kitchen, Amy," Meg called, vastly relieved, then apprehensive again for other, less clear reasons. "Come on back, please. I can't leave the cake icing for a minute."

"We remembered it was about time for Melissa's birthday, Elizabeth and I," said Amy by way of greeting. "I've given her present to Murphy, along with my coat and things. What an absolutely miserable day it is out."

"You were dear to remember her birthday," said Meg, deeply touched.

"Well, but that's not why I came," Amy said firmly, "not all of it. There's been a lot of turmoil at our house since Thursday night; I mean, more turmoil than usual, and more serious. Had you heard Thorne's leaving?"

"Leaving? What do you mean?"

"I don't mean he's going off somewhere to build a new railroad, not for Intermountain, at least. I mean he's going away; even he doesn't seem to know where, or if he does, he's not saying. We thought he might possibly have talked to Murphy about it. Peter Maitland came to our house on Thursday night because he was so upset and troubled about it. Peter is the only one Thorne told, and that was just because he had to tell him in order to make the arrangements he wanted. Oh, I suppose he's talked to lawyers, people at the bank, but I mean Peter is the only one who comes at all near to being family. He's done things with every bit of his stock.

"Elizabeth went to see Thorne yesterday, trying to get him and Ranald together before he goes. She didn't try to talk him out of going or anything like that; just wanted him to see Ran. Well, you can imagine what came of that. Nothing."

"He didn't see Murphy at Christmas time," Meg said, feeling dazed. "Murphy called him and Thorne said—Was he planning to go then?"

"Don't ever ask me what he was planning, or when," said Amy impatiently. She looked troubled. "I've always thought of Thorne as quicksilver. It's hard to touch him at all and impossible to hold onto him. I suppose that's the way he wants to be and it's a good thing he is, or Cherish would have driven him crazy. I came today to ask you a favor. It's the last thing Elizabeth and I can think of to try. This thing, whatever it was between Ranald and Thorne, has just about worried Elizabeth to death. She loves them both like her own sons and it's going to break her heart to have Thorne go, not to mention having it happen when neither of the two idiots will give an inch toward finding some sort of reconciliation. I don't know exactly what happened between them either. The kids and I were away, you remember. But whatever it was, no matter how serious, after all this time, if you were to ask me, I'd say both of them need blistered bottoms. The very idea—two grown men who've been brothers for forty years now won't speak a word to each other when they're about to be separated, maybe for the rest of their lives!"

"He's going that far?"

"Peter said he'd mentioned Alaska and Peru."

Moving without thought of what she did, Meg had taken the frosting from the stove and had begun to spread it on the tall cake. She put her hand to her mouth now, in a quick, helpless gesture, and chocolate dripped from her knife onto her apron.

Pretending to be unaware of the gesture and of Meg's white face, Amy said, "Elizabeth hoped you might be able to talk to one or both of them, try to make them see some kind of reason. I've talked to Ranald until I *stopped* talking to Ranald. For one thing, I told him that if their disagreement was so important as to be treasured and nursed this long, they ought to have a knock-down, drag-out fight and clear the air a little."

"I'm afraid I can't help," Meg said regretfully. "Neither of them would want to see me. It would only—make matters worse. Please tell Elizabeth I'm awfully sorry."

The back door burst open and Melissa ran in. "Mrs. Pratt said I should stay longer, but I couldn't sleep. I couldn't wait to see—" Not all the words came clear yet, but she was very articulate for her age. She had stopped speaking at sight of Amy and cast down her big, dark blue eyes, looking up through the black lashes in momentary shyness. "Pretty cake," she said softly, then exuberantly, "I ran home, all by myself."

"And you got wet doing it," Meg said. "Take off your things. Maybe Murph will put them away if you ask him nicely."

Murphy came in from the living room. Meg thought distractedly that he was pale, his freckles standing out more noticeably than ever. Had he heard Amy, or was it some trick of the dull, watery light from the window?

"Give me the hat and coat, Lissa," he said shortly. "You're dripping all over the place. You weren't supposed to see things before the party. You shouldn't have come back until—"

"Oh, Murph!" She pronounced his name Muff, and hugged him impetuously. "Be nice, Muff. It's my birthday and I love you extra much." Turning to Amy, who was smiling, though her gray eyes had suddenly gone blank with surprise, Melissa said, "Did you know it's my birthday? I'm three."

"Come on," Murphy said gruffly. "You have to change your clothes for the party. I'll get your new dress down for you and button it when you're ready. You're not to look in the living room yet."

There were a few moments' silence in the kitchen when they had gone. With great care, Meg made swirls on the top of the cake.

"She's Thorne's, isn't she?" Amy said quietly.

Color rose into Meg's drained face. For a moment, she could not take her eyes from the cake. Then she looked at Amy for an instant, her expression defiant, proud. She nodded.

"Sometimes I'm pretty stupid," Amy said, a little embarrassed and apologetic. "Sometimes it takes me a long time to see something that's right in front of my eyes. She looks so much like him, and like you too. She's a beautiful little girl, Meg."

"You—you do see then why I can't . . . It's what they fought about, Thorne and Ranald."

"Yes, I see." Amy's voice was kind, thoughtful. "It's why Ranald would never let me invite you to the house, through all this time when you've really needed friends—why you never could manage to come when I asked you. Mama Maria mustn't know?"

"I—I'm not at all sure. Maybe she doesn't, or maybe she just wants to believe she doesn't."

"Well, yes, I can see that. No matter what the circumstances, she'd have a hard time admitting it."

Meg put the frosting things into the sink. Melissa's friends would be here very soon. Could she bear a birthday party now? Of course she could. How could she not?

Amy stood up. "Let me do those dishes. You must have other things that need doing."

"Amy, thank you," she said unevenly. "I haven't even wrapped Lissa's gift yet."

"It looks to me like you need to go off somewhere and cry for a while. I'll just call home, let them know I'll be later than I thought. I'll help with the party if you'll let me."

"But Ranald won't want you to."

"Oh, never mind about Ranald. He's not home yet, and if he doesn't like my coming here, he'll have the rest of his life to recover from it. Meg, don't you want to see Thorne? I mean, if he's going to just go like this, wouldn't you like to talk with him? I could stay with the kids."

"I can't," she said dully. "He'll never forgive me."

"For what?" Amy demanded. "It seems to me you're the one who should do the forgiving."

In a few, brief sentences, Meg told her the facts. It seemed incredible and very sad that all those years could be condensed, disposed of so summarily.

Amy was silent for a moment when Meg finished. Then she sighed, held up her soapy hands in a brief, empathetic, helpless gesture.

"The whole family's impossible," Amy said then, with pretended disgust. "Go and talk to him."

"Oh, Amy, I can't. He'd never talk—"

"Make him mad. *You* get mad. Make him face some truths. Somebody ought to do *something*."

"Melissa's party. I have to—"

"Well, yes, she'll want her mama here, but after that . . ."

"It's too late," Meg said wearily. "I've hurt him too much. I have to think of the children and—"

"I'm trying to get you to do just that," Amy said urgently. She slammed a pan down on the drainboard. "I see now, looking back, he has been hurt all these years. I always thought it was just Angus and Cherish. God knows, those things were enough. Murphy's crazy about him. Melissa's his own child. Yes, think about them, but think of him too, and yourself. It seems to me like the two of you would be about ready to share a nervous breakdown, if nothing else."

"I can't break down," Meg said. "If I ever gave in and let it start, I'd fall into a million pieces, and I wouldn't ever be able to go on. Thanks for doing the dishes, Amy. I'll go and change now."

Meg stood for a long time, trembling, in the corridor of the Fremont. A man walked past, turned back to look at her curiously. She had to knock. Thorne opened the door after a moment and stood there, silent, most of the light behind him.

"Could I—come in?" she said timidly.

He hesitated, bracing himself. He was not really surprised to see her, though he had believed consciously that he would never again do so. He was, rather, shaken, and wondered a little frantically what else he must go through before this was over and he was on his way. He stood back with obvious reluctance.

"What do you want?"

"Amy came this afternoon, to tell me you're going away."

Meg looked about the impersonal hotel sitting room. She saw a small, paperstrewn desk, a suitcase standing by an inner door. This had been home to him, his only home besides a business car, for more than five years. She could not look at his face. Not yet. "Amy and Elizabeth have been—"

"No, I don't want to see Ranald," he said harshly, "or anyone else."

"Thorne—"

"But since you're here, I'll tell you that I've turned my share of the handling of Murphy's trust over to Peter Maitland. Peter or Blessington, the lawyer, will be getting in touch with you fairly soon, I should think. I wanted you to be his guardian, but there are extra difficulties, naming a woman guardian in a case like that. I supposed you'd want to do it."

"You know I'd want to, if you won't or can't."

"Well, I decided Peter should handle it. It's simpler that way. He's a fair man, somebody you can talk to—or Murphy can, later. And they'll tell you, Blessington and the people from the bank, that I've put a third of my holdings, along with the dividends they'll accumulate, into a trust for—for Melissa. The rest goes into funds for Stuart and Clare. I've turned proxies for voting and all the other things the law requires over to Peter. He'll be retiring in a few years, but maybe by then Ranald will be willing to take it on."

"Haven't you kept anything, anything at all?"

"Enough to get where I'm going, to live on until I go back to work. . . . I hope having the money won't be—an embarrassment to Melissa. Maybe all the people she'd have been embarrassed by will be dead when she comes into it."

"Thorne, where are you going?"

"If anyone has to contact me, John Blessington will have some address, eventually."

"You're just going to go down to the station and catch a train and . . ."

"I haven't decided where I'll go yet. But with the new gold strikes in Alaska, they'll be needing roads, railroads, I guess. And they're doing some amazing things with rails in the Andes. I've thought of Canada and Australia, too. All I have to do is choose. There's time for that." He brought himself up short, irritated by talking so much. He said tersely, "Meg, I have to get back to work. There's a report I have to finish."

"Murphy overheard Amy tell me you were leaving. I could tell by the look on his face. He hasn't said anything; there really hasn't been a chance for us to talk. We had Melissa's birthday party right after that, and as soon after supper as I could get Melissa to sleep, I left them home alone to . . . Thorne, it will break Murphy's heart if he doesn't see you, talk to you. It'll be a thing, I'm afraid, that will always make him feel hurt and bewildered, something like the way it was for you, with Mama and Papa and Angus . . . Do you really mean to just break off your relationship with him like this—forever?"

He turned to the window, the dismal darkness. "Maybe when he's grown up . . ."

"He's just a little boy still," Meg said brokenly. "Don't leave him like this. Some of the real reasons can't be explained, but if he could just see you, be with you for a little while . . ."

He would not speak. Slowly, trembling again, she crossed the room to stand beside him, feeling drawn by something outside herself, not really knowing when she moved. She was painfully aware when he shifted to avoid their hands touching on the windowsill.

"What happened to your cheek?" she asked, barely audibly.

"Meg, go home. Take care of Gordon and the kids. Be an admirable, good, long-suffering—"

"Gordon hasn't lived with us for a long while."

"Yes, Murphy told me that, but he will if he wants to. After all, what choice does a dutiful wife have?"

"It's not really about Murphy I've come, not *just* Murphy. It's you and me and—"

"There's no point in talking anymore, least of all in talking about you and me." This was unfair, Thorne thought angrily. If only Peter could have been a man of his word.

"We talked about us," he said, "quite a lot, more than eighteen years ago. That should have been enough. We each knew pretty well where the other stood, especially after you married Gordon. Then we raked it all over again that time in Graham, and before that, when I brought Murphy to Quintana—the whole impossible thing. There can't be anything left to say. There never was very much. I already know you're sorry, never meant any of it to happen, never wanted anyone hurt. No," he said sharply, lifting a hand to stop her from speaking. He struggled, needing desperately to feel real anger now, something violent and caustic that would cleanse him, would, for this present moment, free him. All he could seem to feel was weariness, with only a slight sadness and flickers of dull irritation added to the exhausted resignation within him.

"I can't," he began again, as Meg watched him with those gentle, pleading brown eyes, "I won't go through the thing again, the apologies and asking for understanding. Go home. I forgive you, give you whatever absolution is worth. It's been nothing, really, nothing at all."

"Just listen to me," she said shortly, her low voice tense and shaky.

Turning his head in irritation, Thorne went back to looking out the window, putting up his hands to shield his eyes from the light in the room.

"I agree with you," Meg was going on with difficulty. "It seems as if it's all been said, so many times, but that's partly because I've thought about it so very often. We haven't really talked so much."

"Why should we *have* to talk, now? Do you want some kind of scene of reconciliation—some kind of let's-part-friends-in-spite-of-everything? I won't . . ."

"We're not even friends, then," she said painfully. "All right. I can accept that. And you're right, too, that all the I'm-sorries in the world won't change a thing that's happened already. I understand if you can't forgive—"

"I don't *want* you to understand," he said fiercely, looking at her again. "I just want you to go. Leave me alone. That doesn't seem to me an unholy lot to ask for."

Meg was trying by concentration to rid her voice of its pleading, timorous tremor. "What I'm trying to say is I—I want to believe in—another chance. I know it's a terribly great lot to ask, but . . ."

"Chance for what?"

In a quick, sidewise glance, her eyes not really having time to adjust to the changed light, she saw, nonetheless, that his face had hardened, closed against her.

"I'm not looking for absolution," she said rapidly. "I want us to be together—the four of us—for the rest of our lives. It seems to me that if that were ever to be possible, it could only be so if we—both of us—tried not to think too much about the past. We can't change any of it, though God knows I wish . . ."

"Let's leave God out of it this time," he said shortly.

"All that's ever done is make for longer conversations."

"Yes," she said quietly. "That's true."

Thorne, turning away from her, began to move restlessly about the room, but there was no softening of his expression. Meg felt suddenly weak with longing, with the need to be in his arms, to have his protection, acceptance, understanding, love. If he only could, just this once more . . .

"I don't need to bring God into the conversation, except that I—want one more chance at explaining . . . At your office that time, when you decided to let Murphy come back to me, you said I told things to God or to a priest and turned the responsibility over to them. Thorne, I'd begun to see that for myself, years before. It's hard to give it up. I suppose I may never be able to, completely. I'm just—a country girl from the San Luis, the daughter of a wonderful shepherd. I need—horizons, boundaries that are clear to me, either in sight or in—faith. When I went to live in the East, I'd look out at how broad and vague the horizons were there, without the mountains I'd always been used to, defining my world, marking it out so clearly—I was afraid. Even if it was cloudy and I couldn't look all that way to a blurry, not very well defined horizon, I knew the mountains weren't there. I couldn't *feel* them and I felt so small and lost. . . . I'm saying that the church, God, specific things to believe in, seem to be essential to me. I'm not brave the way you are. I'm afraid I can't live life—uncharted. But I do know now—have known for a very long time—how much I've given up in the name of religion, morals and, all right, martyrdom."

She flung a defiant look at him. Thorne, pacing unconsciously, was waiting; waiting for this to end, to be released from these demands on his time and patience. He felt a compulsion to answer, knowing that that would only prolong her stay, exhaust them both further.

"Are you saying you want to look for—new horizons?" His lips curved in a tight smile that mocked them both.

"I wish—I hope it's not too late to ask you if you'll *be* my horizons."

"Jesus, Meg, you're not putting me on a plane with God?"

"I've told you I seem to need, to have to have things circumscribed, with safe boundaries all around. I'm not strong, not sure enough to be able to just go off on my own, on some uncharted course. I don't believe, anymore, that we are wrong together. I need you; I need to live with you, for a lot of reasons, but partly to strengthen my belief in us. I never have been able to stand up to you, really, in any argument. Now, I don't want to. Your strength has always been a little scary to me. I was afraid of you, in a way, when we first made love, that time before you went to Europe. I was afraid when you came to Quintana about Murphy, and that day in the storm, going to Graham. I knew you could make me to do what I felt I mustn't do, and now I know it was scary because I wanted it so much. That time you came to the house with Mama and Ranald, the night you saw Melissa—oh, Thorne, I'd wanted so much to see you, to share her with you, but most of all, I'd wanted to be with you myself. And because I wanted that so much, I was scared to death of you, afraid you could somehow take her and Murphy and leave me with nothing. I suppose I thought you ought to do that, that I deserved it. I felt so guilty about the way you were being left out of everything."

Thorne looked at her now, his face grown calm and intense. It seemed that less than half his mind heard her words, saw her standing there, twisting her hands together, looking fervent and frightened. The rest of his mind seemed detached, seeking peace, inner and outer silence, rest.

He said, "But life *is* uncharted. No one can plot

another person's course. That's expecting too much. Good parents, I suppose, try hard to give their children directions, guidelines of some kind, but we're damned lucky if we can get even a rough map of the country, some stretch of it."

Meg's eyes had widened in surprise and pleasure. They met his for a moment. "That's almost what Papa said once. He loved you so much, worried about you, always liked talking about you. He said you'd been made to go away, to change your way of living at such a crucial age; and that he, and Angus, had given you so little for the journey."

Thorne felt a small, lonely warmth, hearing Gavin had said that. His face revealed nothing. He lit a cigarette, drew on it deeply.

"You told me, that time at Quintana," she said thoughtfully, "that you almost believed in preordination, and later you said something about our being meant to be together."

"I've tried thinking a little of everything, one time or another. Predestination has looked good because it gives me such an out. If I could really believe I've had no choices, then everything could be rationalized. I'd know, for instance, that my never being able to feel any—any love for Stuart and Clare was not selfishness, cowardice, shirking, but only something that was meant to be, something I needn't keep trying to understand, a thing just to accept, with no blame or credit."

"But you never do that," she said urgently. "You go completely to the other extreme, trying to take on yourself the responsibility for everyone else's feelings and actions. I don't see how you haven't worn yourself out in all these years, just with the sheer weight of it."

"Well," he said thoughtfully, "I believed once that becoming an adult meant you needn't ever again be helpless, not in the face of anything. Along with that, I've thought that any person with some maturity, some knowledge, some degree of strength, ought to be able to control his life, or at any rate himself, his own actions and reactions."

"And you've done that."

"Ah, God, I haven't, Meg. Not ever. The times you've mentioned, when you seem to think I was most in control, those have been some of the worst. When I brought Murph down to you, a strange thing happened to me then. I felt quiet. I thought I'd got everything pretty well in hand, that my mind was giving me a break, some chance to relax. I'd finally left Cherish and the kids. There'd been the fire, Nancy's death; I needed some time. It was something like that too, that day on the mail train. I knew then that we were going to have a chance to be together, somehow. I knew I could make you want to be with me, at least for a while, and I felt peaceful. I took advantage of those times because, as it's seemed so often, I thought I had no choice. I was even pleased about them, about the way I felt, though I couldn't understand it. But then there was another time similar to those. It was when Cherish made that scene, here in the hotel lobby. I suppose Amy or Ran told you about it? My mind seemed quiet then, looking on, and then I—I just passed out. It was the next morning before I woke up. I knew then that those times when I'd felt peaceful, almost sure about some things, or not giving a damn, were the most dangerous of all, times when I was almost giving up—relinquishing control. And that mustn't happen. Why? For God's sake, because there's no one to take over for me."

"Thorne," she said slowly, faintly, "that night in Graham when we made love, I could feel—I thought I could—that you were so . . . open, exposed to me and—willingly so. It was the way I felt toward you, and thinking you were like that made me feel very loved and—special. I trusted you so much, and it was such a beautiful feeling. It doesn't have to be dangerous—does it?—letting go for a while, sometimes.

I know I gave you no reason then to think it was safe to be like that, but . . ."

He had paused in front of her and he said deliberately, "Is it that you want to have another baby, Meg? Is that why you've come?"

"No," she cried, her voice shaking with hurt. A flush came up over her pallor, and with the pain came anger. "I knew you'd believe that Melissa was calculated, somehow. I want—I want you, Thorne. I want, sometime again, to feel the way I felt that night, loving completely and completely loved. And I want it to go on. It could be such a beautiful, wonderful way to live. Couldn't it?"

"No," he said, "because it's too late. I don't want to be thought strong anymore. I just can't live like that any longer, no matter who wants it from me. I haven't got strength enough for one, not to mention two, or maybe even four. I'm tired. I'm so tired . . ."

"Then be *angry*," Meg cried, suddenly furious herself. "Damn us all—Mama and Papa, Angus, Elizabeth, Gordon, Cherish, all the children, Amy, Ranald, Fitz, Nancy, and most of all me. Make it clean. Burn yourself out. Be rid of it. For God's sake, stop taking things. Don't you know that kind of attitude just invites—begs people to let you carry most of the load?"

Thorne had put out his cigarette. Now, unconsciously, he picked up the ashtray, turned it over and over in his hands, spilling butts and ashes onto the rug.

"I've been thinking since I was fourteen of running away. I didn't do it in Pittsburgh because I kept waiting to know things. I wanted answers, some of them to questions I didn't even know. I should have done it, gone away, lost myself, when Angus told me he was my father, and when I knew you'd married Gordon. But I didn't. Now, I'm finally going to do it, when it's too late for anything else, when I know that it won't change anything, won't make me or anybody else different. So much has already happened—is final. If

I could believe, as I suppose I must have, years back, that it *could* mean something—changes . . ."

"Thorne, I want to go *with* you, the children and me. For God's sake, acknowledge that you're hearing me say that, even if you don't want us. Just listen to me then. When we were kids, when your dog Folly came along, big and black in that fine litter of sheep dog puppies so different from him, you asked Papa not to kill him. You said that if something was born into the world, there was surely a reason for it, and it should be allowed to live the life it had been given."

He shrugged. "And Uncle Gavin said, 'It'll be nought but folly, keeping a dog like that.' No, Meg, I don't believe in a grand scheme anymore, if I ever did believe in one. The grand scheme, if it was ever more than a handy argument for me, had to go the way of my expectations for fairness and justice, or even just some kind of sense out of life. That sort of thing, the grand though mysterious Reason for Being, was wiped out, along with silver linings and rainbows and hope—all the childish, dreaming things. Yes, I hear what you're saying. I suppose I'm—grateful for the thought, but I'm afraid that's about all. We'd still be the same people, you and I. There's nowhere far enough to get away from that. We're cousins. You've believed so long in the things you believe. We'd still be going up against the laws and teachings of the church, of your God. You'd be worrying about what our living together—without benefit of divorce, not to mention marriage—was doing to Aunt Maria, to the kids, to—"

"You won't give me the chance I'm asking for," she said hotly. "Of course I'm not going to turn into some other person, or even *try* to lose most of my old self. Even *I* know better than to expect a thing like that. And, yes, I'd keep worrying, searching my mind and heart sometimes, though I'd try not to be tiresome about it, asking you for reassurances every day. But the things that have happened, *have* happened. I'm sorry, for instance, about Gordon. God, I feel so responsible about Gordon; and yet, when I can be honest with myself, realistic, I have to believe what's happened to Gordon, a good part of it at least, would have happened anyway. If I hadn't married him, he'd still have been the weak, sad sort of person he is, because who he was, was well established a long time ago. If I can admit that sort of thing, weak and insecure as I am, why can't you?"

Thorne put down the ashtray, his hands tired of worrying it. "Why can't I what?" he said a little dazedly. "I'm sorry. I've always been bad at philosophy and that kind of thing. I'm afraid I've lost the thread . . ."

"Listen to me," she cried, newly hurt, increasingly angry. "I'm saying things that are terribly important to me. Even if you don't give a damn, please have the courtesy, just for a few minutes, to listen."

Abstractedly, she began her own pacing about the room. "Why can't *you* just try to be realistic and honest?"

"I think I have been."

"Of course you do, but it's not altogether true. You still do believe in all those things: fairness, hope, even love. You *do* think they exist—for other people. You think you've been cheated, singled out somehow, not to have a share in those things. It goes back, I'm sure, to when Angus made you go away without knowing why. You had every reason to be bewildered, confused, hurt. Since that time, you've been afraid of uncertainties; and I think you've believed that other people, almost everyone in the world except you and maybe some of the people whose lives you've touched—that everyone else is happy, has their fair share of justice from life, their hard and fast and never-questioned 'reason for living.' Do you really believe the rest of us are so very different from you? You *are* strong, and you've carried responsibility for people and things anyone else mightn't have felt compelled to touch.

Your idea of dealing with people, with things is, in the end, to dispatch them, get rid of them. Sometimes that is the answer, but not always, not for Murphy, who loves you, not for Melissa, who would love you very quickly if—"

"You're saying let's do it for the children, then? God, what a multitude of sins and wasted years are covered by—"

"I'm *not* saying that. You're putting words in my mouth, and I won't have it. You've made up your mind so many times, what position someone else is going to take, before they know about it themselves. I'm sure that some of the time you've forced people to decisions not of their own choosing with the very strength of your own certainty. I'm not asking you to do anything for the sake of the children. I'm saying they exist. They are entitled to consideration in anything as serious as this. I'm asking you to do this for me and for you. You've said some damned harsh things to me, Thorne, over the years, and I've mostly taken them, felt I had them coming. I still feel that, pretty much, though I wouldn't want to go on hearing those things, having them thrown at me for all the rest of whatever life we might have together.

"But now I'm going to tell *you* something. That thing Gordon says about my being a martyr, and that you so heartily agree with? He wants to think absolutely everything is my fault. He may be right. The thing is, that's been his excuse for everything: his drinking, his not running for election, everything. And I can't go on carrying those responsibilities. I won't. Please don't say anything yet. I know you don't want to hear about Gordon. I'm coming to you.

"You've had your go at it too, at martyrdom. If you were truly honest you'd admit you're no tougher, no more resistant or immune than anyone else when it comes to that kind of temptation. You *have* blamed others at times, *all* the rest of us, just like any ordinary mortal might do. You began, and with perfect justification, thinking, 'If Angus hadn't uprooted my life, if Gavin and Maria hadn't let it happen . . .' and you've gone on along those lines. You've said to all of us, in so many ways, 'You can't hurt me. It's all right; I won't *let* you hurt me.' You've tried, without realizing it, to take away some of the intrinsic decency most people have. You've tried, it almost seems, to *make* us hurt you sometimes, and to make us feel, on the surface, that we needn't bother being concerned about you. You've taken away, in some cases, something of other people's pride. And you've appropriated that to yourself. You've left others hurt, resentful, a little emptier, because so often you won't grant them the right, the obligation of picking up and carrying their fair share of a thing.

"There's Ranald—no, but I *will* talk about Ranald. Don't you know that for more than twenty-five years he's been waiting, wanting to make what he might call a return on your investment? He has got a good many of the things he wanted, starting with moving to Pittsburgh, and that happened for him because of you. You didn't want it mentioned; you got angry, or seemed to, when he tried to express his thanks or wanted to be helpful to you in any way. He began to be angry with you long ago because you wouldn't, or couldn't, grant him the prerogative of returning what he could, in the ways he could. The one time I saw Ran since that night you fought I tried, what little he'd let me, to explain. He said, before he could stop himself, 'If Thorne had only told me in the beginning . . .' I think, and I suppose you do, that he'd have felt, in the beginning, pretty much as he does now. I'm afraid we'll both have to—give up Ranald, for a while at least. The thing is that he wanted so to be your friend, in the ways that he was able to do it. Darling, *I* know he has been. I know he still is. Please understand what I'm saying. You *do* have strength, and what it does partly is to intimidate other people. They resent that, and to *show* you, they give up more and more of their own weight to you—some of them do. I think Angus may have done that, and Mr. Fitzroy, and Cherish. I've done it. I love you. I love you so very much. I depend on your being strong, but I hope I'll never again depend on your strength in such a *using* way. Can't you just admit some things about yourself and the rest of us, accept them? Admit you're as human as we are, and that none of us is any better than we should be?"

Thorne was silent, looking sullen now.

Still vaguely shocked by her own temerity, Meg said, "I truly didn't come to ask you to replace God." She tried a smile, but it did not go well.

Out of ominous stillness, he said, "All right. Just why *did* you come?"

"Because I love you," she said urgently. "Because I want to be with you, wherever you go. It seems to me just now that I don't want to live if I can't be with you."

"Meg, the only thing I've decided for sure about this, besides that I mean to go, is that, wherever I am, I want my name to be MacWinter again. It's stupid, I suppose, to count on a name. What I'm known to people as won't make me any different. It's just that I never wanted to be called, or thought of, as being named Maxwell. In my mind, it never was my real name—my right name."

She said, trembling anew, "I'd like my name to be MacWinter again too."

He said impatiently, "I was trying to tell you that I don't know anything, what I'll be doing, or where. It's no kind of situation to ask anyone else to share."

She said, beseeching him softly, "Thorne, you do still believe. You do still count on things—love, fairness, happiness."

A long silence ensued in which she could not lift her eyes from the rug, a silence full of growing, strangling terror for her.

"Maybe," he said dully. "But I don't mean to go on believing—"

"Oh, you are *so* stubborn!" The words burst from her along with a flood of tears. She had vowed, on her way here that, no matter what, she would not cry. Men always expected that a woman would cry. This was a thing far too important for the helpless luxury of tears. She was furious with herself, and with him.

But she went on crying, uncontrollably. At some point, she sank into a chair because the chair was near and because her legs were trembling so badly. And when, sometime after that, Thorne's hand tentatively touched her hair, she wrenched violently away from it, to go on sobbing, not loudly, but convulsively.

Finally, she felt Thorne's arm around her. He was saying desperately, brokenly, "Meggy, please don't. Forgive me. I . . ."

She tried to stand. He helped her to her feet, picked her up and carried her to the sofa where he sat down beside her. Gently, he wiped her face and neck with his large handkerchief.

"Even your hair's wet," he said tenderly. "Why do I always make you cry?"

"You don't!" she cried vehemently. "Don't flatter yourself—" She broke off, horrified that there could still be anger in her. There was a new, though short-lived, freshet of tears; and then she was looking at him wistfully out of diffident, swollen, reddened eyes, trying desperately to smile. "Please forgive me," she whispered. "I've put all the wrong things first for such a very long time. So many years have been wasted."

He put his fingers on her lips. "Just relax, try to rest a little."

"Will you take us—*let* us come with you?"

In the circle of his arm, she leaned lightly against him, feeling the strength and hardness of his shoulder, the hard, uneven beat of his heart.

"You have a job, don't you?"

"They don't own me."

"I haven't kept back enough money. I don't know

where I'm going or what I'll find, in any of the places I've thought of."

"If things, some things, were cleared up here, would you want to stay, go on with Intermountain? I used to think I couldn't do that, be with you here, no matter what, but I believe now that I could do it."

"No," he said. "I've got used to the idea of going now. I want to do it. What would you do about Aunt Maria and—"

"I'd write her, Thorne, try to explain. She'll never understand, really, I think, and that's probably about all I can do."

He did not move, and she could feel the rigidness of his body. Finally, she lifted her head and looked at the worry and reluctance he could not conceal.

She said softly and with a difficult breath, "You still don't want to do it. Oh, God, it really is too late."

He began painfully, "Meggy, I just don't—"

A sudden movement on her part had stopped his words. He must not say them. She couldn't bear it.

He said, "Do you know how old I am?"

"How could I not know?" she said. Her voice sounded angry, but that was because she could hardly find breath. "You were forty in December. I'm less than two years younger, but we're both healthy. I can find a teaching job almost anywhere, if I need to."

"It's—it seems a hell of a time for starting over."

"It wouldn't be starting over," she said and put her arms around him. "It would be starting new. Can't we all start together?"

He stayed tense for a moment, then started slightly, and she looked up to see some of the tension gone from his face, a small sad smile.

"What is it?" she asked fearfully.

"Nothing. Just that I happened to remember someone's name, a boy I knew when I served my three months at military school. I was thinking of him the other night, and I've been trying to remember his name."

"Well, that's all right," she said dubiously, "but could you forget him again now?"

He kissed her, and after a moment they were quiet, sitting there with their arms around each other, breathing quietly, feeling the gentle warmth of nearness.

They were still sitting like that when Murphy, looking frightened, angry and defiant, opened the door without knocking and led in a big-eyed but smiling Melissa.

He said belligerently to Meg, "I know I shouldn't have got her out of bed. She hated getting up and it took her so *long* to get ready, then it was forever before the cab came, and I couldn't bring her in the rain without a cab. I couldn't leave her home alone either, and I knew Mrs. Pratt would have asked a million questions."

Murphy turned to Thorne then and said with finality, "I've left two bags of mine downstairs."

"You have?"

"Yes. I'm ready to go. Aunt Amy didn't know when you'd be leaving, and all the time I was waiting for Melissa and for the cab and everything, I kept thinking it might be too late and I . . ."

Impulsively, Thorne put out his hand and took Murphy's. "You're cold," he said and his voice was rough. "Suppose you take off that wet coat and cap and sit down a while. Maybe I can get them to send up something hot from downstairs. Chocolate or something."

Murphy looked at them quizzically.

Melissa had been carrying on her own conversation. Backing up to Meg with her arms extended, she had got her own coat and hat off without delay. She began, "Muff's been so cross, Mama. All he could ever say was *hurry*. Mama, have you been crying?"

Then she turned to Thorne. "I don't know you, but I like hot chocolate."

Thorne smiled at her and said shakily to Murphy (who had withdrawn across the room and was watching them sharply), "How would you feel about all of us, the four of us going together—wherever we may be going?"

"All of us?" Murphy's eyes were wide; his face, which had been pale, flushed. "Do you mean . . .?"

To Murphy's surprise, his eyes had filled with tears. "Excuse me, please," he blurted and ran into the bedroom.

Thorne looked at Meg and she called softly, "Murph, darling, please come back soon."

Melissa, after a puzzled glance at Murphy's back, turned cheerfully to Thorne. With her customary assumption that everyone else was aware that whatever she had to say was important, Melissa said, "Today's my birthday. I had a party and then, later, supper. Then I went to bed. Muff woke me up and said we had to come here, but he said this is still my birthday day, only it's night outside. I got presents. I guess you didn't know it's my birthday, but that's all right. Muff tells me about you."

She chattered on, and Thorne watched her avidly, his face revealing more than Meg had seen there in years.

Diffidently, Murphy came back into the room. His shaky smile was tentative, and his face still showed incredulity, half fear at believing what seemed more than he had ever dared hoped for.

Thorne smiled weakly at him. When Murphy sat down across the room, he said, "Come over here, Murph. Do you mind?"

Murphy ran the few steps to sit beside him. "I don't mind," he said, trying to sound casual, but unable to keep the jubilation from rising any longer. "You do mean it! You both do."

Melissa, leaning against Thorne's knees, plunged back into any slightest break in the others' conversation. "You got a hurt on your cheek, didn't you? Mommy kisses hurts like that, then she puts medicine on, and after that they don't hurt, and they get better and then all well. I bet you falled down, didn't you? I do that too. I don't know if my kisses make things better like Mommy's, but I could try. I'd like to give you a kiss."

Thorne trembled as he picked her up and received the healing kiss. She snuggled on his lap then, still talking. He lowered his face against the little girl's hair, trying to conceal his tears. Then suddenly, gladly responding to impulse now, he lifted his head and turned his brimming eyes first to Murphy, then, at last, to Meg.